A TALE OF FOUR PLANETS

A Tale of Four Planets
Book One: Sessions with the Seer, Revised Edition.

A Novel by David Taylor

ISBN: 978-1-951985-76-9(softcover)
ISBN 978-1-951985-77-6 (hardcover)
ISBN: 978-1-951985-78-3 (ebook)
Library of Congress Number on file with publisher.

BOOK ONE: SESSIONS WITH THE SEER

Revised Edition

a novel by David Taylor

"…and the nurse will tell you lies,
of a kingdom beyond the skies…"

-from "The Musical Box," by Genesis

dedicated to my family

Contents

Philadelphia, 2002

A hauntingly vacant row-house was not what the Santiago family expected when they went to visit relatives. Only nine-year-old daughter Samantha received an explanation, though incomplete and bizarre. She also received a task, equally bizarre. For completion of that task, plus a fuller explanation what happened to her cousins and the rest, she would have to wait sixty years.

Not thirty minutes away from facing the enigma, Samantha Santiago tugged at the brim of her Baltimore Orioles baseball cap for the umpteenth time. "So Papa, who built all that stuff?" she asked from the back seat. "I've never seen so many bridges and train tracks in the same place!"

Younger brother Eduardo followed his sister's gaze out her side window, at the vast array of black steel girder trestles and expansive railroad freight yards. Then he was back to his *Star Trek* comic book.

"I don't know specifically..." was as far as papa José Santiago got with his daughter's question when Eduardo exclaimed, "Way awesome, man! It's all right here in *Star Trek*, Sammy!"

"*Star Trek*?" papa chuckled.

"There were these walking plant monsters, and the starship Enterprise destroyed their planet to keep them from spreading elsewhere! But some of their seeds escaped, and traveled back in time."

"Sammy" rolled her eyes then shook head in hands with melodramatic despair.

"The plant-monster seeds dropped on cars like ours, transforming them into these monster metallic weeds that are going to attack Philadelphia! You better hurry, Papa! We have to rescue our aunt and uncle before the monster metallic weeds strangle them!"

"Will you explain this to the police when they pull me over for speeding?"

"The weeds look like railroad tracks and bridges and roads, oh wow! We're climbing one right now! I hope we're off this bridge before it can grab us!"

"Me and my panic attack thank you for that wonderful imagery, Eddie," said Mother Julie rummaging furiously through her purse. "Did someone take my Life Savers? Oh, here…"

"We're on the highhhhway to hell," José sang gutturally as he stomped his foot against the floorboard, the one not on the accelerator.

"Okay, José, that's enough," Julie managed to say clearly, despite a Life Saver knocking against her teeth. "Stop it!"

"Look out!!" José shouted, slapping his hands back onto the steering wheel soon as he lifted them off. Might as well have been doing the wave at a sporting event, where Samantha was concerned.

"Great, you almost made me choke on my Life Saver!"

"Eddie, see how white your mama's knuckles are from gripping her door so tightly? Maybe we should not keep going up and up this bridge like a stairway to the stars?"

"Warp drive 8, Mama," said Eduardo.

"Next time you and your papa go on your own; Sammy and I, we'll take the Marc into Camden Yards for an O's game! Right, Sammy?"

"Totally right, Mama! Maybe we'll see someone hit a homer through the warehouse windows!"

"I'm telling you, Sis'," Eduardo flopped the *Star Trek* comic on his lap for emphasis, "no human can hit a baseball that far!"

"Oh, sure, but these plant monster seeds can time travel to grow metallic weeds? By the way, ever hear of Ken Griffey Jr.?"

"What about him?"

Samantha would have gone on to explain that Ken Griffey Jr. was the guy who once hit the warehouse wall. But even from the back seat, she could sense her mother continuing to struggle with the stark surroundings despite silly banter. So instead, betting the banter had not been silly enough, "Hey Mama?! I was just thinking. Our bodies need a gross part to dump the stuff out of us we can't use. Maybe cities are the same way, and this is Philadelphia's umm...you know... It's not nice, but nothing to worry about!"

"All right, Sis'!!"

"Oh, so we're being mooned on our way into the City of Brotherly Love," said José. "Fantastic!"

"Oo, PU!" Sammy held her nose. "I don't know about 'Brotherly Love,' but that sure smells like brotherly fart!"

"It could be the fart of something big!" said Eduardo.

"No, I think it's the fart of something PIG!" giggled Samantha.

José couldn't help a small snicker himself.

"Yeah, that's fantastic, encouraging our children to use vulgarity."

"Oh, c'mon, sweet stuff, it's not like I'm teaching them to rob a bank!"

"You should have put the air on recycle; here, I'll get it," Julie sighed with exasperation. "Keep your eyes on the road so you don't have an accident or miss the Aramingo exit! Quiet, kids! Your papa needs to concentrate!"

Headed north for a day with José's relatives, the Santiago family found Aramingo Street as they last left it:

unsettling. Soot-grimy street signs and block after block of scab-colored old brick buildings lined a bumpy patchwork quilt of pothole repairs.

The late-summer morning sun still shone heavenly bright in a sky otherwise glowing deep azure. And breezes blew as refreshingly dry as for the most beautiful pastoral settings in the region. Samantha wondered whether such glorious weather ever blessed those horrible World War II concentration camps she'd read about. Black and white photos gave the impression of unremitting, colorless gloom.

Parked cars crowded residential street curbs practically bumper-to-bumper. They included one on flat tires and another duct-taped with clear plastic for its broken-out windshield.   Most, though, appeared in sparkling condition. José figured lots of polishing fended off the dulling effects of city dust, how people showed their pride. Neons, Corollas, Caravans and even two SUVs: they could have been parked at Columbia Mall, just outside Sear's.

The mother pushing her baby stroller, for sure she would not have looked out of place sauntering down the sidewalk past the Santiago's suburban townhouse in Columbia, Maryland. Perhaps she would not have been wearing such a frilly dress. Perhaps her face would not have been blemished with so many whitehead pimples. And just maybe the stroller itself would have appeared more subdued, covered in dark-colored cloth rather than the bright pink and blue plastic set off so noticeably by the scabby brick background. For a softball injury, Sammy's impacted knee was bandaged in comparably bright pinks and blues. Whether or not real healing was going on underneath, sure looked like it ought to have been.

"Oh, great," Julie moaned, "we're stuck behind someone."

A pick-up truck slowed to scarcely ten miles an hour after racing to slip in ahead of the Santiago family. Day laborers sat scrunched together in the rear, their ruddy sunburned backs already sheened with sweat.

"Look out, kids! Duck!"

"What?!? What?!?" cried Julie, twisting around to check that Sammy and Eddie were okay in back. Giggles greeted her, plus Sammy saying, "Come on, Mama, you know Papa's always pulling this stuff!"

"Nooo," José squealed as his wife slapped his head. "Didn't you see in that stroller? The kid is packing heat!"

"I thought the kid was packing poop in his pampers!" giggled Eddie.

"As much as you're packing in yours?" said Sammy.

"No fighting," cautioned Julie.

"You're lucky that Mama and Papa are around," said Eddie.

"So I don't have to worry about getting a scratch on one of my knuckles when I beat up my older brother?"

A guy who stood tall on his row-house front stoop was packing a beer belly swollen out from where the buttons left off on his colorful shirt imprinted with palm trees and turquoise sea. José had more time to contemplate him than he ever wanted, thanks to the red light that halted the day-laborer pickup truck.

Same as the mother pushing her baby stroller, Beer Belly Guy could have been relocated to the suburban setting to which José Santiago was more accustomed. Back home, in fact, José had noticed someone a few doors down who also left his shirt unbuttoned where his imposing gut manifested all the presence of a geologic formation. No tropical imagery colored his attire, but a more important difference accrued.

Beer Belly Guy, Suburban Edition, could be spotted on weekend mornings watering his azaleas and rhododendrons, quiet satisfaction on his face. Beer Belly Guy, Slum Edition might have emanated comparable contentment. He might have been an emperor surveying his kingdom. All the parked cars would have constituted a parade of his military's might, stopped for inspection before his review stand. Instead, though, his regard reminded José of lions at the zoo, the same as day laborers in back of the pickup. It was the regard of creatures resigned to their imprisonment, complete with lethargic scratching at themselves.

"Finally," Sammy's mama exulted with relief on the light finally turning green. Beer Belly Guy, Slum Edition gave her the creeps.

To Mama Julie's further relief, the pickup continued straight through the intersection while the Santiagos were making a right onto North Hancock Street.

North Hancock was named after John Hancock, an original signer of the Declaration of Independence. *But couldn't that just as easily have graced the avenue of some ritzy gated country club community?* Julie Santiago asked herself. *Although what was I expecting? Losers' Dump Lane? Addict Alley?*

Getting out from behind the truck restored José's sense of freedom, his awareness he could have driven anywhere, really. He chose to visit his relatives. The same as at the zoo, he could leave when he'd had enough.

"So what happened to your nephew? He lost his job?" Julie asked with the family encounter looming imminent. Imminent enough for her to oblige refreshing herself on certain what she would have termed soap-opera details.

"Pedro lost everything. The woman who hit him wouldn't give him nothing for the surgery he required. This is what my sister Rotonda says."

"A woman smacked Pedro, Papa?"

"A woman drove her car into Pedro's car, Eduardo, and he was hurt mucho mucho."

"So he's in the hospital? Why didn't he call the police to make the woman pay to fix him? Is he going to be okay?"

"I only know a little of the story from your aunt, Eduardo. You can practice your Spanish and ask her for the details, sí, señorito?"

"I don't know no Spanish, Papadoodledoo! YOU ask her! Then tell me what she says! That is, if you don't want me directing the steel girder plant monsters to eat you, Nya-ha-ha!"

"Well this is just great! Just great, 'Papadoodledoo,'" complained Julie. "It's no wonder you were hired so quickly to teach PE. You're such an effective instructor, with only one example you have children speaking in double negatives!"

"If that wasn't the case, weren't no way I could seduce the sweetest first grade teacher weren't none sweeter, kids!"

"Oh, yuk!" said Sammy.

"Hey, Papadoodledoo, you ain't no PE teacher," said Eduardo. "You told me you're just a pee teacher! You teach kids how to pee! Yeah!"

"Well now you're just trying to get me in more trouble with your mama."

"I'm an expert at that, right?"

"Oh, I don't think your papa needs any assistance getting into trouble," said Julie.

"Maybe your mama should practice HER Spanish to find out more from Aunt Rotonda, sí?"

"Help, kids!"

"Hey Eddie, my bro-ther, I thought you really, really wanted to talk with guys from some other planet. How are you going to learn their freaky outer space language if you won't even learn Spanish? Mrs. Paulson told me Spanish is the easiest language to learn in the entire world!"

"The guys from some other planet are going to meet us, we're not going to meet them! They'll be flying here in their UFOs like we drive to Philadelphia. Their civilization will be hundreds of years older than ours, and they will be so smart, we won't have to learn their language. They'll learn ours first, just like that!" Eduardo snapped his fingers. "Then they'll talk to us through special translator devices like in *Star Trek*."

"Huh!" grunted José Santiago, not meaning to suggest his son made a provocative revelation. Rather, he was struck by peculiar comparisons.

Jose had reached the portion of North Hancock that ran under a black subway trestle. Shops lined an intersecting street in the trestle's shadow to his left. The dinginess of the trestle's cement supports, of the trestle itself, and of the shop signs reminded him of the dark, greasy buildup inside his balcony grill.   Years ago that grill gleamed shiny brand new, moments before he started making his cookout messes. Likewise, going back whatever number of decades, there had to have been a time this slummy intersection also gleamed shiny brand new. Surely, people must have harbored hopes for it turning out far, far nicer than it did, no?

Tables outside the stores displayed a mix of street-merchant ware and sale items from within. Toy trinkets glared bright plastic yellows, reds and greens in the same league as the baby stroller. They reminded José of artificial flowers he saw placed on graves when he visited his father's in Puerto Rico. Those trinkets were doing about as much good to heal the stark, grimy wretchedness of the place as those bouquets did to bring back the dead.

Talk about *Star Trek* or *Star Wars*, José mused to himself that he might as well have been soaring through space in a miniature starship. *We are surely this minute traversing a void of deprivation in our bundle full of love and material abundance.*

At least from what José recalled of previous visits, his older sister made her tenement dwelling an outpost of warmth, a moon colony of caring. Hopefully, it was just one among many that would grow in enough strength and numbers to ultimately overwhelm the crack houses and AIDs and ignorance and prejudice.

"Hey!? Where are the barking dogs?" complained Eduardo as he leaped from the car.

Eduardo's father, José, parked across the street from the relatives' home, beside an abandoned lot overgrown with weeds. There, José espied a discarded syringe and needle.

"Dogs are always barking whenever we visit."

"I hear one dog barking," muttered Sammy tugging down hard on the brim of her O's cap, both to block out the mid-morning sunlight glare and to make extra sure the cap wasn't going to slip off. "I've had to listen to him for an hour, barking about *Star Trek*."

"I think the dogs were out late last night chasing the cats," speculated José in forced jest as he double-checked the sedan doors were locked. The discarded syringe and needle really spooked him. What did such drug use litter say about the goings-on in this field not fifty feet from his relatives' home? Agitated dogs nearby or not?

"I hope your sister-in-law isn't waiting to greet me with a plate full of rice, beans and 'biftec'! I can already imagine her trying to shovel it down my throat while she complains how thin I am!" But Julie actually would have welcomed that happenstance with profound relief. Any other time they'd visited, Pedro or someone would have long since appeared on the front stoop to greet them with uninhibited hugs.

"Don't speak so loudly; you have a big mouth, woman, from correcting all those double negatives in your classroom," José blustered through additional creeps from the whole block seeming abandoned.

Knock! Knock! Knock! Eduardo knocked with the urgency he last experienced seeking shelter from a thunderstorm.

"Oh great! You smell that, José? The beans are simmering, so the rice and 'biftec' can't be far behind!" complained Julie, trying to convey disgust over having to face not her favorite late morning meal, especially on a steamy mid-summer's day. But she couldn't hide her relief. Still no one to the door, yet unmistakable scents were seeping out.

"Try again, Eddie," said his father. "Possibly they didn't hear you the first time because of electric fans and the TV."

While the sweet odor of kidney beans mixed in garlicky, oniony tomato sauce tempered Julie's anxiety, José took comparable comfort from the TV blaring away. Its constantly shifting aural kaleidoscope went from revving race car engines one moment to some megaphone announcement in Spanish set to a disco beat the next.

"Maybe they're doing something in there?" asked Julie, initially more puzzled than alarmed when Eddie's second, more insistent series of knocks also failed to bring anyone to the door.

"Like maybe they're having sex?" Sammy asked, turning sunburn red.

"Samantha Santiago!"

"Is that what we smell cooking in there?"

"Eduardo Santiago!" Julie tried not to let her amusement undermine the sense of shock, of being offended, she wanted to convey. "I'll have to stop letting you two watch any TV besides the news."

"Great, so we'll only be allowed to see how someone was shot, or a bunch of people were blown up by the terrorists," said Eddie. "Or the accident they're trying to clear that's caused a five-mile backup on the beltway."

"Julie, I'm going to find out whether the door's unlocked, but I think you better take the kids back to the car first."

"José?!? Should we leave and call the police?" Julie couldn't help fear heightening her voice's pitch. "Are you sure they didn't step out a minute for errands?" she added, straining so hard not to panic that she forgot about her Life Savers.

"I think their cars are both parked here."

"Couldn't they have walked to a corner mart to buy some pan de agua?" Despite her question, Julie protectively hugged both Eduardo and Samantha to her side; she knew it didn't make sense that more than one or two of José's relatives would have gone out for bread. There should have been plenty of people left inside to answer the door.

"I'm not allowing my papa to get shot or something!" announced Eddie, wriggling free of his mother.

"Stand back, son, while I try the door," said José in a loud whisper.

"Who's that you're calling on your cell phone, Papa?!! The POLICE?!!!"

Enhancing Sam's impromptu bluff were cop sirens wailing away not too far distant.

"Wow! Thanks, Sammy; maybe they'll feature you on *America's Most Wanted*. The bad guys should have scooted out the back by now. But just in case..." BAM! BAM! BAM! José pounded at the door. "THIS IS THE POLICE!! OPEN UP!!" He tried the knob though already resigned to needing to kick the place open, but found to his surprise that it easily turned all the way.

Air agitated by the thrown-open door slapped the banner against the wall in the foyer, the banner that displayed the one-star flag of Puerto Rico together with that island's coqui tree frog. The living room and kitchen fans hummed loudly. And the TV blared heavy metal for a car commercial.

The especially strong, air-thickening smell of simmering kidney bean sauce had José still half-expecting to see his sister waddle out of the kitchen with a smile as wide and welcoming as her embracing arms. At the least, his brother-in-law Placido should have been rising from his easy chair to offer greeting. He should have been returning to full consciousness from his channel-surfing stupor.

"Placido?! Rotonda?!" José shouted to no avail.

"Look here, José. Weren't these shelves full of family portraits?"

"Sí, claro," José shook his head worriedly. "The picture of Pedro in his army fatigues, the girls when they were babies, and over here..."

"I'm checking the second floor, Mama and Papa," said Sammy, already bounded halfway up the stairs.

"Be careful," Julie warned. Had the strange circumstances not so overwhelmed her, she would have insisted her daughter not go off anywhere in the house alone.

"Sis' wants to see if Gloria and Jerri kept their Ricky Martin poster, so she can drool all over him."

"YOU want to drool all over him, my bro-ther, ever since you learned he was gay!" Samantha shouted from her completed ascent. Truth was that she did enjoy groaning in disgust when her cousins Gloria and Jerri talked boys while assaulting her to apply makeup, eye shadow and lipstick. And she also enjoyed checking out their posters of corporate music teen idols like Ricky Martin, to sneer with more disgust. But something else chased her up the stairs, far beyond any desire to indulge more secret pleasure masked as revulsion. Samantha feared for her cousins' safety, and hoped she might find at least a small good-news clue to everyone's whereabouts.

She didn't realize she wasn't alone until the door closed gently behind her. It closed so gently, no one would be the wiser on the first floor. That is, unless they were looking up the stairs at the time.

"Oh!" Sammy let out a little gasp, and held on to her baseball cap for dear life. The next moment she would have screamed for help, if not for an air of peace emanating from the woman who shut the door. Maybe it was the way that unexpected stranger clenched her hands prayerfully together, snug against the waist of her diminutive, frail-looking figure. Her wild lengths of tousled gray hair might have inspired additional terror regardless, if not for her breathless whisperings. "Please, say nothing to your family. I would not harm an ant. Bendito, no. I collect them in a little match box to put outside when they invade my kitchen."

"Are you a witch?"

"If I were a witch, I would place a spell on those ants so they never enter my kitchen again. They really are a problem, you know. I am a chef, not a witch, and I find myself trying to save a peculiar recipe. It's going to take about sixty years to bake, but instead of putting the key ingredient inside an oven, I am handing it over to you."

"Huh?"

"Here, take it fast. Your parents are going to be calling soon, and you will have to go." The woman offered Sammy a small, cylindrical, gold pendant attached to a bracelet-sized chain. "It arrived with a thunderstorm one year ago almost to the day, like the tremendous rain we had here last night."

Letting go the brim of her O's cap to receive the "key ingredient," Sammy noticed unusual engravings. They reminded her of what she had seen in a school social studies text of Egyptian hieroglyphics.

"You know how certain cakes rise while baking, but if you open the oven too soon, they collapse and are ruined? If you show that to anyone before sixty years from now, the peculiar recipe might be ruined too. Only it is more important than a cake recipe, because life and love are at stake."

"So what am I going to do with this in sixty years?"

"You are going to give it to someone close to you after he survives a terrible ordeal, an awful adventure."

Sammy suddenly shook her head, like she was snapping out of a trance. "My Aunt Rotonda and Uncle Placido and their children: Can you tell me where they are? Are they okay? Are they safe?"

"They are caught up in the same adventure. It would take too long to explain before your family calls you downstairs." The mysterious woman was backing away from Sammy ever-so-slowly, towards a window that opened onto a flat, tar-sealed roof. "They are celebrating the beginning of the Great Healing."

"Will we get to see them? Where are they?"

"Sammy?! Sa-mannn-tha?!" Julie called.

"Hey, Sis'?? Where are you?"

There was the thud-thud-thud of someone running up the stairs.

"Quick, hide it in your pants pocket, Samantha; you can examine it more closely later."

The door opening behind Sammy drew away her attention from the woman.

"Ah-HA!! DON'T WORRY, MAMA!! SHE'S RIGHT HERE!!" Then to Sammy, "I knew it, Sis'; you wanted to be alone with the hunky guy posters! C'mon! You scared the willies out of our mama!"

Eduardo was already returning to the first floor, so he missed his sister's double take as she realized the woman was gone and the window locked tight, from the inside.

Chapter 1

Pedro Perez eagerly anticipated getting his wife Ludi alone on the rooftop to discuss new horizons of possibility opening for them, for their family. But that was also when a mysterious item would drop at their feet, the same mysterious item handed over to his cousin Samantha one year later. Had Pedro only known, surely he would have begged off dinner even sooner than he did.

Pedro didn't need to knock when he arrived at his parents' tenement dwelling after work. He still had the key, even though he and Ludi were living with her grandparents two blocks down the street.

Pedro found the fans set high on that muggy early evening in late summer, the same as his Uncle José would find them a year later. Also the same as a year later, garlicky, oniony, tomato-sauce heat further thickened the already thick air. Megaphone style announcements blared from the TV, of an upcoming pay-per-view boxing match "más espectacular." And the Puerto Rico banner slapped against a wall in the foyer as Pedro shut the front door behind him.

Only this time, the experience was not of a mere semblance of thriving life with the life itself eerily absent. This time, well before Pedro would have felt compelled to call out if anyone was home, Don Placido made his presence known. He craned his face round the corner of his armchair rather than stand for his greeting. "Finally!" *Finalmente*, he spoke and continued in Spanish with a deeply guttural voice, some words slurred together. "You arrived any later, and I was going to eat your dinner for you! You stopped for a beer again at *Primitivo's* on your way home?"

"Papi…"

Placido was actually Pedro's stepfather.

"…I have told you I never drink even a spoon full! There was a switching problem at one of the stations, so we had to run extra diagnostics. Possibly there are thunderstorms tonight and we will have power outages!"

"Thunderstorms?! But is already seven and still a clear sunny sky! Yes, I know," Placido chuckled and nodded as he resumed his slouch practically molded into the Lazy Boy knockoff.

Pedro closed his eyes and shook his head over this familiar irritation. When Papi chuckled, "I know," what was he really laughing about? What was he really knowing? Did Placido think it funny pretending not to believe his explanation for being late? Or - what Pedro suspected being the more likely situation – was Placido serving notice he was on to his stepson? He knew Pedro to be a sinner like the rest of them? Certainly like himself before Doña Rotonda finally settled him down taking him to church? So Placido was laughing at what he regarded as a lame lie?

"Mami, I have news," leaped from Pedro's mouth seeing Rotonda waddle out of the kitchen from where the Santiago family would wait in vain one year later for anyone to emerge.

"News!?" exclaimed Papi. *Why didn't you tell me first?*

"Don't care what it is, son; give me a strong hug," said Rotonda, all open arms and cherishing smiles.

"No, Mami, is good news."

Doña Rotonda was already embracing him and kissing his cheek. "Is okay," she said, what he said not registering with her.

While Pedro deeply appreciated his mami's unconditional love, her presumption all news was bad news never ceased to irritate him. It bothered him nearly as much as his stepfather's kidding-that-might-not-be-so-much-kidding. Pedro wanted to terrify her with some concocted horror, give her what she was expecting before he revealed the joyous reality. However, she'd been through so much; what was she supposed to expect ever since her first husband beat the crap out of her? She left that brutality behind years ago, but still...

"Mami," Pedro spoke softly as he allowed Rotonda's expansive hug to pull him bent over so far, his mouth was practically in her ear. "I received the promotion. Philadelphia Electric has made me a substation maintenance supervisor."

"Yes??" asked Rotonda, letting go of Pedro and giving him a *you're-not-kidding-me-are-you?* look. "Ay, son, that is tremendous!" she sighed with hand to chest, straining to catch her breath.

"Substation maintenance supervisor?! Very good, Pedro," said Placido hoping to convey how sincerely impressed he was by his stepson's achievement. "When do you start?"

"Let him eat first, Papi. Here is your salad, my son." Rotonda indicated a plate of pale green lettuce and thinly sliced tomato on the dining room table separating kitchen from living room. "You can start while I bring you the rest."

"Have you seen Ludi yet?" asked Pedro following his mother into the kitchen, ignoring her instruction.

"I am not asking him to play a dominoes match before he eats; I am just asking a simple question: When is his first day as supervisor? Aydiomio!" Placido half muttered to himself, half complained to Rotonda. *Oh my God!*

"As usual, she is probably taking home from church the other 'day care' mothers because their no-are-good husbands and boyfriends stay at *Primitivo's* or worse all night. Ay bendito. Here is lemonade, son, or you want soda?" asked Rotonda in surrender to Pedro shadowing her rather than staying behind with the salad.

"You see any of them at *Primitivo's*, macho mio?" Don Placido spoke loudly enough to be heard in the kitchen.

Pedro sighed with resignation.

"Oh, maybe she is here already," reacted Rotonda to a noise from the foyer, just as she was handing Pedro a plate piled high with rice, beans and fried chicken breasts.

Knob jiggling preceded the front door giving way to an unseen force from beyond.

"Bla-bla-bloo-bla-bloo-bla-bloo-bloo-bloo!" went five-month-old daughter Alexandra safely tucked in Ludi's arms. Her babbles drowned out the Puerto Rico banner's slap against the wall.

Pedro thought his daughter had the funniest look, like maybe she was puzzling over how to get her mouth under control from running off on its own.

Soon as noticing Pedro's approach, though, Alexandra's mouth and eyes alike radiated pure joy. She let out a squeal of delight tinged by a threat to howl grief-stricken if her daddy didn't take her into his arms.

"Hola Preciosa," Pedro said to his daughter as he obliged her apparent demand. *Hello, Precious.*

"I cannot believe what those women accept," said Ludi in a breathless rush. Instead of driving, she might as well have just run all the way home from church.

"You can continue to not believe what those women accept while you are eating," said Rotonda. "Your mami and papi have to eat, sí, Preciosa?" she proceeded to address Alexandra, taking her off Pedro's hands. "Ay que linda!" *How beautiful!*

"Ludi I have news."

Pedro didn't need to say another word. Ludi knew that smile, that smile which drove her wild from the first day they met. It was the smile of someone whose main happiness stemmed from happiness brought to other people.

"You received the promotion?" asked Ludi. And on Pedro's nod, she squealed with the adult-sized version of delight that baby Alexandra had simply required her father's mere presence to prompt.

"Yes, he received the promotion," grumbled Placido, sunk into the slouch mold with which he'd embedded his chair. "Maybe he will tell you when is his first day at the new job."

"Pedro can tell us his first day after they eat. The dinner is waiting for your mami and papi, Alexita bonita, sí señorita!"

"Aydiomio," grumbled Placido anew as Rotonda made her grandchild giggle by nuzzling her tummy.

"Where are Gloria and Jerri? I should tell them my news too."

"You don't hear your sisters?" asked Ludi, backing off from her husband to point upstairs. "They are practicing their merengue. Oo, Chi-Chi Peralta, nice!" She snapped her fingers in sync with her swiveling shoulders and hips.

"You can dance after you eat. You heard what I told Alexita, that your dinner is served?"

"Mami thank you for repeating that. Without your help Ludi and I forget to eat!"

Pedro may have been sarcastic with his mother, about forgetting to eat. But he could hardly wait to have Ludi out on the rooftop, alone, to discuss their future and see what stars they could discern through city haze. So he took only a few mouthfuls of the lovingly offered meal before he stopped to say, "Oh, man, I have a backup in my stomach; nothing is moving."

"What is this, my son?"

"Mami, I think the rice and beans and chicken had a rear-end collision with my late lunch, yes! Need to stop eating until the caca police open a few lanes of traffic."

"That lemonade is a good tow truck for re-opening your highway," grumbled Placido anew. "But don't listen to me."

Sí, don't listen to Papi, Pedro's mama would have said, if not for... "Pedrocito, you are a pretzel stick! You must eat more if you are going to work harder in this new promotion! Bendito, the caca police should arrest you for not making enough of it, true, Alexita? That is the truth?"

Alexita squealed again from more of her grandma's ticklish nuzzles.

"Sí, Pedrocito, your daughter says that is the truth."

"Okay, Mami, we are not bears who have to store fat because they hibernate five months of each year with nothing to eat. My promotion is big news for Ludi and me. We want to discuss it on the rooftop."

"They want to make a barón!" said Placido.

"We need a little privacy," said Pedro.

"Yes," nodded Placido. "You need privacy to make a barón!"

"When we are making a barón up there, Don," said Ludi, pushing back from the dining table, "we will try not to put a crack in the ceiling, okay?"

"For sure," agreed Pedro, joining his wife at the foot of the stairs. "And we will also try not to disrupt any power lines; I do not want to create extra work for myself."

The couple still had to negotiate the bedroom of Pedro's sisters. Their window provided the one safe exit from the home out onto the tenement building roof. So they would have to spend a little time first with Gloria and Jerri. Most likely Ludi would practice dance steps with them. Then all three women would harass Pedro because he wouldn't join in or, as his wife put it, he wouldn't let them help him trade in one of his two left feet for a right foot.

Mami wanted to shovel food down his throat and his sisters wanted to shovel dancing down his legs, as if the substation switching difficulty and the subway ride home weren't enough. Pedro forced himself to smile, at how he had to make it past all these obstacles simply to climb out the window of his sisters' bedroom and discuss the future with his wife under an open sky.

"Of course, *claro que sí*," nodded Pedro after he opened the bedroom door on his sisters.

Gloria and Jerri were dancing separate from one another, arms encircling nobody.

"Yes, in this heat makes sense to dance with a ghost, how they say in English: he is a 'cool dude.' You do not want to be embraced by some macho so hot that he makes M&Ms melt in his hands before he can bring them to his mouth!"

"Yes, and also makes sense for your wife to dance with an invisible spirit. That way she has no problem from you stomping the nails off her toes!" responded Pedro's sister Jerri.

Where Ludi was concerned, Jerri's words could have been sparks, or beads of sweat flying from the plump teenager's gyrations to the bachata beat.

What Pedro's wife didn't expect next was how her husband's sister suddenly abandoned all rhythm to seize her hands and cry, "Ludi! Por favor! You have to help us! We know they are going to play lots of Juan Luis Guerra at the church dance, but this one song 'Rosalia' is impossible!"

"Ay, yes, 'Rosalia,'" Ludi nodded knowingly. "What a crazy rhythm!"

"Please!" Gloria dropped to her knees from her own slow dance with no one. She clenched her hands together in begging supplication, melodramatically like she was asking for her life to be spared. And she displayed her toothiest smile as in: Am I not too cute for such suffering to be inflicted on me?

"Mm," Ludi put forefinger to lips pouted out as though granting this stay of embarrassment-at-the-church-dance execution were a really tough call. But then she nonchalantly shrugged her shoulders, "Okay. However, at a later date you have to help me with *these* two impossible dance steps!" She indicated Pedro's legs.

"Ay, no!" cried both sisters, waving their hands and backing away. They could have been steering clear of two rattlesnakes rather than two left feet, their brother mused. "Ask us for something easier," went on Jerri, "like how to mambo with a crocodile!"

"How come my 'boogie-woogie' little sisters have to wear so much makeup?" Pedro grinned half mischievous, half plaintively concerned. "Appears so thick, is the same if you put on a mask. What are you thinking attending the dance like that, and wearing a dress with the neckline down to your navels? Some Hollywood agent is going to discover you for becoming the next Jennifer Lopez? Is the same if I travel to Florida and parade around Cape Kennedy in an astronaut suit, expecting someone will put me on the next space shuttle."

"But brother," said Jerri, "they *will* put you on the next space shuttle, for sending you back to your home!"

The sisters' insults directed at her husband notwithstanding, Ludi walked them through steps for the odd time signature of "Rosalia."

Resigned to the dance-lesson delay of his rooftop rendezvous, Pedro examined a piece of thin laminated cardboard left on his sisters' shared dresser after the shrink wrap was torn off and cosmetic items removed. The list of contents with an outer space backdrop had him shaking his head disdainfully. *Yes, of course, applying eye shadow, lipstick or whatever other junk will be my sisters' ticket to the stars, their passport to the good life far from this terrible inner city mess. Crowds will go crazy for them. Ay, bendito, my sisters could be mail order brides from the Philippines supposing they will be rescued from poverty by old men more interested in sex slaves than true companionship. Mami has made all the effort she can, but Jerri especially believes dance could fly her to the romance star of luxury. God save her from pregnancy and crash-landing out of high school. And God do what you will with the macho responsible for her pregnancy, if he leaves her for a new conquest!*

"Look, sisters," said Ludi, "appears your brother is too bored. We have some things to discuss, okay?"

"Is not boredom," Pedro shook his head. "I worry for you chicas. All that lipstick is like blood in the water, how it attracts sharks."

"Aydio, no," groaned Jerri, "not another lecture, or I am bored for sure."

"Listen to your brother, he loves you." Ludi wrapped one arm round Jerri's shoulders and the other round Gloria's.

"Ay, no, no!!" Pedro pretended trouble pulling back his leg from being out the window up to his thigh. "One of the land sharks has my foot; someone help me!"

"Eat him, Mr. Shark!" cheered Jerri, her hands cupped together for a megaphone effect. "Eat all of him, especially his mouth so he cannot lecture us anymore!!"

"No, I need him for changing Alexita's diapers the middle of the night! And there is a big spider he has to squish in our bathroom! I come for rescue you, Electric

Man!" shouted Ludi, following her husband out the window.

She caught up to Pedro several steps away, as far away as he could go without approaching too closely an adjoining row-house window. His eyes intently scanning the night sky, she nevertheless latched gently onto his shoulders. No land shark pulled him out the window by his legs, but it was like she was making sure some cosmic monster wouldn't pull him into space by his head. Or that if it did, she would be pulled along with him.

"We need a good thunderstorm tonight for clearing this haze; most stars are lost from view."

So much air pollution made difficult discerning exactly where empty sky shaded off into clouds encroaching from the west. Down along the building-jagged horizon, a purplish-tinged orange glow brightened to what gave the appearance of an extensive bonfire just beyond.

"You see that star there, Ludicita?" Pedro pointed, encircling Ludi's waist as though were that space monster to be taking him, he did want to make sure he swooped her up alongside. "That's the planet Venus."

"Yes, I know; you show me so many times before."

"But this time you see how much it flickers, how they say in English 'twinkle'? Usually only the stars more distant than our sun look like that. But none of them are visible now, because the air is so thick with dirt. That is why Venus wavers so much, as if a candle is going to be snuffed out! And look how orange is that sliver of moon!"

"Cariño," *Heart*, said Ludi, "Venus is not wavering. She is dancing the merengue. Yes! Is true! And the nights we see many stars, those are not connect-the-dots for creatures in the constellations, ay no! Are patterns for where you have to put your feet so you can dance the merengue too! See? Like this- Oh!"

A sudden bang sent Ludi rushing back into Pedro's arms after having swayed away from him, gyrating to the music leaking from Gloria and Jerri's window.

"Is okay," said Pedro. "A car backfired, or possibly a tire blew out."

Or gunshot; the young lovers exchanged looks where neither one had to voice that awful possibility while police and ambulance sirens went off.

"I wonder whether the husbands of Myriam and Carmen have returned home yet," softly spoke Ludi nestling her face in Pedro's expansive chest, her blond-streaked auburn hair giving him something to nuzzle. "I worry for them how you worry for your sisters."

"Their husbands are day laborers, yes? From one morning to the next they have no idea what is their work, or for how long, or whether they will have any work at all. If they have nothing, then how can they show their face at home? So they stay at the bar until closing. Or they obtain a little work and are returned to the pickup parking lot by lunchtime, with a little money in their pocket. But is still too early to return home with any sense of dignity…"

"So they lose even more dignity by spending their little money on alcohol," Ludi commented in disgust. "And when is time for going home, they have nothing to show and beer on their breath, the same as for those with no work."

"Yes, and maybe one of them starts to sell drugs, is what I fear Roberto is doing."

"And what happens with the macho who does have a full day of work? What is his excuse?"

"Ay, Ludi, is no excuse. He still does not know whether there is any work for him the next day. Anyway, he can have work every day, but then also have a boss like one of mine. Mr. Gibbons has a manner of saying what to do that really says, 'I would not trust you to even dig a ditch correctly, if I could find someone better!' You know what he said when he heard Mr. Smith authorized my promotion? He said to me, 'Congratulations! You have to feel good knowing you helped Alan fill a quota.'"

"Ay, yes, Pedro, I am not saying there are not bad people who look down their noses at anyone different from them. I am not saying this is not a difficult life here for us." Ludi looked into Pedro's eyes, her hands twined together behind his neck. "But cariño, for why these other guys cannot make the same effort as you? How you said with your boss, you have to endure the same prejudice!"

Pedro shrugged his shoulders with authentic modesty. "Possibly is the discipline I received from my years in the military. But there are other people I know from the military, and-"

Suddenly, another loud noise; this time someone was revving a car or motorcycle engine. At first, on-edge Pedro wasn't sure it wasn't thunder. He knew the weather forecast, and that an electrical storm could mean having to go back out to work that evening. "Is my good luck, Ludicita," he went on finally, about what they were discussing before. "Sincerely, I am not feeling any superiority to those other guys. Maybe is my mami also. She always said to remember what I am working towards. But my sisters have the same mami, and the only things they work towards are more makeup and worse school grades."

"I think you *are* superior."

"No," Pedro closed his eyes and shook his head firmly. "When we look away from Venus on a hazy night like this, finding it again can be very difficult. But I always do. Distracting noise and heat make no difference, not even this terrible smell of tar that rises from the roof so we cannot stand out here very long.

"That special good fortune has also always been mine, to rediscover where the stars of my dreams are located even when I have looked away from them. You know how I surrendered to my friends' persuasion in high school, and smoked a marijuana cigarette? And watched for police in front of a market while they were shoplifting candy bars and condoms? Other things stupid like that? Desperation led us on searches for easier routes to the stars that were in reality the devil's traps.

"Many of those friends, a thick mental haze thwarted them when they returned to seeking their true dreams. Took so long discovering where exactly they needed to redirect their view for that one faint 'twinkle' still visible, they gave up before they could succeed.

"But again, searching in the right place always came fast and easy for me. Maybe if I could not locate my stars again so rapidly, I would have, how we said in the army, 'thrown in the towel' too. And then you would have found me joining the others on a counter stool in *Primitivo's Cantina*."

As though on cue, Ludi's large eyes caught enough ambient light to twinkle.

"Ludicita," went on Pedro, "there are places where our Alexita preciosa can view many more stars than ever we can spot here. They are places where Venus and the North Star shine brightly even before the sun has finished setting. And they are also places where every time we hear a 'bang,' we will not have to worry over our daughter's safety."

"Are you talking about a house outside the city, mi guapo?" *my handsome*

Pedro nodded with that smile again that drove Ludi wild. Before he could continue, she was drawing his lips apart with hers, plus holding him in a tight embrace. When she finally let Pedro continue, she kept her face close to his, cherishing every feature from his chiseled jaw to his light brown complexion while running her fingers through his shortly cropped, tightly curled hair.

"Mi cielita linda," *My beautiful sky*, he said, running his fingers most longingly through the entire length of his wife's silky hair, "there are three-bedroom houses for sale in an old suburb the other side of the Delaware River. Only a little bigger than this of Mami and Papi, but they have a front yard and back yard. And with the raise from my promotion and our savings, for sure we can obtain a 'VA loan,' and pay the mortgage each month."

Before Ludi could kiss Pedro anew, a rumble caused them to look away from one another.

Pedro closed his eyes and shook his head. "Is thunder," he said as several dogs barked. At first he thought, he hoped, it might be someone else revving their engine. However, there was a quick, short follow-up he'd always likened to someone pushing a piece of heavy furniture across the floor. A big sofa or bed. Moving time for God.

"Okay," Pedro said with an added sense of hurry, "we can explore houses this Saturday? You have no other commitments then?"

"Yes," Ludi nodded eagerly. "Ay, Pedro, I can imagine how we will live! Is too far north for a mango tree in the backyard, like my aunt Filomena has in Bayamón. But I will grow tomatoes and maybe corn and beans. And I will take so good care of our Alexita until she goes to school!"

"And I will take so good care of her in the evenings," added Pedro as he put a forefinger to Ludi's lips. "Saturdays also, maybe; that will depend on your schedule of teacher training classes at a community college."

A sudden, sustained **CRRRRRACK!** reminded Pedro of wood splitting apart, how that sounded beside one's ear. It was accompanied by flashes of lightning and abrupt gusts of breeze.

The storm was getting closer.

"Ay, Pedrocito, is okay, we are not going to have money for my tuition with the mortgage!" From the desperate urgency in Ludi's voice, someone not knowing any better might have misapprehended the young couple was about to be torn apart. They wouldn't be able to communicate again for weeks or months.

"But we *are* going to have money for that, Ludi!" insisted Pedro, struck by the absurdity of how melodramatic he must have sounded. Something instinctive brought on by the approaching thunderstorm? A relic of prehistory, when survival went to those ancestors who responded swiftly to the threat of bad weather?, thereby avoiding being struck by lightning, or so soaked they were subsequently more vulnerable to disease? Or even worse, drowned in a flash flood? Weren't these storms special tests? And what people did to prepare for them during the peaceful times in between, wasn't that what determined how well they endured them? "I looked at the numbers-"

"I will be happy with no classes, mi guapo! They can wait for when Alexita starts school!"

"Cielita, I do not want to see you defer your dreams!"

"But you and Alexita are my dreams!"

CRRRRRRRRACK!!!!!!!!!!!!!!

"Ay!" screamed Ludi, holding on to Pedro tighter than ever. However, terror soon gave way to fascination.

The crashing thunder came almost instantaneously with the lightning. But that lightning! The couple had never seen anything like it before. Zigzagging cloud-to-cloud across the sky, it seemed extra thick. Far weirder still, it split into two parallel bolts.

Streaming out from between those parallel bolts was a dull yet rainbow-colored swirling something-or-another. It reminded Pedro of oil or gasoline swirls he'd seen on gas station cement after a heavy rain. That amoebic whatever-it-was floated drifting right over Pedro and Ludi's heads, then **BANG!!!**, ball lightning. The next thing the couple knew, something dropped to the gravelly roof at their feet. Its greenish glow like a firefly light faded as the first pelting raindrops landed with a hissing sizzle.

"Ouch!" Ludi found it still too hot when she tried picking it up.

"We have to show this to Doña Galleta," said Pedro after briefly torrential rain cooled the mysterious object enough for them to examine closely.

Doña Galleta - Madame Cookie - she was the woman who would be handing over that object to Samantha a year later.

Chapter 2: The First Session

"Everything is the ingredient for a recipe, and everything, each thing, is the product of a recipe. Circles within circles.

"So these chocolate chip cookies are not simply the product of a recipe, no. In addition, they comprise one of the ingredients for the recipe of cooling ambience. They are haunted by a hint of lemon."

Doña Galleta might have added that her voice was another of the ingredients for the cooling ambience; its delicate timbre made Pedro recall wind chimes made from hollowed-out bamboo shoots. Those chimes hung in the lanai of one uncle's home up a hillside overlooking Ponce, Puerto Rico on that small Caribbean island's desert-dry south coast.

"More ingredients for the cooling ambience include spearmint added to your ice tea, and tuna cacti and aloe plants on the window sills. Even fading light from the setting sun is assisting. Waves of refreshing tingles ought to be washing over you, yes."

"Aydiomio," complained Don Placido; he received Doña Rotonda's fierce pinch to keep him from drifting asleep, too refreshed.

"Yes," Galleta nodded, "the recipes are never perfect. Always at least one thing is wrong. The meat might have been marinated for so long that it chews softly tender and flavorful from the grill. First, though, a poor animal had to suffer the ultimate terror and pain. That part of the result is not good. Consequently there are always new recipes.

"I can tell you a little something about this object already," announced Galleta, lifting up before her the gold cylindrical pendant on a bracelet chain. "It is only one of many products from a recipe that ultimately produced a grave tragedy. More than that I cannot say yet, any more than someone who has not tasted one of my cookies can say for certain all the ingredients that went into them. Even someone who has savored my cookies will not be able to say much, if her taste buds are not sensitive enough and she is not sufficiently knowledgeable. But blessed with such gifts, she should be able to accurately reconstruct how they were prepared.

"Likewise, give me enough time for probing with my fingers and deeper spirit, and step by step I should be able to retrieve much of the recipe that accounts for this particular pendant's existence."

"How much time will you need exactly?"

"Yes," nodded Rotonda before Galleta could take up her husband's question, "is urgent to know, because he can't be wasting all evening sitting on this floor. He still has a lot of sitting left to do on his chair at home."

"Aydiomio!"

Galleta tipped her head from side to side, smiling wistfully at both Placido and Rotonda. "For identification of this object's origin," she said finally, "there is a recipe I have to follow. And am not sure how long we will have to keep it in the oven of my intense concentration before we have a well-baked answer. Especially since I prepare them differently each time, have to check my cookies often to make certain they are baked enough, but not too much. Is the same with this object. We have to check often."

"Doña Galleta, have you put the object in your oven of concentration yet? Or were you waiting for our arrival?"

Galleta could hear Pedro's curiosity lift off into excited anticipation when he asked this question. She wondered whether Ludi encircling his arm was merely for keeping him grounded in the figurative sense. Or could there be a more literal meaning, somehow?

Whichever, Ludi also gently rocked Alexandra sucking rhythmically on her pacifier to most dozing effect. And Doña Galleta finally answered, "You should never leave an oven on alone. The same for me; is not safe to make myself the medium for divining the origins of this object without an audience. More important than the danger of something overcooked is the possibility that the oven will somehow catch fire and burn everything. One never knows for sure. A comparable fate could await me if I make this effort unattended. True, certain plant spirits might call out for help. But who would permit themselves to hear their entreaties in enough time?"

"Is interesting," said Ludi's grandma Norma, seated together with the others in a semicircle around Doña Galleta. Norma spoke only after she'd relented from drawing in her lips so much that they couldn't be seen, like someone with their dentures removed.

Pedro sensed Norma was stifling herself, holding back on what she really wanted to say.

"But I have to tell you," Norma went on, "that pendant reminds me of those crazy-large earrings one sees on the street. Could someone have dropped it on the roof? Possibly, Ludi and Pedro, you are not the only people who go there? You have to be careful about maybe encountering prostitutes or drug sellers."

"Abuela," *Grandma*, said Ludi, clearly animate with frustration. "That object," she pursed her lips in the direction of the bracelet with the oversized, mysterious pendant. "I told you where it came from."

Galleta was holding "that object" before her like she could have been a butcher holding up a cut of meat or a fish fillet to make sure it was the one wanted before wrapping.

"There was lightning over our heads that made a big bang. BANG! Like that! Then the object fell from the sky," Ludi patiently recounted.

Norma drew in her lips again before she responded, "I believe you saw ball lightning. I have experienced that sometimes myself. But you know how the thunder rattles the windows when is too near, like in an earthquake? I am only saying that maybe, *maybe* the bracelet was there all the time. You were not noticing it until the thunder from the ball lightning rattled it like maracas, possibly made it dance the merengue with the roof gravel. Then you noticed, yes?"

"Me, I never go up on the roof," announced Ludi's abuelo - grandfather - Típico, like this was one of his proudest accomplishments. Seated on a floor cushion, he tugged on his trousers with the air of a king or sultan. "They can have rats there or who knows what?"

"You should not go on the roof, Tipi. Is dangerous, especially if they see you are so old."

"Ay, caramba, Norma, I just said I never go up there!"

"Yes, yes," Norma patted her hubbie on one knee to calm him down.

"Will we have to pay for using you like an oven, Doña Galleta?"

"Is not psychic hotline, Placido," said Rotonda before Galleta could respond to her husband.

"Aydiomio."

"Me, I never call those 'hotline' numbers. Is too much money for nonsense."

Another grand achievement for Grandpa Típico, Pedro mused.

"You should not call those 'hotline' numbers," cautioned Norma. "They are so expensive. People see these hundred-dollar charges on their phone bills."

"Ay, caramba, I just said I never call those numbers!"

"Yes, yes."

"When something tastes bitter or sour, adding a little sugar works well. A spoon full of honey is even better," counseled Galleta. She was all about soothing and relaxing her guests despite her lack of air conditioning or fans. That was the least she could do for them, an unsettling comparison having occurred to her. Her guests were so many baby birds that she, the mama bird, was feeding. The huge throw pillows and floor cushions were her version of gathered twigs and branches for the nest. But for where was she preparing them to leave that nest?

"You need all of us here to assure you are not starting a fire or something?" Placido asked, wishing a remote control could switch this particular channel of his existence to something else. "You have a TV in the other room where some of us can watch until you finish cooking?"

"Doña Galleta has no TV," explained Rotonda, again speaking before Galleta could offer her own response.

"Aydiomio."

Pedro shook his head and smiled. His stepfather's frustration might not have been expected from his willingness earlier that day to accept Galleta's hospitality. But Pedro knew what lured Placido and most of the others there in the first place. It was the same morbid, shameless fascination by which people slowed down and caused big traffic backups when they were driving past a really bad accident.

Everyone said they joined him and wife Ludi only out of innocent curiosity about this woman who had so insinuated herself into their lives. And in the hope that, as the case turned out, she'd be serving up more of her always delicious cookies. This is what they said. For that matter, Pedro was certain what they also would have said about slowing down as they drove past an accident scene. They would have claimed they were seeing whether they could help. As well, they were insuring they didn't compound the mess by crashing into anyone themselves, the police especially.

Okay, Ludi's husband had to concede, maybe motivation of the decent variety was involved. But he would never forget Placido commenting, "If we smell something strange like a grill that has not been cleaned for years, I hope is not her dead husband rotting in a closet or even her bed!"

"One thing I never do," reacted Típico in an assertive tone to which Pedro wanted to say, *You never leave dead bodies rotting around the house?* But he stifled himself as Ludi's grandfather went on, "I never, never bring food and herbal medicines to people I have not previously met."

"The man is a saint," Pedro whispered, for which he felt Ludi's hand claw deep into his armpit while Grandma Norma cautioned, "Is not a good idea, Tipi, to visit the houses of strangers uninvited, even if you have good food for them. You never know what problem they can make for you."

"Ay caramba, you are not hearing what I just said?"

Yes, Pedro mused, Norma and Típico need to add a spoon full of honey to their recipe, so whatever they are trying to prepare won't turn out so bitter. Although - talk about morbid fascination, talk about slowing down to check for blood at an accident scene - how much less fun would that be?

Anyhow for Ludi and Pedro, Galleta's effort to set an enchanting, refreshing mood was icing on the cake of a Saturday already brimming over with enchantment. Where they were concerned, the second house shown them by the real estate agent could have been plopped down beside Cinderella's castle in Fantasyland at Disneyworld. A low picket fence painted light blue encircled both front and back yard. A driveway meant that no longer would they have to leave their car parked out on the street. No more fear about when the next drunk would sideswipe it then not even leave behind a note taking responsibility. And four bedrooms! "One will be your office, Ludicita, for when you are grading papers and preparing lesson plans."

"And another is for if we ever start work on that barón!"

Something funny happened when they peeked inside one bedroom that felt perfect for Alexandra. "What you think of your new room, Alexita?" Ludi asked her. "You will finally enjoy some privacy, yes precious?"

The whites showed clear around Alexandra's eyes as she cooed and slapped at the air like she actually did understand what her mama said.

For this magical day to conclude with an attempt to solve the riddle of the mysterious object fallen at their feet... Okay, Galleta might have insisted there are no perfect recipes. But Pedro and Ludi would have had a tough time admitting there was the least bit wrong with the particular recipe they'd been experiencing for the past twelve hours. Wouldn't even have mattered, were the mysterious pendant to be explained in purely conventional terms as Grandma Norma proposed.

The young couple did not believe that possible, though. They could have made more of an issue when Norma essentially dismissed their wonderment. However, they were both well past tired of repeating themselves. In fact, they'd lost count of how many umpteen occasions someone scoffed when they recounted the pendant initially glowing whitish green, like a firefly light, and being too hot to handle until rain cooled it off.

Where Ludi and Pedro were concerned, people could scoff all they wanted. Besides, there were the cylindrical pendant's engravings the appearance of Egyptian hieroglyphics. Had that been what they were, well okay, maybe someone bought the artifact at a museum gift shop or some such. However, Pedro gathered from his library research that they definitely were not Egyptian hieroglyphics, or any other known writing system.

Pedro might have conceded that one part of the recipe baked into his day was not so perfect, having to do with his sisters. He took another apprehensive sideways glance at them seated beside their boyfriends. *What are they getting into with these guys? Possibly the reason so many recipes are problematic is that too many people are not looking for as much as they ought to out of this meal of life. When a person is hungry enough, he will settle for worse and worse food instead of holding out for the quality nutrition.*

That's what I fear, that Jerri and Gloria are settling for these machos of the swaggering strut. They know how to pile on men's cologne; can smell them from here. And they also know how to make their shirts seem left unbuttoned as part of their casual attitude, when really they are trying to give the women a "sneak peek."

Of course, Gloria and Jerri complain to Mami they are too uncomfortably warm for anything more than their short-shorts! But clearly they want to sample this recipe for intimacy before its preparation is completed, because their cologne-fueled hunger is driving them crazy! Makes no difference what additional ingredients they mix in, no.

They could as easily be watching a dog chase a cat through an alley, as watching Galleta connect to the spirit responsible for the object from the sky. It's whichever situation permits them to sit nestled together holding hands, ay!

Although – perhaps yet an additional significant imperfection to the recipe for this magical day – Pedro also thought wistfully that maybe his sisters and their boyfriends were enjoying something he and Ludi had lost to an extent. In recent months Pedro noticed how foods tasted blander; he needed them spiced up more, extra pepper and tomato sauce on his beans for the same "kick" they used to give him. Was something analogous to that also happening in his relationship with Ludi? Sharing ever more ambitious new dreams was what they required to light the same spark their mere presence beside one another, holding hands, used to amply ignite?

"Why I need to wear all these bracelets and toe rings, am not sure," commented Galleta already well underway with her mystical task. "But maybe this is like installing an antenna for a TV or radio. Who knows what energy waves are out there not yet understood by even our most brilliant scientists? But, if we were to limit ourselves to only those actions where we understood everything about them, we would not walk, or sing, or see, or breathe, or eat. We would not live. We would not love."

The last toe ring in place on her sandaled feet, Galleta placed a silky, pastel-green blanket center of the semi-circle her several guests made, and unfolded it. "Other time, I remind you that progress towards answers will probably not proceed very rapidly. Like the cookies I prepare, this situation will have to bake slowly at low emotional temperature not to ruin it." On this warning, Galleta made a special point of looking up from her gracefully executed preparations to give Pedro's sisters and their boyfriends a short yet telling stare.

Gloria and her guy averted their gaze from Galleta, holding up their arms protectively as though she tried kicking sand in their faces.

But Jerri held her head haughtily high, sweeping her length of straightened, blond-highlighted dark hair around one shoulder. And how Jerri's guy glanced her way gave Pedro the impression he was deferring to her authority.

Galleta lied down upon the fully unfolded pastel green blanket. Facing the ceiling, she said, "If I am not bringing myself out of the concentration when I start to have problems – and you will know when I start to have problems – please, any one of you, tap me on my shoulder until I acknowledge your presence. Okay? Gracias."

"Aydiomio," Placido complained under his breath; Galleta said "Gracias" before he could answer her "Okay?"

True to her speculation over how her strange feat worked, Galleta lifted and extended her arms and legs straight out at various angles like they were, indeed, television antennas. Then she wobbled them about in the same way, Pedro Perez reflected, a person would adjust television antennas in search of the best possible reception.

Suddenly, Galleta froze with her arms and legs outstretched in odd positions. That's when everyone heard a hissing sizzle like ham or bacon frying in a pan, until Snap! The sizzle abruptly shut off.

Pedro thought he saw a wraith of blue smoke dissipate as quickly as it appeared, about a foot above the pendant Galleta left atop her belly. He recalled puffs of smoke from fireworks flaming out.

Galleta bolted upright to sitting cross-legged on the blanket, and slowly scanned the room with eyes open wide. But when her gaze crossed Pedro's, he was of the creepy notion she did not actually see him.

Somehow, she peered through him.

Then turning her attention ceiling ward, Galleta gaped in wonder. And she reached out as much to grasp as to point at, where Pedro was concerned. "Stupendous glistening sails on spacecraft gliding between the Earth, the moon, and Mars!!" she gasped. "Cosmic clipper ships conducting trans-world trade!"

"When?" Pedro couldn't help blurting out.

"2061," Galleta answered. She could have been on the phone speaking to someone mere miles away rather than decades-of-space-time distant. "A solar-sailed vessel soars gracefully on a wide spiral towards space dock," she continued. "Appears like a flying fish the size of one of those cruise ships that visit Old San Juan. Is beautiful! Solar sails in place of wings! They shine translucent blue from semi-transparent aluminum only two atoms thick held together by electrostatic charge. They are so thin that flashlight-emitted photons make them billow out.

"When the space clipper left Mars a day ago, the force of sun-streamed photons sent it around back of that planet. Then Martian gravity provided a slingshot effect for returning to Earth. After the slingshot, the wings were positioned with their edges facing the sun to minimize photon friction. But now they are slanted like the wing flaps on a jet, to provide braking action. There are tail wings opening up in addition, like a flower blooming. However, they appear comparable to the flukes on a whale's tail. Ay, is so beautiful!" Galleta sighed, pressing her hands against her cheeks in gaping, awestruck amazement. And her eyes could not have opened any wider.

"A transparent geodesic sphere encloses the space station, International Space Station 2," Galleta proceeded despite her visceral reaction. "It protects the station from minor asteroid and space dust impacts. Also, it screens out dangerous cosmic rays, and facilitates easy containment of gas leaks. But now its two hemispheres are splitting open on the smallest hinge, to welcome in the solar clipper.

"Ahh, here is a big, framed photo of International Space Station 2, possibly taken from one of the solar sail clippers. Seeing the space station through its protective sphere reminds me of baby guppies. But rather than internal organs seen through diaphanous skin, there are odd-shaped buildings. Two of them are luxury hotels to where the very rich are transported on a special jet that leaves the atmosphere on gradual ascent rather than shooting straight up like a rocket. Also, a monorail tube connects- Ay, the solar clipper is docking. Its wings have not so much retracted as dissolved with the electrostatic charge shut off. Astronauts have seized Velcro anchors, and are pressing them against winches pulling the ship alongside the dock. Is an incredible sight, those transparent geodesic hemispheres sealing back together in the background."

Encroaching sunset left Galleta's living room increasingly dependent on a corner fluorescent lamp for continued illumination.

Pedro noticed a tiny mobile hung center of the room, featuring various large fish – tuna, dolphin, and swordfish. Lamplight cast their shadows swimming across the ceiling as every tiniest air impact set them in motion.

Pedro wondered: Did those shadows inspire Galleta's flying-fish spacecraft plying oceans of cosmos in a sixty-year-distant future? "Doña Galleta, how are you seeing so many stupendous things?" he asked. "Somehow are you actually inside this 'Space Station 2' of the future, the same time you sit here at home?"

"My host says she is okay, only has a little headache. Possibly is too much excitement for her first space voyage. Another journalist, think he has romantic feelings for her. He is offering to help file her story."

It finally occurred to Rotonda's son Pedro what Galleta's audience was supposed to believe. That somehow, she was experiencing what she described through the eyes of someone aboard the space station. But Pedro was less clear whether she was responding to his question. Or saying what she would have been saying regardless. Did she just coincidentally happen to make a comment that addressed his concern, however obliquely?

Whichever, Placido couldn't hold back any longer. "Caramba," he moaned, as much over finding his left leg asleep as over his frustration with no TV. "Someone can explain for me, please," he went on as he reconfigured his floor cushion seating in search of a more comfortable posture. "What is this, what Cookie Lady is talking about? First there is a sail ship that is a flying fish. Then there is a space station, and someone has a headache. But I hear nothing about the mystery pendant in her lap!"

"Papi, is very strange and maybe very complicated," said Pedro to his stepfather.

Before Pedro could go any further, though, Galleta resumed in Spanish, "Good. This man is supporting my presence better. He has been to the station many times before, and is not preoccupied with a little vertigo."

"And now," muttered Placido, "who is this man who will support Doña Galleta's presence because he has been to the space station before?"

"Ay," gasped Galleta, "people wearing pastel blue uniforms are filing into the room behind this long conference table with a podium at the center. Oh! That's what those clunk-clunk-clunks are from! Magnetic shoes so they don't float in the weightlessness! And members of the audience with camcorder spectacles, they must be journalists. 'Quiet please! We want to make introductions, the captain wants to say a few things, and then we'll take questions. However, the crew is on a tight schedule.'"

Galleta's sudden change in tone included switching from Spanish to English. Pedro gathered she was supposedly channeling the man who was "supporting" her "presence better."

"What 'crew' is this?" muttered Placido anew. "Why Doña Galleta is speaking English? I don't understand!"

"Shh!" Rotonda shished her husband Placido, as sharply as when his snoring woke her up overnight. "You have to be quiet!"

"Aydiomio."

"Everyone is laughing," Galleta continued back in Spanish as though she heeded Don Placido's complaint, "because the last two crew members collided. They arrived minutes ago on the solar sail clipper. The one who entered first, he realized too late he was supposed to come in behind the conference table rather than in front of it. He stopped to turn around while his partner was still hurrying forward. They both dropped their duffle bags when she plowed into him."

Once those last two crew members were seated, the one who entered first craned towards the closest mike.

He said in a deep yet gentle voice, "She's always doing that to me, truly. That's why I'm so thankful we've never been on spacewalk duty together."

After laughter subsided, the other crew member spoke in a voice creamy with Russian accent. "I should have learned my lesson by now. He never knows where he is going."

"Ah, yes, my love, but I make you most comfortable when we get there, yes? Truly, you know I do," he nodded knowingly at his companion.

"Ohhhhhhh," harmonized the press corps in lieu of, *Naughty, naughty!*

"Ladies and gentlemen, welcome to another episode of *Lust In Space*," said the man whose English Galleta resumed channeling. Cathartic laughter in response finally earned him the respectful quiet he required for proceeding. "On behalf of the International Space Exploration and Colonization Task Force, it is my distinct honor and deep pleasure introducing you to the commander for the first manned mission, or should I say the first womanned mission, outside our solar system. Ladies and gentlemen, I give you Captain Helena Taylor and her crew of the Smoke and Mirrors."

Captain and crew stood to a thunderous standing ovation.

*

"She is clapping her hands," whispered Placido. "This means the show is over? She is applauding her own performance so then we can leave? OW!"

"Don't shout like that," scolded Rotonda in a harsh whisper. "You are going to disturb Doña Galleta from her trance before she finishes baking."

"What I am supposed to do when you pinch me so-OW!"

"What I tell you?"

"But- OW!"

"Shh!"

"Aydiomio," Placido complained under his breath.

*

"What a difference five years makes," said Captain Taylor with hand put to forehead, wondering why all the sudden a peculiar sensation had come over her. But she tenaciously resolved to dismiss it as nothing, stage jitters perhaps, as she swept her sandy-shaded hair back behind her ears for the umpteenth time. She could not have known that Pedro and his family were hearing her exact words; Galleta's spirit had moved on to her from the fellow who introduced her. "Five years ago, you couldn't tell my hair was streaking through with gray. But now…" What got the bigger laugh was Taylor adding, "I warned my husband here I'm just no good at standup comedy. No, I'm not ready to introduce him just yet. I'm still thinking of something, um, appropriate." She flashed her beautiful brown doe-eyes his way.

Helena's hubby met the new round of laughter with nods and gestures to the effect of: Yes, he was receiving the grief he deserved.

"In all seriousness," went on Taylor, "five years ago we faced a future full of fear. Had the great English novelist of two centuries ago, Charles Dickens, been present, he might have written: 'It was the worst of times, period. We had nothing before us, period.' Humanity's noblest experiment, the terraforming of Mars into a second habitable planet of our own solar system, failed beyond our most awful imaginings. We populated the newly created Martian oasis with brave pioneers from a neglected inner city neighborhood in the Philadelphia quarantine zone.

"Scarcely three months later, though, a hurricane seemed to blow out of nowhere. We are still struggling to understand. In one terrible night, exactly the sort of storm struck that we thought the carefully cultivated Martian atmosphere had forever made a part of Mars' forbiddingly barren past. Not only did it wreak havoc on the first human settlement, even though situated under a protective dome. That would have been bad enough. But this storm's four-hundred-mile-an-hour winds generated a miles-high funnel cloud. And that funnel cloud sucked out nearly ninety per-cent of the newly generated Martian air, dispersing it to deep space.

"We believe several colonists were vacuumed off the planet's surface as well. We may never know every victim's precise fate. Of course I'm reporting nothing new; for sure, this tragedy has been recounted often enough. But relatives of my husband were among the victims, so we understand how fresh the pain remains for many.

"Of course, the human spirit is endlessly resilient. We endured and survived environmental and economic calamities earlier this century, including a terrible pandemic. And we were prepared to endure and survive again, striving ever forward. Only we received a psychological one-two punch that same year. The dust had not settled out from what little remained of the Martian atmosphere, when an experiment in Earth orbit with an anti-matter photon propulsion system didn't just fail. It also sent an unforeseen radioactive fireball raining down on Europe and wiping out parts of Spain, killing millions. The door on interstellar travel was slamming shut.

"Between the Martian hurricane and the propulsion system disasters, humanity seemed to have cruelly run up against a virtual brick wall. Beyond that brick wall, there would be no going forward. We had reached our limits, portending hopelessness for the steadily increasing number of fellow Earthlings engulfed by wretched living conditions."

*

"Ay Santo," Placido whispered, "I don't understand more than two words. How much more time she speaks in English? And my leg is falling-"

"Sh!" Again, the same harsh "sh" Rotonda used to cut through his snoring at night.

"Ay Santo, what special hell is this? I cannot sleep, I cannot watch TV, I cannot move. I am allowed only to sit, and listen to things I don't understand..."

"You are behaving like a dog," Rotonda whispered admonishingly in Spanish, of course. "A dog sits and listens to people speak in an incomprehensible language for only so much time before he barks to complain of not enough attention."

"Ah, but you know better than a dog, you are superior because you-"

"Sh!"

"Aydiomio."

*

"But there is a saying that probably goes back even longer ago than Charles Dickens. 'It's always darkest before the dawn.' I am proud to call our first officer and lead engineer, Buddy Leung, a close personal friend." Captain Taylor gestured towards Buddy seated beside her husband Chris. He received a round of applause that prompted him to nervously wave hello and laugh like he just got the punch line.

"Dr. Leung and his research team," went on Taylor, "were working on a new aluminum glass alloy. That's when they accidentally discovered an elegantly simple solution to the problem of how not only to travel at velocities approaching light-speed, but considerably faster as well. Dr. Leung's solution is so simple, in fact, that a five-year-old can understand it. Yet our best minds are left thoroughly perplexed.

"As with solar sails, particles of light called photons exert force on the new aluminum glass alloy. But then, Dr. Leung's innovation on the track of something entirely else: He positioned an array of aluminum glass alloy plates at odd angles to one another, forming a maze. Bathing that maze in an electromagnetic field caused the photons to actually bounce through it like they were inside a pinball machine. As a mysterious result, they actually accelerated to astounding multiples of light-speed. At those speeds, those photons pushed against the alloy plates until POOF! The array disappeared to a location an astronomical distance away. A trail of sparklers remained in its wake, like the trail that an activated magic wand is depicted having."

*

"The dogs of Jerri and Gloria have discovered a diversion," Grandpa Típico complainingly whispered this time. "Their hands are tarantulas trying to crawl down the front of our great-grand-daughters' blouses."

"You men are all alike," grumbled Norma, though re-energized by her husband's gripes. That is, re-energized to continue sitting attentively through what otherwise she would have had to concede did seem a tedious waste of time.

"Oh, you want to say," Típico cackled, ready for battle, "none of us men know how to sit doing nothing for-"

"Oh, you men are experts at sitting doing nothing, especially when there are clothes to wash and dishes to clean!"

"Por favor," Pedro said in a loud whisper. "I will translate everything for you later. Is really interesting, but I have to hear the rest..."

"Ay caramba," went Típico's exasperated cry under his breath like the "aydiomio" under Placido's.

*

"Since Dr. Leung's array mysteriously vanished," Galleta went on channeling Captain Taylor, "we have successfully sent mice, a dog, and a chimpanzee out past Pluto and safely back again. As you already know, each of those missions took just a little over a single day. Such research provided the basis for a top secret project over the past three years. With major funding from the Asian, European, and American unions, the International Space Exploration and Colonization Taskforce has completed humanity's response to the dashed hopes and dreams of the Mars Regenesis Project and the European fireball disaster. We have developed the battering ram for what only five years ago seemed the ultimate brick wall barring any future progress in space exploration. Ladies and gentlemen, we intend to rush busting through that wall. If you will turn your attention out the panoramic window..."

Captain Taylor stepped aside, humbly holding wrist by hand behind her back. "I'm sure you're well aware that solar sail clippers and transport shuttles, alike, have been instructed over recent months to studiously avoid traversing a certain region within the space station globe," she went on. "Cloaked security surveillance drones, ghostly unexplained lights, those were among the excuses we spread for that odd protocol. Didn't take a paranoid conspiracy theorist to figure out they were, indeed, excuses for not admitting to something else altogether."

A restless murmur arose like smoke from a smoldering fire. At least that's how the captain's husband Chris would have characterized it.

"Well, that something else was a cloaked spacecraft construction hangar."

Murmurs turned to gasps.

The way Doña Galleta was gazing out on her own audience back in Philadelphia had Pedro straining desperately to somehow see past her.

Forward in 2061, two mag-sail space tugboats emerged from the visible trestle-strewn space hangar. Their compact forms reminded Chris of bumblebees. Both tugboats slowed to a hover over the cloaked construction hangar. They dropped thick cables with splayed-out, flat ends drawn magnetically from random dangling to stopping dead still against an invisible surface. That's when the tugs slowly yet steadily ascended. As they did, their audience realized their cables were lifting an enormous tarp. This tarp quickly resolved from the concealing illusion of star-bejeweled space into the drapery-like wrinkles and ruffles of a dark, shiny-smooth material.

With a sweeping gesture, Captain Taylor said, "Ladies and gentlemen, we give you the Smoke and Mirrors."

The first part of the Smoke and Mirrors into view drew awestruck reactions, even from crew members who twisted around in their seats to look behind them.

"Ay Santo, is so beautiful," Galleta lapsed back into Spanish, setting aside for the moment channeling Captain Helena Taylor's remarks. "I don't know which end I am seeing. But is like a giant rosebud, a rosebud the dimension of an amphitheater. Is even green."

"Zzzzzzzzzzzzzz–"

"Ay, grandpa," Ludi complained in a harsh whisper. "Wake up! Wake up! How you can snore like that while Doña Galleta describes a so-amazing spaceship sixty years in the future?!"

"When is the world not amazing? The beauty of your grandma is always so amazing, too. But at some point I have to sleep, I cannot stay awake admiring her all night."

"Get your nose out of my butt, Típico! When is there not housework? The quantity of housework is so amazing, too, but at every point you have to channel surf!"

"Ow!" exclaimed Placido, pinched crab-claw sharp by his wife Rotonda again.

"You have difficulty sleeping through my beauty?" Rotonda asked.

"Are we not supposed to stay quiet- Ow!"

Slap! Slap! With these two slaps, Pedro's sisters put an abrupt halt to their boyfriends' fondling.

Pedro wondered whether it was just a coincidence, that at that specific time his sisters decided they'd finally had enough. Or... he whispered in Ludi's ear, "I think maybe the ripples from Don Típico's snore are putting in trouble every man within a five-mile radius. Is like a nuclear bomb- Ow!"

"Sh! I thought you wanted to hear the rest of this," harshly whispered Ludi, following up her expertly painful tug on Pedro's ear with mock anger. "You will wake up Alexita. And for the record, your ugliness puts me to sleep, sí señor," although she succeeded this remark with a loving pat on his inner thigh.

"Ay, one end of 'Smoke and Mirrors' is the amphitheater-sized rosebud, and the other is the amphitheater-sized tulip bud," was going on Galleta. "Relative to both buds, the body of the spacecraft is much thicker than a plant stem. They might as well be asparagus buds on both ends of an asparagus stalk. The stalk itself has rows of windows like on a cruise ship, and stabilizer fins like rose-bush thorns."

Pedro scanned the windowsills for a vase of roses. But even where the Doña's numerous plants were cast in shadow, he could not discern anything other than herbs and cacti. Still...

"Ay, is that the prow or the stern? The longer, sleek tulip bud end, maybe that's the prow. And the shorter, squat rosebud end is the stern.

"Ay! This one is leaving for the vacuum toilet. He thinks I have given him a bad case of constipation."

Galleta twitched, appeared to Pedro she experienced the briefest spasm. He sensed she was supposed to have abandoned the constipated person, to resume channeling this Captain Helena Taylor.

"What everyone immediately notices, of course," continued Galleta back in English, "is the remarkable likeness of the mirror array shutdown modes to a rosebud at the rear, and a tulip bud at front. More remarkable still is what you will see when the 'buds' open and the mirror arrays are in full 'bloom.' Those arrays take on an uncanny resemblance to a rose and a tulip.

"The rear end 'rose' provides the power forward, 'pushed' by both sunlight and ambient starlight. During deep-space flight, additional 'push' is provided by an onboard laser hung out the back. Think about how the deep-water lantern fish hangs a chemical light source forward to illuminate its way through ocean bottom darkness.

"Meanwhile, here's the even stranger part. Yes, light is able to make the starship move forward, pushing against its mirror-like glass aluminum alloy plates much like wind pushes against a boat's sails. Plus, accelerating the starship well past light-speed as it bounces through the mirror array maze. But that also means ambient starlight ahead of the starship is actually offering resistance. It's the same kind of resistance you notice when you try walking against the wind or wading against the current.

"That's where the 'tulip' array at the front end of the Smoke and Mirrors starship comes into play. The 'tulip' array acts like a vacuum cleaner. It funnels nearly all starlight ahead of the starship through a cylindrical shaft running the starship's full length, and dumps it out the rear. As a result, inertia is practically eliminated, and the Smoke and Mirrors is sucked forward even faster than the light behind it is already pushing it. Either that, and/or there is some bottleneck effect, like you have when water rushes more rapidly through the narrower portions of a stream bed. The physics are far from fully understood.

"Even less understood is why this funneled light creates a gravitational field.

"Okay, Dr. Spritzer is motioning we have to hurry this along. And I'm getting the feeling many of you want to ask for clarification about the Smoke and Mirrors propulsion system from that five-year-old I mentioned." The captain took advantage of resultant laughter to go on, "I just wanted to note about the rush of ambient starlight sucked through that cylindrical shaft I mentioned, which we formally refer to as the photon exhaust shaft. It solves a century-old problem associated with space flight. It creates an artificial gravity field, albeit only half the gravity found on Earth. To take advantage, we had to design rooms and floors in a pentagonal arrangement around the photon exhaust shaft. Again we're puzzled as to the whys and wherefores, but there you have it.

"Okay, um- Yes, Chris? Ladies and gentlemen, I might as well give my husband his formal introduction now: Officer Christopher Olsen-Taylor, our mental health allsorts specialist."

"My mission is to have fun. Oh, and to make sure my hardworking teamies have a little fun as well. Just wanted to say I was reading about ratios and constants in the known universe. If they'd been some teensy bit different, life would be impossible. It's as though life were meant to be. So maybe this stuff with the mirrors and gravity working out for us is because we were meant to be able to zip about the cosmos."

"Permission to speak freely, Captain?" asked another crew member politely raising his hand. "I can't let that hang out there uncontested… if it's okay with you, of course."

"My command of this crew," said Captain Taylor, surfing on more press laughter, "is already hanging by the most slender of threads. This is Kevin Smith-Park, our second engineer. Have your say, Officer Smith-Park, but keep it brief."

"Thank you, Captain. Chris, I don't mean to give you a public dressing-down," Kevin's voice went hi-pitched with his intensity, "but you really should familiarize yourself with Crueson's extension of the work done by Hawking on alternate universes. The best thinking posits an infinite number of universes, with an infinite number of ratios and constants that don't support life. In that context, the ratios and constants we are experiencing still constitute a random event."

Slap!

"I think," went on Kevin, "my slap-happy better half here, Yoon-hee, wanted to add that I am a random event too, and really should attend spiritual discussion groups with her more often."

"Ladies and gentlemen, this is chief navigator and Kevin's wife, Officer Yoon-hee Park-Smith. Yoon-hee, you didn't request permission to slap your husband; keep up the good work."

"So," Chris proceeded, oblivious to the additional laughter and Yoon-hee's face turning beet red as she tried hiding it in her hands, "isn't it a convenient coincidence we were born into that one universe hospitable to life? Kind-of like buying the winning lotto ticket, isn't it?"

"Yes," said Kevin. "It is positively eerie how our parents didn't give birth to us in a universe where life is impossible."

"Needless to say," said Captain Taylor as a few reporters went, "Ooo," "we won't lack for provocative discussion if any tedium threatens during our mission.

"I might as well finish the introductions. Here are assistant navigation specialist and shuttle pod pilot extraordinaire Tanya Petrovsky and her husband, Ali Magabu, our creature comforts coordinator and general counselor. He'll be in charge of peeling my husband and Kevin off one another if their discussions become, shall we say, *too* entertaining. And last but not least, our medical biochemist Debbie Davis-Murphy and her co-wife Geena Murphy-Davis. Geena is our third engineer."

Debbie smiled faintly with only the smallest nod of acknowledgement.

"The Smoke and Mirrors is built to carry up to five hundred people, but we are going with a skeleton crew on this first mission, just in case there are any surprises our pioneering small critter friends didn't warn us about.

"As for our first mission, we will journey some thirty-two AUs to the Oort Cloud that encapsulates our solar system. There, we will search for a large asteroid where we can establish a combination lighthouse beacon/Hubble Space Telescope 5. This is in aid of extra early warning of any large object on a dangerous trajectory headed towards Earth, as well as preparation for a future mission to another solar system. But in the larger sense, our real task was summed up on the television program, *Star Trek*, nearly a century ago: 'to boldly go where no one has gone before.' We carry the hopes and prayers of humanity with great honor, and greater humility."

*

"Listen, son, will Doña Galleta continue with this spirit transmission for much more time?" Rotonda whispered to Pedro. "What do you think?"

"This Captain Taylor, appears she has completed her speech and is receiving much applause. Maybe Galleta will stop channeling her soon. However, nothing has been said yet that I comprehend refers to our mysterious jewelry from the sky. You are too bored?"

"Ay, no, is our big baby husbands," Grandma Norma shook her head emphatically. "They have the same patience as *una chiquitita* who wakes up hungry. They are about to kick their legs in the air and scream."

"Ay caramba listen, Don Placido," Grandpa Típico half whispered, half cleared his throat, "we obtain no respect even when we are behaving. Here we sit in suspended animation, doing nothing. *Bueno*, if we are going to be accused of committing the crime anyway, we might as well commit it. They think we act like babies? Let us act like babies!"

"I am with you!" nodded Placido. "Let us act like babies!"

"I think that means," Norma whispered to Rotonda, "they are going to leave a little present for us in their diapers."

"What kind of present is that?" Rotonda's question had them both snickering.

"Mami, please," Pedro whispered pleadingly. He wanted his family quiet again so he could continue following Galleta's... What was it? A fabrication? To what extremes did this rare woman go preparing, if it was something contrived? Pedro always had an interest in astronomy, yet never heard or read anything about this "Oort Cloud."

"Why admiring my beauty is not enough for you while we wait for Doña Galleta to complete her recipe?" Rotonda elbowed Placido half joking, half wistfully.

At least that's what Pedro thought while he said, "Please Mami, Papi, a little more time, a little more patience. Then we can judge this experience."

"Aydiomio."

*

"We have to prepare for the final twenty-four-hour countdown," said Captain Helena Taylor as the applause finally subsided and she and her crew retook their seats. "Think there's time to field only a few questions." The captain looked to her crew and Dr. Spritzer for nods of affirmation that she had this straight. She managed this even though a headache was unexpectedly coming on of the sort she was more used to from lots of reading. "Yes," she nevertheless motioned a reporter sitting near the front.

"Captain Taylor, are there any concerns about temporal displacement or other speculated consequences from traveling at light-speed?"

"We found none with our furry animal friends. Onboard video and biorhythm monitors during their test flights did not pick up any signs of undue stress or discomfort.

"I'm sure you've read how physicists have been sent back to the drawing board. Again, what this boils down to is our development of technology having vastly outstripped our understanding why it works. We might as well be those ancient Egyptians, thousands of years ago, who stumbled into inventing the first batteries. They were able to put them to practical use, presumably, while still knowing nothing about electrons. And so..." Captain Taylor shrugged her shoulders and wiped her forehead, wishing she could wipe away an almost dizzying pain as well. "Yes," she nevertheless proceeded to nod and point at another reporter.

"Captain Taylor, a confidential informant has told INBC News that you have received a packet not to be opened until the flight is already well under way. What can you tell us about it? Rumors say it contains instructions for your real mission, that all we have been hearing about is the decoy."

"Oh, that."

Nervous laughter.

"Due to our endeavor's historic uniqueness, I think people are making way more of a procedure considered routine on any other scientific probe where I've played a part. It's not so much a matter of something top secret we can't look at until such-and-such a time. It's too many other concerning details before we can deal with the packet contents. Take the Phobos mission, for example. Kevin, you were with me to Phobos. What was in the packet that time? A high school wind gauge project?"

"Yeah, there was also some crazy stuff about hurling a basketball towards Mars and seeing if it ever achieved orbit."

"So," said the reporter, "it wouldn't be a big deal opening the packet and sharing its contents with us right now?"

"It wouldn't be a big deal if I had that packet in front of me, but I don't. It's already safely tucked away aboard the Smoke and Mirrors, I'm sure. Besides which, I'm not kidding when I say we really do have a lot on our plates. In fact, I think Dr. Spritzer is motioning..."

"Ay, am giving her too much headache," Galleta reverted back to Spanish. "Hope I also don't give her a fainting spell in front of all those people. She is troubled by the last question especially; I am transmigrating to her husband's spirit to see- Ay, he is too preoccupied..." Galleta stood up abruptly, carelessly letting the mystery pendant slide off her lap onto the special blanket laid out on the floor. "Everyone is moving. The reporters are filing their stories on holocams, the crew is leaving and the captain is okay, but I can't concentrate. There are too many at once...I can't focus..."

Galleta took a step towards Pedro, staring wide-eyed directly his way, yet somehow seeing through and past him. Although she then seemed headed for Ludi instead, then Grandma Norma to Ludi's other side. She swung her left foot around in front of her right foot in what appeared like a drunken swagger, her arms reaching out imploringly... "Ay, someone help me; am falling through the tunnel..."

Ludi anxiously rocked Alexita to assure she would remain asleep while Pedro, Norma, Rotonda, Placido and Típico all hurried to their feet.

The two dons excitedly darted their eyes about as they made sure their shirts were tucked in.

Pedro and the two women crowded Galleta to prevent her falling over, possibly hurting herself.

Galleta gripped Pedro's arms. She held on for dear life as Norma and Rotonda frantically tapped her on both shoulders, and Rotonda said, "Is okay, is okay; your friends are here and God loves you." Yet for the panic still possessing her, "I am falling more and more rapidly through the tunnel," they might as well have been tucking in their clothes like Placido and Típico. They felt helpless.

"The pendant! The pendant!" shouted Pedro despite uncertainty whether he was experiencing a flash of insight or sheer desperation. "Someone hand it to me!" no sooner saying this than Gloria obliged. Whereupon he fought Galleta's terror-driven iron grasp on his arms to place the mystery object up against her belly, over where her navel was hidden. A sizzly, electrical crackle ensued, not unlike a cracked whip, followed by a puff of faint blue smoke that dissipated the moment it appeared.

Galleta slumped against Pedro, finally letting go his arms.

"One can say I put myself in the oven but that afterwards, like any other food, I wasn't very well able to let you know when I finished baking," explained Galleta while Pedro gently set her back down on her blanket. She resumed a reclined position, though this time without elevating her arms and legs like they were TV antennas being adjusted to tune in whichever station. This time her limbs, while still outstretched, lay limp. They created an impression for Pedro of Galleta having just been washed ashore, how she might have appeared after fighting tremendous currents.

"Doña Galleta," Pedro knelt down beside her, "you are not needing to answer now if you are too tired…"

"Let her rest, my handsome," Ludi firmly patted her husband on the shoulder in what he unmistakably knew was her insistence they leave.

"Is okay," said Galleta. "Impulsively impatient your Pedro might be, but his gentle nature is still soothing as my aloe plants."

"This can wait if too much for answering now," said Pedro ignoring Ludi's increasingly insistent taps. "But, have you discovered the recipe for what went into preparing the jewelry from the sky? It is something with spaceships in the future? I can assume you are aware what you said while your spirit was, um, investigating?"

A frown compromised the corners of Galleta's smile as this time when she shifted about her limbs, she reminded Pedro of a particular baby chick. He'd seen the poor young thing sprawl about in dirt after having fallen out of its nest, perhaps in a premature effort at flight. "I remember everything, I think," she moaned more than spoke. "But we are not to where we can learn about the jewelry yet. Appears this recipe has many steps. Sorry for saying, I have to cool off for some time before I can safely put myself back into the special oven."

"This is so confusing- Ay, Ludi, these are my final words for now, okay?"

Ludi had latched onto Pedro's shoulder and given it a forceful tug.

"Is no problem," assured Galleta.

"This is so confusing," Pedro repeated. "First, I think that somehow you tasted the pendant to determine its ingredients. But then you are- You say you were baking."

"It is like this, Pedro: you cannot permit one way of seeing the world to preclude seeing it other ways."

Chapter 3

"You filmed this yourself, Shelly?" asked Captain Helena Taylor while reading the handwritten label affixed to an otherwise blank holodisc container:

Route 1 South, Santa Cruz to Santa Barbara

In the captain's study aboard the Smoke and Mirrors, Helena and husband Chris were on a holophone with their daughter before final countdown to launch.

"I'm really impressed," commented Helena, not waiting for her daughter's response. "But hope you weren't biking too close to any of the quarantine areas."

"Mom!"

Helena couldn't hear her daughter's foot-stomp. But she did see the grainy holographic projection of her daughter's hiking boot disappear into the turquoise translucence of her study's rubbery floor.

"How close you think lower San Francisco is to Santa Cruz?" daughter Shelly vented more than asked. "Or east LA is to Santa Barbara? You and Dad are the ones who keep complaining about walling off half of humanity inside those damned no-zones!"

"Okay, sorry!" Helena held up her hands defensively, not having meant to agitate her daughter so much. Moreover, she feared that Shelly could unwittingly scratch at a still-fresh wound, namely the fate of some of Chris's relatives. "You know how a mother worries."

"I know how *you* worry, Mom! You and Dad are the ones hitching a ride aboard a rainbow out past Pluto. *I* should be the one worried sick! But don't stress over my stress. I diverted myself, umm, let me put it this way: Hope you don't run your stationary holo-bike off its stand once you see a certain cetacean menagerie I programmed rising out of the Pacific."

"What about my tape, Shel?" asked Chris in mock despair, turning a different container over and over. "There's no label even!"

"You *did* bring your holo-golf set with you, Dad?"

"Okay, here we go," Helena grumbled.

"Happy early birthday, Daddy: Pebble Beach!"

Chris contorted his lips into a frown like he was going to cry, and with tearful voice wailed, "I love you, man-Whoops! Wo-man!" Then he rushed into an impossible embrace of Shelly's holographic projection.

"Oooo, Daddy, stand back! This is like having my body invaded by a ghost!"

"You know your father won't be able to spend much time holo-golfing. In fact, I might be putting him in charge of a high school project. It's something to do with the effects of long-term artificial gravity on mice."

"But, but 'lena hon', you told me yourself what a big chunk of time physical exercise requires on long-term flights! And I've read that holo-golf works especially well to minimize bone loss under partial gravity conditions."

"Those studies were with zero gravity and gyroscopic low gravity. From the animal test voyages, we know with certitude we will be experiencing steady three-fifths G. Sufficient exercise will not consume nearly so much of our schedule. Certainly not three hours for holo-golf. Also a big relief, we won't have to clomp around in these magnetic boots all day, or worry about a cloud of pee spray drifting into our faces. My biggest concern, Shelly, will be your father ever again roping me into standup comedy."

"That gray hair thing did have Daddy written all over it."

"Just hoping no one took offense; didn't occur to me until after the words slipped out that someone might think I was making light of the Mars disaster."

"Oh, c'mon, Helena. If anybody should have taken offense..."

"Okay, sorry! Um, you know, Shelly," went on Helena, anxious to change the subject, "your gifts remind me of when you were a little girl and we took you to the beach. You must have packed away half your room, dolls and games and what-not. But once at the shore, you left most of it untouched. There were too many other exciting things.

"Well here we are, on our way out of the solar system into the Oort Cloud, what a funny name. And we have all this stuff to bring along, lots of security blankets from home as in: home planet."

"Mom, I hope you and Daddy discover as much fun stuff out there as I found at the beach, so you don't unpack most of your toys either."

"Exactly."

Helena and her daughter rushed into an embrace, laughing tearfully at its impossibility. Absolutely no sensation could be experienced from the grainy holographic image each tried to enfold.

Shelly stepped back first from this cruel ultimate in thwarted closeness. Whereupon she mischievously thrust her hand through her mother's tummy so it emerged out her back. "Boo!" she said. "Daddy, remember you can't do this actually beside Mom like you are."

"The last time I tried, got my hand stuck in her belly button."

"Dare I even ask about your chores, Shelly? Your room and the laundry room?"

"Mom..."

"How many minutes does it take to program the housebot?"

"The last time Howby, uh, you know this: It mixed everything together and my favorite blouse came out looking batiked! I promise you, I *promise* you, once I finish that paper on quarantine rehab models, room cleanup will be my first priority."

"So when we return in two weeks…"

"Two weeks?!?! You'll get all the way out there and back that fast?"

"Don't sound so disappointed! We are provisioned for a year, just in case microid impacts unexpectedly degrade the mirrors to the point we have to limp home on conventional mag sails. But we're not expecting that. Now about those chores…"

"Sorry, Daddy, I tried to change the subject."

"Ah, yes, your father; almost forgot about *his* chores."

"Well played, pal! Well played," Chris slow-clapped daughter Shelly.

"Christopher Olsen, *please* tell me you've at least cleared the living room and dining room of those dusty piles of records and CDs. I seem to remember a few bare spaces left on the floor in your office. And oh, yes, here's a novel idea: Have antique shipments made directly to your store instead of home! Maybe I should program Howby for a search-and-destroy pulverization task!"

"Helena. 'lena hon'. Remember what you said about pretending. Even had I finished sorting through them… and you know when I was on spaceflight training, I had no one to man the shop. But think of it this way."

Helena's long face looked to her hubby even longer as she closed her eyes and shook her head.

"Suppose I had gotten to it," continued Chris. "Suppose I'd taken every last vinyl record out of there and had

Howby do a dust-and-vacuum. That would have been mere pretense of neatness and organization, not the real thing."

"I'd gladly settle for pretense."

"Mom, Dad, I love you, bon voyage. Really have to get back to that paper."

"And miss the rest of this conversation?" said Chris. "We love you too. We'll do voice-only on our return so we don't accidentally come barging in on you and Tony."

"Daddy!!"

Knock! Knock!

As Shelly's image shut off, Chris opened the door. Buddy Leung greeted him with one of his nervous laughs, like it was supposed to be funny that, surprise, he'd appeared at the captain's study.

"Yeah, shouldn't these doors slide open like they do in the old sci-fi flicks, instead of swinging on hinges?!" Chris asked, as usual reaching for something to warrant his best friend's jolliness.

Only to be met, also as usual, with an even bigger outburst.

Chris was left nonplussed, wondering whether Buddy ever really truly enjoyed anything beyond his genius-level fascination with space travel engineering. Were his expressions of amusement an act? Were they a show as illusory as the holographic images? In a pathetic attempt to seem more sociable than he actually felt, did they mask his impatience to be back at work? Or, the other extreme, did he find the work to which he had committed himself pure hellish drudgery? Whenever he got away from it for any social interaction, he really did enjoy himself that ridiculously immensely much?

"Any chance you brought aboard part of your store?"

"Not the store as such," said Chris. "I did bring aboard some new stock for review. And of course all the old stock is on my card in case there's something you want to add to yours. Anything in particular you're looking for?"

"So you're going to be leaving messes all over the Smoke and Mirrors now? It's not that funny," Helena grumped as Buddy guffawed like she'd just hatched one of the better punch lines.

"If there's something you'd recommend, maybe once we're comfortably underway I'll give it a listen. Then who knows..."

"I could make a little money on this trip beyond what the agency is paying us."

"Right," Buddy laughed like the sidesplitting jokes just weren't quitting.

Sometimes, including this time, a creepy question came over Chris. Namely, did Buddy see their friendship, including steady patronization of his used music shop, as a big favor for him? As opposed to Buddy actually getting much out of it for himself? Again, this came under the heading of wondering if all enjoyment and satisfaction was an illusion where Buddy was concerned. That is, once he left the realm of space-travel engineering. *Okay,* Chris told himself like he'd told himself so many times before, *maybe I'm way too paranoid; nobody twisted this guy's arm to enter my shop in the first place, or to buy so many records and CDs over the years when card downloads were so much easier. Eighteen years, and I'm still wondering where I stand with him? And besides all the music stuff, we haven't taken enough golf trips? He even introduced me to Helena and got me aboard this spacecraft over the objections of a whole bunch of very powerful people. With all he's done for me, don't I at least owe him the respect of not doubting his sincerity? It would help maybe if I didn't keep wondering about...*

"Helena, I could come back at a better time. We're leaving so soon, um… Sorry guys, there's no reason I can't just use the flat-screen phone once we're en route; we'll have a few hours before we're out past Mars, um…"

"Buddy, would you like a little privacy to holophone Cathy?"

Captain Helena Taylor sounded to her husband Chris as cut-through-the-crap cool as Buddy sounded absurdly apologetically awkward, especially for a person who invented breakthrough spaceflight technology. She did wince, though, as Buddy nervously laughed, "That would be okay? Here, why don't you stay a minute? I'm sure Cathy would want to wish everyone well."

"You know, Buddy, we always could have used a second geologist," said Helena while her perplexing friend and work associate punched in his wife's phone number.

For Buddy and Cathy's marriage going on ten years, Helena had never known them to be together more than seven days at a time. Months-long separations were not uncommon, with Buddy seemingly seeing more of her husband Chris than of Cathy. There were all his shopping visits to Chris's store, not to mention their golf trips.

Helena didn't wonder much about Buddy's so-easily-prompted laughter, aside from occasionally finding it irritating. However, she did give considerable thought to this conjugal union of his. Why did Buddy end up apart from Cathy so often? Was it more than accidental? Was he, were they avoiding a close-enough look at their marriage to realize they had nothing going beyond sexual compatibility? Their relationship might as well be a holo-image?

On the other hand, especially given Helena's own circumstances, who was she to judge? If Buddy and Cathy's peculiar arrangement made them happy…

"Gee, I think she would have loved that," remarked Buddy, no laughs this time, like the idea of Cathy joining the Oort Cloud mission had never occurred to him before. "But I'm not sure she could have gotten out of her commitment to that Martian tectonic plate- Cathy!" chuckled Buddy.

A typically grainy three-dimensional image of Cathy James-Leung bulged from the sixteen-inch holophone screen, and then ballooned to full adult size.

"Have my shoes sunk into the floor as far as yours?" asked Cathy while eschewing a frustratingly sensationless hologram hug in favor of adjusting her holophone's vertical control knob.

"Always something, isn't it?"

Chris couldn't help suspect that Buddy's laughter expressed relief over having the trivial technical problem to fuss about.

"Cathy?"

"Oh, hi, Helena, *Captain* Helena Taylor! What an honor talking with the captain of the first light-speed spacecraft during the, uh, you're in final countdown, right?"

"A little over an hour and a half left. Cathy, I was telling Buddy we could have used a second geologist for this mission. You know the whole couples' orientation, in case we get stuck..."

Cathy could not have looked more confounded had Helena seriously asked her to eat the holophone, Chris imagined.

"But I wouldn't miss my Buddy if I did that," Cathy said finally, like that should have been obvious.

"I think that was the whole idea," said Helena.

"But I like being missed," said Buddy turning beet red, especially his ears.

"Sorry, guys, I really wanted to give you a few minutes of alone time with Buddy here," Captain Taylor nodded Buddy's way, "to tell you how much fun he's having missing you, Cathy. But our holophone is lighting up from a high priority transmission that's probably- Oh, Mr. President!"

Cathy's image abruptly drained out of view. American Union President Andrew "Andy" Carey swelled off the holoscreen in her place, only his upper half visible, floating mid-air. "You must be Captain Helena Taylor," he said. "I just want to say what a thrill- Oh, done it again, haven't I? So disconcerting to see just part of someone in a holographic projection, isn't it? I received the same queasy look from the French governor yesterday that you folks are giving me."

"It's nothing, Mr. President," said Captain Taylor. "We constantly have to remind ourselves the holophone only conveys what is associated with body heat signatures..."

"Oh, it's something. I might as well punch up graveyards to haunt a few tombs while I'm at it. With the old cell phone, I was so used to sitting behind my desk," the president shook his head. "There, is this better?" Having moved out from behind his desk into full view of his holophone, he was turning all the way around as though modeling his woolen plaid vest.

"Much better, Mr. President."

"Great!" President Carey slapped his hands together and vigorously rubbed his palms. "We know you have to be getting going soon on your final launch sequence. I just wanted a few minutes to chat with some real heroes."

"Wouldn't call us heroes, Mr. President," said Captain Taylor while Buddy laughed like the president had also joined the ranks of top standup comedians. "Those little furry critters sent into deep space ahead of us, they took all the real risks if they but knew."

"Well, maybe there are some things you still don't know."

Oblivious to the dead-serious look Helena and Chris saw flash across President Carey's face, Buddy guffawed anew, treated Carey's remark as yet another hilarious punch line.

"Mr. President, this is my husband, Chris Olsen, and perhaps you've already seen Buddy Leung here nab a few headlines?"

"How wouldn't I know both of them? Buddy, if I can call you that?"

"Of course, Mr. President."

"That's one tight-knit little family you have on board. My chief of staff, Daniela Sanchez," Carey motioned behind himself with his thumb, "she tells me you would have refused signing on this mission unless Helena Taylor was made Captain. Not to say, Captain Taylor, you are anything *but* the best person for this job. I am in awe of your résumé."

"Thank you, Mr. President."

"Mr. President, I strongly urged the space agency," Buddy chuckled on utterance of "urged." "I urged they push Captain Taylor to front of the line. Her extensive flight experience has included, if you remember, the emergency launch of an antique shuttle strapped to those dangerously explosive old booster rockets. More importantly, she alone of all the possible candidates was on hand for every one of the mirror array test flights. She even helped design and implement deep-space retrieval of the rodent-carrying 'donuts' so we didn't have to keep cratering the moon."

"Not to mention avoiding Mickey Mouse graveyards," added Chris.

While Buddy laughed as though comic genius had struck again, President Carey merely nodded and said, "Ah, yes, entertainment director Chris Olsen. Do I understand you connected to these wonderful people through your record and CD store? Speaking of antiques..."

"Buddy stumbled into the shop some twenty years back."

That was another big punch line, where Buddy was concerned. "I was wondering what it was," he stopped laughing for long enough to say, "and the guy wouldn't leave me alone until I bought *Close to the Edge* by Yes."

"Yes?"

"Yes, Yes!" Buddy laughed yet again.

"They were a rock group who informed their music with classical symphonic sensibilities. Must have recorded for over sixty years, and not sure their grandkids aren't still at it. *Close to the Edge* was one of their early masterpieces from the 1970's," explained Chris while Helena checked her watch.

"So Buddy, you got back at Chris by introducing him to Helena? Or you were getting back at Helena for something she did?"

Chris gathered from the president's tone that he'd also like to get back at him. Here they were on the eve of humanity's first flight outside the solar system, at light-speed no less. Why should he, president of the United Americas, have any of that time wasted on a mini-dissertation about an archaic music group few cared much about?

"No," Buddy's laugh petered out on a bit of a defensive edge. "I thought they might enjoy one another's company, and here we are nearly two decades later..."

"Buddy looked around at how neat I kept everything," said Captain Taylor, "and thought he needed to bring a little mess into my life." Sensing Chris's discomfort, Taylor shook his wrist as in: *Don't take any of this too seriously. Snap out of it!*

Chris wished that instead, she had patted his hand reassuringly.

"So here you are, Chris, with these two pretty special people, and again, they've made you entertainment director in charge of 'allsorts.'"

"Yes, Mr. President," said Chris, resisting an urge to add: *They must be pretty special, giving an idiot like myself an opportunity such as this. If you had been in direct charge of the space agency, you'd have had none of it.* "When I'm not showing them card tricks, my better half will have me manage some of the selected high school projects."

"With your interest in 1970's music, don't know if you've paid any attention to popular turn-of-the-century television," said President Carey. "But I was one of the winners, alllll the way back in 2021, of *Survivor*. Think they started their run right around 2000. Learned a lot from that show, about teamwork with a group of total strangers. Good preparation for my service in the navy. The difference, though, my fellow sailors weren't meeting regularly to vote the weakest character off the ship. There was Oscar, but he was the dummy. That's what we named the dummy for the man-overboard drills."

"Yes, Mr. President, sir." Chris wanted to add: *Think I know who would be your first choice for dummy to toss overboard from the Smoke and Mirrors.* He self-consciously rubbed his days-old cheek stubble.

"Chris, *and* Helena and Buddy, your bigger American family is counting on you to make us proud. Like you said, Captain Taylor, you're carrying a lot of our hopes and dreams. And hey," the president threw a hand in the air, trying to look as nonchalant as possible, "your ship isn't armed, so don't run into any of those little green men that turn out to be real bad guys after all."

"Yes, Mr. President, referring to our cultural history again," said Taylor, "we aren't prepared to fight *Star Wars*."

"That's right. No one can accuse us of venturing forth into the cosmos with sabers rattling. Wait! If you can hold for another minute, we have a special treat for you. My in-house techno-freaks assured me this will patch through…"

Buddy, Chris and Helena puzzled over the president appearing surprised over something or someone they couldn't see. That is until suddenly, a second holographic image presented beside him to which he bowed and said, "Ko-nee-chee-wa, President Toyozumi."

"Good afternoon, President Carey. Good afternoon, crew members of world's first starship, Smoke and Mirrors."

"President Toyozumi of the Asian Union," Helena added just in case either of her sidekicks didn't know. "This is a special honor."

Mayuko Toyozumi regaled President Carey and company with her extravagantly appointed outfit. A Chinese-influenced high collar topped off a pastel-blue fusion of the Korean hangbok with the Japanese kimono. Also, her raven black hair hung in ringlets round her ears, what hadn't been woven into a tight bun.

President Toyozumi bowed at Captain Taylor then said, "On behalf of entire East-Asian Basin, is special honor for me wishing you and your crew most pleasant, safe, and productive journey to outer limit of solar system. I so like in your press conference when you speak of carrying hopes and prayers of all people. A successful mission opens way for journey to habitable planets in other solar systems. Maybe there are worlds of more close approximation to gravity of our Earth where terraforming is not so dangerous. However," she held up her right index finger most emphatically, "we must not balance all our wishes on back of possibility that may not be strong enough to carry that weight. We must, I think," spoke the Asian Union president in a breathlessly urgent voice, "work today, tomorrow, and day after that for reintegration everywhere of quarantined communities."

"President Toyozumi," said Carey, "I always admire your lofty goals. They are a beacon of inspiration around the whole world."

"Not so many decades ago President Carey, my goals were not considered lofty. My goals were...status quo. Barriers to advancement for world's poorest citizens were formidable enough in the psychological, economic, and nutrition arenas. They were not also physical, electrified, barbed wire barriers dwarfing the Wall of China in their combined distribution."

"Captain Taylor, I understand your chief navigation officer is Yoon-hee Park-Smith. She came from what part of Korea?"

"Pusan, Mr. President. A beautiful beach resort town, she says. I'd have her tell you herself, only she's poring through the final launch sequence checklist even as we're speaking. But I do know she and her hubby go snorkeling there whenever they have time off, it seems."

"Must talk to her about that, find out how their coral reefs compare to our Florida Keys reefs. Anyway, didn't I hear they adopted a young man from the struggling part of her hometown, and took him out of quarantine?"

"Think his name is Dae Hyun, Mr. President; he's staying with Yoon-hee's parents during our flight."

"And isn't Ali Magabu your counselor guy? He's from Cairo originally, isn't he?"

"Two people saved from quarantine, President Carey. How is expression? Two down, four billion to go?"

"President Toyozumi, you continue to be the planet's conscience."

"That would be if my conscience were all the planet had. But most fortunately, is only one grain of sand on that most important beach."

"Point well made, Madame President, with your usual poetic grace. And I think there are enough grains of sand represented here, between yourself and the crew of the Smoke and Mirrors, to choke an oyster."

"I would hope, President Carey, you are not excluding own self from sandbox."

Once a flourish of diplomatic gestures brought this holographic transmission to a close, Helena, Chris and Buddy spontaneously sighed relief. They might as well have been holding their breath ever since the president's holographic image ballooned out of the holophone.

In any event, they clomp-clomp-clomped their magnetic boots out the door of Helena's office, en route to their respective stations.

Captain Helena Taylor wanted to put the holo-transmission behind her, put everything behind her, and treat this mission almost like she was going on vacation. This should have proven easy enough, as much as she marveled over her circumstances. Simply proceeding down the hallway from her office to the navigation room, she still found the starship's design amazing.

As on any sea-going vessel, floors ran the length of the Smoke and Mirrors, from stem to stern. But they weren't simply stacked one atop the other, from the bottom of the starship upward. Rather, they were arranged hexagonally around the cylindrical photon exhaust shaft, in three concentric layers like tree rings. This meant someone standing the opposite side of the exhaust shaft from Helena stood upside down relative to her.

The exhaust shaft ran centrally through the starship's "stalk," conveying from the "tulip" mirror array in front to the "rose" mirror array in back. Such an arrangement took maximum advantage of the gravity "shed" by photon exhaust. And that exhaust resulted from light bouncing between special mirrors bathed in an electromagnetic field. Somehow, mysteriously, light was thereby caused to favor material particle existence over immaterial wavelength existence.

And how appreciative Helena kept feeling over "shed" gravity! She'd endured weightless spacecraft as well as gyroscopic test modules that employed centrifugal gravity. What special joy was that, no longer needing clumsy magnetic boots? Nor having to float from rung to rung worrying about bumping her head into something? Yet she could still look out a window or at the view-screen on the navigation bridge, and enjoy the view. No more suffering motion sickness nausea inside gyroscopes, as a result of watching distant constellations wheel in and out of sight at a dizzying rate.

Of course there was also the little matter of the mission itself. There was the sense of higher purpose, blazing the path for sooner rather than later exploring nearby solar systems in search of other hospitable planets. Besides Earth, that is. Eventually, maybe such planets would take pressure off the Earth's limited resources from an ever-growing population.

And the more immediate goal continued to loom large, expanding the early warning system for tracking dangerous asteroids and comets.

Between magical marvels and hugely important tasks, Helena should have been able, comfortably, to put the rest behind her. But maybe the Asian Union President's apprehension would turn out well-founded. Rather than playing an important role in the alleviation of human misery, maybe the Oort Cloud light-speed mission would simply amount to a distraction. Another distraction. Aside from dealing with potential asteroid threats, might as well be a vacation, an obscenely extravagant vacation.

To focus on their mission, weren't Captain Taylor and company doing the equivalent of a typical child told to clean their room before going out to play? Mightn't they as well be shoveling toys helter-skelter into the closet? And wasn't Helena's husband leaving their home littered with antiques the least of it? Weren't they leaving for later a far more serious mess of a civilization? Fully half its citizens living in abject misery strictly cordoned off from the rest? When the hi-tech quarantine walls started going up some fifteen years earlier, wasn't that tantamount to throwing a huge portion of humanity into the closet rather than compassionately addressing their needs?

Helena recalled how bitterly her parents complained, especially when several protesters were added to the quarantine. The way her late Dad put it, the prosperous fraction of society had essentially erected one overarching gated community. Meanwhile politicians assuaged their guilt by offering empty assurances that eventually the world would be reopened for everyone. Big whoopty-dos were made out of people "rescued" from quarantine, amnesty offered some protesters, and the occasional act of conscience when someone or a group of people voluntarily "went over the fence."

President Carey apologized about presenting with an upper torso holo-image only, insisting "it is something." But meanwhile, he unabashedly presided over the construction of additional sound-proofing barriers. People outside the quarantine could live that much more oblivious, if they chose, to cries of agony from within.

With as hurried a pace as possible weighed down by magnetic boots, Captain Helena Taylor clomp-clomp-clomped onto the navigation bridge. There she took her centrally located seat. She remembered old *Star Trek* reruns from when she was a kid, watching Captain James T. Kirk take his seat on the Enterprise.

What really lifted, rescued Helena from her earthly cares was contemplation of the panoramic view-screen set before her. That screen displayed images channeled from camcorders mounted behind special one-way mirrors in both the fore and aft mirror arrays. How weird was that going to be, seeing starlight from ahead of the Smoke and Mirrors funneled into the photon exhaust shaft? At light-speed and beyond, was all light ahead of the Smoke and Mirrors going to converge into a central beam?

Captain Helena Taylor knew from test flights that witnesses observed what they labeled stardust. A steady stream of sprinkly, multi-colored flecks of light issued from the photon exhaust shaft.

Yes, there would be plenty to gape and gawk at. But exactly because of that, Captain Taylor found herself reflecting: *We can embrace holographically from thousands of miles apart. Yet the best we can do for the world's teeming desperate masses is essentially lock them away so they don't spoil the fun. Heaven help us if, as the Asian Union's leader frets, the salvaging-humanity aspect of this mission is nothing more than a flimsy, ultimately unworkable pretext. And even if we do discover other habitable worlds, what's next? Are we just going to spread our mess there as surely as Chris has spread his CD mess from his office to the family room?*

Far from being heroes, as President Carey would have it, maybe we are just running away from confronting our problems head-on. We're simply off to play with our new toys. Our great great ancestors ran away from misery and persecution in "the Old World," only to massacre Native Americans and enslave Africans in "the New World." Hmm, maybe there's a pep talk in that mission package we can't open until we're out past Jupiter. For sure, wouldn't the space agency be delighted to know the thoughts bouncing around the head of their mission commander?

Mag-sail tugboats ferried the Smoke and Mirrors outside the space station complex's protective shell.

"EM fields enabled, Kevin?" Helena asked, finally lost in the moment, finally completely distracted by such large-scale toys.

"EM fields enabled, Captain."

"Buddy, are the bud casings peeled open?"

"Tulip and rose mirror arrays are fully exposed, ready for deployment bloom, Captain."

"Yoon-hee, you have charted an unobstructed course for 30 AUs, that away?" Helena motioned forward with an almost dismissive hand gesture.

"All twenty-eight-hundred-million miles, Captain, include a close flyby of Mars, a zigzag around the orbital plain of the asteroid belt, and a close flyby of Neptune."

"Chris..."

Yoon-hee, Kevin, Buddy, Tanya, the whole crew looked Chris's way. They wondered what possible role Helena's hubby could have in the launch sequence.

"...are you behaving yourself?"

"Aye-aye, Cap'n!" Chris saluted.

Laughter quickly subsided, with Kevin shaking his head in a mix of bemusement and disgust. Then Helena took a deep breath, exhaled, and said, "Buddy, give us the early morning bloom, and let's pull the rabbit out of the hat. And any other metaphors we can mix in."

Buddy chicken-pecked his display panel before announcing, "Captain, fore and aft mirror arrays are unfurled twenty-two percent."

"Yoon-hee, fore view on screen."

"Nay," Yoon-hee answered in Korean with *of course* in her voice.

Convoluted, paper-thin "tulip petals" from the mirror array not yet in full bloom framed the fore view of far-distant stars ahead.

"Captain, we don't appear to be accelerating," said Buddy.

"Aft view, Yoon-hee," a rattled Captain Taylor ordered. She resisted temptation to answer Buddy's distressing observation with: *Don't come crying to me; this is your invention.* Not to mention a sinking feeling maybe they'd just gotten themselves cast adrift on a trillion-dollar boondoggle.

"There's our problem, Captain," said Buddy matter-of-fact. "That mag-sail tug has been eclipsing- Wow!"

As the tug, on return to Velcro dock inside the space station dome, got out of sunlight's way, the Smoke and Mirrors lurched violently. Captain and crew would have been thrown from their seats, sent floating about the command center bouncing off the walls, if not for their magnetic boots and seat belts. But no sooner the unexpected turbulence than the photon-powered spaceship shot smoothly quietly forward. The aft view-screen revealed fairy dust exhaust from funneled starlight burying the mag-sail tug silhouette in a foamy cascade of glitter. And as Buddy predicted, initial acceleration to one-fourth light-speed faded down the blinding sun to a beautifuly lavender, rapidly shrinking orb.

"Captain, Dr. Spritzer with a voice only."

"Patch him through on the intercom, Yoon-hee."

The navigation bridge filled with cheers and applause emptying out of the intercom. And then even louder, "Captain Taylor, we don't want to distract you and your crew from this important phase. However, despite the celebrating you hear going on behind me, there's some concern over what we just saw when you deployed the mirror array. Was that a spatial distortion illusion we would require a doctoral thesis to understand? Or were you folks rocked around a bit?"

"It did get more exciting than we bargained for," said Taylor. "Think my first engineer has an explanation. Buddy?"

Buddy's laughter expressed a combo of nervousness and relief. "Through, uh, nobody's fault, a mag-sail tugboat fully eclipsed the sun from our perspective. But of course the tugboat kept moving, just like the moon keeps moving during a lunar eclipse. The changing shadow boundary made for an uneven photon impact against the partially bloomed mirror array. That led in turn to our abrupt jolt."

"Which *was* something we were expecting," Captain Taylor addressed Buddy more than Dr. Spritzer, seeking reassurance. *Please don't tell me the unexpected, unexplained has already happened to us before we've even really started.*

Buddy's laughter this time stemmed from genuine amusement. The punch line, to Helena's continued unsettlement, was her bravado assertion they had anticipated what occurred. As in: *Yeah, right, of course, uh-huh.*

"We did believe, um, I believed..." Buddy picked through his words with deliberate slowness; he was about to contradict the captain, his friend, in front of essentially an entire planet. "I was confident, too confident obviously, that any conceivable unevenness in photon distribution would smooth out quickly. That is, too quickly for any significant hull shudder from either the impulse or braking mirror array modes. At least the event ended before I could try any adjustments. Uh, what we might liken it to, if you're a golfer, ha! ha!" Buddy laughed nervously. "You know how you can think you addressed the golf ball perfectly, but then you have it slice off wildly? That's due to your club diverting ever-so-imperceptibly slightly from the ideal swing path."

"Ah, yes, golf," Captain Taylor sighed with weary disgust unnoticed amidst the amusement over Buddy's analogy both shipboard and at Spritzer's end. Speaking of distractions from really helping the world's teeming suffering masses, how much more distraction could there be than Buddy and her husband's endless chatter over what they did on practically every shot? Not to mention the hours it took them to play a round of that stupid game? So was this what their mission would turn into? Would it consist of nothing but endless chatter over the glitches as well as the trivial minutiae of their accomplishments? Would it simply be a fun story to follow, which incidentally might take certain people's attention off their personal misery just enough to keep them docile? That is, as opposed to erupting through their quarantine barricades? And on the la-de-da side, would it distract people who lived a life of ease from mounting any serious effort to knock down those barricades?

In less than sixty seconds, the Smoke and Mirrors had already flown well out beyond lunar orbit, leaving Space Station 2 and Earth over three million miles behind. Only a fading streak of twinkling stardust remained visible near the space station to show it had ever been there.

Chapter 4: The Second Session

"We are going now. Are you coming? Or will you take all night to complete your masterpiece?" asked Ludi's grandma, Norma, knocking on a bathroom door for her husband to hurry up.

"Ay caramba my little cow, probably I have more fun in here than awaits me out there!" said Don Típico, capping off his response with a machine-gun-fire fart.

"Grandpa!" Ludi exclaimed admonishingly. "You are testing a new propulsion system for the spaceship Doña Galleta described?"

"Ludi?! How large is my audience?!"

"Only half the neighborhood, Grandpa!" laughed Pedro, and Alexita in his arms giggled because her papa's amusement tickled her. "Actually, we are calling from home in New Jersey. We can hear your propulsion system that far away!"

"All of you leave me alone! Caramba!"

The noise from Típico's fart did not, of course, carry anywhere close to the New Jersey border. But earlier that day, Ludi and Pedro's excitement over their house in the suburbs certainly did propel them back across the state line, back into the north Philadelphia row-house of Pedro's parents. As Rotonda waddled out of the kitchen there, drying her hands on a new dish cloth, she could see the twinkle in their eyes. *Perhaps they left a trail of stars streaming in their wake.*

"Mami-in-law," Ludi arched back from Rotonda's hug, "you should see our new home! This morning, we put Alexita in her baby crib for her first morning in her own room, sí! With the walls freshly painted how they say? 'Lavender purple'!"

"I love these names for paint," chuckled Pedro. "Lavender purple, oyster white... why not caca brown or puke orange?"

"I thought you liked painting your daughter's nursery, Señor Guapo (*Mr. Handsome*)," Ludi whined pouty-lipped. "Let me take my Alexita from her nasty papa who is making fun of her walls!"

Alexita relieved from his grasp, Pedro threw his hands in the air, exasperated.

"I am not making fun of her walls! I am making fun of the names people give paint colors!"

"Is okay, is okay." Rotonda took advantage of Pedro's outspread arms to give him a big bear hug with her head nuzzled against his chest. "You treat my son well, chica, or I will repossess him. Anyway, now I know why you were not answering the phone. I called you a half hour ago to meet us at Doña Galleta's."

Pedro's eyes opened wide. "She is finally prepared to search further for the origin of our mysterious pendant from the sky?"

"Look, Alexita," said Ludi, dangling the bracelet pendant not quite completely beyond Alexita's reach. "Your papa gets more excited over this than he got over painting your new bedroom."

Snuggled securely in her mama's arms, Alexita made a grab for the pendant but couldn't more than slap at it, sending it swinging back and forth on its bracelet. Yet she still cooed and squealed with delight, then looked around to assure that her loved ones were sharing in the fun.

"You see, Preciosa (*Precious*)," Pedro said to Ludi, "the pendant intrigues her more than her room."

Preciosa twisted Señor Guapo's ear while retorting, "Alexita is as intrigued, ay no, MORE intrigued by the fish mobile."

Ludi and Pedro hung the fish mobile high above the mattress before setting down their daughter in her crib.

Quickly noticing the slow rotation of the cartoonish toy fish, Alexita had kicked her legs a lot as she reached for them in vain.

"Yes," said Pedro, "those cardboard fish are her mysterious objects from the sky. She understands them as little as we understand the pendant."

The pastel green curtains softened morning daylight in a manner that helped Pedro imagine the sun's rays gently pushing the mobile. Mere illumination could provide the necessary force to propel spaceships across the cosmos, couldn't it?

"Don Placido!" shouted Ludi, playfully slapping Placido on what she could get at of his shoulder since he sank so low into his recliner. "You have to drive your wife to see our house."

"Ay chica, you tell us enough about it; I get the picture."

"You don't want to see the room of your granddaughter?"

"Aydiomio, of course I want to see the room of my granddaughter, and the bed where you are going to make a barón. But you just arrived. You have to eat something. And look." Placido motioned with his remote. "The Phillies are playing in New York. They're only two games out of first. Is almost as important as a playoff, with only three or four weeks left of the regular season."

"The Phillies in New York? Man..."

Ludi slapped the back of Pedro's head not so playfully before he could finish whining. "If you cared so much about that game, you would have noticed it in the TV guide already! It wouldn't have come as such a big surprise!"

"The only reason Don Placido knows is because he stumbled over it during his channel surfing," grumbled Rotonda.

"Aydiomio…"

"Anyway, bendito, I want so much to see the beautiful room of my beautiful granddaughter, but we cannot go this evening, Ludi…"

Placido nodded and grunted the nod and grunt of one who has at last been vindicated.

"…because we have to visit Doña Galleta. All of us! Now! You too, Papi!"

"Aydiomio!"

"Turn off the TV and put on your shoes! Now!"

"Pedro wants to watch the game with me!"

Just in case he was even thinking of saying something about accommodating his stepfather's wish to stay put, Ludi slapped Pedro on the head again.

"Come on, Papi!" said Pedro, leaving out the part about how he didn't want to be slapped a third time. "For sure Doña Galleta will have her special refreshing tea and cookies for us! And she will reveal more of her strange vision!"

At first, Placido appeared to be staring straight ahead at stats shown for one of the New York Mets' pitchers. But then his hands started shaking so much, he almost dropped the remote. Pursuant to which a tremendous trembling radiated from his arms to his entire body. He could have been in an earthquake were everything else not so still.

Pedro thought: *This is like when Mami has left the rice on boil too high for too long. The pot rattles, and bubbly water foams out from under the lid.*

Suddenly Placido crossed his arms, and just as suddenly stopped trembling. That's when he announced, "I am not going! I am staying here!"

"Don Típico arrived so we can all go together," said Rotonda. "You are coming with us to see Doña Galleta!"

Típico popped his head up and looked from side to side like he'd been abruptly woken from a nap. Or like the TV was the proverbial sand where he'd been keeping his ostrich head buried until he could no longer ignore threatening noises from above. "I came here to watch the game," he announced. "I - I was not going to the house of Doña Galleta," he added, channeling his occasional tremor into shaking his head NO.

"This is the first time I hear about this stupid game!" complained Norma. "Don Típico, you are going to the house of Doña Galleta with us, no more about the game!"

"I do not go outside alone when almost sunset. Is too dangerous."

"You should not go outside alone at sunset because in this neighborhood something bad can happen!"

"I said that, Norma! Ay caramba! That is why I am not going!" For special emphasis, Típico gargled to clear his throat.

"You are not going alone, mi bruto (*my brute*)! Understand? We are all going together, only a block down the street!"

"Ay caramba!"

Ludi and Pedro grinned at each other over the ridiculousness of grandpa Típico's ploy. Especially the tone of his latest "caramba" as in *Curses! Foiled again!* Like there had been any chance Ludi's grandma Norma wouldn't pick up immediately on why his alleged concern was not a concern at all; no way did she ask him to step outside alone.

But Típico wasn't finished yet. "A - A gang with guns and knives could approach us! Then what happens?" He couldn't help a smile playing across his face over anticipation he had conceived the ultimate stumbling block to Rotonda's plan.

"Then we throw you to them for a sacrifice!" snarled Norma.

"Ay caramba!"

"Pedro and Ludi can represent us," said Placido, arms still barricading himself into his recliner. "They can share what happened when they return."

"Sí," said Típico. "Why not? They can tell Doña Galleta we will visit next week!"

"Oh, you are truly the grand compromiser, *mi bruto*! And what excuse will you have when next week arrives?"

"Ay caramba!" Another grand scheme, foiled.

"This week, tonight," said Rotonda, "not next week." She shook her head with finality. "Look, I don't understand this any better than you, but Doña Galleta told me she wants us prepared."

"Prepared for what? Prepared for boredom?" grumbled Placido. "Aydiomio!"

"Yes, I am sure," nodded Rotonda. "She wants to take you down softly from the excitement of 'channel surfing' to the boring reality of life outside a TV set! Look, all I know is that this woman gives, and gives, and gives. She gives food, medicines, counseling… Reminds me of a herbalista I knew in the mountains south of Cayey. She never asks anything of us aside from a little bit of our time… Okay, so we waste an hour listening to her crazy story that Pedro has to translate for us. Maybe the truth is simply she wants our company. Maybe she is a very lonely woman since her husband died. But she does not know how to request our company without at least the illusion that actually, she is doing something for us. Is too much guilt for her if she just says, 'Look, please visit me. I am lonely.' However, I suspect her loneliness has nothing to do with her present actions. This mysterious object fell from the sky, at the feet of our precious Ludi and Pedro. And I do not think Doña Galleta knows so much English as she used the first time. All that English has to be coming from somewhere."

"Papi," added Pedro, "I checked on the internet this 'Oort Cloud' that Doña Galleta mentioned. I never heard or read of it before, but it is something real, and astronomers believe the comets originate from there. One internet article says the Oort Cloud surrounds our solar system, like an eggshell. But you don't bump into it until you travel thirty-two astronomical units away from the sun. Bueno (*Well*), I remember something Doña Galleta said in English as the captain of the spaceship. She gave thirty-two AUs for the location of the Oort Cloud. Yes! AUs have to be Astronomical Units! Oh, and the internet article explained that one astronomical unit is the distance from the sun to the Earth, or about ninety-three million miles. How Doña Galleta knows all of this? And in English?"

"Maybe she discovers this information on the internet like you!" cackled Típico.

"That is impossible; she does not even own a computer." Norma slapped her hands together as a substitute for slapping her husband on the head like her granddaughter did to Pedro.

"Ay caramba!" Foiled again.

For the ensuing quiet, all eyes were on Placido. Expectant.

He tried to pretend all eyes were not on him. Or at least that he was oblivious, just innocently watching his baseball game. Inevitably, though, he looked this way, then that. And finally, he made a motion like he was about to stand up. Only, he proceeded to act like his arms that were crossed over his chest prevented him from rising. He sat back into his recliner with a most pronounced Thump! "I am NOT going!" he announced again.

"You ARE going!" Rotonda announced again also.

"You are going too, Señor Lazybones!" said Norma.

"He is not going, I am not going." Típico brusquely flapped his hand like he was chasing a mosquito or a fly out of his face.

"Placido IS going," insisted Rotonda.

"No I am not!"

"Síííííí!!!"

"Síííí!" chimed in Norma. "Both brutes, they are going!"

"I am not going!" Típico bent forward and shook his head 'no.'

Pedro chuckled to Ludi, "They are sitting down for what they believe in."

To which Ludi said loudly enough to assure everyone heard, "The couch potatoes, united, will never be deseated!"

"Is true," nodded Placido.

"Okay, no more with jokes," said Rotonda, waddling over between her Placido barricaded into his recliner by his own two arms, and Típico sitting hunched over on the sofa.

Pedro mused that on the slightest touch from anyone, Placido looked like he was going to curl up completely into a ball like certain bugs.

"Now we all go," insisted Rotonda.

Típico held up his hand in a "no more" gesture, and hunched over a bit further.

Placido turned his head away, though still keeping focused out the corner of his eye on the count for the Phillies player at bat.

"I am not arguing anymore." No more waddle for Rotonda. After pausing for one last look her husband's way, then Tipico's, she spun around and took measured strides back towards the kitchen. By the time she arrived there, those strides had evolved into forceful stomps. She threw open the dishwasher, tossed in some silverware with as much clanging as possible, slammed closed the dishwasher, then threw open and slammed shut various cabinets and drawers. She closed the refrigerator door so hard that juice and sauce bottles inside rattled together.

With no uncertain fury, Norma abruptly convulsed out of her chair in the dining area. She scowled at her husband and Placido both, taking one last stab at shaming them into doing the right thing. But when they continued to remain seated, she rushed into the kitchen, disgusted the men weren't concerned enough to check on Rotonda for themselves. Her frumpy flower print gown constrained her pace, though, in addition to a headache which pounded every time she put down her foot too hard. "Are you ready to go?! I am ready!" She still spoke loudly enough to be heard back in the living room.

"I am ready to go," answered Rotonda stomping out of the kitchen. "Pedro and Ludi, you are coming also, yes?"

"Of course, Mami," Pedro answered quickly, fearing the consequences otherwise.

En route to the front door, Rotonda stopped to pick up a pair of Placido's work shoes left carelessly strewn across the floor. But since Placido pretended to have his full attention riveted to the baseball game, she thought better of holding them in his face. Or saying for the umpteenth time: *Someone can trip over these; they don't belong here.* Instead she yanked open the foyer closet, sending its doorknob banging against the wall. And she threw down the shoes so fiercely hard inside there, one bounced off the floor and knocked against the back wall. And when she swung the closet door closed, some empty coat hangers dingled together.

Placido cringed on every noise, even the coat-hanger dingles. He felt less than certain he wasn't going to feel something crash into his head.

"We don't know when we will return," announced Rotonda after wrestling violently with the front doorknob.

Suddenly, Típico raised his hand to gesture: no more. Then trembling as he struggled to his feet, he said, "Caramba, Norma, I have to use the bathroom first!" as though that were his initial bargaining position all along. So began the toilet stop of such length, Norma would feel compelled to knock on the bathroom door for her husband to hurry up.

"And I am waiting for Don Típico to finish in the bathroom," said Placido as though that were his bargaining position all along, as well. But Pedro saw the look of defeat draw Placido's long frown even longer, and further deepen years-old wrinkles carved across stubbly unshaven terrain.

Placido brought his lounger to the upright position and, after a lingering gaze at the score, averted his eyes to click off the television. Clearly, he couldn't endure watching the image flash down to a quickly fading point at center of the screen. And from sitting for so long, he stooped forward after getting to his feet. With furrowed brows he turned to face Rotonda, and asked, "What happens with Jerri and Gloria? Doña Galleta is not interested in them preparing for whatever-it-is also?" What he really wanted to ask was: *Why are you putting me through this?*

"Yes, of course. *Claro que sí.* Ludi is writing them a note to meet us at Galleta's. They are returning any time from a car wash at their school."

Placido reflexively glanced his recliner's way, overcome by a sudden faint hope he might yet steal more game-watching time there before leaving. "I should wait here until they return, to assure they receive the message?"

No sooner did he feign that innocent inquiry, though, than Jerri and Gloria came bursting through the front door, animate with laughter.

"Oh, good, you are here," said Rotonda, blocking her daughters' path to the stairs as Placido stooped over even further and muttered, "Aydiomio," under his breath like a curse. "I received a call from Doña Galleta this afternoon. We have to visit her, this night, for her second effort to determine from where originated the mysterious pendant of Ludi and Pedro."

"Ay, Mami, nooo," Jerri and Gloria whined as one, their turn to stoop over.

"Please, chicas, Doña Galleta says is very important for all of us to listen so we can prepare. Prepare for what, I do not know. But I think she is trying to help us."

"José and Rubin are coming here after they finish putting things away from the car wash," Gloria continued to whine, her arms outstretched in pleading supplication.

"Ludi is writing a note for them to meet us at Doña Galleta. Sí, Ludi?"

"Of course."

"So there! And I cannot leave you alone in the house with boys."

"Ay Mami," Jerri's continued whining grew tearful, "we do not want to listen to Doña Galleta, okay? Is so boring and stupid!"

"Síííí, Mami," chimed in Gloria. "Pedro can tell us if finally she discovers the origin of their thing that fell from the sky, okay?"

"Okay," Rotonda nodded, her last calm utterance before, "LUDI?! I NEED ANY SPARE PAMPERS YOU ARE NOT USING FOR ALEXITA!! SÍÍÍ!!" She went on, crying tearfully, "YOUR BIG BABY FATHER-IN-LAW AND YOUR BIG BABY SISTERS-IN-LAW HAVE TO WEAR DIAPERS BECAUSE BIG BABIES MAKE A MESS IF THEY ARE NOT WEARING DIAPERS!!! WATCH YOUR BASEBALL GAME! AND YOU TWO CLOSE YOUR BEDROOM DOOR AFTER BRINGING THE BOYS INSIDE, SO YOUR PAPI DOES NOT HAVE TO HEAR WHAT YOU ARE DOING!!"

"Ludi, I will write the note for our *machos*, gracias," said Gloria, careful not to complain any further while Norma stretched a comforting arm round Rotonda's shoulders.

"Gloria, you want a glass of juice before we leave?" asked Jerri likewise abandoning her whine as she headed for the kitchen, but exchanging a look of solidarity with her sister.

"Am okay gracias, *hermana* (sister)."

"Am certain Doña Galleta will have special refreshments for us, like Pedro said. But have a drink now, Jerri, *hija* (daughter). You too, Gloria, if you want. We are waiting on Don Típico in the bathroom," Rotonda explained, not about to apologize for her blowup. But she packed much gratitude and respect into her decidedly more subdued remarks.

This was when Norma knocked on the bathroom door for Típico to hurry up, and he grumbled "Caramba" over not being left alone to finish his business.

Ludi sidled back up beside Pedro rocking Alexita the rest of the way to sleep from her pacifier daze. She pursed her lips towards the bathroom and said, "I wonder: is a boy or a girl?"

Even Norma and Rotonda laughed, and Jerri spit apple juice back into her glass.

"Like Doña Galleta advised us," Pedro responded, "you cannot hurry certain recipes. But I must say," he also gestured towards the bathroom down the hall just past the stairwell, "that is one bakery where the smell does not draw customers."

Placido chuckled all the way back to his recliner for clicking on the remote.

"Hey, what are you doing?" Rotonda asked.

"Don Típico is not finished delivering his baby yet," Placido noted with a matter-of-fact innocence he had perfected over the years.

"Mami, Don Placido is training to become a spaceship captain," Pedro hurriedly remarked, anxious to preserve the break in tension after his mother's blowup. "You have not seen on *Star Trek* how Captain Jean Luc Picard sits in a big chair to monitor a big screen for threats to the universe?"

"Mami" in a single motion swiped the remote from her Placido, and clicked off the TV. "This is like trying to build a sand castle in a hurricane! Everything keeps washing away!" she complained, fury returning to her voice. But this time she checked herself to take a deep breath, and proceed more gently, "Is a *simpático* mission we are on because we are providing company for a lonely old woman. Can you understand?"

Pedro winced, noticing a huffed exhale from his younger sister Jerri that portended her rejoining the battle.

But then the toilet flushed.

Spontaneous applause broke out, ever more thunderous as Típico exited the bathroom.

"Next time," he said, "I will sell tickets."

"As we speak," said Pedro, "the people of Waterland are being visited by a mysterious, monstrous object floating down to them out of a grand whirlpool."

"Sí, brother," said Jerri, "and they will want to mash it all over your belly button so you can tell them more about it!"

"We go," Rotonda said in a forcedly light-hearted tone, anxious not to poison the joviality. "We should not be late."

"Maybe Doña Galleta starts without us?" said Placido.

"Let's find out, my fat one."

"Aydiomio."

"Papi, the Doña will have a problem starting without this," said Pedro, lifting Ludi's wrist to display the pendant hanging from a bracelet there, even as he shuffled out the door.

"Ay, caramba! Is like a furnace out here!" said Típico as he hobbled down the front stoop, careless how he might affect the general mood.

"You were not complaining about the heat two hours ago when I suggested we stop by Placido and Rotonda's place," said Norma. "Felt much hotter then, with less shadow than now."

"Grandpa," said Ludi just up ahead, "I think is part of Doña Galleta's recipe. She is a cannibal who wants us pre-cooked so she can eat the moment we arrive. *Sí!*"

"Ay caramba!"

"Hear those dogs?" Placido asked as in: *The argument over the wisdom of what we are doing is not over yet.* "I hope they are chained and not running free; wherever they are sounds too close. How far we have to walk?"

"Papi, when is the last time you see any dogs around here?" asked Pedro. "Almost never, but only takes someone sneezing, and they all bark like crazy! And how you and Don Típico ever would have made that historic, quarter-million-mile moon voyage thirty years ago? I imagine you with panic attacks, saying 'Aydiomio' every time you saw a shooting star, or heard a grain of space dust go 'ping!' against the hull of your spaceship!"

"And why anyone wants to go to the moon?" asked Placido, stopping in his tracks and turning to face his stepson with a slow but deliberate shuffle. "Look at this place. Is a month since they fix that water pipe, and still they have not cemented back over it," he gestured towards a big square of bare dirt that interrupted the sidewalk across the street. "How about if people take care of what is down here first?"

Pedro looked up from precious Alexita in his arms, for the larger view. "Sí, Papi," he nodded grimly with a wincing eye-blink, "is true."

"Yes, is true," Placido said gruffly as he shuffled back around to continue onward.

Everything Pedro had previously managed to ignore hit him all at once.

The pervasive stench from a virtual sancocho stew of uncollected trash, hot asphalt, and automotive gas fumes blended with the exhaust from so many people living so close together. Before moving to the suburbs, such foul odor didn't use to bother Pedro so much. But now...Outside Pedro's new home, the most noticeable scents usually emanated from spring onions and freshly-mowed grass.

How about the vegetation in north Philadelphia? An empty lot across the street from his parents' tenement row house featured tufts of long, unkempt grass browned out early on by oppressive summer heat. And interspersed plantain weeds wilted under a thin coat of dusty dirt, lots of luck noticing any least fragrance from either plant.

And sure, there were big laughs over Típico's worry they might be attacked on their walk to Galleta's. Clearly, though, empty plastic syringes crowned by hypodermic needles ornamented the paper-dry grass. What crimes might their users commit to finance their next drug-induced flights out of this miserable place? With syringes as falling-away booster rockets from their missions bound for ecstasy that always crashed in hell?

Pedro hunched over, protectively cradling his baby Alexita. He wished he could conceal her under his shirt or Ludi's blouse, a simulated return to the womb until they arrived safely at Galleta's residence.

But where Pedro's younger sisters were concerned, he knew he really should let go. True, despite much complaining they still respected their parents enough to honor Mami's extreme-seeming desire they join the second session with Galleta. Ditto for not allowing themselves any alone time with their boyfriends. Gloria and Jerri did always insist on the presence of a mature adult, far as Pedro knew. But how much longer could they face wretchedly worn brick and cement forests without succumbing to temptation? Despite uncertainty their machos were not just looking to score before they moved on to their next conquests? How much longer would suffice the spirit of the dance and making up to look like J-Lo?

Ay, Santo, Pedro sighed. *Suppose Mami and Papi have been worrying for their children the same as I worry for my sisters and Alexita. Then no surprise they behave like they do. Papi is trying to lose himself in the fantasyland of television; maybe on his remote control surfing, he seeks the impossible channel that will pour flooding out of the TV screen with beauty and harmless fun and excitement! That then spills out into the street and transforms the entire* neighborhood! And Mami, she does not want to give up, so she latches on to how they say in English, the "pie-in-the-sky" of church instruction. If you live your life well, even in the midst of shameful living conditions, paradise will be your reward, eventually. However, her hope now is somehow entangled with the mysterious jewelry that fell at our feet. That is why she hangs on Doña Galleta's every word about it. No wonder she was so adamant about our all attending a new session with Our Lady of the Immaculate Cookies. She hopes that in some manner this will be our ticket to a better life!

Before my military service, special anchors kept me from drifting away on a sea of hopelessness, yes? Of course, that is why I still remember so fondly Mami buying me that new pair of basketball sneakers when I started high school. Their new rubber smell, their fresh bright colors, special thin paper to keep them from scuffing: That cardboard box contained a perfect little world. I could escape there from worn-out buildings, the cinderblock and dry wall of my classrooms and bedroom, the painted-over cracks and crumbles, with the paint itself like so much heavy makeup!

No wonder my real Papi before my stepfather became such an alcoholic. Drunk, he could avoid noticing things such as the unrepaired sidewalk that stepfather Placido complained about.

"You want to wear those out of the store?" the shoe salesman asked. I answered "no," to carry them around a little time longer protected in their box like an unborn child protected in the womb. Was so "cool" running my fingers over intricate tread designs on the soles before actual use started to age those sneakers.

Thank God I was not lured by false promises and self-destructive temptations. Instead, I worked hard to eventually surround myself with a beautiful wife and *daughter who I love more than anything; and a beautiful house for them in a beautiful neighborhood with trees and flowers everywhere; and a clear sky some nights for my telescope to transport me to the constellations.*

I could be the macho in that movie, "Titanic," leaning out over the prow of the boat and shouting: "I am king of the world!" So I also have to hope my boat does not hit an iceberg!

"Mmm," Pedro couldn't help reacting to the strong baking smell when Galleta swung her door wide open in response to Rotonda's knock.

"Yes," nodded Galleta, "just took a batch of pecan and chocolate chip cookies out of the oven...ay..." She fanned her face with one hand, nearly overcome by the heat. "Feels like I am taking you out of the oven too!"

"You see, grandpa?" Ludi laughed. "I told you Doña Galleta wanted us well cooked before she eats us!"

"Ha! She can try," Grandpa Típico's voice cracked. "But there is not much meat left on these old bones."

"No, no," Galleta protested, her eyes wide open with delight and surprise. "Is plenty of you, Don Típico, for a Thanksgiving feast! Yes! But suffices to drink in the mere sight of you, of all of you like the most refreshing gazpacho soup possible! Doña Rotonda corralled you together for this visit, sí?"

Rotonda nodded at her family as in: *You see? I told you!*

"I appreciate the difficult trajectory of most people's lives," said Galleta as she quickly closed the door behind last-entering Norma. "Nothing but the most profound love, admiration and respect flows from me to you. This is the truth. But is the same as for everyone else. When preparing a big batch of gazpacho, just before serving you have to really shake it up to keep the olive oil and vinegar-soaked ground tomato closely associated. Or else the oil settles apart from the rest of the soup. The same applies for people. The great events of your lives - weddings, births, professional achievements, even funerals - they stir you close, they are the recipes for the delicious feasts of love that explain our whole existence. However, between them, during the crucial preparation time, there is a natural tendency for people to separate apart from one another. Takes special chefs like your Doña Rotonda to gather people into the same bowl, as it were."

Placido shuffled up so close to Galleta, his expansive lion's face loomed over her mouse-y countenance when he asked, "Tonight we learn finally why the mysterious jewelry fell from the sky at the feet of Ludi and Pedro?"

"Don Placido, she cannot know how long that will take," said Rotonda before Galleta could answer.

"Aydiomio. Okay then, Doña Galleta, can you at least promise you will speak only in Spanish this evening?"

"Come here, *mi bruto*." Rotonda hooked her arm around Placido's, and pulled him aside. "Doña Galleta cannot possibly promise through what language her spirit trip will take her."

"Aydiomio!"

"Don Placido, I have a suggestion for you and Don Típico," Galleta offered nevertheless. "The elements of a delicious feast find their way together once they are inside your stomach, this is true. But my suggestion flows from understanding those elements are best savored separate from each other, prior to stomach entry. The caramel custard is not served over the rice and beans. And even with gazpacho, is best to keep some chopped onion and green pepper set aside for mixing in at the last moment, instead of grinding it all together with the tomatoes at the start."

"Most of what this woman says makes no sense to me," Placido muttered to Rotonda. "She could be speaking in more English for all - Aydiomio!"

Rotonda sucked in her lips with the effort of digging deep into her husband's belly flab for a twisting pinch.

"My suggestion," went on Galleta pretending she was oblivious to Placido and Rotonda's behavior, "sets you two apart from the rest of us in the side room there, Don Placido and Don Típico. You can exercise off the extra calories from the cookies I am sure you will be eating tonight, because I've turned it into a nursery Alexita ought to enjoy."

"A nursery," said Norma. "So is perfect for our husbands to play without getting hurt."

"Though maybe Gloria and Jerri should still keep an eye on them in case they try putting in their mouth small objects not meant for eating," added Rotonda.

"Aydiomio!"

"Caramba!"

"Actually, I thought your handsome cowboys could share cradling and rocking precious Alexita. And they could also entertain her if she wakes up before I return from my spirit-channeling journey, wherefore the nursery setup."

Rotonda slapped Placido on the arm for brushing at his hair and patting his day-old stubble. Obviously, he was fretting over how much handsomer he might have appeared had he shaved and combed.

Típico did his ostrich-head-out-of-the-sand routine again, like he'd just been roused from another nap. "Huh? What? Uh...entertain Alexita? She is asleep!"

"Think you can handle that?" asked Norma.

"You and Don Placido can take turns holding her in your arms while you discuss quietly anything you want," Galleta said gently.

"I will stay here," Típico shook his head as in: *Not so fast!* "One never knows these days; we leave the room, and some beast might invade to steal Norma from me!"

"Ha!" Norma laughed with a blush. "What you are really saying is, the baby could wake up and then you would have to actually work!"

"Ay caramba!"

"Are you worried some beast might steal me while you are in the next room?" Rotonda asked Placido with another pinch, this time more affectionate than brutal.

"I worry you will still be here when I return!"

SLAP!

Placido took his seat on one of the floor cushions, the slow squat of surrender.

But Cookie Lady Galleta's attention had moved on to Gloria and Jerri. She noticed Jerri check her watch, slump her shoulders, close her eyes, and finally give her sister a pleading look that asked: *What are we going to do?*

"Gloria, Jerri, I see your friends are not here this time," Galleta delicately observed.

"Ay, sí," said Gloria with a touch of whine. "We stuck a note for them on the front door, and have no idea whether they saw it. Maybe some loco took it, or it fell off in this heat." *Is no problem if we go check? And is no problem further if we not return?*

Galleta smiled generously, compassionately, though with furrowed brows. "Maybe watching my spirit-channeling became very boring for you very quickly. At best, was only a little less boring than for your stepfather and Ludi's grandfather, because you know some English. You should not apologize; you owe no apology," she shook her head, pre-empting any protest from Gloria and

Jerri. "I understand. You fear the boys are not coming. You fear they have chosen not to be bored themselves again. Maybe as we are talking, they are looking for fun with other people."

"Ay," Gloria whined anew, "this is so awkward."

Galleta shook her head. "As I told your brother last time, you should not permit one way of seeing a situation to preclude other ways of seeing it. Consider this a test of their friendship. Do they care enough to come rescue you from a tiresome waste of time?"

"Ay, Dios," it was Jerri's turn to whine, "they will think we do not find this tiresome, that we are asking them to join us for another fun evening. We lose them not because they are not caring for us enough, ay no! We lose them because they start to think our interests are too different! They start to think that what excites us does not excite them!"

"Jerri! Gloria! How can you be so insulting to our host?!?" asked Rotonda admonishingly. "I apologize for my children, Doña Galleta!"

"No, Rotonda, you should be so proud of your children. The real insult is dishonesty. And besides, I suspect before much more time passes, the activities of this crazy old woman will prove TOO interesting, for everyone! Yes! But what I want to ask your daughters now is: Buried somewhere in the message you left, could there be a hint you desire being somewhere other than here? And this hint is such that only young men the most deserving of your attention will be sensible of it?"

Pedro couldn't suppress his amusement enough to avoid an arm slap from Gloria. He had shielded what his sisters wrote from his mami catching a glimpse, worried it could set her off again. But that's when he noticed what Jerri scribbled in capital letters: WE NEED YOUR AROUSING

PRESENCE TO KEEP OUR BLOOD FLOWING!! HELP US!! PLEASE!!

Jerri knew she blushed and giggled too much to argue Galleta's point. So instead, she asked, "If they arrive, will they be allowed to rescue us?"

"I will think of something else clever to keep them here."

"Ay," moaned Gloria, "but what if they arrive while you are in outer space? What happens then?"

"Then YOU will think of something else clever to keep them here."

"Ay," Gloria and Jerri sighed in unison.

How tranquilly Cookie Lady convinced my sisters to join us sitting in a circle around her! Did they really put up much more of a fight than a ball of dough when someone spreads it on a baking pan? So that when Galleta smoothed out her pastel green blanket on the floor, she might as well have been covering the dough with sauce? And then she was the cheese, decorated with toe-ring and bracelet toppings?

My God, if I visit Galleta often enough, what even crazier comparisons are going to haunt me? Pedro had to wonder. *As my papi would say, Aydiomio!*

History repeated itself after Galleta reclined on her blanket, with the mysterious pendant left centrally located on her belly, and her arms and legs outstretched at various odd angles. The same as many weeks earlier, a hissing crackle introduced a puff of blue smoke right above the pendant. And once more that puff dissipated the moment it appeared.

From how Gloria and Papi's eyes grew wide, Pedro knew he and Ludi were not the only ones who noticed.

Also the same as earlier, Galleta bolted upright. And though she turned towards Pedro, he sensed her looking through him at something completely else.

"There it goes! They just launched a firefly donut!" Galleta exclaimed convincingly enough that everyone looked the direction she pointed. "The donut hole exhaust is a small version of what the spaceship's mirror array produces! So beautiful! It might as well be the stream of fairy dust you see spurting from a magician's wand in the movies. And now the firefly donut has already flown so far ahead of the Smoke and Mirrors, that stream has faded from view."

"Ha!" Típico coughed as much as laughed, continuing to find the whole thing ridiculous.

"Why are they launching donuts?" said Placido. "Donuts are for eating, not for launching. And why produce donuts for fireflies? Firefly donuts must be so small, no wonder we can't see them."

"That is the diet you need, my fat macho," Rotonda patted Placido affectionately on his big belly. "You need the firefly donut diet."

"For those of you watching from the security of our planet Earth," said Captain Taylor turning away from the ship's panoramic view-screen to face husband Chris's camcorder. "Actually," she changed course to go on, that wry look coming over her that Chris loved so much, "our Earth travels over sixty thousand miles an hour in its orbit round the sun. And it rotates on its axis over a thousand miles an hour at the equator. I should wonder why you're not getting dizzy down there."

Placido and Típico bowed their heads dejectedly, soon as Cookie Lady resumed channeling Captain Helena Taylor in English, of course. "Aydiomio." "Ay caramba," they muttered respectively, earning "Sh!" "Sh!" from their wives.

"Phew!" Captain Taylor wiped her brow. "Maybe, um, well anyway, First Officer Leung and I have been referring to a so-called 'firefly donut.' It's basically a replica of the test vehicle that, to our unwitting surprise, achieved light-speed propulsion. We've adapted it to act as our advance guard probe. But we're already travelling at one-fourth light-speed. So for the firefly donut to do us any good, we had to scoot it way far ahead of us, like millions of miles ahead of us. We accomplished that no small feat by launching it several minutes prior to our own anticipated acceleration to full light-speed. Thereby, hopefully, it can warn us plenty early enough for reacting effectively to any and all potential hazards. For example, there might be an asteroid or other outer space debris we can give a wide berth via evasive maneuver, again provided plenty of lead time.

"After the fast-approaching Mars flyby, our course is set high above the planetary orbital plane. That's double protection, keeping us a more-than-sufficient distance from anything dangerous in the asteroid belt between Mars and Jupiter, and the Kuiper belt out past Neptune. If you're tuning in, Shelly – that's our daughter – please don't worry about us.

"Of course," continued Captain Taylor, craning her face forward, closer to Chris's camcorder, "isn't it curious how our notions of 'high' and 'low,' 'up' and 'down' have come to embrace the entire solar system?"

"Not curious at all," said Chris. "Just ask the thousands of people who fall off Australia every day. A little known fact," he added despite noticing Helena wipe her brow.

Officer Kevin Smith-Park kept his "Oh, jeez" of disgust under his breath, heaven forbid any notice of it by the vast audience for Helena's mission update.

"Of course, Mr. Olsen is joking. Thousands of people are NOT falling off Australia every day..."

"Only a few."

"And you might be joining them."

Tension-breaking laughter erupted on the navigation deck.

Helena nevertheless wiped her brow again. Finally saying something genuinely funny seemed to have taken a lot out of her, far as her concerned husband could tell. "That's the odd thing with gravity," she still pulled herself together to go on, extracting a ballpoint pen from her uniform's breast pocket. "I let go my pen, like this," she said, and released the writing tool from her fingertips.

Galleta's channeled fingertip movement perked up Placido to say, "What?! She showed there is nothing in her hand because she is going to perform magic?"

"Sh! She is going to make your complaining disappear! That is her magic!"

"Aydiomio!"

"Sh!" repeated Rotonda.

"It falls to the floor," continued Captain Taylor, "probably not as quickly as you are used to seeing. We are at only one-fourth Earth gravity, hopefully strengthening to three-fifths once we reach full light-speed. Anyhow, one would think we have established fixed directions for 'up' and 'down.' But if I were to walk around to the other side of the photon exhaust shaft..." Helena bent forward to retrieve her intentionally dropped pen. In addition, though, she extended her right hand for support with fingers splayed, the hand not reaching for the pen. Otherwise she would have fallen over from vertigo.

Standing back up went tentatively slow for Helena. She checked her watch along the way to feign her problem had been nothing more than distracting worry. How much time left for doing her update until she needed to address the next item on her agenda?

Chris would have asked if she was okay, but guessed she wouldn't want that going out on the news feed. Far better to let the viewers and mission control people wonder whether they were imagining things.

"Um, I'm sorry," Captain Taylor smiled wanly into the camera. "Time flies when you're having fun. I'm supposed to be extending holograph greetings to the Mars colony governor soon. And, uh, we are not really equipped for that in this particular room. So I'll, um, Officer Leung, think you know where I'm going with this. Could I impose on you…"

Buddy Leung laughed awkwardly and said, "No problem, Captain. Send Governor Sanchez my best."

"Of course," said Helena. Then it was all she could do to affect a confident stride out of the navigation room. That is, without latching onto a panel or chair for support. But the moment she reached the hall, away from anyone else's scrutiny, she allowed herself a pause to lean against the handrail. *Damn! This happened at the press conference! Must be coming down with something, not contagious I hope. Can't be space sickness issues, can it? Especially now… Here, we've finally achieved substantial if mysteriously sourced gravity aboard ship… Well if I'm going to throw up, at least let me reach my office first…*

Captain Taylor tightly gripped the handrail as she resumed her unsteady trek.

Sensors brightly lit her way ahead, and dimmed to faint fluorescence behind.

"Oh!" she gasped, startled out of her growing nausea by a stream of strange mist swirling diagonally across, from lower left hallway edge to upper right edge, some twenty feet ahead. Might as well have been light passing through windows, how it emerged from one corner and vanished into the other.

Even more distressing, the mysterious ghostly substance assumed corporeal form including head, arms and legs.

Helena ran closer, insistent on discovering her imagination had simply run wild in some form of panic attack. That as with certain clouds, she was reading shapes into the diagonally flowing mist that were mere coincidental likenesses.

Oh, no, this is not good. Helena stopped dead in her tracks, feeling violated by a distinct chill. *God, please let this be a fever chill from whatever I've contracted, a chill accompanied by hallucinatory delirium, and not a hull breach. Oh, crap, a hull breach might explain it. Must return to the control room and seal off the impacted zone until we are able...* "Uhh!" Reversing course, Captain Taylor saw more of the swirling vaporous whatever emerging from the corridor wall.

Only this time, she stood close enough to see clearly that whatever-it-was definitely assumed a human shape. But its face's torment so distracted her, she could not say whether the rest appeared clothed or naked.

Instinctively Helena turned around again, away from this awful specter, only to find herself confronted by several more. Each phantom man, woman and child struck a different pose, but the wide-eyed expressions frozen on all their faces bespoke the same sheer terror. Collectively, they gave the appearance of some explosive force having blasted them flying who knew how far.

Helena spun back around to where she'd been headed originally after her initial bizarre experience...only for one of the specters to get directly in her face, someone familiar.

"DON PEDRO!! AYEEEE!!!"

Galleta's frantic pirouette, round and round, finally left off in a fainting collapse.

"Eh!" Típico grunted, laughter tempered by concern. "She made too much trouble for herself, just to divert us!" he speculated.

Rotonda slapped Placido backside the head.

"Hey!?" Placido howled, "What was that for?"

"You think it is funny too?"

"Aydiomio, I was thinking nothing!"

"Yes, always you are thinking nothing unless there is a baseball game."

"What happened, Doña Galleta?" asked Ludi. She cradled the small, fragile woman's head in her lap.

Doña Galleta's mousey gray hair still grew thick, so thick that cradling her head in her lap reminded Ludi of cradling Alexita. Moreover, the faraway look in the woman's eyes called to mind a similar look from Alexita on one occasion. This had not dawned on Ludi before, seeing Cookie Lady's wild faraway stare as she purportedly relayed outer space events somehow experienced decades prior to their actual occurrence. But Alexita would stare off in the same manner, even cooing, and excitedly kick her legs at what Ludi and Pedro could not make out to be anything more than thin air.

"You said my name," said Pedro, "but it was like I was some monster scaring you."

Galleta gave Pedro her most forlorn look, and bit her lower lip before saying, "I was seeing your ghost, from after you are older than me!"

Chapter 5

"Captain Taylor, all your blood work reads normal. The multi-scanner shows your system clear of any tumor activity. Your inflammation count is close to zero. I can't find a thing wrong with you," concluded Dr. Debbie Davis-Murphy, scratching behind her neck.

"That's a good thing, right?" asked Helena seated on the edge of an examination cushion, her legs swinging wildly with irritated impatience. She found Debbie's clean bill of health issued in a tone of voice that sub-texted: *You poor creature; Sorry I can't tell you something you want to hear.* Making matters worse was the medical biochemist's overdone lipstick lending her pitying frown a clownish quality.

"I know what the good doctor is trying to say, Captain Taylor," boldly claimed Helena's husband, Chris. "You're in the same shape you wanted me to get the house before we literally lighted out for the cosmos. And she just wishes your condition was less boring, more exciting. Like my mess."

"My kind of boredom, Mr. Olsen; I could use more of it."

"Ohhh," sighed Debbie as in: *Isn't this couple's bickering cute?*

"I've got a real yawner for you," Buddy Leung guffawed like he'd let rip his funniest line ever. But to be sure, he was experiencing a huge measure of relief. "The ship's systems are all operating within normal parameters. Sensors don't evidence even the teensiest hull breach, and we're not taking only their word for it. One of our backup fireflies has given us visual confirmation over every square micron of the starship's outer molding. A few striations, albeit less than a millimicron deep, still go to show the impact dust particles have out here when we're sideswiping them at one-quarter light-speed. But that's it; again, no hull breach. Not even close to close."

"Captain Taylor," said Dr. Davis-Murphy sternly, "over the course of your long, illustrious career, have you ever had any trouble with panic attacks or space vertigo?"

"Ali here can confirm," Helena nodded Dr. Ali Magabu's direction.

Ali was taking stock unobtrusively, thumb supporting his chin, and forefinger curled under his wide nose.

"Believe I'm one of only a few mission commanders who have never had to toss their cookies, even when we were experimenting with those awful centrifugal gravity spinning tops."

"Captain Taylor is correct, absolutely," Ali Magabu gestured emphatically with both hands. "And this is not a woman who has panic attacks."

"There is always a first time," parried Debbie. The casual way she inserted her hands in her medical smock's big pockets somehow gave Chris the feeling she wanted to add: *That settles it.* "Humanity's first light-speed mission, humanity's first journey outside the solar system, all that together with a little too strong a cup of coffee this morning... who knows?"

"Maybe," reluctantly conceded Ali. "You're going where the captain is going, too, and I don't see you freaking out."

"Not yet."

"Think it helps, truly, having our sweeties along. Except yours, Buddy. I'm not forgetting you. But your head is always up past the clouds anyway, with your dreams of multiple light-speed propulsion."

"That's okay, Ali, I'm fine," Buddy laughed.

But Chris sensed a touch of defensiveness.

"Excuse me, Captain Taylor," went on Ali Magabu, not insensitive to Buddy's feelings, but more concerned about something else. "What really interests me," he said, "is this chill you experienced out in the corridor. Such a sensation in our present context is truly worrisome. Did anything else accompany that sensation, Captain? Or was the feeling of extreme cold itself your sole basis for fearing a possible hull breach?"

"Not sure," responded Captain Helena Taylor, head in hands. "Think I spooked myself." Counselor Magabu's persisting contemplation of her headache-stricken pose weighing on her, she felt compelled to add, edging closer to full disclosure, "Told myself that maybe I was noticing, umm, some impact from the hull breach. Umm, like a cloudy mist."

"Nothing more than a shapeless cloudy mist, Captain? That's as far as spooking yourself went?"

Magabu's insertion of "shapeless" was not lost on Helena. "Dr. Magabu, I'm sure you're aware of how cumulus cloud formations can assume various forms when one is in a susceptible state."

"Were you in a susceptible state, Captain?"

"I'm always in a susceptible state, Dr. Magabu."

The tip of an iceberg, or a shape I'm reading into my wife's verbal cloud, again? Chris wondered uneasily. He shifted his weight from left foot to right foot then back again.

"So Captain," Ali smiled, "in your susceptible state, what particular form or forms did your cloudy mist appear to assume?"

Helena Taylor could feel, in addition to Ali Magabu's fixed regard, others present ready to hang on her every word. No matter. She fearlessly responded, "Why, I thought I saw you, Dr. Magabu, gagged and bound so you couldn't ask me any more questions."

"Excuse me, Captain," Buddy Leung cut in over the intercom as Dr. Davis-Murphy gasped, Chris snickered, "Wow!" and Magabu nodded and smiled, "Very good, Captain." Buddy was transmitting from the bridge; he didn't call the least attention to his departure from the captain's side after briefing her on the good news concerning the absence of any hull breach. "Hope this is okay, Captain. I went ahead and holophoned Governor Sanchez, sending our official regards to the Mars colony."

"Oh, Governor Sanchez, well thanks for covering that, Buddy."

"I hope nobody needs to shovel after me, Captain, ha! Told the governor you regretted not being able to extend greetings personally, but that something came up as it always does on these missions."

"I don't hear anything yet that requires shoveling after you, Officer Leung."

"Ha! Well here's the rest of it. I said that given our speed, by the time you *were* available for diplomatic chitchat, we'd be well out of holophone range. To add an exclamation point, Sanchez's projection had decayed to a grainy blur by the time he replied with his heartfelt wishes. At the conclusion, we were down to sound only. I said we hoped to honor the memory of the hurricane victims with our lighthouse mission for one day bagging a killer asteroid or comet. If you're still there, Chris, the governor suggested your grand uncle would have been proud of your involvement."

"Yeah, I only got to visit Pedro twice. First time was way back in grade school, before they erected the Philadelphia confinement zone. And of course the second time..." Chris's voice cracked with emotion. "My mom said this was his dream. At least..."

"Captain, you're still there?"

"Yes, Yoon-hee?"

"Dr. Spritzer says he wants a visual so he can see how you're doing."

"Oh-oh, Buddy! If the governor has gone and told on us, better keep that shovel ready! Yoon-hee, tell Dr. Spritzer I'll take his call once I scurry over to the conference office."

"Nay, Captain."

"Come with me, Chris." Helena grabbed her husband by the arm. "I can't face Spritzer alone."

Chris fancied they could have been married for a thousand years, a million years, and he'd still thrill to his wife grabbing his arm. Yet what tempered this thrill, as usual, was grim suspicion Helena could have been just as desperately grabbing any arm; his just happened to be the one available. Okay, she couldn't face Spritzer alone. But a guy who cluttered up her home with old compact music discs and vinyl records wasn't necessarily her optimum choice to make her not alone.

"Captain," said Buddy over the health room intercom, catching Helena just before she exited. "If you want to short-circuit Spritzer's nosing-around, this is not another cheap excuse: We really could use an extra pair of eyes on the bridge to monitor our climb off the orbital plane. We want to make double certain we're following precisely the trail-blazing firefly donut's course, before we attempt a jump to one-half light-speed."

"Officer Leung, you're even better than the Cat in the Hat; you pick up after other people's messes as well as your own. Thank you."

Still locked onto the arm she grabbed, Captain Taylor pulled Chris out the door and down the hall. They were halfway to the conference office before he regained his footing from an off-balance stagger.

"I need to tell you something, Chris."

No, don't do this to me when we're cooped up in a tin tulip headed for somewhere out past the edge of the solar system! was Chris's first heartbeat-hiccupping thought. *Or if you do, don't expect me to manage keeping the whole crew from knowing, to just suck it in until we return to Earth!*

A dozen years earlier, Helena gave him the curious comfort of confirming his feelings weren't all paranoia. Out of the blue she questioned whether she could go on with him. This happened the day after he turned down an opportunity she'd arranged for him. He could have started training immediately for artificial habitat climate maintenance, in turn fast-tracking him to a position on Space Station 2. Instead, he protested he couldn't do that and simultaneously keep his antique music trade afloat. There wasn't enough business for him to bring a partner into the operation, so the maintenance training would mean shutting it down. Either that, or turning over *Unidentified Freaky Discs* to someone who might not share his passion for preserving the most exciting music from 1970 to 2030. Anyhow, while Chris held his ground, he also responded to Helena's threat to pull the plug on their marriage with begging and tears. A sort of reconciling family vacation to the Grand Canyon became the eventual result. Chris suspected Helena's reluctance to put their daughter through the consequences of a separation pulled her back from the edge. Ever after, though, he feared this particular volcano had gone dormant rather than completely extinct. Anyhow, daughter Sherry spent the vacation itself scampering about the numerous hiking trails to her heart's content. And Chris and Helena spent seeming endless hours contemplating the canyon's grandiose beauty, a little something from several epochs saved in several layers of rock, the ultimate diary.

"Hi! Good day, Dr. Spritzer!"

"Hope this isn't a bad time for you, Captain Taylor, and I see your hubby Christopher there," responded Spritzer, his response taking minutes to reach Helena's end of the plain old non-holographic visual transmission. "I know you're edging closer to light-speed and off the solar system's orbital plane, so I won't keep you long. We're expecting the regular progress report in an hour anyway."

"First Officer Leung was just saying they need an extra set of eyes, umm…"

For Helena, the pause seemed interminable until Spritzer held up a "say no more" hand. "I won't keep you. Just wanted to be able to tell the president we spoke and that everything's all right."

"The president?"

"Carey saw what I saw on your husband's cam feed, Captain. You appeared to lose balance bending down to retrieve the pen after your artificial gravity demo. And when you excused yourself from the bridge, you looked pale, like you'd seen a ghost."

"Probably was my amateurish light setting, Dr. Spritzer," stepped in Chris.

"Was that all it was, Captain?"

"After Debbie checked me over, we concluded it was a touch of anxiety. Maybe things were going too smoothly. I do tend to worry a lot." Helena didn't think she could believably pretend nothing had happened. As with Magabu, better admit to a little of the truth rather than face closer scrutiny.

"That's what I was hoping you'd say, Captain. I'm glad you availed yourself of Dr. Davis-Murphy's expertise. We all have our moments, but only the wisest leadership resists pretending otherwise. I think you've provided me enough to reassure President Carey. Check with you in an hour."

"Thank you, Dr. Spritzer."

"Captain," Buddy Leung over the intercom as the visual of Spritzer went blank, "we really do need you pronto. We've got a developing situation."

"What sort of situation, Buddy?"

"A UFO appears to be pacing us, Captain."

"I'm there," but before Helena Taylor turned to leave, she tugged Chris extra close. "It was your grand uncle Pedro," she murmured. "He looked exactly like in the photo you showed me from the Martian storm coverage. He was joined by other people as well, streaming out of one wall and passing through the opposite wall as easily as a hot knife through warm butter."

"Ghosts?! I heard a rumor on the space station that one of the Jupiter moon missions traversing the same region…"

"I knew you'd be thrilled, and now a UFO… Please don't say anything. I've got to process all this. We better hurry."

Chris wasn't sure what was better: that his wife wasn't been about to pull the rug out from under their relationship again, after all, or that she admitted having experienced something exceptionally bizarre.

"I wouldn't want to bet against my having slipped into some anxiety-induced hypnotic state that made me subject to the slightest power of suggestion," Helena said breathlessly on her final long strides approaching the bridge. As if, Chris mused, she was cautioning him: Don't get too carried away.

"Captain," said Kevin Smith-Park, standing out of his seat on Taylor's entrance, "the UFO has been duplicating exactly our speed and course. We should consider the possibility it's nothing more than a reflection of the Smoke and Mirrors realized by some hitherto unknown inversion layer induced by the local amassing of cosmic subatomic particles. On Earth, atmospheric inversion layers occasionally send streetlamps and auto headlights zooming across the sky, fooling some people into believing they are flying saucers."

"Kevin, thank you for what I'm sure is a cogent analysis. But I want to see for myself what this is we're talking about."

"Captain, I've run the image onto our view-screen," noted Yoon-hee.

"Huh," Helena mumbled, pondering the pinpoint of light that appeared to remain motionless while the constellations behind it appeared to whiz by. "I suppose our advance guard firefly donut can't very well zoom up and give a closer look, see if Kevin is right."

"Captain," said Buddy, "we could launch one of our spare fireflies."

"What I was about to order."

"Done in two minutes." Buddy leapt from his seat, headed for the exit. "Let's hope the UFO is still there."

"Or let's not, Officer Leung, if it's thinking about zooming in closer to swallow us whole. By the way, how goes our acceleration off the orbital plane?"

"Whoopsi," said Yoon-hee as Buddy Leung, one leg out the door, did an abrupt about-face and returned to his seat. Not enough time to launch the spare firefly donut before the next step closer to light-speed. Anyway, how was the donut actually going to home in on the UFO, whether it was an inversion layer chimera or something actually out there?

"Officer Leung, I'm gratified to see you knowing better than to obey one of my ill-considered orders."

"No," Buddy demurred, waving his hands in protest.

"And I love how you go into denial whenever your captain hints she might be less than perfect."

"We're coming up on the course adjustment coordinates; you should be seeing the countdown on your screen, Captain," said Buddy. "Initiate?"

"Initiate."

"Countdown is initiated, Captain."

"Seven, six, five, four," Kevin read off the half-second countdown increments as part of the redundancy system; Buddy and Helena were watching that same descending sequence on their own laptop-sized screens. "And we have mirror tilt underway."

"If I didn't know better... Maybe it's this artificial gravity," said Helena. "Doesn't it feel like we actually are climbing? That it's not merely the suggestion from the screen image?"

"Captain, you are noticing this, yes?" asked Yoon-hee. "Our UFO has disappeared."

"Oh, wow, 'lena hon,' did you see?" Chris bounced up and down in his seat as he pointed at the display screen. "It didn't exactly disappear! It peeled off! I saw a distinct-"

"Chris, we've got too much happening at once; stifle yourself. Kevin, what's the timing on our level-out?" Helena really wanted to tell her husband: No more *'lena hon.*

"We are leveling out now, Captain, approximately five million miles above the orbital plane. The advance guard donut shouldn't come across any errant asteroids in need of our avoiding. We go to one-half light-speed on your command."

"And Buddy, you're sure we're still picking up enough sunlight to not need a laser boost yet?"

"I'm sure, Captain. For now, that extra boost we're always receiving from the ambient starlight stream is plenty adequate to benefit the next mirror array adjustment. Thus far, diversion from calculations has been on an order of less than one thousandth of a percent."

"Incredible. I'm still amazed. Okay, Kevin, initiate acceleration."

"Adjusted bloom completes in five seconds, four, three, two, one, complete, and complete for the firefly as well."

"Okay, folks, I suppose we don't get to see the stars streaking like in those old sci-fi films until we achieve full light-speed." Captain Taylor pushed aside her laptop screen and rose from her command chair as she spoke. "Now back to this UFO business..."

"Captain," said Kevin, "excuse me, Captain, but the image vanished coincidental to initiation of the course change. That fact strongly supports the hypothesis we were observing an inversion layer reflection. Just as with any other reflection phenomenon, a shift in perspective instantly removed it."

"But it didn't just vanish," objected Chris. "Didn't anyone else see it peel off from its parallel course?"

"Likely an illusion caused by OUR peeling off from the set course," fired back Kevin.

"There might be something to your cosmic particle inversion idea, Kevin," conceded Buddy. "But I'm puzzled. Assume we were simply witnessing a reflection of the Smoke and Mirrors. Why an oval-shaped reflection? The starlight stream funneled in and then fanning back out of the S and M's photon exhaust shaft should have favored a bowtie-shaped image, I should think."

"Distorted by the inversion layer?"

You have an answer for everything, don't you? Chris wanted to say. But he stifled himself, as his wife would put it, in humble recognition of the physics going well beyond his comprehension. Though he still would have sworn the UFO peeled off in a manner having nothing to do with the spaceship's course change.

"I think it would be useful," said Helena, "to replay the tape from the time frame in question. Yoon-hee?"

"Nay, Captain, coming up on the view-screen in a moment."

"Ah, here we go. Freeze it right there, Yoon-hee. Buddy, when this was a live feed, did you have a chance to run a spectrum analysis?"

"Finishing right now, Captain," said Buddy with his eyes glued to a panel monitor. "Well this is curious. Could be a metal alloy, and then again it could be a gas mixture, or both."

"Both?!"

"Both, Captain. Maybe some sort of quantum field."

"What does this do to your inversion layer hypothesis, Kevin?"

"Captain, I'm not sure a reflection of a hitherto unknown cosmic particle inversion wouldn't assume the characteristics of a quantum field, perhaps give a false reading of such."

"Well I don't know." Captain Taylor crossed her arms and walked up closer to the panoramic view-screen that dominated the navigation bridge. "That thing sure does look oval to me. But you say," she turned her head back over her shoulder at Kevin, "the inversion could be distorting the reflection of the Smoke and Mirrors?"

"Or maybe, Captain, dark matter or a mini black hole between us and the image somehow bent, twisted the reflection to make it appear oval."

"Anyone," said Helena, "do we have a means of measuring how far that thing, or image, was from us?"

"It maintained a precisely parallel course with ours, Captain," said Buddy, "at least up until it left or vanished. So no, we've got zippo in the triangulation department."

"Then what you're giving us, Kevin, is a lot of conjecture.

"Yoon-hee, run the video forward to when the phenomenon either departed or simply vanished."

Kevin inhaled and exhaled to help keep his cool. "What I'm giving you, Captain, are numerous options to explore before we resort to discussing an extraterrestrial spacecraft shadowing our mission, or something like that. That's all I'm saying."

"There! There!" Chris pointed as excitedly as when they were receiving the live feed. "The object veered off before it vanished!"

"Oh, jeez, now it's 'the object.'" Kevin couldn't contain himself.

"Play back that sequence, Yoon-hee. Buddy-"

"I'm processing, Captain; if the phenomenon did veer off, that should give us enough info for triangulating distance."

"But if there was a pint-sized black hole which bent the light when we came even with the event horizon..."

"*If*, Officer Smith!" There was a touch of exasperation in Helena's voice. "And *if* your conjecture doesn't pan out, we need all the data we can collect on this- this whatever."

"Captain Taylor," said Buddy, "there *might* be a problem for Kevin's inversion-layer-plus-black-hole hypothesis. I have already succeeded with triangulations. And they put the phenomenon at increasing distance from us, inversely proportional to the strength of light transmission. I.e. the image grew fainter as it apparently veered off from running parallel to us. Perhaps, if I might throw my own conjecture into the pot, it not so much vanished as sped out of range."

"Or got sucked into the event horizon of the mini black hole; couldn't that have produced the same data from nothing more substantive than a reflected light source?"

"Possibly," acknowledged Buddy, though simmering over Kevin's unwillingness to face reality as he saw it. He kept his eyes glued to the monitor to avoid boiling over.

No matter. Kevin needed only to read the look on Chris's face to himself erupt, "I know what you're thinking, Mr. Olsen-Taylor! You're thinking this is the conclusive proof that little green men are buzzing us!"

"Actually, I was thinking about a principle almost two centuries old, I believe, called Occam's Razor."

"Okay," Helena said in a tone meant to convey: *Everyone keep calm; no fighting.*

"Oh, yeah," said Buddy, "that's where, um, it's the principle of the simplest, most elegant, least cluttered explanation for something probably being the best."

"My understanding also," nodded Chris. "So Kevin, you're positing a hitherto unknown cosmic particle inversion layer nearby a teensy-weensy black hole.
I should think that's a not-so-elegant, complex and cluttered square peg crammed into the round hole of reality."

"Chris...," Helena moaned in a tone both pleading and admonishing.

"Captain, permission to give your husband a little history lesson, which I pledge to drop like that," Kevin snapped his fingers, "should anything develop requiring our immediate attention before I'm through."

Helena shook her head bowed into her hands. But it was about more than just the resurfacing of tension over her relatively untrained husband gaining passage aboard an historic mission. There was puzzlement as well. Why wasn't that tension retriggering those weird feelings from during her gravity lesson with the pen for folks back home?

"Hey Chris," said Yoon-hee, "don't worry. He argues with me all the time about the relevance of the Bible to modern life, and he married me."

"Thanks for the support, sweetie. So here's the deal, Chris; over several decades people thought they were seeing UFOs. Some even thought they were being abducted by aliens."

"Most of the sightings of course were weather balloons, weird clouds and other conventional objects. And most of the abduction cases were bogus."

"*Most* of them, because you believe at least a few were legit, right?"

"I tend that direction, yes," affirmed Chris.

"You 'tend that direction,' okay. That means you 'tend' the 'direction' of believing extraterrestrials have been visiting Earth from some distant star system. And there's the problem. For years now, we've been romping around our neighboring planets, mining the moon, colonizing Mars, establishing outposts on the moons of Jupiter. Weren't we supposed to come across ample evidence of extraterrestrial visitations? Didn't one believer even expect formal greetings? 'Hey, you guys are spacefarers now like us; welcome into the galactic fellowship!' And then what did we find? Nothing! The little green men managed to traipse all over the solar system without leaving so much as a footprint or an accidentally dropped Orion Galaxy credit card! Meanwhile, though, we're constantly stumbling over flotsam-and-jetsam from our twentieth century moon and Mars missions! There's been everything from probe wreckage to a lunar golf ball!"

"Maybe the ETs really know how to clean up after themselves," offered Chris. "They're like the Cat in the Hat before the children's mom returns home. Maybe advanced civilizations advance beyond making messes."

"Well I'm not sure advanced civilizations don't make even more messes," said Captain Taylor. "They've got more stuff to make messes with."

"Oh, so you're finally admitting I'm advanced." Chris couldn't help himself.

"Advanced delusional state," Kevin muttered, unable to help himself either. "Your element will go a thousand more years never admitting that, apart from maybe some poorly understood natural phenomena, there is nothing to UFOs."

"What's really amazing is how often YOUR 'element' is proven wrong, or at least is given reason why you should keep a more open mind. The Io ocean mysteries, for example…" Chris was referring to one of Jupiter's moons.

"What mysteries? Yes, I know how cool it would be for some strange extraterrestrial sea beast to be lurking under that ice! But all we've found are those molten rock globules with gas trapped inside that make them float. Talk about proving someone wrong; it's turning out like what they finally established in Loch Ness half a century ago with those comprehensive sonar sweeps!"

"Interesting how you focus on Loch Ness, and conveniently skip over the pigmy Australopithecus proven to still be romping around Sumatra, the flying reptiles brought to zoos from New Guinea…"

"What was the big deal with those?"

"Oh! Oh!"

"Chris, Kevin, I'm afraid… no, make that delighted to have to cut you off," intervened Captain Helena Taylor, her hands raised for them to stop. "Actually, it's a close call."

Something in Helena's voice was enough to make Yoon-hee and Buddy look up, away from their monitors.

"In a little less than an hour, we'll be cruising past the asteroid belt and almost 'above' Jupiter," Helena elaborated. "If all goes well, that's when Dr. Spritzer will contact us on the micro-firefly hyperlink. We won't have to wait minutes between each end of the conversation. It's our last communication before we jump to light-speed, and Mission Control want to know we are confidently ready to step it up to the next level." Helena paused for a deliberately deep inhale and exhale. "I want 'all hands on deck,' if you will. Someone rouse Tanya and Geena so as an entire crew we can, um, vet all our options."

"Captain," said Buddy urgently, unable to effect he was making a dispassionate inquiry, "is a mission abort one of the options you intend for us to, uh, vet?"

"All our options, Officer Leung."

"Yes, Captain."

"And let's break out some snacks; I'm noticing too many growling stomachs, including my own."

Chapter 6

"Truly, I do not understand how you two women did it," Ali Magabu couldn't help commenting. He was ushering his wife Tanya and Engineer Geena Murphy-Davis onto the bridge. "Here you are, among the first humans to travel faster than light. And yet - how ironic – you were both out like a light not five minutes into the flight. I understand all about the round-the-clock work shifts. However, I would have thought that being at the center of such an historic event, you could not have helped experiencing a bad case of insomnia!"

"You would have konked out in a flash too," said Geena as co-wife Deborah pecked her on the cheek, "had you been up for sixteen hours straight, running diagnostics on every last mirror array mode to assure nothing got stuck!"

"Actually… mmm, yum, peashews and macawalmondias!" enthused Tanya. She noticed the bag of hybrid nuts dangled before her by Yoon-hee, like a hypnotically swinging watch on a chain. "I'll take a bag, thank you. Okay, back to my Ali-papali's comment. I did watch departure from bedroom screen, expecting excitement to forestall any slumber. However, rear view of star stream exhaust soothed me asleep. Next thing I know, Ali is crashing me awake like hypothetical asteroid crashing our civilization awake from quarantine zones."

"Ah, and what a coincidence, truly," said Ali Magabu. He held up for everyone to see where he had just taken a bite out of a globster handed him by Buddy. "I was about to say the same thing precisely about this magnificent concoction. It crashed into my slumbering taste buds like an iced-packed comet, and drowned them awake in a flavor flood."

"You sound like you're ready to do a commercial for them," observed Chris. "But have to admit these honey-sweetened brocciflower globules are something special."

"I prefer the chocolate-covered kelpydoodles." Yoon-hee popped two in her mouth.

"Truly amazing," said Magabu. "The taken-for-granted props of our existence now include a juice bequeathed such extraordinary surface tension, you can hold a large drop between thumb and forefinger like a marble. Yet the slightest contact with saliva collapses it into a totally liquid state. Meanwhile, one of the most popular candies incorporates seaweed with lab-grown whale blubber! Yes, the miraculous novelty of our snack foods has apparently worn off. But far more terribly, as my dear wife suggested, so has the sense of horror, a certain sense of dismay, over the quarantine zones. My experience has been that many people become hostile whenever one mentions them. Reminds me of how grumpy my uncle gets, upon being woken from a nap."

"So come up with a better plan for protecting us from rampant acts of crime and nihilism!"

"Which 'us' are you referring to, Officer Smith-Park, when fully half of humanity is subject to the quarantine?"

Kevin Smith-Park turned his head from side to side, forcing down his instinctive fight-or-flight mode. "Look," he responded finally, "I'm glad you guys enjoy throwing a party for your taste buds while scoring sweeping indictments on social norms imposed for our safety. But we have a situation here. Dr. Magabu, you're surprised Geena and your wife could snooze through the opening moves of this mission. Well imagine my astonishment at how you guys are able to prattle on about globsters and grumpy uncles when any second now, we expect the captain to make her case for mission abort! Anything you can say about that, Chris? I know this places you in an awkward position, but an awkward position is what you agreed to place yourself in when you signed aboard. Any clue you can share as to your wife's intentions before she arrives?"

"That's really not fair to Officer Olsen-Taylor," said Ali. "And mere 'prattle' is a common occurrence when facing anxious moments or dire situations. People try to escape at least temporarily into meaningless chitchat. That was my point about how people react when quarantine zones are mentioned. I applaud you, Officer Smith-Park, for returning us to the matter at hand."

"I applaud my husband too," said Yoon-hee. "But if you answer his question about the captain, Chris, I will have to slap him once we're off duty."

"No, Yoon-hee, that's okay," Chris assured her. But before he could embark on a response to Kevin's question, however awkward, Helena entered. A frown drew her face longer than normal, more horse than deer, thought her husband. Wherefore resumed his self-torture over whether he shouldn't have gone to her side instead of remaining on the bridge to indulge snacks. What didn't help was how she hunched over clutching an envelope to her chest. Chris sensed a massive burden she could just as easily have been bearing on her back instead.

"Here's the situation," Helena said as she took the captain's chair and slapped the envelope down on her lap. "Chris might have already told you."

"No, Captain," said Ali. "Your husband has told us nothing, for what it's worth."

"Debbie, Ali, I'm sorry I was not honest with you when you asked what I thought I saw in the hallway. So here we go. They were human apparitions, seeming ghosts of the

Mars storm victims. Some subliminal power of self-suggestion from subconsciously downloaded news images and rumor? Maybe. I don't know. Yes, Dr. Davis-Murphy, your exam turned up nothing. The fact remains, regardless. During Chris's cam-feed just before my hallway episode, my brain started feeling indescribably weird. And that same thing happened during the space station press conference days ago, when we revealed the Smoke and Mirrors."

"I remember you bathed in camera-clicking flashes," recalled Ali.

"But there were no such clicks and flashes on the bridge, Ali," pointed out Helena.

"Captain," said Debbie, "remember what I mentioned about the potential psychological impact of space travel at unprecedented speeds? I know you have no history of panic attacks..."

"You might be right, Deb," conceded Helena, holding up one hand defensively. "Or maybe I'm losing my mind."

"Not impossible, Captain, but you have no family history..."

"Whatever. If it is possible, I could pose an inestimable risk to crew and mission both."

"Captain," said Ali, "who is to say we ALL won't be seeing ghosts? That this isn't some as-yet-unknown consequence of humans traveling in this manner?"

"Exactly, Dr. Magabu," agreed Dr. Deborah Davis-Murphy.

"So what are you saying, Captain?" Kevin pushed back from his console. "Here we are, sitting around munching on our macawaca doodle globs in a partial gravity situation. Unlike any previous deep space mission I've ever been on, no worries stray crumbs might float into our eyes. And we're riding a photon-propelled system; also no worries over a nuclear reactor meltdown or some such. In short, this has been one of my smoother, more stress-free flights. And yet you're ready to pull the plug over one hallucination? Captain, I'm not trying to minimize your unsettling experience. But at the same time, I'm not convinced it even begins to rise to the level of a mission-jeopardizing crisis. With all due respect, I dissent if that's where you're going with this."

"With that due respect right back at you, Officer Smith-Park, this might well be the smoothest bon voyage ever. But it has not been without significant incident. You know I'm talking about that UFO."

"Jeez, Captain," said Kevin Smith-Park, slapping hand against forehead. "Are you actually afraid we're being tailed by extraterrestrials? I'm the first to admit my explanation for the anomaly is speculative. However, doesn't it forestall jumping to any rash conclusions until we collect more data?"

"I have a speculation of my own, Kevin," said Helena. "What if that entire incident was a case of mass hallucination? What if from here on, none of our perceptions can be trusted?"

"Captain, we do have information about the UFO stored in our databanks," cautioned Yoon-hee. "Remember the video we used to track its coordinates?"

"I appreciate what you're saying, Yoon-hee. But what if we were collectively hallucinating what was on there?"

"Then can't we transmit the video to Earth and have them corroborate our findings?" asked Buddy.

"And hallucinate they've sent the corroboration? Yes, First Officer, we could do that. And I'm not saying I believe one word leaving my mouth," admitted Captain Taylor, holding up her hands as though to fend off a pelting with globsters and kelpydoodles. "What I want to do, what I am going to do as your captain, is evaluate the urgency, the level of urgency with proceeding on this mission presently.

"First off, Tanya Petrovsky, talk to me about asteroids and comets. Of course, there are longer-range goals already ceded to future missions. Especially important is the search for habitable planets in nearby solar systems, of sufficient mass and resultant gravity to preclude another Mars-type storm. There is that. But more immediately, Dr. Petrovsky, there's our Oort Cloud mission you're to commandeer. Have you been advised of a specific threat yet to gain my attention?"

"Umm…"

"A threat of such imminence that postponing the mission for a week would put the Earth in serious danger?" elaborated Helena. "The idea would be to have an even more barebones crew test-fly the Smoke and Mirrors."

"As you know, Captain, the odds of extinction event asteroid or comet in our lifetime has been variously calculated from one in five thousand to one in a hundred thousand. Of course," Tanya went on, shifting to a more reflective mood, "for persons struck and killed by lightning, the odds of one in seven-hundred-seventy thousand are still too great. So the celestial object threat should always be taken seriously. But no, *nyet*, I have not been confidentially apprised of anything specific and immediate."

"Thank you, Dr. Petrovsky, which brings us to this." Helena held up high an oversized manila envelope. She turned it from side to side for all to see the bright red letters stamped: TOP SECRET: NOT TO BE OPENED UNTIL LIGHT-SPEED ACCELERATION PAST NEPTUNE. "We are still hours away from Neptune. Now, I don't expect this to contain much more than directions for a couple of high school experiments. But on the off chance we've been sent out here to save the world within a critical time frame..." Helena shook the envelope like maybe they could guess its contents that way. "I believe we should peak inside immediately to inform my decision-making process. As first officer, Buddy Leung, if at any point you assess I've become mentally incapacitated, I will not resist stepping down for you to assume command. Unless you herewith exercise that option, I intend to violate mission protocol and open this packet right now."

"So far so good, Captain," said Buddy. "You have my full support. I find your analysis cogently far from evidencing the least mental incapacitation."

To which remark everyone else spontaneously stood up and applauded.

Captain Taylor covered her mouth to conceal its quiver. Quickly regaining her composure, though, she went on, "I couldn't hope for a better crew to guide my decision-making. I especially appreciate the support and trust of those of you who think I might be making way too much of circumstances. Part of me feels most partial to that perspective, making this matter even more difficult. So I implore you to further plead your case as you feel warranted. Or on the other hand, give me additional reason to trust where I am headed with this."

"Open the damned envelope, Captain," said Kevin, and everyone laughed.

"Very well, Officer Smith-Park, if you insist."

The top secret "damned envelope" contained a video diskette and papers full of drawings with accompanying texts. Helena dove into the papers as she held out the diskette and said, "Someone put this on the screen, split view."

"Helena-"

"Sh!" she cut off her husband while Buddy rushed the diskette into Yoon-hee's hands.

Once Yoon-hee loaded up the diskette, the Earthlings' window on outer space shrank into the left half of the view-screen. Starlight could still be seen funneling into the Smoke and Mirrors' photon exhaust shaft. Meanwhile on the right half of the screen, President Carey was revealed seated at his desk. "Captain Taylor and any crew members who may be watching this with you," he said, "my congratulations on achieving light-speed velocity. Or if you broke protocol, if you peeked in the closet early at your birthday present, no harm, no foul. Because I'm here to discuss something urgently serious, not quite birthday present material I'm afraid."

Debbie and Yoon-hee gasped, both modestly covering their mouths.

"Months ago, November 2060, the monitor satellite orbiting Uranus picked up an intelligently produced transmission from outside our solar system."

"Holy crap!" exclaimed Kevin.

Ali, Tanya, Buddy and Chris crowded behind Helena to look over her shoulders at what consumed her visual attention while listening to the president's video.

"There were striking similarities to the packages we've sent out announcing our own existence and location. You will notice in the third transmission, for example, a diagrammatic of their solar system. An arrow points to their planet, presumably, fourth from their sun.

"You might be asking yourself, 'So what's the problem?' Extraterrestrial communication is obviously an historic development of such import as to dwarf your achievement of safe light-speed propulsion, as momentous as that is. But didn't the transmission initiate so long ago, for all we know its originators are now extinct? Perhaps they destroyed themselves in a nuclear holocaust or some environmental calamity which makes the Mars storm look like a picnic? Where's the urgency?"

Captain Taylor's headshake in disbelief had more to do with what she'd just read than with the video presentation.

"I am in way over my head at this point, Captain Taylor and crew," the president went on. "So I am turning this over to someone for whom I'm not sure this stuff even reaches his knees. Dr. Aquinas?"

"Dr. Aquinas," repeated Kevin. "I've wondered where he disappeared to. They must have had to slap down the lid extra hard on at least two dozen other people to keep this..." He trailed off as one of the world's foremost applied astrophysics engineers appeared on screen.

"Captain Taylor, First Officer Leung, Second Officer Smith and Engineer Murphy-Davis... I know a lot of you. Anyway," went on Aquinas, making a nervous-tic adjustment of his spectacles, "There was a procedure established decades ago for handling first contact. Short of a saucer vehicle landing on the White House lawn, the intelligence quarantine restricts knowledge of such an event to twenty individuals maximum. And I understand in this case that fortuitous circumstances kept it down to ten, including the president and the head of the Joint Chiefs of Staff. Anyway, you'll notice in your packet a series of time-elapse star charts transmitted to us. They reveal two things. One, they establish near which star the transmission source is located. Two, they facilitate determination of when the transmission was made, within a one-week margin of error.

"I'm guessing you don't need me to tell you which star, if you've been poring over the charts as intensively as we did. But just in case, it's Alpha Centauri C. Alpha Centauri C is a class G sun with 1.1 luminosity and 1.05 mass, approximately five light-years from our sun. No surprises as to the star type we expected could host a habitable planet. And that planet, as President Carey mentioned, is the fourth one out. It is ninety-seven million miles away from Alpha Centauri C, with a .95 mass compared to Earth's."

"The Goldilocks zone," Helena Taylor murmured while on the video, Aquinas went on, "We had long since identified it as one of eighty-seven-hundred planets potentially suitable for carbon-based life forms. And that's where everything we expected begins and ends."

Everyone looked up from the papers in Captain Taylor's hands, to give each other telling glances. They had already figured out a lot from the pictograph transmissions. But presently they were about to hear someone give voice to those figuring-outs, and thereby make them inescapably real.

"The time of transmission: approximately three months prior to this presentation. The mystery, one mystery is how we received it so quickly. As you can see in pictograph transmission number five, vehicles visit their space station from a large pyramid structure erected on their planet. But nothing suggests they have developed anything close to the photon-propelled technology of even our magsails. We have every reason to believe their technological development is at least a good fifty years behind ours. How fascinating, incidentally, their use of 'x' to denote that of which they are incapable."

Pictograph five featured a drawing of rocket-like things. Atop each rocket were depicted tinier, bug-like things, with stick figures beside them. The stick figures were crossed out, suggestive the bug-like things were satellites, perhaps.

"My best guess is that a small-scale wormhole sucked one of their satellite transmissions out our end. Who knows?" Aquinas continued.

"You hear the man?" asked Kevin. "Like I suggested, maybe that's what happened to our 'UFO.'"

"But we're really no closer to definitively establishing the existence of such a phenomenon now than we were a century ago. So I doubt our Alpha Centauri neighbors were counting on it. More likely, they were praying for a chance flyby near their solar system of a civilization as kindly as it is advanced. The important thing is, we received the transmissions in a timely-enough manner, hopefully.

"Anyway, while the central purpose of our transmissions 'out there' has been simply to say, 'Hello, here we are,' clearly their central purpose has been to say, 'Help! Urgent!'

"I refer you now to pictographs seven and eight, both most fascinating in a multitude of ways. Number seven clearly, um, actually there is compelling clarity to nearly the entirety of the transmission. I could probably shut up, and you'd easily digest the rest yourself. But I am sure you appreciate the importance of making absolutely certain we are all of the exact same understanding. You must advise us immediately of even your smallest divergence from our reading of this or any of the other pictographs." Dr. Aquinas paused to clear his throat before proceeding, "Pictograph seven shows a stick figure falling off a cliff-like structure. And next to where you would expect its mouth, a balloon is drawn. That balloon, sure enough, contains special markings one assumes constitute language. They resemble hieroglyphics, but I've checked. They are not at all related to Egyptian, Sumerian or other Earthling hieroglyphic systems. But an arrow is pointing at the balloon. Apparently x's and arrows carry universal semantic import.

"Next we examine pictograph eight. The same characters are scribbled inside its balloon as are scribbled inside the pictograph seven balloon. Apart from that, the number eight pictograph stick figure is depicted caught in the maw of what can only be described as some sort of huge reptilian creature. Whether real or fanciful, we don't know. The commonality between the two pictographs being a stick figure in peril, we deduce that the identical scribbles contained by each balloon signify, 'Help!'

"Help from what, that apparently is depicted in subsequent pictographs.

"Pictograph nine features a star chart, presumably the constellations as they appear from Alpha Centauri C's fourth planet. An arrow points from one star to a saucer-shaped object. We have determined the star is Cygnitaurus, luminosity .87, mass .98, distance from our sun eleven light-years, about seven light-years from Alpha Centauri C. We're talking another class G sun where we would not be surprised to find carbon-based life forms thriving on one of its planets. In fact, a curious binary planet system maintains a steady, eighty-eight-million-mile-radius orbit of Cygnitaurus.

"In pictograph ten, the saucer in pictograph nine, presumably from near Cygnitaurus, appears to have crashed. It is shown embedded at an odd angle on the planet's surface. Pictograph eleven illustrates two figures carrying a third figure away on a stretcher from the crashed saucer. Most fascinating, the two standing figures sport eye slits and oval-shaped heads. The figure on the stretcher, presumably injured, has what look to be antlers on its head."

"Wow!" said Chris, overcome.

"Is this love at first sight, seeing sketches of your first real extraterrestrials? That is, assuming this isn't the hoax of the century?" asked Kevin.

"In pictograph twelve, the balloon emerging from the antlered figure's mouth is large enough to encompass the following four pictographs. We've labeled them thirteen A, B, C, and D. Thirteen A shows a fleet of saucers with an arrow pointing to them from Cygnitaurus. Two additional arrows point from the saucer fleet to Alpha Centauri C, and to a third class G star, Callaway X Centra. Callaway X Centra has 98 percent luminosity and 99 percent mass, and is nine light-years from Earth. And I'm sure you have also noted a third arrow extends from the saucer fleet to our sun."

When Dr. Aquinas paused, Chris sensed an unscripted quiet moment for prayer, or to otherwise draw upon whatever spiritual resources available.

"Pictograph thirteen B," Aquinas went on finally, "portrays antlered figures wielding whips. They are driving numbers of slit-eyed figures into a box at the bottom of one of the saucer-shaped craft. The slit-eyed figures might as well be cattle.

"Pictograph thirteen C shows the body of a slit-eyed figure separated into pieces.

"Pictograph thirteen D is the most disturbing of all. It depicts the antlered figures with body parts in their mouths. And those are clearly meant to be the body parts of the slit-eyed figure displayed in pictograph thirteen C.

Another pause.

"Maybe the antlered figure on the stretcher, presumably from the crashed vessel, came to the Alpha Centauri C system to warn what was coming. Maybe it would have been on its way to our neck of the interstellar woods next, if not for the crash. Or maybe it was part of the advance guard for the invasion, and the slit-eyed figures were able to squeeze this information out of it.

"A hostile civilization with the technological wherewithal to project itself to a solar system seven light-years away might just as easily pose a severe threat eleven light-years away. If they expect to be rounding up people like cattle, they might possess the weaponry and strategies for overwhelming any resistance. We don't really know. Here I turn this back over to President Carey. Mr. President?"

"Thank you, Dr. Aquinas. Captain Taylor, crew, you can probably tell where we're going with this. I know that over the years, there have been whispers, suggestions our government knows more about UFOs than it's letting on. These suggestions have persisted even after extensive exploration of our backyard solar system has turned up nothing you would have expected, had extraterrestrials been visiting regularly."

Kevin nodded *You see?* at Chris.

"I'd love for there to be little green men locked up in some secret air hangar, who we could consult for further insight into this situation. But we've got nothing. Or if we do have anything, I'm not even trusted with such knowledge.

"These are my orders as your commander-in-chief. For now, I want you to shelve establishing a nemesis tracking station inside our solar system's Oort Cloud. Instead, devote your full attention to the feasibility of the Smoke and Morrors safely and quickly leaving that Oort Cloud behind, in favor of breaching the Oort Cloud presumably encapsulating the Alpha Centauri C system. Your new goal is to establish first contact with the originators of the pictograph transmission.

"Officer Leung, Dr. Aquinas is of the opinion there are enough spare mirror array parts on board to retrofit the spacecraft for a light-speed multiple capable of bringing you to Alpha Centauri C within three months."

Helena grimly acknowledged Buddy Leung's cringe.

"Even if the retrofit works out, Captain Taylor, it's your call whether to proceed with this new mission, or return to Space Station 2 for further consideration of our next move. I cannot order you into a situation you deem perilous to a foolhardy extent.

"But should you decide the mission is a 'go,' this is how Dr. Aquinas and I foresee the crew's roles. Ali Magabu, you're the expert linguist. Work closely with Yoon-hee Park-Smith to glean what you can from the sparse written language in the alien transmission. Develop strategies for rapidly building lines of communication with the extraterrestrials once formal contact is established. Dr. Aquinas and I discussed whether you should formulate a reply to transmit in advance with a refitted firefly donut. It would communicate that help is on the way. But we concluded such a transmission posed too much danger. What if your reply fell into the hands, mandibles, whatever of the ETs from the Cygnitaurus system? Obviously, we do not know for a fact yet that the habitable planet of Alpha Centauri C hasn't already been overrun by the supposed enemy. For all we know, the Cygnitaurus aliens are already shipping Alpha-Centauri ground meat back home.

"Dr. Deborah Davis-Murphy, I understand you have extensive training and experience in hazardous biochemical research and accompanying decontamination procedures. Should the new mission proceed, we will depend on you to develop and train the crew in a strict new protocol for healthfully safe contact with inhabitants of the Alpha Centauri C solar system.

"Dr. Tanya Petrovsky, as mission specialist for the original mission, your expertise obviously is still crucial for any safe navigation of Oort Cloud boundaries."

Dr. Aquinas leaned back into view on the video. "Tanya," he said, "I assume you and Buddy will use your extra firefly donuts as scout probes."

"Chris Olsen-Taylor..."

As Buddy slapped him encouragingly on the back, Chris remembered a long-ago literature teacher speaking his name in just such a tone because he wasn't paying attention.

"...your task, should the reconfigured mission proceed, will be as important as anyone's. At minimum, the nine of you will be cooped up together for a good six months. That would be trying under the best of circumstances. Yes, you've got food supplies to last well over a year. But you're going to need someone who is the point person for keeping people's spirits high. Officer Olsen-Taylor, you are that person. I am well aware the mirror array propulsion system provides the spinoff benefit of partial gravity. And that as a result, last-minute launch prep included retrofitting a full oven and cooking ingredients. Officer Olsen-Taylor, if you don't already know how to prepare chocolate chip cookies, you need to learn."

"Is part of the mission to see what happens to us when we sample his baking experiments?"

There was no reaction to Kevin, for fear of missing what else the president had left to say on video.

"Captain Taylor, clearly you understand the explosive nature of the information with which you and your crew have been entrusted. No telling the consequences were it ever more widely disseminated. That being said, I am still hoping against hope you find circumstances far more benign than they presently appear. In fact, wish I could say we were simply dealing with the hoax of the century. But Dr. Aquinas tells me the best we can realistically pray for is that the aliens in the Alpha Centauri C system are crying wolf to get attention.

"For some years now, extraterrestrial contact has been considered inevitable, only a matter of time. But who could have foretold the first message received from outer space being a distress call? Well I'm rambling, three days before your scheduled departure.

"Captain Taylor, please contact me soon as you have reached a decision. The well-wishes and prayers of the world are already with you on this historic voyage as it is generally understood. You know what they would be..." President Carey trailed off with a stiff-upper-lip nod. Then the video went blank.

Whirs and clicks from the ship's computer systems irregularly punctuated the tinkle-tinkle ambience, an ambience first noted on initial acceleration to one-half light-speed. Buddy likened those tinkle-tinkles to distant chimes. And he was convinced he understood their source, the where-from, if not the how. Light was forced to favor its photon particle nature over its wavelength character on its funneled rush through the Smoke and Mirrors central shaft. This was also thought responsible for the sparkly "exhaust" out the ship's "rose" rear.

Kevin's outburst about having to deal with Chris's cooking might as well have not happened. The issue remained: What were to be the first words spoken on this side of a revelation of such enormous consequence, a boundary might as well have been crossed from AD over to a new epoch?

Captain Taylor finally got the ball rolling. "President Carey said no one could accuse us of not going forth into the cosmos in peace," she noted. "Isn't that what he said, Buddy?"

"His exact words, Captain."

"I heard them too," added Chris. *Don't leave me out.*

"He pointedly referred to our being unarmed. Yet the thing is, he already knew. Long before that conversation, he knew."

"Captain, I don't want to promote paranoia," said Buddy most somberly. His nervous laughter like they were all standup comedians might as well have been left back aboard Space Station 2. "But isn't it possible that UFO was a reconnaissance craft dispatched by those antlered guys from Cygnitaurus? Could they be sizing us up already in preparation for an invasion? I can't believe I just said that."

Captain Taylor squinted. "If they're that advanced, they won't be expecting..." She abruptly sprang out of her seat and turned around to face her crew. They had gathered behind the captain's chair to peek over her shoulder at the extraterrestrial transmission printout while taking in President Carey's videotape. "First allow me to reiterate," she went on. "Imagine hallucinations and/or other manifestations of madness overwhelm my ability to competently lead this mission, and I do not voluntarily step down. Buddy, I expect you to forcibly, forcibly end my command and assume full control."

"Yes, Captain."

"In fact I wouldn't mind being told right now that I just suffered from a massive hallucination. President Carey didn't really ask us to make Alpha Centauri C our new destination to answer a distress call, did he? And he didn't warn of antlered creatures from Cygnitaurus about to launch a multiple-solar-system food-gathering expedition? Buddy, shouldn't you be relieving me from duty, forthwith?"

"If you were hallucinating, Captain, so were the rest of us."

"Occam's Razor," said Chris. Unsure whether to add 'Captain' or 'Helena,' he opted for neither. "The simplest, most elegantly straightforward explanation is often the closest to the truth."

"Well," Captain Taylor sighed.

Chris had to wonder whether she was expressing frustration over being stuck with his nonsense.

"If we're all suffering from some hitherto unidentified form of mass hysteria triggered by approaching light-speed," Taylor went on, "the reality check will have to impinge from an outside source. Either ground control will have to ask us what we're up to before, uh... How can we reach Alpha Centauri C in three months, Officer Leung?"

"Forty times light-speed should do it, Captain. That is, if we succeed with Dr. Aquinas's proposed retrofit."

"Okay. Well, either ground control will have to catch us before we really take off. Or I suppose we will get the hint if we find all the planets in the Alpha Centauri C system uninhabitable."

"Unless, Captain," said Ali Magabu, "this hysteria you speak of convinces us, oblivious to reality, that one of the planets is fully populated. In which case, as part of that old song goes, truly, life will be but a dream."

"And for communicating with that dream, Dr. Magabu, you can get to work linguistically analyzing the extraterrestrial transmission. As President Carey suggested, glean whatever you can from the pictographs and the scant language samples. We need a hard plan for the initial back-and-forth on first direct contact."

"I'm honored, Captain, truly."

"Yoon-hee will assist."

"Honored as well, Captain."

"Dr. Davis-Murphy, Debbie, I expect that over the next few months you will devise a safety protocol for close encounter with an extraterrestrial bio-system.

"Buddy Leung, you will head up the team working on the mirror array retrofit, surprise surprise. And maybe you can use a spare firefly donut for the scouting mission to chart a safe course through the Oort Cloud or above it, if there is an above." Helena waved off Officer Leung's acknowledgment to go on, "Kevin, reprogram for a straight course with full light-speed mirror deployment initiating in one hour. That's after our scheduled transmission to Dr. Aquinas. As per President Carey's advice, Yoon-hee, during that check-in we will act like we didn't peek at our birthday presents."

"Nay, Captain."

"We are scrubbing shallow descent back into the orbital plane for the Neptune flyby. But that's obvious from my straight-course order. And Yoon-hee, work with Geena on a firefly application for maintaining contact with at least a Jupiter moon outpost once we leave the solar system.

"Needless to say, I will stay here sifting through all incoming data for any warning signs re extraterrestrial spacecraft, worm holes, dark matter, you name it.

"And Officer Chris Olsen?"

"Yes, Captain."

The other three couples shared amused looks.

"Mr. Olsen, I like my cookies with the extra dark chocolate chips and plenty of crushed walnuts."

"Aye-aye, Captain."

"Tanya, Geena, you two want a little more sleep before-"

"I'm okay."

"We're okay, Captain," said Tanya.

"Then let's get going. We've got some planets to save, maybe, including our own."

Chapter 7: The Third Session

"Look who I bring home!" called out Ludi entering arm-in-arm with Pedro, who leaned against her for support. "Is not a stray dog!"

"My back remains in terrible condition, my little heaven," Pedro mumbled softly. "Probably you are better with a stray dog. Ow! Help! She is torturing me!" he cried from Ludi's twisting ear-pinch.

"Ay Mami! Is Pedro!" exclaimed Pedro's sister, Jerri, who'd opened the door. "I can see my brother is no better dance companion now than before the accident. What a pathetic chorus line he makes with you, Ludi!"

"I know. Is better a palm tree in a strong breeze. At least I can sway to that rhythm! But still I love my big handsome who worries maybe I would be happier with some dog!"

"Do not worry, brother. She can't have my dog!" said Jerri, kissing Ludi and Pedro on the cheek. Then noticing her brother's cringe, she added, "Ay, Pedro perfecto, hurts when you move too much?"

"Hurts when I LIVE too much! We only stay for a short time; need to assure everything is okay back home."

"Ay, no!" protested Rotonda coming out of the kitchen cradling her granddaughter. "Listen, Alexita linda, we cannot permit your mama to steal your macho papa for herself! Sí! Three women are going to compete for him! Sí! Sí! Sí, señor!"

"Look who has returned for his princess," spoke Ludi to Alexandra in a girlishly high pitch. "He is also here to warn you about certain dogs!"

"Hey!? I can call my dog a dog, but you cannot," protested Jerri.

Alexita worked to keep her wobbly head from falling over to one side or the other, or forward onto her chin. Besides which she was taking in the sights, trying to reconcile them with the noises people made. The moment she looked Pedro and Ludi's way, though, all such bother dissolved into a sunburst smile. Lights-turned-on recognition of her parents crossed Alexita's face. Mama and papa, the love that produced her, made plenty enough sense of the world.

Alexita squealed with delight as she reached out for her parents with her tiny yet pudgy arms. Her squeal startled Ludi's grandfather Típico out of his drowsing off to the televised baseball game.

"Ay caramba... Oh!" Típico exclaimed as he saw what brought on Alexita's ear-piercing outburst. "Norma?! Look! Pedro is here from the hospital!"

"Yes, I have noticed," said Norma seated at the dining table not four feet behind Típico. "And three chicas are fighting over him. The two losers can join me to fight over who gets stuck with you! That gives me a chance of not being the one!"

"Ay caramba!"

"Here, sit down here, son," said Placido, suddenly stirring from his adjustable extra-cushy armchair with an awkward scramble, having himself nearly drowsed off. He also offered up the remote control.

"Oh, man, the key to the throne of the king!" Pedro knew how much it meant for his stepfather to hand over his remote control. Ditto for giving up "the throne," which he couldn't bring himself to have Ludi steer him over to accept. Pedro feared becoming a potted plant, only distinguishing himself from a potted plant by making an occasional comment on the game, but otherwise just sitting on Placido's easy chair...like a potted plant. Again, he knew this wasn't any fairer than were he to mock his

Alexita, his little angel, for dozing off in her mama's arms. But if loved ones are life's meaning, aren't you required to work on big dreams for their happiness and security? Isn't it a betrayal how his parents gave up? How they settled on an extra cushy seat and a remote in front of a big TV in what had to be admitted was a barrio, what they called a "slum" in English? Where contraction of AIDs was only a finger prick away? From one of the hypodermic needles still dripping with heroine, carelessly flung into the weedy empty lot just across the street?

But Ludi's clumsy dancer checked himself on too much pride over having secured a detached house out in the suburbs. His mama and step-papa both made tremendous sacrifices, leaving Puerto Rico for Philadelphia to seek a better life. The unjust struggles they subsequently endured, wouldn't those have been enough to send Pedro drinking like Don Placido used to until his mama's love straightened him out? And didn't his mama's love also prepare Pedro well for coping with prejudice and other obstacles to his goals? In an important sense, couldn't that special pair of sneakers she bought him in junior high have been equipped with rockets that launched him closer to the stars he was always trying to discern through the city haze? So that now, out in the suburbs, he enjoyed crystal-clear celestial views with a telescope he'd afforded to buy in addition to the detached home? Even making out the ring of Saturn?

"Ay, Papi, leave him to rest," Rotonda admonished her husband when Pedro at last pivoted around Ludi to head for the "throne." It was as though she sensed her son's inner turmoil. Yet she was also promoting the absurd notion, in Pedro's estimation, that standing engulfed by women was more restful than reclining in a luxury armchair.

"Aydiomio, Rotonda, I am not asking him to wrestle!"

"No wrestling for my poor little rabbit! Still his back is so bad, ay Dios mio!"

"This might be my final opportunity to tackle him to the ground before I am too old and he is too macho!" Placido responded. If his wife was going to take his words the wrong way, he might as well aggravate her aggravation.

"No wrestling!"

"I think I wrestle with you instead, the type of wrestling where we make more little rabbits!"

Knock! Knock! Knock!

Placido cringed. Rotonda stood a far enough distance away, she could not possibly be raining down blows on him for his remark about "more little rabbits." But he wasn't certain he didn't deserve such blows for his crudeness, despite the frustration that prompted it. So the timing of the noise at the front door...he relaxed his shoulders as he realized those knocks weren't on his head.

"Ay caramba!" griped Típico in a gravelly voice as Gloria got the door.

Finally gratefully seated on Placido's "throne," Pedro mused over Típico's complaint. *The way he reacted, someone might as well have spilled a dish of rice and beans all over his lap. He should know what it is for someone to run a red light, coming right at you, so you see your whole life passing before your eyes...*

"Roberto!" exclaimed Pedro, recognizing his old high school friend.

Roberto snaked his way between Pedro's wife, Pedro's mama holding Pedro's baby daughter, and Pedro's step-father Placido looking cast aimlessly adrift without the anchor of his chair and remote. Roberto, all moustache and smiling yet wary, darting eyes...he could have been weaving around traffic cones on an obstacle course.

"How did you discover what happened to me?"

"I know nothing what happened to you, man. We don't see you at the cantina no more. I am just checking to assure you are okay. Appears very comfortable that chair where you are sitting."

Yes, you caught me, Roberto. I have been such a good friend that I have been too busy luxuriating in this chair to see how you are doing. The least I could have done was drop by the corner cantina. Where to go with Roberto, relationship wise, had grown increasingly problematic for Pedro. A two-year army stint succeeded graduation, then vocational training and marriage. But every few months Pedro had made a point of reconnecting with Roberto at Primitivo's. Roberto could always be found there ready for a free beer, and answering each milestone in Pedro's life with a steadily more disturbing, unsettling milestone of his own. Pedro considered Roberto's deepening involvement with drug trafficking to be the worst, by far.

Roberto had neither the grades nor the money for college, even junior college. And he failed the physical fitness test for joining Pedro in the military. So right out of high school, he tried his hand at one of those door-to-door sales schemes. He needed to "sponsor" so many "associates," and they had to do well for themselves before he would start to see any real money. He did sell some cosmetic and hand cream products to Pedro's mama, thanks to his sisters' urging. And of course they confiscated most of it for their own use. But when Roberto argued Rotonda should "invest" in bulk purchase of "inventory" so she could "sponsor" other "associates," she bristled. Other neighborhood women he approached reacted similarly. Moreover, those other women and Pedro's mom soon discovered comparable products at considerably lower cost at local department stores. Thereafter, Roberto couldn't even get them to buy off the remainder of his own "inventory." "Why this company wants to bleed additional money out of our community?" Rotonda asked Pedro. "We are not poor enough?"

Roberto insisted the face cream he sold was far superior to the typical store-bought product. He argued it should cost three or four times as much, let alone twice as much. But he failed to convince Rotonda. And eventually he stopped telling Pedro this was such a tremendous "first floor opportunity" that shouldn't be missed. Pedro never was clear how Roberto got out from under the pyramid scheme.

However, Roberto's next intrigue almost had Pedro wishing he would find another shady sales gimmick instead. Roberto took up with a woman plastered by so much makeup and lipstick, Pedro would have nicknamed her "the clown" were he not concerned his friend's self-esteem had already taken too many big "hits." When Roberto brought her to meet him at the local cantina, she laughed a "tee-hee" Pedro found too affected for a woman in her mid-twenties.

If only that was the worst of it.

Roberto went on about how they should double-date, with Pedro bringing along his then-fiancé Ludi. But Pedro couldn't imagine Ludi finding the least thing in common with her. Maybe if they went to see a movie…

"I tell you, man, this woman Celestina has opened my eyes to things I never consider before. You know how people say the marijuana is no good for you?"

"It's not worse than cigarettes, only because people don't normally chain-smoke marijuana."

"I know, man, I know!" conceded Roberto like Pedro's observation went without saying.

Which put Pedro on guard that Roberto was about to push something outrageous.

"But Celestina confirmed what I heard before, but never stopped to consider," went on Roberto. "She told me how marijuana makes the treatments far less painful for people dying from cancer. There is also less nausea, so they are not throwing up all the time. The problem, though, is that in the U.S. they cannot obtain the drug legally." Here Roberto's voice had softened to a whisper. "She is selling it to these people so they not suffer. Am not sure what to think. I only know is very good money for her."

"Friend, you have to be careful," cautioned Pedro. "The police find that stuff on her when she is with you…"

"I know, man, I know!"

A double-date is definitely not happening.

The next time Pedro and Roberto shared beer with fresh *pan de agua* bread at Primitivo's Cantina, Roberto also shared a discouraging development. Shaking his head, Roberto admitted with a girlishly high-pitched laugh, "You were right about Celestina, man. I found out she is working for a pimp who almost killed her when he discovered she was with me. Now who knows whether her son is his or mine? I still buy him clothes and toys; I take responsibility even though maybe I am not the father, and have terminated relations with the mother."

Pedro really felt for Roberto with his latest humiliating disappointment. But he also couldn't help a wave of hope washing over him, as tangible as Roberto's beer breath. Maybe this particular disappointment would be the earthquake, finally, to change his friend as significantly as earthquakes changed the land.

At long last, maybe Roberto would seek a good path.

Or not; eyes darting from side to side, Roberto proceeded to whisper breathlessly, "I know drug trafficking is very wrong. But the money is so good, and I realized something. If one person is not making distributions in a certain area, another person fills the vacuum. In other words, if I am not doing it, someone else will. That is something I must consider."

"Drug trafficking is as wrong as anything gets, my friend. And you should also consider this: Gangs are always battling over who distributes in a particular neighborhood. A lot of sellers are shot." This wasn't the first time Pedro Perez offered reality checks. However, Ricardo's rationale for selling drugs left Señor Perez far more disturbed than ever before. Afterwards, he just couldn't bring himself to return to Primitivo's ever again, even though that felt like he was abandoning Roberto. But he had a wife and beautiful baby daughter to protect. How could he forgive himself if he got caught up in a police raid that found cocaine and the like in his friend's possession?

"Hey, man, I hope you are not carrying…" Once he got over the shock of Roberto's surprise appearance, the first thing Pedro thought to say concerned drugs, naturally.

"Noooo!" Roberto protested. "No way would I bring that stuff into the home of your family."

"Okay. Well then, I tell you what happened. I was driving home from work…" Pedro easily resolved not to let on about his Jersey suburb residence, about specifically where he was driving home from work *to*. Roberto said "no way" would he bring drugs into his family's home. But where *would* he bring "that stuff"? "…So I am making this left turn on the left turn green light arrow, when this old woman barrels through the red light! She smashes so far into the side of my car… Oh, look! Is a commercial for the insurance company! They are the ones managing my claim against the other driver!"

In the upper-right-hand corner of the TV screen appeared the AllCare logo, people arm-in-arm in a circle. Set to peace-after-the-storm piano tinkling, a woman said, "The sirens gave us barely enough warning to reach our underground shelter before the tornado hit." The video cut to a later portion of the interview where the woman went on, "I found our favorite family photo with miraculously only a hairline crack in the glass." Later still, "The AllCare adjuster wrote up our claim that same day. We were able to plan with the builders before the cleanup had even begun." The commercial concluded with a deep-voiced narrator, "Your care is our care; we all care. AllCare."

"Oh, man," Roberto squeaked his pitying amusement. "How they say in English? You are 'screwed.'"

"Man, no," Pedro scoffed. "Why you say 'screwed'?"

"You hear that commercial, Pedro? They are acting like they are saints because they handled this insured woman's claim when her house was destroyed by a tornado. They are suggesting this is exceptional service when they accomplish what they are paid to accomplish. You believe they are going to think twice about denying a claim like you are making?"

"What do you mean, man, about 'a claim like I am making'?"

"You said there was a left turn green arrow for you to go through when the old woman hit you. But if it is not one of those intersections with cameras, AllCare only has your word about the green arrow. How are you going to prove to them she had the red light?"

"You think I am lying?"

"No, man, I believe you. What I think is that the insurance company will bet it can avoid responsibility."

"No, no. I will tell you what they said, Roberto. Not only are they believing me, they had the excellent idea to post a sign by the traffic light. It asks anyone who witnessed the accident to call them. Such a busy intersection, for sure there was at least one witness, and probably many."

"And if no one calls because they are afraid of the Mafia or something? Then what?"

"Makes no difference, man. The insurance company WILL take care of it."

"Good." Roberto sensed a defensive tone unusual coming from Pedro, so he decided not to press any further. "You okay, man? Clearly from what you say, your car is a wreck, but how about you? Are you a wreck as well?"

"Too much wreck, my friend." With his gentlest voice, Pedro tried to make up for how he bristled at Roberto for questioning whether AllCare would settle. "The doctor says the collision caused a tear in one of my backbone muscles. And the tear sends a pain shooting down my right leg when I put too much pressure on my right foot. I need the insurance money for an operation. In the meantime I cannot go to work."

Pedro didn't reveal the consequences if his health issues weren't resolved in a matter of months. His savings would dry up, and the emergency supplemental union fund would only keep his family financially solvent for a short time beyond. He hadn't been at his job anywhere near long enough to draw disability, and this wasn't even job-related, so... Pedro well knew why he snapped at Roberto over how AllCare might handle his situation if an eyewitness didn't step forward to verify the green light arrow. The possibility so much of what he'd worked for could be lost, thanks to one person's careless stupidity, was too much to take.

With Roberto's questions, Pedro relived for the umpteenth occasion the moments leading up to his fateful accident. And he yearned for time travel, to redirect the course of history like they did in those *Back to the Future* movies.

Completing his routine feeder station inspection faster than expected, Pedro was headed home by late afternoon on that fateful day in mid-September. Having no idea what danger awaited him, he experienced grateful contentment as he quickly approached the three-way intersection where everything would change. The sun setting to his rear cast a pleasant mix of waning light and encroaching shade ahead, instead of glaring in his eyes. He would be getting home early to the Jersey suburbs, to his beautiful wife and precious baby daughter. Maybe they would set up his telescope in the backyard like they'd done the previous night. They could take a closer look at the full moon, and cross-reference it with his lunar map. He would show Ludi various lunar craters, and the spot where one of the manned moon landings took place way back in the early 70's.

Most importantly, maybe the previous evening's magical vibe would be encored.

When the Perez family went outside to their humble little backyard the night before, they found the moonlight bathing everything, everyone in ghostly white. That included a few scraggly yet productive tomato plants tied to the chain-link fence, and coral pink impatiens thriving like robust weeds along the brick wall beside the rear stoop. But even more enchantment awaited them. With a sweep of her arm not cradling Alexita, Ludi cooed, "Oohh, aahh." And Alexita obliged with an "Oohh, aahh" of her own, happily flapping her baby-fat-pudgy arms. *Trying to fly?* Pedro wondered. Whatever, Alexita stared down Ludi, obviously seeking approval of her imitative behavior. Best of all, her "ahhh" swelled into a squeal of bemusement at what she was doing.

Pedro couldn't be sure his daughter's happy face was bathed in lunar glow, or her happy face was doing the bathing.

"Hey, man, I don't know what I was thinking," said Roberto crashing in on Pedro's soothing albeit wistful recollection, though not to the damaging extent that old woman crashed in on it long days ago. "If the old woman who hit you admits she ran a red light, then you are right, man. You don't have to worry about the insurance company paying. That is how this thing went, yes?"

Pedro was always extra careful about turning left on a green light, even when there was a left turn arrow. He adamantly waited until he saw the crosswise traffic stopping on red, including before the accident.

The oncoming car in the lane closest to Pedro's turn lane had slowed way back uphill, in response to the yellow light. But it blocked the next lane over from Pedro's view so that he would have needed extrasensory perception or help from a guardian angel to see what was going on there.

Long after the light turned red, a big olive-colored Cadillac the next lane over from the stopped car was nevertheless continuing downhill at a steady twenty miles an hour, well below the speed limit ironically.

Pedro's split second of terror seared his mind, thereby making it destined to replay over and over. He glimpsed motion where there wasn't supposed to be any, just as he was tentatively edging his Toyota Corolla out past the stopped car in the nearest downhill-bound lane. ***TOO LATE,*** he thought horrifically. Whether he braked or accelerated, an awful collision with the big Cadillac was unavoidable.

The old woman's mouth froze rounded open in shock, and she reacted way too late applying her brakes. Meanwhile, her daughter wasn't keeping her eyes on the road, preoccupied trying to hear someone on her cell phone above the traffic din. She got taken by even more surprise than Pedro.

The dull yet deafening crunch included a boom! of windshield glass shattering into thousands of rounded pebbles.

For Pedro, this accident didn't play in quite the same slow motion typically depicted in movies. Rather, it took on the appearance of a most peculiar sculpture his spirit flit back and forth bothering over. He desperately sought an alternative to having to at last yield to time's free-fall rush forward.

At impact, his muscular frame flung about despite the seat belt constraint felt devoid of sensation for Pedro, an out-of-body experience. He found himself reminded of his sister Jerri holding on carelessly to her Raggedy Ann doll by only one arm as she bounded upstairs. Her doll swung so wildly, after weeks of such treatment its stitching loosened to the point that that arm was hanging on by a mere thread.

Out-of-body could postpone the inevitable for only so long. There came that awful moment when Pedro could not delay experiencing any longer whatever pain was to be experienced. He twisted the very least amount he thought necessary to unlatch his seatbelt. That's when knife-sharp pain shot up his spine into his neck, causing a jarring, nauseating headache. Then he noticed that somehow, thank God, he had already turned off the ignition. Nevertheless, he would have to wait for help, or risk further aggravating his injury.

The last thing Pedro expected was for the daughter of the driver who crashed into him to pound on his window, raging, "What did you do to my mother?!?! Look at what you did to my mother!!!"

Pedro amazed himself for not having automatically shouted, *Go to hell, woman! Look at what your mother did to me!* Sure, preservation instinct might have warned him such response could have led to more sharp pain shooting up his spine. But that it didn't even cross his mind to curse... Instead, his abundant spirit automatically probed deep. He wondered whether the daughter projected her anger, unable to admit personal blame. If only she had set aside her cell phone to give her mama's substandard driving more attention...

Pedro twisted anew, this time slowly enough to avoid more knife-in-the-back sensations. He saw the mother still seated behind the steering wheel, a faraway look in her eyes. A fancy broach concealed the top button of her flowery blouse. Shoulder pads helped that blouse hang as perfectly as though still on a clothes hanger. And her gray hair, elaborately coifed how Rotonda could never have afforded, might as well have been sculpted from marble where Pedro was concerned. So many things perfectly staged in her life, and now she had suddenly made this great big mess.

What was going through her head? Hints her family dropped to which she pretended to be oblivious, that she'd grown too old to drive? Jokes about buying her the Cadillac in lieu of a tank, only because it was cheaper? Her brother saying it would be "good enough" to protect her from whatever accident she might get herself into? Or how about the time she was driving on her own that her family didn't even know about? When someone furiously honking a horn woke her up to having run through a red light on that occasion as well?

Pedro found the sum of all his speculation most surprising. He pitied this woman far more than he reviled what she did to him. Giving up her driving privilege voluntarily or continuing until she crashed into someone didn't really matter. Either way, she was doomed to self-degrading humiliation simply for getting older. Involuntary manslaughter as well, had she killed Pedro. Society, or at least the society within which she moved, had not worked through a graceful enough manner for her to slide out from behind the steering wheel.

When Pedro had finally managed to roll down his window, he said, "I am sorry for your mother." Then he got to hear that response to the daughter's rage used against him with the police. This happened as he tried to tell his side of the story from a stretcher, before he was loaded into an ambulance. "If it isn't his fault, Officer, why did he apologize for what he did to my mother?" the daughter interrupted him to vent.

Presently for Roberto, Pedro would have shrugged his shoulders if not for the pain. He would have affected the nonchalance he wished he could feel in place of nagging dread. "Of course, the old lady and her family prefer not to admit the reality. But this makes no difference. The driver who stopped at the red light in the other lane, he saw the whole thing."

"Oh, then you have an eyewitness?" Roberto's eyes grew wide. "Oh, man, what you worry about? You got no problem for sure. I tell you, that old woman is in big trouble. Very big trouble."

"Excuse me, Roberto," said Ludi, juggling Alexita and two tall glasses. "Alexita tells me she is certain you two men want lemonade, *sí Preciosa?*"

After Ludi set down both drinks on the coffee table, Alexita complainingly extended her pudgy little arms towards Pedro.

"Ay, now she is protesting that she wanted to serve the lemonade herself. Here Papa," Ludi handed her over to Pedro, "you better take her."

Ludi was trying to redirect Pedro's focus to the miracle product of their love. Nevertheless, he couldn't help a grimace from the stabbing pain when he accepted Alexita into his arms.

"Oh, man, you hurt too much," Roberto shook his head in sympathy. Then leaning forward, he added in his conspiratorially soft voice, "Listen, man, I can get something to relieve you, something better than aspirin or Tylenol. Until you have surgery, is better for you I think."

"You see that smile?" Pedro pretended being too enraptured by his daughter to have heard Roberto's offer.

"You better check that smile is not from dumping a load of caca in her diapers, man!" Roberto laughed. But his amusement had more to do with how his increasingly distant friend ignored his proposal than with any caca threat.

"No, man! That smile, the light from that smile is the amazing breeze propelling me through all my work to provide her a happy life, caca or no caca!"

Roberto would have insisted Pedro needed something to reduce the pain enough for his daughter's smile to continue propelling him. But before he could utter another sound, Pedro's sisters made a huge racket giggling and shouting as they galloped downstairs from their bedroom.

Ludi's grandfather Típico went into a fit of "Ay caramba!" followed by complaining to his wife Norma, "I did not need to make such noise when I was young!"

"You make noise now that is more irritating than that, and you never were young!"

"Ay caramba!"

Pedro imagined his sisters swept downhill by a huge avalanche. They were screaming for help rather than enjoying themselves to an almost hysterical extent.

"Hey, Gloria, Jerri," Roberto waved them over like they were old drinking buddies he was waving over at the cantina. "Roachman and Bossaman both say hello. They said they will be looking for you tonight or something."

"We know," Gloria nodded, then darted her eyes towards her stepfather as in: The less said in his presence, the better. But too late.

Placido leaned forward out of his TV stupor to turn around and mumble, "I am not seeing much of those wild horses here lately."

Before Placido could really make his stepdaughters feel put on the spot, the televised crack! of a baseball bat intervened. A broadcaster's frantic shouting ensued, refocusing Placido on the game.

Under cover of din from the homerun excitement, Jerri reacted to her stepfather's comment he hadn't seen the boyfriends recently. "We are seeing too much of them!" she excitedly whispered Gloria's way, and left both sisters giggling and blushing. That was, until Gloria noticed Alexita's looks alternating from her to Jerri and back again. "Ay, how precious! Our niece is so precious!"

"Ay yes," chimed in Jerri.

Jerri and Gloria sounded to Pedro like they were crying in agony, as though pained by Alexita's cuteness. Perhaps regret they weren't that young and innocent anymore?

Whatever, an insistent knock at the front door bespoke the inevitable forward rush of events. Alexita could not remain the little baby forever. Yet Pedro also sensed a tempering gentleness, a hopeful wish for the course of that forward rush. *Doña Galleta!*

Ludi opened the front door, serenaded by Típico's umpteenth cry of "Ay caramba!"

Pedro imagined Ludi's grandfather bracing for a stampede of raging bulls, and Galleta a tiny mouse sniffing around a corner, how she peeked inside. He also thrilled at the prospect of finally another supposed spirit trek into the future. At long last, this mysterious woman would resume her search for meaning behind the strange pendant that fell from the sky. But what caught Pedro's attention next were his sisters suddenly bolting for the kitchen door, like their avalanche down the stairs had resumed.

Rotonda headed off Gloria and Jerri. "Where are you going?" she demanded to know. "That woman always brings the best cookies."

"Ay, Mami, we do not need more cookies," moaned Jerri. She and Gloria drooped over. Their arms hung limp, as though most of the life force had gone out of them. Or, "Mami" Rotonda mused, like they'd turned into a pair of weeping willows.

"What you do not need are more secret encounters with your machos."

"That is not for you to tell us!" cried Jerri in a mix of despair and defiance, though still drooped over.

Before the argument could escalate, Galleta intervened.

She might as well have materialized in the women's midst like a ghost, where Jerri was unsettlingly concerned.

Galleta held her tray forward. "These are dark chocolate oatmeal, including chopped pecans and almonds. You can take some with you, young women. You do not have to stay."

"Ay, Doña Galleta," Gloria whined resignedly with a wan smile while snatching two cookies. "We cannot say no to your face!"

Galleta's diminutive stature had her looking up at the sisters to address them, even though they remained drooped over. "When you feel like you are trapped in a spider web, sometimes you are right," she acknowledged. "It really is that bad." The treebark's worth of lines and creases in Cookie Lady Gellata's face seemed to multiply.

Rotonda wouldn't have been surprised if their neighborhood mystic was reflecting on her own troubled entanglements.

"But sometimes," Galleta continued, "what appear at the time like senseless traps are in reality good, protective. Someone's raft is caught on the rocks, and her jacket is snared on the branches of an overhanging tree. But thereby is she saved from the deadly waterfall further downstream. Tomato plants are tied to a trellis like prisoners chained to a wall. But when they give light to heavy fruit, those ties save them from becoming weighed so far over, they would have broken apart."

"Ay, our tomatoes are not THAT heavy!" Jerri giggled.

"Man, I remember something. Sorry, have to exit."

Pedro saw Roberto's eyes dart to the front door from Rotonda, Galleta and his two sisters congregated by the kitchen entryway. Clearly, Roberto was mapping out an escape route. So Pedro protested, "No, man, you should stay and see this. In August this very strange thing, some pendant with mysterious lettering, fell from a thunderstorm sky. Doña Galleta believes her spirit can travel to its origin. So each couple of weeks she has this session where she communicates to us from sixty years into the future on her search. Maybe she is inventing her story, but I am not sure. She tells about an 'Oort Cloud' and other crazy things I don't think she would know otherwise."

"You have to be careful, friend. That woman is probably a witch!"

"A witch?"

"Yes! Yes!" Roberto nodded emphatically, like what he said was something obvious and well known. "She made this story with me like you say she is making with you. I swear to you on the Bible, this is what she told me: My life is on a trajectory that could result in my grandson conceiving a major terrorist attack! Man, I think she got 9/11 on the brain! You think she comes up with such a thing if there is no 9/11?"

9/11, of course, referred to the terrorist attack on the Twin Towers in New York City in 2001.

"Maybe that is her special way for communicating her concern over certain of your habits. I don't know if it is true or not, that you are selling certain things. Maybe she hears rumors…"

"Drugs??" Roberto opened his eyes wide to suggest he was shocked, taken totally by surprise. But Pedro also detected a suppressed grin, and sensed Roberto was trying not to bust out laughing in embarrassment. "No, that was my ex-girlfriend! She almost she got me killed with that shit!"

"*Bueno*, you said," started in Pedro, about to recall Roberto saying "no way" about ever bringing any drugs into Pedro's house. The point being, that seemed to imply Roberto was in possession of drugs to not be brought in.

But Roberto interrupted, "Have to go; promised my mama I would pick up her groceries." He left at lightning speed.

Coincidentally, Galleta had just set down her cookie tray on the dining table, to retrieve the mysterious pendant on a bracelet chain from her apron jacket.

"I have been keeping this around my wrist at night," she told Ludi. "Although am not sure how much good that is going to do, as far as anchors go. Little more than the equivalent of a four-foot sea would be required to dislodge me and send me adrift."

"Doña Galleta," screeched Típico with a silly grin, "people cannot speak through you from the future, without your green blanket?"

"You need not worry, Don Típico. Whether my best recipes are mixed together in a pot or a bowl makes no difference." This time it was Galleta's turn to give Típico a silly grin. "Likewise, makes no difference whether I channel the future on my green blanket, or on whatever other blanket or towel your family might provide."

"But I don't think we have an extra towel or blanket!" protested Típico, not ready to give up so easily.

"Here you are." Norma moved faster than Pedro ever remembered, pulling a big bath towel from the hall closet and handing it to Galleta.

"Ay caramba!"

Subdued, Galleta unfolded the towel on the living room floor.

Nevertheless, Placido suddenly stirred restlessly where he retreated so Pedro could have his lounge chair.

How Papi is writhing about on the sofa, Galleta might as well have been setting down an arm full of rattlesnakes on the floor, Pedro mused.

"We can watch the game first?" asked Placido worriedly.

"I- I want to watch the game also!" Típico stuttered with excitement over the hope Placido revived. Maybe they could avoid another evening surrendered to this crazed woman prattling on in English about life sixty years from then, supposedly. Enjoy her cookies without the boring séance.

"The game will not finally end for three hours, at least," firmly pointed out Rotonda. "And that is when both of you will complain is too late for what Doña Galleta has come here for!"

"No! No!" Placido shook his head in near panic. "We turn the volume low so Doña Galleta can proceed-"

"Pedro, turn off that TV NOW!"

"Yes, Mami."

"Aydiomio!"

"Ay caramba!"

Galleta rose to her feet from where she'd spread out the towel. Then she folded together her hands in a most prayerful fashion, bowing her mousey head demurely towards Típico and Placido. For Pedro, she radiated a preachy countenance as she said, "Sometimes, the problem with television is like the problem with fishing nets. The net catches many more fish than a single fishing pole. A popular television show catches more audience for the commercial advertisers than a person who goes door-to-door introducing a product. But sometimes, fishing nets fatally entangle dolphins and other precious creatures of the sea that are not those precious creatures on which unfortunately we depend for food. The same goes for cattle-drive calls to 'Must-see TV.' People's talents and dreams become fatally entangled in too much time set aside as mere spectators."

"Doña Galleta," said Rotonda, "thank you so much for this visit. You could not have known my poor son Pedro would be here now, with his back hurt from an accident. But he has been asking when you will continue the search for the meaning of the pendant from the sky. *Sí*, Pedro?" Yes?

"Of course, Mami," Pedro nodded. He was certain Galleta's odd comparison left his mother as perplexed as his stepfather Placido and Ludi's grandpa Típico. That's why his mother went on about how grateful she was for Galleta's timely presence.

"To fulfill the promise of a good recipe," went on Galleta, "requires adding certain ingredients at just the right times. However, do not misconstrue," she waggled a cautioning forefinger. "Do not misconstrue that anything, the story of your future, is already written. Or that the past is nothing more than fossils set in stone. No. When I channel the voices of a half century from now, I am taking the future's temperature. It might change with each visit on our search for the source and significance of this pendant. So if anyone suggests I have predicted what is to come in absolute terms..."

Pedro recalled what Roberto claimed Galleta said about his not-even-conceived-yet grandson, that he would become a terrorist. But before he could ponder further, Alexita in his arms reached upwards and made a coo that evolved rapidly into a screech of delight. Particularly puzzling to her papa was how her attention, her gaze, seemed focused on something not there, far as he could tell.

"As babies are especially prone to do," Galleta observed, "your 'preciosa' is taking in the wider perspective. She is delighting over future possibilities. But with age, of course, our focus narrows to specific goals, to haul in specific fish from the sea of Maybe. Now I must prepare to lift my focus from this place and narrow it on another."

With that, the cookie lady reprised her behavior of weeks ago. In her modestly long dress and plain beige apron left on after her latest baking, she reclined on the light blue beach towel provided by Rotonda. And the pendant once more on her belly, she lifted her arms and legs at all odd angles, what Pedro had likened previously to adjusting old TV antennas. Presently he also found himself reminded of how Alexita wobbled about her pudgy arms and legs when she was placed on her back in her crib. The difference was Galleta held out her appendages straight and stiff, rather than bent so much at the elbows and knees like his 'preciosa.'

Poof! A faint trace of bluish smoke curled a few inches above the pendant, eliciting another joyous, rapturous coo from Alexita.

Then Galleta was back on her feet, carelessly allowing the mysterious object to drop off her belly onto the towel. Wherever she purportedly transmigrated, Galleta looked from side to side with a tentative grin, leaving Pedro and company with the same unsettling impression as before. When Galleta made eye contact, she was seeing through and past them to a different audience. She might as well have been little Alexita appreciatively ogling what no one else in the room could see.

"Is the camera ready, Chris?" Galleta at last said in English, this time channeling Deborah Davis-Murphy.

"She wants the TV turned on?" asked Placido.

"She is talking about a CAMERA!" Rotonda whispered harshly. "And she is not speaking to us!"

"But appears she is watching our TV!"

"Sh!"

"Aydiomio!"

"Sh!"

Billions of miles and sixty years away, Captain Helena Taylor ducked her face in between Deborah, who asked about camera readiness, and Chris's camcorder. "Ladies and gentlemen, girls and boys," she said, "after months of space travel, we've gotten very used to informality. Moreover, our chief medical officer Dr. Deborah Davis-Murphy never expected to be making such an address as this. So let me just say, before she gets started..." The captain took a big bite out of a chocolate chip cookie. "Mmm," she mmed, "This briefing aboard the Smoke and Mirrors is brought to you by Chris Cookies. Chris Cookies," Captain Taylor repeated, licking a few crumbs off her lips, "they are out of this world. And now that I've made a complete fool of myself, I will turn this over to Dr. Davis-Murphy."

"Thank you, Captain Taylor," Galleta laughed, continuing to channel Davis-Murphy. "Before I proceed, must admit that only Captain Taylor would have tried making this occasion less stressful for me by doing what she did."

For Chris Olsen-Taylor, Dr. Deborah Davis-Murphy's thick, glistening layer of blood-red lipstick might as well have been real blood staining her pearly-white teeth. She could have just taken a bite out of someone.

"I am proud to serve aboard the Smoke and Mirrors under the command of Captain Helena Taylor," went on Deborah. "Especially since we face the most serious possible...um, serious as for the historic significance. We all appreciate the history we're about to make, establishing first contact with an intelligent species on a planet outside our solar system."

Oops! thought Chris. *With that "most serious possible" stuff, Deb almost blew the lid off the top-secret part of our mission. I wonder if the powers-that-be now wish they hadn't let the general public know anything at all about our new marching orders. Bet they'll be sweating the commentary after this latest feed. Ideally the talking heads will dismiss Deb's awkward gear shift as the result of stage fright, rather than take it as an inadvertent hint at a cover-up. Really, though, there was no choice but to reveal we were headed for first contact with extraterrestrials. How else to explain why we've been gone for so much longer than the original mission was supposed to last?*

"I hereby announce a safety protocol for initial encounters with extraterrestrial life," said Deborah. "This protocol is based on two principles. One principle is that age-old adage: A gram of prevention is worth a kilogram of cure. The second principle involves erring on the side of extreme caution. Less elegantly put: It is better to look ridiculous than to die.

"These principles in mind, this is one of our special suits normally employed for spacewalks." Deborah lifted a helmet off the floor, revealing a silvery material piled underneath it. "You've probably seen this used for outdoor work on planets and moons characterized by poisonous atmospheres and forbidding temperature extremes. Of course, those are the only other atmospheres encountered inside our own solar system, aside from the artificial one we sustained temporarily on Mars.

"Certainly, the inhabitants of Alpha Centauri C's fourth planet are carbon-based life forms like us. Therefore they enjoy an atmosphere similar to Earth's, probably safe for us to inhale unassisted by any respiratory device. Adapting to their atmosphere should prove no more of a strain than adapting from sea level to, say, the mile-high city of Denver, Colorado. The more significant danger resides in all their microbes and viruses to which we've never been exposed before. This danger runs both ways, because we carry microbes and viruses likewise potentially lethal to our new extraterrestrial friends. Therefore, I recommend this spacesuit for all crewmembers participating in first contact. I've made the principle adaptation with assistance from one of our engineers, my beloved co-wife Geena."

Deborah's pause for Geena to stand and take a bow, sixty years hence, meant that Galleta fell silent as well in the present day.

Pedro whispered to Ludi, "Maybe that spacesuit would also be a good idea for entering a bathroom after Don Típico."

Ludi stifled a giggle, which led to Pedro wincing in pain from trying to suppress his own bemusement.

"A speaker system allows for easy communication between persons wearing these spacesuits," Dr. Deborah Davis-Murphy went on finally. "But Geena has developed a retrofit that also enables clearly hearing outside sounds, and outside entities clearly hearing sounds from inside the suit. That is, unless the suit wearer wants to keep particular sounds to herself, or just between herself and a fellow suit wearer. In which case, she simply needs to flick a switch."

That will come in handy after a bean burrito, Pedro couldn't help thinking. But he did help uttering his little yuk-yuk-yuk aloud, for fear of missing something super important Galleta might soon channel.

Too asleep to care, Placido suddenly let loose with an especially gargly inhale through his hung-open mouth.

"Wake up!" Rotonda hissed harshly, squeezing and twisting one of her husband's ear lobes.

"Ow!"

"Sh! Doña Galleta could be close to revealing the origin of the mysterious pendant, and Pedro will not be able to hear above your snoring!"

"Is that true, Pedro?"

"Sh!"

"Aydiomio!"

"Probably they don't need any special retrofit inside their spacesuits to hear Don Placido snore," Pedro mumbled softly to Ludi in English. And again, containing his bemusement made him wince with pain.

"That's not all with which we have to concern ourselves," Galleta went on, channeling Dr. Davis-Murphy anew. "Our away team can easily conclude first contact, perfectly protected inside their spacesuits from extraterrestrial germs and viruses. But those very same germs and viruses might latch onto each spacesuit's exterior layer. Consequently, our safety protocol requires away team members to perform a routine hull-inspection spacewalk before re-entering the shuttle pod airlock. During the inspection, ambient severe cold plus solar irradiation will quickly destroy any extraterrestrial bacteria and viruses still clinging to spacesuits.

"But let's suppose the shuttle pod itself must land on a planet, rather than making a space-station rendezvous. During the return flight to the Smoke and Mirrors, harsh outer space conditions should eliminate biological hazards from its hull. Of course, under that scenario the away team would have to remain inside the shuttle pod airlock until they can make their spacewalk. And during that walk, the shuttle pod airlock would be left open for de facto cleansing-out by extreme cold and irradiation.

"Okay, let's imagine we have implemented all these procedures. There is something we still need to address, something that follows naturally."

Deborah's persistent, teeth-flashing smile reminded Chris of clips from a beauty pageant. The contestants sustained their toothy smiles through questions about how they want to serve their country and the world. But Deb also wearily rubbed her forehead. Was she furtively trying to wipe away a headache? Her usual look of delight appeared even more plastered on, less heartfelt than normal.

Helena noticed too. "You're doing great, Deb. I'm sure our viewers back on Earth really appreciate your detailed explanations. I remember in most of the old science fiction movies, humans and little green men simply walked up to one another and talked. Or they shot ray guns first, asked questions later."

"I think we are hearing Captain Taylor now," Pedro whispered in Spanish. "Maybe Doña Galleta left from channeling the doctor because she was causing her too much discomfort."

"Time for another snack break!" exclaimed Kevin, ducking his head in front of Chris' camcorder like Captain Taylor did at the outset. And somewhat garbled because his mouth was already full of chocolate chip cookie. "Wait a minute! Ack! Ack!" Kevin melodramatically clutched at his throat like he was choking, opened his eyes wide, and staggered backwards mock-complaining, "These cookies are poisoned! Officer Olsen-Taylor is feeding us extraterrestrial cookies!"

"Ladies and gentlemen, girls and boys," intervened Captain Taylor, "like I said before, we're family out here. Our kidding around is meant to be good-natured fun. But to echo Dr. Davis-Murphy, we fully appreciate the historic nature of our mission. We have been and will be strictly, seriously about our business. There will be none of this silliness in front of the extraterrestrials.

"Deborah, if you want to schedule for later..."

"I'm fine now, Captain, thank you. What I was starting to explain is there are two other crucial elements to our decontamination protocol. One element is what you might term dealing with, uh, sensitivity issues."

Galleta had jumped from channeling the captain back to Deborah. So when Deb went, "uh," so did Galleta. And though Chris and Pedro were separated by sixty years and billions of miles, both were left with the same impression: Whether Galleta or Deb, someone was fighting an impulse to rub her forehead in headache-y discomfort.

"We are confident our new friends will not take our precautions the wrong way," the starship's doctor continued. "When we arrive at their planet, presumably their medical researchers will share the same health concerns. So they shouldn't take offense when we greet them from behind a spacesuit instead of giving them a hearty handshake with our bare hands.

"Some of you, uh, might be worried, uh, saying to yourselves, 'Wait a minute! Forget the health risks! What if these creatures think we are coming to invade? Or what if they want to attack us?' As I think Captain Taylor already explained in a previous transmission, we responded to the extraterrestrials' welcoming message with a pictograph developed by Dr. Ali Magabu. In essence, that pictograph expressed acceptance of their kind invitation. Thanks to an adaptation of a spare firefly donut which has also, uh, been mentioned priory…"

Back sixty years earlier on Earth, Galleta's head wobbled like it was about to tip over. Might as well have been Alexita's, where Pedro was concerned. And 'priory' slurred from Galleta like from someone drunk, Pedro also thought.

"Uh, we transmitted our message to the Alpha Centauri C system in a timely manner. And since their positively, uh, positive response, uh, also made possible by that firefly donut, we've sent pictograph explanations of our- what I developed- uh, the protocol- Dr. Magabu- I worked with Dr. Magabu to design- Excuse me for a moment…"

"Captain..." Buddy Leung rushed into the captain's office where the televised briefing was being staged. "We need you on the bridge; Tanya confirmed our advance scout firefly has picked up a comet, course heading uncomfortably close to intersection with us. We're about to program the mirror array setting with an evasive maneuver."

"Nothing to worry about," Helena Taylor spoke into Chris's camcorder. "We successfully completed one of these precautionary actions three weeks ago. We were located above what you might term a comet nesting area, formally named an Oort Cloud. Anyway, the encore evasion maneuver might prove interesting for you folks back on Earth. And allow Dr. Davis-Murphy some much-needed rest after going non-stop with her safety protocol preparations."

"Thanks, Buddy," softly whispered Captain Taylor whilst leaving her office. So softly, Buddy Leung practically had to read her lips even though he was walking alongside her.

When Deborah's briefing started tumbling downhill, Helena quietly posted a message to the bridge. She requested a distraction to steer the telecast away from the chief medical officer. Fortunately at that very same moment, Tanya really had teased out a dangerous-sized comet from the firefly donut data.

"I am fine, Captain," Deborah called after the departing Helena Taylor. But soon as Chris was gone with his camcorder, she clutched her head and grimaced. Tears ran down her cheeks from holding in the strangeness she'd been feeling. Geena held her steady as she shook her head furiously and screamed, "Get me out of here! Get me out of here!"

While co-wife Geena led Deborah in a panicky sobbing state to the ship's infirmary, Ludi, Gloria, and Jerri were dealing with Galleta in a similar state. They were lowering her back down recumbent on the beach towel spread across the living room floor.

Pursuant to which, Galleta suddenly began thrashing about. Gloria and Jerri strained to hold her still while Ludi instinctively grabbed the mystery pendant. She tried to hold it steady above the cookie-maker's navel.

Seeming the result of Ludi's effort, Galleta's legs and arms abruptly froze at odd angles. They were the same angles at which Deborah's limbs froze on a stretcher in the Smoke and Mirrors infirmary, sixty years and billions of miles away. Faint bluish smoke made a distinct poof! above both women's bellies, succeeded by them collapsing into a deep sleep.

"Ay caramba!" blurted out an extremely agitated Típico. "Whenever Doña Galleta goes into a trance state speaking English, there is more and more danger for her! This should be the final time!"

Were his back not injured, Pedro would have joined his wife and sisters to help Galleta. Despite his deep concern over her well-being, however, he found himself amused at the 'I told you so' tone taken by Ludi's grandfather. Pedro knew what Típico's real "bottom line" was. When they were not at work, they should all just sit around watching television.

"Are you volunteering to spirit travel in the place of Doña Galleta?" said Norma. "I was not aware my macho is so courageous!"

"Ay caramba no!"

"Why can't we live with the mystery?" asked Placido most animatedly, building on what Típico said. "I do not need to know where the pendant came from. Ludi and Pedro, you can simply enjoy it, and we can go on with no danger for anyone. I have seen blue smoke rise like a ghost over Doña Galleta, every time she performs her drama. What will happen next? Will she catch fire and burn?"

"Yes, of course," nodded Rotonda, "no more of these sessions, so you and Don Típico can return to your extensive analysis of TV shows. That will require years more of 'channel surfing' before you can offer the results, yes?"

"Aydiomio!"

"Ay caramba!"

Chapter 8

"All her vital signs are normal," reported Dr. Ali Magabu.

Dr. Deborah Davis-Murphy lay fast asleep on a stretcher, her head cradled and rubbed gently by co-wife Geena.

Kevin looked on with an awkward mix of concern over the physician's condition, and wonder over how he could politely make his exit to resume work.

"Tell me," Dr. Magabu went on, oblivious to Kevin's dilemma, "did either of you see a thin wraith of faint blue smoke curl up from Deborah's tummy, then vanish? Or am I the only one?"

"Ali, we're all getting super edgy here," said Kevin, "but let's keep it real."

"I saw the blue smoke," Geena blurted out albeit softly, trying not to disturb her spouse's sleep.

"I know, Kevin. The last thing we need, truly, is another UFO," Ali agreed. "But we can't ignore our senses, especially when there is corroboration." Ali nodded Geena's way. "There is also Deborah's discomfort somehow leading her to shout, 'Get me out of here!'"

"Yeah, 'Get me out of here!' as in: Get me to the infirmary fast! I'm sick! And get me away from this bunch of wackos who see my belly button belching blue smoke!"

"But you also need to carefully consider Deborah's violent head shaking. I don't know about you, Kevin. But my heart of hearts tells me the 'here' that 'me' wanted to get out of was her body, rather than Captain Taylor's office. And whether you observed the blue smoke or not, wasn't it odd how our dear doctor suddenly dropped into a deep sleep, just like that?" With "that," Ali snapped his fingers in Kevin's face. He seemed to Geena as much about trying to wake up Kevin to the exceeding strangeness of what had occurred, as to demonstrate instantaneity.

"Oh, I didn't realize we were supposed to start collecting data from our 'heart of hearts'! Look," said Kevin, abruptly striking a more conciliatory tone, "didn't Captain Taylor suffer something similar during our Mars flyby, pursuant to her own televised presentation? Maybe going on-stage during hyper-speed space flight causes stress to be expressed in anomalous ways."

"However, Taylor and Davis-Murphy's freak-outs are spaced months apart. And they're not the only ones who have had to go 'on-stage,'" pointed out Ali Magabu. "Besides, I would have thought we have experienced nothing more stressful than the first hard evidence of other intelligent beings in the universe besides ourselves. Especially learning of creatures out there intent on making us their primary food source: Wasn't that more stressful than talking about evasive maneuvers for the folks back home? When the captain shared the top secret packet, shouldn't that have precipitated another freak-out, if not several?"

"Points well taken, Dr. Magabu," conceded Kevin. "For sure, still blows my mind we're engaging back and forth with our blind-date ETs from trillions of miles away while approaching them at forty times light-speed. That is, thanks to Buddy's firefly donuts. So shouldn't be surprised, next thing, should purple bubbles start foaming from my ears. I'm just cautioning against jumping to any wilder conclusions than are necessary.

"Regarding that blue smoke, for example, haven't physiologists found this blue aura around us that's poorly understood? Maybe with certain ailments, that aura takes on a different appearance... still pretty strange, but at least in a known realm, even if shrouded in mystery. As for when Deb said, 'Get me out of here,' well doc, haven't you ever been sick enough or had a bad enough headache, you wished you could jump out of your own skin?"

"Points well taken, Kevin," Ali sighed. "Anyway, we should soon have Deborah's blood work results."

"How is she, Ali?" panted Captain Taylor as she came full stop beside Deborah's stretcher, having sprinted into the infirmary.

"Far as we know, Captain, she's fine, nothing wrong," reported Dr. Magabu, "just like you after your own peculiar episode two months ago. Of course as Kevin has wisely counseled, we should not jump to any conclusions before we learn more. Did you hear her screaming?"

"Screaming?"

"Of course you would have mentioned that, Captain, truly. After you left for the bridge, Deborah shook her head violently and shouted repeatedly, 'Get me out of here!' Once we brought her here from your office, she quite literally collapsed into this deep sleep."

Taylor noted Deborah's closed eyes emanating peacefulness before she said, "Well thank goodness her shouting didn't carry to the bridge. Would have made more difficult leaving our distant audience with smiling assurances all is well. And in case you're wondering, Yoon-hee successfully executed the course correction. Our advance guard firefly donut has already confirmed a clear path the rest of the way across the Oort Cloud."

"Very good, Captain," nodded Ali. "Now about Deborah..."

"Excuse me, Captain," said Kevin. "And believe me. I never take for granted your encouragement for us to speak honestly."

"And I appreciate your holding nothing back. I'm just happy you're able to eat Chris's cookies."

"He's found his calling, Captain. Anyway, don't you think we should revisit your spook-out during the Mars flyby? Shouldn't we consider whether there's any commonality with the good doctor Deb's bum experience?"

"My 'spook-out' seemed connected to that flyby, what with my seeing or hallucinating phantasms of the Martian hurricane's victims. There was no sequel, and I've been feeling fine ever since. But in light of this new incident…Ali, you're basically our backup medical guy. What do you think? Could there be some relation between Deborah's trauma and mine?"

"When Dr. Davis-Murphy wakes up, perhaps she will have some insight regarding what produced her agitated state," said Ali. "As for you, Captain, I truly don't remember your fighting any sort of exhaustion that, if not for sheer willpower, would have had you falling off into our dear doctor's deep sleep."

"The difference might have been what I noted for public consumption. Deb really was awake all hours preparing for the decontamination protocol."

"I can vouch for that." From affectionately brushing back her co-wife's hair, Geena timidly raised her hand like a reluctant volunteer.

"Whatever Deborah experienced could have been plenty to push her exhaustion over the edge. I'm not claiming to have been all that rested before my haunting hallway adventure. But I do recall riding an adrenalin rush from our successful launch."

"Captain," said Kevin, "Ali and Geena both think they saw blue smoke or the like rise off Davis-Murphy's torso after we brought her here."

"When I saw the ghosts, no one else was around to incidentally notice any blue smoke rising off me. Again, let's hope Deb wakes up soon so we can pick her brain."

"Captain," Geena hunched her shoulders, cringing, "I know we decided it was better to give the Alpha Centaurians advance notice we were on our way. We didn't want them to think we were the leading edge of an invasion. But..."

"That's right," Kevin broke in. "And we're defenseless. Isn't that the 'but'?"

Geena gave a clipped nod.

"So for all we know," Kevin continued, "they've equipped a satellite to greet us with nuclear missiles. They'll blow us apart before we can re-blossom to light-speed acceleration."

"We are defenseless," Helena conceded. "Nevertheless, we concluded that arriving unannounced was riskier than trusting the Alpha Centaurians are acting in good faith, or good enough faith. And of course, our communication with them might have been intercepted by 'the bad guys' from Cygnitaurus.

"Historically, though, we know that so-called 'evil empires,' at least on Earth, are weaker, more easily defeated, than would appear at first glance. Such systems are inherently unstable. The spaceship that crash-landed on Alpha Centauri C's fourth planet, maybe those were not ETs warning of a coming invasion; they *were* the first wave of that invasion. Their spacecraft are constructed so poorly, most of them shear to pieces before they ever reach their destination."

"Excuse me, Captain," Kevin bristled. "My great great grandfather died on an aircraft carrier struck by a Japanese Kamikaze pilot. At that time, the Japanese war machine sure as hell didn't look 'easily defeated.' Neither did the Germans, for that matter."

"As you must have read, Kevin, those 'war machines,' as you call them, were employing brute force technology," lectured Captain Taylor, sounding unflappable to Chris. "As the military technology grew more sophisticated, totalitarian dictatorships such as the Soviet Union simply could not keep up with progress in the free democracies. While the United States was landing men on the moon, the U.S.S.R. was drowning in vodka. The cold war was being fueled by political and intelligence agency ideologues wildly exaggerating-"

"Captain, would you say the atomic bomb German scientists almost developed for Hitler was part of that 'brute force technology'?"

"But the free democracies co-opted those scientists."

"Captain Taylor, Engineer Smith, I truly don't believe Geena had in mind a debate over twentieth century world history." Ali figured if he didn't intervene on Geena's behalf, she wouldn't find her way past her timidity to be heard.

"I'm sorry, Geena," said the captain. "You were saying?"

"I was just wondering, Captain, whether we are mixing an apple with an orange. Maybe your difficulty on the Mars flyby did have something to do with the hurricane disaster, and you *were* seeing ghosts. But in Deborah's case, maybe we're learning just how advanced a nasty civilization can get. Maybe the ETs with antlers intercepted our transmissions with the Alpha Centaurians, and subsequently sent a probe our way we haven't been able to detect. Yet somehow, it tapped into Debby's mind for information to use against us. And then it debilitated her. And soon they're going to debilitate all of us. We'll all drop off to sleep, and wake up in a spaceship cattle cart."

"Dear Geena," said Ali, "we should not succumb to paranoia. There might be something to what you fear. But for your scenario, we don't have nearly enough to go on yet. Actually, I am more interested in pursuing a possibility raised previously that would mean we are dealing with two apples, as it were. Perhaps for some, one consequence of hyper-speed travel-"

"Captain, you better come to the bridge," Yoon-hee's voice suddenly flared from a ceiling speaker. "We lost our advance guard firefly donut."

On the captain and company's sprint down the hall, Kevin said, "We may need to just get the hell out of here, return when we're better prepared!"

"If that's what we need to do, we will," Helena Taylor panted.

Taylor focused on the panoramic view-screen as she took her seat on the navigation bridge. She visually bored into what there was to see, hoping against rational hope to pick up some clue as to what happened.

Widely scattered stars dominated the deep space vista, save for where they clustered in the lower right-hand corner against a hazy backdrop. Of course, that backdrop was comprised of millions more stars at far greater distance, closer to the center of the Milky Way Galaxy.

One star shined brighter than the rest, just south of dead center.

"Captain," said Buddy, "Yoon-hee is about to replay the last seconds of feed from the advance guard, posting right half of split-screen."

The deep space vista shrank into the view-screen's left half. A different deep space vista, filled with far fewer stars, expanded into the right half.

"Captain, I am slowing down the feed," said Yoon-hee.

Already, Helena noticed those fewer stars in the right half of the split screen being rapidly snuffed out, like black ink was spilling over them. A slow-motion burst of twinkles like a fireworks display lit up the ensuing total darkness. And transmission "snow" followed immediately thereafter before the screen went completely blank.

"Yoon-hee, I assume the fireworks resulted from the collision of whatever it was with the firefly donut's mirror array."

"Captain, you couldn't tell with unaided eye because available starlight was too weak, but the reflectivity level and pattern were consistent with a 'V' class comet," said Yoon-hee, typing on her control panel to replay the feed through an ultraviolet filter.

"Let me get this straight," said Kevin, walking behind Yoon-hee to peer over his wife's shoulder at her monitors. "One of these firefly donuts can provide all the information we need to assure we're not crossing paths with some errant rock, and plenty of time to change course if we are. But it's virtually defenseless against something headed straight at it?"

"Not the least bit surprising," said Buddy. "It's traveling at a light-speed multiple. But given its small size, the odds of such a collision were, um, how else to put it? The odds were astronomical."

"What we have to conclude, people," said Helena with her eyes still glued to the screen, "is that this firefly donut's lotto number came up."

"Captain, isn't that kind-of like getting struck by lightning twice?" asked Kevin. "Didn't our lotto number just come up earlier, when we had to make an evasive course correction? The odds were astronomical like you said, Buddy, against such a close encounter for the firefly donut. What were the odds that firefly and starship both would wind up in the bull's eye within such a short time frame? Or any time frame?"

"Actually, Kevin," answered Buddy with studied calmness, "odds were that the other comet - it does appear to have been another comet – the odds were that it would have missed us by thousands of kilometers. We made the maneuver to lower the odds from one in forty thousand to zero. Moreover, we possessed scant probe data before crossing the Oort Cloud boundary, as regards the prevalence or scarcity of celestial objects inside there."

"But haven't we been traveling above the orbital plane of the Oort Cloud, Bud? And aren't we nearing the back edge of it? You see Alpha Centauri C is already looming larger on the forward monitor. Moreover, doesn't one of our surviving advance guard firefly donuts show a dramatic drop-off of asteroid and comet frequency further 'down' closer to the orbital plane?"

"It certainly does," confirmed Yoon-hee, intently eyeing her monitor. "But Mr. Smith, sir," her favorite form of address for Kevin even when they were alone, especially when he needed reining in, "Buddy is absolutely correct. We have meager data to work from. For all we know, we are skirting an asteroid belt like the one between Mars and Jupiter."

"Buddy, Yoon-hee," said the captain, "I appreciate your keeping us from slipping into panic mode. Yet shouldn't we concede Kevin's basic point until we know more? Isn't it ridiculously unlikely both our ship and the advance scout would have come under fire, not much more than an hour apart?"

"We 'came under fire' by objects which in both cases, Captain, demonstrated all the refractory characteristics of plain old comets," Buddy couldn't help bristling.

"Captain, you heard Geena," said Kevin, nowhere near ready to let Buddy's reassurance stand uncontested, bristled or not. "What if she's right? What if those ETs, the ones supposedly out to feed on other-world steaks, intercepted our communication with Alpha Centauri C's fourth planet? And now they're trying to cut us off from Earth by destroying our fireflies with missiles they've disguised to look like comets? Or maybe they've figured out how to corral comets and send them at targets like in those old westerns. Remember bad guys rolling boulders down hills to crush their intended victims?"

"Kevin," Captain Helena Taylor smiled and shook her head, "Kevin, if our cowboy bandit aliens want to grind us up to make people burgers, I can understand their knocking out our probes. However, why would they also try to destroy our ship and risk losing us savory morsels in the process?"

"Maybe, Captain, the comet we changed course to stay away from, maybe it was set on a path to merely disable our ship, make fetching us easier. Look, I'm not saying I necessarily buy any of my own speculation."

Helena stared off into the panoramic view-screen again, and thoughtfully stroked her chin.

Only mechanical whirs broke the silence, plus eerie tinkle-tinkles from the electromagnetically juiced light-stream through the spaceship's photon exhaust shaft.

Husband Chris sensed wistful regret fueling his wife's decision-making delay. If only she could postpone announcing a course of action indefinitely, or somehow escape this situation altogether. What to do seemed way too far from obvious. Chris's heart went out to Helena; he wanted to sidle up behind her and affectionately, supportively rub her shoulders. From past experience, though, he knew she'd recoil. She'd shake him off with a fury that left him wondering whether it was only a matter of her considering such a public display of affection way too inappropriate. Was it that, or was there something terrible, another issue she wanted to escape facing?

Finally, Helena spun about in her captain's chair and stood to face everyone. "Buddy, I want you to see Ali about preparing a special SOS message. Two special SOS messages, actually. One worded in English, the other expanding upon the universal pictograph system Dr. Magabu and our Alpha Centaurian blind date have been developing. Both messages will be ready to send on an instant's notice if we come under attack. I'm still far from convinced we are dealing with interplanetary cattle rustlers. However, we are so far into the unknown at this point, it is clearly imprudent to assume anything."

"Helena," said Chris, "does your plan involve the communications firefly donuts? Once they oscillate back this side of the Oort Cloud from their latest run to within contact range of our home solar system?"

"I know where you're going." Helena held a silencing hand towards Chris. "The bad guys could destroy them the way they did the other one, IF they did destroy the other one. Buddy, I want you to jack up our spare firefly to its ultimate speed capability, on the outermost theoretical reach. I'll have Geena join you once she's more certain Deb is okay. If our spare finds no other fireflies left operating in the relay zone, we can just have it continue all the way home, transmit our SOS directly. Again, that's assuming we ever do come under attack."

"Understood, Captain. But we're already pushing that theoretical outermost speed capability with forty times light-speed. Okay, yes, there is some room left for play." Buddy couldn't help this concession under Helena's withering, don't-tell-me-it's-not-possible look. This, despite knowing how little sleep he could expect over the next couple of days, assuming they had that long. Although his gut told him the threat was not really so imminent.

"That's all I'm asking you to do, Dr. Leung. Play. From what we know, maybe we already can easily outrun whoever-they-are. They apparently haven't launched their full-scale invasion of the solar system we're entering, yet. Maybe they need a lot longer to cross seven light-years from Cygnitaurus than we've needed to cross five from Earth. But I'd like to virtually guarantee, if we could, that we can get out a distress signal. Thank goodness we have the extra firefly, especially were our communication link firefly to fall prey to a third lightning strike."

"Oh!" Buddy Leung gasped, suddenly remembering something.

"Hey!" Yoon-hee coincidentally did a double-take on her routine monitor scan. "Who has something in countdown? 11-10-9-"

"That's okay." Buddy reached out a leave-it-alone hand as he rushed over beside Yoon-hee. "Display the rear view."

"What's this?" Captain Taylor's attention alternated between the panoramic view-screen, and Buddy seated with Yoon-hee.

The screen had been split display, the right half blank because of the failed firefly donut transmission. But on Buddy's command, photon "exhaust" often likened to fairy dust took up the entire transmitted view.

"3-2-1-now what?" asked Yoon-hee.

"That's our extra firefly donut! What are you doing with it, Bud?" said Kevin.

On countdown's end, the ship's last remaining firefly donut floated out amid the photon stream. A sparkly diamond bounced about by smaller twinkles like a beach ball tossed by surf, so Chris imagined.

"Captain, regarding my presumed free rein to play with mirror array capabilities..." Buddy's face turned beet red.

"Yes, yes," Helena impatiently conceded. "Can you abort whatever experiment- Oh, there it goes!"

From one instant to the next, the firefly donut vanished into a thin, bluish-white wisp like a comet's tail.

"Captain, what's that?!?" Kevin pointed urgently at the screen.

A new sparkly light had suddenly seemed to materialize beside the trail of the departed firefly donut. Where Chris was concerned, it could have been a second firefly answering the call of the first, blinking on and off just like one of those curious bugs.

"Wo!" Buddy laughed.

"Bring us up to speed, Dr. Leung." Captain Taylor sounded a combination of panicked and annoyed. "That thing is getting much closer with every blink! Are we too late for an evasive maneuver?"

"No need, Captain," Buddy said as he reached in front of Yoon-hee to access her keyboard. "Um, that's our spare firefly I launched just a minute ago. We are going to net it into the launch bay like we do any other firefly."

"So that's not a different firefly donut, returning in record time from reception range of the Saturn moon station to forward our latest public broadcast?"

Mechanical whirs from the deployed retrieval net punctuated Kevin's question as it scooped the firefly donut into the launch bay.

"No," confirmed Buddy. "That firefly should still be well on its way."

"Wait," said Captain Taylor, suddenly doing a double-take. "Our spare firefly donut made an insanely tight U-turn? And then caught up to us for retrieval even though we were going at forty times light-speed?"

"I did engineer record-fast acceleration for it," acknowledged Buddy Leung. "But there was no U-turn. The spare firefly donut returned roughly the same time it left."

"'roughly the same time it left'?! You mean to say," said the captain, "you sent it into the past?"

"That is exactly what I suspect happened, Captain," nodded Buddy.

"What?!?" Kevin got the most twisted, contorted expression on his face Chris had ever seen.

"Oh my my!" gasped Yoon-hee. "What is your next experiment? Trying to talk with God?!" The way she leaned away from Buddy, he figured he might just as well have cut a loud and smelly fart.

"This is what happened, Captain," said Buddy. "Poring over our flight data from the Mars flyby, I noticed something exceptional. We experienced an anomalous, momentary acceleration, right around when you experienced a parade of apparitions streaming diagonally through the hallway."

"Yeah, I remember seeing that data. We just shrugged our shoulders and moved on," admitted Kevin.

"After our shoulder shrugging, Kevin, I recalled a paper Gómez published in '55. She postulated that certain tragedies and disasters cause rifts in the space-time continuum. She speculated we're surrounded by uncountable nicks and cuts from every experienced pain, down to an ant smashed underfoot. But her most inflammatory suggestion, by far, was that the big rifts, rifts in the continuum big enough to fly a spacecraft through, were torn open by epic loss of life from epic cataclysms. Such events disrupt four-dimensional objects across the time axis, the same as sawing off a branch creates a three-dimensional rift between that branch and the rest of the tree."

"Dr. Leung," Captain Taylor held up a cautioning hand, "I am completely sincere when I say 'unfortunately.' And unfortunately, we're way too busy now for an entire dissertation defense. We're headed into the twenty-four-hour countdown for first contact. Jump to the conclusion, what you think happened, and believe me I do want to hear the rest, eventually."

"Yeah, me too," nodded Kevin.

"Okay, Captain, so I programmed our spare firefly to accelerate into the rift from the Mars disaster. My calculations were based on where the Smoke and Mirrors was located when you experienced the apparition stream. I sent in the firefly at an entry angle from above the postulated rift line. Remember the entry angle for those old space shuttles to re-enter Earth's atmosphere?"

"Of course," nodded Helena. "We had to deal with that personally for a rescue mission. Too steep an angle, friction would have burned us up. Too shallow and we would have bounced off into deep space."

"Exactly," said Buddy.

"But let me get this straight," said Helena. "Here we are light-years away from our solar system, and you sent that firefly donut all the way back to Mars, to enter a space-time rift there. And then somehow it did all of that and returned here within minutes of leaving."

"Right again, Captain. The spare firefly was retrofitted to collect star chart data once it breached that rift. We were looking for key star coordinates at dramatic variance from present coordinates, i.e. where the stars were located pre-Mars-disaster. Once those coordinates were identified, the firefly was programmed to return the way it came on a mirror-image speed-profile trajectory."

"In other words, Buddy," said Helena, "you ordered the firefly to retrace its steps exactly, once time-travel was confirmed."

"Not quite exactly, Captain. I was curious about the skipping stone effect, without which we would have no chance of welcoming back that spare firefly until weeks from now. So for the firefly's return to the present, I figured: Why not finish off a second experiment?"

"Let me guess, Buddy. Once the firefly donut returned to the present, you 'asked' it to zoom in at the rift again, but at a shallow-enough angle for skipping back to us like a stone across water. That's why it appeared to wink on and off."

"Imagine the firefly donut leaping from curve to curve in the space-time continuum, leaving much of the intervening space not actually traveled through. We're talking multiples of light-speed far exceeding any imagined in those ancient TV shows and movies."

"*Star Trek*," said Chris.

"Incredible," said Captain Taylor.

"The issue for us here, however, Captain," went on Buddy, "is if we're talking about making an ultra-fast getaway. There's a problem, even if we just want to send out an ultra-fast distress-signal firefly donut. The problem is that we don't have a clue where any local time rifts might have been torn. Of course if Deborah thinks she saw a ghost, we could retrace our steps. But the furthest the Alpha Centaurians appear to have gotten off their planet is to their space station. We'd probably have to locate an epic disaster down on the inhabited planet."

"That is, unless our Cygnitaurus cannibalistic rustlers-"

Before Kevin could complete his thought, they were hearing Ali over the intercom, "Captain?"

"Dr. Magabu?"

"Yes, Captain. Dr. Deborah Davis-Murphy has just woken up. If you want to ask her some questions..."

"Thank you, Ali, but please assure Deborah- Deb? If you're listening, please don't force yourself to stay awake on my account. If you need to fall back asleep on me, as your captain I order you to fall back asleep on me."

"If it's the same with you, Captain, I think she'd rather fall back asleep on Geena, truly."

"Tanya, I didn't know your husband is a frustrated comedian."

"Yes, Captain, Ali can be frustrating." She looked up from data she was studying concerning a newly identified comet on a harmless path. "But comedian? No."

"Kevin, I'm leaving you in charge on the bridge, and that's no joke. Double-check all the diagnostics for the laser shutdown and mirror array re-alignment; I think that's coming up-"

"One-hour-thirty-seven-minute countdown, Captain," said Yoon-hee, "with deceleration re-alignment on a six-hour-fifteen-minute countdown to initiation."

"You've programmed the mirror array adjustments required for keeping above the orbital plane until we're closer to the fourth planet, Officer Park-Smith? Since we're essentially flying blind without our advance-guard firefly?"

"Nay, Captain; I started on that the moment we realized we'd lost the firefly."

"Thanks, Yoon-hee.

"Buddy and Tanya, I'm sure this will come as no surprise."

They were both already nodding.

"As soon as you download all the data from your time travel experiment, Dr. Leung, I want that firefly donut immediately redeployed as our new advance guard."

"We won't retire for the day until that's done, Captain," said Buddy.

"And Buddy?"

"Yes, Captain?"

"No more tinkering around with the laws of the universe, at least until after tomorrow."

"Yeah, Bud," said Kevin, "you can wait for your chitchat with God until after we schmooze the aliens."

*

Excerpt from Captain's Log,

October 7, 2061

I just finished stationary biking through Big Sur, courtesy of Shelly's holodisc program. Nice not worrying someone might inattentively clip the bike lane, especially on those hairpin turns. Instead, it was all about mountainous terrain making steep descents into a deep blue Pacific punctured by the occasional whale breach. And special hats-off to the programmers for their sea-air simulation.

All the same, still felt stuck in the middle of some extra-fancy postcard.

Eventually, I suppose special software will replicate parking off Route 1, sticking bare feet in the sand, and then dipping them in icy cool surf.

Working with these good people aboard the Smoke and Mirrors, I've never felt so alone despite a certain someone's presence. No one else here really understands my responsibility to answer for whatever mess-ups, whoever is actually at fault. Maybe a co-captain would help.

Something a little easier for those seafaring captains, long ago. Far from their loved ones, they had the wind-blown sea spray in their face, the rocking and pitching of their ships tossed by mighty swells. They could viscerally experience their travels. And oddly enough, they could also still feel connected to home, even from halfway around the world. Drenching mid-ocean rains might have evaporated from thundershowers on the backyard garden. And at night especially, the moon and stars were the same wherever you looked up at them.

Out here in the depths of space, though, if we start feeling anything exterior to our high-tech galleon, we'll die. And whatever moon or moons orbit Alpha Centauri C's fourth planet certainly won't be ours.

Even when we make first contact tomorrow, hopefully, Dr. Deborah Davis-Murphy's safety protocol will rule, as well it should. Consequently, however, we won't be experiencing the feel, the touch of an extraterrestrial's handshake, or whichever other greeting involving physical contact. Okay, maybe they simply bow to one another.

But we also can't allow ourselves to sniff at the extraterrestrials or their planet. Our lucky mice, that opportunity will be made available with their counterparts. Hopefully they won't instinctively go at each other's throats in a death struggle, or succumb to illness from the other's viruses and bacteria.

Curious what the ETs offered for their version of a rodent. Those two eyes on the same side of the head remind me more of a flounder or sand dab than a mouse.

I suppose all the new sights and sounds will prove stimulation enough for us. Probably just as well to be spared the full sensual bombardment.

Before concluding this entry, formal note should be taken of the mirror array's successful realignment into what is termed the daisy petal arrangement. The "tulip bloom" fronting the Smoke and Mirrors still funnels ambient starlight through the photon exhaust shaft. But the aft "rose" has been "bloomed" into two "daisies," one behind the other.

The rearmost "daisy" blocks much of the photon exhaust from escaping into deep space. Then via its mirror maze, it accelerates that exhaust back towards the closer-in "daisy," impelling the starship forward. Thereby Alpha Centauri C's ample sunlight is ingenuously U-turned. The Smoke and Mirrors is able to continue speeding away from less light towards more light, towards a star, rather than experiencing a slowdown due to photon friction.

Amazing how solutions to the various problems involving speed-of-light travel have turned out so elegantly aesthetic, manifesting as metallic flowers. I guess beautiful is the only word for it. Wish this was true across the board!

Not sure why I bothered going on at such length about the daisy petals. Probably reads like so much gibberish, especially for lay readers with no expertise in light propulsion, which I'm not sure doesn't include everybody who is not Buddy Leung.

These are the last words I'll be recording before humanity enters a new phase via first direct contact with an intelligent extraterrestrial species. Maybe that's why I'm lingering over this entry, glomming on to any excuse to extend it.

I remember my last night at home before college. It felt similar to the outset of this mission, even prior to the involvement of extraterrestrial life forms. I was leaving behind a big mess that included unresolved issues with high school friends and my parents, and the literal mess in my bedroom. There was all the stuff piled in the closet from my first eighteen years. One day I'd need to resolve what should accompany me to my first new home after college, and what should get trashed or given away.

But ahead lay a fresh start, new stuff, new relationships, possible romance...

Chapter 9: The 4ᵗʰ Session, Part One

"Mami, thank you so much for letting us use your phone number. As soon as this thing is totally resolved..."

"Ay, son," said Rotonda on her waddle out of the kitchen balancing two plates piled high with rice, beans, and ham, "was very prudent of you to suspend your cell phone service! Somehow the world used to survive without cell phones. Now, you and Ludi eat while I feed Alexandra."

"Ay, Mami, we came to tell you how well the hearing went this morning. We did not come asking for a meal!"

Ludi nodded enthusiastically, "The judge ruled for Pedro. Our insurance company should call this afternoon with details. Maybe inside a week we bring our big guy here to the hospital for his operation! Yes, Alexita, your papi will be able to toss you into the clouds soon."

Alexandra smiled and cooed, and flapped her arms like a bird. She was feeling the happy excitement.

"I want to hear more, but sit. There is no reason you can't eat something. You know the hospital food is terrible."

"Thank you, Mami." Pedro wanted to say they already ate lunch an hour earlier; they really didn't need another meal, himself especially. With his back trouble, he couldn't cut the lawn or do other forms of exercise. As a result, he was growing chunkier and chunkier. Concealed underneath the belt buckle, he'd started to leave the top of his trousers unbuttoned. Moreover, his expanded waistline had stretched the elastic band on several of his boxer shorts to the breaking limit. But he sensed how desperate his mom was to help. She would have traded her own back broken for his if she could have. But since she couldn't, she stuffed him full of home-cooked meals instead. Besides, the cool, late-autumn air stoked Pedro's appetite. And his extra fat seemed to cushion his injury so sitting, lying down or moving about didn't prove quite so painful.

Nevertheless, Pedro's first spoonful of his mother's latest offering he paused halfway to his mouth, to say, "After I am better and return to work, I want us to join one of those gyms, Ludi. At least, I have to go." He censored himself, leaving out: *We are too old to be carrying around all this baby fat besides Alexandra's.*

"That is a good idea, mi Pedrocito," said Rotonda. "Don Placido? After this problem is settled for our son, we should also join an exercise gym, sí?"

Placido jumped in his lounger, Pedro mused, like he'd received an electric jolt. "Ay, Rotonda, those gyms are so expensive! People pay thirty, forty dollars a month! And if the company goes out of business, you lose all your money!"

"Yes, I hear that too," Típico chimed in.

"Gyms closing used to be a problem," said Pedro. "But they have become so popular, that is not something to worry about anymore."

"Yes," nodded Ludi, "and you only pay a month at a time. If your exercise place closes, you cannot lose that much."

"What are we paying a month for cable TV? Wasn't the last bill forty-five or fifty? Plus twelve extra so you could see a fight that was over in twenty seconds?" Dawning realization informed Rotonda's voice, to Pedro's mischievous delight.

"Aydiomio!"

"In truth," said Norma, "I am not so interested in the gym."

"Hmm," Típico hmmed approvingly.

"I would like my big old rooster to take dance lessons with me. Merengue and salsa, maybe."

"What?!" It was Típico's turn for an electric jolt. He suddenly went thrashing about on the sofa, Pedro mused, like a fish flung onto a pier. "Look - Look at Gloria and Jerri! They are going to a dance all the time! They have to wear such short skirts, and they put on- You see how they apply so much lipstick and makeup?"

"I promise you, Don Típico," said Norma walking over and lovingly placing her hands on his shoulders. "No one will make you wear a mini-skirt and use heavy lipstick and makeup."

"Maybe some eyebrow liner?!" Pedro laughed.

"Ay caramba!"

"So tell me, Pedro..." Rotonda sat down at the dining table beside her son. She was rocking Alexandra, whose eyelids looked heavy with her pupils disappearing up into them. "...is true? The judge considered your situation despite your absence from the first hearing?"

"In English is called a 'continuance,' Mami." Pedro couldn't help irritation leaking from his voice. The undercurrent of worry in his mom's voice spooked him. "He not only heard my case, he ruled against the other driver. His exact words in English were, 'I find Elizabeth Lansing predominantly culpable for this accident.'"

"The attorney from AllCare was there early for the first hearing date," explained Ludi. "He took our call from your cell phone, when we said we were going to arrive too late. When he alerted the judge, she even commented she had heard on the news about the shutdown on the metro line, and the water main break blocking traffic."

"Sí, Mami," added Pedro. "I think we were not the only ones who had to reschedule."

"Yes, I remember you told me all of this. So this Ms. Lansing, she had to appear in court two times?"

"Her daughter brought her the second time, Mami. She was the one too busy on her cell phone to notice the red light when her mami ran into me. We saw her driving into the parking lot. I bet the daughter drove the first time, too. The family was not going to trust that older lady after what happened." Pedro wanted to avoid sounding defensive, but couldn't. That persistent nagging hint of doubt in his mother's tone maybe wouldn't have mattered much, if not for some unsettling incidents at the hearing. He kept telling himself he was reading too much into them. And yet...

There was the daughter coming over to him before they entered the court room. With as much intimidating belligerence as she could muster, she asked, "Haven't you caused my mother enough suffering?"

Then there was the attorney from Farmland Insurance. Pedro imagined he should have appeared rattled, perturbed when the judge declared his client "predominantly" at fault. (*Why not completely at fault? Why predominantly?*) But he took the judge's ruling stoically. That insurance rep simply shrugged his shoulders. Then he whispered something to the daughter and mother which left them both appearing not especially upset either.

Lastly, there was their AllCare attorney. He did offer congratulations, how the ruling would keep any points from going on Pedro's driving record. But after saying AllCare would call later in the day, he rushed off surprisingly fast. But maybe he had lots of other clients to attend to?

"Doña Rotonda, I would not believe it if I had not seen it." Ludi was wide-eyed with her lingering amazement. "This woman who crashed into Pedro, when came her time to speak on the witness stand, their attorney had to wake her!"

"Ay bendito! So she fell asleep during a court hearing about an accident she caused? Ay Dios!" Rotonda shook her head. "That had to make a bad impression on the judge."

Ring! Ring!

"Is for you," Rotonda confirmed, before handing over the phone to her son while still cradling Alexandra.

"Yes? Hello, Mr. Caplan!" said Pedro happily. His heart still beat a mile a minute because This Was It. But what did he have to worry about? *Mami was right, Dios mío! That could not have gone well with the judge when the woman dozed off like she was my baby daughter, right in the middle of a hearing into an accident SHE caused! I am being too paranoid!* "'70 percent at fault,' that is good, no?... They will not pay?! Nothing?! Not even 70 percent?... Bueno, while you are fighting this,...Okay, while you are petitioning them to re-evaluate, can't you take care of my car and my back surgery?... I hear this is how you insurance companies are supposed to operate. After you take care of people, you fight among yourselves, and then if the premium of someone has to be raised,...mm-hmm,...mm-hmm...For only one car?... Fifteen hundred a year? How can I afford that if my back remains in too much pain for work?... Look, how you have these commercials where you say, 'We care at AllCare'?" Pedro hunched over further and further on the couch, and his voice went high-pitched from trying not to cry.

Ludi brought Pedro's head close to her chest, where she comfortingly stroked his shortly cut, tightly curled hair.

"How you are caring now?... No, nobody answered... Yes! My wife posted those cards all around that intersection! On every telephone pole!... This is unbelievable! At the time you said this was no problem, the judge said no problem. How I perform a miracle?!; we were supposed to hire a flying taxi or a helicopter to take us there?!?! What about that woman?! How could they say she was not one hundred percent at fault after they see her sleeping- Hello? Hello?" Pedro dropped the receiver on the floor. His hand was trembling too much to hang onto it.

"Aydiosmio, Pedrocito, what happened?" Rotonda would have recovered the phone and helped Ludi physically comfort Pedro, had her arms not been full with Alexandra.

Pedro signaled "stay back" even though he was still allowing Ludi to cradle him. "That was the AllCare agent," he spoke finally, lifting his head away from his wife like he'd just woken up. "He said the Farmland Insurance Company decided, based on the judge's use of the word, 'predominantly,' that their client was seventy percent responsible for the accident. But then they said that meant I was thirty percent responsible, even though I had the right of way. They argued I should have looked up the road and seen the lady was coming so fast, she wasn't going to stop."

"So they're not going to pay for the accident and your injury because they think you are thirty percent responsible?" asked Rotonda incredulously. "How were you supposed to see around the car stopped at the light, in the lane closest to you?"

"Mami, you remember those fliers Ludi posted around the intersection? The AllCare insurance agent said it would have helped if even one witness had responded."

"But I thought he said that wasn't going to matter!" Ludi fumed.

"He said he was not thinking it would matter. But when we had that terrible luck unable to reach the first hearing on time...! I said I did not know what the company thought we were supposed to do! Maybe rent a helicopter to fly over the stalled traffic?"

"I still do not understand, Pedro," said Rotonda. "If that woman was seventy percent responsible, Farmland should pay at least seventy percent of the expense, yes?"

"This man, Mr. Caplan, he says they told him the responsibility has to be eighty percent at minimum. Basically, it is my word against her word because no witness has come forward to corroborate I had the green arrow for a left turn."

"Didn't I hear something about petitioning?" asked Ludi desperately.

"Mr. Caplan said AllCare is going to petition Farmland for re-evaluation of their decision, but not to get my hope up. He said in the meantime AllCare would cover the car repair minus the two hundred dollar deductible. However, they will have to raise the premium to fifteen hundred a year!"

"Aydiosmio!" exclaimed Rotonda, rocking the asleep Alexandra with increasing fervor. "I never hear of this before, where a person owes nothing because some people decide she is 'only' seventy percent responsible! Seventy percent sounds plenty enough to me! What makes the big difference if one person is mostly to blame or completely to blame?"

Placido had been twisted about in his lounger for several minutes, to take in the upsetting mix of fear, anger and frustration. "Pedro," he motioned finally with his remote, "sit over here and watch any program you want!"

"No thank you, Papi, is okay." Pedro gave his stepfather the most affectionately appreciative smile he could force to shine through his mental and physical anguish.

"These people are sharks," growled Típico. "I never trust any of them! I stay far away from them!"

Reason number thousand-ninety-two why you sit in front of a TV most of the day, Ludi wanted to comment, but her grandma Norma went a different route: "You can make an exception this time, and go fight for Pedro! Also for your granddaughter and great granddaughter!"

Típico spread his arms apart as though to say: I am going to fight with this frail body?!? And he muttered, "They are not going to listen to me!"

"That would be me," snapped Norma, "who is not going to listen to you!"

Unable to hold it in any longer, Pedro cried, "We are going to lose our house!"

Ludi once more cradled Pedro's head, and ran her fingers through his hair with extra firmness. "We will keep our house!" she choked out through her tears. "We can do it! They always need overtime at the store!"

"I can be fine with no cable," added Placido. "They show the most important baseball and football games on regular TV anyway."

"Papi, you keep your cable," Pedro smiled despite his eyes welling up. "We have fifteen-hundred-dollar monthly mortgage payments. An extra forty is not going to make so much difference. But Mami, give him a big hug for me because he is offering the ultimate sacrifice!"

After handing off Alexandra to Ludi, Rotonda approached Placido to deliver the hug on behalf of Pedro. A knock at the door sidetracked her, though. Nevertheless, she did make sure to give her husband a loving brush across his shoulders when she passed by him.

This is just what we could use if it is Doña Galleta, Rotonda couldn't help thinking. *Is early in the day for her, however.*

Still wishing for Cookie Lady, Rotonda in her distracted anxiousness forgot to check through the peephole before opening the door. Too late, she recognized the people presenting before her. Normally, they sent the whole family into hiding, to wait for the danger to pass. Even Placido would turn off the TV without having to be asked, and then conceal himself behind furniture as fast as anyone.

There were two smartly dressed young men. They wore freshly pressed black pants with suspenders, and freshly starched shirts that virtually glowed bright white whether sunny or cloudy. Their backpacks matched their pants, as well as did the thick rims of their eyeglasses. Rotonda guessed they were a year or two older than Gloria and Jerri. Nevertheless, she wouldn't have wanted these guys for her daughters' boyfriends, any more than she approved of those two strutting roosters with whom she feared Gloria and Jerri were spending too much time. The shorter one cradled a Bible, and looked on reverentially at the taller one who flashed his most winning smile to say, "Good afternoon, *Señora*. Are you looking for a miracle in your life?"

"Yes, yes," Rotonda nodded emphatically. "There is a miracle I want in my life! That miracle would be if you never came to our door, ever again! No! Here is a better miracle you can perform!" She grabbed the tall guy by one arm, pulled him off balance as she impulsively dragged him inside. "Here are my son Pedro and his wife and daughter!" she shouted, pointing. "My son has been a good boy! He has worked hard all his life, but now he could lose his home thanks to a lady too old to drive! Her family should have taken away her license years ago! She crashed her car into his, and gave him a back injury too painful for working! And what is worse, the insurance company will not pay for the surgery he needs! They say the woman who caused the accident is seventy percent responsible! But seventy percent is not enough! They also say my son is thirty percent responsible because he doesn't have x-ray vision like Superman! He could not see through another car that this woman was coming and would not stop at the light! Yes! You make a miracle for that!"

"Mami, is okay," insisted Pedro, hating to see his mother so upset.

The shorter door-to-door evangelist went paging furiously through his Bible until he settled on something. "This is from Daniel, Chapter Ten," he said. "In Chapter Nine, Daniel confessed his sins, so in Chapter Ten he receives a vision, 'O Daniel, a man greatly beloved, understand the words that I speak unto thee, and stand upright: for unto thee am I now sent. And when he had spoken this word unto me, I stood trembling. Then he said unto me, Fear not, Daniel, for from the first day that thou didst set thine heart to understand, and to chasten thyself before thy God, thy words were heard, and I am come for thy words!'"

"The word of God," nodded the taller one. "Tell us, Pedro, so maybe we can pray with you: Have you confessed your sins, and asked God to send Jesus into your heart? When you accept Jesus as your personal savior, wonderful things become possible."

"I am sorry," Rotonda spoke before Pedro could open his mouth, "but I am not very impressed with this Jesus of yours!"

The two young men quickly crossed themselves.

Ludi mused they would have donned oxygen masks as well, had that been possible.

"I work in a soup kitchen once a month, and bring a meal to someone who is sick, and you can see we are not especially wealthy. But when I do those things, I am not first requiring people to accept me or say something good about me, and I am no Jesus Christ! I pray in church and out of church every day for the forgiveness of my sins! So you tell me why this Jesus of yours demands all this worship before He can show His love! If demonstrations of His love are conditional on people accepting Him, whatever that means, sounds like blackmail to me, and I am really NOT impressed!!"

"No, no, no!" the tall one shook his head. "Jesus loves everyone whether they love Him back or not!"

"Yes, but according to your group, He will not lift a finger for you unless you love Him back! AND, if you don't love Him back, He makes sure you go to hell after you die! How is this son of God as you believe in Him any different from some ultra-macho who shoots a woman because she will not return his love?"

"Lady," said the tall one, "we will pray for your soul, and pray for God to give your family the help it needs. Maybe you can join in?"

"That is not necessary. I am here to give this family some of the help it needs."

The two young men looked outside, then at each other. And then they made way for Galleta as they shouted, "Alleluia, Jesus! You have sent us a powerful sign of your love before our prayer even begins!! All praise to our savior!!"

Pedro mused that Galleta might as well have been riding in on a donkey, though she was carrying a tray full of fresh-baked cookies. There was a most diminutive manner to how she entered, head modestly bowed and long mousey-gray hair pinned up in a bun.

"Part of the help I am here to give them-"

"Sweet Jeeesus!" interrupted the tall one.

"A messenger sent from the Lord, like the archangel Gabriel! Amen!" said the short one.

"I am sent here, if you like," Galleta smiled wryly, "to help them by driving you away."

The tall one greeted this soft-spoken pronouncement with visible terror. He suddenly cowered behind his short partner, who tremblingly held his Bible before him like a shield.

"I believe the creative force of the universe is more concerned with people behaving nicely with one another, than with whether people bow down to a particular manifestation of its existence. You can take one of my cookies before you leave."

Both young men seemed to shiver more than shake their heads "no," where Pedro was concerned. "The Devil is trying to trick us!" the tall one declared. And as they both fled, the short one could be heard shouting, "We will pray for the salvation of your souls!"

"Huh!" grunted Típico. "They are not even trying a cookie! I tell you, nobody would ever get me to go from door to door like that!"

"Nobody would ever get you to do anything like anything!" said Norma.

Típico turned on the couch towards his wife, and gestured animatedly, "They could arrive at the door of someone who pulls out a pistol and shoots them!"

"Is true? Let me see if they will wait a minute so I can have you join them!"

"Ay caramba!"

A lot of what comes out of Don Típico's mouth, Pedro reckoned, does seem to center around reasons for him to just remain seated, watching the world go by.

"Ay, how beautiful," said Ludi. "Look who slept through everything!"

Little Alexandra safe in her mother's arms did not need to explain or justify why she was doing nothing. She yawned and stretched, little mouth and little limbs, so helpless, *Mami is right; those evangelists' idea of Jesus not helping anyone until they pray to Him is ridiculous! Is like if Ludi and I were not going to care for our daughter until, unless she told us how great we are! But my Alexita could pee on my face and it would make no difference. I want to provide her a safe and prosperous life, regardless, and I am not Jesus!*

"This is our miracle they did not recognize," said Ludi as she unbuttoned for breast feeding.

"Please, Doña Galleta," Placido unexpectedly burst out, "you know about my son's serious injury in the car accident. His operation will probably cost twenty thousand or more, but now he discovers the insurance companies will not pay one cent to help!"

Galleta looked down at her cookie tray; Pedro could tell she was pondering the inadequacy of what she offered. *How ironic this is, after Mami lectured those evangelists that if Jesus is so great, He won't condition his help on someone begging for it.*

"I already asked about a second mortgage on my home," said Galleta finally. "But since I have no collateral and am too frail to work, and it is not for home improvement or a relative's education..."

"Don Placido!" Rotonda exclaimed admonishingly. "Doña Galleta, please excuse my husband. Don Placido, when you accept the joyous beauty a blooming flower brings into your life… Okay, in your case we are talking about an adjustable lounge chair. You are not asking your 'Cushy Max' to also brush your teeth for you, besides relaxing you! And I do not ask a beautiful blooming flower on the window sill above my kitchen sink to also wash the dirty dishes for me! That is what we ask you men to help us with sometimes!"

"Aydiomio!"

"But we are beautiful flowers ourselves," creaked and croaked Típico. "Should be enough that we sit here for you to admire!"

"Ay caramba!" said Norma for once.

"Doña Galleta," said Pedro ignoring the older couple friction, "I have done nothing for you! Yet you do so much for me, bringing your delicious cookies at just the right times, like today. Plus you carry us on a voyage sixty years in the future, to seek the origin and purpose of our mysterious pendant from the skies. Believe me, my back will feel far worse if you push yourself even further!"

"Ay, yes!" nodded Ludi. "We appreciate if you just bake the cookies and stop channeling future voices! Remember last time? You gave the impression you were stuck somewhere! You kept shouting, 'Get me out of there!' until Pedro thought for us to hold the pendant against your stomach! I think we prefer living with the mystery over seeing you suffer more like that, yes Pedro?"

"Yes, is true." Pedro strove to keep wistful regret out of his voice.

"I think they are right," piled on Típico.

"Yes, you always think is a good idea for someone not to do something," said Norma. "I think maybe we force you down to the floor on your back, and stick the mystery pendant in YOUR navel!"

"Ay Caramba!"

"I appreciate all your concern," said Galleta. "And I am flattered by your comparing me to a flower, though I consider myself somewhat wilted. I started this voyage as you aptly termed it, Pedro, reviewing the recipe to learn the pendant's origin. But clearly, I have become a crucial ingredient in a larger recipe. Circles within circles, as mentioned before. I can no more avoid leaving myself vulnerable than a caterpillar can prevent being eaten or otherwise destroyed during its cocoon stage. Of course, I have more choice than the caterpillar; I could decide not to channel today. Clearly if unexplainably, though, such a choice leaves an important matter tragically unattended. Which matter? I have no idea. But I suspect, dear Ludi and Pedro, that your pendant fell through a rift, a wound in the very sky itself that you supposed was cloud-to-cloud lightning.

"Anyhow," Galleta continued, "here is my pledge so you will not need worry over my safety during the session today. I will change perspectives frequently. In other words, I will not channel any one person for so long that he or she feels the ill effect from two spirits trying to inhabit the same physical presence. I will not wait for someone to become over wrought; this is what got me in trouble before. I need to be more careful anyway. Some of my primary host's associates suspect something beyond the ordinary, and my intrusion is that something, of course."

Even Pedro wasn't clear what Galleta meant, only that she had to do another session, but would be playing it safer.

Someone unlocking the front door-knob with a loud jiggle finally broke the silence over Cookie Lady's latest cryptic remarks. Then Gloria and Jerri were taking stealthy cat steps up the stairway to their bedroom, trying to escape notice. And for the first time Pedro could remember since they were girls, they were holding hands. He wondered, *Are they trying to steady one another after getting drunk mid-day?*

"You girls want a cookie?"

"Doña Galleta!" Startled, Gloria and Jerri disengaged their hands. "Yes, those look good. I will take one." "Me too."

Pedro sighed aloud with relief to see his sisters were not drunk. In fact if he didn't know better, he would swear their voices expressed appreciation. Were they actually happy over Galleta's presence?

"I was just explaining to the rest of your family that I made a choice, with this voyage to discover the origin of the mystery pendant. And now I must endure to completion of the recipe."

Neither Gloria nor Jerri could evade Galleta's penetrating gaze, even to focus on not dropping big crumbs when they bit into her cookies.

"We know our mami will want us to stay for your session," said Jerri, "so we will sit with Don Típico."

"Ay, yes," sighed Gloria.

Pedro and Ludi gave one another significant glances. Pedro's sisters expressed resignation to their fate, but more feigned than real. Unaccountably, they appreciated getting caught trying to evade Galleta's new session.

Pedro sensed something really odd going on. He knew his sisters too well. But he held his tongue. His mama worried enough about him with his back injury and the house; she didn't need to also be agonizing over whatever trouble his sisters might have brought on themselves.

"Out the rear window of our solar sail pod, we enjoy a nice view of the Smoke and Mirrors parked in high orbit," said Galleta, wasting no time getting to her feet and speaking. That is, once the correct positioning of her outstretched arms and legs produced the telltale poof! of faint bluish smoke gone as fast as it appeared above the mystery pendant. In contrast to other sessions, however, she took no step without clutching at the edge of furniture, whether chair, sofa, or dining table.

Galleta's audience could not have known Captain Taylor was operating in the first weightless environment since mission launch.

"You can see the fore and aft flower bud configurations have re-concealed the mirror arrays. And note the golden solar sail deployment. That is giving our nearly depleted photovoltaic systems a much-needed recharge. Also, if you look closely, you'll notice an occasional glint of reflected light some distance from the spaceship itself. That's nicknamed the soap bubble. It's an electrostatically maintained micron layer of a special plastic alloy. The soap bubble protects the Smoke and Mirrors from space dust and micro-asteroid impacts when parked, so to speak. The only unprotected area is the pod bay hatch; if the entire soap bubble were visible, the shuttle pod would appear to be exiting from its belly button, so to speak."

Galleta paused on her way into the kitchen. Pedro surmised she was giving her audience, whoever wherever they were, a moment to take in the view he would have loved to have had with his own eyes. Then she spun around and, still awkwardly clutching from furniture piece to furniture piece, returned to the living room. "We are headed for docking with a space station in orbit around the planet," she said. "It's depicted in this transmission from our extraterrestrial contacts."

Galleta lifted the mystery pendant beside her face how someone in a television commercial might lift a product to be sold, Pedro imagined. But trillions of miles and sixty years away, Captain Taylor held up a paper-thin screen displaying select pictures sent by the extraterrestrials. And Taylor's husband, Chris, was filming both her and screen together, on the camcorder clipped to his felt-covered headband.

"This is the fourth planet from their sun," Galleta went on channeling Captain Taylor. "Their sun, which we know as Alpha Centauri C, is a bit larger and brighter than our sun. However, their planet is also a little further away from their sun than our planet is from our sun. 97 million miles, as opposed to the 93 million miles our Earth is from our sun. And their planet is about 97 per cent the size of Earth, so less gravitational pull. You can't make hundred-foot leaps like you can on our moon. But if you're trying to lose weight, might be the place for a flattering reading."

What Pedro could not have known was that during Galleta's pause, Chris remarked, "Maybe I will finally have my tee shot go three hundred yards."

"Yes, there might be incidental, um, advantages for various sports," Galleta channeled Captain Taylor continuing. "Now you will notice here, beside the transmitted depiction of their planet, um... We're still unsure whether boundary lines indicate only a few immense lakes amidst vast land masses, or only a few Australia-sized continents amidst vast oceans; we should learn within minutes. Anyhow, check out these hieroglyphs unlike any from Earth, whether from the Egyptians or other civilizations thousands of years ago. According to our brilliant resident linguist, Dr. Ali Magabu, they very likely display our extraterrestrials' name for their planet."

"Ay Santo!" burst out Pedro, thunderstruck. Galleta pointed at the mystery pendant's markings the same time she channeled Captain Taylor talking about strange markings on an extraterrestrial transmission! "Mami, everybody, the host of Doña Galleta is talking about hieroglyphs not from our Earth! Based on my library research, the hieroglyphs engraved on our pendant are also not from Earth! Maybe they are one and the same language! Maybe our pendant contains a message from extraterrestrials!"

Típico shook his head and waved his hands dismissively with a grunted chuckle. "If I see something like that fall from the sky, I will not touch it! I will leave it on the ground!" He raised his hands to demonstrate not reaching for a fallen object.

"You hear this?" said Norma. "Don Típico boasts what he will not do! *Bueno*, maybe there is something *I* should not have done! When we met for the first time, Típi tripped over himself and fell at my feet. Maybe I should have left him there!" Norma also raised her hands to demonstrate not reaching down.

"Ay caramba!"

"Sh! Look!" pointed Pedro.

While they were talking, Captain Taylor had gone on, "We would love to utter their planet's name aloud. Up 'til now, though, neither their computers nor ours have been able to transmit sound. Due to system incompatibility issues, their vocalizations, music, any noises they might make have remained a mystery. But one of our many exciting expectations from this imminent historic encounter includes finally hearing what accompanies their words and pictographs. Speaking of incompatibility, another- Wait..."

Galleta abruptly stopped talking. She dropped the pendant on the towel where she'd laid herself down for this particular session, and looked towards the Santiago family's front window. By the time Pedro said "Sh!" she was headed closer to that window, totally transfixed. Her mouth dropped open as she stumbled forward, clutching at furniture for balance. "Chris," she said, "can you direct your camcorder over here?"

In the silence that followed for Pedro's family, Chris was saying some sixty years and trillions of miles away, "You've got it, Captain."

Placido hobbled over beside the entranced Galleta, to also look out the window. They heard and saw a late-autumn wind gust blow dry fallen leaves down the street.

"Hey Papi," said Pedro, "are you expecting to see a little green man?"

"I do not know," he said as, scratching himself, he u-turned back to his lounger. "There is a gutted-out car across the street, left on cinder blocks. Maybe it is really a landed spaceship, but very rusty from the trip."

"That was from flying through the rust belt, maybe."

As his mom, wife and sisters giggled, Pedro "shh!"ed them again because Galleta resumed.

"That long, thin crescent of light arcing from top to bottom of the screen: You see how it's steadily widening to quarter phase?" Doña Galleta asked. "Uh, that's the daylight side of the planet we're approaching. Uh, we used Alpha Centauri C's photon rays to billow our solar sails and, uh, propel our shuttle pod around the dark side. Uh, our descent to their space station is taking us much lower from where we left the Smoke and Mirrors in high orbit. So, uh, we're seeing more detail…"

All those "uh"s…Oh-oh, Pedro thought. Galleta is rubbing her forehead anew, looking bothered like she did before she had a lot of trouble previously. I thought she was going to…

"Uh, Officer Leung, would you like to take over the narration from here? You were making lots of worthwhile observations…"

"Of course, Captain," said Buddy Leung, vigorously motioning Helena over to the co-pilot's seat Geena had already vacated.

Captain Taylor practically collapsed into Geena's seat, head in hands.

"Those observations Captain Taylor referred to, though am not so sure of their worth... Oh, wow," Buddy practically gasped. "In high orbit aboard the Smoke and Mirrors, we were expecting clusters of pin-point lights visible on this planet's night side, especially through our magnification screen."

Pedro and his family were hearing nothing from Galleta, but at least she had stopped acting like she was dealing with a painful headache. Típico wanted to cynically suggest she was at a loss for what to say next. But before the first word could leave his lips, she went on, channeling Buddy, "Of course, such clusters would have been artificial lights from population centers. Exactly what one would anticipate from a civilization advanced enough to send pictograph messages outside their solar system. Not to mention the space station where, if we understand correctly, they have asked us to rendezvous for our first direct contact."

"Ay caramba," Típico muttered under his breath.

"From high orbit, all we could detect on the dark side was darkness," Buddy laughed nervously. "But now, I hope Mr. Olsen-Taylor's camcorder is picking this up for you. There are these faint yet clearly discernible blotches of greenish tint. Uhhh, what do you think, Officer Petrovsky?" Buddy unexpectedly found himself rubbing his forehead due to a sudden, insistent headache.

"Naturally occurring luminescence, perhaps," speculated Tanya.

Chris kept his camcorder focused out the shuttle pod's cockpit window. He well knew to divert attention from his crew mates as they played pass-the-hot-potato with the trip narration.

Of course, the real hot potato was the sudden headache mysteriously bouncing from person to person.

"Definitely originates there," went on Tanya. "No moon is in evidence to provide reflected light for the planet's surface."

With Tanya's conclusion of her remarks concerning greenish tints that blotched the planet's dark side, Cookie Lady went quiet anew.

"Doña Galleta is leaping to another host again," Ludi commented softly. "This time, she really is being more careful about discomforting anyone for too long."

"Maybe is better if we call her back," said Típico as Galleta's mute period extended. "If she leaves them alone, she will not give those people of the future so many headaches."

"Can someone call YOU back to end *our* headaches?" said Norma, wiping her husband's silly I-don't-believe-any-of-this-anyway grin off his face.

"Ay caramba!"

"Sh!" said Pedro. "I think she is about to resume!"

"We can speculate," Galleta continued finally, this time channeling Officer Tanya Petrovsky-Magabu, "the greenish splotches are bioluminescent nocturnal releases from planet's eco-system. Yes, this would be comparable to activities of some aquatic algae and plankton in a few locations on Earth. But on much broader scale, mostly land-based."

"I think they are flying a smaller ship launched from the mother ship named Smoke and Mirrors," Pedro whispered loudly enough for his entire family to hear. "They are describing what they see of the planet they are visiting in another solar system."

"Or," Galleta channeled Tanya further, "maybe we ARE viewing artificial lighting of the extraterrestrial civilization we expect to contact. However, it manifests in different manner than anticipated."

"A fascinating possibility, Officer Petrovsky," said Buddy, fully recovered from the mysterious relaying headache. "In other words, maybe those blotches are concentrated population areas, their version of urban centers. But they are blanketed by domes on a far larger scale than our Mars domes destroyed by the storm. And those domes subdue and suffuse the artificial light observed even from low orbit!"

"Intriguing speculation, Officer Leung," nodded Tanya. "Now, on to what we *are* certain of. Preliminary spectrograph analysis indicates an atmosphere very similar to Earth's. As a result, our away team's own air supply brought to the extraterrestrial space station might prove a needless redundancy. But we don't know yet. There are dangerous microbe possibilities for which Dr. Davis-Murphy has prepared her safety protocol."

"Officer Petrovsky!" exclaimed Buddy Leung. His astonishment propelled him out of his seat at the shuttle pod control panel. "Do you see what I'm seeing along the boundary between night and day? Or am I hallucinating?"

"No hallucination, Officer Leung!" Tanya tried to maintain her enthused tone even though the marauding headache had finally afflicted her. "I see them too, if you are talking about green blotches turned olive and brown by reaching dawn interface."

"Good!" said Buddy as off-camera, he motioned furiously for Tanya to take a seat, her growing distress clearly evident despite her stoicism. "Even better, we're also solving a riddle posed by the extraterrestrial black-line sketches. Is this planet covered by vast oceans punctuated by Australia-sized islands? Or is it covered by vast land pock-marked with large seas? Those sparkling blue ovals we're observing argue for the latter scenario."

"Yes," agreed Tanya, feeling better already, "which might account for so little evident cloud cover."

"Hope our camcorder is allowing our fellow Earthlings, so many trillion miles away, to share our sense of wonder over the awesome view spread before us," resumed Galleta after another silent spell, this time returned to channeling Captain Taylor. "If my eyes aren't deceiving me... My God! Officer Smith," Helena called from the shuttle pod back to Kevin on the bridge of the Smoke and Mirrors, "what is your magniview showing?!"

"Looks like an epic line of dust storms traveling the sunset interface, Captain! Should you guys abort out of there?"

"That storm-line does appear threatening," conceded Buddy. "However, our sensors detect its highest altitude at no more than twenty thousand feet. Mighty impressive, nevertheless!" he laughed. "Oh! There's the pyramid! Wo! That's enormous beyond anything built on Earth!"

"Yes, Officer Leung." Helena made a special effort to keep her cool while Buddy came unglued. "I was wondering why they made a point of depicting that particular structure. Now we know.

"Anyway, if you look above its apex, you can see a flashing light. That's probably mounted on a tower too thin for discerning from this distance. My guess is we're viewing our first extraterrestrial lighthouse. Again, hope our fellow Earthlings are enjoying such an extraordinary sight.

"Officer Petrovsky, what would you estimate are the pyramid's base dimensions?"

"Unbelievable, Captain! Pyramid's base would have to be several miles across on each side for it to look so large at this distance! Wonder what will happen when that structure is engulfed by dust storm?!"

"Not simply a dust storm now, Captain!" Buddy broke in. "Look at those thunderheads popping up behind the leading edge!"

"The question becomes whether we are witnessing a normal weather phenomenon for this planet," spoke Captain Taylor with studied cool, trying to establish calm for facing the unknown. "If so, the pyramid should stand up quite well to the onslaught. Otherwise we happened to arrive, coincidentally, on the verge of a disastrous calamity taking our extraterrestrial contacts by as much surprise as it's taking us."

"If you mean something on scale with the Mars tragedy, Captain," said Buddy Leung, "wouldn't we have received a pictograph transmission to that effect by now? Incidentally, we're approaching so close to their space station, should be a visual any second."

"Thank you, Officer Leung," Helena exhaled with relief, so much for her studied cool. For terrorizing moments, she feared the antler-bearing extraterrestrials might somehow have made weather manipulation a form of attack.

"Having said what I said, Captain," Buddy laughed nervously, "wow and more wow! As the dust storm accompanies sunset, those thunderstorms keep popping up behind, dissipating into the darkness!"

"Do you think, Officer Leung," Tanya asked, "this weather phenomenon could be common daily occurrence along sunset boundary?"

"Wouldn't that be amazing to always have nightfall heralded by thunder-bumpers kicking up dust storms? Okay, let's see what happens with the pyramid!"

No sooner said than rapidly billowing thunderheads ushered in a dust storm that engulfed the pyramid. The flashing red light could still be espied above the turmoil, though sporadically upstaged by greenish-blue lightning flashes.

The violent weather's sunset-synchronized advance reminded Chris of yeast bloom suffusing warm water when he prepared fresh bread. He wondered whether the thunderheads' amazingly rapid climb heavenwards could be attributed to the slightly lower gravity compared with Earth's.

"This must be what is meant by that poetic term, 'terrible beauty,'" commented Helena Taylor. "But at least the architectural wonder of our extraterrestrials' world appears unscathed."

"And there's the space station, Captain, right where it's supposed to be." Buddy pointed at an unusually dense concentration of glitter and twinkles. It might have been mistaken for a distant star cluster by less careful observation.

"Captain," Kevin broke in again from the Smoke and Mirrors, "we're receiving a new pictograph transmission. Can you turn on your telescreen?"

"On, Officer Smith."

"We're splicing this through to your telescreen from ours, Captain. How is that?"

"We're good. Officer Olsen-Taylor, can you direct your camcorder at our telescreen for our audience in other-solar-system abstentia? There. So Dr. Magabu, am I looking at a more detailed black-line sketch of their space station?"

"Apparently so, Captain. Follow the arrow. Truly fascinating, how the arrow works as a universal symbol for pointing. I believe it indicates where you're supposed to dock. Wait…"

The telescreen suddenly went blank.

"We're receiving another pictograph, filling in quite nicely," Ali went on from back aboard the Smoke and Mirrors. "Captain, I believe this is a close-up from where the arrow was directing our attention. Clearly, it shows where our shuttle pod should dock."

"I see that, Dr. Magabu, along with lines drawn around the pod. They stem from small apertures on the space station hull."

"Captain, I'm guessing those are tethers normally used for spacewalk inspections and exterior space station repair. Our extraterrestrial friends must be improvising since truly, their normal docking mechanisms are likely incompatible with our shuttle pod."

"Think you're right, Dr. Magabu. Does makes sense that we would have to dock alongside their space station rather than within its shuttle hangar."

"Notice a smaller arrow on the second pictograph, Captain? Pointing at a circle right above where they evidently want us to park our shuttle pod?"

"We see that, Dr. Magabu," said Buddy. Aboard the shuttle pod, he and Tanya were joining Chris to look over his wife's shoulders at the navigation console telescreen. This, despite having trouble holding still thanks to near-zero gravity.

"I believe that's supposed to be the airlock. Ah, we're receiving a third pictograph, truly amazing."

"I'm receiving word… Are you getting this, Officer Smith?" asked Captain Taylor, clutching at her earphone.

"Yes I am, Captain. Sounds like the folks at home enjoy our show. What's that they're reporting? Yesterday, people rolled out of their beds middle of the night in China and Japan to watch? Practically the entire planet is awake?"

"Let's hope they see this third pictograph, Dr. Magabu. Shouldn't need any explanation, I would think."

"Neither would I, Captain."

"But just in case none of these pictographs go through...We won't know for sure until, well, the firefly donut takes twenty hours to oscillate from transmission range of our solar system back to us near Alpha Centauri C. Um..." Captain Taylor's touch of headache was bad enough, from Galleta lingering too long before jumping to another host. But what also ground Captain Taylor's narration to a halt was an emergent realization. Ever since an asteroid apparently wiped out one of their firefly donuts, the others had become all the more precious. *Yes, sharing a history-shattering experience with home certainly rates high priority. But how high, given the risk entailed by constantly sending one of the remaining two fireflies back and forth across an Oort Cloud? Especially since Buddy Leung employed the other remaining firefly for his time rift experiment? Shouldn't both fireflies be kept safely corralled inside the shuttle pod hangar to ensure our safe navigation back home after first contact? After all, even traveling above the Oort Cloud plane en route to Alpha Centauri C required two midcourse corrections, to avoid dangerously close space-rock encounters.*

Okay, maybe the Alpha Centauri C extraterrestrials possess adequate technology for constructing additional firefly donuts. However, every indication suggests their chemical metallurgy lags a good fifty years behind Earth's.

We still do have two fireflies, so we really can afford one more loss. But if that happens, I will definitely shut down our interstellar pony express. Ditto for Buddy's rogue experiments. There, that's settled!

Buddy had long since picked up Helena's narration while she was wrestling with the firefly donut issue. "Since the visual portion of our transmission might not go through, let me give this a shot," he had gone on. "The captain and the rest of us are seeing a line-drawing close-up of that small circle above where our shuttle pod is supposed to dock. Sure enough, as Dr. Magabu expected, a black oval is drawn beside that circle. Presumably that's the opening to an airlock chamber. And to remove any doubt," Buddy laughed, "there's also this remarkable… must be an extraterrestrial's guess as to our appearance."

"Not to take away from the momentousness of their communication, Officer Leung," said Magabu. "But I believe they simply used the sketch we sent of how we expect the three of you to look, climbing out of the shuttle pod in your safety protocol gear."

"Maybe they can tie balloons beside the airlock," proposed Chris, "pretend it's the mailbox for someone having a birthday party."

Buddy Leung interrupted the ensuing cathartic laughter by pointing out the shuttle pod's panoramically expansive cockpit window. "We don't need drawings any more, people; look how close we're getting."

"Officer Leung, solar sail tacking appears nicely decelerated; can you confirm?" asked Helena, having collected her wits enough to resume duties.

"Autopilot program's right on pace, Captain."

"Switching to manual, Captain," added Tanya. "We are on three-minute countdown to docking."

"Mr. Olsen-Taylor, of course you have your camcorder directed at the extraterrestrial space station?"

"Searching for those party balloons, Captain."

"Yes, well…" Helena was the only one not chuckling at her husband's remark. "Time to suit up; can you attach your camcorder to the navigation console, looking out the cockpit window? As we approach docking, perhaps the insomniac portion of our audience can drift off, lulled asleep by the extraterrestrial space station's exquisite beauty."

"Done, Captain."

"Dr. Magabu?"

"I'm listening, Captain."

"Can you continue the narration? And maybe fellow officers on the bridge will pitch in?"

"No worries, Captain. Truly, I have plenty to say. But first, can you or your husband, or Officer Leung, describe the excitement of donning gear for humanity's first direct encounter with an extraterrestrial intelligence?"

"Officer Olsen-Taylor?" laughed Buddy. "I don't want to put my good friend on the spot, but I bet his travelogue will rival his chocolate chip cookies!"

"Sure," said Chris, ready to go. "When my parents took me to the beach, my favorite part happened right after hotel check-in. We changed into our swimsuits. It's that kind of thrill."

"Truly wonderful, Officer Olsen-Taylor," said Magabu. "So let me turn to my fellow officers back here aboard the Smoke and Mirrors. Any thoughts on what we're seeing through the magniview?"

"I have," offered Yoon-hee. "Very unusual."

"Yes, Officer Park-Smith?"

"Those different-colored domes… At least they appear different-colored, tinted. I assume they're windows. They give the space station an antique look like something owned by an emperor or royalty, studded with emeralds and other jewels."

"Hey, she's right," said Kevin. "I'm just thinking of this amazing sheath we saw at an archaeology museum."

"Nay," Yoon-hee nodded. "That dark slot for their space shuttle vehicle docking, that's where the sword would slide in!"

"Something eerie, though: If those domes are their windows, doesn't look like anyone's home," said Kevin. "Shouldn't they be lit up or something?"

"May I propose, fellow officers," said Ali Magabu, "that those various dome tints protect the creatures stationed there from harmful rays? Perhaps they are comparable to especially dark sunglasses?"

"Dark sunglasses, exactly! It's a fashion statement, Doc," said Kevin. "Our extraterrestrial friends are trying to project coolness at the cosmos."

Light patter from officers aboard the Smoke and Mirrors accompanied amazing views of the alien space station provided by the shuttle pod, its solar sails deployed for final approach. Pedro and his family were not privy to any of this, however. They had to settle with the odd spectacle of Galleta quietly lifting one foot then the other while making a variety of motions with her arms and hands.

"I think she is channeling one of the people putting on their spacesuit for a visit to the aliens' space station," said Pedro. "Looks like, how you say, pantomime."

"Ay," Típico grunted with a dismissive wave, "I hope she is not going to undress!"

"I am sure she will not want you too excited, Grandpa," said Ludi.

"Ha!" Típico coughed more than laughed. "Listen, you will not see me pretend like that."

"That is true," said Norma. "We will not! We will look the other way!"

"If I do something like that, you will lock me in the crazy house!"

"We WILL lock you in the crazy house!" agreed Norma. "So do not try it!"

"Ay caramba!"

"Maybe we lock you in the crazy house anyway!" Norma added, but immediately thought better of this particular needling of her husband. Before Típico could let loose with another *Ay caramba!*, she came up behind him and lovingly rubbed his shoulders. "If that happens, I will stay there with you."

"Ah!" Típico's silly grin returned.

"I think the visiting hours are only from two to four. I can spare that!" She playfully twisted his ears.

"Yes, and then the rest of the time," said Típico addressing Gloria and Jerri seated beside him, "she will dance with strange men!"

"Ay, sí," nodded Norma. "Forget about J-Lo. Is me they are after!"

"Chris? Buddy? You can hear me?" Galleta abruptly blurted out after lifting her knees high to take two steps towards Pedro and Ludi's family. She gave Pedro the clear impression that wherever she was channeling from, her host had entered some passageway.

"We can hear you," Gloria whispered, prompting Jerri's giggle.

"Maybe she is testing her cell phone," Pedro speculated, wanting to promote the lightened mood. But for fear of missing something, he added, "We should be quiet now."

"I'm hearing you loud and clear, Helena," said Buddy, standing close beside her and Chris in the shuttle pod's airlock. All three were suited up for the spacewalk over to what they presumed was the airlock of the alien space station.

"Eek! Eek!" squeaked Chris, then, "Oh! Our two mice Ferdinand and Magellan must have heard you as well."

"You did double-check their chamber is properly sealed? And that their temperature and air controls are operating properly?"

Chris gathered from Helena's severe tone that her more important communication was to the effect of: This is all super serious now; no more funny stuff. "You can read the gauges yourself, Captain," he subsequently responded, holding up the mouse container for his wife's inspection.

Where Captain Helena Taylor was concerned, Ferdinand and Magellan's home away from home might as well have been an over-sized, insulation-padded lunch container.

"Captain," said Tanya, her voice emanating gently from tiny speakers inside the away team's suits, "air drain is complete. Anything else before I open outside hatch?"

"I guess we should have tried our exterior mikes before the drain."

"I can refill the airlock if you want. That would only take seconds."

"Please, Tanya. I would hope our extraterrestrial hosts understand the delay, especially in the name of thorough preparedness."

"I hear hissing, Captain," said Buddy. "Tell me you've flipped the switch to the exterior mikes, and that's coming from Tanya refilling..."

"Calm down, Officer Leung." Captain Taylor raised a cautioning hand while trillions of miles and sixty years away, Pedro reflected on how awkward Galleta appeared.

Doña Galleta was holding out her arms to her sides, plus her legs stretched further apart than normal. Properly outfitted, she could have been a gunslinger ready to draw her pistol, Pedro mused. "Ah," he sighed, finally realizing, *what she said about sucked-out air, Galleta must have put on a spacesuit. Her previous movements were more than mere pantomime!*

"Captain," said Chris, careful not to call his wife by her first name even though the broadcast wasn't back on yet, "should I resume filming with our supplemental camcorder for the folks back home?"

"Not yet. Let's stay with the other camcorder view from the shuttle pod's navigation console. There's something I want to discuss without worrying our vast audience."

"Hey, what are you doing?" asked Chris; as Helena told him not yet with the supplemental camcorder, she was feeling where his helmet attached to the suit, and then his gloves and boots.

"You've never done a spacewalk before. So I'm checking that everything is sealed tightly. Anyhow, we have a new development regarding our roving headache."

"Excuse me, Captain, are you ready for me to re-drain the air?"

"Everything checks out fine, Tanya, but wait. I want you in on this conversation also."

"Yes, Captain?"

"About that headache we've been experiencing except for you, Chris, correct?"

"Correct, Captain my captain."

"Of course, Chris is the only one who hasn't been providing narration for our broadcast back to Earth," observed Buddy, "by virtue of his always being the cameraman."

"Okay, well," Helena made an awkward motion to trying rubbing her forehead, impossible constrained by helmet and suit glove intervening between head and hand. "So much for the marauding headache necessarily linking to whoever narrates. I'm feeling it coming on again, but I'm not center stage for narration this time. Hoping that as before, it leaves before turning unbearably uncomfortable."

"Which might make one of us the next victim, anew," said Buddy. "I am correct about there not yet having been experience of this headache by more than one person at the same time?"

"That seems the case," Tanya confirmed. "And there is chicken-egg question. You have in America, how it goes? Which came first, chicken or egg? When we notice someone feeling distress in front of camera, one of us makes a quick substitution. However, it is not clear whether headache relief results from not having to continue in front of the camera, or... Last time I was star of the show, I felt discomfort diminishing before you took over for me, Officer Leung. So which comes first: headache relief, or getting relieved from having to narrate? If nuisance headache ebbs and flows regardless of who is narrating, maybe we have chicken that doesn't need egg."

"Yes, yes," nodded Buddy; he would have snapped his fingers if they weren't constrained by the spacesuit glove.

Galleta suddenly squatted down before Pedro, and opened her eyes wide for looking deep into his. Then with a jerk, she blinked and shook her head.

Only Pedro's fear of further aggravating his back injury kept him from a reciprocal jerk.

"I hope that was not making you too uncomfortable," Galleta said. How she rose back up on her feet and turned away from Pedro left him unclear whether she was addressing all of them, or him only. "The astronauts were comparing notes," she went on. "That brought them too close to maybe remembering research into spirit channeling that will take place forty years from now. So I had to focus on one of you to pull myself out. Is better if they suppose their discomfort from my presence actually stems from speaking before a film camera. Hopefully they will conclude their captain's headache, when the camera was not operating, is the exception that proves the rule. In other words, I want them to believe her headache had no special origin."

"So you are stopping for now?" asked Típico with a silly grin, making no effort to conceal his delight over the prospect he raised.

"Only for a few minutes."

"Ay..."

"I am waiting until our friends of the future make direct contact with the extraterrestrials, because that is also when they will resume filmed narration."

Chapter 10: The 4th Session, Part Two

The spacewalk went as anticipated. Helena, Chris and Buddy linked arms to drift across from the shuttle pod airlock hatch to the extraterrestrial space station airlock hatch.

Chris easily kept the mouse container from floating out of his grasp. And closer to the space station he avoided bumping against one of the docking tethers, which might have dislodged important items from his suit.

"Your hearts are racing, blood pressures elevated," reported Dr. Deborah Davis-Murphy from monitoring equipment aboard the Smoke and Mirrors. "Well within safe parameters, but I'm going to release a hint of stress-reducing lilac scent."

Just then, the space station hatch popped up and rotated aside, revealing a pitch-black entrance.

"Thank you, Deb. Most soothing, and most unexpected!"

"That's the whole point, Captain, for maximum effectiveness."

Buddy grabbed hold of the opened hatch's rim first, and gently swung Helena and Chris into a crouch down around it.

"Everyone's feeling okay?" asked the captain as she anxiously pondered the alien space station's pitch-black entrance, lilac scent notwithstanding. Though she did remind herself the shuttle pod's airlock entrance could also appear very dark.

"Still blissing out on the lilac, Captain," said Buddy. "And you?"

"Floral accents always help. Um, Chris, suppose I take the mouse container off your hands. Can you wield our extra camcorder to document what comes next, and where we walked from, without losing it?"

"Without losing what, Captain: the camcorder or my sanity?"

"Both."

"How about I also provide a little narration? I promise the briefest observations, captions for what we're observing. Who knows? Maybe the marauding headache won't afflict me, speaking from behind the camera instead of in its crosshairs."

"Chris's plan is good, Captain," said Buddy. "But when we're in actual contact mode, Ali should do the narration honors from back aboard the Smoke and Mirrors."

"Oh, which reminds me," said Captain Taylor, chicken-pecking at a keyboard built into the left arm of her suit. "Is everyone on the bridge hearing this? Especially Tanya?"

Tanya did the honors, confirming reception of audio as well as visual feed from Chris's camcorder. Tanya also confirmed that broadcast transmissions Earthwards would be resumed via firefly donut oscillating between Alpha Centauri C and Pluto. With such details settled, Captain Taylor followed by Buddy and Chris carefully descended feet first through the presumed airlock of the alien space station.

"That hiss you're hearing," narrated Chris, "should be their air, what the extraterrestrials breathe. It's filling where we've entered, which you probably can't see for the darkness."

"Not untypical of airlock chambers on our space stations and spacecraft," Helena hastened to add, stretching the truth. She didn't want the Earth audience stressing over a lack of lighting, however much she might. Curiously, though, neither the unexpected darkness nor Chris adding to her nerves ignited any least headache.

Sheer wonderment evaporated any and all jitteriness once the airlock door slid aside. In fact, Deborah aboard the Smoke and Mirrors saw away-team blood pressures drop back to normal.

Captain Taylor didn't even have to worry about what might come out of her husband's mouth next. He couldn't find any words. And he had a lot of company in that regard on the Smoke and Mirrors' navigation bridge to where his camcorder was feeding.

Soft-glowing luminescent bulbs dimly lit the room outside the airlock chamber. And for some unfathomable reason, they were embedded in the soil of big, porcelain pots.

The pots were planted with tall ferns looming over the glowing bulbs.

The away team marveled at the potted soil staying put, not floating about the near-weightless environment. Helena figured a nutritional sticky goop was mixed in, comparable to back home for Space Station 2 foliage.

The extended ferny branches curled at their tips, reminding Chris of a Halloween goblin reaching out to grab someone. They also conjured a bent-over fortune-telling gypsy encircling a crystal ball to coax visions of the future from its swirling smoky inners.

Starlight shone brightly through one of the domed ceiling windows that from outside the space station looked like tinted jewels embedded in some ancient ornate artifact.

"Well," Captain Taylor said finally, "everyone's mag-boots are working?"

"Fine, Captain."

"I'm okay Helena Captain, sir."

Both Buddy and Chris took two march-steps in place, but were careful not to stomp on the floor. Rather, they lowered their feet gingerly slowly.

"Well is this it, or should we stand here all day admiring the present view?"

"Funny thing, Captain," said Buddy, "they've yet to peek in at us. Maybe they're going through our same last-second hesitancy. Listen."

Soft shuffling noises emanated from outside the airlock, accompanied by… *mumbled whispers?* Chris wondered.

"Go ahead, Captain; we're here for you," said Kevin Smith-Park, his voice coming across the away team's headsets with unexpected force.

Without their magnetic boots for zero gravity, Helena and company might have hopped in surprise at Kevin's intrusion. But instead they lost balance, taking awkward steps that sent them bumping into each other. Chris imagined they looked as silly as the Three Stooges in century-old movies.

A sudden yet faint rustle ensued from outside the airlock.

Buddy suspected the extraterrestrials had their own clumsy moment, reacting to abrupt noise from their as-yet-unseen visitors.

"Gentlemen, you heard Officer Smith-Park," said Captain Helena Taylor. "Turn on your exterior speaker systems, and let's do this."

Helena squeezed Chris's gloved hand, a squeeze he would treasure for the rest of his life. Then she lifted her right foot to an exaggerated height, and announced, "One small step for woman, one big blind date for humanity with the universe!"

From outside where the three Earthlings stood, they could hear someone finish an utterance full of soft vowels, especially lots of ahs.

Buddy and Chris intuited an extraterrestrial announcement comparable to Helena's, as to the occasion's momentousness.

The Earthlings still didn't see anyone else present once they left the airlock chamber. They were getting used to the darkness, so no slightest motion would have gone unnoticed. They had one more corner to turn, however. Helena approached that corner taking the softest steps she could, slowly, slowly…

"Oh!"

"Ee-ee! Ee-ee!"

Helena and the extraterrestrial exclaimed simultaneously because they peeked around the corner at the same time, nearly bumping their heads together.

The extraterrestrial's exclamation reminded Chris of shrill monkey cries at the zoo.

Earthlings and extraterrestrials alike quickly concluded no harm no foul, and finally stepped out into full view, no more peekaboo.

Nevertheless, the Earthlings could not help certain disappointment. The extraterrestrials clearly did not heed Dr. Deborah Davis-Murphy's suggested protocol, as portrayed in her transmitted pictograph. They wore no protective suits, not even a face mask. Rather, they simply presented in long-sleeved, knee-length gray tunics with bow-tied rope belts, and shoes comparable to the Earthlings' magnetic boots.

"They must be exceedingly confident the spacewalk wiped out any viral and bacterial contaminants on your suit, Captain," said Deborah from back aboard the Smoke and Mirrors. "Either that, or they didn't understand my pictographs."

"Hopefully, they at least brought along a flounder mouse for an encounter with Ferdinand or Magellan," said Buddy.

"Zah?" said the lead alien, tilting his head quizzically to one side.

Buddy realized the extraterrestrial thought he was addressing him, so he shook his head "no." Then he gestured towards the captain, to indicate she should be the focus of communication.

"Wah," the alien nodded, undoubtedly understanding.

"Truly fascinating," commented Ali Magabu from back aboard the Smoke and Mirrors. "Nonverbal signs are evidencing universal application. Their pictographs incorporated arrows for pointing, and now we have his simple head nod. *And,* did you notice the rising intonation on his question?"

Captain Taylor nodded quietly even though Ali couldn't see; Chris's camcorder was directed away from the astronauts, focused on the extraterrestrials.

For the longest subsequent while, the humans and extraterrestrials silently scrutinized one another. At least it felt long for Chris.

The Earthlings' initial shock might have concerned their other-world hosts presenting so vulnerably unequipped with safety gear, not even face masks. But now their attention turned to the extraterrestrials' extra-large eyes. Could have been owl eyes, where Chris was concerned.

"Captain, would you ask our new friends to turn on the lights down there?" pled Kevin. "We're having difficulty seeing anyone or anything."

Captain Taylor quietly shook her head "no," which again no one saw on the bridge of the Smoke and Mirrors.

"Captain?"

"Officer Smith-Park," intervened Ali, "I believe the captain is temporarily forgoing any further utterances. A truly wise choice, I would guess. You know how nervous and suspicious some people on Earth become when surrounded by others conversing in a language they don't understand."

"Gotcha, Dr. Magabu. No rush on my request, Captain."

Chris suppressed an urge to exclaim *Oh my gosh!* Kevin wanting better lighting brought to mind that owls are nocturnal creatures. They sleep during the day and feed after sunset. Their big peepers evolved for darkness. *Good grief, these extraterrestrials must also be nocturnal!*

Buddy also realized these "new friends" were likely creatures of the night. What's more, he noticed two of them with long, mousey whiskers, the third without. He speculated that ancestors found those whiskers useful to help feel their way prowling in the dark. Presently they might be a sex indicator, sometimes shaved off like Earth men's beards.

Meanwhile, Helena noticed the extraterrestrial tunics all of the same dull-gray color. Space station uniforms, she assumed initially. Yet closer inspection revealed quite varied surfaces, not so uniform. Crisscross creases distinguished the tunic of the whiskered fellow who stepped furthest forward. Another tunic featured spiral creases of varied sizes, and the remaining tunic sported several small, randomly-spaced pyramid and box-shaped creases. Clearly, anatomical features had nothing to do with any of these designs. Helena gathered they were simply extraterrestrial fashion statements.

In the away team's estimation, the extraterrestrials appeared remarkably similar to human beings. That is, apart from their exceptionally large eyes, rodent-like whiskers and oddly creased tunics. True, dim light could have been casting shadows over other significant differences. However, from what Captain Taylor and company could discern of their ears, noses, mouths, general body proportions, hair…

The rearmost extraterrestrial peered through something on shoulder mount that could have been a television news camera from Earth's twentieth century.

Chris turned his camcorder on that presumed counterpart burdened by far more cumbersome equipment. "I believe he's filming for their audience," he said, "the same as I'm filming-"

Chris halted abruptly, having realized his alien counterpart was talking as well. Narrating for fellow extraterrestrials, like he was narrating for fellow Earthlings?

The extraterrestrial also halted abruptly, and looked over at Chris to find Chris looking over at him. Extraterrestrial and terrestrial, alike, instantly surmised what happened, and busted out laughing.

Chris's chuckles were recognizably human, the alien's high-pitched "hee-hee-hee"s like from monkeys. This ice-breaking moment incited howls and screeches from the other two extraterrestrials.

Buddy and Helena broke into the kind of laughter terrestrials make when they are as relieved as they are amused.

"Sounds like a nuthouse down there, Captain!"

"Don't worry, Officer Smith-Park; we'll at least keep our envirosuits on!"

"The time has come for me to lie down again," noted Galleta, sixty years and trillions of miles away.

"Officer Olsen-Taylor, as we continue let us know if you wish to be relieved from narrating," said Helena Taylor, mindful of the mystery headache which had plagued everyone else who took on that task.

"So far so good, Captain," Chris responded, still feeling okay.

*

"Why not let me lie down there instead?"

"You, Don Típico?" Pedro laughed sixty years ago.

"Yes, the pendant can be put on my stomach as easily as on Doña Galleta. That was your suggestion, Norma, yes?"

"But the problem," responded Típico's wife, "is that we will learn nothing from hearing you snore! You lie down there, is three hours later when you wake up. And then your only information for us is that you have to go to the bathroom!"

"Ay caramba!"

*

The two extraterrestrials unencumbered by a camera motioned the astronauts like they wanted to show them something. Then the taller one bent at the knees, and leaned forward to rub the top of his head against the smaller one's tunic. The shorter one reciprocated. Chris was reminded of a cat rubbing up against a person's legs.

Helena wondered whether these other-world beings derived any special pleasure rubbing their heads against their clothing's patterned topographies, such as the swirls and tiny pyramids.

"We have maybe just seen how these extraterrestrials typically greet one another," said Chris. "And now Captain Taylor and Officer Leung are being asked to mimic them."

Helena and Buddy took turns rubbing with the aliens. Then Buddy extended his right hand and made an up-down motion.

"Officer Leung is inviting the extraterrestrials to try a typical Earth greeting known as the handshake."

The taller alien approached Buddy. However, rather than reach out *his* hand (and the Earthlings did strongly suspect the extraterrestrial welcoming committee was all male), he lowered his head and rubbed his hair against Buddy's gloved palm.

Again, the alien's motion appeared very feline to Chris.

"Whoops!" laughed Buddy. "Looks like Captain Taylor and I will have to shake hands to model the behavior!"

First official greetings successfully concluded between Earthlings and extraterrestrials, the taller alien initiated something new. He brought forward an easel magnetized to the floor, supporting a large notepad.

The shorter alien flipped open to the notepad's first page, where three columns of seeming hieroglyphics were printed in phosphorescent, light-green ink. No two characters were the same.

"Are you seeing this clearly enough, Dr. Magabu?"

"Clearly enough, Captain. Truly, they understood our transmitted pictograph quite well. That was, of course, the pictograph about making language sharing a priority item on the first-contact agenda," Ali Magabu added for the audience back on Earth.

"Ladies and gentlemen," Chris resumed narrating, "we are apparently about to receive our first lesson in an extraterrestrial alphabet."

*

"Ludi, pronto give Doña Galleta a paper and pencil. Maybe she can write..."

*

A pause in the shorter alien's presentation impressed Captain Taylor and company as meant for Chris and his alien counterpart. They could catch up on reporting for their respective folks-at-home. And time also, perhaps, to admire the phosphorescent printing.

Finally, the shorter alien pointed at the seeming hieroglyph atop the first column and said, "Rah."

"Rah," his fellow aliens repeated.

"Rah," Chris and company belatedly followed.

"Lah."

"Lah," the away team Earthlings repeated in unison.

"Ay, Pedro," sighed Ludi, "maybe those are sounds that go with the strange letters engraved on your pendant, but Galleta is not writing down any of them."

"Is okay; maybe she will remember which sounds go with which letters."

Once the sound represented by each seeming hieroglyph was exemplified, the extraterrestrial teacher tore off the page and handed it rolled-up to Captain Taylor.

"Thank you," said the captain bowing slightly.

"Oy?" responded the alien, his tilted head conveying puzzlement. Then he shrugged his shoulders and bowed with a huge flourish, sweeping his right hand down diagonally to alight on the left side of his rope belt.

Captain Taylor sensed he was communicating "you're welcome," but not necessarily to her. She hoped nothing more than her paranoid imagination had her thinking he directed his gesture past her at Buddy. "Officer Olsen-Taylor, don't we have souvenirs for them?" she asked. "Let's start with something small." Curiosity fueled her request, beyond simply wishing to reciprocate receipt of a page full of extraterrestrial hieroglyphic-type characters. Would her concern find justification as more than just paranoia, or refutation?

Chris unzipped a compartment stuck to his spacesuit's left leg, and extracted a zero-gravity ink pen imprinted with the United Americas flag. "Weren't we going to give them one of these, Captain?"

"That will be fine," answered Helena, grabbing the pen. She nodded towards the rolled-up paper in her left hand, nodded towards the pen in her right hand, then turned over the pen to the shorter alien.

"Pama," the alien said, unmistakably directing his utterance past Helena to Chris.

As much as he wanted to make the "You're welcome" gesture demonstrated by the alien, Helena's husband understood she'd been slighted. So he pretended too much preoccupation with his camcorder to notice he'd been thanked.

That's when Captain Helena Taylor purposefully stepped between her husband and the shorter alien. Pursuant to which she held high the rolled-up paper full of extraterrestrial printing, pointed at it, and said, "Pama, thank you, pama." She tilted her head from side to side as she went from speaking in the extraterrestrial tongue to English, then back to extraterrestrial.

"Wah," the extraterrestrial creature nodded, sneaking a side glance at his taller companion, the one unencumbered by the big camera. After which he held up the zero-gravity pen and said, "Tahhnk yah."

The captain responded how Chris had wanted to, with the alien's grand sweeping "you're welcome" bow. *Hopefully,* she thought, *that "Wah" wasn't only about his understanding "Thank you" meant "Pama." Hopefully, it was also about his understanding I am more than just a pretty face.*

What fascinating arrogance either way, Helena thought further, assuming she intuited correctly the other-world males judged her female. How could they so casually assume the child bearers of a never-before-met extraterrestrial species were second-class citizens? Of course, if you went back far enough in Earth history, many women **were** second-class citizens. Most despicably, even in 2061 such inequality still persisted, especially within certain quarantine zones.

The shorter alien made an ear-piercing whistle to refocus attention on the easel, where tearing off the list of extraterrestrial language characters had revealed fresh paper. Painted there was a phosphorescent-green-tinted orb back-dropped by star-filled darkness. Could have been the same painting transmitted through space like a bottle thrown in the ocean, including the same hieroglyphic caption.

"Fafama wawa," said the shorter alien.

"Fafama wawa," the away team wondrously repeated.

"Are you getting this, Ali?" Captain Taylor asked over her headset. She had temporarily turned off her suit's embedded speaker system so the aliens wouldn't hear what she was saying. And for additional good measure, she moved her lips little more than a ventriloquist.

"Captain, so far there's a truly fortuitous direct correspondence between hieroglyphs and sounds. Not unlike Spanish or Korean, for example. Which means the hieroglyphs are hieroglyphs in appearance only," said Ali. "Of course, they could have other language characters that are true hieroglyphs, actually depicting various objects. Anyhow, I've already loaded a basic linguistic algorithm program into the pocket translators Tanya and Yoon-hee have so generously donated. Regarding what we just heard, though, I'm truly unclear which sounds signify their planet's name, and which merely play a supporting role. Or maybe..."

"Got it," said Captain Taylor, having conceived a plan for clarifying "Fafama wawa." More importantly she sensed that where their alien hosts were concerned, she'd gone too uncomfortably long not trying to communicate further. That's why she made a point of turning back on her speaker system before asking, "Officer Leung, how about sharing our own chart?"

"We'll compare planet names, Captain?" said Buddy, already unzipping a square compartment across his chest. Once he unfolded its contents, the half-inch-thick plasma screen measured a full four square feet.

"Yes, but allow me to do the talking," said Helena. "I want our hosts to understand I'm the boss," she went on most frankly, trying not to worry how every last word would be received back home. Who cared? So long as she didn't leak the real reason for dumping a cautious test-run of first-ever light-speed propulsion in favor of pushing poorly-understood physics applications to the limit?

On the top-secret video informing Helena and crew of the extraterrestrials' hi-tech message in a bottle, there had been an addendum. That addendum warned against any secret communication between Earth and the Smoke and Mirrors. Whether a ham radio operator embedded with the remaining Mars colony, or an exobiologist on the Europan Ocean research mission, someone was certain to eavesdrop. Someone was certain to monitor all such transmissions for anything the least variance from official briefing updates.

Therefore, all contact was to be treated as worldwide public broadcast, comparable to the press conference prior to departure from Space Station Two. Assuming, of course, the Earthlings did survive their unprecedented acceleration to light-speed multiples.

Only the United Americas President and select few others knew the true mission of the Smoke and Mirrors. That it was answering a cry for help, not merely an invite to an extraterrestrial getting-acquainted social. They would receive Captain Taylor's private debriefing upon her return to Earth. And hopefully she would bring good news. Namely, that there wasn't an extraterrestrial civilization intent on filling their sandwich buns with chopped-up humans and other intelligent creatures. Rather, an innocuous misunderstanding had occurred, as one might expect between civilizations from two different solar systems at the outset of their relationship. Instead of preparing for extraterrestrial invasion, an exciting new chapter in history, galactic history, would open on a most tranquil note.

Of course Captain Taylor couldn't stop fretting over what might set off Earth-wide panic, not to mention panic on the destination planet. What if the big-eyed, shadow-loving extraterrestrials displayed those frightful pictographs of antlered beings cattle-driving people onto their flying saucers? And they did that during a public broadcast with no advance warning?

Days earlier, Ali Magabu transmitted two pictographs for the extraterrestrials.

One pictograph illustrated a camera broadcasting the first encounter between the civilizations. Ali drew comic book conversation balloons containing x'ed-out antlered creatures. Ali also populated those balloons with handshaking and other nice-to-meet-you pleasantries, not x-ed out.

In the conversation balloons of the second pictograph, the antlered guys were not x-ed out. But the camera outside those balloons was.

Ali hoped he made the message clear. The antlered creatures would be for private discussion only, out of public reach.

Mere hours before the Smoke and Mirrors entered high orbit around the nocturnal extraterrestrials' planet, Yoon-hee received a response to Ali's pictographs. Both were returned with a check drawn beside each one.

Ali grinned with delight at seeing the check join the arrow as a universally understood communication mark.

And so, both parties agreed to a meeting for public consumption, followed by a private encounter with no cameras allowed. At the private encounter, they would get down to the real reason Earth humans rushed their unprecedented first contact with an extraterrestrial intelligence. Maybe Captain Taylor and company would even be allowed to meet the antlered aliens who brought news of an impending invasion. Hopefully they survived their crash landing as drawn on a pictograph.

Presently, Earth as photographed from space came up on Buddy's portable plasma screen. Captain Taylor pointed at the planet, at her own self, then at the planet again, and said, "Earth."

"Ahhhth," the extraterrestrials hesitantly repeated.

Buddy pushed a button on the back of the screen, and the word "Earth" appeared in big yellow letters underneath Antarctica.

The aliens squinted.

Buddy figured they were reacting to the big letters' added brightness. Far more oddly, out the corner of his eye he caught a partial curling-up by one of the potted ferns.

Chris might have noticed squints and curling-up, both, hadn't the roving headache at last come home to roost with him. But he resolved to wait on sharing this news with his wife until the public broadcast concluded. His head didn't feel all that strange, so he couldn't automatically dismiss the possibility of simply a plain old headache. What he didn't know was that Galleta had already jumped back to Captain Taylor.

*

Galleta pointed at a photo of Alexandra hanging on the wall, taken when she was a month old. Helena pointed at the bright-yellow, one-word caption Buddy materialized under Antarctica. Then, separated by sixty years and trillions of miles, both women said, "Earth."

"She *is* our whole world," Ludi whispered to an agreeably nodding Pedro.

*

"Okay, Buddy, give us split view: Earth captioned the left half, Mars the right half."

"Like this, Captain?" asked Buddy. He couldn't turn around the plasma screen to check for himself, without breaking the extraterrestrials' focus on what was displayed there.

"Perfect, Officer Leung." Captain Taylor pointed at the captioned photo of Mars and said, "Mars."

"Mahs," echoed all three aliens.

"Now add 'This is,' Captain?"

"Great minds think alike, Officer Leung."

After Buddy Leung made the captions read "This is Mars" and "This is Earth," Helena pointed at the Earth photo and said, "This is Earth."

"Wah" and "Wah" nodded the shorter alien followed by the taller alien. What's more, their film guy craned his head out from behind his camera lens to also nod, "Wah." All three pointed at the picture of Earth and said, "Ahhth wawa." Next, they pointed at Mars and said, "Mahhs wawa."

Captain Taylor walked over beside one of the orbiting extraterrestrial space station's domed windows. As she pointed out there at the extraterrestrials' home planet, Galleta pointed out the Santiago family's front window and said, "This is Fafama."

"Bingo, Captain!" shouted Ali Magabu, excited.

So thrilled herself, Helena didn't even much mind the prowling headache's return aggravated by Ali's loud voice in her earpiece.

"Not exactly enough vocabulary to discuss the most pressing issues," Dr. Magabu went on. He hadn't intended to hint there was a reason why first contact wasn't prefaced by a good year's worth of careful preparation. However, he realized his misstep soon as the words escaped his mouth. "Of course," he hastened to add, "those issues carry a certain joy, truly. They have to do with our civilizations from two distinct planets establishing relations for the betterment of all."

"Yes, Dr. Magabu," said Captain Taylor, straining to stifle a sigh of relief. "Very eloquently put."

Buddy noticed the buzz over their communication breakthrough already starting to die down on the extraterrestrial side. To preclude another awkward silence, he pointed down over top of his plasma screen at the Earth photo, and said, "Earth wawa." Then he pointed at the Mars photo and said, "Mars wawa." And for the grand finale, he pointed out the same domed window as had Captain Taylor, and said, "Fafama wawa."

The extraterrestrials applauded.

"Folks, we're having another universal communication moment," Chris ventured to comment. "Clearly, applause means the same for our new friends from Fafama as it means for us."

The short and tall aliens unencumbered by a camera joined Buddy at the window and said, "Thahs ahz Fafama."

Putting an exclamation mark on Chris's observation, Buddy and Captain Taylor broke into applause as best they could, slapping together their envirosuit gloves.

"Captain," said Ali Magabu from back aboard the Smoke and Mirrors, "this is truly a great start towards mutual understanding. To build on that, hopefully our new friends will provide us an extensively illustrated picture dictionary for our translators."

The shorter alien lifted a hard-bound book from the shadows, and he approached Buddy. But suddenly, he froze. On reflection that stirred a bemused grin, he pivoted towards the captain, and presented her with the book instead. When she accepted it into her gloved hands, he bowed slightly and held his arms high. Chris Olsen-Taylor thought the alien might descend those arms into hugging his wife. And he realized the alien's odd pose imitated the tall, potted ferns. Their branches reached out like spindly goblin arms, high above the dimly glowing bulbs buried halfway into the soil at their base.

Rather than drop his arms to embrace Helena, however, the extraterrestrial backed away.

Helena said, "Thank you, uh, pama."

"Pama," the extraterrestrial nodded approvingly, then added most loudly, "Woonana."

Captain Helena Taylor sensed the extraterrestrial thought if he spoke loudly enough, she'd understand him. But he could have screamed "Woonana!" at the top of his lungs, and she still wouldn't have been clear whether it meant "book" or "you're welcome." So she held up the bulky tome before her and said, "Book. This is a book."

The shorter alien pointed towards the book and said, "Phew. Phew wawa."

"Hey Captain," said Kevin Smith-Park over the earpiece from back aboard the Smoke and Mirrors, "I guess that's a relief. I mean, that's a phew!"

"Very funny, Officer Smith-Park," said Helena, transfixed paging through the "phew." So transfixed, she was even able to keep ignoring her nagging headache. "Officer Park-Smith," she went on finally, speaking to Yoon-hee instead, "remind me to be amused by your husband's wit once we're back on board. Dr. Magabu, wait until you see this. If I'm not mistaken, umm, you can confirm, Officer Leung..."

Buddy Leung was peeking over the captain's shoulder. Ditto for Chris, who also held his camcorder high over both his fellow Earthlings' heads to give the "folks" back home precious glimpses of the extraterrestrial book.

"This looks like a children's picture dictionary."

"I believe the captain is correct, Dr. Magabu," chimed in Buddy.

"You see, Dr. Magabu," added Captain Taylor, "you only needed to make your wish known, and it came true."

*

"Why Doña Galleta pantomimes leafing through a book?" asked Rotonda miles and years away.

Pedro responded obliquely by translating into Spanish what Captain Taylor said as channeled through Galleta.

Típico reacted, "So if I say I want this *tonteria* to end, my wish will come true?"

"That magic did not work for us, my brute," said Norma. "I tried, and you are still here!"

"Ay caramba!"

*

The captain marveled at illustrations and letters alike, glowing phosphorescently. They really stood out for her in the dim light, even though she lacked the extraterrestrials' extra-large pupils evolved over eons of living nocturnally. "I'm just thinking," she remarked to her fellow Earthlings, "it's very wise we used a plasma screen to share our visual language. Next best thing to phosphorescent lettering, whereas our old-style book print probably can't be discerned in this darkness, even with their specially adapted eyes. And I suspect that were we to ever insist on showing them something in full daylight, they'd probably squint themselves blind."

"Oh, that's right." Buddy suddenly felt around his suit for the compartment where he'd stored a special present for the extraterrestrials. It was a second, smaller plasma screen, loaded with illustrated and sound-accompanying dictionaries from a variety of surviving Earth languages.

"Captain," spoke Dr. Deborah Davis-Murphy from aboard the Smoke and Mirrors, as heard through Helena's earpiece, "one more reason why our safety protocol has been so important: I am concerned about the source of their phosphorescent lettering. We can hope it's as innocent, as intriguing, as a firefly's light. However, until we take measurements, we must assume there is a potentially hazardous radioactive component."

"Yes, Dr. Davis-Murphy," Captain Taylor responded noncommittally. Her head was spinning from a damnably persistent headache despite the precious marvel in her hands of an extraterrestrial children's dictionary. "Isn't it fortunate that thanks to our envirosuits, we are perfectly safe?" she went on. "We should reassure our audience back home, shouldn't we?" Captain Taylor labored not to sound irritated, as she well knew that Deborah's tactless remarks didn't cause her headache. Neither did the phosphorescent print; there was no way its ill effects, if any, could penetrate her envirosuit, could they? Wasn't that Deb's whole point when she talked up the safety protocol? For certain, this same suit clearly protected her from all manner of known cosmic rays when in spacewalk mode.

But why was her headache lasting so long this time? And why, creepily, did she feel compelled to page all the way through the dictionary? Was her subconscious searching for...Why stop on this particular page? Why her déjà vu with this particular assortment of hieroglyphic-type characters? Why so intently study the accompanying illustration... Was she seeing a "word" already noticed on one of the extraterrestrials' pictograph transmissions, but just not recalling it on a conscious level?

"Captain," said Yoon-hee, again like Dr. Murphy-Davis from back aboard the Smoke and Mirrors, "we've finished putting our orbit in sync with their space station's orbit. And we've spotted something headed your way."

The something headed their way distracted shorter and taller alien alike from Buddy's proffered plasma screen.

A glint of light shone through the same domed window where Captain Taylor pointed at Fafama.

For a better view, the two extraterrestrials clomped over beside the window in their own magnetic boots. The taller one's cell-phone-type device erupted with chattering fah-lah-lahs, and he responded with his own stream of soft vowels.

"Captain," said Buddy having also clomped over beside the window, "you'll want to see this. And Officer Olsen-Taylor, you'll want to bring over your camcorder so our viewers at home can share. Looks like our new friends have their own version of a gradual-ascent, planet-to-orbit shuttle vehicle."

Captain Taylor felt her steadily intensifying headache suddenly lift away. Did the spirit responsible for it make a hasty exit? Whatever, such unexpected relief staved off a fainting spell that would have gone most awkwardly, given her mag-boot floor anchor. Instead, she affected a casual folding-shut of the illustrated extraterrestrial dictionary to join everyone else at the domed window. "Can we assume, Officer Leung," she said, "their cell phone conversation concerns their arriving shuttle's docking maneuvers?"

Before Buddy could respond, the shorter extraterrestrial motioned everyone back over to the tripod easel outfitted with a paper pad.

Helena and company wanted to continue observing the shuttle's approach. But they well understood it behooved them to follow their host's lead.

Having been left unattended, pages of the giant notepad had leisurely, weightlessly floated ceiling-ward. They were prevented from floating off altogether by whatever glued their common edges to the notepad spine.

For Chris the effect was of gentle currents waving seaweed. That is, until the shorter alien grabbed those pages, and draped them back to fully reveal a blank one.

The shorter alien used his light-green phosphorescent marker to draw a platform. He depicted a tall figure astride that platform, dressed in flowing robes as opposed to his tunic.

Down in front of the platform, he drew several circles. Attached to each circle were what the captain took to be outstretched arms, curved like two parentheses.

Helena was reminded of how the shorter alien held his arms after presenting her with a dictionary.

Captain and crew both surmised that the several circles depicted an audience in adulating mode.

Meanwhile, the marker-wielding extraterrestrial pointed from the robed figure on stage to the domed window.

"I'm guessing that robed figure is coming here aboard their space shuttle, Captain. Someone important, a political leader, perhaps?" suggested Buddy.

*

While the alien shuttle was arriving to the space station, Galleta went silent. She was channeling Chris, who had nothing to say.

"Is possible," Pedro said softly, taking advantage of Galleta's quiet spell, "Doña Galleta found the pendant's markings in that dictionary to which Captain Taylor referred. If so, she might finally be able to tell us what it says after she returns."

Ludi lovingly ran her fingers through Pedro's short, thickly-curled hair, sending a message he appreciated to bottomless depth. Galleta might never learn what the pendant's engraved characters signified. His back might never return to functional normality, meaning they might lose their house. But none of that mattered; Ludi would always be there for him, to lovingly run her fingers through his hair.

Alexandra made a long yawn in grandma Rotonda's arms. Still, her mouth opened little wider than an uncorked wine bottle. Típico taking note grunted approvingly, and said, "I agree with her."

Alexandra's tiny action received adoring contemplation. Perhaps even more marvelous, though, was the innocent wonder she exuded over reflected lamplight. It glimmered off the mystery pendant left fallen from Galleta's stomach onto the pastel blue wool blanket spread out across the living room floor.

*

Captain Taylor and crew experienced innocent wonder as well, awed by the approaching extraterrestrial space shuttle. From aboard the extraterrestrial space station, they saw it become fully bathed in sunlight from Alpha Centauri C.

Miles below, Fafama's sunset boundary raged onward, cluttered by billowing dust clouds and anvil-shaped thunderheads. But presently, the Earthlings were too captivated by the space shuttle to notice. And if asked, all of them would have likened that extraterrestrial vehicle to a huge sword in flight, its hilt for wings.

With the space station having looked so much like a jeweled scabbard, no surprise what transpired next. The shuttle slid into the space station as smoothly as Buddy Leung imagined a warrior sheathing his sword. He had to wonder whether this effect was intentional, achieved at the cost of efficiency and maybe even safety. But he would delay sharing his concern until which time everything said wasn't being broadcast light-years away.

"Wow," said Chris, heard channeled through Galleta trillions of miles and decades away.

Helena and Buddy experienced varying degrees of couldn't-put-their-finger-on-it discomfort with the spectacle, but opted to remain silent.

*

"Mami," said Pedro, "I think maybe Doña Galleta noticed your curtains for the window, and she was so impressed."

"Pinch your husband for me, Ludi."

*

Meanwhile back aboard the extraterrestrial space station, the taller alien turned away from the domed window, and gestured for Captain Taylor and company to follow him.

Fafamans and Earthlings alike stepped through narrow doorways and passageways, then down one flight of metal stairs to a more open area.

There, a transparent wall slanting overhead provided dramatic views of the sword-shaped shuttle in dock, at least for the Fafamans. As elsewhere aboard the space station, their nocturnal nature meant minimal artificial lighting. But shafts of sunlight entering from somewhere helped the Earthlings discern the shuttle cushioned by what appeared to be tractor-sized tires polka-dotting the slanted wall. Buddy was absolutely convinced they were tires, like used back on Earth to cushion large seagoing vessels in dock. Just another reminder, where Buddy was concerned, this civilization lagged behind technologically.

Anyway, the taller and shorter aliens clomp-clomped over beside sealed elevator doors, the accompanying stainless steel elevator shaft interrupting the slanted transparent wall. With arms elevated they bowed slightly, mimicking the goblin-like way the alien ferns' branches loomed high above those curious, dimly glowing bulbs half-buried at their base.

The third alien set down his camera to join in, and waved for the Earthlings to follow suit.

Chris clipped his camcorder to his envirosuit, unobtrusively focused on the elevator door which he expected to slide open any second.

Any second indeed, with a hiss the elevator door slid upwards out of sight.

*

But for Pedro's family trillions of miles and sixty years away, Galleta stood uneventfully motionless at a first-floor front window.

"Aydiomio," Placido finally blurted, "now she channels a vulture waiting all day for a mouse to crawl by?"

"You will never get me to do that," Típico grunted, and gestured towards Galleta with an air of indignity.

"Yes," nodded Norma, "I think one day we need to make a list of all the things we will never get you to do."

"Ay caramba!"

Suddenly, Galleta leapt backwards.

*

Years and miles away, Captain and crew were startled by two uniformed extraterrestrials wielding machine guns. Without warning, they literally hopped from the slid-open elevator door. They peered through infrared scopes for sweeping the perimeter, special attention given to especially dark nooks and crannies.

Captain Taylor wondered: Are the officials protected by these guards really this afraid their enemies could have stolen aboard the space station? Or was the infrared sweep the type of ritual to be expected from creatures who engineered their spacecraft and space station to look like a sword and scabbard?

When Chris's camcorder attracted the guards' attention, Chris's extraterrestrial counterpart intervened to explain. The Earthlings understood this without knowing one extraterrestrial word spoken.

Satisfied Chris posed no threat, the guards laid down their arms to join the waiting reception line beside their fellow extraterrestrials and visiting Earthlings. Of course, they also assumed the looming-goblin posture with arms held high.

Soon thereafter, the elevator revealed two additional extraterrestrials attired in gray tunics like the captain and crew had seen worn by other Fafamans. Once they cleared the elevator, backing out slowly, they adopted the same, odd, looming-goblin posture of everyone else.

A tall figure followed in flowing robes, clearly the same figure the shorter alien depicted earlier as someone important about to arrive.

Captain Taylor noticed the tall figure's right hand clasped firmly, tightly round the hilt of a sword sheathed by a scabbard belted to his waist. No surprise that the scabbard bore a striking resemblance to the space station.

Buddy noticed the tall figure's flowing robes glowed with the same, light-green phosphorescence of the bulbs buried partway into soil beside the potted ferny plants. That pale glow helped Earthlings discern hundreds of small adjoining pyramids creased into his robes.

Inevitably, the Earthlings' attention was drawn to the tall figure's face, especially his meandering lips. Did they bespeak the special thrill he anticipated dealing with creatures from another planet? Or the pleasures that awaited him afterwards? Or rather, world-weary wariness mixed with condescending glee at the royal greeting he received?

Helena's heart went out to him, feeling here was someone with whom she might, ironically, really communicate. Another leader weighed down by historic responsibility. Youthful vigor conveyed by his nocturnally-adapted, extra-large eyes only lent him further appeal despite encroaching age wrinkles.

Chris's heart did not go out to this majestically enrobed extraterrestrial ruler nodding from side to side in acknowledgment of the looming-arm greetings. Rather, he felt the Fafaman's condescending-glee quotient reach stratospheric heights over the envirosuits he, Helena and Buddy were wearing.

Two other Fafamans followed directly behind the exalted extraterrestrial, holding high between them a bulky, dull-green material. Could have been a huge bed comforter where Buddy was concerned, possibly woven from the potted ferns.

By this time, geosynchronous orbit had brought the space station flying across the day-lit half of Fafama.

Shafts of sunlight stabbed through a domed window opposite the slanted wall. The window's tint colored those radiant shafts pastel purple. However, they remained bright enough for the Fafamans bringing up the Fafaman ruler's rear to spring into action. They lifted the bulky comforter-like material even higher than before, intent on providing shade for their evident superior. But before they could carry it over top of him, he raised a cautioning hand, the one not gripping his sword. Whereupon they backed off and lowered it quickly. So quickly, Chris sensed more ritual than any authentic springing-into-action-to-protect-the-throne.

Odder still was the effect of the lavender sun beams on one of the potted ferns. The plant's olive-green goblin-arm branches and backbone-like trunk curled together, rolled up into a sandy brown ball. Then its roots retracted out of the soil, and wrapped around it like string or rope around a package for delivery. However, once it started drifting off in the weightless environment, a single root unwound, and burrowed back down through the soil for re-anchoring.

Chris gathered the Fafamans couldn't care less, obviously used to this plant's behavior.

The advance guards retrieved their weapons, and resumed heading up the Fafaman ruler's entourage.

*

This at least gave Pedro's family back home on Earth something of more interest to contemplate. Galleta channeling Helena Taylor paraded through the dining space to the kitchen and then back out to the living room again. She held her arms looming-goblin high for the entirety of this odd trek.

*

Before the arrival of the sword-shaped shuttle craft, the captain, her husband and Buddy Leung had felt relatively free to converse with one another. That was, when they weren't trying to bridge the communication gap with their extraterrestrial acquaintances. But the arrival of weapons and, for all they knew, the king of the entire planet, intimidated them out of saying a peep. This went double for the Earthlings still aboard the Smoke and Mirrors at a plenty safe distance, and Tanya piloting the shuttle pod. Yet Chris knew he couldn't cut off the camcorder's transmission back to Earth. The home crowd might worry they'd gotten in way over their heads.

No sense bothering them with the truth.

The Fafaman ruler squinted from ever-more-pervasive sunlight, however much dimmed by the colorfully tinted window domes. Nevertheless, he headed without hesitation for an especially ornate chair. Guards plus two other members of his entourage took their positions either side of that extraordinary furniture piece clearly constructed from wood. Exquisite carving gave its arms the appearance of two immense ferny branches, partially coiled.

The extraterrestrials laden with the bulky, comforter-like material stepped around behind the ornate chair, ever ready to provide shade. Once they took position, the still-standing Fafaman ruler queried the shorter ambassadorial extraterrestrial, including a nod towards the Earthlings.

The shorter alien shook his head "no."

Captain Taylor grasped not one extraterrestrial word, but still gathered meaning. The Fafaman ruler asked whether some specific matter had been shared with the Earthlings, and the shorter alien answered, *Not yet.* To which Buddy would have bet the ruler's curt, harshly intoned response would have translated: *Do it now!*

Whatever, the Fafaman ruler finally settled in on his royal chair with a dramatic flourish of his phosphorescently glowing robes.

Wielding a phosphorescent writing tool, the shorter alien hastily went at a notepad easel the Earthlings hadn't noticed until then. His first pictograph illustrated ten separate pie slices, and an arrow pointing to them reunified.

"Okay," nodded Buddy in the first words any Earthling dared utter since the shuttle craft's arrival, "their demonstration of tenths of a whole. We've gone through this already in our pictograph transmissions before we even entered their solar system."

Ditto for the following pictograph, having to do with the amazing similarity of Fafama's atmosphere to Earth's, a similarity confirmed by spectrographic analysis once the Smoke and Mirrors reached Fafama. The pie slices represented relative percentages of oxygen, nitrogen and the rest.

The third pictograph offered something new, a decent rendering of the envirosuit presumably occupied by an Earthling. A typically large-eyed Fafaman stood beside it. His wavy mouth lent a quizzical look, while dotted lines trailed from his eyes to the envirosuit helmet.

A hieroglyph-type figure (Ψ) accompanied both sketches.

The shorter extraterrestrial stepped aside so the Earthlings could digest his drawings, but he quickly realized they were totally mystified. So he opened his eyes painfully wide, painfully on account of the brightening if still-tinted sunlight, to focus on Captain Taylor. Once he had engaged her full attention, he shrugged his shoulders and, with elbows bent in against his gray-garbed torso, faced the palms of his hands ceiling ward.

"Captain," said Ali Magabu, "his pose resembles the written character."

Coincidentally, the shorter extraterrestrial pointed at the Ψ he'd drawn, and then resumed imitating it.

"So that's their *I-don't-get-it* hieroglyph question mark, Dr. Magabu? Looks like a letter from the Greek alphabet."

"Yes on both counts, Captain."

Captain Taylor nodded knowingly and, remembering how the extraterrestrials expressed *ah-ha*, went, "Wah." *Okay*, she thought, *so now what?*

The shorter alien nodded encouragingly. Next, he referred back to the atmospheric content pie chart enhanced by molecular representations including electron, proton and neutron signifiers. Then he mimicked lifting off a helmet, followed by a deep breath.

"I see," nodded Helena. "The question is: Why don't we take off our envirosuits to kick back and relax?" *So, their leader wants a better look at us.* "Buddy, can you punch up the viral-danger pictograph?" That was the pictograph designed to coax the extraterrestrials into embracing Dr. Davis-Murphy's safety protocol.

Once Buddy retrieved the requested pictograph on his plasma screen, the shorter extraterrestrial nodded "Wah" knowingly after giving it only a cursory glance. Then he explained for the important one, clearly making reference to it.

The Fafaman ruler nodded "Mm-hmm" frequently, his arms hooked round the arms of his throne so he wouldn't float off in the near-weightlessness. No telling how much he actually understood. However much, Captain Taylor sensed he strained to project intent consideration of the pictograph as described by his adviser.

When his adviser fell silent, the extraterrestrial leader turned to Helena. However dimmed by the tinted dome like light through a stained-glass window, the sun's rays made narrow slits of his squinting eyes. Yet he still managed to smile his meandering smile. Pursuant to which he unhooked his throne's arms, and pointedly displayed the palms of his hands.

What, is he telling us there are no dangerous viruses or bacteria hidden up his sleeve? Captain Helena Taylor asked herself, stunned.

Not exactly disabusing the captain of her bothersome notion, the majestically enrobed Fafaman inclined his head and pursed his lips in what could only be described as a forlorn, pouty expression.

Buddy noticed the other extraterrestrials avoiding eye contact with anybody, their presumed leader included.

"Hey Captain," said Kevin from back aboard the Smoke and Mirrors, "you don't think their Grand Wazoo, or whatever they call him, seriously wants to ignore the potential health risks of you guys taking off your suits? Looks to me like he's blowing off what the adviser just explained to him. You don't have to respond if you think that's going to complicate matters, but jeez Louise!"

Chris clicked off his speaker system to keep the extraterrestrials from hearing him respond, with as little mouth movement as possible, "You notice the 'Grand Wazoo's' sidekicks suddenly acting like they're strangers waiting for the next bus?"

"Yeah," chimed in Yoon-hee. "Why doesn't one of them reiterate how hazardous that could be, actually talking the captain into removal of her helmet?"

"They know better, Yoon-hee," said Kevin, "than to contradict their Grand Wazoo."

"In fairness to them," said Buddy who, like Chris, was with speaker phone off and mouth movement reduced to a minimum, "their planet's prevailing climate might be so warm and arid, harmful bacteria and viruses are not a big issue for them. Must hastily add I doubt that's the case. But you do have a situation on Fafama of limited, circumscribed bodies of water and minimal polar ice caps. Not to mention the low humidity maintained on this space station. Okay, so maybe their scientists aren't especially impressed with the health threat they could pose, fully exposed to us. But I should still think that after our pictograph explanation, they'd be VERY concerned about the threat we could pose, fully exposed to THEM. Maybe you're right, Officer Smith, about their not wanting to contradict their Grand Wazoo! Maybe they're even more concerned about that!"

"I would love to discuss this further," said Captain Taylor, pointedly speaking loudly with her own speaker phone left on. Happily as well, unsure the extraterrestrials could discern her forcedly broad smile through her helmet's face shield.

Taylor wished she could have muzzled Kevin before he vented over the "Grand Wazoo" trying to coax them out of their envirosuits. But obviously, second guesses would have to wait until later. So she went on, "What we have here, people, is an awkward moment, an impasse. Neither our new friends nor we are sure of our next move."

*

Snort! "Aydiomio! What was that?" Placido jerkily jumped in his seat.

"That was your thunder nose. Is worse some nights than a lightning storm passing through," hushingly whispered

Rotonda. "So disrespectful of you when Doña Galleta is resuming her search for the origin of the pendant from the sky!"

"But- But," Típico got all trembly with his fluster, "she was not speaking for several minutes!"

"The way you like people: doing nothing! Sh!" Norma snapped with her own hushing whisper.

"Ay caramba!"

"Sh!"

To be fair, Rotonda was paging through a fashion magazine her daughters left lying around, and Norma was admiring a framed family photo. And when Galleta finally erupted again in English, channeling Captain Taylor about the impasse, even Ludi was caught inattentive, her nose buried in a home improvement magazine. But at least she didn't admonish anyone for giving less than their full, quiet attention to Doña Galleta for all the long while that the Doña stood mute.

*

"Ah, look and listen," continued Captain Helena Taylor while sixty years and trillions of miles away the women were shushing the men. "You see that fellow speaking into the film camera held by Chris's counterpart? He's probably telling the audience down below on Fafama the same thing I'm telling you, that we've reached an impasse."

The Fafaman ruler nodded and smiled at Helena, and she reciprocated, though doubting her facial expression could be discerned through her obscuring face shield. "Until we overcome the impasse," she soldiered on, "it's important we exercise all available nonverbal signs of friendship. In case you're still wondering, here's the issue: Our extraterrestrial host wishes we would remove our protective environment suits, while we are concerned about possible health hazards if we humor him."

Kevin back aboard the Smoke and Mirrors wanted to comment, *Thank you, Captain Obvious.* But he knew Helena Taylor was addressing a larger audience back home on Earth.

Chris worriedly imagined the nods exchanged by Helena and the Fafaman ruler as the first, subtle stage of a mating ritual.

*

Meanwhile sixty years ago down on Earth, Ludi and Pedro whimsically reciprocated Galleta's nod, which of course was Captain Taylor's nod channeled. Then they nodded at each other. And to their surprise, Placido and Típico appeared to return Galleta's nod as well. But then they snorted each other awake, making clear they'd not been simply nodding. They'd been nodding off, the second time for Placido.

*

"Captain, our flowchart is ready to transmit."

"Excellent, Dr. Magabu. Let's hope we can amicably break the impasse," added Captain Taylor, already motioning towards the plasma screen.

Buddy had attached the plasma screen to his envirosuit's breastplate, thus giving his arms a rest from holding it up for display. On the captain's cue, he pressed a few buttons, and it flickered to life with Magabu's transmission.

Magabu's flowchart started with two boxes. One contained a mouse, the other a comparably small, furry creature of Fafama.

Weeks earlier when Buddy Leung first saw the Fafaman creature's transmitted image, he nicknamed it Flounder Mouse. Flounder Mouse lay flat like a flounder, two eyes the same side of its pancake-shaped body.

"Namalumala," the Fafaman ruler said as he pointed at the boxed flounder mouse. Helena read a hint of condescending chagrin in his smile. Was she imagining things, or was this guy struggling to remain pleasant about her and her fellow humans' refusal to shed their suits? Moreover, was he steeling himself to take in stride their defense of that refusal?

One hand firmly entwined with his royal armchair, the Fafaman ruler pointed with his other hand at the flounder mouse drawing. But helped by his magnetic boots, the entwined hand easily kept him anchored despite the weightless space-station environment.

When Captain Taylor's attention wandered from this particular Fafaman's face, she noticed his entwined hand drumming the wooden armrest's underside. Simply a nervous tic, or impatience to wield his sheathed sword? Restrained only by tremendous self-control?

Whichever, the second flowchart image depicted mouse and flounder mouse (or namalumala) together, sniffing at each other.

"Okay, Magabu, ready for the next part," rushed Helena, sensing growing restlessness from the ruling Fafaman's nod.

The next part shrank the mouse depictions to the screen's left half. From there, arrows pointed at new boxes filling the right half. The top new box showed the animals continuing their sniff encounter. However, the bottom box showed the Earthling mouse on its back, and the flounder mouse eyeless side up. Their little limbs were splayed out stiffly lifeless.

An accompanying photo sequence of Fafama's day-night phases underlined the possible outcomes with a clear message. Namely, assessing the safety of unprotected contact between Earthlings and Fafamans would require at least two full days of mouse and flounder-mouse interaction.

Before Magabu could reveal more of his flowchart, the Fafaman ruler rose from his throne, and he clomp-clomp-clomped on his magnetic boots over beside the plasma screen. There, with an imperious swirl of his phosphorescently glowing robe he pointed at the screen, drawing attention to the dead mice images. Then he mimicked two boxers, one landing a blow that sent the other reeling, the other boxer returning that favor. But he concluded with a dismissive gesture as in: No fighting between Earthlings and Fafamans. Pursuant to which he produced a clownishly exaggerated frown, and made motions suggestive the Earthlings remove their envirosuits.

"Good grief!" exclaimed Captain Taylor, shocked. "I thought they understood our main concern was over viruses and bacteria, not over our mouse doing battle with their flounder mouse! And how could they possibly think we would regard those creatures' behavior towards each other as predictive of Earthling-Fafaman relations?!"

"I could resend the virus pictograph, Captain, truly," offered Magabu from back aboard the Smoke and Mirrors.

"Wait, Ali," said Taylor. "I think one of the leader's minions is explaining to him, though maybe not for the first time."

After groaning "Wahlahwah" to gain the Fafaman ruler's attention, the shorter extraterrestrial forced a sneeze into his own hands. From whence he walked over beside his easel, and drew particles spraying from his nose. Narrating the whole while, he went from pointing at the icky goo sneezed on his hands to a sketch of particles leaving his nose for someone else's.

Additional narration centered on the mouse depictions until the Fafaman ruler finally nodded "Ahhhh" as in *now I get it.* Only, he still gave Captain Taylor another forlorn look with his clownishly exaggerated frown.

Taylor pretended not to notice as she said, "Continue unveiling your flowchart, Officer Magabu."

Two new depictions shrunk the previous depictions to half the screen again. A new arrow pointed from the mice still enjoying a good sniff to a smiling person with his protective helmet removed, standing beside a smiling extraterrestrial. From the dead mice, the other arrow pointed at the person keeping on his helmet, but still with a big smile beside a grinning extraterrestrial.

The Fafaman ruler acknowledged the flow chart with a shrug. Presumably he finally understood that viral infection, not violence, was the issue. Whatever, he turned his attention to Captain Taylor, and with a generous yet sly-looking smile spoke in his soft-vowel-ridden tongue, fah-lah-lahs aplenty. But his words spoken in an extraterrestrial tongue were not meant for her.

He's following my lead, Helena concluded. *While talking shop with his fellow extraterrestrials, nonverbally he's assuring me things are okay between us. Hope he caught at least a glimmer of my smile through the face shield. If so, wonder if he found it at all...enticing?*

The shorter extraterrestrial, of the ones not brandishing weapons, produced a terrarium from the shadows to set on a table. Inches deep with wood shavings, it reminded Helena of the terrarium daughter Shelly had for her pet hamster when she was a little girl.

"Dr. Magabu, Earthlings back home," said the captain, "I think we've made progress. Our new friends appear to have accepted research on whether unprotected exposure to each other's germs poses a significant risk. Officer Olsen-Taylor, will you release one of our tiny explorers from their container, whether Ferdinand or Magellan?"

The Fafamans clearly made no effort to follow the originally proposed safety protocol as explained in flowcharts transmitted well before the Smoke and Mirrors' arrival. They were supposed to have greeted the Earthlings wearing their own protective gear, but didn't even bother putting on face masks. Moreover, the furry little creatures were supposed to have had weeks rather than forty-eight hours to incubate possibly lethal viruses and bacteria. Which meant unprotected exposure of humans to aliens was not supposed to have happened until the Earthlings' second mission to Fafama. *Deb must be freaking*, Captain Taylor couldn't help thinking.

Chris Olsen-Taylor froze midway unzipping Ferdinand's special portable container, awed motionless by an occurrence in the flounder mouse terrarium. The short-furred, pancake-shaped extraterrestrial creature was suddenly glowing brightly with green bioluminescence, after having formerly assumed the color of his surrounding wood shavings.

Coincidentally, the space station's orbit cast the flounder mouse terrarium in darkness after having illuminated it with sunlight filtered violet through a tinted dome.

"Captain," said Buddy, "the glowing orb planted beside each fern-type plant: Could those be stand-ins, or maybe it's more proper to call them dig-ins, for the flounder mouse? They've got the flounder mouse's same, greenish glow."

"That greenish glow we noticed splotching Fafama's night side," said Chris, "can it be that a third of their planet is covered with these critters?"

"Putting poor Ferdinand in a cage with one of them, hope that glow won't prove toxic for him," fretted

Captain Taylor. "Bad enough that for all we know, we might as well be caging two scorpions together. Um, Officer Chris Olsen-Taylor, we better move this along lest our hosts misapprehend we are having second thoughts."

"Oh yeah!" Chris snapped out of wonder over the animal from another planet, a wonder not the least diminished by its humble size.

"Captain, fortunately none of your sensors are detecting radioactive or other known hazardous signatures beyond the normal background stuff," observed Kevin.

By then, Ferdinand had been gently, gingerly set down inside the flounder mouse container by the shorter extraterrestrial.

Reactions were immediate.

The flounder mouse's green fluorescence shut off as abruptly as had someone turned off the lights. And the small extraterrestrial creature started doing pushups at a manic pace.

For his part Ferdinand hopped all around the flounder mouse, comparable to someone doing a Mexican hat dance, Chris thought. Due to weightlessness, however, Ferdinand's very first hop should have sent him bouncing about the flounder mouse cage like a marble in a pinball machine. But it didn't; he arched his back for each hop, thereby pulling himself down as soon as he leapt. Doubtless this trick was learned from prior space-flight experience.

The flounder mouse's own anxious behavior would also have sent it careening, if not for sticky soil similar to that used in Earthlings' space-faring rodent cages. That's what kept the wood shavings from floating like imitation snow in a snowflake water ball, the rodents floating with them.

Anyhow, the flounder mouse and Ferdinand eventually settled down from the pushups and hat dance, respectively, for a good sniff snout to snout. The sticky soil provided their tiny paws ample anchor so that, again, they wouldn't drift uncontrollably about.

As the flounder mouse's comfort level rose, it resumed glowing with bioluminescence. This set off Ferdinand with a jump backwards, succeeded by a new hat dance. Then the flounder mouse went lights-off again, opting for more pushups. When they finally calmed anew for more sniffing, the flounder mouse's bioluminescence freaked out Ferdinand anew, and they were back to the manic behavior. This cycle repeated over and over.

During the creatures' curious spectacle, the Fafaman leader motioned towards them as he gave Captain Taylor a teeth-baring smile. (*You see? Exactly how I expected!*) Taylor knew his squinting resulted from his nocturnal eyes' trouble adjusting to even what little light remained with the space station headed orbiting back around to Fafama's night side. But she also sensed, or hoped, he was trying to espy her expression through her helmet's face shield, despite its reflectivity. Anyhow, when he snapped his fingers, he spoke in a tone that conveyed giving orders.

Two of his entourage moved quickly, returning into the sword-shaped spacecraft. They were back not a minute later, bearing clear plastic bags filled with what impressed Helena, Chris and Buddy as being fully-loaded kabob skewers.

The Fafaman ruler unzipped one of the bags handed to him, and fitted it over his mouth like some rancher fitting her horse with a feeding bag. All the while, he did not take his eyes off Helena.

The bag stayed put without having to be held there. A Velcro-type innovation, Buddy remarked to Helena, where the material clings to skin yet can probably be peeled off easily enough.

Whatever, the Fafaman ruler held onto one end of the apparent kabob skewer as best he could with the plastic bag intervening. And at last he left off from eyeing Helena, to focus on eating one of the impaled items.

At first glance Helena thought, *Looks like he couldn't wait to snack until later. And isn't that sweet how his entourage gets to stand around like we do, watching him munch away? At least I don't see anything slithering. In fact, if I didn't know better, I'd guess that's a chunk of green pepper, followed by a mushroom... Wo!*

When the Fafaman ruler bit into the green-pepper-type object, something pink and fleshy-looking like a tongue emerged and quivered rapidly. It made the same sound as a stuck-out tongue caused to flap noisily fast. Though once he chewed it completely off the skewer, both quiver and noise stopped with an abrupt "Wank!"

Even worse, with only one bite into the mushroom-type object, two eyes shot out on long stems from what would have been the cap of an actual mushroom. Chris was reminded of sand crab eyes. They gave Captain Taylor the distinct impression of frantically looking hither and yon, even at one another, until a second bite left them drifting limply in the weightlessness.

Once the important one finished eating the second item on his skewer, eyes and all, he pulled both skewer and feedbag from his face.

At first, the captain was relieved to see him set his snack aside. Especially with her nagging mystery headache, she was wondering how much longer she could watch this guy eat before nausea set in. But then he motioned for one of his entourage to bring one of the unopened bags over to her, and clearly gestured her to try it.

Helena shook her head "no" without hesitation, and walked over to point at the flow chart still displayed on Buddy's plasma screen.

Again, this flow chart illustrated the Earthlings taking off their suits in the extraterrestrials' presence only provided one important condition was met. Namely, Ferdinand Mouse and Flounder Mouse had to keep their good health after unmediated exposure to one another.

The Fafaman ruler gave a perfunctory glance, then reacted anew with his combination of woe-is-me eyes and clownishly exaggerated frown.

"Music!" blurted out Buddy. "Captain Taylor, what about the amplet we were going to gift them? Wouldn't a snippet of something Chris selected, wouldn't that be a cultural experience we can all enjoy without health issues? Maybe they will even reciprocate with some of their own music, and wouldn't that be fascinating!"

Officer Leung didn't have to elaborate this much for Helena; he could have stopped after, "What about the amplet?" He had gone on at such length for their vast audience back home on Earth. Chris mused it was the sort of explication some inept author would have had issuing from the mouth of a poorly realized character, for want of a better plan.

The Fafaman leader grasped clearly the hopeful tone, if not the content, of Buddy's utterance. He gave Captain Taylor a look communicating that whatever Buddy said was well worthy of her consideration, certainly. Perhaps a means by which, he misapprehended, the captain could find her way to remove her helmet for sampling Fafaman delicacies.

"That is something we talked about before we arrived," acknowledged Helena, also for the benefit of their light-years-distant audience. "Officer Olsen-Taylor?"

Chris extracted the amplet from a zipper compartment on the right leg of his envirosuit. Its tiny yet powerful speaker dishes might as well have been robot mouse ears, he fancied.

Nobody had to engage in artificial conversation to explain the amplet for folks back home. Everyone, or at least everyone on the comfortable side of the quarantine zones, knew it was the latest, hottest, must-have gadget of the twenty-first century. True, devices that responded to commands for certain music, weather reports, dinner recipes, etc. had been around for decades. But they usually required hyper-net access. The amplet's special charm was its state-of-the-art music storage, millions of recordings. No need for hyper-net access if you were billions of miles away on a deep space mission. And on Earth as well as in space, it had become all the rage for exploring tuneful nooks and crannies across multiple cultures and centuries.

Chris set down the amplet on the table where bags full of skewers were left for the Earthlings. "I have selected a song six decades old, co-written with the guitarist Carlos Santana," he announced. "Entitled 'Africa Bamba,' it demonstrates our planet's rich, enduring music heritage by succinctly blending several different sensibilities."

Hmmm Captain Taylor hmmed to herself. *I wonder if that was the best place to put the amplet, right beside the food the Fafamans set out for us. I hope my counterpart doesn't think we're irradiating his skewered delights to make them safer for consumption, if not more palatable.*

"So with no further ado," said Chris, poking a single blue button atop the amplet, "amplet play all listen Santana, 'Africa Bamba.'"

The "all listen" command directed "Africa Bamba" through the amplet's speakers instead of Chris's earpiece.

A suspenseful moment later, Spanish acoustic guitar, string synthesizer and jazzy percussion accompaniment burst from the amplet with definitive, cumulative force.

The extraterrestrials, even the ruler, jumped. Security instinctively seized their weapons and trained them on the curious-looking little contraption that was producing the music. But instead of blowing it apart, they surrendered to the soothing rhythms and relaxed their aim.

*

"Ay! We have that CD!" exclaimed Gloria and Jerri in unison, trillions of miles and sixty years away. Thanks to Gloria's quick action, "Africa Bamba" burst from their CD player nearly simultaneous to it bursting from the amplet, where Doña Galleta was concerned.

"Ay caramba!" "Aydiomio!" complained Típico and Placido, roused from drifting off by something other than their snores.

Carlos Santana sang in Spanish about dancing with calm and singing with love, in dialogue with his acoustic guitar and propelled along by the driving rhythm.

*

Helena noticed the Fafaman ruler tapping his fingers on the arm rests of his throne-like chair. Next thing she knew, he was nodding his head from side to side to the bass beat, and giving her a playful smile.

Helena smiled back and tried nodding, but her helmet proved most restrictive. So she started her hips swaying even though her envirosuit also proved a restrictive nuisance.

No matter, her motion was obvious enough for the Fafaman ruler to step down off his throne and do some swaying of his own while Santana's trademark electric guitar wailed in ecstatic response to the refrain, and the pulsing beat was coming more to the foreground.

"All right!" said Kevin. "Their Grand Wazoo knows how to boogie!"

While Gloria and Jerri mirrored each other's dance moves back in Philadelphia some sixty years earlier, the important one came up close to Captain Taylor. He encircled his arms high above her head and made experienced, practiced steps around her. She answered in kind, as he obligingly sank low on bended knees so her arms could encircle high above *his* head. For Ali watching from the Smoke and Mirrors, the clomp-clomp-clomp of their magboots added a flamenco touch.

Then Helena turned her back on the alien, and attempted an antique dance move called the submarine, inspired by a recent newscast about its improbable comeback. But constrained by her envirosuit, she couldn't apply fingers to nose through the helmet lens, let alone wriggle and writhe sinking to her knees.

Something had to give.

Trumpet blasts ushered in an instrumental break dominated by Santana cutting loose on his guitar. But they also unknowingly ushered in Captain Helena Taylor unlocking the air seal in three different locations on her suit, thoughtless of possible consequences. Her husband and Buddy were too late getting past their shock to protest or otherwise move to stop her. She had already removed her helmet, and was shaking her long hair free from being bound up in a bun. All that, whilst crumpling down her envirosuit to more easily step out of it for uninhibited dancing. Her liberation from self-consciousness complemented perfectly the wonderfully wild vamp that concluded "Africa Bamba." She spun clomp-clomp-clomp, round and round, into a swooning faint that could have seriously hurt Doña Galleta had Ludi not caught the small, frail woman in her arms.

Chapter 11

Aboard the Smoke and Mirrors, lights flared up and faded down on a programmed cycle simulating Earth's diurnal twenty-four-hour cycle. Only the bridge, the infirmary, and Buddy's applied hyper-physics workshop were kept brightly lit round the clock.

Midway through the away team's first "night" back from the Fafaman space station, an onset of nasal congestion bothered them awake.

Blowing into tissue failed to dislodge the least stubborn bit of mucous. Helena and company decided, though, to leave chief medical officer Deborah undisturbed for what remained of her own sleep cycle. Unless someone's condition turned worse than nuisance, they would stoically endure the discomfort for a few more hours.

However, the "morning" after first contact with extraterrestrials, Helena, Chris and Buddy faced a disturbing sight in a long mirror set above four side-by-side washbasins. Slimy bioluminescent green gunk dripped hanging from their nostrils, as if they needed any more reason for quarantine.

Subsequent to Captain Taylor discarding her protective suit for a less inhibited dance with the Fafaman ruler, the Earthlings had made quick exit from the extraterrestrial space station. But Buddy pieced together another pictograph for the extraterrestrials, letting them know the Earthlings would be back soon, equipped to communicate in far more depth.

On the away team's return to the Smoke and Mirrors, Captain Helena Taylor had convened the rest of the crew to tender her resignation. "Before any questions, I have a statement to make," she said, addressing Yoon-hee and company through a panoramic window from inside the room where she and fellow away team members were immediately quarantined. "I don't understand what came over me down there. I'd like to blame the recurrence of that bothersome headache, but can't with any honesty. Plainly, my stupidly careless act may have jeopardized our safety unnecessarily. So I am offering to step down as captain of the Smoke and Mirrors. Yoon-hee or Ali should take my place for the mission's duration, but that's up to the rest of you."

"Captain, I am curious about your husband and Buddy," reacted Ali Magabu, thoughtfully stroking his chin with forefinger and thumb. "Why did you both remove your envirosuits as well? I gathered you were seeking a better look at the captain in her distress. But truly, I wonder just what went through your heads."

"She's my wife," answered Chris. He ventured a protective arm round Helena's shoulders, but relented because she sidestepped further away from him. She wasn't trying to avoid public displays of affection between them, was she? She was merely bending forward to read digital displays on the quarantine room monitor, yes? Chris couldn't help worrying, but he continued, "My envirosuit's cumbersomeness impeded rushing to her side when she went into her fainting swoon. Thank goodness, um, their Grand Wazoo was able to catch her before she hurt herself. So you see I sought more flexibility were she to require more help on our way back to the ship. And how was I to achieve that without removing my envirosuit?" *While we're at it, Helena, I wasn't too keen on the Grand Wazoo holding you in his arms.*

"I think, uh, what Chris is saying, uh, it makes sense," said Buddy, though all those "uh"s nearly belied his defense.

"We were better able to monitor the captain's condition, um, unimpeded by our suits."

"I see," nodded Deborah. "So if I can paraphrase, Officer Leung, you believed you would make a better diagnosis free from the protection of your envirosuit. Only you are not a trained doctor, are you?"

Ali Magabu understood why the chief medical officer snapped like that. She worked so hard developing a safety protocol for the first encounter of humans with extraterrestrials. She went to all that trouble, only to see it carelessly tossed aside by their head honcho. But Ali wanted to lecture her that this mission, this historic adventure, was about far more than protecting the turf of any one individual's domain of expertise. He wasn't sure yet, though, the extent to which the captain's behavior ought to be excused.

Meanwhile, though, what Kevin was sure about had him blurt out, "What I don't understand, Officer Olsen-Taylor, is your music selection. I mean what the fried fish?!?! Who's ever heard of Santana? If you wanted something cosmic to send the solar clippers careening, why didn't you go with more recent tunes, like from this century?"

"That piece was from the turn of the century."

"Oh, the turn of the century, that was only sixty years ago. I mean something most people would know, like 'Surfin' the Sunbeam.' But I suppose the Almost Stinks are too contemporary for you. You favor all that antique stuff."

"It's what I explained for our fellow terrestrials back home," protested Chris. "'Africa Bamba' seemed a good introduction to our civilization's vast music diversity. So much is incorporated, of course no one four-minute piece can fully encapsulate..."

"Yeah, yeah, yeah," Kevin nodded as in Enough Already. "But if you were going that route, why not one of those timeless masters like Beethoven, Mozart, or one of those other guys? Maybe you'd run the risk of putting the ETs to sleep, but at least that Grand Wazoo guy might not have treated a minuet like a mating call."

"Actually, Officer Smith," Ali Magabu weighed in, "we know nothing about the inescapable physiological changes possibly incurred by stirring music into the extraterrestrial contact mix. For all we know, even the slowest movement from Beethoven's Pastoral Symphony might incite a reaction even more pronounced than that from the Santana piece. Which I quite truly enjoyed, incidentally. Nevertheless, introducing music at this beginning stage might be comparable to introducing pizza to a one-month-old infant."

"A mistake, in other words," had said Kevin. "And now we're just hoping our dancing fool and her two sidekicks aren't going to grow tentacles out their butts during quarantine. But I guess our real concern is over how we're going to play all this for our audience back on Earth. Assuming, of course, the firefly donut dingy is even getting our transmissions through."

"You're not forgetting…"

"Okay, Buddy, so we'll receive confirmation of that within another day."

Buddy Leung programmed the firefly donut to "hang" home side of the Oort Cloud for several hours after transmitting the extraterrestrial encounter footage. Only then would it make its way back to the Alpha Centauri C side. In other words, someone aboard the Saturn moon station would have plenty of time to load up at least an acknowledgement of receipt.

"So when and if that happens," Kevin went on, "here's the problem: Everyone is going to expect a quick follow-up report on Captain Taylor's condition."

"And by the time we hear back, we should have a pretty good idea how she and the rest of the away team are doing," Yoon-hee said, intent on minimizing her husband's worry.

"I'm guessing we will be able to confidently report Captain Taylor is in good shape after her dance encounter with the extraterrestrial," counselor Ali Magabu added. "She suffered merely from too much boogie on too little sleep. And regarding questions anyone might have about her violating Dr. Davis-Murphy's safety protocol, we can credibly argue for suspending judgment until later."

"Just wondering," said Kevin defensively, turning aside with shoulders hunched like he was bracing for a physical blow.

"Umm, uh, guys?" Captain Taylor had tapped on the panoramic window separating her and her contaminated "sidekicks" from Kevin and company. "My resignation?"

"Again, CAPTAIN, none of us," started Magabu, pausing to stare down Dr. Deborah Davis-Murphy, "NONE of us understands yet what came over you. At least not so much that we could guarantee we wouldn't have done the same thing in your shoes. In fact, I am especially concerned Kevin would not have stopped after he removed his envirosuit. That might have only been the start."

"You have to remain Captain, Captain," laughed Yoon-hee. "I don't want to see my husband performing some strip-club routine."

"Moreover, Captain," Magabu piled on further, "are you expecting your husband Chris and Officer Leung to resign from their respective posts, since they also broke protocol?"

"That would be- Ow!" Yoon-hee twisted Kevin's ear before he could finish. Nevertheless, Chris knew he was going to say that would be a good idea in the case of the captain's eminently disposable husband.

"People of the Starship Smoke and Mirrors," said Magabu putting on a mock-official air, "are we unanimously agreed that, as Officer Smith so eloquently articulated, anyone's resignation here would be totally, truly 'Ow!'?"

"Ow!" laughed Yoon-hee while Deborah and her wife, third engineer Geena, exchanged chagrined looks which Helena read as: *We're outnumbered.*

Deborah gave Dr. Magabu a severe regard as she said, "Let's just hope the away team will continue to experience nothing more than relatively benign impacts on their autoimmune systems from their first unmediated exposure to an extraterrestrial biological environment." She did stifle herself from characterizing the exposure as reckless.

"Let's truly hope, Dr. Davis-Murphy," agreed Ali Magabu, though he returned Deborah's regard with what Helena read as an admonishing glare. He was thinking what the captain was thinking: The first medical officer's real hope was for her fury over the decontamination protocol violations to be vindicated by one of them burping up a kidney, or experiencing something else equally horrendous.

"I don't know about you, Captain," said Tanya taking a stab at reducing the tension caused by the face-off between her husband and Deborah, "but were I in your shoes, dancing with extraterrestrial hunk would have been worth it for me, especially to make my husband jealous."

"Ahhh," Ali nodded, "for that, a resignation would have been expected, truly."

Tanya and Ali gave one another an I'm-just-kidding chicken-peck kiss.

Chris wished Helena would follow suit. Instead, she bowed her head and smiled faintly. *What was she concealing?*

When Helena, Chris and Buddy presented next "morning" with the weird glow-in-the-dark nasal discharge, Deborah successfully collected samples for analysis. ("Okay, Officer Olsen-Taylor," said Kevin, "I have to concede you've verified the existence of Unidentified Snotty Objects, if nothing else.") Deb's wife, third engineer Geena, was able to retrofit an analysis equipment package into one panel below the quarantine chamber's panoramic window. Included were gloves for handling toxic materials. Still, the weird nasal discharge proved too slippery for Deborah to get a good grip. Unlike normal nasal discharge, it demonstrated amazing elasticity and resistance to being pulled free from Earthling nostrils. Ultimately it took Chris's long bare nails to so glom on to his own and others' nasal discharge as to break off samples. And at that, the green gobs he handed over to Deborah ended up ridiculously small. Once broken off, they abruptly shrank with a distinct snap!, as though they were rubber bands let go after being stretched nearly to the breaking point. What was left hanging from the away team's noses also shrank, back up inside their nasal passages. Consequently, they were still afflicted with the congestion which woke them middle of synthetic night.

Nevertheless, Deborah asserted, "So far, so good, Captain."

"You need your nails clipped," said Helena addressing Chris.

"If I had already," said Chris, "how were we going to obtain any of those snot samples? I don't see any scissors lying around."

Helena didn't mean to snap at her husband. But she had to direct her irritation somewhere, the way Chief Medical Officer Dr. Deborah Davis-Murphy said, "Captain." Sounded to her like Deborah was saying: *See how magnanimous I am, still addressing you as captain? Despite my conviction your offer to step down not only should have been heartily accepted, you should have been forced to resign if you didn't volunteer?*

Before Captain Taylor could wonder whether she read too much into the special emphasis Deborah put on "Captain" when she said, "So far so good, Captain," Deborah was hurrying on. "Your white blood cell counts and other autoimmune system indices have remained well within healthy parameters. Antiangiogenesis is occurring at normal, uncompromised rates. As for the phosphorescent discharge, that does seem to result from dynamic, synergistic interaction of your regularly produced mucous with an unknown biological pathogen we can presume originated on Fafama. That unknown pathogen seems content transforming your mucous, is not demonstrating any invasive properties beyond that. At least not yet."

"Captain, please allow me a less clinical characterization of what is taking place." Dr. Ali Magabu rushed to Deborah's side with papers and three identical small gadgets in hand. "Fafaman biochemistry is throwing a party over the introduction of extraterrestrial biochemistry. We are witnessing the antithesis, truly, of our bodies attacking replacement organs from fellow humans without the mediation of anti-rejection drugs. The Fafaman microbes lodging in your nostrils have, in a sense, embraced your snot, derived inspiration from your snot. You might even say they have collaborated with your snot to produce something entirely new. Indeed, in a truly similar way, extraterrestrial microbes frozen aboard comets striking our Earth billions of years ago are believed to have inspired the proliferation of the life from which we evolved. I'm not saying there won't be any medical challenges ahead stemming from this stumbled-into historic interaction. And I'm certainly not saying, Captain, we can safely go ahead now and mingle with you unprotected by the quarantine chamber. Come our next orbit of Fafama, I would not want to bet your odd green secretions won't grow fangs and tear into you. I'm only suggesting that maybe, maybe there is some prospect for you, Chris, and Buddy to emerge relatively unscathed."

"For the moment, as you note with the fangs scenario."

You can always hope Captain Taylor stifled herself from bitterly adding to Deborah's cautionary note.

Unfazed by Deborah, Dr. Magabu enthused over some important developments the quarantined away team missed while they were trying to sleep.

For starters, oral translation devices donated by Tanya and Yoon-hee were reprogrammed to handle the extraterrestrial language. For that process, Magabu leaned heavily on Fafamans' gifted picture dictionary as well as their introductory language lesson.

Thereafter Magabu exposed the reprogrammed translators to snippets of the "Grand Wazoo's" dialogue with fellow Fafamans. This quickly revealed much to be desired. The translators did spit out entire sentences, albeit riddled by drop-out silences most likely due to

Fafaman names for which there were no English counterparts. But certain nonsensical-seeming passages could have resulted from most anything, whether homonym confusion, idiomatic expression, something unimagined, or a combination thereof. "You want me to order you into a (drop-out) leaf?" went one of them uttered in a threatening tone.

Naturally when the translators were fed English, subsequent fah-lah-lahs in the alien tongue were also littered with silences and seeming nonsense. Probably. With nobody fluent in both Fafaman and English, who could know for sure?

For the time being, Captain Taylor and company would need to keep their syntax and content as basic as possible so that maybe the translators would work well enough.

A pictograph was already transmitted to the Fafaman space station, explaining the possibility of oral and written translation issues. In that pictograph, characters turned angry because an expression of friendship mistranslated as a challenge to fight. Ali lost hours of sleep constructing that pictograph, including an oral accompaniment he could be certain was accurate. But there would have been no sense bothering hadn't the extraterrestrials successfully installed a network compatibility program arranged by Buddy Leung. It enabled successful transmission of sound in addition to text and illustrations between Fafaman and Earthling computers.

"Truly," Ali concluded his briefing for the away team in quarantine, "I hope that someday, communication with an extraterrestrial species will approach the level of ease always assumed in *Star Trek* and other old space opera. But for now, at least our translators achieve rudimentary dialogue. There's one translator for each of you, in case you get isolated from each other during your return visit."

"Our return visit, Ali?"

"Truly the most exciting development I have to share with you, Captain. We received a pictograph that includes simple captions in English, making precisely clear the Fafamans expect your return, the return of all three of you. You're to meet with survivors of the spacecraft that crashed on Fafama a few hundred days ago. Apparently they are hospitalized."

"Survivors who might be invaders on a people-herding expedition, the reason we set out for Fafama with such reckless haste in the first place," Captain Taylor nodded, feeling obliged to restate a painful if obvious reality. They'd experienced exhilarating historic first contact with intelligent extraterrestrials, including first dance. Who wanted to face the fact they were responding to a distress call concerning a threat of potentially apocalyptic proportions? Couldn't they just savor the adventure? Couldn't their biggest worry remain that mysteriously glowing, elastic green snot up some nostrils?

"My fondest hope is that who we call invaders now will prove to have been completely misunderstood. Then we can rejoice, led by Chris. He'll play some more Santana so we can all lose ourselves in the spirit of the dance," concluded Ali Magabu, gesturing emphatically ceiling-ward.

Chris mused to himself that Dr. Magabu would have launched his gesturing forefinger into orbit if he could have.

"In the meantime," said Ali moving on, "what should prove most fascinating is the ride on their dagger-shaped craft down to Fafama for a meeting with those crash-landed ETs."

"So they will transport us to the surface of their planet?" asked Captain Helena Taylor, unable to help sounding alarmed.

"Captain," said Buddy Leung, "those crash-landed ETs might have suffered injuries leaving them too fragile for travel up to the space station." Officer Leung guessed Helena was reluctant to trust extraterrestrial space flight technology, especially since the Fafamans seemed a bit backward. No matter her surrender to the spirit of the dance inspired by a Santana song, in total disregard for the safety protocol.

"I suppose we don't have much choice if we want to more directly check out the invasion threat for ourselves," Helena conceded.

"One Fafaman pictograph also showed the three of you being their supreme ruler's guests at a parade, perhaps a welcome-to-our-planet parade," said Ali, holding up to the quarantine room's panoramic window the pictograph in question.

The pictograph showed marchers beating on drums, followed by other marchers playing various guitars. People of clearly feminine form came next, one leading the rest, and all striking the same dramatic pose.

Someone stood tall in a review stand to the side of the parade, his arms held high like a looming ghoul, Chris imagined. Three shorter figures flanked him, looking like bulky robots complete with square faces. *It's the Grand Wazoo, accompanied by his three silly outer space friends wearing their silly envirosuits because they're afraid of a little green elastic boogersnot.*

"Captain, it's interesting they drew us envirosuited," said Buddy.

"But I would truly hesitate to read into that any endorsement of our precautionary behavior," warned Ali before Buddy could go on. "The Fafamans might simply be using our envirosuits as handy markers to identify us. In like manner, they gave the other figure those looming arms to portray their 'Grand Wazoo.'"

"Which leaves us with the question," said Helena, "to envirosuit or not to envirosuit?"

"Do what you think is best, Captain," said Deborah Davis-Murphy.

In how Deborah uttered *Captain*, Helena again detected a nasty edge.

"But remember," the chief medical officer went on, "no one gets a rash the first time they're exposed to poison ivy. I really hope Dr. Magabu is correct about the biochemical party going on. Our data is so scant, we can't be sure a second unprotected exposure to the extraterrestrials won't have unexpectedly more dire consequences than the first."

"Dr. Davis-Murphy, truly I would not suggest there is little or no risk," said Ali Magabu. "In fact for all we know, our away team's fate might already be sealed without another molecule inhaled from the Fafaman ecosystem. They might already be doomed to horrendous suffering and death, thanks to their break with your most carefully considered safety protocol. They're not even disputing that."

Helena, Chris and Buddy received Ali's assertion with grim-faced nods.

"The real question is," continued Ali, "what's best for assuring we obtain full access to the oddly antlered fellows supposedly crash-landed from another solar system? I don't know how the rest of you saw it. Especially you, Captain. But the Grand Wazoo's amusement over your refusing to sample choice Fafaman delicacies truly seemed to stray perilously near profound irritation."

"My same impression exactly," nodded Captain Taylor. "And I did subsequently remove my envirosuit to dance, and fellow officers removed theirs to check on my condition. So I'm wondering how he'll take our resuming with our sensible protection. We could be perceived as purposefully anti-social, however unreasonable such a perception would be."

"But you can pictograph, or we can simply send photos of you guys with the stringy green glop hanging from your noses," said Deborah, unable to help sounding defensive. "Certainly the Fafamans won't change their minds about offering you access to the crash-landed aliens because you try to protect yourselves from potentially more lethal health effects."

"For all we know, the Grand Wazoo and friends have been dealing with some green slime of their own," Buddy added supportively. Under less onerous circumstances, he might have laughed at his own conjecture like he'd just told the funniest joke. Instead, though, he eked out a wan smile as he went on, "They might be about to greet us wearing their own protective gear, and then treat us as lepers."

"When on Fafama, we'll do as the Fafamans," Captain Taylor said with finality, seizing on Buddy's point. "If they're suited up, we'll remain suited up. Otherwise...Dr. Magabu, before I forget, any response from home yet to our last transmission?" Helena Taylor was concerned about hearing from Earth, at least receiving confirmation the firefly-donut com-link worked. But she abruptly raised this issue out of desperation to head off, postpone more unpleasantness with Deborah.

Were the Fafamans planning on finally implementing the chief medical officer's safety protocol, they most likely would have indicated that already. Since they didn't... Helena could sense Deborah simmering, with glistening lipstick and heavy eye shadow highlighting her severe countenance.

Captain, to suit up or not to suit up should not be held hostage to the whims of the Fafamans ran through Deborah's mind. But she bit her lip instead of speaking up, determined not to offer more advice unless asked. Especially since Captain Helena Taylor obviously wasn't interested.

It actually made no difference if Helena didn't head off a protest from Deborah. Deborah could even have called her an ignorant, mentally deranged incompetent. But no way would Helena risk giving such offense to the Fafaman ruler, he denied them an audience with the extraterrestrials who crash-landed on Fafama. Sure, the Fafamans had issued a distress call, calling all planets, about the threat they feared those antlered guys represented. Nevertheless, a big enough challenge to Fafaman pride - HIS pride – might seriously cloud HIS judgment.

"Captain, Officer Buddy Leung has received a holo-message from his wife, but that's all there is," said Magabu in answer to Captain Taylor's question whether there had been any response from home yet. "Of course, Buddy, we will accommodate a private viewing for you."

"Hopefully Cathy knows better than to send something THAT private," Buddy laughed flippantly, for a blessed moment not feeling the weight of circumstances.

"Hmm," hmmed Captain Taylor. "Maybe our fearless leaders wanted to assure us the firefly donut was getting through. But they're not exactly comfortable telling us to keep up the good work."

Deborah gave the captain's assessment a stiff-upper-lip nod. Where Helena was concerned, she might as well have asked: *What did I tell you?*

"We don't know that yet," said Magabu. "Perhaps our fearless leaders gave Cathy a message to pass along to the rest of us, and we will receive our 'job well done' approbations after all. That is, once Cathy has finished delivering to Buddy whatever scandalously personal thing meant for his reddening ears only."

Deborah crossed her arms and rolled her eyes.

*

"So did Cathy say anything fit for public consumption?" Captain Taylor asked Buddy Leung at the outset of their shuttle pod flight from the Smoke and Mirrors back to the scabbard-shaped Fafaman space station.

Helena and Chris boarded the pod early to give Buddy privacy for his wife's holo-message.

"I know this isn't the time or the place..." Cathy had started.

"So why are you?" Buddy's interrupting voice cracked with upset as he challenged the flickering three-dimensional image recorded six trillion miles away.

"Bud..."

Officer Leung's heart skipped a beat over Cathy James-Leung's pause after voicing her nickname for him.

"...I just keep wondering how you can endure these long separations, if... When you return, we'll have to talk. In the meantime, everyone here prays for your mission's safe completion. Take care."

Buddy did breathe a little easier after the "have to talk" bit. There was nothing ominously new, after all. Assuming their next talk went the way of the previous ones...There was always that edge of uncertainty. When they were apart, he fretted over how SHE could stand their extended periods alone, if... But he didn't dare make a move to facilitate their working side by side, for fear she'd get so sick of him she'd file for divorce. He always said this when they reunited, and then she always shared with him how she harbored the same worry. Such confessions never failed to prompt their rush into one another's arms, igniting a week of unbridled passion.

What traditionally ensued was a dispassionate, logical reflection on their situation. Buddy's precedent-shattering breakthroughs to achieve light-speed propulsion through poorly understood physics applications required long journeys far away. Meanwhile, Cathy's calling as a geophysicist went more ground-bound directions. Love would always keep them connected, but like the known universe, they both needed to keep expanding.

Albert Einstein's "spooky action at a distance" described how one subatomic particle could instantly impact another particle, no matter how far removed. So naturally, one of Buddy's hyper-physics colleagues labeled his relationship with Cathy "spooky romance at a distance."

"Umm, not too much, Captain," responded Buddy, answering Helena's question about what was fit for public consumption from his wife's holo-message. "It's the usual. Cathy hopes I'm okay, and everyone else at home joins her in wishing us continued safety." Making clear he had nothing more to say, Buddy turned away from Helena to peer outside the shuttle pod's cockpit window.

The shuttle pod happened to be approaching dock with the Fafaman space station for a second time, so it wasn't like there wasn't a lot to see. But for Buddy's purpose, they could have still been inside the Smoke and Mirrors shuttle pod hangar, not due to launch for hours.

In any event, not five minutes disembarked from the shuttle pod flown by Tanya Petrovsky, a most ominous development really rattled Captain Helena Taylor's cage. She felt nearly ready to abort their second visit, return to the Smoke and Mirrors at once.

Helena, Chris and Buddy had just shed their envirosuits, and were giving Helena's translator a most promising debut. "Thank you for allowing our second visit," said Helena. "We like the plan on your pictograph." Captain Taylor carefully repeated the sentences word-for-word that she practiced aboard the shuttle pod. And the same as during rehearsal, her translator's synthesized voice spit out a succession of fah-lah-lah soft syllables.

The Fafamans delightedly clapped their hands and hee-hee-heeed like howling monkeys. And when the shorter Fafaman spoke, Helena's translator crackled, "We are happy because you like our plan. We will introduce ourselves. My name is Wafalawa, and this is (   )." Exactly as programmed to do, the translator repeated the unrecognized clump of sounds that followed the phrase translating as, "My name is."

"Nice to meet you, Wafalawa," said the captain. Then she pointed at the taller one and went on, "But can he say 'My name is' before his name? The translator went silent when you introduced his name with 'This is.'"

The taller extraterrestrial was just about to oblige Helena's request when the ominous something happened. It started with the mysterious bioluminescently glowing green gunk that plagued the Earthlings with nuisance congestion. A strand of the stuff bloomed iris-shaped out Captain Taylor's left nostril, trumpeted, "Wank! Wank!", and then retreated back deep inside her sinus passageways.

Captain Taylor couldn't help sneezing, so tickled were her nostrils.

Before anyone could comment, iris-shaped green gunk shot elastically from Chris's right ear, went "Wank! Wank!", then returned deep inside his head.

Buddy experienced the trumpeted "Wank! Wank!" next, out his nostrils like Helena, with the ensuing retraction also causing a sneeze.

"Wank! Wank!" here, "Wank! Wank!" there, Chris could imagine rewriting "Old MacDonald Had a Farm" as "Old MacDonald Had Elastic Green Snot" despite his being so personally impacted. He couldn't keep his camcorder steady, but Dr. Magabu and others were able to marvel nevertheless at the weird spectacle from back aboard the Smoke and Mirrors.

While both doctors were too alarmed for comment, Kevin said, "Hey, looks like the green snot is playing hide and seek!"

Stranger yet, violet-glowing counterparts suddenly shot from Wafalawa's nostrils. Curved and slender like two, small Alpine horns, they went, "Toot! Toot!" before leaving Wafalawa in the throes of a sneezing spell.

Popping from the tall one's ears, two more horn-shaped mucous-like substances also went, "Toot! Toot!" If Chris didn't know better, they were answering the first horns' calls.

The next thing Earthlings and Fafamans knew, toots and wanks popping in and out of nostrils and ears coordinated almost like a fugue, Chris mused. That fugue played faster and faster, drizzled with sneezes. Until suddenly, all the bioluminescent goop leaped free from their bodily orifices, went "Ta-daaa!!", and fell into lifeless, gray puddles on the floor.

"At least you guys didn't have the runs with this extraterrestrial germ stuff," commented Kevin, heard only through the crew's earpieces. "Wouldn't have been a pleasant sight watching elastic shit play peek-a-boo out your asses."

Thank goodness, Captain Taylor sighed with relief, *the translators aren't accessing Kevin's remark.* Also lowering her stress was an overwhelming sense the health crisis was past. They wouldn't have to short-circuit their second direct encounter with the extraterrestrials, after all.

"Nobody would have seen that with their pants on, Kevin," grunted Yoon-hee as she put some muscle into twisting her husband's ears.

"You're right," Kevin himself grunted with the effort to wriggle free of his wife's playful yet painful assault. Then facing her on the bridge of the Smoke and Mirrors, he added, "They would just see these bulges coming and going in the back of their pants, like some guy's-"

"Oh no, you don't!" shouted Yoon-hee, getting her hands past Kevin's defensively raised limbs to cover his mouth.

The extraterrestrials were alternating between shocked contemplation of the lifeless puddles on the floor, and an exchange of puzzled looks. But then Helena, Chris and Buddy busted into giggles over Kevin and Yoon-hee's struggles heard over their earpieces. Said extraterrestrials misapprehended those giggles as delayed reaction to the toot-toots and wank-wanks, so they erupted in their shrill, howling-monkey hee-hee-hees.

May all our big problems be resolved in such an amusingly innocuous manner, the captain wanted to say. But trying to keep her communication as simple as possible for the translator, she went with, "I hope the next big problem has a funny answer also."

Tugging anxiously on his whiskers, the taller alien mouthed lots of fah-lah-lahs in his native tongue, and Captain Taylor's translator crackled, "What is the next big problem?"

"I don't know," answered Captain Taylor, shrugging her shoulders. Then baring her palms, she strained her face into the most quizzical expression possible to reiterate, "I don't know what the next big problem is."

The three extraterrestrials exchanged glances. Then the smaller one strung together more fah-lah-lahs. What the translator made of that utterance was, "There is the answer to your question, Nanofafo, about what is the next big problem. The next big problem is: We don't know what the next big problem is! Well done, person from 'Ahth,' supplying the funny answer you hoped for!"

The extraterrestrials laughed their hee-hee-hees alone; the Earthlings' hearts weren't in producing even a forced chuckle for diplomacy's sake. They'd travelled light-years on the possibility of an impending invasion from a civilization technologically superior to Earth's. That really could be the next big problem, a whopper. And how likely would some hardy-har-har make it go away?

Traveling from the space station down to the Fafaman surface posed a more immediate concern, however. Nanafafo, the taller extraterrestrial, brought that into focus by suggesting the Earthlings leave their envirosuits aboard the space station for retrieval on their return.

Captain Taylor spoke for the away team. Another flow chart supplemented her translated explanation why they had to lug along their envirosuits. Should they suffer unanticipated bad side effects from the Fafaman atmosphere, they could quickly resort to a safe air supply from those suits. And ditto for food and personal articles, should their stay prolong unexpectedly.

"That is your decision," Nanofafo's fah-lah-lahed reaction translated, uttered with a wan smile plastered across his long-whiskered face.

For Helena and her away team, the synthesized translator voice felt imbued with Nanofafo's same lack of enthusiasm. This set them to reflecting anew on the enormous risk they were about to take, letting the Fafamans fly them down to the planet's surface in the sword-shaped vehicle. They were putting their safety completely in Fafaman hands.

"We should be okay, Captain," Buddy still assured Helena while shorter alien Wafalawa strapped them to their seats. "Establishing a space station must have required working through re-entry issues to an acceptably safe level. And Fafama's slightly lower gravitational pull compared to Earth's gives them a larger margin for error in that regard."

"You like the shuttle blade's contours?" asked Wafalawa. He paused from tightening Chris's straps to search Buddy's face at discomfortingly close range with his overgrown nocturnal eyes.

Officer Leung reminded himself not to squirm. That most likely, these creatures customarily got in each other's faces for conversation. And so he nodded with all the casual enthusiasm he could feign, to remark, "The design is fascinating." He figured the translator wouldn't find a Fafaman word for "fascinating," but that Wafalawa would conclude it was a flattering term.

Sure enough, the extraterrestrial reacted, "Since we have better spacecraft, you want to trade your two vehicles for our shuttle blade?"

Buddy doubted he successfully concealed being taken aback by Wafalawa's boastful question. Surely these extraterrestrials weren't blinded by pride to their outer space visitors' clear technological superiority, were they? Now Buddy had to wonder, even though the Fafamans did send out a distress signal. Originally, he believed that showed lack of confidence they could tackle the potential other-worldly menace on their own. *But what if that threat was all made up, to lure whoever into a trap?*

On the other hand, Buddy couldn't be quite sure Wafalawa's question wasn't just some face-saving tactic.

Buddy knew the debate still raged in academic circles, over how to cope if super-advanced extraterrestrials ever made their presence indisputably known on Earth. The general consensus was that such creatures must have progressed beyond the use of violence. Otherwise they would have self-destructed well before reaching any planet outside their solar system. But the fear was that an encounter with such creatures might prove so demoralizing as to mentally paralyze humanity. Quarantine zone or not, most human beings would sink into a morass of drunken, drugged-out stagnation and decline.

"Our leaders will be mad if we return in a different spaceship," said Buddy finally, in answer to the offered vehicle exchange.

Buddy's answer sent Wafalawa away to the shuttle blade's cockpit. Presumably he would tell the pilot how impressed Earthlings were with Fafaman technology.

Wafalawa and the pilot out of hearing range, the away team shut off their translators. Then Buddy whispered, "Having said what I've said about our probable safety, be prepared for a wild ride. We know from its exhaust trail signature that this horse and buggy runs on hydrogen fuel only. I'm expecting atmospheric re-entry to be comparably, um, antique."

"Yes," nodded Helena. "I noticed their Grand Wazoo isn't here for us. Yesterday might have been his first-ever trip into space, and re-entry might have proven too much for him to even consider a second round."

His wife's speculation got Chris thinking: *Yes, but you're certainly willing to take this risk for another look at him, perhaps another dance even.*

Backing out of its space station berth, the shuttle blade shuddered like an old-fashioned jet taxiing down an old-fashioned macadam runway. But the questions Chris found himself pondering tempered his anxiety over their safety, at least temporarily. *Where can Helena and I travel, what adventure can we have, that will actually get at the festering sore in our relationship? Or leave that sore far behind? And what hope is there anyway, when she appears willing to strip down for the Fafawazoo, regardless of health risks?*

And what is this whole mission about anyway? Okay, so we're investigating a potentially unimaginable threat out here. But I believe the best academics have it right. Any civilization that continually embraces war inevitably self-destructs before it can achieve interstellar travel. The Fafamans' fear is not well-founded. So what will this voyage to Fafama really accomplish? Okay again, we're establishing contact, we're opening diplomatic relations with an extraterrestrial intelligence for the first time in human history, at least in official human history. But is that going to take down the quarantine barriers? Is glowing green elastic booger-snot dancing out of our bodily orifices going to bring us world peace? In fact, how is this mission any different from a long vacation at an amusement park?

Guess I shouldn't underestimate the value of vacations, and extraterrestrial contact might end up having considerable spin-off value. So get a grip on yourself.

That's as far as Chris got with all his pondering before the rough spaceship ride occupied his full attention.

Deafening rocket engine blasts punctuated the shuttle blade's gliding descent closer to Fafama's outermost atmospheric layer, in aid of safe re-entry. With too shallow a re-entry angle, the shuttle would have become like a stone skipping across water, and gone careening into deep space out of control. Too steep an angle, it would have burned to cinders like a shooting star.

What brought the shuttle blade's constant shuddering to a whole new terrifying level for the Earthlings was deployment of its umbrella shield. Heat sensors caused it to emerge popping open from the shuttle blade's nose.

The umbrella shield took the brunt of re-entry, enough to protect the shuttle blade from heat damage. But the metallic hull shook so much, Helena and company could easily imagine it coming apart, their fear further aggravated by rapidly intensifying warmth. In fact as the umbrella shield burned away, the Earthlings experienced sheer terror. They misperceived seams separating when actually the intense air friction was producing blinding light shining through portholes. None too soon those portholes went dark. And short hydrogen-fueled rocket blasts steadied the shuttle into a smooth, shallow, cooling-off descent on a wide spiral path.

Night side of Fafama, Captain Taylor and her Earthling companions strained to see familiar asterisms such as the Big Dipper through shuttle blade portholes. No luck, unsurprisingly, since their current perspective varied greatly from home, light-years away. But before they could wonder about Fafaman asterisms, a flashing red light seemed to drift ever-so-slowly upwards.

"Captain, I think that's the warning beacon atop their wondrously enormous pyramid," said Buddy, assuming Helena knew what he was talking about. "As we descend, it appears to ascend."

On the shuttle blade's continued descent into the Fafaman atmosphere, other lights came into view ornamenting the pyramid apex. They illuminated the trestle tower on which the warning beacon was mounted.

"Okay, the Fafamans are nocturnal creatures who usually make do with faint luminescence at night," said Chris. "Would you guess those bright flood-lamps are for assuring no aircraft collisions with their giant anthill?" Chris shouldn't have had to frame his suspicion as a question. But he always felt so ignorant in the presence of both his pilot-trained wife and hyper-physicist friend.

Before Helena or Buddy could respond, Wafalawa left the cockpit to rejoin them, prompting reactivated translators. After coincidentally confirming Chris was correct, he provided a narration so carefully scripted, the Earthlings experienced few translation drop-out silences. He explained pyramids were the building structure of choice because they proved best able to withstand daily sunset storm-line impacts. "You have a sunset storm-line on Earth?" he subsequently asked.

"Um, late-day thunderstorms are a common feature of places with very warm temperatures and high humidity," offered Buddy with his usual nervous laugh. "But there is nothing of this regularity and latitudinal extent."

Wafalawa tilted his head with a quizzical look, as the translator couldn't handle "latitudinal extent."

Buddy asked whether Fafaman scientists could explain why every single day, the sunset storm-line swept virtually the entire planet save for its north and south poles.

"Apparently, it has something to do with the fifty-five to forty-five ratio of dry land to water cover. Fifty million solar orbits ago, an unusually large volcanic eruption dramatically changed that ratio from the earlier one, when water cover predominated. And coincidentally, geologic and paleontological records indicate the sunset storm-line became a daily occurrence starting likewise fifty million solar orbits ago. That's about all we know. But hopefully, comparative studies with your 'Ahth' weather will cast some shade over this blinding glare of mystery."

Wafalawa volunteered additional pyramid info before anyone could ask. Thousand-year-old pyramid ruins were located just outside a vast cave not far from the Great Pyramid. They were built around far smaller pyramids believed by Fafaman archaeologists to date back at least an additional two hundred years. Doubtless, everything had to be built piecemeal between storm-lines, using sandstone mined from within the cave.

Pyramid and grotto complexes, both, secured the safe space necessary for Fafaman society and technology to flourish despite the sunset storm-line's daily onslaught.

And by far, the Fafamans' miles-high Great Pyramid constituted their most significant achievement. About one-tenth of the planet's entire population lived and worked there, wherein the shuttle blade would be landing on level four. Moreover, central to its base stood a pyramid believed to be the very first one erected on Fafama, anywhere. Tourists could visit centuries-old layers accreted over it. But Fafamans considered that seed pyramid, as translated, sacred holy ground into which no one save the Fafaman ruler could ever be admitted.

Helena noticed the shuttle blade's brief rocket bursts kicking on more often. They leveled off its spiral descent into a circle round the Great Pyramid's lower part, evidently so Wafalawa could extend his guided tour.

"You see those vertical and horizontal dark crevices with dark-green rectangular shapes moving through them?" Wafalawa asked. "That's the transportation network between and within levels.

"The black holes set off by phosphorescent glows are openings to wide-diameter tubular shafts. Those shafts allow storm-line wind passage from the Great Pyramid's two east-facing sides all the way through to exit out its two west-facing sides. Fans located within some of them produce windmill energy."

All that Kevin could think about, listening to the translated narration from back aboard the Smoke and Mirrors, was the size of those pyramid holes. *Good God, in full daylight that thing must look like a monster-sized triangular block of Swiss cheese, albeit shiny metallic!*

"Question, Wafalawa," said Buddy. "Your transportation vehicles moving through the dark crevices, they are not damaged by the sunset storm-line?"

Wafalawa explained that prior to each sunset, metal shields slide down protectively over the crevices.

But Buddy ended up only half-listening, distracted by a long rectangular slit growing wider and wider in the pyramid's vast southeast-facing wall. Framed by glistening domed windows, again like precious gems studding a museum piece, that was where the shuttle blade would finally come in for a landing.

"Amazing," remarked Kevin from back aboard the Smoke and Mirrors, enjoying a full view courtesy of Chris's camcorder. "We have to share this with the folks back home. Just too bad the Fafamans do all their stuff in the dark. Of course, I do all my best stuff in the dark. Ow!"

Another pinch from Yoon-hee, who added, "I didn't know you thought so highly of your snoring. Though I will admit it's probably loud enough to drown out those hydrogen fuel rockets!"

"Yeah, whatever. Hey Chris?"

"Uh-huh?" asked Chris only half-attentive to Kevin as heard through his earpiece, thanks to the spectacle taking place outside the shuttle blade.

After a very bumpy landing, the shuttle had come to welcome rest beside a panoramic window through which Chris beheld said spectacle. Even with only dim pastel green lighting, he could see hundreds, thousands of

Fafamans pressing their noses against thick plexiglass. *Obviously they're all here for their first close-up look at visitors from another solar system, in other words us.*

"You haven't seen any of those UFO spacecraft you were expecting, have you, Officer Olsen-Taylor?"

Kevin's snide question gained Chris's full, bristly attention. "This is only one planet out of maybe thousands that are habitable. And- And for all we know, the extraterrestrials who crashed here have been buzzing the Earth for a century, sizing us up before they cattle-herd us. Maybe they even account for that UFO early in the mission."

"So you do your best work in darkness as well, when you're dreaming up-"

"Enough, both of you!" reproved Captain Taylor.

Stepping out of the shuttle hangar, Captain Taylor, Officer Olsen-Taylor and Officer Leung received a huge welcome. The Fafaman multitude created a deafening, echoing racket, hopping up and down in unison.

Security guards armed with imposing-looking guns moved ahead of the shuttle entourage to make way for the guests from another world.

Wafalawa took short yet proud strides up to a microphone. There, he let loose with an ear-piercing "Eek!" that quieted the crowd.

Press cameras flashed with distinct clicks, numerous times. Each flash was so faint, though, neither Helena, nor Chris, nor Buddy felt compelled to even squint, let alone blink. Chris recalled distant lightning in a night sky, while Buddy thought on his flickering-lights sensation whenever he awoke from dreaming.

"This is a translator" erupted from the translator Captain Taylor loaned Wafalawa for holding up so the audience could see. "It converts simple sentences from (gap) into their planet's primary language. It also converts back to our language. They call their planet 'Ahth'." What Wafalawa said next was littered with gaps. But Helena and company could tell it concluded with the Fafaman equivalent of, "Let's give a warm welcome to..."

The Fafaman multitudes reprised their thunderous hopping up and down, succeeded by Wafalawa extending a hand to Captain Taylor. "This is how they (gap)," he said, but Helena demurred. Instead, bending at the knees she bowed into what struck Chris as a feline motion. And rubbing her head against Wafalawa's tunic at chest level, she said, "Pama."

The crowd went nuts. They howled their hee-hee-hees, and made more jumping and stomping thunder. An audience storm-line, Chris mused.

"Wahwah Officer Olsen, Wahwah Officer Leung," Captain Taylor gestured towards her husband and Buddy once the ruckus died down.

Chris experienced a visceral reaction to Helena leaving off the Taylor part of his last name. So visceral, he instantly pointed at himself and said, "Wahwah Officer Olsen-TAYLOR." Then he put his arm round Helena's shoulders, and added, "Wahwah Captain TAYLOR."

Captain Taylor awkwardly ducked and wove away from her husband, with a clump-clump-clump of her magboots still on from dealing with outer space weightlessness.

Buddy Leung could tell that Chris was marking his territory.

"'Cahptahn Taylah,'" said Wafalawa, "you or another 'Ahthlahn' can answer questions from our news organizations?"

"Wah," Helena nodded, which sent the crowd into their howling monkey frenzy yet again.

Standing center of the extraterrestrials' attention long enough, the Earthlings started to notice certain things. In particular, a three-floor edifice recalled shopping malls from before holographic commerce made them obsolete back home on Earth. Looming behind the welcoming crowds, it featured several places that looked like storefronts. For their presumed names, soft pastel fluorescent lettering appeared to float mid-air in the pitch-black darkness above each dimly lit entrance.

On their next mission down to Fafama, Buddy swore that he and his fellow Earthlings needed to wear night-vision goggles.

"You like Fafama?" asked the first reporter on whom Wafalawa called.

"Fafama is a beautiful planet," answered Captain Helena Taylor. "Yes, we like it."

Chris and Buddy nodded along.

"What is the first new thing you want to learn about Fafama?" asked the second reporter.

"Um, Wafalawa explained many things about the pyramids and the sunset storm-line. But what is the first new thing we want to learn besides all that?" Helena asked, inviting Chris and Buddy to have a crack at the second reporter's question by looking towards them.

Of course they would avoid any least reference to the real reason they were there, a reason kept from the general Fafaman population as much as it was being kept from people back on Earth.

"Uh, everything," nervously laughed Buddy. "We want to learn everything."

"Music," said Chris. "The music of Fafama," but his response got drowned out by shrill hee-hee-hees over Buddy's answer.

The third question suffered lots of translation gaps, but among the words spit out were "dancing with," "wife," and "appropriate."

A sudden hush fell on the crowd.

Chris sensed they wanted to make sure they heard every last word the captain spoke in response. Maybe even the English before the translation.

To the away team's relief, Wafalawa called an end to the press conference before Helena could open her mouth. Way too many drop-outs in the last question's translation, and besides, "Our visitors from another planet are exhausted because on their planet, they sleep during stars-out and are awake during blinding-light."

On such bizarre news for them, the Fafaman crowd gasped as one while a monorail whisked away the Smoke and Mirrors away team.

Also accompanying Captain Taylor and company were Wafalawa and the tall, silent, whiskered Nanofafo, together with the armed security contingent.

As monorail doors hissed shut, Captain Helena Taylor said, "If your leader, the male who danced…"

"Fafamafalafama," said Wafalawa, soon as he heard the translation of "leader."

"Fafama-fa-la-fa-ma," Helena haltingly, tentatively repeated, receiving an approving nod from Wafalawa. "If he wants to see us now…"

"The Fafamafalafama is very busy with the business of the country!" Wafalawa snapped with his eyes bulging, before the translator could finish with Captain Taylor's remark. "He would have been back aboard the space station, first to welcome you on your second visit! Far from scaring him, riding the shuttle blade thrills the Fafamafalafama immensely! But he has too many responsibilities to indulge such pleasure more than once!"

"On Fafama," joined in Nanofafo stroking his twitching whiskers reflectively, "we have an expression: No more for the task than the task requires. Otherwise, you see, important work is neglected."

Wafalawa and Nanofafo stole sideways glances at the security guards a few seats down the monorail aisle from them. Those glances were received with subtle, approving nods.

Helena, Chris, and Buddy had to wonder. How sincerely did their extraterrestrial hosts defensively bristle on behalf of their so-called Fafamafalafama? Might it be no more than show so the guys with guns wouldn't for one second doubt their loyalty?

"Jeez Louise," exhaled Kevin into the Earthlings' earpieces. "King Fala-lalala must have been puking his guts out with motion sickness aboard their space shuttle!"

"Interesting speculation, Officer Smith-Park, but please don't shout," cautioned Captain Taylor. "If the translator ever picked up your vents..."

"Gotcha, Captain."

"While you await an audience with the Fafamafalafama, we could bring you to one of the interior pyramid museums," spoke Wafalawa in his most gentle voice.

"That would be wonderful!" effused Captain Taylor, clapping her hands together. However, just in case "wonderful" did not compute for the translator, she more disinterestedly paraphrased, "That is a very good idea."

"We understand," Wafalawa nodded while Nanofafo cut loose with "Hee-hee!"

"But something before we go to the museum," said Captain Taylor plastering her face with a nonstop smile, wishing she could avoid the uncomfortable topic she inevitably needed to raise. "Is there a place we can urinate and defecate, then eat what we brought in our envirosuits?"

Wafalawa and Nanofafo exchanged puzzled looks, gave Captain Taylor a puzzled look, and exchanged puzzled looks again.

Helena didn't notice the translator leaving any gaps in what she said. So she braced for perplexity turning bristly defensive as she added, "We can use our envirosuits for urinating and defecating." *Maybe I should have had Chris or Buddy do the honors instead. For all we know, these creatures find female discussion of such matters highly offensive.*

"We assumed you slept before this visit," said Wafalawa, oozing bafflement.

"Of course," the captain confirmed, also oozing bafflement.

"So your urinary and intestinal cycles were completed, no?"

"Captain," cautioned Magabu back aboard the Smoke and Mirrors, "I think you're talking past each other, truly. Somehow, they must take care of such bodily functions in their sleep." Ali gave chief medical office Davis-Murphy a sidelong glance, wondering whether his admittedly weird conclusion had occurred to her.

"Ohhh," said Captain Taylor as the import dawned on her, at the same time Wafalawa and Nanofafo "Ahhed" at each other.

"Your urinary and intestinal systems operate at random intervals, the same as those of our crash-landed extraterrestrials, yes?" fah-lah-lahed Wafalawa.

"And your urinary and intestinal systems, um…" Captain Taylor ground to a halt. She was suppressing a rare mischievous impulse to say: *What, you guys soil your beds every night, err, every blinding-light?* She went on finally, "Can you tell us how *your* systems operate?"

"I think the best plan is our original plan." With this non-sequitur response, Wafalawa slowly bared his teeth like Chris once saw a chimpanzee do at the zoo. "Use your envirosuits if you must," Wafalawa went on, at least as expressed by the translator. "But you will each receive a (gap). Choose for yourselves how to evacuate your bladders and bowels while we leave you resting until stars-fade."

Captain Taylor found herself mysteriously struck by a most peculiar notion. *The Fafamans are treating their itinerary for us as inflexibly as were it an exacting recipe for some special gourmet dish.* A most peculiar notion, indeed, but at least she wasn't suffering another of those unsettlingly chronic headaches. *Maybe the Fafaman air is actually doing me some good?*

The smooth monorail ride blurred whatever dimly-lit features along the way for Helena and company. But then it stopped deep inside the pyramid, and they experienced the last thing any of them expected.

Exiting the monorail, for fleeting moments they couldn't help the impression they were stepping out into a starlit night. Only after focusing on a particular "constellation" did Helena, Chris, and Buddy realize teensy light bulbs had been artfully wired onto trestlework support beams across the cathedral ceiling.

Of course, the illusion of expansive outdoors must be meant to take a little edge off these filing cabinet living quarters, Chris thought to himself.

A key opened the door to the away team's designated filing cabinet drawer, as Chris might have put it.

Inside, a centrally located television could have been a religious shrine, Chris mused. Not untypical back on Earth, but its knobs glowed with that pervasive green fluorescence. And when Nanofafo surfed the variety of programming available, images proved uniformly difficult to discern for Earthlings. Chris was reminded of century-old black-and-white horror films, people chased down dark corridors by some evil force. At times, he couldn't make out much detail in those, either, especially if he was watching in a brightly-lit room. *Guess this is to be expected of television for nocturnal creatures.*

A sofa and chairs glowed faintly as well. Foamy material, well-rounded arms and backrests, no legs...on Earth they could have passed for beanbag furniture. Chris wondered: Were Fafamans prone to stumbling over things in the dark, despite their nocturnal nature? Did they learn the hard way the need for furniture safe from hard edges?

The Fafaman version of a refrigerator proved weirdest of all. From outside, it didn't appear too different from an Earth refrigerator. However, when Wafalawa opened it, a light inside went off rather than going on as normally the case back home. And no Earthling felt any draft especially cooler than room temperature. Moreover, instead of trays and compartments displaying various foods in still-life poses, wire screen mesh predominated.

From a long metal rod, Wafalawa plugged a cord into a wall socket virtually indistinguishable from its Earth counterpart.

That's when noises started to emit from the refrigerator, reminding Buddy of bugs and frogs making mating calls from a swamp at night.

And the screen mesh rattled like something was trying to rip it away, Chris thought.

All three Earthlings stepped back from the refrigerator, unsettled.

Wafalawa, however, exuded nonchalance as he opened a small gate in the mesh to intrude his metal rod. A distinct, electrical buzz culminated in a sharp zap! Then the extraterrestrial withdrew his rod and, continuing nonchalantly, reclosed the mesh gate followed by the refrigerator door.

All manner of squirmy stuff enrobed the metal rod. Chris recalled cotton candy enrobing a paper cone circled inside a cotton-candy-making machine. Only, the cotton candy hadn't been writhing about.

Wafalawa continued to appear engaged in routine behavior when he held the critter-heavy rod over a big bowl. Another zap! and said critters all dropped into the bowl, convulsing once or twice before settling into shock-induced stasis.

Helena thought she recognized a few of the Fafaman life forms from her first encounter with the Fafamafalafama, when he nauseated more than tempted her with them.

Anyhow, Wafalawa picked up one shell-shocked morsel and unceremoniously plopped it in his mouth like he was eating popcorn. On its dying gasp, that hapless critter managed to protrude something out the extraterrestrial's nose that went, "Oooeeeoooeeeoooo!" Might as well have been on a roller coaster ride, where Chris was concerned.

Wafalawa passed the bowl around for any Earthling to sample.

"Pama, but no pama," said Captain Taylor.

"Pama," feebly echoed Chris and Buddy, sheepish over the prospect they might be committing a diplomatic faux-pas.

"We want to try your food," Helena added with unabashed forcefulness, "but we have suffered from strange sinus mucous. And so we seek a better understanding of how our biochemistry interacts with

Fafaman biochemistry before taking such a chance. For now, breathing your air unfiltered is risky enough."

"We would offer you some of the food we brought in our envirosuits," said Buddy Leung providing backup for Helena. "However, on the same basis that we are declining your generosity, for now, we are also refraining from any such offer."

"It is all about keeping everyone safe," concluded Helena.

Despite numerous translation drop-outs, Wafalawa and Nanofafo got the gist. Earthlings were scared of sampling Fafaman delicacies due to strange activity in their sinuses. And for that same reason they didn't want the extraterrestrials sampling Earth food yet, either.

Both Fafamans found the Earthling position perfectly reasonable, having been forced to consider it. But they worried over armed Fafaman security sulking in the wings. No doubt, those guards were wondering how long Earthling males were going to let a female order them around before they took charge like real males, like their Fafamafalafama.

Wafalawa finally reacted, "We say the same on Fafama: Thank you but no thank you. You two, though," he indicated Chris and Buddy, "this is your decision also?"

"We take our orders from Captain Taylor, but we agree with her assessment as I tried to emphasize," spoke Buddy assertively, sensing the chauvinism issue. "On our own we would have made the same decision."

"Yes, we agree," Chris nodded with continued feebleness he could not rise above despite also sensing the chauvinism issue.

Nanofafo had no idea where to go with the Earthling males' clear unwillingness to assert dominion over the female. Therefore, he simply drew the away team's attention to a cloth pyramid centrally located in the temporary accommodations they were being provided. He explained that all *respectable* Fafaman dwellings contained such an object in tribute to the original pyramid that made Fafaman civilization possible.

As Nanofafo explained, the original pyramid used to protect even the most fragile pieces of glassware from destruction by the sunset storm-line. And it lay in tact at the bottom center of the Great Pyramid, forbidden entry by anyone other than the Fafamafalafama.

But back to the cloth pyramid, Nanofafo detailed its practical uses for insomniac Fafamans. The middle of blazing-light, it provided enough shade for writing letters, or composing a poem inspired by the Fafamafalafama.

However odd the entire cloth pyramid thing struck Helena and company, though, was as nothing compared to where Fafamans retired for sleep, sex, and bladder and bowel evacuation.

"This dwelling conveniently contains four tralalafas, one for each of you with one left over," said Wafalawa, gesturing towards the extraterrestrial plants.

Four holes in the cement floor were colorfully rimmed by ceramic-glazed decorative tiles glowing pale lavender. A squat smooth-barked trunk grew from each hole, topped by an enormous olive-green leaf thicker than the thickest bed comforter Chris had ever seen.

"We have a word for the special relationship between people and tralalafas," Wafalawa continued. "Other plants and animals enjoy a similar interdependency that has origins, we believe, in the first sunset-storm lines of fifty million solar orbits ago. Plants give off oxygen we need for breathing, and we respire carbon dioxide they need for photosynthesis. But this special relationship (gap, but the away team were certain the words not translated constituted an expression meaning, "goes farther")."

"On Earth, we call such a relationship symbiosis," said Buddy. "We have flying animals named birds that eat particles on the teeth of meat-eating animals named crocodiles. Because the birds clean crocodile teeth, the crocodiles are not eating the birds."

"Here on Fafama, the name of this relationship is mamapapa."

"Mamapapa?" burst out Helena, Chris and Buddy, all at the same time.

The translator provided Fafaman for "Mother" and "Father," leading Wafalawa to a nod of dawning realization. "Ahh," he said, "so this is why the 'mama' is not eating the 'papa'! Hee-hee-hee!" More somberly he went on, "At sunrise, what we term stars-fade, many animals crawl for safety into the center of spread-open plants. While blazing-light blinds the land, those plants curl protectively closed around them.

"Other animals, the flounder mouse in particular, remain half-buried in the soil. Shortly before the next storm-line, though, they completely submerge themselves. And at stars-out once the storm-line has passed through, they resurface shedding light generated by solar energy collected during the day.

"Flounder mouse light is absorbed by the ferny fronds of plants like those planted aboard the space station. Those plants and the others unfurl open only at night, when the others let go various creatures that slept in them during blazing-light. Of course, those other plants always benefit from absorption of wastes excreted by their furry occupants.

"Tralalafas have evolved specifically favoring people," Wafalawa continued further. "If a creature other than a person tries entering a tralalafa, it releases a fume no animals besides us can tolerate, and the intruder leaves quickly. And plants adapted to other animals spray an awful fume that chases away people who mistakenly seek refuge in them.

"The most dangerous plants imitate the tralalafa and other such plants in appearance, but are really different. We call them trap plants, and they enjoy relationships with some of the most dangerous animals on our planet. The creature named the 'ahaha,' for example, camouflages to look like one of its selected trap plant's leaves. When an animal becomes tightly enrobed by that trap plant at stars-fade, imagine its horror as digestive juices secreted by the 'ahaha' quickly burn into its flesh. Usually the 'ahaha' and host have finished sharing their meal long before the sunset storm-line arrives.

"Walk in a forest close to stars-fade, and you will hear the muffled cry of some hapless creature that accidentally took refuge inside a trap plant."

"If one of you wants to sit there..." Nanofafo gestured towards one of the unfurled tralalafa leaves.

That's when Captain Taylor realized she had seen these things before, in their uprooted, bundled-up state. Two of Mr. Fafamafa-whatever's entourage carried them behind him on their stately procession out of the shuttle blade into the space station. Or maybe those were manufactured imitations inspired by the real thing.

"Hey, Chris, why don't you volunteer, and go take a poop in that thing? Yow!" Kevin intruded from back aboard the Smoke and Mirrors.

Acutely sensing Earthling reluctance to give the tralalafa a try, Nanafafo nervously stroked a whisker and added, "We know you are not used to execrating in your sleep like us. For you, execration is a voluntary function, not an involuntary function. But if you still would like to give the tralalafa a chance, remove all clothing from relevant body parts. Otherwise, please feel free to employ the execratory function you mentioned your envirosuit having."

"Should your envirosuits be good for resting as well, please also feel free to place them on the floor beside the tralalafas," added Wafalawa, anxious over the developing awkwardness. "We promise they will not disturb you."

"Um, when people, uh, when you execrate inside a tralalafa," Chris hesitantly forced himself to say, "you use something to, uh, clean where your, uh, execration, uh, exits?"

"After millions of solar orbits, evolution has resulted in the tralalafa absorbing every speck, every last drop of solid and liquid excrement."

"Well, maybe I will not avail myself of that particular, uh, function. However…"

Wafalawa and Nanofafo showered Chris with encouragement after he removed his magboots for approaching a tralalafa.

"Just try it for a 'nininana,'" suggested Nanofafo, his long whiskers a-twirl with anticipation.

"Just one 'nininana,'" chimed in Wafalawa. "Here, allow me to tie this end of a string to your finger. The other end is tied to artificial blinding-light controls. You can tug on it at any time to switch back to artificial stars-out, and the tralalafa will automatically unfurl."

There were no surprises when Chris lay down on the tralalafa. Wafalawa turned a knob on one wall, and bright light flared out of recessed ceiling bulbs. Pursuant to which, the three tralalafas curled into shapes suggestive they were all packed full of something, not just the one Chris chose.

Helena found herself reminded of pale green magnolia blossoms on the verge of blooming. Only, those blossoms would have had to have been the size of canoes.

"It's actually quite cozy and restfully comfortable in here," Chris commented before tugging on the string to activate light-fade and thereby unfurl his tralalafa.

Translation of the one word, "comfortable," was all the extraterrestrials needed to nod knowingly. Wafalawa commented, "The result of millions of solar orbits of evolved adaptation."

Forthwith the extraterrestrials left the Earthlings alone to do as they chose, provided they remained within dwelling confines. About five nanas from then, what equated to five-and-a-half hours, they would be brought to the Fafamafalafama for a parade followed by completion of their mission, hopefully.

"The crash survivors are on your stars-out sleep schedule, and the Fafamafalafama and his assistants are working a long day to accommodate you," were Nanofafo's last words before the Fafamans parted.

Captain and crew gathered this was his diplomatic way of saying: *Don't even think of proposing any least change to the schedule we have planned. We could have taken you to a pyramid museum, but your request for a place to eat and rest only reconfirmed the wisdom of our original decisions.*

"Clearly," commented Captain Helena Taylor after the extraterrestrials left, "this would not be my first choice, to cool our heels before we can do what we came here for. But let's regard this as part of a recipe for success; we're at the step where we have to be marinated in Fafaman atmosphere for so long before we'll be ready to be cooked." Helena shook her head. "I don't know where that metaphor comes from. Maybe something in the Fafaman air is getting to me."

"A truly odd comparison indeed, Captain," said Ali from aboard the Smoke and Mirrors. "However, allow me to extend it a bit further as a caveat. The likelihood seems strong to me, that the tralalafa's utility has been completely explicated, nothing left out. On the small chance, though, there is something sinister afoot, that we are being bamboozled, I would suggest not using those fascinating plants for the time being. Two hours from now, we wouldn't want to find out they've begun digesting you along with your excrement, like the monster version of a Venus flytrap.

"Besides, there's also the small possibility of some adverse reaction unanticipated by our Fafaman hosts. They have already shown themselves blissfully unconcerned about the possibility of unfortunate exo-biochemical reactions, even in the face of their unpleasant encounter with tooting elastic mucous. For example, Chris, how were they to know the tralalafa wouldn't release its stink on you? They made a truly breath-taking assumption, that the plant would be able to mistake you for a Fafaman primate despite your other-world biology."

"This small chance we're talking about, Dr. Magabu," Captain Taylor said worriedly, Ali Magabu having played to her worst fears. "When you use the term, 'bamboozled,' are you not entirely certain other extraterrestrials have crash-landed here? That it might be a ruse broadcast across the universe like a piece of deceptive junk mail?"

"Highly unlikely, Captain," Ali responded without hesitation. "But not impossible. There is another question I'm now thinking should have received far more attention from me, truly. How are these ruling elite of Fafama handling their realization of our significant technological superiority? Clearly they have been made so insecure, they are trying in ways both big and small to send us the message: *We have our pride. You are not going to push* us around, just because you can cheat the speed of light. Yes, we are the ones who called out for help. However, if we decide to make you wait on us for whatever amount of time, we will, and you can do absolutely nothing to stop that."

Chapter 12

"The Fafamafalafama will not permit one-on-one communication with you until after the parade," Wafalawa announced to the Earthlings before he left them alone on a privileged review-stand perch.

When not in use, bleachers and review stand alike were retracted into the northeast face, protected from the sunset storm-line's daily ravages by a metallic shield.

We should be bundled up in big black furry parkas, Chris mused. *Then we could mimic Stalin and his gang in the U.S.S.R. over a century ago, waiting on an arms parade.*

Chris, Helena and Buddy found their selves loftily seated four stories up the northeast-facing side of the city-sized pyramid, enjoying unobstructed vistas.

The intensifying glow of approaching sunrise, what Fafamans termed stars-fade, shed light on a road system woven across flat terrain. A surprisingly elaborate road system given the storm-line's daily assault, the Earthlings thought initially. But further scrutiny quickly revealed what made such a system usably maintainable, if still surprising. All streets were lined with the same ferny trees curled by sunlight into so many olive question marks aboard the Fafaman space station.

"Of course!" Buddy exclaimed. "Their plants keep enough storm-blown dirt and debris off their roads for street-sweeping machines to do the rest."

"Maybe they don't even bother with street sweeping. You see the front of their roadsters?" asked Chris, pointing.

"Those look like... What were they called on antique trains?"

"Cowcatchers, Captain." Buddy had already been wracking his memory for the term. "I see debris buildup down the center, like snow on the road back home where traffic hasn't yet melted it away. But how about that: they drive on the right side."

"Assuming those aren't giant beetles crawling well-worn paths," cautioned Chris. Yes, he did label them "roadsters" initially. But since their bodies concealed any wheels, and whatever they were burning for fuel didn't leave visible exhaust out the rear...

"Giant beetles that evolved cowcatchers? Definitely not," said Buddy. "People are emptying out of one parked at a mini-pyramid."

"I see," said Chris. "And appears they're sheltering it in advance of the next sunset storm-line."

"Oh, yeah," Buddy nodded.

Someone was tossing a dark-olive tarp atop the pastel-purple vehicle that oddly did look like a monster beetle outfitted with a cowcatcher.

Chris was reminded of an experienced fisherperson casting a net. But the tarp was tied to hooks cemented into the driveway.

"Wo!" Chris couldn't help emoting when his attention strayed up a hill just past the suburb of small pyramids. There, a ferny tree rivaling a typical California redwood's height curled up while at its base, green fluorescence faded to sandy brown. *Did a flounder-mouse colony just switch from light shedding to light absorption mode, in advance of full sun? Or was that some single, half-buried monstrosity? And does it matter either way, if the Fafamans keep jerking us around?*

Chris's thoughts anxiously returned to Wafalawa's parting remark before he left Captain Taylor and company alone in their privileged seats. Again,

Wafalawa advised them the Fafamafalafama would allow no direct conversation until after the parade. In other words, the Fafamans were dictating the terms for a second close encounter with their leadership.

Ali Magabu believed that such controlling behavior was how these other-world creatures handled their insecurity over dealing with extraterrestrials of clear technological superiority. Assuming this the case, Chris wondered worriedly, what next?

Suppose Captain Taylor abruptly announced she'd had enough, that the Fafamans needed to return her and her away team to the Smoke and Mirrors pronto. Would the Fafamans immediately oblige, and fire up their shuttle blade? Or would they say in effect: *You will leave when we decide you can leave*, and then hold the away team hostage until certain demands were met? In other words, were the Earthlings being victimized by an extortion scheme? What's more, without any weapons to threaten military action, how could the Smoke and Mirrors crew respond effectively?

Chris's apprehensions were only heightened by ensuing events.

Below the review stand, bleachers filled with several people escorted by armed guards. Were they compelled to drop whatever they were doing to attend?

Review stand seats above and behind the Earthlings were also filling up, presumably with dignitaries and the like who knew better than to await being forced to attend.

Once the place was packed, trumpet fanfare emitted from an unseen location, quieting the hum of fah-lah-lahs. That's when the Fafamafalafama rose out of the floor of a special box seat down front of the Earthlings. He rose on a circular dais, attired in a rose bloom's worth of flowing robes.

Shine a laser on the Fafama-whatever out in weightless space, Chris mused. Then watch him shoot off at some significant fraction of light-speed like the Smoke and Mirrors, impelled by photons pushing against his regal wear.

Encroaching sunlight all but washed out the faint glow from the Fafaman ruler's robes. Nevertheless, thousands of Fafamans rose to their feet, holding their arms high in an encircling gesture.

The Earthlings concluded they'd better join in. For Fafaman society, clearly, the Fafamafalafama was the Ultimate Flounder Mouse, the go-between from Alpha Centauri 3 to Fafama. He provided warmth and energy in comforting fashion, neither searing nor blinding. He was their moon, their son of their sun reflecting its brilliance in soothing form.

With flowing extravagance, the Fafamafalafama unsheathed his sword and lifted it pointing skyward.

Chris couldn't help imagining the fellow had whipped out part of his anatomy instead, assuming Fafamans were so endowed.

The extraterrestrial ruler slowly turned around until he went full circle, until he'd directed his weapon everyone's way. His shaded goggles kept the Earthlings from ever telling whether he made eye contact. But he did temporarily lower his sword to roughly a forty-five-degree angle as he slowly yet steadily swept it past them.

Chris tormented himself wondering: Did he lower the sword to honor their presence? Or...was this his imagination, or did he lower it just for Helena? And was that pursed-lip smile for all of them, or only for her?

His sword ritual completed, the Fafamafalafama paused.

The ensuing quiet enabled Chris hearing another protective tarp being slapped down over another distant beetle-shaped vehicle,

and the Fafamafalafama's sniffle.

Oh-oh thought Buddy and Chris, their memory still fresh of gooey elastic mucous. On their second visit to the Fafaman space station, it had played peekaboo out their nose and ears, followed by a "Ta-da!" expiring leap.

The Fafamans' own strange nasal discharge had gone "Toot! Toot!" instead of "Wank! Wank!" And it had shaded purple instead of green. But clearly it had proven every bit as embarrassing and uncomfortable.

Were those same exo-biochemical interactions about to afflict the Fafamafalafama, leading to his public humiliation in a most grandiose setting?

They were not, thanks to his quick reflexes. And thanks also to Wafalawa and Nanafafo giving advance warning, Chris figured.

With the first trumpet-shaped protrusion of purple mucous out his royal left nostril, the Fafamafalafama grabbed hold tight. "Toot-ow!" rather than toot-toot went the mucous, yanked completely from his sinuses. Slashed into several short strips with a blur of swordplay, it fluttered harmlessly floor-ward like so much tossed confetti.

Fafamans jumped up and down to show their approval. They made the chairs shake where the Earthlings sat, like there was an earthquake. That was, until the Fafamafalafama raised his sword pointing skyward again. This settled the crowd instantly, to raise their hands in mimicry. Then the Fafamafalafama swung down his sword at a diagonal with such speed that the Earthlings could hear its swish! He could have been chopping off someone's head instead of slashing air, Chris thought with a shiver.

Fafamans collectively lowered their hands, and waited dead quietly.

A second trumpet fanfare prolonged the crowd's silence, thereby ramping up suspense.

Only then did Buddy realize not even a bird tweet was to be heard. He wondered whether sunset storm-line regularity suppressed flying creature evolution. Although where certain bugs were concerned, the slightly lower gravity compared to Earth's...

Finally the Earthlings heard creaky grating, what Buddy concluded was a huge rock moving, grinding against another huge rock.

At first the Earthlings couldn't tell from where the harsh noise emanated. But then they noticed a slit developing at one end of the empty boulevard they faced.

Dark asphalt was lifting like a drawbridge, opening for a ramp from underground.

Syncopated drumming echoed from deep below. Louder and louder it grew, gradually less echoed, until percussionists emerged off-ramp onto the boulevard. With sticks and mallets, they beat on drums of various sizes and shapes.

The five Fafamans who emerged next were playing a march on electric guitars wired to amplifiers nestled on their heads.

During pauses after every six-note phrase on guitars, the percussionists played a special off-kilter rhythm.

"This place rocks, apparently," commented Chris, not worried how his remark might translate in Fafaman. He trusted the amplified din to drown out his device for anyone not seated beside him.

Soon, thunderous noises from deep belowground were competing with the drums and guitars; Chris imagined very, very heavy vehicles rolling along ponderously.

But after the guitarists came Fafaman women marching and pausing to the syncopated beat. On each guitar pause for the off-kilter percussion fill, they struck provocative poses somehow reminiscent for the Earthlings of models on a Parisian fashion-show runway, their clothing skimpily revealing.

Chris was especially struck by the lead marcher. From his four-stories-up distance, he could not see her nocturnally adapted eyes thanks to her protective goggles for dealing with daylight. But he could easily imagine their oversized nature making her beauty all the more striking.

Plus there was something else for Chris to wonder about, something else to torture himself over like when the Fafawazoo dipped his sword Helena's direction. The pose struck by the lead marcher on her pause before the review stand: Was Chris's imagination playing tricks, or did she crane her head ever-so-slightly forward? And if the latter, was she attempting eye contact enhanced by her smile of the flirtatious sort?

"Nanawa habba-habbasa," said the Fafamafalafama after he turned his head half way around, giving the Earthlings his profile. Was he making sure his words would reach their translators?

But at least the Fafamafalafama didn't turn all the way around, Chris thought with relief. He wasn't going to get in Chris's face and menacingly rumble: *What are YOU looking at?!?! Better not be leering at our women!!*

"My wives," crackled Captain Helena Taylor's device strapped to her belt.

Darting looks at Chris and Buddy either side of her, Helena asked, "Did I hear...?"

"'My wives,' Captain," nodded Buddy definitively as in: *No question about it.*

Chris stifled an urge to say: *I hope you're not jealous.*

Meanwhile the subterranean thunder grew deafening loud, its source ponderously rolling up the ramp.

Chris recalled his earlier thought that he might as well have been joining Joseph Stalin or Adolph Hitler for reviewing a military parade.

Tanks shaped like behemoth snail shells rumbled forward with their treads hidden from view. Unlike the wives, they paused only once, and on that pause turned to face the Fafamafalafama. But neither monster snails nor crabs subsequently poked their heads out from underneath. Rather, what the tilted-up bodies revealed were the enormous muzzles of missile launchers, three each.

The Fafamafalafama greeted this spectacle with additional diagonal slashes of his sword. His blur of motion seen from behind, long robes a-swirl, lent Chris the oddest impression. Namely, that the Fafaman ruler might as well have been trying to fight his way out of the all-embracing beauty of an impossibly huge flower blossom.

Following the Fafamafalafama's swordplay, the launchers were retracted back inside the snail-shell tank bodies, and those bodies returned flush to the ground. Then they all pivoted away from the review stand to rumble off like they'd been vanquished by one male wielding his sword.

Reinforcing such a theme was what transpired with the next vehicles. They emerged from underground in two sets of three, each set including two helicopters and a jet slung between them on thick cables. The helicopters reminded Helena of old military transport copters, while the jets suggested antique stealth bombers because the wings tapered all the way to the nose a la paper planes.

The first set parked just past the review stand, and the second set parked just before.

Helicopter blades began rotating slowly. Then they picked up speed until the copters lifted off towing the jets skyward with them. From a momentary hover the copters quickly initiated forward motion. That is when the jet engines kicked in with shrill howls.

Once the jets were going faster than the copters, all cables disconnected from them, writhing about wildly like four monstrously long flying serpents, Buddy mused. But they couldn't writhe about wildly enough to keep from being rewound inside the copters while both jets accelerated to ever higher speeds.

The jets came together, side-by-side formation, a far distance from the Great Pyramid's northeast face. But they had circled around so they were headed straight back towards the review stand.

With concern that froze them immobile, Helena and company realized the rapidly approaching Fafaman vehicles couldn't have been flying more than two stories off the ground. Their air turbulence shook some of the curled-up ferny trees as though the sunset storm-line were passing through.

Nevertheless, the Fafamafalafama struck a defiant pose with his sword held high. This was the last image Captain and company, and most of the Fafaman audience too for that matter, could handle before instinct had them cower their heads and crouch low.

Deafening noise from the approaching jets more than drowned out the Fafamafalafama's air-slashing swordplay. Indeed, Earthlings and Fafamans alike thought their eardrums might burst, even with hands cupped over ears.

But no consciousness-obliterating crash resulted. Rather, at the last possible moment the jets broke formation to arc steeply skyward, barely avoiding deadly if only glancing sideswipes of the pyramid face.

The crowd stomped their approval as Chris reflected: *So this is their Moses. With his sword, he causes the tanks and jets to part rather than the Red Sea to part with a summons to God.*

"Hey, Captain, that parade down there has been real fun and all, especially... Hey Chris, Officer Olsen-Taylor, you should have held your camcorder high over your forehead. I wanted a better look at those hot Fafaman babes. OW! What I meant was, you should have stuck it where the sun don't shine, so we didn't have to see those ugly bow-w-OW! OW! There's no pleasing you, Yoon-hee!"

"You keep talking like that," Yoon-hee snarled at Kevin, "and there will be no pleasing YOU!"

"As I was saying, Captain," said Kevin, resigned to no more funny stuff so as not to provoke any more ear-twisting from his wife. "We've enjoyed the macho display, but how much more before your hosts finally grant access to the mystery extraterrestrials? Or how much more should we put up with before it's time we just pull the plug and head for home? Or otherwise decide what next?"

"What I'm wondering... perhaps Officer Leung here has an idea," said Helena Taylor, artfully dodging Kevin's question. "Why didn't their jets simply use a runway for takeoff, instead of that whole awkward thing with the helicopters?"

"I'm guessing it has to do with the sunset storm-line, Captain."

As Buddy spoke, Chris thought to himself, *Admittedly, I don't have the guts, or reckless confidence, or whatever, to face down those oncoming jets by swinging a sword at them, and then trusting they can pull away before crashing into me. But if I had half a spine, now would be the time to say: I believe the captain is infatuated with the Fafamazoo. So infatuated, she'd be willing to wait a whole week for an audience with him, especially a private audience.*

"Aircraft runways here would probably have to be too wide and too long for keeping clear of storm-line debris on any regular basis," went on Buddy. "Excepting, of course, the runway designed into the pyramid; that ought to be plenty long and wide enough for jet liftoff and landing. It's sure large enough for the shuttle blade. Hmm… Maybe they were putting on a show."

Kevin wanted to reiterate his still unanswered questions. But before he could, next up in the military parade drew all attention.

Ferny trees appeared wrapped into balls the size of giant boulders. They reminded Chris of tumbleweeds he'd seen in a travel film about the desert southwest. But they emitted another ponderous mechanical noise similar to that from the snail-shaped tanks. And they rolled up-ramp out from beneath the boulevard with no wind to blow them along. *However they move is cleverly concealed,* Chris concluded.

Buddy wondered why one ball followed so closely behind another ball that it seemed to be nudging that ball along. But the other balls quickly distracted him from this puzzle. Soon as they rolled to a halt before the review stand, they uncurled open thanks to petals of bolted metal.

Four armed troops stood ready for action at center of each "bloom." They leapt out and turned to face the Fafamafalafama, who greeted them with yet more diagonal sword slashings. However, before the Fafaman ruler's carefully ritualized vanquishing of the foe could be completed, something off-script happened. From the bloomed-open ball that seemed to have been nudging another ball up the ramp, an armed trooper fired into the sky.

Next thing anyone knew, a diaphanously thin yet opaque material hung mid-air, roiled as shapeless as an amoeba, Chris imagined. On its ever-so-slowly drifting, floating descent, Earthlings and Fafamans alike realized it was headed for the one boulder-sized ball that hadn't opened yet. Which was also the same ball seemingly pushed up the ramp by the ball that contained the renegade who unexpectedly shot the thin material skyward in the first place.

Troopers from other balls surrounded the renegade, and trained their weapons on him. But most audience attention focused on the diaphanously thin material casting a dark shadow over the unopened ball.

Once the material descended to within a few feet of blanketing the unopened ball, the ferny plants of which that ball entirely consisted started unfurling, nothing metallic concealed within.

Several Fafamans went, "Wawa, wawa, wawa, wawawaaaaa!"

"Captain! You see that?!" Buddy pointed.

Two long, jointed, spindly legs were emerging from amidst ferny tendrils. Before Helena and Chris could focus on them, however, they were blanketed by the diaphanously thin material finally touching down.

The spindly legs' owner was not to remain concealed. It hopped out from underneath the blanketing material in a manner that launched said material skyward again, albeit for a much shorter descent.

Thereby did Helena and company behold a cow-sized spider the appearance of a behemoth black widow thanks to its bulbous rear abdomen gleaming ebony.

"Fafama's lower gravity, just low enough for exoskeletons to grow that large," Buddy said so softly, no one around him could hear. His consuming fascination left him oblivious to the chaos already well in progress.

Security guards seemed to materialize out of nowhere. They hustled away the cowering Fafamafalafama, while the soldier responsible for the diaphanously thin blanket took aim at the review stand and started firing. Cohorts who emerged from the same metallic ball joined in that attack.

Fafaman troops loyal to the Fafamafalafama would have picked off the renegades in seconds, if not for the monster spider. Blinded into a panic by bright early-morning sunlight, its abdomen arched like a threatened scorpion's stinger arching, and sprayed the boulevard with sticky webbing.

While many loyalists found themselves and their weapons entangled by that webbing, non-entangled loyalists ignored the renegades to fire at the monster instead. This sent it scurrying towards the bleachers, already a teeming, screaming, jumbled mess from everyone trying to evacuate simultaneously.

The monster spider sprayed a new stream of webbing it lost no time gathering up by four front legs, to pull stuck Fafamans towards its pincer-parenthesized maw. Persisting panic sped its crushing of skulls followed by the sucking out of body fluids.

Before guards shoved her inside the pyramid, Captain Taylor's last awful view recalled her mother knitting a sweater with the rapidity that came from experience. However, this speedy knitting was done by four spindly legs, gathering up more hapless beings stuck in the randomly aimed, fear-induced webbing.

"I'm guessing their parade was not choreographed to turn out that way," said Ali Magabu, hoping his understatement would help the away team regain their composure. He asked himself, though, whether indulging such a bit of wit wasn't callously tasteless.

"Yeah," nodded Kevin seated beside Ali back aboard the Smoke and Mirrors, "I like how Mr. Fafamazoo faced down ten snail tanks and two fighter jets, but then ran and hid from an oversized spider. You okay, Captain?"

"Officer Smith-Park," said Ali Magabu before Captain Taylor could respond. "Judging from what we see and hear through Chris's camcorder, this might not be an opportune moment to engage the away team in conversation. Truly, they're experiencing a tempest's worth of shouts and screams while being hurried along."

"Bingo," affirmed the captain, as heard through the navigation bridge intercom. Back down on Fafama, she was seeing security forces pull passengers from a monorail car with violent haste, clearing that car for the Fafamafalafama. Those passengers were left strewn across the concrete monorail platform, moaning from sore and broken limbs.

*

"Most esteemed Fafamafalafama, maybe you heard sounds emitting from this during the parade," fah-lah-lahed Wafalawa, pointing at the pocket-sized translator strapped to Captain Taylor's belt.

Captain Taylor sat between Chris and Buddy, facing their extraterrestrial hosts.

"A fluorescent glow manufactured into this device would certainly make it easier to discern," the translator continued as Wafalawa proceeded in his native Fafaman tongue. "Still, it converts our language to their language, and their language to our language. But when lacking sufficient data about a certain word or phrase, it goes silent. And we have to remember that sometimes it can make mistakes. So we should choose our words carefully as always comes easily for you, my glorious Fafamafalafama."

"The translated parts not to your liking, those are the mistakes," said Captain Taylor.

The Fafamafalafama, still breathing heavily from what he knew was a close brush with an attempted assassination, looked from Helena's translator to Wafalawa. Then his gaze wandered towards one of his security guards, standing ready to fire at a sliding entrance door even though the monorail was in motion. After that, his extra-large nocturnal eyes returned to contemplation of the translator. His respiration having finally slowed, he threw back his head to laugh, "Hee-hee-hee-hee-heee!"

"You see, the other two creatures from 'Ahth' have the translator device also," reacted Wafalawa, pointing towards Chris and Buddy's belt-affixed devices.

Captain Taylor wondered whether this small talk about translators was meant to distract her and her fellow away team members. Maybe Wafalawa didn't want them to think about the monorail taking them deeper and deeper into the pyramid, rather than just straddling its perimeter.

"You know I am the Fafamafalafama," said the Fafaman ruler, looking Helena straight in the eye. His protective goggles for blazing light had been long since removed by a security guard. "Now you tell me your names."

"I am Helena Taylor, captain of the faster-than-light space vessel Smoke and Mirrors. This is Officer Olsen-Taylor, our stress management director, and this is Officer Leung, our first engineer."

"'Stress management.' That is such an interesting phrase for your translator to succeed with converting to our language. Officer 'Olsahn-Taylah,' the music you played for us, that is part of your 'stress management,' yes?" asked the Fafamafalafama, tapping his fingertips together underneath his chin.

It was all Chris could do to spit out, "That is part of it, yes." His mind was racing. Why didn't Helena mention he is her husband? Did the Fafa-whatever notice part of her name and part of his name were the same? *Is he contemplating what to do with me, like feed me to that spider monster, so he can add Helena to his wife collection?*

"Wafalawa, get me my own director of 'stress management'! Hee-hee-hee-hee-heee!"

"Say guys, feel free to ignore me, disconnect me," intruded Kevin on the away team's earpieces, straining to remain circumspect. "But, hope I'm helping keep you anchored even when you can't respond. What I want to say is: You have to really wonder about a guy who can laugh like the Fafamazoo, mere minutes after an attempt on his life and- Jesus! We're seeing an enhanced replay of a snippet from Chris's camcorder, showing that monster spider crush someone's head between its pincers!"

"You are not amused?"

The Fafamafalafama's question so startled the captain, Chris, and Buddy, all three shook their heads liked they'd been suddenly roused from deep slumber. Anchor indeed, Kevin's voice had had them longing to grab hold of it like a lifeline pulling them to safety.

Captain Taylor wasn't sure what to make of the Fafamafalafama's question, while her husband found something else to long for on their spiral path deeper inside the city-sized pyramid.

Right after the Fafamafalafama's question intruded abruptly on Kevin's commentary, Chris Olsen-Taylor noticed an apparent multi-story shopping mall. It provided backdrop to a station they passed through without stopping.

Were the monorail to have been travelling at full speed, everything would have been a blur. But coming into the station, deceleration allowed Chris to discern several people waiting on the platform, and storefront windows behind them.

Moreover, neon sign fluorescence, far fainter than any back on Earth, nevertheless highlighted manikins sufficiently for Chris to notice. They were positioned to appear pushing against the storefront windows, from inside of course. Were they supposed to be bracing themselves against the sunset storm-line? Chris wondered.

A Fafaman pondered the display, perhaps also wondering what the manikins were supposed to be doing. What Chris wouldn't have given, to be suddenly miraculously transported into the shoes of that window shopper! To be contemplating potentialities at a safe distance instead of being spirited away heaven-knew-where in the wake of a deadly terrorist attack!

While Chris succumbed to wistful escapism, his captain wife anguished over a response to the Fafamafalafama's question about their not being amused. Did he sense their discomfort over his monkey-like laughter? And the laughter itself, was that an act for testing how honest they would be with him? Maybe he wasn't any more amused than they were? Either way, did he have his own concealed listening device? And through that device, were his servants feeding him translations of what they'd picked up of Kevin's clearly expressed concern?

Helena resolved to sound firm, not the least bit apologetic or hesitant, as she at last said, "We are deeply worried over the deadly event that interrupted your parade. What can you tell us about the people who instigated such an attack?"

The Fafamafalafama narrowed his larger-than-life eyes, or at least larger than Earthling human eyes, to thin slits. Their emanated intensity reminded Chris of alien eyes depicted in an ancient science fiction movie, when lethal rays beamed from them.

"Ask the victims of the attack," the Fafaman ruler's grumbled fah-lah-lahs translated. "Especially ask the victims whose skulls were crushed by the 'ahtpah.' Ask the victims what they think of the attackers.

"The attackers come from the desert to destroy our progress. They hate progress. If their rule had been ascendant, rather than the long line of Fafamafalafamas, sunset storm-lines would still be sweeping us across the land, until we all got swept into the Grand Basin and drowned.

"The attackers are like debris that clogs our streets after each sunset storm-line. If we don't clear it away with our street brushers, vital transportation between fixed living sites becomes impossible! That is why we had to develop our weapons and weapon delivery systems. We need them to keep the desert people from clogging our progress!"

Chris was struck by the odd thought that somehow, what the Fafamafalafama really railed against was death. His simmering rage concerned the inevitability of his own demise, foreshadowed by those first dimly-perceived signs of aging. That's what fueled his vehemence so every utterance seemed nearly the sonic equivalent of those lethal sci-fi-movie eye-beams.

"You have any idea how some of the desert people infiltrated your military?" Captain Taylor asked.

Once the Fafamafalafama heard the translation of Taylor's follow-up question, he nodded. Was it an approving mod for her care terming the military "your" military rather than "the" military? Or was it mere acknowledgment of a legitimate enough inquiry? Captain Taylor couldn't tell, but he did go on to answer, "They are people who claimed they renounced desert life. Why would we not believe them? Anyone from the desert who leaves behind the ways of the 'ahtpah,' we give them the same opportunity as everyone else. They are free to find their place in our society, to enjoy all its blessings. But we have learned from history that we have to be forever vigilant, we have to be forever prepared to fight, with special weapons for our defense. Sometimes a supposed renouncement of future-hating attitudes is really an infiltration to destroy from within."

"So all of those responsible for the attack today originally came from the desert?" asked Chris after Captain Taylor nodded he could "go for it."

"We do not know that yet. There have been occasions when a person's mind has been poisoned by an infiltrator much as though the 'ahtpah' has injected its venom."

*

"I wonder what the real story is on Fafaman insurgents," said Tanya back aboard the Smoke and Mirrors from her second shuttle pod trip to drop off the away team at the Fafaman space station. She was careful to cut out Helena and company, allowing her feed to only reach the Smoke and Mirrors navigation bridge. This, due to fear of Fafaman eavesdropping.

"That's simple," said Kevin, wishing he could blare his response in the Fafaman ruler's face. "They are pure evil who do not respect the Fafamazoo's ability to scare off an army with his slick swordsmanship!"

*

"Permission to speak, Captain," said Buddy. He would have taken Chris's route, and sought the captain's okay nonverbally. But he was growing to suspect that the sooner they built up Helena as their most powerful authority figure, the better.

"Permission granted, Officer Leung." Sensing why Buddy bothered asking her, and convinced that reason made sense, Helena packed all the sternness in her voice she could muster.

The Fafamafalafama made a big production out of looking from Helena to Buddy, then back to Helena. Then with his eyes so wide that his forehead wrinkles multiplied, he gave Chris a penetrating, admonishing glare. Shame on this "Ahth" creature for not first asking his ruler for permission to speak, like this other creature just did!

Buddy would have waited on speaking until the Fafamafalafama broke off glaring at Chris. However, he feared the Fafaman ruler's evident displeasure could turn the corner to perilous obsession if somebody didn't snap him out of it. So he just went ahead, "On our planet, some psychologists think…" Buddy paused to sigh with relief at the Fafamafalafama finally quitting his stare-down of Chris, to focus on himself instead. "On our planet," he started over again, "some people grow up in poverty, and other people grow up in great wealth surrounded by great poverty, like an oasis in a desert. There are people in both groups who come to suspect the great wealth caused the great poverty. That makes a few of those particular people go crazy. Umm, maybe their suspicion feeds on underlying mental problems, so that is why it makes them go crazy.

"Anyhow, they often turn to violence, thinking that can somehow rectify matters. That's not an excuse. Um, that doesn't excuse the awful actions they take. Um..." Buddy was reduced to stammering by intensifying discomfort.

The Fafaman ruler's eyes had narrowed to those piercing slits again, as focused on Buddy presently as they had been focused wide open on Chris.

Buddy concluded he better not go any further addressing the root causes of terrorism.

"Officer Leung correctly describes some thinking about these matters on our planet," stepped in Captain Taylor. "For my own part, I am troubled by the quarantine zones we have set up world-wide, on Earth that is, on our planet. I'm not sure we are not making matters worse, walling off half our population from the rest."

"So you have this same problem on your planet?" asked the Fafamafalafama.

"We have people who believe violence can rectify unjust situations, yes. Again, I fear our quarantine zones constitute an additional form of violence that will incubate even more violence eventually."

"Yes, we must use violence to end this problem," said the Fafamafalafama. He nodded at Buddy and Chris as well as at the captain, suggestive they were all in agreement.

Chris noticed the Fafaman ruler's smile curl the right side of his face only. He had to wonder whether Helena's voice charmed him, amused him like the flounder mouse night glow made Fafama's fernlike trees unfurl.

Helena had to wonder as well, though in a different direction. Did the Fafamafalafama genuinely misconstrue - or get misled by a faulty translation into believing - she advocated violence for dealing with terrorists? Or did he slyly, intentionally twist her remark, henceforth that sly half-grin?

*

"Maybe their terrorists are ticked off at the Fafamazoo for hogging so many wives," said Kevin. "I'd want to ask him myself, 'Hey, Mr. Fafamazoo, how about sharing a few of your hot babes with'- OW!"

"The great Kevinkeveena only gets one wife," said Yoon-hee as she finished twisting Officer Smith-Park's ear.

"Yeah, that's brilliant, guys," grumbled Deborah. "By all means, do keep trying to make our away team bust out laughing during what is obviously a very tricky stage in their discussion."

"Dr. Davis-Murphy," said Ali Magabu, a touch of lecture seeping into his voice, "truly you must be aware that my better half Officer Petrovsky shut off that little buzzing bee we had in the away team's ear."

"And so it's a good habit to get into, Dr. Magabu, ridiculing the extraterrestrial culture, when any time now we may have to reactivate that little buzzing bee? And we're one hundred percent certain they can't eavesdrop on in-ship communication?"

"Don't worry, Deb. With the ear torturer back on patrol, saying anything else outrageous will be too painful," assured Kevin, still favoring where Yoon-hee made her most recent twisting pinch.

*

"On Earth and on Fafama," Captain Taylor meanwhile went on, oblivious of course to the nonsense back aboard ship, "people seek the end of violence."

"The end of the terrorists, yes," nodded the Fafamafalafama, again with his half smile verging on a smirk.

Captain Taylor all the more strongly suspected he was intentionally twisting what she said. He was pretending to a different understanding than what she meant. Was this because he could not bring himself to respect any woman as an authority figure? Even though he was dealing with what he had to know was a clearly technologically superior civilization from another planet?

"I think we share a hope that the people who crashed here- They crashed here, correct?"

"They crashed here, correct, Captain," the Fafamafalafama nodded. "Though assuming the translation is accurate, I must take issue with calling them 'people.' In our pictographs, you noticed the maze of horns that make permanent erections on their heads?"

*

"OW! Hey Yoon-hee," said Kevin, "the World Consortium outlawed pre-emptive tickles years ago!"

Officer Park-Smith kept squeezing and twisting one of her husband's earlobes, heedless of his complaint.

*

"We have similar animals on our planet," Captain Taylor responded to the Fafaman ruler's question. "We have deer, antelope, moose and others with growths on their heads we call antlers. Yes, they do not grow on us, but that is not to say..."

"Our biologists say it was not practical for land-bound animals of this planet to evolve such erections," stated the Fafamafalafama, incidentally grabbing his sheathed sword's jeweled hilt in both hands. "During sunset storm-lines of millennia past, they would not have been able to avoid ripping apart the nomadic plants in which they sought shelter. But sea-bound we have creatures named Faboompa. Male Faboompa horns are used for battle over who will sire the next generation.

"So on your planet as well as on my planet, we have male animals that display immodest, permanently non-deflating erections. But that is not a characteristic of people, any more than it is for people to walk around naked. Yes, the creatures who crashed here from afar wear clothing, and we can see they construct things, even interplanetary vehicles. But we can NOT consider them people," the Fafamafalafama concluded with a diagonal sword slash for extra emphasis. "My science adviser Wafalawa acknowledges this fact, yes, Wafalawa?"

Wafalawa squinted for his most uncomfortable nod in the affirmative.

Captain Helena Taylor wondered whether the Fafaman leader had even the slightest inkling his advisor backed him up only to avoid perhaps fatal trouble for himself, not because he really "knows this fact."

"We earnestly hope," reacted Helena, steeling herself to stay fearlessly on point, "those creatures from another planet will prove not nearly the threat your data presently seems to suggest. Clearly, you already have plenty enough difficulties with the desert people. We-"

"We must also all be clear," interrupted the Fafamafalafama, "that the desert people are people only in the (gap, but Captain Taylor and company confidently assumed he employed some idiomatic version of 'loosest sense'). And of course, I am talking about those desert people who are irreconcilable to our lawful social order. Our best scientists will tell you they are the intermediate forms between people and the chagwa, which are nearly extinct."

"Very interesting," said Captain Taylor agreeably. But she noted Wafalawa again nonverbally assenting to his boss's version of things with about the same enthusiasm of someone experiencing a gun to their head. "Umm, what we want to say is thank you, pama, for the opportunity, your permission to communicate with the horned creatures."

"No," the Fafamafalafama firmly disagreed, sword-slashing diagonally anew. "Your officer here," he went on, pointing at Buddy, "he will be taken for that on his own. Wafalawa, Nanofafo, one of our language specialists, and one of my groups of security guards will accompany him.

"And you, Officer of the name 'Ohlsahn-Taylah,' you will stay in one of my guest units until stars-out. You can sleep in a tralalafa, listen to our music, or watch our television, your choice. At stars-out, my first wife and her security guards will fly you across a special region. There, you can form an opinion regarding one of our most interesting legends.

"And you, 'Cahptahn Taylah' not 'Olsahn-Taylah,' correct?"

The Fafamafalafama's fuss over whether Helena was 'Taylah' or 'Olsahn-Taylah' alerted Chris Olsen-Taylor that he was wrestling with the connection between himself and the captain. Chris could only hope one of the Fafamans' most interesting legends didn't involve hurling one's rival for a mate - in this case another mate for the ruler's harem - out of a plane into the mouth of an active volcano, or some such.

"'Cahptahn Taylah,'" the Fafamafalafama repeated, not waiting for Helena Taylor's response, "we have much to discuss, how we can benefit one another."

"Yes, how our planet can help yours, and your planet can help ours," Helena agreed, though pointedly recasting the Fafaman leader's remark.

"Captain, we have to assume, truly, he is personifying our societies and not referring to only you two," opined Ali Magabu, his gentle voice filling Captain Helena Taylor's earpiece since the "buzzing bee" had been reactivated. Sensing Helena's creeping paranoia, the starship counselor strove to help her stay calm despite his own concern over what the Fafamafalafama was about exactly.

"That, yes," meanwhile said the Fafamafalafama.

Yes, Chris thought to himself on hearing the Fafaman ruler's ambiguous, noncommittal-seeming response to Helena's interpretation of his statement. *He might have time for "that" after he finishes seducing her, to add her to his collection. Have to hope the translator is missing the guy's intent by a light year.*

That infernal translator! We might have been better off not understanding more than what we could draw for each other. Maybe then, we'd already have been meeting those antlered, crash-landed aliens! And Mr. Fafamazoo's effort to entrap Helena would have been shut down before it started!

"Esteemed Fafamafalafama," said Captain Taylor, curling her head in most feline manner as though she were an unfurling Fafaman fern. That was her way of showing respect for Fafaman cultural norms, in hope of appreciation by the Fafamafalafama. "I most sincerely believe that when Officer Leung meets with the antlered creatures, my presence will hasten our civilization's assistance if indeed their fellow beings pose a real threat."

"We have a saying on Fafama, 'Cahptahn.' 'No more for the task than the task requires.'"

"Yeah, except when it's a parade to show off your army and your wives, not necessarily in that order," Kevin scoffed after double-checking his reaction wouldn't reach away team ears. "Then you're okay making everyone cool their heels watching your damned procession."

"Officer Olsen, hand over your camcorder to Officer Leung."

Is that "Please understand" in my wife's eyes? Chris hoped he wasn't imagining Helena's affectionate regard as he detached a tiny camera from his sky-blue uniform's lapel. Where was the additional camcorder to keep an eye on that guy once he got his wife alone to "benefit one another"?

"You are going to have a transmission from that thing back to 'Ahth'?" asked the Fafaman ruler. "Everyone on your planet will see Officer 'Lahhuhng' encounter those other-world animals?"

"Only a few people on our planet Earth know of those, um, animals' existence, and that they are the primary reason for our mission," responded Helena. "But for the time being, not even those few people will be allowed to see what the camcorder films. Access will be limited to a few crew members aboard our spaceship. And as a result of their viewing, each will be assigned a different task. For example, let's assume a camcorder clip features the animals' crashed-vehicle wreckage. One of our engineers will work from that clip to assess their technology. Hopefully she will determine the physics behind how they got all the way here from wherever they came."

The Fafamafalafama displayed his half smile again, leaving the away team to wonder: Did he appreciate Captain Taylor trying to demonstrate respect for the Fafaman expression: no more for the task than the task requires? Or was he merely amused? Whichever, he went on, "In the present situation, assuring your safety will be easier if you are separated than if you all remain together. Not that we are overly concerned, but we assume nothing."

Chris had a creepy feeling the Fafaman ruler's attempt to lessen anxiety was directed more at him and Buddy than at Helena.

"The important thing is that after our visit we can return to our space vessel without incident," Captain Taylor said pointedly.

Chris thought, *at least that doesn't sound like she plans on sticking around, however smitten she might be with this guy. No, stop it with the paranoia!*

"We will act as we must," nodded the Fafamafalafama.

"One false move, and WE will act as WE must," said Kevin, making sure the away team could hear his bluff, and hoping the Fafamans were eavesdropping. "We tell them it's bye-bye for their precious pyramid. And of course, that will be after we take out their jeweled scabbard of a space station as a demonstration shot."

"Sounds like a plan," Captain Taylor responded to both the Fafamafalafama and Kevin. On the Fafaman end, though, her all-purpose utterance was eclipsed by the Fafaman leader suddenly rising from his seat since the monorail noticeably decelerated.

The destination must be upon us, Chris concluded. *For adoring fans awaiting his arrival, maybe the Fafamafalafama needs to pretend having stood defiant, cutting a regal pose, the entire trip. But hmm…*

The monorail made a jolting lurch, hurling the Fafamafalafama forward. He avoided falling flat on his face by grabbing one of the metallic poles that extended from floor to ceiling. But then he unexpectedly grabbed at the next pole, swinging around it to latch back on the first one, which he also swung around to leap mid-aisle, landing in a ready-to-pounce athletic crouch. Two of his security had long since taken up positions, weapons drawn, both fore and aft of where he made those face-saving moves.

"I need to see…no." The Fafamafalafama's glance towards Helena seemed to make all the difference between the meekness with which he fah-lah-lahed that "no," and the spewed rage preceding it.

Chris wondered whether the Fafamafalafama was trying to impress the starship captain by showing self-restraint.

"Tell the engineer I do not need to see him. Yes. Tell him he is experiencing the mercy of the Fafamafalafama."

"Very good," said the guard.

"Okay, as your captain, I have to say something," Helena suddenly blurted out.

Chris could tell from the Fafamafalafama's raised eyebrow that he was thinking: *What's this?* Too, the Fafamafalafama's twitch in one corner of his mouth betrayed a certain glee. *How cute,* Chris imagined him thinking. *This woman from another planet who declares herself "cahptahn," does she really think she can control a situation where **I** am in command?*

"Officer Olsen-Taylor, Officer Leung, at some later time feel free to second guess what I am about to order. No promise I won't eventually second-guess it myself. But for now I ask that we reinstitute the safety protocol, and re-don our envirosuits. Other Fafamans and the, uh, animals who, uh, crash-landed here will soon be exposed to us."

"Of course, Captain," Buddy hurried to assent.

"Probably less cumbersome than continuing to carry them around in our arms," Chris added. He was anxious to join Buddy showing Helena lots of respect.

The Fafaman ruler looked from Chris to Buddy. They could both easily tell he was searching for any least dissenting note on which he could build, to argue with the captain. Not finding it, he merely said, "As you wish," implying the final decision still remained his.

Well, Dr. Magabu thought to himself, eavesdropping from miles in space aboard the Smoke and Mirrors, *now we've got added tension, like there truly wasn't enough *already. But Chris and Buddy uniting behind Helena's order to re-don their envirosuits is a good thing. It puts the Fafaman ruler on notice that while they might acquiesce to his splitting them apart, they aren't going to just roll over and play dead.*

As throngs made two lengthy lines to welcome the Fafaman ruler off the monorail, Buddy Leung wondered how much their enthusiasm was compulsory. And Chris Olsen-Taylor strained to recall what he was reminded of by the prevailing darkness inside the pyramid only minimally mitigated by patches of faint green fluorescence. But watching the Fafamafalafama's greeters unfurl like Fafama's ferny trees as he strode past them, it finally occurred to him. In his dreams, nightmarish dreams especially, everything gradually darkened until he awoke. Everything gradually darkened to what he was presently experiencing. This comparability gave Chris a cruel false expectation beyond conscious control, an expectation he would wake up even as he left the rail car, and beheld the Fafamafalafama's royal palace.

Chapter 13

Buddy Leung could tell the captain and Chris struggled as much as he did, not to treat their forced parting as the last time they might ever see one another alive.

Helena and her husband were to be ushered off with the Fafamafalafama, while Buddy remained aboard the monorail with Wafalawa, Nanofafo, and a security guard. Wafalawa and company were taking Buddy to the hospital caring for antlered creatures supposedly crash-landed from a planet neither Earth nor Fafama.

"However deep inside this pyramid we've gone, here's one good thing anyway," crackled Captain Helena Taylor's voice from both Buddy and Chris's earpiece, Chris standing beside her on the monorail station platform. "Our private line with the ship, and amongst ourselves, hasn't faded noticeably."

"Captain, I'm sure Kevin would have alerted us had there been any signal degradation, noticeable or not," responded Buddy, pointedly weighing in with his own reassurance.

"I'll do my part by trying not to let a tralalafa digest me."

"Shouldn't be hard, Chris," said Kevin from aboard the Smoke and Mirrors. "You're so full of- OW!"

The Fafamafalafama's palace stood recessed way back from the monorail platform, underneath a dramatically vaulted ceiling. Shadows obscured several of the royal residence's architectural details despite ever-present, softly-glowing green fluorescence. But Buddy could easily discern its more impressive features.

From the palace's roof cascaded a twenty-foot-wide waterfall glowing with bioluminescence, and emptying into a narrow moat at ground level. Gargoyle-like projections down the palace face foamed it into an even more turbulent, bounding flow.

Several narrower streams descended diagonal, stepping-stone paths, feeding into the waterfall's upper half from both sides.

Midway down the palace face, diagonal rivulets branched back off, leading to several narrower waterfalls for the final ten feet or so. *Liquid pillars glorifying the Fafamafalafama*, Buddy Leung mused.

Making the biggest impression of all on Buddy was his final look at Helena and Chris as the monorail started transporting him away. They accompanied the Fafamafalafama and his entourage heading directly into the waterfall it seemed, and vanishing there without a splash. *They might as well have become ghosts.*

"An illusion," Wafalawa assured Buddy, knowing exactly what the Earthling thought he saw. The Fafaman adviser draped an elbow over the backrest of Buddy's seat, and propped his chin atop it to continue, "Faced head-on, the waterfall looks like one continuous liquid wall. But inspected more closely from certain angles, you realize it splits into five streams. Those streams alternate between three making a straight descent, and two redirected on short, slanted conduits before they resume the shortest path down. Watch your step over the narrow moat, and you can remain dry on passage between streams."

"What is the significance?" awkwardly laughed Buddy Leung, having just realized how little attention choosing his words required to not stump the translator. Dr. Magabu's synergistic linguistic algorithm had succeeded beyond wildest expectations. Although, Buddy thought on a less jubilant note, too bad the away team didn't bring just a single translator rather than one for each.

Helena and company could have argued the impracticality of splitting apart.

"The central stream represents the virility of the Fafamafalafama. The streams joining it during descent, those are his wives' fertilities infused with his essence. And so of course, the streams that diverge further down represent the resultant new life providing additional pillars for our civilization."

The guard seated beside Wafalawa nodded with an all's-well-with-the-world smile.

Squeamish over what to say about the palace's immense water feature as explained to him, Buddy changed the subject. "Instead of going to the hospital first," he said, "ummm…maybe we should start with an examination of the creatures' space vehicle wreckage. Umm…"

Nanofafo, the tall Fafaman seated facing the Earthling, held up a say-no-more hand. "We understand," he fah-lah-lahed. "But the antlered animals' health is so precarious, we do not know whether they have five 'nininana,' five 'nana,' or five 'nanala' left to live. Meanwhile, the wreckage isn't going anywhere."

The Fafaman linguist Safasafala met Buddy and company at the hospital entrance abuzz with injured Fafamans carried on stretchers off the preceding rail car.

Those Fafamans moaned and groaned, monstrous web strands having tangled them into painfully contorted postures as if their cuts and bruises weren't enough.

Safasafala eschewed any formal greeting as he ushered Officer Leung and company through the front entrance to a closed-off side room. Marble walls either side of the glass door entrance bore large hieroglyphic-type engravings difficult to discern from any distance in the prevailing dim lighting. Appropriately located deep within a massive pyramid, Buddy thought. And they looked far more pictorial than other Fafaman hieroglyph-seeming inscriptions that turned out to be composed of a Fafaman alphabet.

The engravings composed an epic tableau of special fascination to Buddy.

Left of the glass door entrance, straight lines emanated like sun rays from a pharaoh-type figure. More explicitly, a fountain gushed from his- Well this confirmed that Fafaman males shared something most significant in common with Earth males.

Far left of the glass door entrance, various large-eyed figures were depicted doubled over in pain or lying on their backs, hand to head and clear distress carved into their facial expressions. Similarly distraught figures were bathed in the pharaoh-like figure's rays, and rained upon by his bodily fluid.

Right of the entrance, a third set of engraved figures walked away with big smiles on their faces. Obviously the pharaoh-like figure had healed them with his heavenly glow and not-so-heavenly ejaculation.

I suppose this is tolerable enough nonsense, if in exchange the Fafamafalafama allows real doctors to conduct real medicine.

"I've switched off my exterior speaker so they can't hear me," Captain Taylor's voice suddenly crackled from Buddy's earpiece. "Let's check in with each other whenever we have a chance. I'm okay. The Fafamafalafama is talking with the guards, something about how things are going with the injured spectators. But I'm not clear whether he is genuinely concerned or just trying to impress me, because he's raising his voice. Maybe the guard is hard of hearing. Any event, we are riding a roller-coaster-car-type vehicle. That's the only way to describe it. Said they're taking us into the center of a pyramid constructed ages ago. What I'll try to do..." Helena's voice suddenly decayed to silence.

"Chris? Buddy? Anyone?" pleaded Kevin. "Did the captain's voice just drop out? Are the rest of you incommunicado too?"

"I'm still here," Chris responded finally. "Last thing heard from Helena, they're taking her center of the pyramid. Maybe too many walls block her signal from the rest of you, but why did I lose it? I'm deep inside here too; the signal doesn't need travel through nearly as much..."

"I would not panic, Chris, truly not," said Dr. Magabu lathering on the soothing comfort since he sensed husband Chris's deep worry. "Some pyramid layers might be surrounded by special protective material which also incidentally blocks most transmission frequencies. Helena certainly did not sound concerned."

"Sorry, but have to say something about your envirosuit," spit out a digitized voice from Buddy's translator, heard by virtually everyone except Helena.

The crew aboard ship along with Chris fast realized Buddy had opened a line so they could eavesdrop on his conversation with the Fafamans. What they could not know was they were hearing the translation of something from Fafaman linguist Safasafala, upon first meeting Buddy.

"Nanofafo and I were among the first directly exposed to the 'Ahth' people," Wafalawa interrupted Safasafala before he could "say something." "We, and they, experienced bizarre, synergistically mutated mucous secretions. You might have noticed even the Fafamafalafama had to deal with this problem at the 'Pama' Parade."

"We realize concealing ourselves with these awkward outfits detracts from our historic communication," Buddy said, building on Wafalawa's remarks. "But for now, at least, they seem a wise precaution."

Buddy went on to formally greet Safasafala with the Fafaman diagonal arm-slash across his chest.

Safasala kept his arms folded together, far from any attempt to reciprocate with a human handshake. But he did fah-lah-lah, "Yes, those mucous secretions became most animate. But they also proved ultimately innocuous. And I would add that we've witnessed no such synergistic mutations emerging from the crash-landed creatures. Act as you will, but on Fafama we say, 'No more for the task than the task requires,' and in my estimation, the task is not requiring an envirosuit."

"Do what he wants unless he asks to see your undies," suggested Kevin.

"Wish the captain had not gone off like she did so she could weigh in," said Dr. Deborah Davis-Murphy. "It is my considered opinion, Officer Leung, you would be acting recklessly to abide that Fafaman's complaint."

Like Helena had any choice but to be "gone off," Buddy fumed to himself, wondering whether Chris's present circumstances had distracted him from hearing Deborah's complaint.

"Pama, thank you for your understanding," Buddy Leung said to Safasafala as he unzipped and pulled off his flexi-helmet in preparation for removing the rest. He actually agreed with Deborah that this was a reckless action. Who knew what else could be brewing of far greater danger than those dancing boogers, as a result of his continued uncontrolled exposure to Fafaman viruses and bacteria? Given the potential stakes, however, smoothing the diplomatic path far outweighed any personal risk, Buddy decided. "I just have to reattach this translator to my belt...ha!" he let loose with another of his awkward laughs.

With his nocturnally sized eyes, Safasafala eyed the nervous Earthling intensely. And he twirled together his mousey-long whiskers like they constituted a handlebar moustache, Buddy imagined. *This guy might as well be a villain in one of those hundred-forty-year-old, black-and-white silent films, about to tie his captive on railroad tracks.*

"Is the translator still functioning?" Safasafala asked finally in a dubious tone.

"It must be functioning, Safasafala. Otherwise I couldn't answer your question. Ha!" answered Buddy Leung with another awkward laugh.

"Actually, I would like to practice my 'Ahnglahsh,'" reacted Safasafala.

Before the translator kicked in, Buddy heard Safasafala's pronunciation of "English" stand out from the rest of his fah-lah-lahed utterance.

"But I cannot yet convert directly into your language from the language of the crash-landed creatures," the Fafaman linguist continued. "So when we meet with them, I must translate into our language first. Then we will trust your device to produce the 'Ahnglahsh' version from my Fafaman translation."

"Here is a question," went Buddy Leung, trying to sound as matter-of-fact as possible despite his heart pounding. Nervousness over a trust issue he needed to explore was bad enough. But his fear this already testy Fafaman would sense that and take it the wrong way made him even more nervous. No matter that his translator's digital voice expressed everything in monotone, the great leveler. "The people, um, the crash-landed creatures," he toughed out continuing, "maybe they brought a dictionary or some such? Like the text-and-sound dictionaries we supplied you, and your fellow Fafamans supplied us, on our first encounter?"

"Here is their photograph dictionary," fah-lah-lahed Safasafala, holding up a book in the hand not busy twirling his whiskers. "We had to reprint it with our fluorescent lettering so we would not go blind reading in sun glare."

"That is good, because we were thinking something. Our expert linguist, like your own self, is Dr. Ali Magabu. From a copy of that dictionary, in a few hours, uh, make that a few nanas, in two or three nanas Dr. Magabu could program a three-way translator. That translator would handle our language, your language and their language. And so, um, if I could borrow that, I should be back quickly from our spaceship equipped for three-way translations."

Safasafala exchanged looks with Wafalawa and the security guard who accompanied them. Buddy wanted to believe they were considering whether his proposal made any sense. But he fearfully imagined them telepathing each other: *This guy is trying to escape!*

Finally, Safasafala left off from whisker twirling to wave his hand side to side and say, "Too many problems. Most importantly, we are told the crash-landed creatures are in such fragile condition, they might not survive one more complete nana. There is a big possibility you return with your new translator, only to find them dead. No, I have studied their dictionary extensively, and I communicated with them at length. I might already have their answers to many of your questions. Most assuredly my translation service should rival, if not surpass, your imagined three-way device that not yet exists."

"If their health is seriously compromised...If they are dying, we are fully equipped with a health care program built on hundreds of years' research and medical practice," verbally tiptoed Buddy, careful not to simply come out and say Earth's health care probably beats Fafama's health care by several decades. "I am sure we could arrange safe transport to our ship…"

"Such a move would kill the crash-landed creatures in their present state," Safasafala waved dismissively. "And our medical practice also goes back many solar orbits. In short, we have done all we can!"

"I truly fear, Officer Leung, no good will come from pressing them on this point any further," Dr. Magabu gently whispered in Buddy's ear, as transmitted from the Smoke and Mirrors.

"Yeah," Kevin followed not so gently, "I don't know why we don't have them fly us home. They obviously know so much more than we do. Yeah, yeah, Maggybu, I know! Have to be careful not to hurt their freakin' pride!"

Buddy wanted to ask what changed Fafaman minds. They previously said they weren't sure how long the crash-landed creatures would survive. So wherefore this professed near-certainty their demise was imminent? Calming down, though, he realized it could simply be a matter of late-breaking information. "Okay, then let us go," he said resignedly, heart no longer pounding. But he did omit mention that if he came to distrust any part of Safasafala's translation, he would whip out his computerized pictoscreen for some more comic-strip-style communication.

Arriving at the door to where the seriously injured aliens were being treated, Safasafala pointed at the translator attached to Buddy's belt. "Can you lower its volume?" he asked, his fah-lah-lahs produced softly prior to their translation. Though not so softly that his desire proved any less than deafening, to cast aspersions on the translator.

Officer Leung stifled an urge to respond, *Can you also lower your insecure ego's volume while we're at it?* Instead, he adjusted a knob and asked, "How is that?"

"Please turn it off until I can explain its function. Then after reactivation, we must watch that it does not upset the other-world creatures too much in their critical condition." *Such a device invented by me or a fellow Fafaman would have been far superior.*

Buddy experienced entering the hospital room how Chris had experienced entering a guest room in the Fafamafalafama's palace. Scattered, pale-green fluorescence only dimly illuminated the pervasive darkness, replicating Buddy's most eerie dream settings.

Buddy's first look at the two injured aliens sprawled out on tralalafas only added to the eeriness. He guesstimated the aforementioned fluorescence supplied roughly the same illumination as a full moon. In that faint light, the tralalafas appeared as enormous lily pads burdened with deer lying sprawled out across them. Under more conventional circumstances back on Earth, Buddy would have guessed they collapsed there after being hit by a car.

Buddy was reminded of a years-ago, early-morning commute to the Greenbelt, Maryland space center. In predawn darkness, he espied a family of deer standing as motionless as stone statues amidst pine trees off one side of the road. They stayed put, but he had feared they would make a sudden run for it, too sudden to avoid a bloody collision.

Presently, the crash-landed antlered beings from another world were in no condition to suddenly leap out in front of Buddy, if only for their intravenous feeding tubes. And unlike any deer he ever saw on Earth, they wore clothes. Similar to Japanese kimonos, but Buddy had no idea whether those clothes were their own, or patient gowns supplied by the Fafaman hospital.

Whichever, the crash-landed beings were not so preoccupied by injury that they could not notice visitors. Once Safasafala started fah-lah-lahing to the attendant physician, they lifted their antler-burdened heads off their respective tralalafa beds to take a look-see.

Sight of the Fafaman linguist didn't produce any noticeable reaction. But once the crash-landed beings made eye contact with Buddy, they reached for each other's hands or hooves. Or maybe they were articulated hooves, hand-hooves, squeezed together bracing for whatever next. Officer Buddy Leung couldn't tell for sure in the dim green fluorescence. But his heart went out to them all the same.

"Hey guys!" It was Chris through Buddy's earpiece, and over the speaker phone back aboard the Smoke and Mirrors. "Sounds like you're about to meet with those injured ETs from behind door number three, Buddy. Good luck with that! And I'm sure the rest of you are doing everything possible to re-establish communication with Helena. Just wanted to let you know I'm okay, then shut up so you can focus on those higher priorities. They have me where there's this large cylindrical hole in the wall that conveys air directly from outside the pyramid so that, um... They said if I want to experience the fury of the sunset storm-line while enfolded by a tralalafa..."

"We're going to collect on that shut-up offer, Officer Olsen-Taylor," said Kevin. "You can let us know later, if surfing the storm-line inside a tralalafa is any better than a roller coaster ride."

With the flick of a switch, instead of Chris's voice, Kevin and company were hearing a sequence of tongue-clicks that reminded Ali Magabu of Morse Code. Those sounds were limited to ticks and tocks.

Buddy had had no problem ignoring Chris's intrusion, about not wanting to be intrusive, like it were so much background static. He cared profoundly about his friend staying safe, and returning to the ship fast as possible. But he could hardly give a second thought to seeing his wife again, let alone Chris. That is, until he better understood what was going on with the crash-landed creatures. Ideally, Buddy Leung would learn they were NOT sounding the alarm for an imminent invasion of apocalyptically dire import. There had simply been a huge misunderstanding.

Officer Buddy Leung met Safasafala's gesture for him to reactivate the translator with a simple, earnest, "Pama," thank you in Fafaman.

Buddy could have gotten confrontational, saying he reserved the right to reactivate his pictograph and cut out Safasafala as the middle man at any point felt necessary. He also could have lectured Safasafala about hogging the antlered creatures' dictionary rather than sharing it with fellow Earthling Ali Magabu. How many critical insights were thereby being lost?

For the time being, though, Buddy just wanted to quiz the purportedly other-world creatures quickly as possible. Again, with any luck at all he would learn no outer space invasion was on the horizon. Safasafala got the message all wrong, hopefully not intentionally.

But Safasafala wasn't finished testing Buddy's patience yet, not by a long shot. Next on the Fafaman linguist's agenda, prior to direct communication with the crash-landed creatures, was an introduction to the attending physician, Mafakakala. Mafakakala droned on about concocting "the perfect nutrient drink for these other-world animals" after confirming they were carbon-based life forms. He stirred together water and electrolyte fluid with a liquefied portion of the antlered creatures' food supply not ruined in their space vehicle crash. "We have done all for their survival anyone could possibly do," his concluding remark translated.

Officer Leung figured Safasafala told the Fafaman doctor this arrogant Earth creature boasted to disgusting excess. That he claimed his crew would have worked medical wonders if only the Fafamans had turned over the crash-landed creatures to them.

Anyhow, incidentally continuing to postpone Buddy's encounter with the crash-landed creatures, Safasafala said, "When we speak with them, you should notice something immediately. Their language consists of two sounds, 'tick' and 'tock,' a binary communication system unlike any spoken on Fafama."

"Also unlike any language on our planet I'm aware of, except for computer language, plus something with dots and dashes we used a long time ago called Morse Code."

"Fafaman computers also depend on binary code," Safasafala nodded. "But they do not make binary noises like these creatures do when, for example, they call their home planet Tictoctic which means 'father.' Mother for them is Toctictoc, by the way."

"Might as well be yinyangyin and yangyinyang, like men are imbalanced one direction and women the other," said Kevin back aboard the Smoke and Mirrors.

"You shouldn't read too much into so little information, Officer Smith-Park," cautioned Dr. Magabu standing beside him. "But that is a truly fascinating... One might hypothesize the antlered creatures' language system somehow welled from their male/female chromosome markers and/or neuron synapse operation. Or perhaps even from the negative and positive charge nature of electrons and protons."

Magabu came through loud and clear in Buddy's earpiece. But Buddy was too caught up in his own thoughts to be bothered. He said to Safasafala, "Our planet's name, Earth, refers to its soil we can gather in our hands. But throughout our history, many of us have also called our home planet Mother Earth. A long, long time ago, in fact, some of our people named it an all-powerful woman, Gaia."

"Yes."

Buddy knew he shouldn't read too much into Safasafala's minimal response. But he couldn't help sensing arrogant dismissiveness.

"These pathetic animals," Safasafala waved towards the tralalafa-ridden creatures, "they admitted their vehicle was not designed for dealing with gravitational pull. Still, they thought it could glide in spiral descent all the way ground-ward for safe landing, not unlike our shuttle blade..."

"And similar to our space shuttle of a long time past..."

"Yes," nodded Safasafala.

More dismissiveness, Buddy felt certain.

"But they really had no idea what they were doing," the Fafaman linguist went on. "Our telemetry data indicates they entered our atmosphere at too sharp an angle. Is a wonder their craft did not burn up altogether before crashing, let alone luck onto a landing area soft enough for survivable impact. Wreckage inspection revealed how woefully unequipped they were for a spiral descent on minimal power. Our shuttle blade, of course, is a very different story, as you must know from your own experience landing inside the Great Pyramid." *You see, Fafaman technology is superior.*

Officer Leung might have further indulged his irritation over Safasafala's incorrigible arrogance, if not for his heart going out anew to the injured creatures. Throughout Safasafala and Mafakakala's pontifications, they kept shifting attention from themselves to their visitors. Worry-laden loving looks for each other alternated with plainly anxious regard for their visitors. And frequent wincing suggested they were dealing with numerous bouts of pain.

Buddy tried to convey his most sympathetic regard with blinking eyes, tilted head, and wistful smile.

No good. Pursuant to Buddy's nonverbal efforts, the purportedly crash- landed creatures were becoming more agitated, writhing about restlessly. They even accidentally bumped their antlers together with a clunk!

Officer Leung had to wonder if he hadn't unwittingly produced the Tictoctic facial expression for, "You're dead meat," or something equally cruel. But more likely, their evident distress had nothing to do with him.

Safasafala was not oblivious to the two hospitalized creatures' change of behavior. He engaged them with a flurry of tick-tocks which sounded by turns reassuring and inquisitive. Then Buddy's translator caught him saying to Mafakakala, "You can increase the painkiller dosage?"

"More hemorrhaging is only going to hasten their deaths. And that's what too much jamamba might cause. They could enter a coma in niniwahininana of administration."

"But at least then they will be out of pain."

"Wait," said Buddy, holding up a hand. "Aboard ship we have recently-developed medical technology which dramatically reduces internal injury bleeding. It even neatly walls off aneurisms. And whether you want to accept this help or not, I need your other-world patients conscious for at least a few minutes more so I can ask them-"

"We have performed surgery on them five times already," interrupted Mafakakala, "incorporating our very latest medical technology."

"What other questions about them might you want answered before we leave them alone to heal?" asked Safasafala, resuming whisker twirls.

The inventor of mirror-array light-propulsion technology could have burst into a rage. Wasn't it enough power trip for this guy, being the translator on whom both sides had to depend for communication? Did he really need to stave off direct questioning with this excuse that the crash-landed creatures needed time "alone to heal"? *Time alone to die is more like it!*

"Hey Buddy," Kevin's voice in his ear, "now you wish we had weaponed up so we wouldn't have to take this Fafaman moose crap?"

Actually, Buddy wished Wafalawa or Nanofafo were in the room so he could appeal for intervention. They had seemed less set on proving Fafaman superiority.

"We keep these beasts in permanent stars-out," Mafakakala explained, presumably answering one of Buddy's other questions. "When we first started to extinguish room darkness, the enfolding tralalafas sent their blood pressures and pulse rates soaring dangerously high."

And so, Buddy had to bite his tongue to keep from shouting, *that's everything else I need to know about these "beasts"?* Instead he bluntly asked Safasafala, "Did they answer your questions willingly? Or were threats necessary?"

"These beasts cooperated fully. They said everything they had to say, we have assessed," Safasafala nodded, eyeing Buddy suspiciously as he continued twirling his overly long whiskers.

"So if they cooperated, were they here, um, why did they say they were here? Were they the advance scouts for the invasion? Or were they acting on their own to warn you what was coming?"

"I repeat: They cooperated with us fully."

"So they WERE acting on their own to warn you?"

"We have to assume they were advance scouts, and we disrupted their plans."

"Wait," said Buddy holding up his hand again, in an effort to forestall Doctor Mafakakala administering more pain-killer to the crash-landed creatures. He didn't care whether it was the higher dosage Safasafala recommended, or not.

Coincidentally, said creatures appeared to have settled down. And they were following the back-and-forth of conversation with considerable curiosity even though they couldn't understand a word spoken.

"If you are assuming they were advance scouts for an invasion," went on Officer Leung, "you also have to assume they had no problem flying their spacecraft. So how would they have crash-landed? Wasn't such an outcome far more likely if renegades hi-jacked the spacecraft? Or maybe you caused their spaceship to crash? Was that how you disrupted their plans?"

"Of course we did not cause their spaceship to crash! And cooping them up in our hospital certainly would have disrupted any nasty plans they might have had! That is, had they been in any shape to execute such plans!" Safasafala blustered, though the translator delivered his response in the same digital monotone as everything else he fah-lah-lahed. And he took such umbrage to Buddy's question that his twirled-together whiskers un-twirled themselves.

"So you asked them who they were and why they came here?"

"Okay, maybe you will be more satisfied hearing from them directly."

Buddy Leung bit his tongue anew, this time stifling himself from saying to the Fafaman linguist: *That is a saving-face, phony-baloney substitute for admitting the simple truth: You never got around to asking them point blank why they came here, whether to prepare for an invasion or to warn about it! Which raises the additional question of whether there really is any invasion in the offing, or you night owls made up the whole thing just to lure someone here, like ourselves!*

Officer Leung also stifled himself from pointing out he wouldn't be hearing anything from the injured creatures' own mouths directly. He had to trust Safasafala's translation. And for all Leung knew, Safasafala wasn't that good at being interpreter, was in deep denial on account of his misplaced pride. Maybe he made up most of what he claimed they were tick-tocking. *If that were the case, though, Safasafala could just as easily have concocted an answer to my question. No need for a charade where he pretends to be interpreter.*

Picking his words extra carefully, hoping against hope Safasafala really was adept at conversing with the creatures from Tictoctic, Buddy said, "I am not from this planet. I come from another planet."

No sooner did Buddy pause for translation than Safasafala said, "I have already informed them of that fact."

"Did he also inform them of the fact he's an arrogant bastard?! I don't care if they overhear me!" Kevin continued to shout when Ali Magabu shook his head 'no' and gestured for him to calm down. "We need to remove this investigation from their ratty hands! Maybe a demonstration shot where we take out a few of their snail tanks!"

Kevin hoped the Fafamans heard his bluff by eavesdropping on Buddy Leung's earpiece. The Smoke and Mirrors came unarmed, of course, no demonstration shot to give.

Meanwhile Buddy Leung walked over beside one tralalafa to gently hold a crash-landed creature's hand-hooves, unless that creature recoiled from his touch.

Neither Safasafala nor physician Mafakakala tried to stop him, though anxiously darting looks from side to side.

Officer Leung would have revisited why the creatures crashed on Fafama. Were they shot down, or did their craft otherwise experience catastrophic failure? For example from their lack of experience flying it? He strongly suspected, though, this query would never get past Fafaman ears for translation into the injured creatures' tongue. So he stuck with the question, "Why did you come to this planet?"

Safasafala produced tick-tocks clearly directed at the antlered creatures, who had settled down a bit from their writhing about. Buddy could only hope they received a faithful translation of what he asked. At least they attended to Safasafala's tongue-clicking in a manner suggestive they could understand him.

Once the Fafaman linguist fell silent, the creature responded whose articulated hoof Buddy Leung held comfortingly. Throughout that creature's own tongue-clicked tick-tocks, he kept his eyes on Buddy. Were those eyes watering? If so, due to mental anguish as much as physical pain? Buddy wondered.

Accurate or concocted, what translated into English from Safasafala's fah-lah-lahs went, "We came here to warn you. Kindred animals are planning an invasion of planets including your own. The purpose is to expand our food supply."

Buddy was certain the injured stag-like creatures would never term themselves "animals." But before he could further second-guess Safasafala's translation, he felt his hand squeezed, accompanied immediately thereafter by additional tongue-clicking. "We want to stop the invasion," insisted the antler-bearing creature, again assuming Safasafala's translation could be trusted, "but we do not know how. We brought a star chart showing all the solar systems our kindred animals have targeted. Maybe that will help?"

The creature from Tictoctic tongue-clicked something else, but Safasafala greeted that with a puzzled, whisker-twirling expression. "I am not sure exactly what it said next," he fah-lah-lahed.

Such unexpectedly humble candor might have been mere pretense to trick Buddy into accepting fabricated parts of the translation. But when the Tictoctic creature purportedly lamented not knowing how to stop the invasion, he shook his head "no," a nonverbal evolved across the universe from babies avoiding more food. This coincidence of gesture with supposed meaning inclined Buddy towards accepting that Safasafala was rendering more-or-less-accurate translations.

In any event, Safasafala went on, "There was something about a sister planet, but too many other words the beast tick-tocked are not found in the dictionary they provided."

"So this guy learned their dictionary so well," grumbled Kevin, "he doesn't need it at hand to know Antelope Man said some stuff not contained there. He memorized how every damn word is spoken, or should I say tick-tocked!"

"Understand, Kevin," cautioned Ali Magabu, "we truly have no idea how long - perhaps months - since the crash-landing. Even without a photographic memory, the Fafaman linguist might have had more than ample time to absorb every square inch of the dictionary's contents. And perhaps it's another children's dictionary with limited vocabulary."

Buddy easily tuned out this conversation heard on his earpiece because of something sinking in from the Tictoctic creature's translated utterances. That something concerned one of the pictograph transmissions included with the Fafaman distress call that prompted the Smoke and Mirrors crew to upend their original mission plan. Antlered creatures herding non-antlered creatures like they were cattle... As Buddy opened his mouth anew, he could already feel his stomach sinking, an awful sensation prompted by dread over what he was about to learn. "You talk about your, uh, kind expanding the food supply. What types of food do they, uh, you eat?"

"On our planet, we have to eat meat. We eat the meat of our sister planet. Our parents ate other things, before... Here is where I can't translate again," claimed Safasafala. "But the animal continues about needing new food sources."

"What was the chemical makeup of the food found aboard their crash-landed spacecraft, Mafakakala? You said some was used for developing a serum..."

"We discovered a name - your name - for that food in your dictionary. We have a similar product, a cured meat you call 'jahkee.' "

"'Jahkee'? Oh," Buddy nodded, "Jerky. Never had any, but have heard of it. Have you analyzed their jerky?"

"Has a different signature from biopsies we have conducted on these animals," reported Mafakakala. "Beyond that, though, no idea whether they processed another animal from their planet, or from the sister planet it mentioned."

Doesn't sound like Fafaman biochemists have gotten very far with genetics, DNA and the like, Buddy thought. Surprised Deborah hasn't jumped in, although the entire situation probably still has her too freaked out. Guess it's on me for now. "If we could secure a sample of their jerky," Buddy subsequently ventured to say, "and from that biopsy, uh... Aboard ship we can quickly determine, um... Within one rotation of your planet, we will know whether the tissues are from the same or different lines of evolution."

"That is an accurate statement, Officer Leung," confirmed Dr. Davis-Murphy.

Buddy would have relayed to the Fafamans what he heard crackling in his ear from the chief medical adviser aboard the Smoke and Mirrors. But he didn't want to remind them how closely they were being monitored from several miles above the planet's surface.

"We need time to discuss your offer," Safasafala responded after he and Mafakakala exchanged significant looks.

"And discuss this is all they'll do, because they're holding you hostage," said Kevin. "Just so you know, Bud: Yoon-hee and Tanya have left the bridge to work on that show of force I alluded to earlier. We intend to help the Fafamans reconsider dragging out this whatever-they're-doing for so long."

Before Officer Smith-Park finished, the creature Buddy tried to comfort by holding hands suddenly stretched his limbs stiffly straight. He also tightened his own grip on Buddy's hand, like he was holding on for dear life. And a frantic look on his long, narrow face became a glassy stare into the abyss.

The antlered creature's vital signs monitor went beeping wild as Buddy concluded he must be suffering a seizure.

The creature's fellow traveler brought over her other hand-hoof to join the hand-hoof already holding on to her companion, to give him a full embrace. Buddy imagined she was trying to anchor her loved one so he wouldn't fly away to death. Or if he did fly away would take her along, somehow.

Mafakakala made his robe swirl, checking that a feeding tube was operating properly.

The episode was already subsiding, though, with blood pressure and other parameters returning back to normal.

"I would administer a muscle relaxant," said Mafakakala. "But we are uncertain our biology is compatible with theirs, beyond the basics."

No sooner did the Fafaman physician finish speaking than the distressed creature's companion presented with identical symptoms. Her second arm brought around to hold on tight abruptly swung aside, swinging her flat on her back again. She went stiff as a board, with arms and legs rigid and the glassy stare nowhere. Her companion gently yet urgently disengaged his hand-hoof from Buddy so that this time, he could try to provide anchor.

"Has this happened before?"

"The episodes have been spacing closer and closer together over the past rotation of Fafama," the physician Mafakakala answered Buddy Leung.

Officer Leung left the male creature's side to stand facing both of them, hoping to regain their attention. "The Fafamans have made good progress in medicine," he started diplomatically, "but the medical facilities aboard my spaceship are far more advanced, might be able to do a lot more for you. Would you like us to take you there?"

"I am sorry, but I can't translate that."

"He means he WON'T translate that," commented Kevin.

Sharing Kevin's anger, Officer Leung finally had to vent. "Listen," he said, "we appreciate your efforts to keep these creatures alive. But there are a lot of actions you have not taken. For example, there clearly has been no quarantine protocol to protect you and these creatures from potentially harmful exo-biochemical interactions."

Buddy's severe tone had the two Fafamans stepping back.

That's when Nanofafo, Wafalawa, and the security guard who also had been part of Officer Leung's hospital escort burst through the door.

Ah-ha! Buddy thought. *So the Fafamans have been monitoring this situation closely as we have.* He noticed the security officer's itchy finger on his gun, but continued fearlessly, "Until now, Earth and Fafaman exo-biochemical interactions have proven more curious than dangerous. But for all we know, these beings are nearing death because you've done nothing to isolate them from Fafaman bacteria and viruses."

"When their vehicle crashed, they were exposed to our atmosphere, complete with all those bacteria and viruses. A full quarter of the planet's rotation elapsed before we could reach their coordinates," Mafakakala blustered. He wasn't going to let this arrogant Earthling, as he saw Buddy, continue any further with his patronizing, condescending assessment before he provided major pushback. "The beasts sustained torn ligaments and broken bones; you cannot see the casts underneath their clothing. But to date, we have not noted any reactions that could be traced back to biochemical incompatibilities. In fact, our antiseptic washes protected them from infection during surgery.

Moreover, they have yet to present with even that curious nasal discharge you and certain of us have experienced."

"Yes, all they have are these life-threatening seizures you say are coming closer together."

"We suspect some organ damage and internal bleeding issues. Now if you think your medical technology is so far advanced, you can do organ and vascular repair on animals from worlds other than your own…"

"I am not saying we can do complex surgery on aliens with only a few sunset storm-lines to prepare! I am-" But this is as far as Buddy got before both creatures' monitors started beeping simultaneously.

Their hearts beat out of control.

Next thing anyone knew, both antlered beings, holding one another ever tighter, were tick-tocking in unison. Buddy could tell they were repeating the same thing over and over, until they both appeared seized by some final, stiffening spasm. With a long "baaaaa" like two bleating sheep or two deflating balloons, their bodies went limp, and their antlers clunked together one last time.

But that was not all. Fluorescent green protuberances peeked out from their nostrils. Then they shot out so far, they landed on the floor beside Buddy. Linking together sudden protrusions like two arms linked together for a square dance, they proceeded to circle one another do-si-do style. This went on for endless-seeming seconds until finally they collapsed into lifeless, rapidly shriveling gray puddles.

"What were they saying?" asked Buddy Leung.

Safasafala met Buddy's helpless countenance with a condemning stare. He steamed with resentful suspicion the agitated atmosphere caused by this Earthling somehow contributed to the animals' death, even faster than it might have occurred anyway. And his whiskers twirled on their own as he said, "Their last words were: 'Do not become us.'"

Chapter 14

"What just happened there?" asked Kevin from back aboard the Smoke and Mirrors in orbit around Fafama. "Buddy? Can you talk to us? We saw glowing boogersnot leap from the antelope people and perform a do-si-do swan dive. But it's too dark for us to tell...Are they dead?"

"The creatures from Tictoctic are both dead," Buddy Leung finally responded. "Incidentally I've turned off the translator, and am holding it near my lips like a walkie-talkie. Told our hosts I'm giving you an update. The less we remind them they're under constant surveillance, the better."

As Buddy Leung indicated, he wasn't speaking to Kevin via his translator. That was pretend for the Fafamans. In reality, Kevin was hearing from Buddy, plus seeing everything around him, courtesy of the nondescript camcorder inconspicuously pinned to Buddy's lapel.

"Looks like you're on the move. Where are they taking you? Need to pull a rabbit from our hats sooner rather than later?"

"Just a minute." Buddy reactivated the translator and asked, "Where are we going?"

Once this question fah-lah-lahed out the translator, Safasafala sighed in exasperation. Didn't the Earthling know already?

Wafalawa stretched an arm Safasafala's way, gesturing the linguist needn't trouble himself. Then he took long strides over beside Buddy, and said, "If this experience has been more uncomfortable than any of us would have preferred...Of course nothing could have made pleasant the other-world animals' demise from their crash injuries. Please understand, though, the extra effort we've made to accommodate your biorhythms. Among other sacrifices, we have profoundly disrupted our normal sleep schedule, staying up well past stars-fade. Safasafala and Mafakakala have already gone several days on very little sleep, ever since the animals crash-landed here. Their patience is less than optimal." Wafalawa spoke of inadequate patience so softly, had he not sidled up beside Officer Leung, Leung's translator might have drawn a blank. "While you were contacting your crew in orbit," the Fafaman adviser went on more loudly, "we concluded a short rest is in order. We will set our artificial storm-line to assure not oversleeping. After reawakening, we will take you to the hangar containing wreckage from the Tictoctic spacecraft."

"Thanks for that explanation, Wafalawa! Ha-ha!" Buddy laughed nervously. "I'm just going to let my crew up in orbit know.

"Officer Smith? Wafalawa told me they are so wiped out-"

"You don't have to repeat everything, Officer Leung. We heard!"

"Are you forgetting, Kevin?" intervened Ali standing beside him on the Smoke and Mirrors navigation bridge. "Officer Leung needs to pretend the only way we keep abreast is by him checking in with us on a walkie-talkie."

"Oh, right, sorry."

Albeit haltingly, Buddy kept going with his latest redundant update despite Kevin's complaint and Ali's reminder ringing in his ear. Once he finished, Officer Kevin Smith-Park really let loose.

"This is unbelievable!" Kevin complained. "If the picture painted for us is accurate, those Tictoctic antelope guys could descend on Fafama any time now for a cattle roundup! But they want to postpone helping us help them because it's freakin' NAP TIME?!?!?!?!"

"Of course, unless they do a lot better piloting job, other Tictoctic spacecraft are going to meet the same fate as the first one."

"Hey, Buddy, let me paint a dramatically different possibility," spit out Kevin. "The Fafamans can't take you to see the spacecraft wreckage yet because they're still assembling it from scrap metal! And as for the antelope guys, they heavily sedated some antlered critters native to their planet. Then they dressed them to pass off as so-called other-worlders."

Buddy shook his head "no" even though Kevin wouldn't see that through his camcorder as again, it was attached to Buddy's lapel. "Their hooves weren't really hooves," he said. "They were these hoof-hand hybrids, articulated cloven hooves if you will. And the way one held my hand and looked in my eyes, the way they held one another…There was some real affection…"

"Animals don't show real affection?"

"Yes, but what about their tick-tocks when Safasafala tick-tocked to them? Intelligent communication really did seem to occur."

"Jeezy-peezy, Buddy, if you quack-quack at ducks, sometimes they quack-quack right back!" exclaimed Kevin. "Listen, those tick-tocks didn't sound much different from the clicks dolphins make. Maybe their antelopes are intelligent like our dolphins, and the Fafamans have learned about their communication like we've learned about dolphin communication…"

"So you really think the Fafamans could be perpetrating an epic hoax?"

"Why would they do this, Officer Smith? Why would they cry 'wolf' to the universe?" asked Ali Magabu, unable to conceal his astonishment over Kevin's conjecture.

"Sorry, Chris, if you're still with us..." This was all Kevin could think to say, trying to include Officer Olsen-Taylor stuck somewhere else besides wherever Buddy presently found himself located. That is, within the enormous pyramid down on planet Fafama's surface.

"No problem," responded Officer Chris Olsen-Taylor. "I'm busy figuring out how to flip the switch on this thing that looks like a television. They've left me alone in a room guarded front and back. But what are you sorry to me for? I'll be relieved if the Fafamans are perpetrating your suggested hoax, and other extraterrestrials are not set on herding us to slaughter."

"Your wife is incommunicado," not-so-gently observed Kevin as in *There's plenty to feel sorry about for you, Chris.* "King Fafawazoo, we know he keeps a harem and practically runs the whole show. Maybe he's tired of Fafaman women and ordered his worker ants to go fishing for outer space babes."

"I suppose until we better understand Fafaman culture, Officer Smith, we truly cannot yet rule out anything completely," said Ali. "But on first consideration, your suggestion strikes me as utterly preposterous. And I'm not just saying that, Officer Olsen-Taylor, to keep you from despair."

"Yoon-hee must be out of the loop, else she'd be twisting Kevin's ear already," said Chris.

"Ouch!" exclaimed Kevin, favoring the ear last victimized.

"Officer Olsen-Taylor," said Ali striking a seriously officious note, "please understand two things, and understand them well. One, we are trying everything possible to reestablish contact with your wife. And two, while your brave front certainly eases our focus, don't hesitate to cry on our shoulders, so to speak, should the need arise. After all, we are like family."

Ali's remarks were met with a long silence where he wasn't sure a faint whimper couldn't be heard Chris's end.

Meantime Captain Helena Taylor could have whimpered as well, if she let herself. Riding a roller-coaster-like car deep into the Great Pyramid, she suffered a brief dizzy spell. Such had been her panic when her earpiece went totally dead, shutting her off from the Smoke and Mirrors.

For fellow Earthlings' ears only, she had been talking about gathering the maximum possible information. To that end, she would soon remove her envirosuit again, "No dancing, I promise you."

Buddy had also removed his envirosuit again when Mafakakala made such a big fuss over it.

Anyhow, once Helena unsuited, the Fafamans would hear everything she said. And her translator would remain on to avoid her Fafaman hosts' paranoia rising dangerously high over conversations they could not understand.

In fact, as Captain Helena Taylor explained, she wouldn't speak directly to her fellow Earthlings at all, once shedding her envirosuit anew. Rather, she would keep her utterances directed tacitly at the Fafamans, but embed them with valuable information her crew could glean simply by eavesdropping.

That's as far as Helena got sharing her plans when sheer terror nearly consumed her. The Fafamafalafama's roller-coaster-car entourage entered a granite tunnel after passing through several hundred feet of porous, plastic-looking material. Realizing then that she hadn't heard a peep in some while over her earpiece, Helena said, "Chris? Buddy? Yoon-hee?"

Rather than any response, a solid granite wall dropped down behind the motorcade, sealing the passageway with a booming thud!

Helena found herself sharing Chris and Buddy's same awful thought, if she but knew: This extended experience of dimly-lit rooms and passageways was the stuff of nightmares.

Soon thereafter, the roller-coaster-type cars slowed to a halt. Captain Helena Taylor had to leave her seat for procession through a narrow, low-ceilinged tunnel bringing her that much deeper into the Great Pyramid. Escape seemed near impossible.

Helena still told herself over and over, like some meditative mantra, she could rest assured her crew was making a superhuman effort on her behalf. And with their vastly superior technology, in only a matter of time they would re-establish contact. Moreover, they would also make the Fafamans an offer they couldn't refuse, for safe delivery of the away team back to the Smoke and Mirrors. Wouldn't they, even if they had to bluff?

The low-ceilinged tunnel finally opened onto a wide catwalk where Helena found the view fascinating. So fascinating, in fact, it temporarily transported her out of rising concern for personal safety.

The catwalk's square configuration hung suspended from a pyramid-shaped vaulted ceiling. Ample railings assured no special attentiveness required to avoid falling off.

A pyramid poked ten feet up through the catwalk's center, and spread down below for another twenty feet. Its sides did not gleam metallically smooth, as could be said of the city-sized pyramid within which Helena had been taken. This pyramid was more of the Egyptian sort, though on a far smaller scale. Long ago, stone blocks had been hauled into place by slaves under starlit skies.

From what Helena could see, the thirty-foot pyramid could still be easily climbed at least halfway. But towards the top, too many blocks had been worn smooth by sunset storm-line wind and rain, long before it was subsumed by a larger pyramid.

"This is the first pyramid ordered by the original Fafamafalafama twenty-five-hundred solar orbits ago," said the current Fafamafalafama. Up to then, he had maintained absolute silence begun soon as they boarded the roller coaster lookalikes. And for the duration, he had held his head high.

Helena was reminded of a dog sticking his head out the window of a moving car. Clearly he relished the breeze. Yet he also, Helena sensed, wistfully longed for freedom to frolic about the scenery passing by, unfettered by any leash.

Whatever haunted the Fafamafalafama's head, Captain Taylor had appreciated his prolonged silence. Part of her nearly overwhelming anxiety concerned what he might say when he finally did open his mouth. Perhaps he would announce the additional change of plan to once and for all make clear she'd been lured into a life-threatening trap.

"Once our ancestors realized how effectively such structures withstood the force of the sunset storm-line, a new age began. Pyramids protected the creation of manufacturing facilities underground. This led, in turn, to the affluent civilization you see on Fafama today, preparing to explore the stars."

"Is the original Fafamafalafama buried here?" asked Captain Taylor grateful for Fafaman history as panic-relieving distraction. Not that she was naïve. Helena well knew the museum tour was carefully calculated to put her at ease, lull her into complacency. But that would have been the case no matter what, no matter whether the Fafamans were up to no good, or had the noblest of intentions. The important thing was to keep on the alert.

Anyway, the Fafamafalafama gave Helena a most quizzical look, and responded, "The same as for his successors, his body was cremated, and the ashes left to fly with a sunset storm-line."

"So how have subsequent Fafamafalafamas been chosen, including yourself? And, uh, what made the original Fafamafalafama the original Fafamafalafama? Did that have to do with his presiding over construction of the first pyramid?"

Despite dim lighting, Helena could espy a wry grin, one corner upturned. Did the Fafaman ruler secretly share her skepticism over any one ancient Fafaman having been truly more special than the rest, apart from dumb luck? Or did his wry grin stem from frustration? From feeling the futility of trying to earn her respect for his sacred beliefs as any more than ignorant superstition?

Whatever went through the Fafamafalafama's head, he responded, "The original Fafamafalafama built the first pyramid, with only his two hands."

"With only his two hands? I thought you said he ordered this pyramid built by others."

"There is no contradiction, Captain Helena Taylor. This IS the first pyramid ordered built by the first Fafamafalafama. But it is not the first pyramid built. Again, the first pyramid was built by the first Fafamafalafama with only his two hands. It is located inside the first pyramid *ordered* built that you see before us.

"Once the first Fafamafalafama completed the first pyramid, he occupied it to face the next sunset storm-line alone. He was determined to die or be glorified for his conviction such a structure would free us from tumbling across the land cushioned by tralalafas every sunset.

"Of course that tumbling was only for the lucky ones, the ones who didn't accidentally seek shelter in lookalike trafafalas wherein hid baby ahtpah and another hideous creature, the masacasa. The masacasa wraps round its victim to absorb him through rows of suction cups so slowly, death takes several nana."

"So he was declared Fafamafalafama for inventing the pyramid?"

"The story goes that he was greeted by deafening cheers when he emerged from his edifice unscathed by the sunset storm-line."

"And have subsequent Fafamafalafamas been chosen for their own achievements of great use to your people?"

"All achievements since the pyramid have been blinded from sight by the tremendous shade it casts across them. So a special process has been established for selecting which aspirant will become the next Fafamafalafama. The first step in that process involves taking a far greater risk than the original ruler took. All aspirants must face the sunset storm-line strapped naked to the Great Pyramid."

"How are aspirants chosen?"

"Any male can choose himself."

"Any male," grumbled Captain Taylor, pointedly crossing her arms.

"You will understand - not agree, perhaps, but understand - after you hear the rest. Many aspirants are killed by objects hurled by the storm-line. There were twenty-one others besides myself for the last selection twenty-five orbits ago. Only six survived, besides me. A dead flounder mouse (namalumina) asphyxiated the candidate on my right, blown against his face for the storm-line's duration. His bound hands could not remove its smothering corpse."

Helena kept reminding herself of two things. One, the Fafamans had done nothing, yet, to prove her safe return back aboard ship wasn't a mere request away. And two, certainly the Smoke and Mirrors crew would concoct a rescue plan should she and the rest of her away team turn out to be actual captives. "So including yourself, you were down to seven surviving aspirants," she said finally, having fought down her anxiety like she might as well have been fighting down acid reflux.

Helena's royal host figured her delayed reaction was simply difficulty digesting a way of life probably better understood, and appreciated, by Earthling males. *But if she is going to insist on being a leader, she really needs to either deal with this, or let some other Earthling take over.*

"Did your remaining competitors also have to die?" Captain Taylor went on. "Were you the sole survivor of, um, I assume there was at least one additional task?"

"Only two other aspirants died in my selection, Captain Taylor. We met down there for the final task." He pointed below the catwalk at the pyramid's base, one side anyhow. "To initiate that concluding step in the selection process, wives of the previous Fafamafalafama gather one last time along this catwalk. They are told they will be dispersed back into the larger community, and ordered never to mate again, under penalty of death. Incidentally, no one tries to enforce that, long as the widows are secretively discreet with any illicit liaison."

You see, Earthling, we are not as barbaric as you would apparently wish to judge us, was the message Helena got.

"With a nod from the first wife," the Fafaman ruler continued, "the wives finally let loose their grief held in until that moment. Of course we are talking about grief over loss of the most recently deceased Fafamafalafama. Their collective anguished cry becomes, we believe, the planet Fafama's cry for a new husband to nurse from her wellspring of nourishment, and thus arouse new fertility.

"No sooner than the last forlorn whimper dies away, the surviving aspirants begin their ascent of the pyramid. They struggle and strain for who will plant his mouth over her apex, and draw in liquid mysteriously expressed there every stars-out. The apex is dry at the moment. But take a look after the sunset storm-line passes outside our Great Pyramid, and you will see it glisten until stars-fade."

"So the two more who died…"

"They lost balance and fell backwards during the struggle."

"Does the Fafamafalafama have to come here regularly to, um, draw in more liquid from the planet?"

"The Fafamafalafama only draws in Fafama's life-giving milk once. The very next day, he takes his first wife. She becomes the first of many, chosen once every solar orbit until the Fafamafalafama perishes. He becomes a fountain of great fertility contributing significantly to the general population. In fact, we believe it no accident that Fafamafalafamas are often the children of previous Fafamafalafamas."

"Often means not always?"

"The first Fafamafalafama acknowledged the good fortune being credited with invention of the pyramid. 'I am the Fafamafalafama,' he wrote. 'However, who knows how many of my contemporaries could also have filled that role? Males will surely come along born into families other than my own, males as worthy as my most worthy sons of a chance at becoming the next Fafamafalafama. But there still can only be one

Fafamafalafama, even as a nakana herd can only have one katakana.' These are the words of the first Fafamafalafama."

Each attendant security guard clasped his hands together over his head, and bowed.

Helena wanted to say something to the effect of: *This is all most fascinating, but we've got serious business at hand.* However, she couldn't work up the courage for fear what the Fafaman ruler might say if pressed. Maybe he would confirm that she, if not the entire away team, was in mortal peril. Instead, therefore, she went on with, "The Fafamafalafama selects, um, you select a new wife every solar orbit?"

"Only the first wife is chosen that way. Additional wives are decided through a series of competitions taking fully one-third solar orbit. Families always feel honored to enroll their daughters to compete, beyond the benefits that accrue if their daughter is selected. Viewing the competition has become so popular that it comprises our most-watched television game show."

Don't think I'll be playing, Helena Taylor told herself, not about to utter such a sentiment aloud. But as captain of the Smoke and Mirrors, she also feared shirking her duty any longer. It was time to refocus the Fafamans on why Earthlings had put themselves at Fafaman mercy in the first place. So Helena reacted, "Your civilization's history will be of great interest to us in the future. And we will certainly look forward to reciprocating with information about our own history. You may find it as, uh, unique as we find yours. With the potential crisis we both face, however, I am sure you appreciate the importance of returning to our more immediate tasks."

As the translation fah-lah-laed from Helena's translator, the Fafamafalafama's already large nocturnal eyes bugged out even more.

In nervous reaction, Helena added, "The background information you have supplied will prove useful in future discussions. That is safe to say. I appreciate how we move along." She wished Dr. Magabu still had her ear, to guide her across the diplomatic tightrope. Did the Fafaman leader sense her patronizing him with the "how we move along" stuff? That in fact she was growing steadily more impatient and worried?

On translation's completion, the Fafamafalafama's eyes receded into their sockets. Raising his chin high, he broke into a full smile. "Very well," he said, nodding at his guards as he continued, "we will proceed to a visitor suite for presentation of the agenda."

Helena and company reached the visitor suite through a different tunnel off the catwalk from the one they traversed originally. They arrived quickly at a plain wooden door set into the tunnel wall, bearing more hieroglyphic-type lettering.

"My wives' interior quarters are next door," fah-lah-lahed the Fafamafalafama. "From there, my wives can freely transport to rooms with scenic views constructed along the outermost pyramid walls. No matter their location, though, they receive other family members as honored guests, and assist with our children's education and upbringing."

On the Fafamafalafama's subtle gesture, one guard opened the door for him and Helena. The other guard assumed a watchful, on-duty position, weapon held diagonally across his chest.

Door closed behind her and the Fafaman ruler, Helena easily imagined the guard who enabled entry joining the other one, both ready to defend the throne.

Alone with the Fafamafalafama, Captain Taylor regretted she didn't remove her envirosuit earlier. Perhaps she could have on their journey to the center of the pyramid, what wouldn't surprise her to learn was the largest pyramid in the galaxy.

Deborah warned that future exo-biochemical reactions might not be as benign as what Helena and company had experienced thus far. Such a possibility figured into Helena re-donning her envirosuit after a terrorist attack ruined the Fafamans' military parade. Nevertheless, she worried that that protective gear posed a substantial psychological barrier between her and the Fafamans, be they hosts or captors. To succeed at extraterrestrial diplomacy, she might have to put her personal safety at risk. Yet how was she to "take it off" now without leading the Fafamafalafama to think she was auditioning for next wife? Especially since she had insisted on her away team suiting back up after the military parade?

"Before we discuss anything else," the Fafamafalafama's fah-lah-lahs in a low booming voice translated, "I wish to discuss the matter of your protective gear, 'Cahptahn Taylah.' My science advisers assure me my assessment is correct. Any substantial health risk from our mutual physical exposure would have announced itself within the first several nana. Yes, we have all been inconvenienced by animated nasal discharge. But inconvenience falls far short of substantial risk. Therefore we come to a concern I must state in no uncertain terms. Suited as you are, I can hardly discern your face to take full measure of your sincerity and honesty. But I must take that measure if we are to cooperate in meeting the large matters before us."

"I appreciate your expressing so frankly what is on your mind," said Helena. "Oh, I'm sorry," she shifted gears to say, having noticed the Fafamafalafama's head twitch like someone snuck up behind him and yelled *Surprise!* "Had you not completed your remarks before I spoke?"

He bowed his head appreciatively. *Thank you for acknowledging and repenting your transgression.* "Proceed."

How can this guy be so arrogant as to minimize the "animated nasal discharge" as mere inconvenience? How can he, and purportedly his science advisers as well, ignore the possibility of serious long-term side effects? All thanks to his blowing off Dr. Davis-Murphy's safety protocol, and my surrendering to the spirit of the dance? Helena Taylor wondered. She really wanted to ask whether the Fafamafalafama intimidated his science advisers into assuring him his health risk assessment was correct. "If I might also speak frankly," she went on instead, "there is a sense of rising unease over my envirosuit. More and more, it feels like a high wall barrier to our communication. Therefore please allow me a nininana, as you say, to shed it."

Captain Taylor turned her back on the Fafaman leader. If he moved on her while she took off her envirosuit, or afterwards, she was determined to beat him away with it, even were he to wield his sword.

"Some other details might interest you, 'Cahptahn Taylah.' We are inside the second pyramid constructed under a Fafamafalafama's direction, completed five hundred solar orbits ago. To this day, it remains the central living space of the Fafamafalafama, his wives, his guards, and most other attendant services. Two hundred orbits ago, however, work was begun on a third, much larger pyramid. That ultimately led to the magnificent fourth accretion, the Great Pyramid, you beheld on entering our atmosphere for the first time.

"As mentioned earlier, we believe in no more for any task than the task requires. We also believe in no greater an achievement than the achievement required.

"Well, innumerable Fafamans had compelling reasons to make the Fafamafalafama's address their own. And so, the required achievement attained epic proportions, the most epic ever. Relatives of royal wives wanted to live near their daughters. Unrelated loyalists conducting essential business could best serve the Fafamafalafama and his family by also living near. And in recent decades, we realized an immensely proportioned pyramid would be the perfect place to base our aircraft, and ultimately launch a space exploration program.

"Last and foremost, there is the official palace of the Fafamafalafama through which we entered, before we boarded rail cars to my family's current living quarters. Its design required vast room for construction.

"Of course, not everyone could live and work in just this one location, however enormous. That is why you see smaller pyramids outside this one. Many of their inhabitants commute over nearby hills to operate a vast manufacturing and mining complex."

At least the Fafamafalafama didn't try to sexually assault Helena now that they were completely alone and isolated, and she had removed her envirosuit. Her relief over that made her amenable to his expounding at length on Fafaman history. However, as the Fafaman ruler went on and on, she grew anxiously restless to move matters along. So she seized at his pause for catching breath to gently interject, "You spoke of an agenda?"

"An agenda," he fah-lah-lahed, with his wry grin again.

That grin made Helena nervous enough even in the company of her husband and Buddy. But alone with him...

"Yes," the Fafamafalafama said, pacing the room as his flowing robes cast more luminescent glow than the dim floor lighting. "First," he went on, spinning round on the heels of his moccasins, and jabbing a forefinger ceiling-ward, "you will eat your midday meal while I share a sample of our music. I could also order a Fafaman delicacy for you. But from your previous uncomfortable reaction, I gather you would prefer to continue with food from your planet, for now. Such food is packed inside your envirosuit, yes?"

Helena briefly contemplated lying, saying she needed to re-establish contact with her spaceship to have the crew send down something. But she dumped this idea soon as she thought of it. Odds were that the Fafamafalafama would search her shed envirosuit. Then discovering food packets, he'd rightfully become extremely insulted by her distrustful fear. *(Why didn't you just ask: Can I speak with my crew?)*

Moreover, if something sinister **was** going on, Helena behaving like she suspected that might only make matters worse. For sure, she didn't want to risk sabotaging whatever contingency rescue plan her crew was concocting back aboard the Smoke and Mirrors, weren't they?

Far from any appetite, Helena could feel panic rising like acid reflux again. If only the Fafaman ruler hadn't added two little words, "for now," to his comment about her favoring food from Earth. Nevertheless, though, she at last responded, "Yes, we packed plenty of food inside my envirosuit."

"Well here is the situation, then. Someone else might have already told you. Normally, blinding-light is our sleep time. But we are aware your biorhythms have you awake then. For your sleep cycle, you favor stars-out, and blinding-light is when you eat. So for agenda item one, I will simulate blinding-light in this room. Sitting atop a tralalafa after it has curled shut, you can fill your stomach while I fill your ears with Fafaman music.

"Item two," he continued, stabbing two fingers ceiling-ward.

Helena wondered whether no pause between detailing item one and detailing item two was meant to preclude her wedging in any objection.

"Much as I might accommodate your biorhythm, blinding-light remains sleep time for us. Is also time for other activities that happen naturally when we recline upon our tralalafas. Item two, for a portion of blinding-light I will leave you alone so I can meet my wives' conjugal needs. During that time, you might avail yourself of Fafaman television. I assume your translator will help with understanding our shows.

"Item three," the Fafamafalafama said with a new swirl of his luminescent cape, and holding up three fingers. "On return from my wives' quarters, I will simulate stars-out long enough for the tralalafa to unfurl, and for you to recline restfully upon it. Then I will reset to blinding-light so you might enjoy the tralalafa enfolding you most comfortingly.

"AND, there's a special feature of this guest room. You see the cylindrical hole in that wall? It extends all the way out the Great Pyramid's side that faces the sunset storm-line's daily path. Look here, the wall opposite: A companion cylindrical hole, all the way out the other side.

"Most rooms have to settle with fans to artificially suggest the storm-line. This is one of precious few locations where the effect is real, although still requiring enhancement by embedded fans. You will learn directly how Fafamans have been awakened since time immemorial. Allow me to add: Should you desire my lying beside you to share the experience...

"Item four," he went on, his breeziest robe swirl yet, to bring up four fingers. "We discuss and write details for our peoples, on how we can help your world, and your world can help ours."

So there it was. Offering to lay beside Helena, the Fafaman ruler dropped the first big hint he might have something unthinkable in mind. But as much as that terrified her, she couldn't help smiling. What a preposterous agenda he'd presented, with all the naïve self-centered innocence of a three-year-old! She labored to sustain this smile, despite her terror, as she responded in a soft voice, "You have your expression about no more for the task than the task requires. Well, we have our own expression: Work now, play later. My crew and I, we have a dangerous trip ahead, returning home across a distance light takes several years to travel. Between here and there, we need to dodge miscellaneous rocks, and possibly even the advance guard, another advance guard from Tictoctic. We have risked our lives on our experimental space-flight technology, to assess the threat described in your distress call. Later, I am sure our peoples will want extensive cultural exchanges to understand one another better. But that is the play-later part. For now, isn't it time to work?"

"I am not sure I understood so much of what you say. But we have another expression: The sunset storm-line cannot arrive before the sunset storm-line arrives. You will take out your food while I share our music with you," commanded the Fafamafalafama striking a defiant pose, and firmly gripping the handle of his sheathed sword.

Helena hoped he used his sword for added emphasis only, not meant to threaten her. It was all she could do to keep from trembling, appear casual about searching her envirosuit for food packets.

The Fafamafalafama let go the hilt of his sword to sift through what looked like compact discs piled beside a compact disc player. What thereafter calmed Helena was imagining Chris trying to play Fafaman CDs on an Earth CD player, see if they were compatible.

Anyway, dramatically brightened lighting had Helena squinting after so long trying to discern objects aided only by faint, moonlit-style glows.

"This is the most popular group on the planet today: Faboompa Washed Ashore," said the Fafamafalafama while the tralalafa's comforter-sized fleshy leaves gently curled together. "Hear their most recent song everybody has to have: 'Storm-line In My Feet.'"

Helena noticed noises eerily familiar from Chris playing music on his older equipment. A click preceded the distinct hiss of a spinning compact disc. But something far more unsettling occurred to Captain Taylor, kept her from any least amusement over the music group's name and song title. It had to do with the Fafamafalafama turning up the lights.

On Earth, setting a romantic mood often involved turning down the lights and playing soft music. Not something Chris ever did, but whatever. On Fafama, people retired from wakeful activity in the morning rather than at night. So didn't it naturally follow that Fafamans would try creating an intimate atmosphere by lighting up a room instead of darkening it? Which meant that the Fafamafalafama...

Captain Taylor kept her head low, feigned complete preoccupation with retrieving food packets from her envirosuit. She feared the briefest eye contact with the Fafamafalafama might be read as "go" for him to sexually assault her. Her meal finally in hand, she also foreswore sitting on the curled-up tralalafa. Instead, she crossed her legs to sit directly beside her shed protective gear.

"Storm-Line In My Feet" opened with syncopated rhythms on bass guitar.

Helena marveled at how any number of nondescript dance tunes on Earth could have opened that way. What she wouldn't have found back home, however, was how the Fafaman ruler moved to the beat.

Helena's dread persisted over what the Fafamafalafama might do, should he notice her paying him the slightest attention. But she couldn't help stray glances his direction, sufficient to monitor his behavior.

The imperially dressed Fafaman was swaying his arms one moment, then flapping them the next like baby bird wings still too weak for flight.

Meantime, Faboompa Washed Ashore's layered-in percussion reminded Helena of middle-eastern folk music. Fascinating, yet it was not fascinating enough to spare the starship captain from anxiety laying siege on her. Would dread over the Fafamafalafama's ultimate intent reduce her to a trembling mess? Or would his absurd dance start her giggling irrepressibly?

Debating her best course of action kept Helena from succumbing to either fear or amusement, or a combination of both.

On the one hand she could bluff about what would happen if the Fafamafalafama didn't get down to business pronto, and then release her. She could threaten violence that the Smoke and Mirrors was not at all equipped to dispense.

On the other hand, she could keep acquiescing to the Fafamafalafama's ridiculous agenda and just hope for the best. This is the course she favored. That is, assuming her crew hard at work reconnecting with her, and planning out various contingencies.

A bass profundo male voice entered wailing dialogue with a violin in Fafama's hit tune. Strangely unsettling, but Captain Helena Taylor kept telling herself to remain patient. For all she knew, Yoon-hee just piggybacked a message to her through a Fafaman transmission line, and she'd be hearing it any second.

Moreover, maybe Yoon-hee and company were about to hatch a bluff of their own. If Helena bluffed as well, odds were that both bluffs would be in something less than perfect sync, giving away the game. The Fafamans would quickly realize they were facing an empty threat.

But just when Helena finished convincing herself the best action was inaction, a new possibility tormented her. And out the corner of her eye she noticed the Fafamafalafama sinking so ridiculously low on bended knees, she couldn't help an uptick in anxiety.

The new possibility was quite simple, really. Why not plainly state to the Fafamafalafama she'd been out of touch with fellow Earthlings for too long? And that therefore, she wanted him to facilitate their reconnection?

If only Helena could summon the courage. The Fafamafalafama's dance moves had her newly afraid she'd bust out laughing if she tried to utter a sound. So she kept sucking on her freeze-dried ice cream, munching on her nut packet, and taking sips from her hydration packet.

But it seemed to Captain Taylor that the more she ate, the more extreme the Fafamafalafama's behavior, like he was a child competing with her meal for attention. He writhed about the stone floor, a slithering serpent whose hissing issued from maracas joining "Storm-line In My Feet" rather than from a tail he did not have.

Helena Taylor had to wonder: Was this what drove Fafaman women wild?

Stifling a giggle inadvertently produced a snort as though Helena were clearing her nostrils. Pursuant to which her sudden dread dampened any further amusement. What if this ruling Fafaman noticed her being more tickled than turned on by his behavior? Could such an affront to his ego turn him loose from civilized self-restraint? If so, heaven only knew what would be her fate.

Suddenly, the Fafaman leader got back on his feet and re-strapped his sheathed sword round his waist. Then he stomped over to turn off the CD player before "Storm-line In My Feet" ended. "You can look up now," his bitterly morose-sounding monotone fah-lah-lahs translated as he dimmed the lights.

Only faint, green-tinted luminescence remained, embedded in the floor like so many flounder mice.

With an uncontrollable shiver, Captain Taylor wondered whether the Fafamafalafama noticed her suppressed giggle. Or was it mere coincidence he so abruptly gave up trying to arouse her affection or lust even? And maybe he wasn't even trying to do that? Maybe she read waaaaaaaay too much into his behavior; he had merely reached the end of his cultural demonstration? And she misapprehended a bitterly morose tone?

No. When he said, "You can look up now," forget his tone of voice. How could the Fafamafalafama be expressing anything other than sheer bitterness? *You can stop worrying I'm out to seduce or rape you. Or maybe I'm sorry you find our song and dance so repulsive.*

"Thank you for playing that," Helena said, all her concentration focused on concealing her nervousness.

"The song was very interesting. I'm sure my... I'm sure Chris will also want to hear it, as he is a music collector."

"I am going to check on my wives. If any problem arises while I am gone, my guards can summon an entire army with a snap of their fingers. So you should remain protected," the Fafaman ruler said while opening the door.

From the bit brighter hallway luminescence, Helena noticed his wry grin again. Was he amused by her condescending fear over what he might do next? She did that lousy a job hiding it?

Still in all, Helena bit her tongue to keep from responding: *Thank you for relieving me from fear my crew might rescue me! Thank goodness I'm safe from that!*

*

At the same time lights dimmed for Helena, they still shined brightly in Officer Buddy Leung's location. But they shined less so inside the tralalafa where he considered himself stuck while Safasafala and Mafakakala napped soundly inside two other tralalafas.

Buddy did diplomatically volunteer to bed down for his own nap on the enormous Fafaman plant. But before he could climb onto one of its comforter-sized, comforter-textured leaves, Mafakakala asked him the oddest question. Would he mind removing those clothes that concealed his anal and urinary tracks? In aid of learning whether a tralalafa could nourish itself on bladder and intestine evacuations of someone from another planet?

Buddy elected not to, fearful his waste-collection organs might not handle very well the tralalafa's nutrient-seeking intrusion. Could the Fafamans guarantee his intestines would not be fatally vacuumed from his body?

"Thanks anyway," Buddy responded politely without elaborating on his concern. Moreover, he stepped back inside his envirosuit to take care of his human waste elimination needs before he braved the tralalafa. Though as he learned most uncomfortably, might as well have not bothered. In fact, might have been better off waiting seated on the floor for his two Fafaman hosts to finish napping.

Reclining upon the tralalafa, Buddy imagined a behemoth, flat, thorn-less, needle-less cactus, pleasantly soft yet firm. For the first few moments, though, he also worried that he might as well have been some bug landed inside a Venus Flytrap. Triggered by mere detection of his presence, might not the Fafaman plant close firmly round him, to hell with whether it was day or night?

No such thing happened. In fact, when simulated blinding-light did trigger the tralalafa to enwrap Buddy's torso, he felt anything but suffocated. And despite it also covering his head, he felt as free to wriggle away as had he snuggled under a warm blanket, at least initially. Moreover, the tralalafa let in so much light, Officer Leung fancied he could just as well have been trying to snooze in the shade of a beach umbrella.

All too soon, though, Leung experienced a really disturbing sensation. At first he discounted it as nothing more than his underpants uncomfortably wedged between his buttocks. Maybe they got pushed there by some unusual unevenness on the fleshy plant leaf's wide surface. When he pulled at them, though, he felt something intruding deep enough to be a proctology exam. *Wo!!! Underpants be damned, this plant is trying to feed off my bowels!*

"Hey, Safasafala?!" Buddy shouted to be heard while concealing his panic, he hoped. "Could my tralalafa be trying to, uh, absorb my nutrients despite my, uh, keeping my orifices concealed? Been any research on that?"

A brief pause after the fah-lah-lahed translation, then Safasafala in his tralalafa called to Mafakakala in his, "Have you thought of that, Doctor? Oooo-ahhhh, speaking of which..."

"Oooo-ahhhh, yessssss...None of us would ever imagine NOT uncovering our waste-eliminating orifices when we rest inside a tralalafa," Fafaman physician Mafakakala elaborated, a tralalafa having finished evacuating his bowels and bladder. "From time immemorial, the symbiotic relationship with tralalafas has been considered unquestionably healthy for everyone from babies to the elderly. Where such research as you propose is concerned, we might as well have tried not breathing for a nana or two!"

"Owww!!"

"Are you okay, Officer Leung?"

Buddy could hardly believe how his tralalafa's enormous fleshy leaf forced his bowels to behave, especially since he had completely relieved himself, so he thought, inside his envirosuit. But at least his urinary track seemed to have escaped attention from its strange tendrils. "I am fine, thanks for asking!" he answered finally, guessing he was in no real danger. Yes, the tralalafa had somehow made him soil his underpants, but nothing more. So he pulled them down, hoping the tralalafa would vacuum away the mess.

"Hey, Buddy!" shouted Kevin in Officer Leung's ear. "Contacting us is a covert operation for sure. Have to avoid reminding those bug-eyed Fafamans about the extent of our surveillance. But first chance you get, please explain why you went, 'Owww!' All we're seeing on your camcorder from inside that tralaladingy are indistinct shadows."

"I'm fine," Buddy whispered. "I'll tell you more once they're asleep." He hoped Kevin and company couldn't hear the tralalafa's steady slurp vacuuming excrement from his undies. Ideally, he'd avoid any mention of this embarrassing unpleasantness until hearty laughter wouldn't seem so inappropriate.

"Rest assured, Officer Leung," said Ali Magabu, "and you as well, Officer Olsen-Taylor. Tanya and Yoon-hee are still piecing together a rescue plan on the hopefully remote possibility our Fafaman friends will reject civilized persuasion."

Shortly after Officer Magabu's comforting words, Safasafala and Mafakakala started snoring loudly. They alternated with each other like a relay snore, Buddy mused.

Ali whistled in amazement while Kevin said, "Wow. This is another first, listening to damned extraterrestrial snoring! And Yoon-hee thinks MINE is bad! Anyway, Buddy, if you want to fill in the blanks for us…That racket should drown you out from the guards overhearing."

"Actually… I know this is outrageous, having to wait on their siesta. The time lost might leave us responding too late to the threat from Tictoctic, if there is one," Buddy acknowledged. "But I've been going nonstop so long, might not be a bad idea for me to, uh…"

"Say no more, Officer Leung," said Ali. "Sitting safe aboard the Smoke and Mirrors, we should not be causing you to, shall we say, lose any sleep over catching up on your own rest. The Fafamans' rigid insistence on repose before working with you any further simply clinches the deal."

"My circumstance is similar," Chris weighed in.

"Your circumstance, Officer Olsen-Taylor, and I would truly guess your wife's circumstance as well. The only difference is she's been transported so deep inside the pyramid that we haven't been able to reconnect with her yet.

"And so, Officer Leung, if you can imagine those snores as the lullaby ebb and flow of ocean surf..."

"And my flatulence as the scent of sweetest honey roses..." Kevin Smith-Park couldn't help adding.

"Since your better half is not present, Kevin, I will stand in for her by observing that truly, there is some question over from which end your flatulence emits."

Buddy Leung affected a snorted snore that had Chris remarking, "Fellow Earthling, we might be hearing Officer Leung's nose reaching out for exo-sinus communication with Fafaman noses."

"Yes! Absolutely!" said Ali, delightedly clapping his hands together. "And how truly wonderful if we find Earthling and Fafaman noses speak the same language!"

"You little boys might as well all go to sleep," Deborah remarked disgustedly.

Buddy welcomed the chief medical officer's severe tone putting an end to further banter before it could take an embarrassing turn. The Fafamans still snoring away, someone might have soon realized that was as good a time as any for him to explain what his "ow" was about. But he wanted to avoid ever mentioning what the tralalafa did to him, though he knew that was inevitable sooner or later. The Fafaman plant did vacuum-clean his underpants. Nevertheless they remained damp, so damp that the stain had soaked all the way through. How would his fellow Earthlings not notice? Ditto for a foul odor?

Buddy wondered when the Fafaman nap would end. Mafakakala and Safasafala's persistent relay snore together with his growing diaper rash discomfort left him hopeless over enjoying even the briefest doze.

Soon after Buddy resigned himself to his sleepless state, though, a simulated storm-line marked the end of simulated daylight. A distinct click activated the giant fan recessed deep inside the southeast-facing cylindrical hole in one wall. From turning slowly, it accelerated until howling with the ear-piercing whistle of an antique jet engine, so Buddy thought.

Once the fan blew strongly enough to jostle it, though, the tralalafa's resultant behavior proved far more disturbing. No more the comfortable sleeping bag, it went from gently cradling Buddy to constricting him from the neck down. He feared being crushed as by a boa constrictor.

Buddy reminded himself the tralalafa likely had evolved the good sense not to kill off creatures whose excrement nourished it. He might have kept reminding himself, only his main concern became trying not to vomit.

The simulated storm-line sent the tralalafa rolling end over end, colliding with other tralalafas and the wall. And even once lodged against one corner of the room, it rocked wildly from side to side.

Artificial hurricane-force winds finally subsiding, Buddy was thankful for at least having avoided soiling himself with vomit. But a remarkable realization quickly left his gratitude in the rear-view mirror.

The Fafamans were still snoring like nothing had happened. What's more, Buddy Leung wasn't sure he didn't hear them snore throughout the storm-line simulation, unlike bugs and frogs pausing from their ruckus during thunderstorms.

No sooner did the Fafamans' persisting snooze occur to Buddy, though, than that snooze climaxed on an abrupt snort. Following which, the faded lights triggered simultaneous uncurling of all three tralalafas.

At long last, Buddy was on his way to study wreckage from the crashed Tictoctickian spaceship. But could anything about that extraterrestrial vehicle surprise him more than what just occurred to him?

It wasn't the simulated storm-line tumult that roused Safasafala and Mafakakala from slumber, like an alarm clock. Rather, the cessation of that tumult was what stirred them awake!

Chapter 15

Have to keep myself cool, calm and collected until Yoon-hee and company re-establish contact, Captain Helena Taylor counseled herself. *Especially if I think of something not requiring their assistance, although can't imagine what that would be.*

Noises from next door seized Helena Taylor's attention not long after the Fafamafalafama left her alone. She heard mumbling between the Fafamafalafama and a female. Small talk with one of his wives, she presumed.

The female end of the conversation quickly devolved into titters successively spaced closer and closer together until they became full-out giggles. That's when the Fafamafalafama's cavernous "ha-ha-ha"s set in. *Like Santa Claus grew tired of "ho-ho-ho,"* Helena mused.

All too soon, the giggles went from being interspersed with an occasional moan to nothing but moans, his and hers, ebbing and flowing most rhythmically.

No mystery what was happening. But Captain Taylor did have other questions, starting with room acoustics. How did noises from the Fafamafalafama's sexual conquest carry that easily through a rock wall? Or did a microphone and speaker convey direct aural access to the wife's boudoir? And was Helena supposed to become jealous, desiring a piece of the male extraterrestrial's action for herself?

Okay, Helena thought, *let's say there is no threat to Earth and Fafama from a third world. The Fafaman interstellar message in a bottle was totally unnecessary. Let's say the deer people of Tictoctic simply want to make friends. Or that the Fafamans dressed up animals native to Fafama, made them involuntary participants in a giant hoax.*

Okay, fine. But how can this guy dance his crazy dance, then whoop it up with his wives, not two hours after a terrorist attack during the ceremonial display of Fafaman military force? Complete with a cow-sized spider?

Moreover, let's assume the whole distress call from Fafama WAS that giant hoax, meant to lure unsuspecting do-gooders. Still, how can he cool the heels of a first-ever visitor from another planet, someone whose civilization clearly has demonstrated technological superiority? How can he leave me in seeming captivity while he gets it on with his harem? What is going through this guy's head? For all he knows, Earthlings are the real bad guys, intent on incinerating his planet any minute now!

Tired of overhearing Fafaman intimacies, Captain Taylor coursed restlessly about the guarded room. She checked the tunnels drilled so far into opposite walls, they emptied out on southeast and northwest-facing exteriors of the Great Pyramid. Could she escape crawling through one?

No she could not. The penlight she brought along revealed a giant fan recessed into each tunnel. They reminded her of a century-old jet engine's several-bladed interior. I.e. it would be impossible to safely squeeze her way past either one.

Captain Taylor consoled herself with a grim realization regarding had there not been such an obstacle. She would have had to crawl for miles, and reach the exit before another storm-line hit. And also before security realized she'd gone from where their ruler left her.

The tunnel-to-freedom prospect squelched, Helena pondered various curiosities contained within her imprisoning location.

When the Fafamafalafama operated the Fafaman compact disc player, it looked typical of antique players back on Earth. But seen up close, Helena realized it was set into a leather-looking pillow bound against the wall. And bound against the wall beside that pillow was another pillow, a transparent pillow encasing a pile of compact discs in cushioning gelatinous goo.

Sounds from additional sexual conquest providing an unsettling backdrop, Captain Helena Taylor also noticed a television set, a small full bookcase, and what she intuited was a refrigerator. All were padded with the same, leather-looking material cushioning the CD player.

Helena didn't dare open the refrigerator, for the eerie ruckus emanating from inside.

Helena recalled what she observed after a beetle-shaped vehicle parked beside a mini-pyramid some distance from the Great Pyramid. One of that vehicle's occupants draped a tarp over it, tied down to the driveway. Clearly, the tarp would shield the vehicle from sunset storm-lines.

Didn't reason suggest the padding provided for Fafaman CD players and the rest was likewise meant to protect against sunset storm-lines? Or rather, to protect against sunset storm-lines simulated indoors?

A soft yet firm rap on the door ended Captain Taylor's stress-reducing contemplations.

One guard entered before she could make a move either to ease his way or block him. The monotone digitized voice of Taylor's translator replaced his pleasantly intoned fah-lah-lahs with, "Good news. Your crew says you have a lot of time for your visit."

"Was that my crew aboard our spaceship, or the crew who accompanied me down here to your planet's surface?"

"On one of our frequencies, someone from your spaceship sent the message that you have a lot of time. He also asked us to relay this message to your crew who accompanied you. He assured us there is no problem for you to stay a full rotation or rotations of Fafama."

"Who was he?"

"He was one of your crew aboard your spaceship, like you said."

"But he gave his name? He identified himself?"

The guard had seemed ebullient to Helena, or feigning ebullience. He behaved like a surgeon reporting to an anxiously awaiting family that the operation went really well, the tumor turned out benign. On her question about the identity of the Earthling crew member who bore good tidings, though, he froze. Where the captain was concerned, he might as well have been a robot experiencing a short circuit. "I am sorry," he finally fah-lah-lahed. "When this information was conveyed to me, I did not think to ask who sent it. I can find out for you, however."

"Actually, if I could be allowed re-established direct communication with our spaceship, I could find out for myself."

"I am sorry, but that is too dangerous. Our reconnaissance team is still securing the area. They are still making sure neither more insurgents nor 'ahtpah' were set free in our neighborhoods."

"No," Captain Taylor shook her head. She tried to maintain a friendly smile despite the bottom dropping out of her stomach. "I am not talking about traveling outside the pyramid. I am only asking…"

"Somebody from your spacecraft said you can stay for a lot of time. I will find out who it was." With that the guard was gone, well before Captain Taylor's translator could finish fah-lah-lahing, "Wait, please."

Captain Taylor shivered anxiously, nearly collapsing onto the room's lone tralalafa. The guard, or whoever spoke to him, had to be lying, flat-out lying, about the supposed "good news." Unless, it occurred to Helena, the Fafamans made an offer the onboard crew concluded they could not diplomatically refuse. Maybe Wafalawa or some other Fafaman said something like: *To fully grasp the situation here, your away team needs to remain with us a few rotations of our planet. Will that be a problem for you? Also, we had to put the antlered other-worlders and their wreckage in extra-secure locations. To see them, your away team might fall out of communication range temporarily. Okay?*

Just what were Kevin and company supposed to have said if the situation was presented like that? Probably, though, the Fafamans didn't ask her crew a thing. And the message from someone whose name conveniently escaped attention was a total fabrication. *My God, do they think that convincing me there's all the time in the world will make the Fafamafalafama's amorous advances more acceptable?*

Captain Taylor's stomach resumed sinking.

As Taylor curled into a fetal position on the tralalafa, she told herself another fearful possibility. Maybe the Fafamans wondered: *What if these people we lured here from another solar system are also up to no good? What if they pose a worse threat than the one we faked with the antlered creatures? If that's the case, shouldn't we best hold some of them hostage?*

The more she thought on it, the more satisfactory that explanation seemed for the away team's treatment. A certain conviction lifted Taylor's spirits, that Dr. Magabu would reach the same conclusion. And henceforth navigate the psychological course necessary to convince Fafamans they were under no threat from Earthlings. He might even have a few brought aboard the Smoke and Mirrors to show them that if anything, their extraterrestrial visitors were defenseless. *No, the Fafamans might see that as weakness, and lose any respect for us, which could prove equally dangerous...*

...Helena wished she could shut off her mind long enough to take a catnap. She felt absolutely exhausted. No doubt, she would benefit from whatever sleep she could get before heaven-only-knew-what-next.

She reminisced about biking with daughter Shelly along beaches in Oregon and northern California. Scanning the Pacific for humpback whales... But an awful memory intruded, of ghostly apparitions during the Mars flyby. Especially the one she recognized: Chris's great uncle Pedro. Sheer terror had left his eyes wide open on a worn face that emerged from one wall only to quickly disappear through another...

The door rattled from someone unlocking it.

Helena recognized the Fafamafalafama's deep-throated fah-lah-lahs, perhaps affectedly deep-throated. While he conversed with the guards just outside, she clicked off her translator, and resumed a fetal-curl recline on the tralalafa.

It was all Helena could do to keep from trembling. What if the Fafaman ruler turned up the lights so the tralalafa enfolded her like a Venus flytrap enfolding a bug? But wouldn't he know that Earthlings sleep in the dark, blanketed by bed sheets not plant leaves? And seeing her appear sleeping, wouldn't he just tiptoe away, quietly closing the door behind him?

What Helena heard next made her tense up stiff as a board.

She found nothing bothersome about swishes from the Fafamafalafama's flowing robes. But there was also the unmistakable sound of buttons unfastened slowly, painstakingly carefully, to make as little noise as possible.

Helena feared she would soon have to object in the strongest possible terms. Only a last slim thread of lingering doubt held her back from already jumping to her feet in a wild rage. Wasn't she misreading the Fafaman ruler's intent? Exhausted by his wifely conquests, didn't he scheme simply to nap on the floor beside the tralalafa? And even if he boarded the plant's gigantic leaf, wouldn't he lie down as discreetly far away from her as he could get?

Yes, Helena could go ahead and accuse the Fafamafalafama of something dreadful. But if she was wrong, she would do immeasurable harm to a relationship already maximally strained.

Aggravating Helena's concern, she overheard a bottle opened quietly, followed by a pill shaken out. *Please, please, please*, she prayed silently, *please may I be wildly off-base on what I fear his medication is for.*

The Fafamafalafama ever-so-slowly lowered himself down upon the tralalafa. Helena could feel his tentativeness. That if and when she objected, he would spring back off.

Finally something happened so shocking, Helena's tension unwound if only for a fleeting instant. The Fafamafalafama cuddled behind her, gently molded his body against hers. And he draped an arm round her waist, holding on just below her breasts. He was spooning her.

Helena couldn't help appreciating the warmth and comfort. But before she could snuggle, sheer disgust and rage took over. She yanked off the Fafaman ruler's arm with all the fury she would have hurled away a snake, had she woken to find one slithering across her. Then clicking back on her translator, she sat up and faced the Fafamafalafama reduced to his boxer shorts.

He suddenly grabbed his head in both hands, and his fah-lah-lahs came groaning out as they translated, "You have to understand, 'Cahptahn Taylah.' I've had to deal with the new threat from Tictoctic in addition to longstanding threats from desert barbarians. And now, all the sleep I have lost, wondering whether I can be honest with you! Asking myself how much we can trust your arrival is as pure of motive as you would have us believe! And, and not knowing your culture, really... Abetted by music supplied by your officer, our dance aboard the space station led me to a certain supposition in my exhausted state. That maybe the unspoken strain in our negotiations stemmed from your offense at my NOT attempting your seduction. Even now, how you initially responded to my behavior...-"

The rest of the translation was lost to Helena. Despite still being seated beside the Fafamafalafama on a tralalafa, she could only take so much before bursting out, "The desert people have staged a deadly attack where obviously they infiltrated your military! At the same time, you are hosting people from another planet who risked their lives on virtually untested technology to answer your distress call!

"But what do you do? WHAT DO YOU DO?!?! After isolating me from the rest of my crew, you take me on an historical tour better left for another time! Then you make me wait endlessly while you socialize with your wives! At least if you had been playing with your children instead!

"Meanwhile, for all you know, the antlered creatures from Tictoctic are entering your solar system as we speak! And they are less than a day from launching an attack on your planet! But the main thing on your mind is finding out whether I want to be SEDUCED?!?!"

The Fafamafalafama leapt off the tralalafa and shouted, though the translator still reduced his fah-lah-lahs to a digitized monotone, "AVERT YOUR FACE, WOMAN!!!" Then he stabbed his arms and legs back into his clothes, and refastened the shirt buttons with staccato speed.

When he unsheathed his sword, he made diagonal sweeps so rapidly that Captain Helena Taylor could hear the air swish. Swish! Swish! She wanted to demand return within communication range of her crew, but feared the Fafamafalafama might lose so much more control that he would set about lopping off her head. What Helena did find the courage to say, though, was, "Have you received any reports on how the tasks are proceeding for Officer Leung and my husband, Officer Olsen-Taylor?"

The instant his name left her lips, Helena regretted mentioning her husband as husband. She meant to re-emphasize, however obliquely, there was no way the Fafamafalafama could add her to his string of sexual conquests. Too late, it occurred to her she might have put Chris in great, or greater, danger.

The Fafamafalafama swung his sword swish! through the air in seeming response to Helena's question. But the wry half-smile expression that flashed across his face had her wondering whether his severe countenance was more feigned than heartfelt. Was that half-smile an involuntary reaction he hoped she wouldn't notice, as he enjoyed keeping her terrified? He enjoyed making her wonder whether he might decide on a whim to lop off her husband's head?

After more swishes, the Fafamafalafama at last said, "Not long from now, you would have experienced sunset storm-line conditions conveyed inside this room. However, let me spare you..." He pressed a button beside the entrance, causing metallic covers to slide down smoothly across the two round-holed tunnels that emptied into the room. "...because you have more important matters on your mind.

"I will check on Officer 'Lahuhng' for you. But as for your husband, Officer 'Ohlsahn-Taylah'... Ah, yes... 'Cahptahn Taylah,' 'Ohlsahn-Taylah'..."

Did the Fafaman ruler only just then realize Chris shared Helena's last name? And was he also drawing a larger inference? That Chris sharing the Taylor while she did not share the Olsen meant a matriarchal society where women ruled?

"Officer 'Ohlsahn-Taylah' will be accompanying my first wife to witness our response to the desert people attack. And then he will enjoy a front-row seat to the legend of the ephemeral dragons. Although you might consider that another waste of time..."

On such sour note, the Fafamafalafama slammed the door shut, and stomped off.

Chapter 16

"Amazing, Kevin," Buddy Leung said breathlessly. "The Tictoctic vehicle's hull fragments give every impression they incorporate the same hybrid alloy we formulated for the mirror array. Won't know for absolute certain until the full analysis, but wow! And what's even more amazing is an undeniable implication of the debris field. Yes, crash impact shattered apart their spaceship so completely, no idea how our good Samaritans from Tictoctic survived for even seconds, let alone days. But that debris field..." Buddy shook his head in wonderment at the wreckage spread before him. Then he went on, "The Fafamans assure me this display replicates the crash site, and they've got the photos to prove it."

"Spit it out, man!" said Kevin Smith-Park back aboard the Smoke and Mirrors. "What's the big deal with the freakin' debris field?"

"The 'big deal,' Officer Smith-Park, is that it strongly implicates a saucer-shaped design!"

"Saucer-shaped?! Chris will be thrilled. Oh, yeah! That's how Fafamans depicted the bad guy spaceships!'"

"Yes," said Buddy. "Apparently the Tictoctic beings found a different yet still successful approach to mirror array technology."

"Only, the Smoke and Mirrors hasn't crashed into a planet. At least not yet," added Kevin. "But if you've got that right about the special alloy, Buddy, so much for the Fafamans tricking us here," he conceded with a shoulder shrug Buddy would not see. "So much for drugged-out reindeer dressed for failure, and random scrap metal spread out in a provocative arrangement to help perpetrate the hoax."

"Instead we face some fearful implications," lamented Buddy Leung, squatting on the floor of an underground hangar somewhere near the Great Pyramid. He held a translucently thin yet rigid, subtly-warped metallic piece of spacecraft hull presumably from Tictoctic.

For Buddy's examination of the wreckage, Fafaman hangar crew provided abundant light usually reserved for sleep time. Especially generous of them since they subsequently required glare-reducing goggles to service their copters and jets.

Thanks to such a well-lit hangar, Leung could indulge his endless fascination with the peculiar, poorly understood effects of photon pressure. To his delight, the fragment of alloy in his hands produced a prismatic, arrow-straight rainbow. And other fragments strewn across the hangar floor sporadically flopped about like fish thrown onto a pier. Or they rustled like so many fallen leaves stirred by a breeze, all due to the force of light shining on them.

Buddy Leung remained in contact with the Smoke and Mirrors by means of his earpiece. It was sensitive enough to pick up every sound within a twenty-foot radius, the same as his camcorder he had tucked away for being too noticeable. But he pretended to communicate through his translator as if it doubled as a walkie-talkie. He hoped what Safasafala overheard him saying would hasten the away team's return to the Smoke and Mirrors.

"From here forward, your end of our conversation should be geared towards influencing your Fafaman eavesdroppers," suggested Kevin, unwittingly in sync with Buddy's scheme. "This situation is starting to scare the crap out of me, so it's time they felt the same."

"Copy that. It's starting to scare the crap out of me as well."

"If those antlered freaks from Tictoctic possess star-hopping technology comparable to ours, isn't it possible their invasion will arrive sooner rather than later?"

"That's right, Officer Smith-Park," Buddy agreed. "For all we know, they're entering this solar system as we speak. They could be here before another full rotation of Fafama. And they are unlikely to make their predecessors' mistake.

"The creatures from Tictoctic who did this..." Buddy made a sweeping gesture with his hull fragment like he was introducing the debris field for the first time. "Those creatures probably never received formal training how to pilot an interstellar spacecraft. They just stole it, and learned on the fly, literally. And thank goodness they took such courageous action to warn us about their fellow creatures' plans. However, if those fellow creatures have any idea what they were up to, the invasion schedule might have been moved up dramatically sooner. Possibly there's next to no time left to prepare."

"So the best course of action," Kevin reacted, intent on feeding Buddy lines for their Fafaman eavesdroppers, "is our return to Earth immediately. Back there, we can gather weapons for Fafama's defense."

"Great minds think alike, Officer Smith-Park," said Buddy. "You're right; we should return to Earth immediately, where we can pick up our asteroid-busting laser cannons. Don't think our government would mind the Fafamans keeping some of them for a permanent defense shield." Buddy could sense that behind his anti-glare goggles, Safasafala's already big eyes were growing even bigger, simulated blazing light be damned.

"Are you hearing this, Chris?" asked Kevin. "Oh, that's right. The Vara-what's-her-face is having him see justice meted out to the bad guys; he's probably in no position to talk. But I hope whatever his position, especially if it's horizontal, he remembers he's a married man and a homo sapien. Okay, Bud, this is it! Am I right, Ali? He's nodding. Time to tell them we need to round up our away team, pronto."

"Yes, I'll make sure to thank them for their hospitality," Buddy assured Kevin. "And I will also tell them we need the captain and Officer Olsen-Taylor for our hasty return to Earth. And, bringing along some of this mirror array wreckage would not be a bad idea. We've already lost one firefly. And the two we have left assumes, of course, that the one in active use doesn't collide with a comet or some such."

"I have been empowered to speak for the Fafamafalafama," said Safasafala, impatient after what he'd just overheard. "Here is an idea so you may continue to enjoy our hospitality. Send home a message about the threat from Tictoctic. Then ask that a second interstellar spacecraft bring us the laser cannon you mentioned."

"There is no second interstellar spacecraft yet," Buddy shook his head. "The Smoke and Mirrors is the only one, a prototype. We took a major risk flying it out here after we received your distress call. We originally were not planning to voyage much beyond the outer fringe of our own solar system. That's why I also ask to bring some of this wreckage with us. Looks like the creatures from Tictoctic travel light-speed multiples on the same technology we use. So these hull fragments could prove critically helpful if, for example, an asteroid were to damage our mirror array. But back to your suggestion, building a second interstellar starship will take a half-year or longer."

Safasafala inhaled and exhaled with an exasperation his anti-glare goggles could not conceal. "Well, then," he said at last, "could you leave us with…could you detach weapons from your spacecraft? Something we could retrofit on our space station for the time being?"

"Removing weapons from our spacecraft would also require refurbishing its hull," Buddy asserted, shaking his head NO. "And that would take almost as long as building a second interstellar ship. Weaponry is integral to the design of the Smoke and Mirrors." While speaking, Officer Buddy Leung made the strongest effort possible to look unflinchingly, unblinkingly into Safasafala's goggles. Buddy assumed the Fafaman linguist well-versed in nonverbal communication. So he fought an urge to look down, lose himself in the spaceship wreckage, lest Safasafala surmise he was lying. Which could lead to suspicion the Smoke and Mirrors came totally unarmed.

Of course Buddy *was* lying, and the Smoke and Mirrors *did* come totally unarmed.

Fafaman linguist Safasafala made an even more exasperated-sounding inhale and exhale. During his subsequent pause to process the Earthling's dismissal of his suggestion, Buddy had to keep straining not to squirm under his scrutiny. "I will convey your concerns to the Fafamafalafama," Safasafala fah-lah-lahed at last. "Then we will see what he wants to do."

"I know about your expression, the storm-line cannot pass before the storm-line passes. But we have a saying I respectfully submit is more pertinent to this situation: Time is running out."

*

Chris Olsen-Taylor caught snatches of Buddy's tense conversation on his earpiece while the Varalawa strapped him into a plush seat beside her on a jet-powered glider. He appreciated Kevin and Buddy's valiant effort to diplomatically ease Fafamans into allowing the away team's return aboard the Smoke and

Mirrors. He wanted to learn more, maybe even make some input. But he feared the first wife, the Varalawa, would not take kindly to his distraction, to his not giving her his full attention. Couldn't her reservedly guarded demeanor suddenly turn the corner to dangerously suspicious?

"We will be escorted by jets above, below, and both sides of us," said the Varalawa, strapping herself into the pilot's seat. "As we approach the rebel stronghold, two will peel off for conducting a retaliatory mission."

Chris reflected wistfully on how he could have taken an active part in his fellow Earthlings' most urgent discussion. That is, if only it had gotten going before the first wife arrived.

Crew back aboard the Smoke and Mirrors had kept in contact with Chris as much as possible throughout his stressful tedium essentially imprisoned by the Fafamans. Nevertheless, he felt left to rot in a media center while the Fafamafalafama took his wife who-knew-where.

Only Buddy got to do what the away team came for in the first place. He met with the antlered creatures from Tictoctic, and sorted through wreckage of their crashed space vehicle. But before any of that happened, even he had had a lot of his time wasted enwrapped by a tralalafa while his hosts took a nap. And heaven only knew what the discomfort was about that he didn't want to discuss. Moreover, Officer Buddy Leung's meeting with the creatures purportedly crash-landed from Tictoctic didn't go exactly as hoped for. Safasafala insisted on translating, and denied direct access to the dictionary purportedly brought along by the injured Tictoctickians.

Anyhow, Chris easily gathered that Buddy's remarks to Kevin were meant for Safasafala's eavesdropping. The Fafaman linguist was to be persuaded that letting go of the away team Earthlings was in Fafama's best interest. Back home, their spaceship could be outfitted for interstellar war! All dreamers step aside! No need for a dealer in obscure antique music!

While the Varalawa finished strapping herself in, Chris realized it was probably just as well he felt inhibited from contributing to Buddy and Kevin's dialogue. He was liable to have said something distractingly stupid and unhelpful, maybe even throwing off their game plan.

Earlier that day, the trivial nature of what Chris had to deal with left him too embarrassed to say much. How could he take up Kevin and company's time describing a television show for selecting the Fafamafalafama's next wife? They were busy scheming re-established contact with Helena, plus the away team's escape from Fafama if it turned out they were indeed being held hostage. Did Kevin and company really need an interruption to learn about the tralalafa-suit competition like a beauty pageant swimsuit competition? About the suits being bottomless as opposed to topless? And about how next-wife contestants answered a question put to them afterwards?

The question, incidentally: What is the most important thing you can imagine doing as the Rafafaranalana, as the twenty-second wife of the Fafamafalafama?

Most contestants initially greeted that question with a tittered giggle. Then the audience added howling monkey hee-hee-hees, their thoughts obviously on the newlywed's first expected activity once alone.

Anyway, fellow Smoke and Mirrors crew could hear everything through a teensy surveillance mike clipped inside Chris's shirt collar. What more was there for him to add?

One contestant said, "The most important thing I can imagine doing, besides THAT, tee-hee!, is showing the desert people how life inside the pyramid really isn't so bad."

"Isn't so BAD?!?" complained the host, his facial expression sending the audience into more monkey-howl hee-hee-hees. "Sounds like you are not very sure yourself!"

"Oh, I am sure." More titters.

"Sure of what?"

"I am sure this is a great place, this is a great society, and this is a great time to be alive! Especially since we now have visitors from, um, out there! Tee-hee!"

Thunderous foot-stomping and howls of approval ensued. Again, what commentary could Chris have added that would have mattered as anything more than needless distraction? At least until contact was re-established with his wife?

Then there was Fafaman music Chris sampled on what bore a remarkable resemblance to an antique CD player, recessed into a cushioned wall aperture. Sure, some chord progressions sounded very middle-eastern, and most vocalizing didn't seem to rise beyond erotic moaning. But big deal!

There was also how Chris surprisingly found himself preferring the dim, greenish luminescence of his detention room kept dark. That is, as opposed to its daylight simulation, what the Fafamans referred to as blinding-light or stars-fade. The place somehow felt more soothing, less threatening, no longer the stuff of nightmares despite its few features being left shadowed. Occasional unsettling thumps and scratches continued to issue from the small refrigerator, but no matter.

Striking yet an even more bizarre note was the sunset storm-line simulation supplied by jet-engine-type fans recessed deep within large cylindrical wall apertures.

Chris might have fussed about that experience possibly endangering him. But Wafalawa's intervention put him at ease.

Moments prior to the fans kicking in, Wafalawa explained Chris's options. He could ride out the turbulence enwrapped by a tralalafa, or securely zipped up inside a padded comforter wedged against one corner. The comforter's transparent material would let him watch simulated storm-line winds roll and bounce the tralalafa about.

Since Chris chose the comforter, the Fafaman science adviser didn't bother explaining how that odd plant could have taken care of certain bodily functions. However, Wafalawa did mention the psychological impact from ancestors seeking refuge in tralalafas over millions of Fafaman years. Namely, each present-day Fafaman required snug enwrapping by a tralalafa to doze off, and the cessation of the storm-line to wake up.

Even had Officer Chris Olsen-Taylor wanted to share Wafalawa's history lesson with Kevin and company, there wouldn't have been any need. His earpiece picked up the entire translation.

Of course, Chris's earpiece couldn't show the simulated storm-line winds knocking the tralalafa about the room like clothing inside a drier. Nor could it pick up Chris wondering how even a million years of riding out the storm-line in one of those things could ever have become habit-forming, let alone sleep-inducing.

Anyway, Chris unpacked himself from the protective comforter once the simulated storm-line was done.

That's when the first wife strode in alone, having ordered her security detail to wait outside.

Chris immediately recognized her as the woman who headed up the parade interrupted by a terrorist attack. Who conveyed the odd feeling he had attracted her attention, even from behind her sun-glare goggles a great distance away.

Presently her outfit included baggy pants that came down just below her knees, modestly enough. So much for her figure-revealing garb worn during the violently interrupted parade!

Then there was the first wife's round, nocturnal-eyed face. Chris was bowled over seeing it up much closer than during that fateful parade, and no longer obscured by sun-glare goggles. Framed by ringlet curls, with the rest of her abundant raven-black hair bunched in coiled braids, he couldn't help feeling its striking beauty concealed some deep dark secret.

As Chris scrambled to his feet beside the transparent comforter, she snuck a top-to-bottom glance at him, or did she? Then she struck a pose, hands to hips, and looked up away from him to announce, "I am the Varalawa, the first wife of the Fafamafalafama. I will take you on a flight to see how we deal with the desert insurgents for their deadly attack, and to experience a great mystery of our planet." Her haughty-toned fah-lah-lahs had Chris thinking she might as well have been someone else introducing her and her plans.

Chris also wondered: Was she behaving this way, coming off like this, in her struggle to suppress, conceal feelings she was having for an extraterrestrial she'd only glimpsed from afar up to then? Not to mention her disgust over having to share the "Fafamazoo" with twenty other women? Or were there no such feelings? Was the disgust enough by itself to account for her affectedly extreme formality? Or was this simply how she handled tiresome assignments in what she otherwise found a most satisfying role as first wife?

Whichever solution fit, Chris awkwardly slung his right arm down diagonally across his chest, bowed, and said, "Pama."

Still looking away from him, the Varalawa nevertheless returned his bow and, if Chris Olsen-Taylor wasn't mistaken, flashed a bemused grin. Though she then spun around on the heel of one of her moccasin-type shoes, to face the exit. Her abruptness left Olsen-Taylor expecting her to march goosestep. However, she just as abruptly melted into a relaxed saunter, fah-lah-lahing, "Follow me, please. And bring your envirosuit if there is anything in it you might need."

The Varalawa's security attachment fell into place behind Chris. So he kept his eyes off her figure, fearing he might be made to answer to the Fafamafalafama himself, were his lustful attention noticeable. A sword duel, perhaps.

And who knew but that the Varalawa didn't share a comparable fear of her husband? That she kept Chris in tow behind her for a specific reason? To avoid the risk of succumbing to the temptation of ogling him were they walking side-by-side?

"You are Officer 'Ohlsahn-Taylah,' correct?" asked the first wife in a monotone from which the translator's deadpan digitized voice subtracted nothing.

"Correct," answered Chris as she led him into a monorail headed for one of the launch hangars. He tried to keep his own voice as emotionless as possible.

"And the captain, she is a 'Taylah'?"

"Yes," confirmed Chris, wondering what kind of immoral fool he was not to elaborate on how that meant they were married.

"There is another 'Taylah' aboard your spacecraft?"

"She is the only other one."

The first wife turned around to give Chris a wide-eyed look, which with her nocturnally evolved eyes meant extra wide-eyed. He was reminded of the searching look daughter Shelly used to give him on her birthday, expectant of a most delightful surprise. It was the sort of look he couldn't remember the last time Helena gave him.

The Varalawa avoided eye contact altogether while strapping Chris into the seat beside hers on the jet glider. She focused intently on certain locking mechanisms instead. So intently, Chris thought better of continuing to regard her oversized eyes with a thought to garnering reciprocal attention. How did he know such effort for too lingeringly long wouldn't suddenly turn her dangerously hostile?

On the other hand, she leaned into Chris so close, he could hear her breathing, and detect a flowery scent with a hint of peppermint. While she finished adjusting his straps, he labored to keep his own breathing measured, not reveal a nervous apprehension she might suddenly press her lips to his.

Having strapped in the Earthling without incident, the first wife flopped back in her own seat. Chris wasn't sure her subsequent exhalation of relief didn't match his own. Though relief from what? From having gotten so close to such an ugly, foul-smelling, other-world creature? Or from having succeeded in not throwing herself at him?

Whichever, the Varalawa backed the glider away from the service terminal, halting it aimed towards a slanted wall the opposite end of the launch strip. Fah-lah-lahs ensued between her and ground control, pursuant to which said wall slid up into the ceiling, revealing star-studded night sky.

A small jet engine roared to life, and the first wife's personal aircraft glider accelerated rolling down the launch strip. Already inches off the ground when it reached the exit, it made no use of the extra thousand-foot macadam tongue that slid out.

"This is a nice day!" the Varalawa shouted above shrill engine hum as she banked the glider arcing heavenwards, and Chris adjusted the volume on his translator.

After being cooped up so long inside the pyramid, Chris found flying high above Fafama overwhelmingly exhilarating. Worry dissipated regarding what awaited him, what was happening between Helena and the Fafamafalafama, the invasion threat from the antlered third party…He might as well have arrived back out to a beach on Earth after a long absence, freed from anxiety by contemplation of the ocean's vastness.

As the first wife's glider approached a gradual elevation east of the Great Pyramid, several escort jets hove into view all around. Engine racket additional to what issued from the glider announced their presence. How ironic, Chris thought. Those aircraft were supposed to provide extra security, but actually reignited his anxiety.

Chris still managed to keep potential panic at bay by bothering over something first noticed from the Great Pyramid's review stand. "There is a big green glow down there! To the left! Off to your side of the glider!" Chris shouted so the translator could tease out his vocalizing from ambient jet-engine drone. "Is that a flounder-mice infestation?!"

"No!" the Varalawa shook her head. "We call it the 'lamanacasa'! A monster version of the 'namalumala' (flounder mouse)!"

"That is one creature!?!?!?"

"They are a problem!" The Varalawa continued shouting for the same reason as Chris, to be heard about the aforementioned jet-engine drone. "Right after birth, they burrow deep below ground for a nineteen-solar-orbit-long sleep! Then they tunnel back near the surface, where they lie in wait for an unpredictable number of days! Whenever they are ready, without warning they lift their wide, flat bodies as far off the ground as their four legs will stretch! And their rectum emits a poisonous gas that paralyzes any living thing within a hundred-thousand square 'tahtah'!!

"Soon thereafter, they check if their gas has paralyzed an 'ahtpah' so they can suck body fluids from its shell! If no such luck, they release more gas! They keep doing this until either they catch an 'ahtpah,' or they run out of gas!!

"Our ecologists have located most of the 'lamanacasa' in the developed zone! Subsequent underground explosives have removed those threats! But this must be one they missed! And you see we have walled it in with our excavation machinery!

"Maybe our scientists are going to feed it the 'ahtpah' from the attack during the parade! That particular 'lamanacasa' is in a residential area where they can't blow it up without destroying some homes! So the best hope is probably to send it burrowing back below ground for another nineteen Fafaman years! Surely we will think of something better to do about it before its next emergence!"

"So if your people feed it an ahtpah soon enough, it will not emit any poisonous gas?!"

"That has worked in the past!"

The Varalawa's glider encircled by her jet entourage flew over a mountain ridge worn down to gentle hills, until it was making way across a valley. There, Chris beheld row upon row of small pyramids. From between some of them lazily curled wreathes of smoke, bluish-gray in the starlight, while flames sporadically shot out from between others. Chris imagined some unimaginably enormous crocodile, its scaly back smoldering from having caught fire inside.

"This is our manufacturing center! Our agricultural center lies west of the Great Pyramid, apart from what is grown and raised within the pyramid itself!"

"Was this location chosen for a particular reason?!" Chris asked while his thoughts shifted from burning crocodile to peering down into the darkness of a charcoal grill after a cookout. Maybe the flames given off by Fafaman manufacturing processes reminded him more of the orange-red glow from a briquette not yet turned completely ashen. Or did a lava field only partially cooled make for an even better comparison? Thanks to streams of molten rock shining bright orange and red between cracks in the hardened lava?

Whichever, Chris concluded intelligent life on Fafama comprised a mighty force of nature not to be taken lightly, the same as on Earth.

"An aquifer runs from this region to the Great Basin much further east!" shouted the Varalawa, starting in on her answer to Chris's question. "Thanks to inventors inspired by the Fafamafalafama, it supplies not only most of our drinking water! It also supplies hydroelectric power plenty adequate, together with fuel burning, to operate everything from factories to televisions! Moreover, as residential use for carrying away waste has risen, we have had to construct a capillary network to actually reverse the tendency for underground water to flow seaward!"

For Chris, the translator's monotone delivery complemented perfectly the sterile content of the first wife's response. His fault for asking what he asked in the first place, yet he still couldn't help wondering why she didn't play him a tourist guide tape or some such instead.

But they were leaving the vast manufacturing valley behind for a second mountain ridge also worn hilly by millions of years of daily sunset storm-lines. And the Varalawa was saying, "We are approaching a stronghold of the desert barbarians!"

"Think I see a small pyramid here and there! Is that them?!" asked Chris. Even in the bright starlight of a cloudless, haze-free night sky, he had difficulty discerning features. Back in the manufacturing zone, industrial-furnace-fire glows were abetted by plentiful flounder-mouse bioluminescence filling those few spots still left undeveloped. But presently, not only was the land devoid of manufacturing activity. Scarce bioluminescence was on offer from any source.

"Many of them live in caves and underground tunnels! But yes! There are a few pyramids!"

"We were told they had rejected civilization altogether! That they slept only inside caves and tralalafas during your stars-fade blinding-light!"

"There is nothing consistent about them! They are a mass of contradictions!"

Chris found the agitation in the Varalawa's voice obvious. But agitation over what? Agitation over having to explain to him? Or was she still ticked off at the "barbarians" for disrupting the show-of-force parade? Or was there something else altogether?

"And now," the Varalawa's fah-lah-lahs translated as she continued, "they will suffer consequences for their latest attack!"

Two jets peeled off from the glider escort formation. Both showed their underbellies as they tilted left to descend arcing towards their assigned targets.

"How do they know this is where to strike?!"

"This is an insurgent area!"

"But, do they know the attack during the parade came specifically from here?!"

"We are certain they all endorse the perpetrators' actions!"

"Are you certain their children endorse those actions?!"

With that question from Chris, the Varalawa went mute. She turned towards flashes of light from the ground, followed seconds later by faint booms like distant thunder.

Before Chris could think what to say next, or whether he should remain quiet, one of the two attack jets burst apart in another flash of light. This flash revealed a spiral smoke trail from the ground all the way up to the jet, to where the jet had been.

"YOU SEE?!?!?!" the Varalawa's anguished fah-lah-lahs translated. "They install their missile launchers in around where their children live!!! But what choice do we have other than to bomb those launchers where they are installed?!?!"

An intercom set into the ceiling over the first wife's seat erupted with a flood of urgent-sounding fah-lah-lahs. They came out so slurred, the translator spit random syllables sounding more like static to Chris.

"They have launched another heat-seeking missile!" the Varalawa shouted as she banked the glider steep right. The remaining escort jets locked into that exact same maneuver.

BOOM!

The glider wheeling wing over wing, Chris found himself still of enough presence of mind to realize it wasn't hit, despite his total vertigo.

The first wife regained control, brought her aircraft back to level, right-side-up flight. As she did so, Chris craned his head around just in time to see a crashing fireball. Had to have been the jet flying below them, he figured.

"No need to suspend the rest of your itinerary, most esteemed Varalawa!" fah-lah-lahed from the intercom distinctly enough for Chris's translator to handle.

"Pama."

Two of the remaining jets took up positions either side of the glider while the other two peeled off. Chris gathered no additional danger was anticipated to approach what they'd just gone through. But maybe the peeled-off jets were scouting about just to make sure.

Anyhow, for a long while the Varalawa remained quiet, made no further effort to be heard above the jet-engine hum. That didn't keep her near-hysterical cry from echoing in Chris's head, though, again and again from when the translation went, "What choice do we have?!"

As the terrain flattened out beneath the powered glider, with large expanses glowing from flounder-mouse bioluminescence, Chris realized the obvious. Far from smug satisfaction over how the insurgent problem was being handled, far from regarding Chris's questions as stupid, the Varalawa had expressed authentic frustration.

Did it stem from having to give him a guided tour? Maybe she wasn't exactly looking forward to showing him this mystery the Fafaman ruler had hyped? Maybe there were innumerable other things she would have preferred doing, vain things like getting her nails done?

And since the rocket attack downed two of their escort jets, what was her silent treatment about? Upset with this new tragedy? Guilt spurred by the Earthling, over the killing of innocents that might have resulted from the jets' retaliatory bombing? Or again, was she simply fuming over being stuck playing tour guide? Plus having to risk her own neck to show this ignorant intruder from another planet what civilized Fafaman people were up against? And for all her efforts receiving insulting questions while he leered at her lustfully?

Well, Earthling Chris finally decided, *if her frustration is of a humble, searching sort, she will appreciate my inquiring further. But if she is frustrated about having to deal with me, and/or having to face some of the unpleasantness her husband presides over, my inquiring further is a kick in her baggy pants she deserves!* "Do the desert insurgents, um..." Chris trailed off momentarily, sensing the Varalawa grip the steering stick harder with his opening his mouth anew. "...do they draw their water from the same aquifer as your civilization?!"

"They complain our industrial waste is fouling their water supply! And that our factory exhaust is making some of their cavern network unlivable!"

"Well, are your people addressing those problems?!"

"I have heard of projects, experiments, but nothing possible yet on a large scale! Why can they not leave behind their archaic settlements, and come join us?!?!?" the Varalawa turned Chris's way to shout. She even took one hand off the steering stick to gesture emphatically.

"Has the question ever been framed that way for them?!"

The Varalawa shook her head no, adding, "Too few barbarians have ever wanted to abandon a way of life that has been theirs for hundreds of solar orbits!"

"So they have lived on that land a very long time?! Their ancestors did not invade it?!"

The Varalawa offered no answer. In fact, she acted like Chris hadn't said a word. So he went on, "If they have always lived there like that, why should they need to change?! Maybe they feel like *they* are the ones being attacked, when your people's manufacturing pollutes their habitat?!"

Most unexpectedly, the first wife reached over to lay her right hand gently on Chris's hands, where they were clasped together on his lap. With an urgent squeeze, she gave him a teary-eyed look, and fah-lah-lahed what translated as, "This is what I have grown up with!" *Don't make this any more painful for me than it already is.*

When the Varalawa withdrew her hand, to resume peering forward into the starlight, she said, "Soon we arrive to the Great Basin! Then with any luck at all, we will behold the ephemeral dragons!"

Chapter 17

"I have good news," said Safasafala grinning broadly on his return to the hangar strewn with Tictoctic spacecraft wreckage. Also, he was tapping the top of his head as though playing bongos, as Buddy saw it. *That must be what Fafamans do when they have something happy to report. Guess it's better than banging one's noggin against a wall.* "The Fafamafalafama tells me your 'Cahptahn Taylah' has much enjoyed her tour of the Great Pyramid's nipple. That is good news, yes?"

"That is such FREAKIN' good news, let's break open a bottle of champagne and shove it up Safawazoo's ass!" shouted Kevin through Buddy Leung's earpiece.

"Uh, I am glad to hear that," Officer Leung responded diplomatically, with Kevin's remark still ringing in his ears. "But, uh, what did the Fafamafalafama say about the urgency of our departure to obtain more help? And did he address the possibility of our taking along certain pieces of this wreckage?"

"There is more good news. When your captain was apprised of the situation, she and the Fafamafalafama agreed there is enough time."

"'Enough time'?!" exclaimed Kevin. "Enough time to shove a second bottle up his ass?! Well hot diggity dog!"

"How is there enough time?" Buddy asked wanly, straining to keep smiling. "As I think we discussed, for all we know the invasion from Tictoctic is on its way here even as we speak!"

"Ah! I think my words were mistranslated!" snapped Safasafala, though he still grinned broadly. "What your captain actually said was that she is going to share her recommendation with Officer 'Ohlsahn-Taylah' soon as he returns from his glider flight with the Varalawa. And that recommendation is for you, Officer Leung, to commandeer your spacecraft back to your planet 'Ahth.' There, you will quickly secure for us the equipment we need to defend ourselves against the animals from Tictoctic."

"Okay, maybe we won't shove the second bottle up this guy's ass. But how about we hear from Captain Taylor DIRECTLY??"

"I am certain Officer Olsen-Taylor will be in full agreement with that proposal," commented Buddy, straining to sustain his feeble smile. Nevertheless, he puzzled over why the Fafaman framed things in terms of Taylor having a recommendation to share with Chris Olsen-Taylor. Was this some chauvinist thing where Safasafala assumed the husband could veto his wife's decision despite her being the captain?

"Yes, and even more good news! 'Cahptahn Taylah' will advise Officer 'Ohlsahn-Taylah' they are asked to accept full Fafaman hospitality while you and the rest of your crew secure that necessary equipment from 'Ahth'!"

"Shove that second bottle back up his ass, with a third to follow!"

"I am sorry," Buddy Leung laughed, shaking his head in disbelief. "We took the minimum possible number of crew on this mission. This is the first time sending ourselves at faster than light-speed. Uncertain how that would turn out, we risked the minimum number of lives necessary. Like you say here, there were no more for the task than the task required. In other words, we cannot afford to leave Captain Taylor nor Officer Olsen-Taylor behind. We need them both when our spacecraft departs."

"That's right," said Kevin, back in Buddy's ear. "Officer Olsen-Taylor is the ballast we have to throw overboard if our ship starts sinking into their freakin' atmosphere!"

"And so, uhh, your offer of hospitality is very kind, but..." Buddy showed Safasafala the palms of his hands as in, nothing to hide.

"I think your captain said there are enough others of your kind for the trip."

"That surprises me," said Buddy looking the Fafaman linguist right in the eye. Safasafala had given him a comparable look when Buddy spoke of the Smoke and Mirrors' nonexistent weapons. "Could I speak to Captain Taylor directly?"

"You do not believe what I am telling you?"

Buddy wondered whether Safasafala huffed and puffed that question out of indignation over having his truthfulness challenged. Or was it frustration over not being able to get the Earthling to unflinchingly accept a falsehood? And was there special punishment awaiting the Fafaman for failing to accomplish this dissembling feat? Whichever, Buddy shook his head, "It is not that," as he frantically waved his hands like he was trying to ward off a wasp attack, he imagined. "You said yourself there seem to be, uh... given our translator has a ways to go before full fluency in your language, it might occasionally lead to troublesome misunderstandings. All I am saying is that a direct conversation with Captain Taylor will help assure no confusion about our next moves."

Safasafala made one of his exhales of exasperation. His grin looked increasingly plastered on, less authentic as he said, "I think your captain is still busy with the Fafamafalafama. I will have to check." He turned like he was about to leave, presumably to discover whether Captain Taylor was available yet. But then he paused, hint hint; Buddy could do the right thing diplomatically by calling off Safasafala going to check.

*

"So maybe the captain is really getting 'busy' with the Fafamazoo after that dance they put on for each other?"

Ali rolled his eyes and shook his head over Kevin's newest sweet nothings in Buddy's ear. But Deborah said, in a severe tone conveying, *Look guys, this is serious*, "Receiving so little information, and cut off from contact with Helena, one does have to wonder."

*

"Wait," said Buddy, gesturing at Safasafala while trying to ignore the provocative remarks heard over his earpiece. "Were you or someone else able to ask about our taking some of the Tictoctic spacecraft wreckage with us? It could prove critically important if our own vessel experiences any damage on the round-trip flight you propose we make from here to Earth."

"Ah!" Safasafala slapped the palm of his left hand against his head. "That was the other good news. As an expression of gratitude, the Fafamafalafama has made a pledge on behalf of our civilized peoples. After you return from your planet with the equipment we need for defense against the Tictoctic beasts, he will let you take all the Tictoctic spacecraft wreckage you desire."

Buddy couldn't help sincere, if bitter, amusement enhancing his grin before he reacted, "Uhhh, I hope we are having more translator problems."

"Why would you want more translator problems?" asked Safasafala, open-mouthed astonishment crumbling apart what little remained of his gleeful façade.

"I understood you to imply we cannot take any spacecraft wreckage until our return from Earth. But we need that wreckage NOW, if it is to help us," insisted Buddy. "As I mentioned before, we did not set out from our home planet expecting to make this particular trip. On our return to you, we will come far more prepared. We will no longer need such wreckage for replacing broken parts."

Buddy thought on how useless his plea had become, especially since he was certain nothing went wrong with the translator's performance. And Kevin was in his ear anew, this time with, "I say bottles to shove up ALL their freakin' asses."

Meanwhile Safasafala pasted back together his gleeful façade to say, "We are looking forward to showing our gratitude on your return." If Officer Leung didn't know better, the Fafaman linguist's subsequent bulging-eye stare challenged him, dared him to speak even a syllable more on the wreckage matter.

Before Buddy Leung could formulate a response, Nanofafo rushed in holding an opaque bottle and what looked like wine glasses. Where Buddy was concerned, Nanofafo's whiskers lent him a walrus aspect despite their incredible curling and uncurling on their own, and despite the absence of walrus-type tusks. "An apology, and a celebration," this Fafaman panted in a breathless rush. "An apology, Officer Leung, because of what happened during our effort to secure a compatible communication line with your mother spacecraft. We inadvertently intercepted private conversation. We apologize, and assure you we are not eavesdropping on that com-line henceforth. However, before we realized what was happening, we couldn't help overhearing an especially joyful reaction by one of your crew. Translating that reaction forthwith, we found it expressed unbridled delight over the good news Safasafala brought you.

"'Bottle up your anal orifice' strikes us as a strange expression. But doubtless many of our own behaviors strike you as equally strange. Thanks to materials with which you have so generously provided us, however, we have detected some common ground. Apparently you toast significant good events with glasses of fermented fruit juice, the same as we do."

Nanofafo was already pouring purplish, bioluminescent liquid from the opaque bottle into the long-stemmed glasses. "And so," his fa-la-las translated while handing full glasses to Safasafala and Buddy, Buddy having returned to his feet from being crouched amidst the Tictoctic spacecraft wreckage. "We thought that indulging your way of putting things was the least we could do, to make you feel a little more at home." Lifting high his own glass, Nanofafo said, "Bottle up your anal orifice!"

"Bottle up your anal orifice!" repeated Safasafala, clinking his glass against Nanofafo's.

Lastly, Buddy lifted his own wine glass to clink against theirs. "Up yours!" he chimed in with a mischievous grin.

All this time, distinctive ticking in his ear replaced Kevin's rude vents mercifully misinterpreted by the Fafamans. Static, he thought at first. Either Yoon-hee shut off transmission the moment she overheard Nanofafo say it had been inadvertently intercepted. Or the Fafamans themselves were flooding the transmission frequency with noise to further isolate the away team. Maybe such noise was all Captain Taylor had been receiving as well, ever since the other Earthlings lost contact with her.

However, Buddy suddenly realized he was hearing Morse Code. He got the full message after a second round of ticks. *Meet Chris in the glider hangar when he returns, and accept the hospitality.*

Buddy Leung knew exactly what "accept the hospitality" meant. Once he rejoined Chris, the emergency escape plan concocted by Tanya, Yoon-hee and Geena would commence.

Chapter 18

"Back on Earth, we have long stretches of beach like this! People line them with homes, hotels, restaurants, amusement parks...! However, global warming caused by our air pollution is raising the sea level! And so, many of those vacation edifices periodically require relocation to higher elevations! Imagine an army in retreat but still refusing to give up altogether, if that makes any sense!" Chris shouted for his translator to hear him above the powered glider's jet-engine hum.

Fah-lah-lahs emitted from said translator at amped-up volume for the Varalawa to also be able to hear. But despite that, Chris noticed strange static from his earpiece just as the glider was heading out over the Great Basin coastline. He wasn't familiar with Morse Code, but embedded in the static were enough regularly spaced clicks and pops for him to figure out there was SOME kind of code. *Kevin and company must be hatching a plan, so the best I can probably do is keep playing tourist with the first wife.*

"Anyhow, I am surprised!" Chris went on with the Varalawa. "Why are there no signs of civilization along such a beautiful white-sand beach?! Too dangerous to travel here from your Great Pyramid because of those desert barbarians in between?! Or do certain deadly shore creatures ruin the swim?! Or are beach vacations simply not a thing on Fafama?!"

Chris thought he glimpsed a smirk as the Varalawa responded, "Maybe you forget about the sunset storm-line!"

"Ah!" exclaimed Chris, suddenly feeling stupid.

"The storm-line always sends a flood surging way inland! The buildings you spoke of would be undermined daily! You are right about one thing, though! Swimming here would prove most dangerous, even without the storm-line! The 'faboompa' live too close to the shore!"

"The faboompa?!" Chris thought he had heard this name before.

"Look down deep into the sea as we execute an altitude-lowering turn!"

Like geese flying in formation, the glider and its jet escort banked steeply for making a spiral descent. When they flattened out headed along the coastline, Chris wasn't sure their altitude was more than fifty feet.

As for the water near shore, darting-about bioluminescent creatures might as well have been falling stars in a night sky reflected by a turquoise-tinted mirror.

"There are two 'faboompa' now! They are probably fighting for rule over that nearby colony of them!"

Chris reckoned the two faboompa must have been the size of blue whales to appear as large as they did from so far skyward. Several yards underwater, they were repeatedly charging at one another, knocking together enormous antlers. Oh, yeah, the Fafamans did say something about the antlered Tictoctickians reminding them of faboompa.

"The faboompa colony over there!" shouted the Varalawa, pointing. "How interesting, that they are rooted upside down in the sand by their antlers! Our marine biologists say that is their resting mode when not mating, fighting, or in search of food. Firmly entrenched there, the sunset storm-line cannot inadvertently wash them ashore and leave them stranded on a beach to die!"

The faboompa colony amazed Chris. Rooted by their antlers upside down into the sea bottom, their bodies undulated with the surf's ebb and flow. The Earthling was reminded of sea grass, only sea grass ballooned to the size of palm trees minus the palm fronds, and obesely fat.

"So they are dangerous to people when they are feeding?!"

"Their mouths are large enough to swallow a person whole!"

"Those ephemeral dragons you are taking me to see, are they dangerous also?!"

The Varalawa definitely grinned as she kept focused straight ahead to assure her glider continued on course. "The ephemeral dragons have never been known to attack anything other than solid rock!" she fah-lah-lahed. "And even that might not be an attack, if they are not real!"

"If they are not real?!"

"Judge for yourself! Most people who see them are convinced they are what they appear to be! But there is a vigorous debate among our scientists over whether they are living organisms, or peculiar geologic phenomena!"

"Geologic phenomena?!" Chris had wanted to paraphrase, reiterate what the first wife said for Kevin and the gang, assuming they were still eavesdropping. However, the unrelenting oddness of what she mentioned, taken together with the faboompa spectacle, left him practically speechless beyond clipped exclamations.

"Some scientists theorize- Ah, there are the first ripples! I am activating our floodlights for a better view! There! You see those three parallel trails of ripples up ahead?!"

The pale green floodlights provided little more than dim luminescence where Chris was concerned. But issuing from underneath the glider, they were enough for him to clearly discern three V-shaped ripples, the center one larger than those on either side. He mused they might as well have been wakes for invisible motorboats. As fast as they developed, though, was not fast enough to keep the glider and escort jets from rapidly gaining on them.

"Uh, maybe there is enough air turbulence from your glider and escort jets to produce those ripples! Is that what some of your scientists are arguing?! Although what is the connection to geology?!"

"No! Nothing to do with air turbulence! Some of our geologists theorize gaseous emissions from underwater volcanoes periodically bubble up along a fault line on the sea bed! There they go!"

Just as the Varalawa pointed and exclaimed, Chris saw what certainly appeared to be three shapes lift from the sea, shedding droplets. They sparkled with yet more pale-green bioluminescence. He was reminded of animal shapes drawn around such star constellations as the Bear Nebula and Scorpio. Only these were not drawings. They slowly, gracefully flapped their behemoth-sized wings, reminding Chris of flying reptile wings, or bat wings. Long tails trailed behind them like so many celebratory streamers. Iguana-type frills ran down their necks and backs. And their snake-like heads, adorned with horns, gently swayed from side to side.

Flickering, silvery pinpoints of light suffused the so-called ephemeral dragons like they were, indeed, constellations fallen from the sky.

"Whatever they are, they are completely invisible during blazing light!" said the Varalawa. "Those scientists who believe we are seeing what we think we are seeing theorize life evolved in a universe parallel to ours! In that parallel universe, the thinking goes, matter associates much more loosely than in our universe! Moreover, it is layered atop our universe like a transparency lending additional detail to a picture or diagram!

"Most scientists, though, think that all we are seeing are clouds of volcanic gas, expelled from the sea and floating across it! The shapes are only imagined, like sometimes imagined in approaching storm-line clouds!"

"But you say that people see the same thing every time with these, um, they really do look like dragons!"

"Ahh, the explanation for that is called crystallized gas! Just like rock crystals, crystalized gas would have the ability to suggest regular design, the symmetry of life, where it was actually lifeless! Also, the crystalline lattice would hold such a special cloud shape together while the wind blew it along! Only one problem: There has yet to be any evidence to support such a hypothesis!"

By then, the ephemeral dragons flew or crystallized gas clouds floated in amidst the glider and jets, like they had joined the entourage.

"What you are describing sounds similar to debates still raging- Wo!"

"What?!"

"Uh, it was just that one of those dragons, or gas clouds, came close beside us!"

"A common occurrence fueling another point of debate for the vast majority of scientists who believe they are nothing more than gas clouds! Wouldn't actual creatures' survival instinct steer them way clear of our intrusion on their habitat?! Many marine biologists say yes! Real dragons of any sort would be extremely reluctant to rise from the sea when an aircraft is flying so low overhead!

"On the other side, those few scientists pushing the parallel universe hypothesis argue that these creatures have no reason to fear us. We have never attacked them, so they are simply expressing their natural curiosity whenever we fly by!"

"Hmm!" Unsure where the Varalawa came down on this controversy, Chris was reluctant to admit the real reason for exclaiming "Wo!" Yes, he was astounded by how close one of the two smaller things got to the glider, if only for a moment. But the main surprise was it seeming to turn its seeming head at the end of its seeming long neck, followed by no seeming about it. The creature made eye contact with him.

Chris sensed a connection formed, as much as with any human or domesticated animal he had ever met. Had breathing Fafama's extraterrestrial atmosphere so crazed him, he could imagine he'd had connection-making eye contact with a cloud? "How many of those scientists have actually ventured out here to see these things?!" he asked finally.

"I know of at least a few, but look there! That is the other amazing thing about them!"

With leisurely majestic flapping of their monstrously sized wings, the three creatures had suddenly broken off from the Varalawa's flying entourage. They were arcing towards a stretch of coastline characterized by abruptly steep, craggy features.

Chris thought those features obviously resultant from long-ago volcanic activity, cutting black silhouettes against the bioluminescently lit land beyond.

More importantly, Chris wondered how scientists who scoffed at the notion of ephemeral dragons would explain their suddenly peeling away from the aircraft. That is, if they were just clouds blown about. Would those scientists argue they were magnetic in addition to crystalline? Magnetic rock thwarted where the prevailing breezes would otherwise have carried them?

One after the other of whatever-they-were opened their mouths - if there were mouths to open - and fire as from a lit torch issued in three successive blasts. Incredibly, that fire incinerated portions of rock, which then appeared drawn streaming into each mouth.

The next thing Chris knew, the three ephemeral dragons nose-dived, one by one, back into the Great Basin. Their pinpoint sparkles continued descending until they were lost from view altogether, as though three constellations crashed into the sea.

Three groups of concentric circle ripples remained on the surface.

"Uh, what is your own opinion of the ephemeral dragons?!" Chris finally recovered enough from this experience to ask as the glider turned back inland. "What do you think they are?!"

"I am still not sure what to think!" the Varalawa answered, freeing her right hand from the steering column to stretch out resting gently atop Chris's left hand dangling from an arm rest. "Is there nothing more occurring than a unique combination of geological, meteorological, and non-biological chemical activity?! Or," she went on, squeezing Chris's hand, "are there hints at a larger, living mystery?!"

Officer Olsen-Taylor kept his eyes focused straight ahead.

Chapter 19

Buddy Leung had his doubts about the escape plan. But Safasafala unwittingly squelched any thought he might have given to one last stab at diplomacy.

Escorting Officer Leung to the hangar where Chris would soon return from sightseeing with the first wife, Safasafala added some more "good news." Like the rest of his "good news," it left a bad taste for Buddy that rivaled the bad taste left by the fermented juice for the "up your anal orifice" toast.

"To speed up the process," Safasafala said, "we will not wait for your 'Cahptahn Taylah' to finish her audience with the Fafamafalafama. You will surprise Officer 'Ohlsahn-Taylah' with the good news that he and the 'cahptahn' get to enjoy Fafaman hospitality for an extended time. And then the Varalawa's escort will ferry you to our space station. From there, your shuttle craft can return you to your mother ship for as fast a departure back to 'Ahth' as possible."

"You copy that, Officer Smith?" said Buddy. In his furious anger, he couldn't trust what would have exited his mouth had he responded directly to Safasafafala. But he also felt all the more thankful for having only taken the teensiest sip of Fafaman wine during the aforementioned toast. Given what he was finally resolved to go along with, he didn't need his reaction time impaired.

"I am thinking, Officer Leung: As many bottles up his ass as possible when this is all over," answered Kevin, plenty furious himself.

Safasafala led Buddy into a long, narrow hall adjacent to the Great Pyramid's aircraft and spacecraft hangar. Through that hall's panoramic window, they watched a metallic panel slide open like some behemoth garage door, Buddy imagined.

"I will leave you soon as they land. You can enter through here to greet your crewmate," said Safasafala, indicating a doorknob.

At least, Buddy thought as he scrutinized the hangar setup, *doesn't look like we will have to deal with many people here, even if extra security arrives. We could probably pull this off with their whole populace watching, but the fewer the better.*

Helpfully, the escort jets did not accompany the first wife's powered glider into the pyramid. Rather, they peeled off for return to an underground hangar.

Safasafala didn't even wait for the glider to finish touching down. As its wheels made screeching contact with the landing strip, he fah-lah-lahed, "Good luck flying back to Earth. Hope to see you again soon." Then he was gone before Buddy could say, "Pama." Off on something urgent? Or was he anxious to leave the sight of someone whose presence irritated him? Or on the other hand, did he react to a sense his company wasn't wanted?

Already through the door, Buddy ran over where the glider was parking, grateful to see ground crew waving it stopped. They could convey the threat at an appropriate time.

The Varalawa and Chris lost no time climbing out of the glider, down onto the macadam floor. Rather than greet them, though, Buddy raised his hands and shouted, "STOP!" And to the Fafaman ground crew he said, "Fast! Have the hangar reopened! Both entrance and exit!"

The ground crew dropped their softly illuminated batons used for guiding aircraft into parking spaces. Before those batons finished bouncing off the runway, said crew drew weapons aimed at Buddy.

"Why?" one Fafaman's angry fah-lah-lahs translated.

"In a few 'nininana,' a demonstration of our fire power will soar through here! If the hangar is not open for both entry and exit, the impact against whichever closed door could send your pyramid's full weight crashing down on us!

"Do not alert anyone else! Aside from your other colleague up there in the terminal booth! Or we will blow your space station out of the sky! Shooting me will also result in your space station's destruction! My crew in orbit knows just what to do! And they are monitoring everything!"

Both ground crew lowered their weapons and anxiously waved for Buddy to calm down. Accompanying those frantic gestures, the one who spoke previously said, "I have received word in my earphone from Tatadata, who you see signaling you from the terminal booth! He is opening both ends of the hangar! And he has cut off our contact to the outside! There was no need for any such demonstration! We understand your weapons must be very advanced! After all, you traveled here from another planet!"

Chris wasn't sure what to make of the Varalawa's silent regard of him as hangar doors slid up opposite faces of the pyramid. Was she expressing unmitigated scorn for his having given no hint what was coming? Or was her scorn tempered by admiration, lust even? Lust for this extraterrestrial who could spend so much time cooped up with her, yet not shed a clue about the awful power his fellow travelers were about to unleash?

Chris was going to say he had no idea specifically what his crew, what Buddy, had in mind. And he was going to add that the Earthlings' frustration had been mounting steadily over how the Fafamans dragged out the away team's visit. That it felt like the away team was being held hostage, when they were anxious to take action against a possible mutual threat as fast as possible.

Chris was going to talk about all this, but before he could utter his first word, it happened. What looked like a fireball appeared at one end of the hangar, and it whooshed through incredibly fast. Despite such blurring speed, he discerned a heat shield protecting whatever-it-was from the extremely high, atmosphere-igniting friction.

Upon brief reflection, the Earthling realized what he just witnessed. A firefly donut was jury-rigged with a heat shield to not burn up in a bluff demonstration of firepower the Smoke and Mirrors didn't have.

The Fafaman who did all the talking for his fellow ground crew indicated just how effective that demonstration was, when he said, "I am confident that whatever you want from us can be most expeditiously accommodated! Most lamentable, though, that a terrible misunderstanding must have led to misapprehension you creatures from 'Ahth' needed this to obtain our cooperation. There was a most inaccurate translation, perhaps?"

"Good!" Buddy barked. "Now you and your partner here must resume training your guns on me. But not just me! You must also train them on Officer Olsen-Taylor and the, uh, Varalawa! Order them over beside me! Yes, the Varalawa has to join us! She has to clasp her hands together behind her head, just like us! Like that! So far, so good!

"Now tell your friend up there in the control booth that he has to open a communication link directly to the Fafamafalafama! Wait! Before you tell him, this is what you are going to say to him:

"You are going to tell him that you are more infiltrators for the desert people! You have come to blackmail the space aliens for a machine to convert the Great Basin into drinking water! You think we are advanced enough to have developed a desalinization device. And in exchange for that device, you will spare the life of our captain, whose fate will be in your hands once she is turned over to spare the life of the Varalawa!

"Meanwhile, your companion up there will come down here to refuel this jet glider! We need enough to cross the Great Basin! That is possible, yes?!?!? YES?!?!?!" It was all Buddy could do to continue his even-toned, I'm-in-charge demeanor despite the audacious immensity of the bluff he was attempting.

"More than enough fuel capacity!" replied the Fafaman, his legs shaking visibly despite his having a weapon trained on Buddy's head.

*

Yoon-hee cupped a hand, presumably her own, over her right ear so she could better hear the receiver in her left ear. "It's coming through faint, but the Fafamafalafama is saying there's a big problem."

"A big problem, huh?" said Kevin exchanging knowing winks with Ali. "Patch it through the intercom amped up. Tell him we're having everyone listen so we can all try to help with whatever it is, ahem."

"Who is in charge up there while your captain is down here?" translated the booming series of fah-lah-lahs into a passionless digitized voice.

"I am Officer Kevin Smith-Park. Our chief navigation and communications engineer, Officer Park-Smith, tells me you are the most esteemed Fafawa-Fafamafalafama." Kevin noticed Deborah wince and shake her head over his accidentally starting to address the single most powerful person on Fafama by his pet name for him, the Fafawazoo.

"Officer 'Smahth-Pahk' and Officer 'Pahk-Smahth': A situation I would like to explore further, when we have the time. But ruthless desert barbarian infiltrators have begun a seven-nininana countdown to shooting some of your people plus my first wife if a certain condition is not met."

The countdown was Kevin's idea. If it elapsed before the Fafamafalafama capitulated, the ground crew were instructed to shoot Buddy in the leg, followed by allowing a three-nininana extension.

"What- What condition needs to be met, esteemed Fafamafalafama?" asked Kevin, hoping his reaction to the Fafamafalafama's "news" conveyed shocked hesitancy. If the Fafaman leader were to somehow see through him and call the bluff, then announce there was no way he would accede to the terrorist demands...

"They want us to give them unrestricted leave in my first wife's glider," the Fafamafalafama explained, telling Kevin what he already knew. "Then once they bring your captain and two other officers to their headquarters, they said they will coerce you directly. They will threaten to kill your away team if you do not provide them with technology for desalinizing water from the Great Basin."

"I know time is running out," conceded Kevin, wondering whether he shouldn't have planned a longer countdown. Waiting out the Fafawazoo's fah-lah-lahs for translations seemed to drag on interminably. "But if you could wait a moment for me to consult with other officers here."

"But I thought you were the acting captain."

"You know, esteemed Fafamafalafama, you are correct. Allow me a moment to ponder this situation."

"Of course."

Soon thereafter, a nod from Ali confirmed the ensuing silence had gone on long enough for that "moment to ponder" to have occurred. That's when Officer Smith at last directed, "Turn over the hostages to the desert barbarians, and give them secure leave from the pyramid. And rest assured we have the means for implementing their safe rescue."

"Ahhh," went untranslated before succeeded by, "I trust your means do not involve any of the desalinization technology the barbarians seek."

"Esteemed Fafamafalafama, our means could not involve that even if we wanted them to. We are still struggling with such technology back home on Earth. But a subsequent visit could certainly focus on dealing with Fafaman water shortages to help ease tensions."

The Fafamafalafama erupted, "You cannot ease tensions with evil that simply seeks your destruction! But back to the immediate problem! If you already have a plan to rescue your crew and my first wife, why wait for the barbarians to fly off with them?! Why not act now?!"

"There is not enough time to implement our plan before the deadline ends. And even if there was enough time, everyone else in your pyramid will be much safer if our plan takes place far away."

"Ahh, so you are saying the desert barbarians might experience some collateral damage from such a plan?"

"Unfortunately for them, yes."

After the fah-lah-lah translation of Kevin's response, a long pause ensued during which onboard crew exchanged frequent, anxious glances, save Deborah. She wouldn't even look her own wife in the eye. Rather, she stared off into space, shaking her head angrily. *If they had only listened to me...*

There couldn't have been more than two nininana left.

"Ahh, I have received a report," said the Fafamafalafama, finally breaking the silence. "There were several witnesses who say they saw a strange fireball, either entering or exiting the pyramid aircraft hangar. What are your thoughts about such a phenomenon?"

*

Buddy Leung wished he could remind Chris directly to not make even the slightest whisper about what he knew was on both their minds. Which was this: They should have instructed their feigned hostage takers to set a longer deadline than what amounted to about fifteen minutes. But any such talk overheard would surely give away the bluff, with unknown but most likely dire consequences.

Every few seconds the captain's husband gave Buddy a forlorn, I'm-afraid-you're-really-going-to-get-one-leg-shot look. And Buddy limited his reaction to a negative head shake that could have been mistaken for a nervous tick.

Less than a minute to go, one ground crewman nodded at the other. Then the other peered through his weapon's gun-scope to aim at what Buddy hoped was the fleshy part of his leg's lower calf, as painful as that still promised to be.

"The time has expired."

It was all the gun-aiming crewman could do to keep his nerve for following through as directed. What horrific destructive power might these outer space aliens unleash from their mother ship if they didn't get their way? Just how ruthless were they, that they would have the Fafamans shoot one of their own just to make a point?

"The time has expired," the other crewman repeated.

The crewman assigned to shoot Buddy's leg set the trigger with a click which echoed throughout the hangar. Other than that, the place had gone so quiet, even the Varalawa was taken by surprise when a voice shouted, "Officer Olsen-Taylor! Officer Leung!"

"Captain Taylor!" Chris answered as Buddy buried his head in his hands with relief, and Helena ran towards both of them.

"You have what you asked for! Now free the Varalawa, and leave!" the Fafamafalafama's fah-lah-lahs boomed with cavernous rage over the loudspeaker before Chris's translator crackled with the digitized, robot-voice English version.

"We will let the Varalawa parachute out after we are clear no aircraft are in pursuit!" one crewman hastily responded.

Buddy thought to himself, good thing he'd prepped these two Fafamans on every possible contingency, so nothing the Fafamafalafama said would leave them suspiciously dumbstruck.

Helena grabbed Chris's hand as the crewmen motioned with their guns for her to stay by her fellow Earthlings' side, not approach her Fafaman faux captors.

Despite typically poor lighting, Chris noticed the nocturnal-eyed Varalawa noticing him holding hands with Helena, then turning away most rapidly. Jealousy?

Whatever, as they boarded the glider, Helena tossed aside Chris's hand, it felt like. Was she thinking about the Fafamafalafama? Or had she sensed something between him and the Varalawa? Or most likely, was she simply refocusing her attention on the business at hand? She couldn't responsibly allow herself more than the briefest indulgence of an affectionate response to reunion with her husband? He really shouldn't read anything more into it?

Chris had to wonder.

Meanwhile, Buddy asked the Fafamans, "Uhh, can we carry along our envirosuits?"

One crewman gave Buddy a look that read, *What are we supposed to answer?* So Buddy gave him an encouraging nod which prompted him to fah-lah-lah a mere, "Yes."

"The Varalawa will parachute to safety, or total devastation awaits you!" abruptly fah-lah-lahed the Fafamafalafama. For Chris, his deep voice thundered as from a stray lightning bolt after the storm was long past. "Only by the mercy of the Fafamafalafama are all your settlements not completely destroyed by now!"

One of the Fafamans forced to play gun-toting terrorist rolled his eyes.

Not the reaction towards the Fafaman ruler that Chris would have expected.

But the other responded most solicitously, "Besides letting off the Varalawa in a safe area, we will provide her with an emergency flare so you can more easily locate her, es-uh..." He cut himself off before he could fah-lah-lah past the first syllable of the Fafaman word for "esteemed."

Both gun-toting Fafamans nearly committed a potentially more serious goof when boarding the Varalawa's personal glider. They unwittingly tried to step ahead of the Earthlings, like they were being ordered onto the aircraft at gunpoint rather than the other way around. Helena, Chris, and Buddy hurried past them, hoping no one in the terminal booth was paying too close attention. That they wouldn't notice the supposed captors momentarily left off from training their guns on their supposed captives.

Once aboard the glider, Fafamans and Earthlings alike sighed with relief, except for the Varalawa. She looked clearly stumped, especially when her fellow beings handed over their weapons to Buddy and Helena.

"To learn how this contraption operates, I need to look over your shoulders," Buddy said to the disarmed

Fafamans, who had already buckled themselves in at the cockpit. "Should not take long, then you can parachute. My real concern is with our present total payload capacity. Captain, maybe we drop off the Varalawa before we leave, under cloak of some bellicose statement?"

"I know the appropriate acceleration sequence for the estimated weight we are carrying. There should not be a problem," said the Varalawa, setting aside her passenger seatbelt to approach the cockpit.

One of the seated Fafamans scrambled to unbuckle like he'd suddenly been roused from daydreaming for response to an alarm.

Making no effort to keep the Varalawa from resuming control of her jet glider, Captain Taylor remarked, "We did not wish to show so much disrespect."

Chris couldn't help thinking his wife might want the Varalawa to pass along that message to the Fafamafalafama, about not wishing to show disrespect.

"However," Helena continued, "we fear too much precious time will be wasted that we need for dealing with the, uh…" Helena suddenly realized these Fafamans were very likely shielded from knowing the threat potentially headed their way from another planet. "We believe the sooner we return to our planet, the sooner we can provide you resources and strategies for, uh, reaching a solution regarding the desert people.

"As for a possible payload capacity issue," Helena added, "here is a suggestion. Officer Leung, until we are certain the acceleration sequence is working, maybe you could stand on one foot only."

"Ay, Captain."

"And if that sequence doesn't work," Chris managed to interject despite wonderment over what got into Helena with her comedic remark, "we can step off the glider just before it crashes."

Fortunately, the Varalawa's acceleration sequence launched her glider smoothly into the Fafaman night sky, easily handling its load.

Hundreds of feet below, sprawling landscape glowed pale green from flounder-mouse bioluminescence.

Captain Helena Taylor imagined herself one with the glider, soaring like a bird above the extraterrestrial topography on several warm updrafts, wonderfully exhilarated over freedom at last from claustrophobic conditions inside the Great Pyramid. In odd reaction, though, she found herself having to consciously resist an impulse to re-establish radio contact with the Fafamafalafama. The idea being she would apologize even more than she did to his first wife. Pursuant to which she would urge returning to the pyramid. That way he'd surely understand. No...no, no, no, Helena shook her head.

The Varalawa gracefully yielded to Buddy taking her seat at the cockpit while Helena recalled something she'd read about kidnappers. Their mental grip on captives could grow so strong, chains were unnecessary for enslavement. In fact certain captives could be let loose to pick up groceries, with complete confidence they wouldn't even dream of exploiting that chance to escape.

Regardless of what she'd read, Helena continued to feel strange empathy tugging at her for the Fafamafalafama's circumstances. So she forced herself to focus on challenges yet to be faced in pursuit of returning safely back aboard the Smoke and Mirrors.

Among those challenges, the glider had to reach the other side of the Great Basin. Then rugged terrain might make a safe landing not the easiest thing. And who knew what dangers might be posed by Fafaman wildlife until Tanya could rescue them via shuttle craft?

Helena's husband Chris wanted to give Helena and Buddy a certain heads-up right after dropping off their Fafaman hostages. He wanted to strongly advise they take a roundabout heading coastward to avoid becoming a target for the so-called "barbarians." But the Varalawa and two hangar workers were not one minute evacuated from the Varalawa's powered glider when an attack began. Before Chris could get even one word out of his mouth, a loud WHOOSH succeeded by a plume of billowing smoke flanked the glider.

It was a guided missile's near miss.

"The Fafawazoo's men couldn't have caught us THAT quickly, even if his first wife contacted him soon as we let her free!" shouted Buddy.

"They didn't!" Chris shouted back above the glider's jet-engine hum. "I should have said something earlier! Desert people shot at us, me and the Varalawa, with ground-to-air missiles!"

Captain Taylor gave Chris a significant regard upon his elaborating what "us" meant. Then she unbuckled to join Buddy at the cockpit.

"You might want to head southwest!" Chris went on. "Search for a canyon or deep valley or ravine where we can fly low!"

WHOOSH!!

Air turbulence from a second missile nearly sent the glider into a tailspin, throwing Helena to the floor before she could reach the empty cockpit seat.

"Must be heat-seeking missiles to come that close!" said Buddy.

"I think they are!" said Chris. "Oh no! Behind us!"

"Hold on!" Buddy cautioned as Helena grabbed one arm of the co-pilot's seat to drag herself closer.

Fearing a third missile would latch more firmly onto its target, Buddy risked stalling out by steering the glider directly skyward. Then he let it drop sideways into a dive.

Captain Taylor's feet practically hit the ceiling as she clutched tightly at the co-pilot seat.

The third missile couldn't keep up. However, the concussion from its midair blast sent the glider spinning into a nosedive from which Buddy pulled out less than twenty feet before they would have crashed.

"Without- Without night vision goggles or the Fafamans' owl eyes, I- I cannot fly too low!" Buddy cautioned as he labored to catch his breath, and Captain Taylor finally crawled into the seat beside him. "But I think that's a- that's a," he repeated, his heart still pounding, "that's a hillside to our left! Hopefully we're not coming in low enough over a renegade settlement, they- they could knock us out of the sky with just a skillfully thrown rock! Ha!"

Chris and Helena found Buddy's nervous laughter over not-so-funny material curiously comforting.

"Are you okay, Helena?!" asked Chris, terribly embarrassed. Panic over his own safety had left him useless for his wife while Buddy's evasive maneuvers were tossing her about the glider. There had also been his selfish insecurity worrying that Helena left his side for a cockpit seat over how he mentioned the Varalawa. Clearly, her focus had been on helping Buddy if possible.

"I'm fine, Chris! Is that a hillside coming up on our left, Buddy?!"

So she can't hide her irritation with my too-little-way-too-late question, Chris fretted, making him feel extremely petty given their potentially perilous circumstances.

Ping! Ping! Ping!

"Wo!" exclaimed Buddy as the pings seemed associated with the glider's sudden jostles and slowdown.

"Is it the structural integrity?!" asked Helena, trying not to scream.

Ping! Ping!

"The glider shouldn't be coming apart from my maneuvers…"

Ping!

"The 'G' forces weren't strong enough, I don't think…"

Ping!

"Something's pulling us down!" Buddy shouted as he tried to coax the engine without stalling out. "Brace for impact! Duck your head between your knees!"

"Are you banking us into a spiral?!" Captain Taylor shouted desperately, seeking any least bit of assurance Buddy could give as she sensed the glider falling into a sharp right turn.

Fearful they were going to be killed crashing into a planet light years from home, Chris still couldn't transcend the petty. He wondered whether Helena would tell him she still loved him, once she realized their doom was inevitable. Although maybe her not telling him would mean nothing one way or the other since she was duty-bound to not give up hope until struck unconscious or worse. And what would *he* say if sensing the end at hand? Shouldn't he just keep his mouth shut so as not to distract from whatever miracle Buddy and Helena might yet be able to pull off?

"No idea how this is happening, Captain!! Nothing wrong with the engine, but we clearly are in a steeply descending spiral!"

A large area of bioluminescence loomed closer and closer until the glider's descent leveled off still quite airborne. By then, the three Earthlings became aware they were circling round an enormous one of those fern-like trees unfurled to full height in the Fafaman night. And Buddy realized they'd slowed so much, they should have been nose-diving into an utterly fatal crash, even with Fafama's gravity slightly lower than Earth's gravity.

That's when the glider slowed to a complete halt, the jet engine rocking it about like a penned-up bucking bronco, Chris mused totally perplexed.

Impossibly, so it seemed, the glider was stuck in midair.

"Should I cut off the engine, Captain?"

"No sense wasting fuel, Buddy," agreed Helena trying to discern whatever she could through the cockpit window. "Don't want to belabor the obvious, but this can't be good."

"Wish I could disagree, Captain," said Buddy as the jet engine whined to a halt, and something continued to jostle the glider in almost rhythmic fashion.

"Oh, no!" complained Chris, his eyes growing nocturnal wide with his dawning realization. "Think I know what's happened!"

Before anyone could say another word, the leg-sized mandibles and eight saucer-sized eyes of an elephantine ahtpah, Fafama's monster spider, dropped into direct view out the cockpit window.

All three Earthlings screamed in uncontrollable terror.

Helena and Buddy scrambled to unbuckle themselves, and fled behind the cockpit to join Chris still strapped into a passenger seat.

They moved none too soon.

The ahtpah's powerfully enormous mandibles clicking against both windshields crashed right through all their protective laminated layers, sending shards flying everywhere. Then those mandibles clasped the metallic support frame in between them, anchoring the ahtpah for curling its enormous bulbous rear under itself. A several-foot-long, dagger-shaped protrusion emerged, thrust violently through one of the shattered-open breaches. So violently, the few jagged windshield fragments remaining round the left windshield frame broke off.

An ejaculated milky substance splattered all over where Buddy and the captain had been sitting. Before the protrusion finished retracting back inside the ahtpah's bulbous rear end, both cockpit seat cushions sizzled and hissed. Rising smoke shed fumes like from burning rubber as those cushions quickly turned to creamy mush.

"Thinks it's paralyzed its prey and initiated the pre-digestion process, so it can return when convenient to suck out the insides," explained Buddy. "So now it's going to finish weaving a cocoon around the glider. Well, maybe 'thinks' is too strong a word. More likely, the ahtpah is on instinctive autopilot."

Chris and even the captain struggled with hyperventilating. But Buddy Leung had calmed down, detached himself from personal peril by wallowing in fascination over what was transpiring.

"So what do you suppose, um, what do you suppose happened exactly, Buddy?" inquired Helena, recognizing his strategy for getting a grip might not be a bad idea for all of them.

"Well, let's see," said Buddy with affected nonchalance, feeling panic just around the corner from the new state of mind he was trying to sustain.

The ahtpah's web-weaving didn't help, continuing to jostle the glider.

Instinct kept urging Buddy as he felt certain it was urging Helena and Chris, to crawl out one broken-open window and flee. But he knew that would mean instant death, whether from the fall or from getting caught in the web.

Getting caught in the web, their ensuing panicky flailing-about would certainly send the ahtpah scurrying over to lop off their heads. Then probably it would insert that dagger thing where their necks were left wide open.

"Maybe the ahtpah spotted us from afar," Buddy speculated finally, "mistook us for some behemoth Fafaman dragonfly we don't know about yet..."

A cool, refreshing breeze wafted through the broken-open windshield frames.

"So," Buddy went on, somewhat soothed by the breeze, "it scrambled up a hillside near where we would be flying. There, it squirt a web filament at the glider's fuselage for hitching a ride like a cowboy lassoing a wild horse. That was the first ping we heard. Then it sent out more filaments to strengthen its hold, ah-ha!" Buddy snapped his fingers. "Of course! It also shot an anchoring filament at the fern tree trunk!"

"That must have been quite a sight for Fafaman kids on their nature walk," Chris finally breathed calmly enough to comment.

"Ha!" Buddy Leung laughed, too late slapping a hand over his mouth.

In the wake of Buddy's careless outburst, the jostles from web-making stopped. And all too soon thereafter, the eight ahtpah eyes loomed back into view, upside down from over the cockpit.

Chris, Helena, and Buddy froze still, hardly breathed. They feared the ahtpah re-inserting its dagger-like protrusion through the shattered-apart cockpit window. With a bit different aim, that protrusion's unbelievably corrosive milky ejaculation could be all over them. All over.

After what felt like several minutes, but was really less than thirty seconds, the eight eyes torturously slowly lifted back up away from view. And web-weaving resumed, including what sounded like occasional plucking of a bass guitar string.

From something read about Earth spiders, Chris guessed the ahtpah was dispersing droplets of secreted sticky material at even intervals along various web filaments. Tugging at that filament like indeed plucking at a guitar accomplished the task.

Only then did Buddy feel safe resuming conversation, albeit softly. "My guess," he whispered," is that it cast more web-lines at the tree, plus some ground-ward. And it kept casting web-lines until it finally stopped our flight altogether even with the jet engine still going strong."

"So here are our options," said Captain Taylor with as much dispassionate calm as she could muster. "We could radio the Fafamans for help. That puts us back in their control, more beholden than ever. And probably means, Buddy, you return to Earth short two hands since they've made clear that Chris and I are to be held hostage until they receive weapon goodies.

"The other option is that Tanya or someone concocts a rescue plan using the shuttle pod."

"Captain," said Buddy, "if Tanya can perform what would have to be some spectacular maneuvers, the shuttle's anti-matter exhaust might burn through the ahtpah web."

"Officer Leung, if anyone can perform spectacular maneuvers, Tanya can. And yourself, of course."

"If we gather correctly that the ahtpah is active at night, and curls up into a ball or whatever during the day..."

"Yes," Helena nodded, "we probably should set the rescue mission for after sunrise. And hope that in the meantime, a Fafaman search party doesn't find us first."

"Doubt they possess the wherewithal to home in on our location," said Buddy, "even when I communicate our predicament in Morse Code. Probably will sound like so much meaningless static to them."

"Well just in case, use the echo function to make your transmission seem emitted from a distant hill ridge. You can Morse our actual coordinates."

"Of course, Captain."

"That leaves us with the small matter of surviving the remainder of this night," observed Chris, even as the web-suspended glider grew ominously darker.

The ahtpah's cocoon-weaving around the Varalawa's private aircraft was blocking out more and more starlight and flounder-mouse bioluminescence.

"Should one of us stand guard while the other two try to sleep? Then change shifts every hour or so?" Chris continued, in his effort to finally offer something useful.

Helena and Buddy traded looks that did not escape Chris's attention, before Buddy responded, "That's a good idea, Captain. But might I recommend only one of us sleep at any one time, while the other two remain alert? Uh, one person on their own might miss something crucial that the other, uh..."

"Those are both excellent suggestions."

Chris suspected neither Helena nor Buddy trusted him to wake them in time before a tentacle or whatever made way into the glider and carried off someone. *But don't be ridiculous! Given the deadly peril, of course it makes no sense for more than one of us to sleep at a time!*

Chapter 20

"Captain?"

"I've been awake the whole time," said Helena, sparing Buddy the least concern he'd woken her.

Hours earlier, something happened that made sleep impossible. Hissing like a tire going flat, the ahtpah inserted a long and narrow protuberance through where one of the cockpit windows used to be. The straw-like protuberance alighted on one of the seat cushions turned bizarre mush by the ahtpah's corrosive venom. With a steady whoosh, it vacuumed up that mush leaving only metallic framework behind. Then it did likewise to the mush on the other cockpit seat.

Imagining their fate had they not dodged the ahtpah's corrosive venom, Helena and company couldn't have been more terrorized.

"Captain," Buddy went on presently as Helena sat up from where she had tried to sleep reclined across two back seats, "and Chris, uh, I want you to check this out as well. See if you have the same impression."

Chris suspected his music-trading friend only included him as an awkward afterthought. Didn't want him to feel left out when in reality, he didn't need his input the least bit.

"Am trying to discern web strands, individual discreet web strands, from this side passenger window," Buddy continued. "Wherever starlight and bioluminescence still shine through..."

"Think I see them. Yes, this is not a totally futile exercise," Helena concluded after peering out the same window.

"Captain - and again, Chris, I would appreciate your confirmation - do you notice large nodules crowded along some web-strand silhouettes?"

"Not really. Oh, there they are. Oh-oh." Helena's shoulders slumped as a realization set in.

"Thinking the same thing I am, Captain?"

"Are we talking ahtpah eggs?" asked Chris, somehow knowing without his own look-see.

"Might take days to hatch, or we might have only an hour," said Buddy, straining to remain in a detached frame of mind, keep the lid on panic. And hopefully help Helena and Chris keep the lid on their panic as well. "The better part of caution suggests we cover where the windshields were so they can't come crawling in after us. Whatever can be improvised..."

"There's special tape in our envirosuits for patching leaks," said Helena. "Not going to provide lining all the way around the windshield frames. But, are you having any luck there?"

Buddy was already down on his knees behind the rearmost seats, rummaging through a compartment set into the passenger cabin's back wall. "Well look at this," he whispered, extricating something bulky that looked like a bed comforter. "This must be an artificial tralalafa. For those who can't afford the real thing, I guess. Even found the tube you have to blow into for inflating it. Anyway, folded open it should be plenty wide enough to cover both cockpit window frames."

"If we're climbing over there to work," Captain Taylor said, pointing forward, "we'd better suit up in case of any remnant ahtpah venom."

"Hey guys," said Chris peering out the passenger windows on one side, concern in his voice. "My imagination, or is that particular bioluminescence, what little shines through the cocoon, getting brighter? Or are we approaching sunrise already?"

"Too much night left to go," answered Buddy while Chris moved aside for him to look. "But definitely is brighter out there."

"When the Varalawa took me on a guided tour in this glider, we, uh, I noticed bioluminescence that struck me a bit different from flounder mouse bioluminescence. She called it a lamana-something, a monstrous-sized beast that sleeps underground like a cicada. Every nineteen years it nears the surface, glowing all over. And when it uncovers completely, it expels flatulence so poisonous that every creature within range is killed or paralyzed. But it only sucks out the body fluids of a gassed ahtpah before burrowing under for another nineteen years. And if an ahtpah hasn't been gassed, it keeps farting until, uhh…"

"So that's why we'd better dress up anyway," said Buddy, already drawing his envirosuit up over his legs.

"Let's keep our head gear off until absolutely needed, to conserve the oxygen supply," cautioned Helena.

"If all that light is shedding from a lamana-whatever," said Chris, "from what I understand we will receive ample warning before it, uh, cuts loose."

"I better Morse-Code Yoon-hee regarding these additional complications," said Buddy, "so Tanya can work them into her simulation models."

Affixing the artificial tralalafa leaf to the cockpit window frames proved both tedious and heart-pounding tense.

But at least the ahtpah had finished weaving, so the glider was no longer continually shaken. Most likely, though, this also meant the monstrous spider being fully attentive to any least vibration trembling through its web.

Subsequently trying to move ever so slowly only added to the Earthlings' stress.

"One has to wonder what might be flying around out there," commented Buddy, 'when you have the ahtpah building such an enormous web, and successfully going after the glider."

General despair set in all too soon, over ever getting their nominal protection completely taped up against the potential baby spider threat. However gingerly the Earthlings climbed about the cockpit, resultant disturbances still proved enough to send the ahtpah scurrying about its web.

At one breath-taking moment the ahtpah made its close presence known, blocking out what little starlight and bioluminescent light still penetrated the cocoon woven round the glider. In the resultant pitch-black darkness, there was just the steely glint of its eight eyes, peering through where the Earthlings hadn't yet finished covering over the cockpit windshields.

Helena and company were just about resigned to leaving their protective work unfinished. They would have to hope the baby ahtpah didn't hatch before Tanya rescued them.

But could bleak become even bleaker?

A distant drone intensified to deafening loud extent, then cut off abruptly as Helena and company received a tremendously jostling jolt.

Clearly, something enormous flew into the web, something that continued to jostle that web about.

Under cover of the resultant turmoil, Helena and company finished taping the artificial tralalafa leaf over the cockpit windshield frame.

But what manner of large flying thing had been caught in the ahtpah web? Buddy wondered while he Morse-Coded another heads-up. Tanya needed to know some hapless other object was trapped beside the glider, perhaps a monstrous bug akin to the ahtpah. That is, assuming the shuttle pod wasn't the hapless object, Tanya stuck inside.

The sickening crunch from the ahtpah stabbing its venom-filled dagger deep inside something ended the jostling. And also ended any doubt for Helena and company that an insect the size of a small biplane had unwittingly flown into the web.

"By the way, you're going to love this," Buddy whispered softly, hoping his new information would encourage anger in lieu of hyperventilating panic. "Yoon-hee reported that the Fafamafalafama said he couldn't reconnect her with us yet because we'd been lulled into a deep nap. And he wanted to respect our biorhythms!"

"I was just thinking about some research I'd read before we left Space Station 2," Chris said without any least attempt to segue from Buddy's report. "It had to do with insect consciousness. Apparently, various wasp and arthropod poisons provide them a moment of bliss for their transition to death. But there was no real need for venom to evolve like that because no advantages are conferred to the venom producers."

While Helena shook her head in her hands, Buddy commented, "Good thing Kevin isn't with us, else he'd probably throw you to the ahtpah. I can hear him saying he wanted you to experience that moment of bliss for yourself."

Helena and company strove to stay alert while remaining crouched down behind two rear passenger seats. To that end, they checked regularly out one side window or the other, especially concerned that Chris's lamana-whatever might break surface. Such was their exhaustion, though, that they soon drifted into a half-asleep stupor...

Helena's last clear thought was: At least the behemoth bug caught in the web would provide plenty of food for the baby ahtpahs.

When a thunderously loud drone disrupted his dreaming, Chris momentarily forgot all about that sickening crunch heard overnight. In place of such an awful memory, he wondered whether whatever got trapped in the ahtpah web was struggling anew. The drone's intensity finally bringing him fully awake, though, he panicked at all the light pouring in the side windows, and screamed, "Pull on your head gear!"

In early dawn sky, Tanya Petrovsky had already made one pass of the ahtpah's web, gasping at its size.

The web stretched on a diagonal from top of a nearly hundred-foot ferny tree all the way ground-ward. Suspended, stuck to it was not only the glider, but also a grasshopper the size of a small sports car, with wings splayed out.

Tanya sent the shuttle pod soaring skywards to circle back around for the first of what she expected would have to be at least four risky maneuvers. But she noticed something urgently ominous enough to com-link with Captain Taylor sooner than originally planned. And in her estimation, there was no time for Morse-Code static imitation. If the Fafamans successfully eavesdropped, so be it. "Captain! Heads up! I'm initializing first maneuver! But you have to know monster spider eggs are hatching!"

"We see them, Tanya!" Taylor shot back immediately, also dispensing with Morse Code. "Don't worry! We've put up a protective cover! And we think they'll go after other prey the ahtpah trapped before they mess with us!"

But even as Helena spoke, she saw an incredible number of cat-sized spiderlings seeming to practically pour from the eggs. She guessed there were a hundred or more.

Tanya started her second descent towards the ahtpah web. This time, though, she pulled up on the shuttle and decreased power until it flipped upside-down on a diagonal dive backwards, its rear leading the way. Then at the last possible instant she powered to full force, sending a blaze of super-heated fiery exhaust at the uppermost extent of the ahtpah web.

Seared to black cinders, web strands and fern tree branches alike tore off from near the top of the tree trunk, leaving the web hanging partway over.

The damage was enough to awaken the adult ahtpah from daylight slumber, shooting new silky filaments at the fern tree to try re-stabilizing its web.

After bringing the shuttle pod back to topside up, Tanya made a second flyby to see what she'd accomplished before starting her second maneuver. "Captain," she said, "first maneuver was great success!"

"Hurry, Tanya! Those babies are knocking at our door!" screamed Helena, peeking from behind the passenger seats alongside Chris and Buddy.

All three Earthlings looked on helplessly at the taped-up comforter roiled like a restless sea by ahtpah spiderlings scurrying about its other side.

A few spiderlings kept still, tearing at the comforter with their clicking mandibles.

They must smell us Buddy opted not to vocalize. He didn't want to compound his friends' panic.

Tanya's even-riskier second maneuver involved diving the shuttle backwards much closer to the ground than before. The idea was to burn off web underneath where the shuttle was suspended, and maybe even torch some spiderlings into the bargain.

As with her first maneuver, the trick would be returning the shuttle's hybrid engine to full blast soon enough for the shuttle to reverse course before it could crash. But it had to be not so soon that the craft didn't dive far enough to sear more ahtpah web.

The second maneuver succeeded barely in time. Just as the shuttle pod racket grew deafening for Helena and company, a few of the spiderlings made holes in the comforter.

One baby ahtpah was even pulling off a taped-up corner. And another cat-sized spiderling was about to break through completely, leading a charge certain to doom the Earthlings.

Fortunately, the seared-apart web directly underneath the glider let it drop down abruptly several feet. All the baby ahtpah lost their footing, and got stuck on un-seared web strands.

One complication Tanya didn't expect: The adult ahtpah shot a filament at the shuttle before she could attain full liftoff thrust. So with a monster spider in tow, an especially wobbly ascent ensued.

Shortly thereafter, however, the ahtpah severed its connection to the shuttle pod. And simultaneously it shot out a new filament, to swing back aboard its web. This precluded a potentially deadly free-fall.

Tanya figured the ahtpah sensed her shuttle's vastly superior thrust as compared to the jet-powered glider. Pursuant to which, instinct counseled that trapping the shuttle like the monster had trapped the glider posed too perilous a challenge.

Nevertheless, the ahtpah left behind a troublesome variable Tanya would have to reckon with on her final two maneuvers. That variable was a cable-thick web strand stuck to the shuttle hull.

Meanwhile Helena, Chris and Buddy felt hope fading rapidly after that welcome jolt of optimism from the spiderlings losing balance. Yes, said spiderlings had fallen backwards, getting stuck on their mother's web. But with instinctive ease they drew web strands to their sharp mandibles for snapping apart. In no time they set themselves free, albeit with bits of web remaining essentially glued to their bulbous backs. And many of them were scrambling over to the windshield cover to resume tearing away at it.

"We can't hold on much longer!" Helena announced for Tanya plus crew back aboard the Smoke and Mirrors.

The first baby ahtpah had fully breached the imitation tralalafa leaf. Tar-and-feathered by cottony comforter stuffing sticking to those aforementioned already-stuck-on bits of web, it scurried first one direction then the other.

The Earthlings feared the baby ahtpah's zigzag route must surely bring it to the passenger cabin's rear where they cowered.

One or two of those things, Buddy thought, *we might be able to fend off. But once they swarm here...and for all we know, the first one we harm could send out a dog-whistle-type distress signal...*

Tanya had to cut off her third maneuver midstream. For the longest while she discounted the large luminescent area underneath the ahtpah web as simply a flounder mouse infestation. Innocuous despite how the brightening, clear-sky dawn wasn't diminishing its greenish glow one least little bit. Yes, she'd received Chris's warning about a possible monster, but that was forgotten in her focus on so many risky flight maneuvers.

All the sudden though, the luminescent ground heaved upwards dramatically, sandy soil falling away like water from a surfacing submarine.

Tanya circled the shuttle around, wondering what to do next beyond responding desperately to Helena, "Please, Captain! You must give me a few more minutes!" She realized that whatever-it-was took up the size of a football field, or of a large golf-course green. With four stumpy legs, one each at its four rounded corners, Tanya imagined the monster being an animated coffee table for Godzilla. Two eyes set close together topside, it could have been a flounder mouse bigger than the biggest whale, but flattened out.

"That must be the lamana-whatever!" shouted Chris to explain the tremendous turbulence experienced aboard the web-bound glider.

Of course the cocoon woven round the glider obstructed a full view of what was going on outside. This, even as a second, third, and fourth baby ahtpah were tearing the windshield covering partway off.

The lamanacasa reared up its back end, giving Tanya a clear view of an anus nearly the size of the adult ahtpah busily repairing its web. From the center of that pinkish, squishy-looking orifice issued what sounded like a trumpet blast put through an electric amplifier turned to the highest setting.

Within seconds the adult ahtpah fell limp where it was weaving. And just before several ahtpah babies would have swarmed Helena and company, lamanacasa gaseous emissions poisoned them as well. Most abruptly they froze, then their legs folded up under their bodies and they rolled over harmlessly onto their backs.

"We're okay, Tanya! We already re-donned our head gear, and have been breathing from oxygen tanks for the past several minutes!" reported Captain Taylor.

"Is wonderful thing you tell me, Captain! But stay put! Don't move!! The monster underneath you is doing I don't know what!"

The lamanacasa was sidestepping like a crab out from under the web and away from the giant ferny tree. Tanya hoped it would continue sidestepping a safe distance off so she could simply land for retrieving captain and company. That would have spared them from dangerous maneuvers three and four.

No such luck, leaving Tanya to think, *that Murphy's Law they speak of is especially cruel.* The lamanacasa reared up on its hind legs, only marginally larger and stumpier than its front legs. And its bioluminescence shut off abruptly, casting a dark shadow across the web-entangled monster grasshopper and powered glider. Not to mention the motionless adult and baby ahtpah in who-knew-what condition.

Horrifically where Tanya was concerned, not one but two mouths were migrating across the lamanacasa's underbelly. She would have likened them to two canoes, were they moving about an enormous bowl of thick vanilla pudding.

Tanya realized she would have to execute a maneuver even riskier than the ones she planned originally.

Originally, she was going to fly her shuttle pod directly into webbing on one side of the glider, to drag the glider free. Then she was going to land several thousand feet past, to quickly transfer Helena and company. If need be, she would also torch away any web strands left stuck to her shuttle. That way, they could easily fly back to the Smoke and Mirrors before the ahtpah could do anything more to them.

What became clear to Tanya, necessitating a lightning-fast change of plans, was sensing the lamanacasa intent on falling over atop the web. Perhaps its migrating mouths were then going to gobble up every living and formerly living thing they could.

Tanya took the shuttle two miles high for a severe nose dive from which she would level out at the last possible moment, flying directly for the web. Ideally she would thread the eye of the needle between cocoons woven by the ahtpah around the glider and the monster grasshopper. She hoped to drag the cocooned glider out of there before the lamanacasa could topple over like a ton of bricks.

"Captain! Everyone!" shouted Tanya into her head set at the start of her nosedive, "Buckle in if you can! Now! And hold on!"

The lamanacasa was already swooning…

VROOOOOMMM!!

Tanya felt all the displaced air from the lamanacasa's belly-flop give her shuttle pod a big kick accompanied by a deafening THUD!

She steered the small vehicle soaring skyward, wobbling erratically side to side from what it dragged along behind.

"Captain?!" Tanya called anxiously. "Are you alright?!" *What if I only pulled out giant grasshopper while leaving away team to be squished then consumed by monster coffee table?*

For an awful moment of silence, Ali's wife feared the worst. But then Helena groaned, "Was that you, Tanya? Oh! We're getting knocked about pretty badly here! That giant insect cocoon keeps bumping - Ouch! - into our glider with its own cocoon, like we're two tin cans tied to the rear bumper of a 'just married' car!"

A cheer went up aboard the Smoke and Mirrors, but Kevin was all business. "Tanya?!" he shouted. "Can you find a landing place to untie your tin cans?!"

Just then, a missile sizzled past Tanya's cockpit. She said to no one in particular, "I can't believe this! Where did that come from?! Was that ground-to-air from desert people?!"

"Air-to-air!" shouted Buddy. "I caught a glimpse! We're being followed by two jets, possibly dispatched by the Fafaman government! And we've got the dead mother ahtpah in tow!"

"So much for landing!" said Tanya. "Buddy, you can see if webbing is sufficiently tangled on shuttle for extended flight?!"

"Looks like it! How extended?! Ouch!"

"Tanya??" Ali called from back aboard the Smoke and Mirrors, of course. "Can you head out over the Great Basin?! We're working up a new rescue option!"

"I can, if we're not shot down!"

"Umm, Tanya!?" Buddy's voice crackled tentatively over Tanya's earpiece. "Can you manage at least a ten-degree tilt left?! We're baking in here!"

"Is that better?!"

"Perfect! That's keeping us out of your exhaust trail, and more good news! The other cocoon, monster grasshopper and all, has been burned off!"

Whoosh!

Another rocket fired from one of two pursuit jets passed within yards of the shuttle pod's left wing.

"This is extra fun, trying to avoid spiral descent from flying at this tilt! AND executing evasive maneuvers!! I'm not complaining!!" Tanya added quickly.

Glider and motionless ahtpah still in tow, the shuttle pod was closing in on the Great Basin coastline.

Chris found himself preoccupied bracing against being tossed about the passenger cabin, not to mention fending off waves of nausea from motion sickness. Even had that not been the case, though, no way was he going to bother his fellow travelers with the ephemeral dragon stuff.

"Are those pursuit craft following you out over the sea?"

Whoosh!

"Does that answer your question, Officer Smith-Park?!" Tanya answered.

"Ayee!!"

"We're still okay back here, Tanya!" Buddy shouted reassuringly, not waiting for her to ask what Chris's Ayee was about. "Your last missile-dodging maneuver dislodged a dead ahtpah baby tangled in the cockpit! It flew back in Chris's face, but Helena's already removed it!"

"I'm fine!" reported Chris. "The important thing is: no tear in my envirosuit!" He had considered removing his helmet just long enough to vomit away his motion sickness. However, the grotesque scare of that cat-sized, curled-up-dead ahtpah baby against his face mask somehow curiously freaked the nausea out of him.

"Officer Smith!?" cried Tanya. "Don't know how much longer our luck can hold with evasive maneuvers! Each fired missile comes closer to hitting us! And if Fafamans think to send two missiles simultaneously...! No! I see their jets crisscrossing in rear view! Probably means-"

BOOM!

BOOM!

"TANYA!?! TANYA!?!" screamed Ali, high-pitched hysterical.

"I'm okay, Ali! Something incredible happened! Those noises you heard, that was one jet then the other flaming out! The crews are parachuting from crash dives!"

"Must be that superior Fafaman technology!" Kevin chuckled with relief. "Probably lucky you all didn't get killed when you flew aboard their shuttle from their space station down to Fafama's surface!"

"We still have big problem, Kevin!"

"Way ahead of you on that, Tanya! We know you can't land safely! The captain and company would have an only one-in-a-thousand chance of survival, best we can calculate! So we're feeding special instructions to your autopilot! But you still need to climb twenty thousand feet manually!! Captain?! The three of you have on your envirosuits, correct?"

"Yes, of course! But what are you up to, Officer Smith?!" asked Helena, unavoidably emoting grave concern.

"Captain," went on Kevin, "we ran this contingency through our small-scale simulator even before Tanya left shuttle bay."

"Oh, THAT one!" nodded Tanya in the shuttle pod cockpit. "It is okay, Captain!"

Helena suspected disapprovingly what they were going to try. But rather than voice any objection, she offered an alternative, albeit with despair; she figured they'd already rejected it for compelling reasons. She said, "Can't Tanya make a gradual ascent out of the atmosphere, then we spacewalk over to the shuttle and torch off the webbing?"

"Captain," said Kevin in lecturing mode, "it's highly likely that the extreme cold will make the monster spider web strands so brittle, they snap apart well before you reach minimum orbital altitude. In other words, your glider will lose its attachment to the shuttle pod and go into a multi-mile free-fall. And we KNOW you can't survive that!"

"I'm sorry, Kevin! I can't allow you to put the entire ship and crew at such risk to rescue us! Tanya, we'll take our one-in-a-thousand chance with that surface landing! Maybe-"

"Captain, I don't want to become obnoxious about this, but you know the protocol," responded Kevin. "Until either Buddy or you return to the bridge, I'm in charge! Your job is to hang on tight, avoid being bumped around too much!"

"You're right, Captain Taylor! Listen to her, Kevin!" Tanya heard Deborah Davis-Murphy shouting in the background. "God help us all!"

Deb left out her complaint about how they wouldn't be in such danger if Helena hadn't put herself at risk travelling to Fafama's surface in the first place. Also, would have helped if they'd come armed. When would they drop this ridiculous no-weapons-in-outer-space business? But at least the threat from TicTocTic would serve as a giant wakeup call, she consoled herself thinking.

The Smoke and Mirrors jockeyed millions of miles away from Fafama, and that many millions of miles closer to star Alpha Centauri C.

An ideal distance attained, Yoon-hee worked the starship's mirror arrays to gently U-turn back towards Fafama again. The new course heading would send the Smoke and Mirrors into the Fafaman atmosphere at the safest possible angle, neither too shallow nor too steep. It would neither bounce off from a too-shallow angle, like a stone skipping across water, nor burn to a cinder from a too-steep angle.

With a small forefinger gesture, Kevin motioned Yoon-hee, "Let's bloom, Officer Park-Smith."

"You're making me blush, Officer Smith-Park!" Yoon-hee responded, surprised at herself for such an intentionally mischievous misread of her husband's directive, especially with so much at stake. "Mirror array bloom sequence initiated," she continued, though, back to serious. "Already confirming lock-in at point two two three light-speed."

No sooner did Yoon-hee report this than sunlight electromagnetically bounced about the mirror array, photons in a pinball machine. Thereby was the Smoke and Mirrors pushed close to one-quarter light-speed, at least according to theory. And mysterious shimmering photon exhaust comprised the starship's wake as Fafama swelled rapidly from star to planet in its panoramic viewscreen.

"Heat shield deployment underway," Yoon-hee reported, her fingers playing across the control panel like a concert pianist performing a lengthy solo, Ali mused. "Fore and aft petals are retracting."

Mirror-array petal retraction for plunging into the Fafaman atmosphere left the starship's cylindrical shape modified by only its umbrella-like heat shield.

"We've reached twenty-thousand-foot altitude, Kevin!" reported Tanya. "Now what?" Receiving nothing in return but crackly static, she added, "Are you there, Officer Smith?! I've achieved target altitude!"

"We've just entered the atmosphere and retracted the heat shield, Tanya!" Kevin finally responded. "You're soon going to see us approaching from the rear."

"Yes?!"

"You're about to feel the autopilot gunning your ignition for further acceleration! When we pass you, it will help you guide the shuttle into the photon exhaust shaft! We've retracted the mirror array petals to leave the chamber wide open!

"Once you're inside, both rear and forward cover 'leaves' will seal over! Then as the Smoke and Mirrors descent steepens, resultant weightlessness will allow the captain, Chris, and Buddy to float over to you from the Fafaman aircraft!

"Meantime I will be attaching a mile-length cable to the rear of your shuttle pod, already attached to the Smoke and Mirrors for space-tugs! Then the forward 'leaves' will reopen, letting you fly out the front of the photon-exhaust shaft dragging us after you! Once you've pulled us clear of the atmosphere, you can decouple the shuttle pod from the cable, circle around to dock, and then we're off!"

"And you're saying that's the safest option?!?!" asked Captain Taylor, incredulous.

"Our simulator rates the success prospect at sixty-five percent, Captain!"

"According to quick calculation, we're not going to have much anti-matter left after these maneuvers for any other shuttle missions before return to Earth, Captain!" said Tanya. "But at least there's enough for Kevin's scheme!"

The shuttle pod piloted by Tanya successfully pulled the web-entangled glider the full way into the Smoke and Mirrors photon-exhaust shaft. Then it decelerated to exactly the starship's shallow descent rate.

The curled-up, presumed-dead mother ahtpah was left hanging on by a lone filament, just outside the chamber.

Thank God, Tanya thought to herself as metallic "leaves" re-emerged from where they'd been retracted alongside the mirror array "petals," which remained retracted. *Those leaves should finally slice off that final strand of web and free us from... Oh, no!*

The leaves had not gotten very far sealing both ends of the photon-exhaust shaft when a new web filament flew in from the ahtpah, then another and a third. Those new filaments attached to the shaft's cylindrical wall, followed quickly by the mother ahtpah using them like a mountain climber. Obviously, the lamanacasa gas had only temporarily anesthetized her, instead of out-and-out killing her.

"Holy crap! Stop the seal-up sequence, Yoon-hee!"

"It's stopped, Kevin! Saw that thing the same time you did!"

Tanya was at a complete loss what to do while the ahtpah picked her way across her new lifelines. Helena, Chris, and Buddy had already exited the glider for floating over to the shuttle pod, so the ahtpah's steady approach found them vulnerable as could be…

….when suddenly, all three web filaments burst into flames. Resultant black cinders crumbled apart, totally unmooring the ahtpah so she flew out the exhaust shaft rear before she could launch another silky strand.

"Seal-up sequence resumed, Kevin!" Yoon-hee assured her husband.

"Good! Hopefully that little delay didn't throw us off schedule in any critical sense!"

It threw us off just enough to seal our doom, Deborah thought to herself as she and wife Geena gave each other significant looks. Strapped in on the navigation bridge, they squeezed their hands together.

"What do you think happened, Officer Smith?" asked Ali as Kevin unstrapped himself and grabbed the nearest railing because he started floating weightless. "Was there some unknown friction phenomenon peculiar to the Fafaman atmosphere?"

"We'll discuss it later, Ali! Am already late for attaching the cable to the shuttle pod!"

"Careful, Kevin! Seal-up sequence is complete!"

"Thanks, Yoon-hee!"

Kevin wasn't too far off the bridge when he ran into Helena. Pulling herself along the same railing as Kevin, she was clearly headed *for* the bridge. And she had removed her envirosuit helmet as well as her magnetic boots to make her weightless progress fast as possible.

"Captain?!"

"That's right, Kevin! Captain! Especially now that you're off the bridge and I'm headed there! Listen up, everyone on the bridge!! Hurry to the exhaust shaft airlock with your own envirosuits, NOW!! You're joining everyone else aboard the shuttle pod!! If the ship goes down, your captain and your captain only goes down with it! If it becomes clear the shuttle pod can't tow the Smoke and Mirrors out of the atmosphere, I'm releasing the cable! And then your mission becomes to survive on Fafama until a rescue mission can be deployed! Why aren't you moving?! LEAVE NOW!!" Captain Taylor literally flew through the air onto the bridge before grabbing the next length of railing.

"Yes, Captain!" Yoon-hee, Ali, Geena and Deborah said in unison as they launched themselves flying weightless off the bridge. None of them had bothered re-donning their cumbersome magboots after the Smoke and Mirrors decelerated into the Alpha Centauri C system.

Five minutes later, the shuttle pod was crowded full of crew save Helena. Then soon as the retracting prow-end "leaves" opened wide enough, Tanya accelerated the shuttle pod to emerge zooming from the photon exhaust shaft.

"You didn't want to go with your wife?!" Deborah asked Chris, who sensed she delighted in making him feel guilty.

"She wouldn't let me."

Pulling the Smoke and Mirrors out of crash-dive required an especially tricky maneuver. Tanya actually had to race the shuttle past the Smoke and Mirrors on its accelerating plummet. Then she had to swing back skyward, pulling taut the lone cable connecting both vehicles.

Tugging upward on the Smoke and Mirrors slowed the shuttle so much that Tanya and company experienced an illusion of falling into reverse. Also not helping anyone's confidence were peculiar noises emanating from the shuttle's antimatter hybrid engine, like it was straining not to stall. Mercifully soon, though, the engine sounded less whiny, and everyone felt pressed back against their seat. The shuttle was regaining speed even with the Smoke and Mirrors in tow, for a steady ascent.

A collective sigh of relief suggested to Chris he wasn't alone holding his breath.

Tanya, though, found new reason to hold her breath nearly as soon as she'd relaxed, with others quick to follow. "Captain," was all she could spit out while Helena Taylor rattled on about operating the starship, oblivious to a new threat.

"Fore and aft leaf retractions are complete," Helena happily reported. "Maybe the Smoke and Mirrors will even receive extra lift from all that air running through the exhaust shaft, as if it were some gigantic box kite."

"No, Captain, I mean that's good, but have you noticed what's approaching on the eastern horizon?"

Helena had never seen a tsunami tidal wave before. Yet if she had, she imagined that what was approaching was what it would look like...if it were brown. She could only gape at how the sunset storm-line loomed even from so many miles distant, and with her at such high altitude.

Helena wondered if she should say something to Chris. Some final thing.

"Captain?"

"The sunset storm-line, Tanya; didn't occur to me what it was until now!"

"Same here!"

"Can you make enough of an ascent before we reach it, or it reaches us? Probably easier without the Smoke and Mirrors as ball and chain..."

"HELL NO, CAPTAIN!!!!" Kevin exploded. "If you decouple, we'll dive back down after you!"

"HELL NO, CAPTAIN!! HELL NO, CAPTAIN!!" the crew chanted in unison.

Chris hoped his voice could be heard above the others.

"Captain?!" called Tanya in the ensuing silence.

"I'm here," Helena finally calmed enough to say after wiping away a tear. Very well, she wasn't going to argue with them. But if the storm-line tumbled them about, plus they started losing altitude, that would be it. She would cut loose without a goodbye, and surely reason would prevail aboard the shuttle. They wouldn't really try to save her, on a pursuit as suicidal as it would be hopeless. Would they?

"Going to be uncomfortably close I'm calculating, Captain. Maybe we should swing around for heading opposite direction."

"Bad idea, Tanya," said Buddy while Chris felt the weight of judgmental onlookers.

Chris suspected Deborah and others of thinking: Fine, so he didn't insist on riding out the helpless starship with his wife. Couldn't he at least say something to her, make a final profession of undying love?

Chris kept telling himself that to get through this crisis, the last thing anyone needed was him injecting that emotional element...

"It's like sailing through rough seas," Buddy Leung went on for Tanya, oblivious to the drama centered on Chris. "You're better off going at the waves full frontal, because turning the boat around risks a sideswipe rolling it upside down!"

The steady, smooth ascent suddenly turned bouncy.

"Speak of the devil! I believe we're already experiencing outer turbulence the storm-line sets off way ahead of itself!" shouted Officer Leung. "Might even provide that extra lift Helena spoke of, leaping into minimum orbital altitude!"

The sandy-brown storm-line kept rebuilding, re-blossoming ahead of advancing night as the shuttle pod, starship dragged behind, was climbing towards it. The idea was that if the shuttle pod gained a certain altitude quickly enough, the Earthlings would avoid Fafama's signature daily weather event altogether.

They're not going to make it, Captain Taylor grimly concluded. She reached for the lever that needed flipping to detach the tow cable from the Smoke and Mirrors.

But suddenly, the brightest lightning accompanied crashing thunder. Concussion waves shook starship and shuttle alike, well beyond what the displaced, roiled-up air ahead of the storm-line could induce. Then a powerfully enormous updraft hit the Smoke and Mirrors so abruptly and with such force, Helena's hand flailed away from where she'd been about to flip the lever.

As for the shuttle, while one moment the crew thought the storm-line had engulfed them, the next moment the brown clouds were rapidly dissipating. In their place stretched starry firmament as the sunset storm-line passed well below them. Hurled by a freak updraft, the Smoke and Mirrors had pulled the shuttle pod into the relative safety of outer space.

Tanya still had to tow the starship further away from Fafama's gravitational field before the mirror array could provide light-speed propulsion.

No cheers or sighs of relief this time, as people had variously passed out, thrown up, or come close to cardiac arrest. But Buddy recovered quickly enough to say what Chris would have said first if not for debilitating nausea. "Are you okay, Captain?!" he asked.

"To a most miraculous extent, Officer Leung, and am patching through a transmission from Fafama so we can all listen together!"

"This is the Fafamafalafama, the supreme ruler of Fafama," translated the Fafamafalafama's fah-lah-lahs via robotic-sounding digitized voice. "Is your own supreme ruler, 'Cahptahn Taylah,' returned aboard your space vessel where I can converse with her?"

"This is Captain Taylor speaking."

"'Cahptahn Taylah.' There seems to have been a category of enormous misunderstanding. When we retrieved the first wife and our hangar crew, they explained what your people asked them to perform, your charade. The word, disappointment, does not begin to convey how strongly I feel over your lack of trust that you could simply say, 'Please let us return to our vessel.'"

"Members of my crew explained to your people that not one of us could afford to remain behind while the rest returned to Earth. But they were met with resistance which implied that at least Officer Olsen-Taylor and I were to be held hostage. If that is incorrect we apologize, I apologize, because all decisions came down to me.

"But having said this, please explain why your jets fired on us."

"'Cahptahn Taylah,' I personally ordered those jets out there to provide assistance. The squadron captain reported your escape vessel got entangled by ahtpah webbing occupied by an especially large ahtpah. On hearing this, I commanded missile attacks to free you from such dangerous encumbrance. Only the ahtpah and its webbing were targeted."

"Your squadron captain did not mention your first wife's glider was also entangled? Two of my crew and I were trapped inside there."

"That must have been obscured from view by so much ahtpah webbing. My people probably mistook the glider for typical ahtpah prey. But on their behalf, thank you anyway for the mercy you showed. Had you blasted apart our jets rather than only making their engines flame out, obviously their crew would not have survived."

"We were relieved to see them parachute to safety, Fafamafalafama."

"So where does that leave us, 'Cahptahn'?"

Will there be a second date? Chris couldn't help wondering bitterly.

"That leaves us on course back home to our Earth, where we will concoct a plan for protecting all of us from the threat potentially posed by Tictoctic."

"Then may I wish you and your crew a safe and speedy journey. We anxiously await your return."

Once Tanya parked the shuttle pod, and everyone rejoined Captain Taylor on the Smoke and Mirrors' navigation bridge, a quiet group hug ensued. Because what could any of them have said that such a hug did not communicate far more eloquently?

Chris would have preferred the couples hug separately, so he could have seen how Helena would have behaved with him in that regard. Yes, Buddy would have been left standing alone, his wife busy on Mars. Nevertheless...

Even past the hug, every couple except for Chris and Helena remained arm in arm until having to uncouple at their various bridge stations.

Helena slipped away from Chris before he knew what happened. "I think we need to give Tanya special thanks," she said so soon as planting herself in the captain's centrally located chair. "We ended up owing our lives to her extraordinary flying prowess."

"And that means I'll have to prepare her favorite dinner tonight if we have the ingredients," commented Ali, stirring laughter mixed with applause.

"So tell us, Captain," said Deborah, Chris again unavoidably likening her toothy, lipstick-heavy smile to a monkey aggressively baring its teeth. "Before I take you one by one for minor patching up, we're headed home now, correct?" Home was where the chief medical officer could hardly wait to unload about the reckless lack of judgment Helena had demonstrated.

Helena exchanged a significant look with Chris before responding, "If things had gone more smoothly with the Fafamans, if we could be more certain they were, um... Under other circumstances, we might have been able to comfortably close out this particular mission. But as I am sure you are aware, too many troubling aspects remain. Moreover, long before our arrival here, we identified another planet clearly sharing life-promoting characteristics with Earth and of course Fafama."

"Located in a solar system directly between Alpha Centauri C and the solar system home to Tictoctic," inserted Yoon-hee supportively. "A straight line would bisect all three stars."

"Not only that," continued Helena, "but the two antlered creatures who crash-landed on Fafama, presumably from Tictoctic, they identified this other planet as a potential third target in addition to Earth and Fafama. By no means am I closing the door on working with Fafamans. Obviously there's a lot to sort through. But I have concluded we need to check out this other planet, if only for a brief while, to get a more complete picture.

"Yoon-hee," Captain Taylor went on hardly pausing to catch her breath, pointedly not allowing Deborah a split second for response. She sensed Deb's misgivings, but had already gone over the situation enough times in her head and with Buddy, Ali and Yoon-hee to be firmly resolved. "Yoon-hee, set a course above the orbital plane out of here, the same way we came in. Buddy, redeploy that advance guard firefly donut. Deborah, I know you've got your hands full with decontamination issues; Geena, help her. Kevin, help me finish charting our course to the other star system."

"Mirror array blooming, Captain," reported Yoon-hee.

Where the Smoke and Mirrors had been drifting, sparkles sprayed like Disney cartoon fairy dust until they winked out.

"Oh, one more thing, Buddy," said Helena, spinning around at the last moment from leading Kevin off the bridge.

"Yes, Captain."

"Before you redeploy that firefly donut, take a shower and change your pants. Now! I don't want to know."

"Yes, Captain."

Chapter 21

Captain's Log, Smoke and Mirrors Mission 1, February 28, 2062:
Captain Helena Taylor could have uttered these words aloud, and fast as they left her mouth they would have appeared on the screen of her quaintly old-fashioned, quarter-inch-thick laptop pad. Fearing a slip of the tongue, however, she opted for chicken-pecking the keyboard.

True, de-slipping her tongue was easy. She simply had to say "edit shmedit" followed by a reread of the passage to be removed, then "edit shmedit" again. In the privacy of her soundproofed office, not even Chris would know.

But what if Helena's slip of the tongue accidentally revealed something she did not want to face? Edited out or not, wouldn't it keep echoing in her head, haunting her in her own voice? How could she ever edit *that* out? And what was it exactly she so feared facing?

Fortunately, we've achieved a high-enough altitude flight-path "above" the orbital plane to avoid Oort-Cloud debris. So our advance-guard firefly donut has had an easy go. Let's hope it survives our descent into the Callaway X Centra System.

When I suspended the firefly-donut communication feed, Dr. Davis-Murphy thought I was avoiding Mission Control, or the President even. That I didn't want them trumping my judgment to order us homeward bound immediately. And yes, in my heart of hearts as Officer Magabu says, am not at all certain that taking this detour closer to Tictoctic was wise.

However, our data strongly suggests that returning directly back to Earth from Alpha Centauri C will prove far more perilous than returning home from Callaway X Centra. Something to do with an uneven distribution of Oort Cloud hazards, even though both flight paths take us high above the orbital plane.

In any event, we need to assure that future missions are more plentifully stocked with firefly donuts.

Captain Taylor left out any musing over whether they should shift to some *Star Trek*-type star-date calendar system for log entries. Hopefully Buddy got his test flight data straight, and they weren't going to land at Kennedy Space Center in year 2300 with everyone they knew long since deceased.

We also need to keep the Smoke and Mirrors full to bursting with all the ingredients for Chris Olsen-Taylor's chocolate chip cookies. His big batch has been perfect comfort food for many crew persons still suffering post-traumatic stress over our death-defying escape from Fafama.

Helena could have mentioned Dr. Deborah Davis-Murphy's complaint the chocolate chip cookies were really cookie chip chocolates. She also could have noted the doctor's bizarre comparison of those cookies to civilization-ending asteroids. That Deborah considered them riddled with fat that crashed into people's bodies, blocking their blood vessels. However, she had already mentioned Deborah questioning her judgment. When her superiors examined her journal entries as part of the debriefing process, she didn't want them to misapprehend she had a vendetta against the woman.

As it was, Helena questioned the purity of her motives for bringing up the cookies in the first place. Would she have done that if Chris wasn't involved baking them? Weren't there are other matters of far higher priority for her mission log?

Chris's presence had been challenged as adding nothing more to the starship mission than a crucial member's spouse. Who probably would have been kicked off hadn't Buddy threatened to terminate his own involvement.

Unfortunately, no number of cookies have been able to alleviate us from experiencing an especially unnerving something at the most inopportune times.

Only happened to me once, and granted, was nothing compared to the horror of ghostly bodies streaming through walls on the Mars flyby. But there were these metallic glints succeeded by the creepiest feeling of something very long sliding past me in the hallway.

Officer Kevin Smith-Park tried replicating the phenomenon by making several lighting and air-vent adjustments. But to date, he hasn't even come close to what he himself experienced. Nevertheless, his confidence remains high there's a conventional explanation. Buddy's report bolsters that confidence, of nothing unusual showing up on any shipboard sensors.

Ironically, those shipboard sensor findings also bolster one possibility Kevin won't accept. Namely, according to Dr. Deborah Davis-Murphy we might be experiencing a mass-psychosis hallucination. Could have been brought on by unknown effects from travel at light-speed multiples. Or the culprit could be additional unknown medical conditions in league with the comical if bizarre nasal discharge. In other words, according to our chief medical officer, exposure to an extraterrestrial ecosystem might be wreaking additional havoc.

Either way, Deborah insists we have all the more reason to forego detouring to Callaway X Centra, and head home the most direct route possible.

Frankly, I'm uncertain whether I've made a sound decision. Deborah might be right. Helena paused from her entry to reflect on this admission, on how it should make clear that vindictiveness regarding Deborah was not her intent.

Moreover, there might be an additional reason we'd be better advised to hurry home pronto. For all we know, a Tictoctic warship like something out of an old sci-fi movie is mere hours from discovering our presence and then blowing us to bits. Of course, that would totally refute everything we'd calculated about the horizons of possibility for an advanced alien species.

And yet one prospect feels even more uncomfortable than lingering long enough to vet the potentially habitable planet in the Callaway X Centra system. And that's the prospect of NOT vetting it.

"Captain Taylor?"

"Officer Leung?" Helena reacted, setting aside her laptop in anticipation of Buddy raising an important matter on his intercom call.

"Captain, we're fast approaching orbit of Callaway X Centra's second planet. Calculations did prove accurate, that it is 1.005 Earth's mass."

"So we shouldn't have to deal with any more cow-sized insects. I'll be there in a flash, Buddy, for a ringside seat."

As Helena headed for the hallway, she wondered how Earthlings would be greeted this time around, were there an intelligent species to greet them. Far as she knew, starship sensors hadn't detected satellites, artificial lighting, or any other artifices of a civilization well underway. If the second planet from Callaway X Centra was populated by creatures comparable to humans, they kept their advancements well-hidden. Or they were still living in the Stone Age.

The troublesome question regarding Fafamans might prove even more urgent. Namely, what psychological harm might an encounter with technologically more advanced creatures inflict on less advanced creatures?

For all Helena knew, Tictoctic weaponry would soon overwhelm anything the Earthlings had. Humanity's most brilliant ecological modelers were about to be proved miserably, naively wrong. So why drag creatures into this who might not even have invented the wheel yet? Why not leave them blissfully ignorant? Then hope that either their planet is mercifully bypassed, or adequately protected by whatever defenses Earthlings could provide?

If only those two, antlered Tictoctic creatures had crash-landed on Earth instead, wouldn't that have been much better for the Fafamans? Kept them blissfully ignorant as well?

Welcome to Oomb.

"What did you say, uh, did you say something, Officer Leung?" asked Helena Taylor, paralyzed by anticipation she already knew the answer.

"Not 'Welcome to Oomb,' Captain," Buddy responded through the voice-activated intercom.

"Has everyone heard what we heard?!" shouted Captain Taylor breaking into a sprint for the bridge.

"Captain, we're looking at one another wondering, 'What next?'"

We don't mean to frighten you.

"I'm hearing it in Korean, Captain," said Yoon-hee as Helena burst onto the bridge, making for the captain's chair.

"Russian for me," added Tanya.

"The truly most fascinating thing, Captain," said Ali, "I don't know about you, but sentences have been entering my mind so gently, they might as well have been of my own conjuring. Like whenever I carefully consider an utterance, rather than simply allowing it to pop from my mouth, if that makes any sense."

"That makes perfect sense, Officer Magabu."

We are sorry for causing any additional anxiety. We wish you the safest possible return home after your visit here.

The Smoke and Mirrors having orbited around to Oomb's day-lit side allowed Helena a gloriously epic view from the navigation bridge.

Fafama had appeared more landlocked than Earth. Australian-sized seas pockmarked vast regions generally brown by day and bioluminescent green by night. But dominating Callaway X Centra's second planet...*The voice in my head did welcome us to Oomb?*

Yes, Captain Taylor, we did name our planet Oomb.

Vast seas dotted by assorted archipelagos dominated Oomb's surface. Widely-scattered plumes on a few islands suggested volcanic activity.

Given the planet's slightly larger size and consequently stronger gravity compared to Earth, Buddy had already long since expected a virtual water-world. Over the millennia, far less water vapor would have escaped into space than was the case on Earth, whether "homegrown" or from micro-comets entering the atmosphere.

The absence of ice caps met another expectation based on Buddy's earlier findings about the planet. Oomb's axis of rotation constantly shifted so that daylight in any one location could fluctuate between four and twenty hours. Where Buddy was concerned, this planet might as well have been thrown like a knuckle ball into its orbit round Callaway X Centra.

Snow did grace a few higher mountain peaks, but that was it for wintry cold. Most weather systems drifted aimlessly hither and yon, consisting of gentle showers save for a rare, embedded thunderstorm.

Contemplating our planet, all of you are thinking Hawai'i multiplied several fold.

Helena rose from her chair to address the panoramic vista revealed on the navigation bridge view-screen, for want of a sentient being. "I am Captain Helena Taylor of the light-propelled starship, Smoke and Mirrors," she announced loudly, firmly, despite having already been called Captain Taylor by the voice in her head. "We've arrived from a solar system seven light-years distant, on our maiden voyage. Guessing you're already aware of this and far more, I want to make a special plea. We are not accustomed to mind reading at more than the most rudimentary, error-prone level. Our foremost psychic researchers are still at the baby step phase, analyzing what a few of our more clairvoyant individuals can accomplish. As a result, I suspect that your telepathic powers are making my crew feel as mentally raped as I'm feeling."

Helena Taylor's crew all nodded in the affirmative, leaving no doubt she was correct.

"I can't ask you to pretend you haven't learned what you have already learned about us," Helena continued. "But if you could, please, I respectfully implore you to constrain your telepathic communication with us. Limit your mentally transmitted messages to reactions to what we vocalize. We might perhaps better manage that."

There was a long pause that left the crew exchanging puzzled looks.

"Anybody experiencing telepathy, don't be shy…"

"Yes, Captain, we know."

"Why Officer Smith-Park, it's like you can read my mind."

Yes, we can do that just as requested. We can limit our thought projections to interaction with your vocalizations. Not something we are used to, which is why I had to delay my response. I only ask that if we wish to initiate a communication, we might do so by prefacing it with: Captain.

"Acceptable. Now when you say 'we,' who exactly are 'we'? Is there some collective consciousness?"

I am the representative chosen to initiate this contact, Captain. My name is Oodle-Noodle.

Chris covered his mouth to stifle a giggle. Kevin buried his face in his hands. A wry grin blossomed on Ali's face. Deborah and Geena rolled their eyes. And Yoon-hee, Tanya and Buddy exchanged more puzzled looks.

Oodle-Noodle caught herself about to comment on how laughably ridiculous the Earthlings found her name. From which she would have proceeded to express hope that such unintended hilarity helped lower their stress. But she strove to honor the captain's plea, and react only to what was vocalized. (And how fascinating, she thought, that this visitor from another planet so unwittingly accurately assumed she COULD perceive when vocalizations occurred.)

So in response to Helena's question about who were the "we," Oodle-Noodle telepathed, *There is much for you to understand about our communication, especially since you are not so very far along with mental telepathy yourselves, by your own admission.*

All thoughts of everyone on our planet are available for all to share. But they are like vast landscapes you might see, for example when you are viewing our planet from outer space. We choose the details on which to focus. Or, someone's thought projection calls us to focus on certain details. In this way, curiously, we still maintain a sort of privacy amongst ourselves. Of course we've had several generations' practice at this, evolution over thousands of years.

Having essentially zero practice at it, you Earthlings were sure to be dangerously overwhelmed by the telepathic flood of which we were capable. So on sensing your arrival, we took the precaution of choosing one Oombian only, my own self, to initiate this contact.

"I appreciate, Oodle-Noodle, that, um, I'm assuming you could have projected your thoughts to only one of us, and left the rest out of the loop, as we say…"

Naturally we understand all your idiomatic expressions in all your languages.

"Uh, yes. Anyhow, telepathing all of us is a good thing. It lessens possible suspicion or doubt, limited in our mind-reading abilities as we are. So please continue that."

You are conveying what we expected to be the Earthling consensus, Captain.

"So, um, are we the first? Have you had any other extraterrestrial contact prior to our arrival?"

You are the first we can confirm, Captain. In the past, some of us have claimed pre-emergent abilities to mind-read intelligences several billion miles away from our planet. Purportedly those intelligences have been clairvoyantly detected skirting our solar system. We have explained most of these instances as non-intelligent anomalies and, in a few cases, fraud. But just like your UFOs, a couple of cases remain unexplained, except as what their perceivers thought them to be.

"Which brings you back to us, your first confirmed contact, Oodle-Noodle," said Captain Taylor trying not to grin too much, as though Oombians could see her face as well as read her mind. "I hope you don't take offense at how silly your name strikes us."

We understand, Captain.

"So tell us what you understand about why we're here."

You were on an historic mission to the outskirts of your own solar system. You were to set up a more thorough system for detecting incoming comets, asteroids and other such objects potentially hazardous to your planet. But shortly after embarking, your political leadership warned of an urgent distress message from another solar system. Further investigation revealed the possibility carnivorous creatures only a few light-years away from here were planning a multi-solar system conquest to replenish their food supply.

The urgent distress message originated from the planet Fafama, but erratic behavior by that civilization's leadership raised serious doubts. Could Fafamans really prove constructive allies against such a threat?

You were headed home to work out a plan with your political and military leadership. However, Captain Taylor, you argued for a detour here because our planet might be one of Tictoctic's targets for their interplanetary cattle roundup. At least that's what the crash-landed antlered creatures claimed, correct?

If our Oomb had been found uninhabited by intelligent beings, you were going to recommend it for staging both an early warning system and a retaliatory base.

But Oomb is inhabited by such creatures. So now you must explore whether they, meaning I and company, will make more dependable partners than the Fafamans for dealing with the potential invaders.

"Well?" reacted Captain Taylor. "Are you authorized to share your leadership's thoughts on this entire matter?"

Yes, Captain, I am. On your mental landscape, we have identified certain high-profile figures from your civilization's history of particular interest to us. They seem to have argued a perspective not held by too many members of your species.

"And those figures are...?"

Buddha, Jesus, Mohammed, a few select others... Whether real or mythic, their lives have led to religious faiths. However, to varying extent those faiths have proven as lifeless compared to the figures that inspired them as empty shells left behind by certain sea creatures.

Then there are relatively recent figures such as Mahatma Gandhi and Martin Luther King Junior, and your music group The Beatles singing "All You Need Is Love."

Like hermit crabs, they tried to re-inhabit those abandoned shells by revitalizing a concept most fundamental to our own civilization.

Captain, I'm not saying we don't have our own problems to deal with. I'm not saying that horrible, terrible things don't still continue here on Oomb, especially in what you term "the natural world." But a huge majority of us believe that caring for others is such a strong force in the universe, no matter the continuing extant of violence. We find violence useless, and unequivocally renounce its value for accomplishing anything really worthwhile.

"Is there no history of war in your civilization's history? Have there been no major acts of aggression to deal with?"

The last significant aggression on Oomb was countless solar orbits ago. And it was defused in a miraculously wonderful manner we continue celebrating to this day. I hope you'll experience our celebration.

"Permission to jump in, Captain."

"Go ahead, Officer Smith."

"Thank you. Listen, or whatever it is you're doing, Oodle-Noodle," said Kevin, unable to say her name without laughter in his voice. "This whole routine of yours has me extremely nervous, as I guess you already know. But which might be news for my non-mind-reading fellow crew members. What I also want those folks to know is how I'm wondering whether we shouldn't just hop the next rainbow out of here pronto. That is, before it turns out you're seducing us into a trap which will have us begging for the tender mercies of the Tictoctickians or whatever-the-hell we should call them!"

Officer Smith, we can only hope that enough time will elapse, no trap sprung, to finally convince you I'm not giving any false impression.

"Okay, well whatever, look, I think there are a lot of Beatle fans aboard here. You can count me among them, and I know the captain's husband keeps a collection of their vinyl discs. Good tunes, and the thought of a world full of hugs and kisses appeals to most people.

"Now, I obviously know little about your world. Maybe you've experienced a kinder, gentler evolution. But that's not how things have worked out for us back home on Earth. We've had people in our planet's history who didn't think they needed to protect and defend themselves from bad guys. As I'm guessing you've already picked our brains to know, among them were the Taino Indians. Soldiers came to them in the name of that guy Jesus you mentioned, and wiped them out. More recently, this other guy named Hitler was conquering countries one by one. I don't know if you have countries on Oomb..."

We did. We don't any more.

"Well, the leaders of other countries tried to make peace with Hitler. They believed they could stop his aggression without going to war with him. One in particular, Chamberlain, the thanks he got was England being carpet-bombed. If our country and others had not stepped up for war, we'd all be speaking German. That is, those of us with blond hair and blue eyes who weren't sent to the gas chambers."

In two of your crew members' minds, Captain, a fragmentary memory is stirring. They're wondering if there's anything to it, or just a trick of the imagination wrought by wishful thinking. Permission to raise it since neither of them is willing to?

"Permission granted."

Again, maybe there's nothing to it, a romantic legend as you might say. Apparently, though, a story circulated about a small, isolated French town surrounded by the German occupation. It was something about openly yet peacefully resisting the persecution of Jews with some success.

"Look, Oodle-Noodle," said Kevin, "I might have heard that one myself. It's what we call the exception proving the rule. And had Hitler and his closest associates chanced upon the little town themselves, am not sure that exception wouldn't have been squelched." Kevin paused, overwhelmed abruptly by the astounding extrasensory nature of the dialogue he was having.

Officer Smith, we do not wish to meet the fate suffered by several of your fellow humans over your planet's recent history. But violent tactics are simply not one of our options for avoiding it.

"Okay, what if we exercise violence on your behalf? Will you at least allow us to fight the bad guys if they invade your turf?"

We plea for you not to, but will not obstruct such efforts. Yes, we could flood both you and the hypothetical invaders from Tictoctic with our thoughts, to incapacitating effect. But we are convinced such incapacitation would prove lethal, thereby constituting deadly violence.

"Let me try to understand," said Captain Taylor. "So if we aren't here, aren't present when the creatures from Tictoctic arrive, your actions will be...?"

We will offer them our fruit, and invite them to play our game, the same things we offer you now.

"Your game?"

It bears a remarkable similarity to one of your games. Although from what we have grown to understand about it, this is to be expected. And you do not orbit so high that your telescopic magnification cannot give you a sense of it. Yes, Officer Leung, that will work. Whoops! Excuse my violation of the pledge not to react to any of your thoughts before they are verbalized.

Buddy Leung jumped in his seat like someone had given him an electric jolt, Chris mused.

"Uh, I can have this down to a one-foot resolution, Captain," spoke Buddy in as deeply serious a voice as he could muster while playing his fingers across his control panel at lightning speed.

"Thank you, Officer Leung," responded Helena, already squinting to try discerning some telling detail on the panoramic screen.

"Any second now, Captain."

Magnification revealed turquoise blue and emerald green waters, and a coastline of beautiful white-sand beaches. In one location, curious black dots moved back and forth from land to sea, in and out of the surf.

The view gradually panned inland, where amoebic and kidney-shaped pale green patches were set amidst lush forests and open plains. Leading up to each pale green patch was a wide stretch of darker green lawn, irregularly punctuated by foliage, ponds, streams and sandy brown patches. Those sandy patches bordered some of the pale green patches. Small buildings were also scattered about, though there were no signs of any roads or rail systems.

"Golf courses, Captain?" asked Buddy.

Chris would have spoken first, but was afraid he'd start laughing hysterically.

Golf courses, Officer Leung, though we call our game Oof. Fascinating how close that is to your name for it.

"Oof," Helena repeated aloud as she thought to herself, *My God, are the rest of Oomb's island archipelagos this covered with golf courses? Is that all these people ever do?* "The question occurs to me, Oodle-Noodle: Why do you bother with names for things and for yourselves, or with any language at all since you're able to mind-read? Why a symbolic system when thoughts can be shared directly, unmediated by vocalizations?"

Captain, this is the state of our knowledge on that particular matter: Long before the Grand Merger to which I've previously alluded, our ancestors required noises for communication. Though instead of speaking, they played themselves like drums; this should make more sense once you actually greet us face to face.

Anyhow, as their mind-reading capabilities expanded, percussion went out of use except for playing music. But language remained, despite being regarded by some as a useless vestige.

However, a general consensus is emerging among many who study this matter, and I happen to agree with them. Where total mind-reading is concerned, language as a symbol system provides far more focus than no language. And that in turn prevents us from being overwhelmed by the vast mental landscape to which I also referred earlier.

Incidentally, we knew that were extraterrestrials to visit, our thought transmissions would translate automatically into their respective languages. We have determined that the translation happens in the receiver's mind. The thought transmitter might think he or she is sending the message in his or her language. In reality, however, only the message's pure essence is sent, stripped of any symbolic representation. Then the receiver's mind automatically encodes that essence with whichever language he or she feels most comfortable. This happens to that language's best ability, as the receptor has learned it, to accurately represent the message's content. If this were not the case, mental telepathy across the breadth of our planet would have been impossible, because hundreds of languages evolved on Oomb.

"Okay. Wow," Helena shook her head, stunned. "So, as for this 'Oof': How many holes? Those of us who play, they play eighteen in a round. Eighteen holes. That's what my- what Officer Olsen-Taylor plays."

Eighteen holes here as well. What is more, the rules for your golf and our oof would appear to be nearly identical. All differences are of the most minor nature.

"Captain Taylor, since you told them I play golf, doesn't it make sense for me to join the away team down to their planet's surface? Um, that is if you are sending down an away team." Chris couldn't keep a silly grin off his face, however successfully he fought away any giggles.

"Captain..." Deborah made this utterance into an exhalation of resignation. "...the safety-"

"Hold that thought, Officer Davis-Murphy," said Helena. "Chris, uh, Officer Olsen-Taylor, we didn't come out here to play golf, oof, whatever. Besides, the only clubs you've got on board are virtual. Remember? You left your real ones at home, on the reasonable supposition we weren't going to come across any golf courses. Guess I was wrong. But maybe you can bring them on our next mission. Sorry, but can't believe I'm even having this conversation," Captain Taylor shook her head. She had to wonder why those unsettling, odd headaches which afflicted her so many times at the mission's outset weren't afflicting her presently, especially with all the crazy going on. Was she acquiring her space legs, as opposed to sea legs?

"They probably have clubs I could borrow."

We have enough clubs and balls for everyone on board your vessel, Captain.

"Captain, I wouldn't mind, uh, I could tag along with Officer Olsen-Taylor to make sure he stays out of trouble," offered Kevin. He tried to sound less interested than he really was.

"Okay, here we go," said Yoon-hee, exchanging eye rolls with Helena.

"I've always had a curiosity about that sport myself, truly," said Ali. "Perhaps we could complete the foursome, Officer Leung?"

Helena warded off any response from Buddy Leung as she turned to Deborah and said, "Your thoughts, Officer Davis-Murphy? I trust you won't hold back. Oh, and Oodle-Noodle, I'd ask you to step outside while we reach a decision. But I understand that with your mind-reading ability, there really is no outside to where you can step. I suppose much of your planet is eavesdropping as well…"

This must be admitted, Captain.

"So I'll just ask you to please hold your thoughts until I formally welcome you back into our conversation. Sit back and enjoy the show."

Of course, Captain.

"Deb?"

"Captain, there is so much wrong with the notion of any visit to the surface of Oomb, I hardly know where to begin."

"What if the away team conscientiously keeps their envirosuits on?"

"The envirosuit will mess up my swing," Chris couldn't help complaining.

"Ah, yes, I almost forgot," Helena Taylor deadpanned. "If someone promised that feasting on a pile of maggot-ridden elephant dung would help your golf swing, you wouldn't think twice. You'd be sampling small portions drenched in ketchup and pickles, see whether the taste could be made tolerable."

Captain Taylor was surprised at Buddy Leung's silence, given his own golfing addiction. *To his credit, he must be too focused on the only other addiction that trumps his golfing addiction, namely his fascination with cheating the laws of physics!*

"With the suits, without the suits, Captain, I understand there's an even bigger problem!" Deborah erupted. "The shuttle pod has hardly enough anti-matter left for a direct, uncomplicated touchdown and liftoff from an Earth-type planet. The least detour wasting the least bit of fuel, the additional thrust required for departure from Oomb due to its slightly larger size…The away team's luck could finally run out this time.

"Even if that's not the case, you still can't be certain we're not being lured into a trap. I'm sorry, Oodle-Noodle, but you know it's true!"

Oodle-Noodle refrained from reacting since Dr. Deborah Davis-Murphy didn't specifically ask her to react.

"Maybe the Oombians have hypnotized us into seeing their planet how they've mind-read we'd like to see it," Deborah went on. "That's Hawai'i everywhere, with no climate extremes anywhere! With golf played exactly as we play it! Including the same number of holes! Far more likely, our away team will fly smack into the cosmic equivalent of a Venus flytrap! Incidentally, Venus flytraps also attract prey with the promise of something strongly desired!

"Wait, Captain, I'm not finished," Deborah continued without pause, not wanting to lose her opportunity to keep venting. "If you do send down an away team, at least order them to leave their envirosuits on. A messed-up golf swing isn't the end of the world."

"Oh, but it is," Chris couldn't help reacting.

"You're lucky!" Deborah snapped, not at all amused. "We're all lucky that at least up until now, direct exposure to Fafaman bio-systems has proven little more than a comically benign nuisance.

"And yes, Oombians might turn out to be as friendly and kind as Oodle-Noodle portrays them, nothing like a Venus flytrap. And their planet might really be paradise. At the very same time, though, exposure to one another's biochemistry could still prove fatal.

"Moreover, Captain, time might be of the essence for returning to Earth, whatever Oomb has in store for us. We don't know that a Tictoctic invasion force isn't headed for our solar system this very moment!

"Okay, that's it. Thank you for hearing me out."

"And thank you for not holding back, Officer Davis-Murphy. You wish to respond, Oodle-Noodle?"

Captain, Oodle-Noodle telepathed for everyone's consumption, *where that Venus flytrap possibility is concerned, proving a negative would be impossible until after it was too late. Must admit that's true from your limited perspective. With your poorly developed telepathic abilities, you cannot read our minds beyond faint, elusive glimmers of perception.*

As for biochemical compatibility, we have mined sufficient information from your cranial storehouses to confidently conclude our lives and yours are a good match. In fact, we are a better match than Fafaman life forms, meaning health-related difficulties should prove even more benign.

Deborah shook her head with eyes closed and lips drawn in, making them appear very thin. Chris sensed she was trying to contain herself, keep from blowing a fuse. "Even within the confines of our home planet," she said, "a person can experience serious health issues when exposed to viruses from a different country, let alone a different planet."

We doubt there's anything fatal in the offing for either you or us, Doctor, with all due sincere respect for your impressive knowledge and experience. We realize your imagination must stagger beyond belief that any amount of mind-read information could possibly substitute for laboratory testing. But such is the reality. Meta-analysis of your mental storehouses has allowed us to confidently ascertain the safety of exposing your bio-system to ours without the least protective measures.

"Anyone else wants to weigh in?" asked Captain Taylor. "Buddy, what do you think we should do?"

Yes, I've spoken my peace, Deborah thought to herself bitterly, and now it's back to that small inner-circle clique to decide.

"Captain," said Buddy, "our sensors have not detected even the most minor anomaly that would hint we are seeing some hypnotically altered version of Oomb. But I also share Dr. Davis-Murphy's concern over further unnecessary recklessness. We definitely should not expose ourselves to another new extraterrestrial environment before we can corroborate the Oombians' meta-analysis. Yet I would still argue we not leave here before first building more rapport with these creatures.

"So here is my proposal: Send your husband only down to Oomb in the shuttle pod operated by Officer Petrovsky. More than enough anti-matter left for a two-person payload, even allowing for that extra thrust required on their return. But let's say unforeseen circumstances do deplete said anti-matter, even before they land on Oomb. The pod still contains plenty enough compressed hydrogen fuel for a conventional round-circuit trip.

"Officer Olsen-Taylor, of course, would be wired for us to eavesdrop on his round of oof, should he elect to play. Whether to remove the envirosuit and make himself guinea pig a second time would be his choice. But if he did, Captain, I would strongly recommend enforcing Officer Davis-Murphy's safety protocol in its strictest sense. And do that from the moment he re-enters the shuttle pod."

"Hmm," hmmed Captain Taylor crossing her arms, her amazement undiminished at oof course after oof course sliding by on the panoramic view-screen. Long stretches of white sand beach and wide expanses of turquoise and emerald seas provided occasional variety. One small region featured volcanic, snow-capped peaks, smoke issuing lazily from one of the craters. "Oodle-Noodle," Taylor said at last, for the first time too weary for worry over whether she came off as amused over that name. "What do you suggest, and why?"

You should visit us to share our fruit and play our game, because you are not nearly as happy as we are, not any of you.

Captain Taylor waited for more; surely Oodle-Noodle knew she expected elaboration. But she soon realized that was all the creature of Oomb had to offer.

After another minute contemplating Oomb on the view-screen, Helena turned to Dr. Deborah Davis-Murphy with, "I'm sorry, Deb. Buddy's proposal makes the most sense to me. Gear up the full safety protocol assuming Officer Olsen-Taylor is going to expose himself down there, so to speak."

"I'm sorry too, Captain."

Helena thought better of reprimanding Deborah for her way-out-of-line remark, and went on, "Tanya, discuss landing coordinates with Oodle-Noodle. I'm assuming that will be little problem."

No problem, Captain.

"And Officer Olsen-Taylor?"

"Yes, Captain?"

"Try not to hit any balls into the water, at least!"

"Thank you, Captain."

Chapter 22

"Dr. Magabu, Officer Petrovsky, I'm so deeply grateful for your presence to gain your perspective. For everyone's presence, really," added Dr. Deborah Davis-Murphy, pivoting to Yoon-hee and Kevin seated together on a futon. Then she winked at her co-wife Geena.

Geena made herself just another of the attendees by keeping a discreet distance from Deborah. She'd left the edge of her and Deborah's bed for Magabu and Petrovsky, favoring a chair instead.

"Such formality, truly, after all we've been through together; well as you wish, Dr. Davis-Murphy," Ali observed with his gentlest grin.

"I appreciate your understanding, Doctor. Formality sets a tone where none of you should feel forced to choose between your professional duty, and your personal loyalties."

"No worries there, Dr. Davis-Murphy," Ali nodded soothingly.

Behind Deborah's teeth-displaying smile, she thought, *How condescending, humoring me like otherwise I might fly into some irrational rage. For certain he'll debrief Helena on everything said here; well so be it.*

Deborah had grown used to people not appreciating her efforts. Many did not know she grew up with an alcoholic father whose daily abuse near killed her mother. Her proudest achievements remained getting her father locked away by the authorities, and then nursing her mother back from the grave.

"Well!" said Deborah, nervously slapping her hands together to rub them back and forth. "If anyone on the navigation bridge took mind-reading lessons from Oomb, suppose I could find myself in big trouble."

Ali went, "Hmm," while others let out a clipped laugh.

"Report me to the captain after this, if you must. I am prepared to face the consequences. But I feel a certain moral obligation."

"I don't know why we would report you," Yoon-hee said after modestly concealing her small gasp. "You've made no secret of dissatisfaction with many of Captain Taylor's decisions. I'm sure she's well aware."

"There's more you need to consider, Officer Park-Smith, before we're back to Earth."

The Smoke and Mirrors had already reached the outer edge of the Callaway X Centra system, climbing above the orbital plane on its flight home.

*

The visit to Oomb ended as unexpectedly early as it had proven exponentially mind-boggling. Not early enough where Deborah was concerned, but at least her fear proved unwarranted, of their having been led into a trap.

Oodle-Noodle telepathically guided Tanya to landing on the coast of Oomb's largest land mass, about the size of Borneo.

Tanya and Chris didn't have to wait long for a clear sign they were in for an extraordinary experience, far surpassing anything they could have imagined. Leveled out at a thousand-foot altitude, the shuttle pod made final approach to what welled into Tanya's mind as being a hastily improvised landing strip. That's when Chris noticed one of the apparent trees in an apparent forest suddenly levitate and fly off as effortlessly as a butterfly leaving a flower. "Do you see that tree helicoptering away?!?!" he exclaimed, pointing.

Tanya might have questioned whether the captain's husband suffered from some "way freaky" optical illusion. But before she could open her mouth, a virtual forest suddenly lifted into the air directly ahead, recalling for her a flock of birds scattered by approaching humans.

"Help us out here, Oodle-Noodle," pleaded Captain Taylor, her and other crew sharing the view through Chris's camcorder.

You might be astounded by our flying capability. But believe me, Captain. We are no less amazed by the spectacle provided by two of your species occupying the same shell or exoskeleton for descent to our planet.

"Um, wow," Helena shook her head as she realized what the telepathic creature of Oomb was suggesting. "With all that you surmised from our history, guess I'm surprised by your present misapprehension, if I understood you correctly. The shuttle craft isn't a natural secretion like a crab shell. We had to consciously design and construct it."

Oh! We were wondering how your planet's prehistory would have favored evolution of such a protective covering that could safely leave and enter a planet's atmosphere! What you say actually makes more sense! With our mind-reading capacity, I'm rather surprised myself we didn't ascertain the reality before you specifically focused on it! Whoops!

Chris followed Tanya out of the shuttle pod onto the flat stretch of beach where they had a smooth landing. He also followed Tanya's lead wearing an envirosuit. "When I take this off for playing oof," he cautioned, though, "suppose we'll want to clarify I'm not like a snake shedding his skin."

"Think they'll get the idea if they haven't read our minds about it already," Kevin's voice crackled through Officer

Olsen-Taylor's earpiece. "Either that or they'll keep scratching their heads, or whatever they've got to scratch, about the envirosuit zippers. They'll wonder endlessly how those would have evolved naturally."

"Am not sure zippers are more improbable than many biological structures which supposedly did just evolve 'naturally.' If anything, by comparison with zippers..."

"Okay," Kevin sighed, "let's not rehash THAT argument!"

Chris and Tanya found themselves alone on the beach save for a few teensy seagull-type creatures...and a curious column of curious-looking trees.

While said seagull types continually ran back and forth with the gentle surf's ebb and flow, Chris marveled at said curious trees. At how they were lined up just where he would have expected a welcoming committee to line up. Their roots also proved notable, sprawled across the white coral sand. Did other roots grow anchoring-deep below surface? Or did strong winds blow these trees about like tumbleweeds? Always landing them back on their "feet"?

What most amazed Chris and Tanya was the tall plants' surrealistic mash-up of palm tree with deciduous tree elements. Three enormous palm fronds dominated each treetop. Yet the rest of the way down featured leafy-branched, bark-covered trunk of the wrinkly kind.

Chris wondered whether the palm fronds could spin like helicopter rotor blades, sending the trees flying like he and Tanya had seen during shuttle pod descent. For sure, those fronds radiated from a smooth, bamboo-like stalk poking out of the main trunk like a shaft out of an electric motor.

Fruits hung from the leafy branches like so many Christmas ornaments, Chris fancied. They assumed every possible likeness whether to apples, pears, oranges, strawberries, tomatoes, green peppers, or even cashew fruit, and hybrids thereof.

Once we come a few steps closer, wonder whether they're all going to take off like so many startled birds? Chris wondered just before…

Now that you've grown at least somewhat accustomed to our appearance, hopefully, we will open our eyes slowly.

The wrinkly bark wrinkled further in certain spots, revealing pairs of eyes even larger than the Fafamans' nocturnally adapted ones.

The tree person closest to Chris and Tanya shuffled forward, her shallow roots stirring up small clouds of sand and leaving striations on the beach in her wake. Then she extended a branch sporting five wooden fingers. *Welcome to Oomb. I am Oodle-Noodle* she telepathed while shaking the Earthlings' envirosuit-gloved hands.

"Thank you, Oodle-Noodle. This is extraordinary surprise," said Tanya.

This is an extraordinary surprise for us as well, even after reading your minds. These are some of my friends and colleagues. Oodle-Noodle gestured expansively towards several other tree persons, all rustling their branches to wave hello. No mouths apparent on any of them while Chris could have sworn their eyes were imbued with a gentle sheepishness.

I would tell you their names, Oodle-Noodle went on telepathically, *but we figure mine is enough for now. Doubtless you will find theirs equally ridiculous, and so similar as to confuse matters needlessly. But we would like to hear yours.*

"So you do hear, even though you do not speak," Tanya concluded in a tentatively faint voice.

Of course; how would our ancestors have communicated percussively otherwise? And how would we continue to enjoy music?

"Please pardon my, err, am very nervous. I'm Officer Tanya Petrovsky."

There is no need for nervousness.

"And I'm Officer Chris Olsen-Taylor. Listen, on a future visit we would love to learn more about your music, and share some of ours. But as am sure you also have already mind-read, we can't stay too long this time." Chris wondered whether the way some of the tree people subtly bent forward constituted nodding agreeably.

Yes, of course. Now one thing before we play oof. Whenever wherever we greet one another, we always do this. Oodle-Noodle turned this way and that, her branches and leaves spread apart to more fully reveal the various fruit hanging there.

Chris was reminded of an old video wherein some fashion model turned this way and that. She flipped a small curl here, a skirt edge there, calling attention to her outfit's special features.

Please pluck off a fruit of your choice. I know about your reluctance to actually take a bite until you've run tests back aboard your starship. That's okay. But please.

Chris went for one that looked like an orange. Then raising it close for better inspection he said, "So with no mouths, how do you eat these things? Or don't you?"

No mouths in your conventional sense. But our way that evolved to eat them does include taste buds. This is in addition to absorbing water and nutrients through our roots, yes. I will demonstrate the eating part. Oodle-Noodle plucked one of her own fruit, what looked like a green pepper. Then she pulled apart a slit in her bark, and stuffed it in there.

Tanya's skin crawled, watching Oodle-Noodle's stuffed leg go through contortions suggestive of chewing. Yet she still collected herself enough to reach forward and pluck off something that looked like a pear. "Umm, I sincerely hope our biochemistry is safely compatible for this," she said.

Oodle-Noodle and company bent subtly forward again, confirming for Chris that that was how they nodded approval.

Now we wish to take you to the nearest course for a round of oof. Will both of you be trying our game with your swing constrained by your envirosuits?

"Actually," Tanya nodded Chris's way, "Officer Olsen-Taylor will play while I watch and learn!"

"And here," started Chris, unhinging the airtight seal on his face mask. "I'm removing this envirosuit; otherwise my swing is going to suffer." He hoped his willingness to hazard direct exposure to the tree creatures' habitat would soften the edge of Tanya choosing not to play. Buddy had already established that Oomb's atmosphere bore a remarkable resemblance to Earth's, so with any luck...

We are honored you will try our game, Officer Olsen-Taylor, and honored you will watch, Officer Petrovsky, Oodle-Noodle telepathed, making a deferential bow. *But well aware you have so little time left to spare, we propose flying you to the nearest oof course rather than walking there.*

"By fly, you mean, um," Chris tentatively pointed towards the three palm fronds atop Oodle-Noodle that reminded him so much of helicopter rotor blades.

Yes, with you safely entangled by our branches, we can spin our tops fast enough to lift off for our destination, and arrive a brief while later. Untold generations of practice have made such travel nearly as safe as walking. Indeed, we've carried everything from our children to building supplies across vast stretches of sea, island to island. Calamitous incidents are so rare as to have become the stuff of tragic legend, none happening in my lifetime.

Flying in Oodle-Noodle's leafy embrace proved a far cry from the terror and motion sickness experienced in the Fafaman ahtpah-damaged glider. But Chris still struggled to keep panic at bay. And so, as mysterious extraterrestrial forests slipped past below his dangling feet, he pursued conversation with the Oombian tree creature more for distraction than anything else.

"I can understand how a bird starts flapping its wings!" Chris shouted to be heard above the whup-whup-whup of spinning palm fronds, temporarily forgetting Oodle-Noodle's mind-reading ability. "I can flap my arms, even though that doesn't help me fly! But how do you start something spinning that sprouts from your head?!?!? Doesn't that feel strange?!?!?"

Certainly you understand, Officer Olsen-Taylor, that when you grow up with something and it's all you know...

"Yes, you're right!"

Now there is a big anatomical difference involved, from how your arm fits into your shoulder, for example. We have no real connective tissue between our uppermost rotator trunk socket and our main trunk, only a cartilaginous substance. For flight, we flex our main trunk muscles in a rippling manner that interacts with the rippled surface round our trunk socket, sending that socket spinning. And that in turn sends its attached fronds spinning for easy lift-off.

Like teeth interacting for transferring movement from one gear to another, Chris imagined.

Yes, you understand. But as we age, the cartilaginous substance starts drying out and hardening so that spinning our top feels more painfully creaky. Fortunately, redistributing sap secretions from our lower trunk effectively re-greases the gears, as it were.

"So you do have to concentrate on flying or, um, if you lose your concentration…"

No more than you have to concentrate on walking, Officer Olsen-Taylor, while carrying something or talking to someone. We believe our flying ability evolved as a survival response when, in our planet's prehistory, certain islands became uninhabitable for one reason or another. Those ancestors who could quickly pick up and leave…

"Maybe that also has something to do with your ability to crawl across the ground as well as fly. That is, while plants on our planet usually stay anchored where they are. Or at best, they're blown or swept about by air and water."

Ah, we have several permanently anchored flora as well, including most of who you see below us. Many of them enjoy a rich mental state with which we regularly engage. Comparably, I have mind-read of your people's efforts to communicate more profoundly with dolphins, pigs, and other of your planet's creatures.

Tanya also used conversation to try keeping calm while soaring across an alien planet's sky in a flying tree's embrace. "Given your ornamentation by so many varieties of fruit," she said, "is there regular time of year when you and fellow Oombians flower?"

Our blooms are wondrously synchronized, planet-wide.

After touchdown beside an oof course clubhouse, both Earthlings found plenty more to marvel at.

Vines from what looked like a cross between a giant sunflower and a weeping willow suddenly seized a cat-sized rodent. They turned the frantically struggling creature over on its back while other vines tickled its tummy and neck, making it cackle, "Re-re-re-re-re-re-re-re-reeeee!"

Defecation of small, round, ebony-black pellets succeeded the creature's cackle while the sunflower seemed to watch.

Continuing to behave like octopus tentacles, Chris thought, the tickle vines promptly seized the pellets and smeared them against the soil. Then the sunflower face ejected seeds the shape of sunflower seeds, and the other vines let the rodent go.

Said rodent nibbled up some of the ejected seed, then went calmly sniffing about like nothing especially threatening or out-of-the-ordinary had happened.

Other Oombian nature tableaus might have caught the Earthlings' attention. However, they forthwith put on their blinders, focusing exclusively on the clubhouse.

"Umm…" Chris mumbled, wondering later why he worried over coming off impolite. After all, the Oombian tree creatures could read every last disgusting thought that entered his mind. "…where did you obtain wood for constructing such a building? And does it mean you don't always stand around outside come rain or shine, like our trees back home?"

We used to cut apart wood from trunks of permanently anchored trees. But as we grew more aware of their resultant pain, we wanted to show compassion. Those few people on your planet who still kill animals to use their hide for coats, belts, etc., we didn't want to act like them. And so we bred some of our permanently anchored trees to grow especially thick branches from the base of their trunks. Those trees have since assured us that harvesting such branches inflicts no more pain than when we saw off upper branches for carving oof clubs. The sensation they experience is probably comparable to what you experience clipping your toenails.

"Wow!"

As for where we "stand around," yes, that usually is outside. When we nap, we temporarily root ourselves into specially formulated patches of soil. But we still need buildings for sheltering our three-dimensional musical instruments, our instruments for conducting scientific research, our oof clubs, our oof balls, and numerous other precious artifacts. They simply last longer and better when provided such protection from the elements.

The clubhouse featured an actual door, a very tall and wide door the size of a castle drawbridge. Tanya and Chris marveled at Oodle-Noodle opening it, as they had never seen a tree open a door before, let alone such an immense one. Its archway proved plenty high enough for Oodle-Noodle to pass below without even having to duck down.

Allow me to introduce you to our special playing partner, Oinkle-Doinkle. He produced the oof balls we will be using.

"Oinkle-Doinkle?!" exclaimed Kevin into Chris and Tanya's earpieces, Oodle-Noodle having made his telepathing available to everyone back aboard the Smoke and Mirrors. "Let me know when you meet Tweedledum and Tweedledee!"

"He produced the oof balls we'll be using?" Chris repeated slowly, as he scanned the clubhouse interior for any comforting similarity to the content of golf clubhouses on Earth.

All illumination appeared the sole benefit of enormous skylights, no artificial lighting in evidence. And so with numerous tree people standing around, both Chris and Tanya felt like they might as well have been wandering through a dense forest.

An Oombian tree creature standing behind a counter, at least conceptually Chris could relate that to an Earth clubhouse. But no cash register was in evidence, ditto for any glass case displaying boxes of oof balls and the like.

Oof clubs did appear remarkably similar to golf clubs, including drivers, woods, irons, and putters. Yet aside from their black, rubbery grips, they consisted entirely of wood, including light-colored grain for shafts, and mahogany shades for club heads. And they were grouped in barrels similar to how Chris remembered different varieties of apples being displayed at a farm market.

Ah! Oinkle-Doinkle is entering. He must have just completed a ball-laying session.

Oinkle-Doinkle exuded a pleasant fragrance not unlike eucalyptus, Chris thought. And he cradled a straw nest brimming with pearly-white oof balls which he emptied into a barrel full of them. *These have finished curing,* he telepathed while the Earthlings further noted his bark's smoothness in stark contrast to the rough corrugations of his fellow tree people. *And I am happy to report my latest session having been most productive. The rest should harden before nightfall. So we can afford several others flying into hazards, much as we want to avoid that. In conclusion then, Earth guests, play relaxingly.*

"I appreciate that," said Chris, bowing slightly in the manner Oodle-Noodle had greeted him and Tanya.

"Excuse me, Oinkle-Doinkle..."

Oinkle-Doinkle is correct, Officer Petrovsky-Magabu, Oinkle-Doinkle hastened to confirm.

"Yes, thank you. I want to be clear. You excrete oof balls? Are they unfertilized eggs? Or, um..."

No, they are not eggs. But my colleagues have been rummaging through your memories for a meaningful comparison. So far, pearls produced by oysters come closest. Only, my body's secretions around an ingested irritant are infused with a rubbery, sap-like substance, not something that is stone hard.

The beauty of our naturally excreted balls is in their near-perfect sphericity, and how easily they decay back into the soil when lost in a hazard. To produce consistent quality, I eat special foods. There is some disagreement as to which diet produces the very best oof balls, for greatest carry, spin, and feel. So you will notice slight differences in appearance and performance dependent on who the ball-excreter was.

We know you don't have much time, Officer Olsen-Taylor, Oodle-Noodle acknowledged, taking over from Oinkle-Doinkle. Do you want to select a club from each barrel that feels like the appropriate length? And then select a bag from over there to carry them? Of course you will also want to secure tees and balls.

"Umm, do you use scorecards?"

We will provide you with paper and pencil. Yes, we do have paper and pencil, though usually for other situations. We are not in the habit of writing down our oof scores. Our perceptions allow us to reflect upon the flight paths of an entire round, even produce music with them, whenever we wish. Yes, playing oof serves a duel function. Beyond its sporting aspects, oof also sculpts four-dimensional strummables. Oh, my my my, that is not making much sense. "Strummable" isn't even a word for you, yet.

Tanya and Chris exchanged what-in-the-world-was-that-about looks while hearing Captain Taylor through their ear pieces say, "Believe me, that just riveted my attention, and I don't even care for golf. And you should see Buddy's rabbit ears popping up. But keep in mind the clock is running out. Need to leave 'strummables' for a future, hopefully less stressful occasion, if at all. Maybe we're better off not knowing."

Chris could think of something else maybe better off not knowing. Namely, how did Oinkle-Doinkle excrete all those oof balls? Out a butt that Chris formerly would have bet was not part of any tree's anatomy?

Helena's husband did have to concede, though, that careful examination did find the oof balls perfectly spherical.

The selected oof course started with a par five Chris estimated ran only about three-hundred-fifty yards. On Earth, par fives typically ran from four-hundred-fifty to six-hundred-fifty yards. But ah, yes, he remembered, Oomb's bit-larger size meant more gravitational pull and consequently shorter ball flight.

Chris's selected driver certainly felt heavier than what he was used to. Although he feared muscle mass deterioration from occasional weightlessness during the mission might also be involved. So as he took practice swings, he resolved anew to make more frequent, regular use of exercise equipment aboard the Smoke and Mirrors.

You will be teeing off with a driver instead of your ass? Oodle-Noodle telepathed.

"What?!" exclaimed Chris, wondering whether Oodle-Noodle was kidding.

A driver would be my preference as well, but watch Oinkle-Doinkle. He finds his rear end the club of choice, especially after sitting on an oof ball nest for any length of time.

Oinkle-Doinkle took a while working a tee into the ground so that his ball would stay balanced atop it, some three feet up.

Back in the clubhouse, Chris didn't even realize a barrel of four-foot-long tapered sticks were tees. He just assumed they were surplus club-head shafts.

Anyhow, ball-layer Oinkle-Doinkle got into position with his hands intertwined prayerfully together, inches below his eyes. Then he set himself in what Chris guessed was a proper enough posture for a golfing tree, albeit no club in wooden hand. His backswing appeared conventional, again given no club in hand. But at the point he should have stopped turning, where Chris was concerned, Oinkle-Doinkle kept going. He continuing rotating until his trunk coiled into a corkscrew.

Oinkle-Doinkle followed his slight pause with a rapidly accelerating uncoil that caused his rear to smack the oof ball with a loud Boink! The ball was sent flying out about a hundred yards where it sliced hard right, hopping into a stand of thick bushes.

Oh, no! Oinkle-Doinkle's leaves rustled in despair. *That was my typical evil off the first tee, what I do until I settle down!*

The tree person's characterization of his shot as evil jolted Tanya visibly.

"Wow!" said Chris, equally stunned. "Admittedly that was not, uh, the shot you wanted. You must have swung your, uh, you must have come across the ball from the outside in. But I wouldn't call that 'evil.' It looked more like, 'Whoops, made a mistake!' than 'Nya-ha-ha! My plan to have a terrible round is starting perfectly!'" Chris rubbed his hands together for that last utterance, like he was some cartoonish bad guy.

Ah, but here is what happened, Oinkle-Doinkle telepathed. *I noticed bushes on the right, just off the fairway. So I aimed way too far left and as a result, like you pointed out, I cut across the ball, doing exactly what I wanted to avoid. In short, my lack of faith I could hit the ball straight produced my slice. Such an error resulting from lack of faith we define as evil. We believe there is nothing worse...*

"Back home on Earth when I've seen a mishit like yours," said Chris, "sometimes the player reacts by throwing their club in anger. But guess you can't very well throw your, uh..."

I've seen non-butt-swinging partners toss their clubs in anger here on Oomb as well Oodle-Noodle nodded. They are cries for help when faith has been lost, even if that loss lasts only a moment.

"Tanya?! Chris?!" Captain Taylor's voice suddenly crackled with urgency in their ear pieces. "We have to cut this even shorter than planned. Tell Oodle-Noodle we need you both back to the shuttle pod immediately!"

Captain Taylor, we're taking the liberty of not waiting for your away team to inform us what you just told them. Oodle-Noodle had already dropped her bag of clubs and encircled Tanya with several branches.

"Thank you, Oodle-Noodle. Officer Leung has been tracking what we initially thought was an asteroid skirting the outer edge of your solar system. But it's suddenly made an impossible right-angle turn. Have you or your fellow Oombians, Oodle-Noodle, read any minds from there?"

None I know of, Captain, Oomb's chosen ambassador telepathed while she and Oinkle-Doinkle were flying Chris and Tanya back to the beach where they landed. *We were only able to home in on your presence once your starship had flown well inside our solar system.*

"Due to our worry over the possible threat from Tictoctic, we've had a firefly donut prowling the perimeter. Hopefully all we've picked up is a benign, unrelated extraterrestrial presence who could even help. That is, if it's not some weird, non-intelligent phenomenon presently beyond our understanding. But just in case it is the leading edge of an invasion force, hope you understand how defenseless we are. And that consequently you're better off with us not anywhere near here, perhaps attracting attention."

We understand you, Captain.

"In the worst case scenario, you might want to pretend you're trees only. That whatever civilization was on Oomb mysteriously abandoned all its buildings and golf, uh, oof courses."

Thank you for your concern, Captain. We wish you a safe journey back to Earth, no hooks or slices off your planned flight path.

The shuttle pod made a smooth departure from the surface of Oomb, marred only by having to rely totally on momentum for its final hundred miles back to the Smoke and Mirrors. Shortly after leaving Oomb's atmosphere, it lacked enough energy to even deploy solar panels or electrostatically constituted solar sails.

Yoon-hee charted the Smoke and Mirrors course out of the Callaway X Centra system far away as possible from where the UFO was detected.

Soon after leaving Oomb way behind, just one more star in the firmament, Captain Taylor gave everyone but Chris and Buddy a fourteen-hour rest break. And that's also when Deborah discreetly asked other crew to convene in her and Geena's quarters.

"Yes," chief medical officer Deborah Davis-Murphy went on while rear-mounted lasers kept the mirror array working light-speed wonders back out in deep space. "Captain Taylor has done and condoned actions I consider dangerously reckless, quite frankly.

"Yes, I wasn't on the Fafaman space station when she disrobed from her envirosuit to dance with the Fafamafalafama. I really don't know how it felt there.

However, I have trouble accepting she couldn't have controlled herself enough to desist from violating the safety protocol in such a major way.

"Of course there were other matters as well," Deborah added, deliberately vague. She didn't want to get into her disagreement with putting themselves at risk flying the Smoke and Mirrors like a huge paper airplane into the Fafaman atmosphere. While that had been the norm for those old rattletrap space shuttles, at least they were outfitted with wings like a paper airplane. They weren't in much danger of nose-diving like a cigar-shaped craft many times their size. "At the end of the day," Deborah finally continued, "I understand that people of good faith examining these matters won't necessarily agree with me. They'll take the captain's side. I understand. But shortly after we left Oomb orbit, any of you notice her wiping her brow then leaving her post?"

"She let us know she needed a break. A restroom stop I assumed, truly nothing suspicious," said Ali.

"Yes, I was there. I heard," Deborah snipped, regretting her testy tone soon as the words left her lips. "Shortly thereafter," she nevertheless plowed forward, "does anyone remember Buddy announcing he wanted to examine the spare firefly donut?"

"No offense, Doctor," said Kevin, "but I'm exhausted. Can you more quickly melt down this ice comet to what actual hard rock you've got?"

"You're right," conceded Deborah, hoping her trademark plastered smile masked her strain to remain pleasant. "I left the bridge myself, to see how Tanya and Chris were doing in quarantine. Well, I wasn't halfway down the hall when I heard the captain and Buddy speaking in hushed whispers round a corner. Buddy said he thought the captain's proposal would work, 'as amazing as it sounds.' Those were his exact words. But he wanted to make an additional test before final implementation, and wasn't optimistic Mission Control would approve. Then Captain Taylor said, 'I'm willing to plead the case directly to the president if I have to.' Again, those were the exact words. Kevin," Deborah said, gesturing for him to hold his fire. "The comet rock is this: Captain Taylor went on in an even softer whisper, in Buddy's ear for all I know, that this plan of hers came from a voice in her head. She didn't want anybody else to know because she wanted it judged on its own merits, not on its source."

"Maybe the voice was from somebody on Oomb, Dr. Davis-Murphy?"

Deborah nodded the reasonableness of Ali's question. "That's what Buddy asked Captain Taylor. But she purportedly heard it while we were high over the Oort Cloud that envelopes the Fafaman star system. And had been thinking about it ever since."

"Okay, two things, Doctor," said Kevin, holding up two fingers. "Thing one: What is this plan the voice told Captain Taylor to implement? Do we know that? And thing two: What exactly do you suggest we do? Fit her for a straitjacket before reaching Space Station 2?"

"Officer Smith-Park, I didn't hear the actual plan. But don't think that matters. After everything else we've gone through, what really concerns me is her following the lead of a mysterious voice in her head. Maybe we should have taken more seriously her offer at this mission's outset. Remember when she proposed being relieved from duty for having thought she saw ghosts on the Mars flyby?

"Once we're home, I suggest we ask for a private audience with Mission Control. We can explain the situation, and suggest keeping Officer Leung and Captain Taylor apart for any future missions. Officer Leung clearly doesn't have the gumption to see past their long history working together, to challenge her judgment."

"This is what I think, if I might," said Ali Magabu.

Deborah offered a tight, thin-lipped smile as she reluctantly nodded approval for Ali to continue.

"Regardless of its source, Captain Taylor's idea will truly get evaluated on its own merits by the powers that be. However, Dr. Davis-Murphy, you are perfectly entitled to seek this private audience of which you speak, to air your concerns. Accompanied by anyone else here who feels as you do, of course."

"Okay," said Deborah, slapping her hands together to keep calm and collected. About to ask who was with her for complaining about Captain Taylor, she wanted to seem just as likely about to ask who was with her for an ice cream cone.

That's far as Dr. Davis-Murphy got before a loudly beeping alarm accompanied Captain Helena Taylor shouting over the intercom, "Red alert! Red alert! All hands on bridge! We need to be strapped down before impact! Red alert! Red alert! All hands on bridge!"

Everyone was out the door, racing down the hall to the bridge, before Helena finished repeating her urgent command.

"What the hell's going on, Captain?!?" Kevin shouted over the alarm as he strapped himself in at a control panel.

Seeing the last person sprint onto the bridge, Helena shut off the alarm and said, "Check out the fore view, people."

The panoramic screen showed dust streaming rapidly into the photon exhaust shaft, as recorded by a firefly donut from out ahead of the Smoke and Mirrors.

Ali imagined an impossible lava flow of sparkling diamonds.

"What, is this the contrail from an asteroid that strayed way far off the Oort Cloud path? Whoa!" Kevin exclaimed, taken by surprise when a shuttle-pod-sized rock emerged from the darkness amidst the sparkly dust.

Said rock quickly vanished into the photon exhaust shaft, exiting the rear an instant later.

"Probably, Kevin," Captain Taylor answered. "Soon as our lead firefly donut noticed, we took evasive action. But we were too late for a phenomenon not previously anticipated. Somehow the photon exhaust shaft is vacuuming up the asteroid contrail. And we don't know how to stop that without damaging the mirror array."

"So somewhere out there ahead of us is Big Mother Asteroid shedding this stream of dust. Good God!" Kevin exclaimed again, slapping his forehead.

"Hopefully there are not too many more of them out there, Officer Smith. Anyway, we've retracted the mirror array as you can see, so at least we'll continue decelerating into our encounter with 'Big Mother.'"

"Can we deploy our soap-bubble shield to cushion the blow? And, uh, exactly what sized rock are we talking about?"

"Buddy?" said Helena, deferring to Buddy Leung.

"Waste to even try, Kevin. That steady dust stream with the occasional embedded larger rock won't let the bubble completely coalesce. And as for Big Mother's size, I've calculated approximately equal to the photon exhaust shaft diameter. Going to be close whether it can slip through. We also considered sealing the 'leaves' over the fore 'tulip' array. But at the speed we're still going, our impact with Big Mother Asteroid would smash everything to bits, us included."

"So all we can do is hope either that asteroid can just squeeze through the shaft, or not do too much damage as it gets stuck. Great," Kevin muttered, reaching out to Yoon-hee the same time she reached out to him.

"At least we've been able to fully retract the mirror array petals and their protective leaves. Hopefully that will keep them out of harm's way," said Buddy, trying to remain upbeat even though he feared there was a good chance they were doomed. "One benefit conferred by this unpredicted vacuum effect, at least, is that it's sucking in all micro-debris as well. The outer hull shouldn't be undergoing any function-compromising weathering."

"The asteroid should be appearing on the screen shortly," reported Helena. "It has been an honor to serve as your captain." She started to reach out, thought better of it, and then hugged herself instead.

Was she reaching out to me? Chris wondered in the final seconds before they would learn their fate. *Oh, no, there it is…*

The Earthlings could clearly discern the large asteroid tumbling end over end, once it was in range of the starship's searchlight. All along, this rock conglomerate had been heading the same direction as the Smoke and Mirrors. But the Smoke and Mirrors easily caught up to it, even though the Smoke and Mirrors continued decelerating well below light-speed. And as with the shuttle-pod-sized rock earlier, an illusion played out, of the asteroid approaching the starship rather than the other way around. Its disintegration tail appeared to have dragged it into the shaft, rather than trailing behind.

There was a moment after the asteroid vanished from view into the photon exhaust shaft, a peaceful moment. It lasted just long enough for Chris to hope that maybe the asteroid could pass through without damaging the starship.

All too soon, though, a tremendous jolt occurred simultaneous to a sickeningly shrill screech from metal-plastic alloy being scraped, bent and warped.

Shoulders ached and heads throbbed from bodies' momentum straining against various seat restraints.

A half-eaten bag of kelpydoodles suddenly floated free from Yoon-hee's station, its remaining contents gently spilling and spraying everywhere like in a slow motion video.

The Smoke and Mirrors had lost all gravity.

The still-operating searchlights picked up nothing, not one speck of dust, from ahead of the asteroid presumed wedged stuck inside the photon exhaust shaft. And the panoramic view-screen otherwise revealed nothing more than star clusters and distant galaxies.

"Is everyone okay?" asked Captain Taylor, finally breaking the eerie ambience of control panel whirs, clicks and beeps.

After an "okay" popped from everyone, Buddy said, "Captain, at least the sensors are indicating no damage to any of the tucked-away mirror array. Assuming we can dislodge the asteroid from the photon exhaust shaft, though, not sure what impact any denting of that shaft might have on acceleration performance."

"Would it make any sense, Buddy, to launch our remaining firefly with a distress message?" Helena grabbed floating-about kelpydoodles as she spoke, to zip into her blouse pocket for the time being. "We have a five-month food supply. So maybe Mission Control could go on a crash course to build a rescue vehicle, especially since they already have all the mirror array specs. That is, just in case we have any trouble getting out of this predicament on our own."

"Captain, that crash course will likely take them at least five months. Less than half the time needed to construct the Smoke and Mirrors, true. But then they will require two more months to get out here, seven months in all assuming everything goes smoothly. We can maybe stretch out our provisions to six lean months, including maximum possible greenhouse garden output. In other words, we won't last long enough." Buddy wished he could do a better job of keeping whiny despair out of his voice as he continued, "On a more positive note, let's say we are able to dislodge the asteroid to be up and running again, relatively soon. At least we still do have one last firefly donut for our advance guard the rest of the way home. If it hadn't given us advance warning, we wouldn't have had time to decelerate the Smoke and Mirrors enough to keep the asteroid from pulverizing us."

"Before we speculate any further, Captain," said Kevin, "shouldn't we check exactly what we've got with that rock stuck up our butt-hole?"

Under other circumstances Yoon-hee would have unstrapped herself to propel over beside Kevin in the newly weightless environment, and give him a painful ear twist for speaking so crudely. But under the circumstances, she could only smile appreciatively.

"Kevin's right, people," said Captain Helena Taylor. "We have to clear our heads, think lucid thoughts about the objective rather than give way to dark fears or panic."

Deborah Davis-Murphy shook her head slowly at Geena.

Chris couldn't tell if Deb was only reacting to the obvious peril of their situation, or also expressing no confidence in how Helena would handle matters. For his own part, he determined the best thing he could do was place a fresh batch of chocolate chip cookies in the oven. *Thank goodness I prepared extra batter before we reached Oomb! Rots of ruck doing that in these weightless conditions, especially adding flour!*

Chris hoped a thin layer of oil would keep batter stuck to the baking sheet by providing just enough adhesive capillary action while it cooked. Perhaps with parchment paper put overtop as well.

Tanya and Kevin reported to shuttle bay where they hoped, via spacewalk, to better understand the magnitude of what they faced.

Meantime, Yoon-hee deployed what they termed the soap bubble, to protect the Smoke and Mirrors from microdust degradation. They had done the same thing while parked in orbit around Fafama and Oomb.

Buddy begged off contributing to either endeavor by claiming important starship integrity parameters needed checking. He especially wanted to confirm no significant hull breach through the exhaust shaft. What he left out was discovery of a massive comet not too far away. It lurked closer to the orbital plane they steered clear of, the hell of a lot of good that had done.

With everyone else off the navigation bridge, Buddy recruited Yoon-hee to assist with data input and calculations.

It didn't take long for both to realize a deadly reality. Exchanging grimly silent looks, neither knew what to say. How were they going to keep panic and dark thoughts at bay, as the captain urged, when their spacecraft was slowly but inexorably coming under the gravitational influence of a moon-sized comet? How were they going to share that the Smoke and Mirrors was only thirty hours away from drifting crashing into it? And that far less time than that remained for the mirror array to work effectively? Not fatally compromised by said gravitational influence?

Chapter 23

"I want to understand something, Captain."

Chris wondered whether he was not the only one who found Dr. Deborah Davis-Murphy's utterance of the word, captain, laden with contempt. Soon as it left her lips, all eyes did turn her way on the navigation bridge.

"Had you forbidden the shuttle landing on Oomb," Deborah continued, "its anti-matter and hydrogen fuel reserves would not have been depleted, correct? Then at least it could have towed us away from the comet's gravitational influence."

Helena Taylor made a big inhale and exhale, trying to keep cool before she responded, "I made a big mistake authorizing that mission, Dr. Davis-Murphy. Really don't know what else to say."

"Captain, please allow me."

"Of course, Ali."

"Deborah, many of us, I for one, thought the captain's reasoning made perfect sense. The Oombian tree creatures seem exceedingly reluctant, if not completely opposed, regarding any military option for protecting them from an extraterrestrial invasion. The greater rapport we established via face-to-face contact might soften that attitude down the road. But even if you disagree, I truly, truly fail to see how this rehash brings us any closer to effectively dealing with our present dilemma."

"Thank you, Dr. Magabu. Let me just reiterate what I said after experiencing, uh, certain difficulties on the Mars flyby. Suppose a majority of you decide I'm incompetent, unfit to continue my command. That another of you is more psychologically fit. Maybe even you, Deborah," Helena added with no trace of bitterness or spite. "In such an eventuality, I will relinquish this dubious throne without the least resistance. And pledge to do my utmost carrying through on whatever orders thereafter. Once Kevin finally makes it back up here,-"

"Sorry, Captain!" Kevin burst onto the bridge as if on cue. "I hoped to have good news, but our monitors were accurate. Aside from our firefly donut's insufficiently weak micro-beams, all other lasers have been knocked out by the asteroid impact. And I doubt we'll finish getting even one of them back on line any earlier than three days from now. Way too late, given we only have twenty-eight, twenty-nine hours left before we crash into the comet.

"Chris," Kevin went on, abruptly swinging his weightless self around to face Helena's husband. "I understand the stress and fear getting to you but jeezy-peezy, how did you burn that new cookie batch so badly?"

"I didn't burn them, they came out perfect!"

"Perfect, huh? I have to admit, en route back to the bridge I stopped by the kitchen expecting a chocolate chip morale boost. Well imagine my surprise when I see these burnt cinders."

"They were not- Holymamoomoo!" exclaimed Chris, his eyes lighting up, grown nocturnal large like Fafaman eyes. "Did they look smaller than my usual cookies? Um..."

"Of course they looked smaller! The sublimation of that carbonized material in a weightless atmosphere..."

"I'll be back," said Chris, unstrapping to propel himself for the exit regardless of any protest.

"Don't burn them this time!" Kevin called after him. "Dying man's final wish!"

"We'll have no dying wishes," admonished Helena. "Yoon-hee," she went on, temporarily forgetting about her renewed offer to step down, "I understand that a single laser beam giving the mirror array a push should be all we need to dodge the comet, yes?"

"Correct, Captain."

"Well if enough of us pitched in, if there was something each of us could do to shorten the process, um…?"

"You know what they say about too many cooks, Captain," responded Yoon-hee. "No more than two of us, tops, should work on bringing the first laser back on-line."

"Captain," jumped in Buddy Leung. "Kevin and I could start the process, and hope that we or someone peering over our shoulders soon enough realizes there's a faster way, something we overlooked…" Buddy trailed off, unable to help a tear welling in the corner of his eye, stuck there with no gravity to pull it dripping down his cheek.

*

By the time Chris re-entered the ship's galley, the tray full of cookies left outside the oven to cool was empty save for a few black specks.

Those charred remains couldn't have sublimated that quickly! Chris swore to himself before reheating the oven and putting a lone scoop of greased cookie batter on the tray. Back to the bridge ten minutes later, he said breathlessly, "Helena, you've got to see this."

Helena looked up from where she joined Yoon-hee to study an operational manual. "Chris," she said, "if this is only about satisfying Kevin's dying wish,"

"It's about maybe not needing a dying wish!"

Helena and Yoon-hee might as well have been Oombians telepathing each other, *I hope he's not delirious*, before the captain said, "Tanya, you join me; Yoon-hee, please keep searching."

"Nay, Captain."

"Helena, Officer Petrovsky, just wait out here," Chris cautioned as he swung open the galley door and slipped inside. Then while the captain and Tanya gave one another puzzled, doubtful looks, he pulled out of the oven a second lone cookie he prepared. He set it on the counter for an unobstructed view through a window beside the galley entrance.

"Watch closely," Chris advised once he rejoined his wife and Tanya.

Just when Helena was going to insist that Chris explain why he was wasting her time, flames abruptly flared from the cookie. She and Yoon-hee alike did a double-take as the fire quickly died down to reveal a charred-black mound that shrank before their eyes.

"You know what caused that, Chris?" asked incredulous Tanya, unable to wait for the captain's reaction.

"Think so. I was going to postpone discussing any of this until the full debriefing back on Earth. But, um, the Fafamafa-whatever's wife took me on a guided tour to a large body of water named the Great Basin, where she told me about these, um, they're controversial because nobody's really sure what they are. But they're called ephemeral dragons, and starlight has to shine especially brightly to see them.

"Whatever they are, they left behind ripples as they rose from the sea. And they sparkled like maybe from bioluminescence that clings to them underwater. And, well, they did look like dragons, or our prehistoric flying reptiles. Anyway, I lost sight of them along the coast where there were these jagged, towering rock outcroppings. But then the tips of some of those outcroppings burst into flames like what you saw happen to the cookie.

"The Varalawa, um, the first wife explained that some of their scientists believe the ephemeral dragons evolved to survive harsh desert dryness, the sunset storm-line, and who knows what else. That they're a loose assembly of molecules or some parallel universe ether that has to burn regular matter for its food supply."

"So you believe one of these, uh..."

"Ephemeral dragons, Helena."

"You believe one of them has stolen aboard our ship, and is enjoying your chocolate chip cookies in its own special way?" asked Captain Taylor while telling herself: *Patience; you've experienced so many incredible things on Fafama and Oomb, not to mention that spooky stuff on the Mars flyby. Hear him out.*

"It makes sense," Chris insisted, struggling not to sound defensive. "When we were fleeing Fafama, remember how the jets pursuing us suddenly flamed out mysteriously? And then, when that ahtpah finally had us trapped inside the photon exhaust shaft?"

"Yes, I remember," answered Tanya, feeling hair standing on the back of her neck. "Its web-line unaccountably burned to cinders. We figured at the time there was odd friction phenomenon."

"But ever since leaving Fafama, every once in a while..."

"One of us has felt unexplained creepy something slide past," said Tanya, finishing Chris's sentence for him. Pursuant to which she and Helena exchanged looks that this time said, to his considerable relief, he really might be on to something.

"Okay, so presuming this ephemeral dragon, uh... If such a creature really has stolen on board, how does that help us avoid the comet?"

"If we could lure it into the photon exhaust shaft with a trail of cookie crumbs, then wedge cookies into place between the asteroid and the shaft wall...I mean there must be nooks and crannies."

"When the creature goes after your cookies," said Helena, "how is it going to manage an outer space environment? We can't very well fit it for an envirosuit. Or don't these things need air since they are, uh, ephemeral?" *I can't believe what I'm discussing seriously.*

Chris misread the look his wife Helena gave him, thinking it revealed she was humoring someone who'd lost his mind. So he couldn't help bristling, "Maybe you two need more proof I've not simply made up something to account for what happened to my cookies!"

"No; if I believed that, I wouldn't be wasting another split second here."

"Helena is speaking for me too," added Tanya. "Actually, I have idea-"

"Okay, but you both need to experience this in case there's the smallest doubt," Chris insisted, holding open the galley door for Captain Taylor and Officer Petrovsky to enter.

"Chris, is this really necessary?"

"It's really necessary. Not only to remove any lingering doubt, but also to show you why there's a chance our stowaway could unclog the asteroid from the exhaust chamber."

Chris no sooner finished speaking than Tanya let out a squeak. "Eek! This is first time I feel anomalous coolness sweep past me! That's the ephemeral dragon? Captain?"

"Yes, Tanya, I'm feeling it too," confirmed Helena sounding irritably weary, which she was.

"The way it rubs against me reminds me of that cat," observed Chris. "Remember, Helena? Kept coming over to our townhouse from next door? Begging for food by rubbing against our legs? Then we left it a pan of milk? In fact, can't swear Effy hasn't actually purred!"

"Effy? You've given it a pet name...Oh, for 'ephemeral,'" Helena nodded, trying to remain matter-of-fact even though wondering whether they'd all lost their cookies. "Okay, so Effy would toast cookies after you wedge them around the asteroid, maybe do a few marshmallows as well..."

"Look at this baking sheet," said Chris, holding it in Helena's face. "You see how the metal has been melted and warped? Especially if the asteroid is really a dirty comet...I overheard Buddy speculate that might account for it streaming such a long tail of dust and stone. A couple hot breaths from Effy could melt enough ice and deform enough of the rest-"

"To shake loose the asteroid from exhaust shaft!" Tanya completed Chris's sentence excitedly. "Captain, your question about how the ephemeral dragon can manage outer space environment, think I know! We can seal shut rear photon exhaust shaft with the aft mirror array's protective 'leaves.' Then we boost the protective soap bubble's tensile strength around entire starship. Then in between sealed-shut aft mirror array and the asteroid lodged stuck in front part, we fill exhaust shaft with heated oxygen. We must assume some air will leak, of course, because asteroid clog is not completely airtight. Eventually that leaking air will pop protective soap bubble. But if bubble lasts sufficient time, and I can boost oxygen level to twenty-three percent for greater combustion..."

"Buddy?!" Captain Taylor shouted at the intercom.

"Captain?"

"Did your spectroscopic analysis of the asteroid turn up much water?"

"Twelve percent, Captain, confirming it is a dirty comet through and through. Why? Wait, Kevin has something."

"Captain, for what it's worth, our diagnostic sensors didn't get things entirely correct," said Officer Kevin Smith-Park. "One laser, just one, did remain undamaged for the aft mirror array. It could limp us out of harm's way, were the asteroid not stuck up our ship's ass."

"Thank you, Officer Smith-Park. Get that laser ready to go."

"You have something, Captain?"

"We'll let you know.

"Chris, make a big batch of cookies."

"When they're done, I'll crumble up a few for distraction while I bag the rest."

"Tanya, let's work up some calculations on the highest air pressure the soap bubble can sustain before it pops, for the approximate time this stunt will require."

"Da, Captain."

Kevin suggested they seal off the photon exhaust shaft's front end as well via the "tulip bloom" mirror array's protective "leaves." This would guarantee no oxygen escaping out either end of the photon exhaust shaft while the ephemeral dragon was toasting the asteroid loose. But Tanya nixed this plan. Her calculations indicated the resultant air pressure rise inside a perfectly sealed photon exhaust shaft would easily shatter the front and rear mirror arrays as well as their protective "leaves." Such a tragic result could not be avoided, even were the mirror arrays retracted into concentric spaces around the exhaust shaft.

Moreover, Effy's dragon fire heat would only further accelerate an air pressure increase. At the same time that heat was burning loose the asteroid, it would also leave less time to accomplish such a wondrous feat.

And so, Helena ruled that only the aft bloom would be sealed shut. The fore bloom, at the front of the Smoke and Mirrors where the asteroid first entered, would remain open.

Unbeknownst to anyone else, Buddy also considered sending the remaining functional firefly donut back through time with a distress message. Hopefully that message would be received on Earth soon enough for Mission Control to launch the newly-constructed second starship on a rescue mission.

The more Buddy thought on that possibility, though, the more difficulties occurred to him. Sure, he'd successfully retrieved a firefly donut from the earlier, first-ever time travel experiment through a rift opened by the Mars disaster. However, he hadn't learned enough yet to target the destination time with satisfactory accuracy. The firefly donut could pop up decades earlier, where it would likely be treated as a controversial matter. Unsure whether it was a hoax or real, no one would be willing or able to commit sufficient resources to act. And that was assuming it even made it back to the Mars rift before a collision with other wandering flotsam and jetsam pulverized it.

Speaking of which, what if they DID pull the asteroid rabbit out of their photon-exhaust-shaft hat? That remaining functional firefly's surveillance system had degraded from overuse. And the other firefly donut required serious repair from one-too-many pony express runs across multiple solar systems. And so, the flight home would have to be made essentially blind, gambling THEY wouldn't be pulverized by wandering flotsam and jetsam.

Hmm, Officer Leung concluded grimly, *I suppose there is something else I could do if all else fails. It would have to be about two minutes out from impact, so the light propulsion isn't overwhelmed by the comet's gravitational pull. I could send off the firefly donut on a time-travel quest, and hope we can be resurrected after we've already been destroyed. Unless... now why didn't I or anyone else think of this earlier?*

*

Captain Taylor reassigned Officer Geena Murphy-Davis to assist her husband on his cookie-planting venture in the photon exhaust shaft. She would parcel out cookie pieces to keep the dragon busy, hopefully, while Chris wedged the remaining batch in between the asteroid and the exhaust shaft wall.

All this of course assumed Chris would succeed in luring the ethereal creature into the photon exhaust shaft with a cookie-crumb trail. Also assumed was that they weren't dealing with some equally bizarre, nonliving phenomenon, accidentally sucked into the Smoke and Mirrors from Fafama.

Whether the phenomenon in question was living or nonliving, Captain Taylor had to hope Chris's cookies would cause it to emit the hot flames necessary for dislodging the asteroid. And that this would happen before the soap bubble burst from air pressure.

On a practice run, the bubble burst before the photon exhaust shaft could reach even fifty percent of target pressure. So Tanya was pulled from helping Kevin with a salvageable laser, to assist Geena reformulate the bubble fluid for enhanced tensile strength.

Trial and error ate up several precious hours and lots of fluid. When the final bubble was blown around the ship, not enough fluid remained to blow any others. That was it.

Besides, there was little time left before the moon-sized comet would start pulling the Smoke and Mirrors into a final, fatal free-fall.

The Earthlings had to hope that the target air pressure would suffice for the ephemeral dragon. For sure, it was still going to be so thin, Chris and Geena would have to wear their envirosuits, regardless.

Standing outside the galley with a Santa Claus bag full of chocolate chip cookies, Chris said to Helena, "Well, wish me luck." He wished his wife would kiss his envirosuit helmet, at least, but all she did was nod and wave impatiently, "Yes, good luck. Now go. We don't have much time left."

The likely imminence of their death, if his plan didn't succeed, helped Chris to easily force down a dejected feeling, and remain focused. He broke off half a cookie from his bag and let it loose to float in midair. Then he and Geena clomped down the hall in their magnetized boots while Captain Taylor pulled open the galley door.

An anxious minute elapsed, waiting for Effy to incinerate the first bait.

If it's already had its fill of cookies, or for some other reason just doesn't want to leave the galley, this gambit is over before it even begins, Helena reflected ruefully. *Maybe we should try forcing it out by creating an airless vacuum in the galley.*

Just before Helena could make her forcing-out proposal, the floating cookie fragment burst into flames like a teensy fireworks display.

Then Chris let go another cookie fragment, further down the hall towards an airlock for the photon exhaust shaft. Fifteen minutes later he was floating inside that shaft, trying to latch hold of an outcropping from the asteroid without tearing his envirosuit.

Meanwhile Geena picked up from where Chris left off having successfully lured the ephemeral dragon into the photon exhaust shaft. She sprinkled a floating cookie-crumb trail towards the shaft's sealed-up rear. And happily, whatever-it-was kept incinerating that trail, crumb by crumb. Clearly the amount of oxygen satisfied the creature's requirements, if creature it was.

Planting chocolate chip cookies around the asteroid proved a tediously long and arduous task. But once completed, Chris easily shook remaining cookie crumbs out of his Santa's bag, leading where Geena had distracted Effy.

Moments later both humans were back to the exhaust shaft's maintenance entrance, keeping a watchful hopeful eye.

The cookie-crumb-trail incineration reminded Chris of fireflies making their way across a grassy field on a warm and muggy summer evening. The first ignition of a full-sized, comet-wedged cookie proved altogether different, though, sending a reverberating blast throughout the exhaust shaft. Fragmented rock sprayed from where Effy torched the dirty comet asteroid, reminding Chris of an old video played in slow motion, of a surface-mining dynamite blast.

"Captain, we need to retract the aft array before any of that debris can scratch or crack it!" Kevin's voice thundered in Chris's ear piece.

"NO!!" shouted Chris as he leapt back through the maintenance hatch into the exhaust shaft. "If you do that before Effy finishes, one of those stones is likely to burst the bubble and then there won't be enough air! Here! I'm catching them!!" Just as Chris said this, two more flaming blasts came one after the other, sending out more debris than he could possibly seize before they reached the closed-in mirror array.

"Look, Captain! It worked!" exclaimed Yoon-hee, applauding. "The asteroid is drifting towards the photon exhaust shaft's front exit!"

"I'm sorry, Chris, but we have to retract those aft mirrors now!"

To his horror, Chris could already see a starfish-shaped opening steadily growing in the exhaust shaft's rear.

Meanwhile, the ephemeral dragon's cookie incineration continued vaporizing ice that laced the asteroid. Resultant blasts propelled what still remained intact of that giant space rock towards exit, out the photon exhaust shaft's front entrance. It went tumbling and bumping against the exhaust shaft walls, shaking the Smoke and Mirrors as though caught in an earthquake.

Chris slapped desperately at larger asteroid bits to stop them hurtling towards where the mirror array was retracting. The whole time he shouted, "Please close the array!" But too late; one softball-sized rock had already gotten past him, exiting the exhaust shaft fast enough to easily pop the starship's protective "soap bubble."

Meantime, another especially big rock caught Chris by surprise. It tore across his left shoulder, ripping open his envirosuit. He quickly lost consciousness from oxygen depletion. Fortunately, Geena had followed him back out into the exhaust shaft. Pulling him to safety, she revived him inside the airlock.

By then, Captain Taylor was gasping, "God save us all." Via view-screen, she saw the exiting asteroid take an unfortunate last bounce off the photon exhaust shaft's cylindrical wall. Then she looked on horrified as that bounce sent it careening into one side of the fully bloomed-open mirror array of the Smoke and Mirrors.

A huge section of the array shattered apart, fragments sprayed everywhere like so much dust, dirt and sand sprayed by a strong wind. Yes, the mirror array petals and their protective leaves were retracted into the starship's hull to avoid damage when the asteroid was sucked into the starship's photon exhaust shaft. However, they were bloomed back out into the open before executing Chris's plan, on the certainty the ephemeral dragon's cookie-torching blasts would have vibrated them to pieces in their retracted state.

"Kevin, please," cried Helena, her tearful voice full of desperation, "any luck at all with-"

"No luck, Captain, but we're still working on it."

"Uh, if you want to- Tanya, if you both want to just drop it, and come here to be with Yoon-hee and Ali..." Helena trailed off in frightful awe of the comet presently taking up two-thirds of the view-screen.

"Dammit, Captain, send Ali and Yoon-hee down to us!" cried Kevin. "We're not giving up!"

The looming comet dwarfed the dislodged asteroid tumbling away from the Smoke and Mirrors.

In sick bay, Deborah ignored the distraught ravings of Chris revived. He was complaining tearfully about Effy being given up for dead. Deb ignored him to snuggle in Geena's comforting arms as they contemplated the comet steadily blocking out star-filled deep space on the sick bay view-screen.

Captain Taylor is getting us all killed with bad decisions to the very end, the chief medical officer concluded bitterly. *She could have imposed more order. She could have, she ought to have had all the physics-savvy crew work together on the single most practical plan. Instead, she let everyone go off and do their own thing. Now thanks to her lack of real leadership, we've lost the propulsion we'd need to not turn into a floating tomb out here, even had we dodged the comet.*

"Ali and Yoon-hee, stay put! Everyone else, to the bridge and strap yourselves down immediately! No time to explain, Captain!"

"Buddy!" Yoon-hee exclaimed hopefully as she tried unsuccessfully to wipe dry her eyes.

No sooner did the last person, Geena, finish buckling up than the Smoke and Mirrors lurched abruptly.

The comet started to recede, first slowly then at an accelerating pace. It shrank out of sight altogether in the lower right-hand corner of the view-screen from where it had loomed into view originally. Just a swirl of stars remained.

Everyone sat still, dumbfounded with astonishment until Buddy weightlessly propelled himself onto the bridge. That's when general applause broke out, albeit grudgingly from Deborah and Geena.

"Captain, the solution was almost too obvious," Buddy panted breathlessly. "And had it occurred to me even a minute later than it did, well that would have been too late. The comet's gravitational pull would have neutralized our electromagnetically enhanced light propulsion before I could act. As it turned out, though… We're piggybacking a ride on our firefly donut!" he busted out laughing, this time others joining in like he really did finally say something gut-busting comical.

"Of course," Helena gasped, awestruck by the simplicity of it. "The Smoke and Mirrors is virtually weightless in space. Wouldn't slow down the firefly donut any more than those mice we loaded inside it for a test flight!"

"There's more," added a beaming Officer Leung. "Emptying that nasty asteroid from the photon exhaust shaft also helped. And we're benefiting if only a wee bit from what's left undamaged of the mirror array. Yoon-hee, you should find the firefly donut operation linked to your control console."

"Here it is," Yoon-hee confirmed most cheerfully, her fingers hopping and skipping across her keypad.

"Captain, our lone remaining firefly donut is basically out of order. Would be useless sending it on ahead for detecting other asteroids and the like soon enough to give advance warning. So I would suggest Yoon-hee chart a course as far above the orbital plane as we dare go without running the risk of encountering dark matter. Once we reach our solar system, we can safely descend back on plane for the remaining leg. Most everything from Pluto on in has been charted.

"The only hitch: Hope everyone doesn't mind that clearly, we're going to be zero gravity until we're home. You'll all need lots more exercise."

Chris silently unbuckled, and made for the exit.

Ali and Helena exchanged understanding looks.

An hour later, Ali was gently pushing Helena to go find her husband, try to console him over the likely demise of Effy. But that's when Chris reappeared on the navigation bridge. Grinning from ear to ear, he held up a cookie incinerated down to pea size. "Guess who's safe?!?!" he asked.

"Great!" Kevin exclaimed, tossing his arms in mock exasperation. "That means fewer cookies for the rest of us!"

"Captain," said President Carey, "let me introduce you to Michael Spinner, the secretary of defense."

"I'm honored, Captain Taylor."

"A pleasure, Secretary Spinner," said Helena, feeling quite the phony as she shook Spinner's hand.

Since before Carey's election, Michael Spinner had played a big role in toughening up laws for anyone passing in and out of the quarantine zones. Captain Helena Taylor believed his influence festered from his combination of Santa Claus beard, charmingly jovial folksy character, and African American descent. He could implicitly argue, and be used to argue, that quarantine zones had nothing to do with segregation.

But two years after Carey welcomed him into his cabinet, Spinner had to fight off being removed. On a "hot" mike he was overheard saying, "Hey, you never know. Keep white trash cooped up with ghetto folk for long enough, and they might learn from one another." He "ate all kinds of humble pie for that," as he said most flippantly. Nevertheless, ever after Helena heard whispered: *There might be something to what he's saying, and he should know.*

People like Spinner, Helena often thought, offered yet another excuse for the well-off to ignore deteriorating conditions the wrong side of the quarantine walls. This despite sociologists warning those conditions could soon erupt to everyone's harm, both sides of the walls.

"I can tell just by looking at you... Mike's not on is it?" asked Secretary Spinner, shooting a mischievous glance right and left. "Ho! Ho! Ho! Despite all you've been through, Captain Taylor, it's obvious to me you've still held on to a lot of your youth and idealism! That's a good thing, as long as we temper it with a pinch of reality. There's almost no limit to what you can build in nice packing snow. But if you're not bundled up against the wintry cold, you're not going to last long enough outdoors to even finish making one snowball. Restrictive as a thick coat and good gloves might seem, you still need them. After your space walks, of course, you know better than me about restrictive clothing."

"Not sure about the youth part; think what we went through added considerably to my gray hairs," reacted Helena, wondering whether Spinner's "Ho! Ho! Ho!" and snowbound lesson were really part of who he was, came to him naturally. Or did he cynically craft them to play up his Santa Claus likeness?

Or more complexly, could they be trace relics left over from the guy's true self? Maybe his folksy stuff about dealing with the world as it is and not as we'd like it to be, maybe that hinted at the compromises he made? Maybe he'd traded in his metaphorical reindeer and sleigh for a suit and tie?

Anyhow, the situation being alone with these people in a White House conference room made Captain Taylor extremely nervous. To keep appearing poised and at ease, she reminded herself repeatedly that nobody there was directly threatening her life. This was a piece of cake, (Talk about being folksy!) compared to the predicaments she'd navigated on Fafama and in deep space. Yes, she would have loved calling in fellow crew for backup. But there was nothing President Carey and company could throw at her that even began to approach cushion-corroding ahtpah venom, for example.

"Captain, this is Dr. Louisa Entroper, a systems analyst for Space Station 2, and herself a former astronaut."

"Well if you think YOU'VE got an extra gray hair or two, let's see!" said Louisa seated across the oval conference table from Helena, too far away for a hand shake. Instead, she was patting her white mop-top.

"Dr. Entroper," nodded Helena, recognizing her name, "we haven't met before."

"Captain Taylor, I am in complete awe of what you and your crew have accomplished. Complete awe," affirmed Dr. Entroper, shaking her head from side to side. "I'm not sure I could have done it!"

"Thank you," said Captain Taylor. From the way Louisa looked around, however, she creepily sensed the woman expected someone to take exception and interject, *Nonsense, Dr. Entroper! From your amazing work on Space Station 2, it's clear you could have done all that and more!*

"Captain, of course you already know Dr. Spritzer and Dr. Aquinas."

"Yes," Helena nodded, and they nodded back. If she couldn't have any of her crew present, at least there were these gentle scientists she absolutely respected and adored. She doubted they'd offer her much support when this albeit not-life-threatening dialogue nevertheless inevitably turned squeamishly rough. Their extreme timidity would surely stifle them. Yet based on private conversations Buddy had enjoyed with Spritzer and Aquinas, she suspected they would exude most sympathetic vibes.

Of course, back when Dr. Spritzer was introducing the crew of the Smoke and Mirrors to the world, his timidity didn't seem to matter. He fearlessly faced down a host of reporters and flashing cameras.

"Finally, Captain, this is General Sandy Warlor, head of the Joint Chiefs of Staff."

"A real honor, General Warlor," Helena couldn't help enthusing as she heartily shook hands with the head of the Joint Chiefs. As much as Santa Spinner continued rationalizing a need for quarantine zones, Sandy Warlor had been sounding cautionary notes in recent months. Yes, she did go along with prevailing currents to ultimately reach the top military post. But clearly, the increased cordoning-off of people troubled her profoundly.

"This is a real honor for all of us," Louisa said.

Helena felt reprimanded by Louisa's correcting tone despite her accompanying warm smile and affirming nods. *Perhaps she's hurt over my not having offered her the same effusive greeting I gave Warlor.*

"Captain," said Warlor, sensing Helena's sincerity, "you're looking so fit and trim. Maybe it's time I skipped some briefings to go dance with the Fafamafalafama myself."

"Well one thing's for sure, Sandy. Every bit the same as Captain Taylor here, you make the briefings you do attend easier on the eye! Oops! Can I say that? Ho! Ho! Ho!" ho-ho-hoed Secretary Spinner, checking under the table for a hidden mike.

"So, Captain Taylor," said President Carey, his evident discomfort and awkwardness not helped by Spinner's remark, "your husband and rest of crew, you enjoyed the ticker tape parade?"

"Amazing to learn the Fafamafalafama became popular as a Halloween costume."

"The deluxe set came with a glow-in-the-dark cape and a sword-shaped spaceship," said Secretary Spinner. "My grandson went berserk, swinging that thing around and declaring in his deepest voice, 'I am the Fafamamapapa!' Never did get the name right," Spinner shook his head, this time his comments actually drawing genuine tension-relieving laughter.

"Guess imposing that blackout for the rest of our mission was a good thing. Else you would have had monster spiders and golf-club-wielding trees running through the streets for trick-or-treat."

President Carey took advantage of additional amusement over Helena's response to say, "Well, that might be the best segue I'm going to get into why we're gathered here. Captain, this is an opportunity to weigh proposals for the Smoke and Mirrors second mission before I make the final call. We'll start with Secretary Spinner. Mike?"

"Thank you, Mr. President. Captain Taylor, I read your full report from stem to stern. Have to agree with Louisa here about being in awe of you and your crew. Think it's fair to say we're all in awe."

Heads nodded emphatically.

"Some might wish to dispute a decision here, a decision there," Secretary Spinner went on. "You indicated there was dissension even within your own ranks. But that's how these things go, especially when we're taking a plunge so deep into the unknown. You might have made a mistake or two. Frankly, think I'd make a better dance partner than the Fafamafalafama! Ho! Ho! Ho!" said Spinner as an aside, as though Helena was the only other person in earshot. "But I wasn't there, so easy for me to judge.

"Now we're sitting in the comfort and security of the White House, however. Decisions to make, orders to give, aren't coming at you, Captain, like bullets from an attacker. There's calm to consider and reflect.

"So okay, here goes: I am puzzled, frankly, that in all your recommendations, you wrote not even one little weapons upgrade for Mission Two. Now I understand you've got these fun-loving tree people on Oomb. But there was all the bluffing you had to do on Fafama when you could have fired a real demonstration shot instead, not that nonsense with the firefly donut. And then of course we have the threat from Tictoctic making this conversation necessary in the first place. Are you seriously proposing we send a crew back out there again essentially defenseless?" Then back to his aside manner, just himself and Helena, he added, "Remember what I mentioned about needing that coat for playing in the snow?"

The way Spinner framed "we" sending "a crew" rattled Helena for its clear implication: The second-mission crew wouldn't necessarily consist of herself and company. She nevertheless expected Spinner's question, so took no time answering albeit shakily, "B-Buddy and I thought, um, I agreed with my colleague that any defense retrofit proposals should come from you. Then we can see what we're comfortable with."

"'What we're comfortable with,'" repeated Secretary Spinner, looking aside with bulging eyes. "In that case, guess it's a good thing I thought to bring along such proposals. Please, no reflection on you," Spinner cautioned with a raised hand as he opened the folder he'd set before himself. He didn't want to be accused of insulting the captain, especially after struggling so visibly with her "comfortable" remark. "Post-traumatic stress disorder from what you've gone through, I probably would have forgotten about, skipped this meeting altogether. Anyhow, here's a copy for everyone."

Once the papers were passed out, Spinner went on, "The proposal comes down to three top-priority items. First priority, deploy a laser mesh shield around Oomb and Fafama. They don't welcome our missile launchers and such on Oomb, fine for now. Any craft besides ours that intrudes on Oomb's orbital space won't possess the passcode wiring for running a current uninterrupted through its hull. So it's going to break off at least one mesh beam, and next thing you know nuked out of existence."

"That's assuming the spacecraft isn't impervious to nuclear missiles and their explosions. And that its crew doesn't detect the laser mesh before intrusion."

Spinner's grin reminded Helena of the Cheshire cat in *Alice In Wonderland* as he pushed back, saying, "Captain, based on Officer Leung's analysis of the wrecked rogue vehicle from Tictoctic, no need to worry about impervious spacecraft. And as for detecting the laser mesh: how? Those cloaking mirror arrays Officer Leung invented - you know, the same ones he accidentally discovered could produce light-speed propulsion - those cloaking arrays make the mesh and its associated weapons satellites invisible as well as undetectable by any known means."

"Except for the means we have developed, from learning how to deploy them. Any other civilization could do the same thing."

"Yes," Spinner nodded irritably, closing his eyes. Being forced to make such a concession by Captain Taylor did not sit well with him. "But," he jabbed defiantly with a forefinger, "even if they detect the mesh, without the passcode what are they going to do? If they try knocking out the system, that will be the same as a mesh breach, and send missiles flying their way. They'll have to leave the solar system to dodge them, and maybe not even then, if we can retrofit those firefly donut do-hickeys.

"But Captain, you raise an excellent point that brings us to the plan for Fafama, Priority Two if you will. What if, somehow, these deer but not dear creatures from Tictoctic, if you catch my drift, Ho! Ho! Ho! What if they successfully breach the mesh? From what you report, our tree friends on Oomb just want to arrange golf foursomes, and have the invaders pick their branches clean of fruit.

"Fafamans, on the other hand, sound more willing to set up a second line of defense. So we're proposing to provide them with a suite of ground-based, air-based, and sea-based launchers. Those launchers will be armed with enough nukes to scare off anything short of a thousand-saucer invasion.

"And of course we'll send along the technical personnel needed to help them use the equipment. They'll be armed with those wonderful translator dingies Officer Magabu jury-rigged.

"Captain Taylor, you agree with me don't you? That this interplanetary cattle-rustling operation most likely doesn't include more than a few hundred cowboys horseback-riding maybe a dozen starships?"

Helena nodded, "That's probably the case."

"You don't seem too comfortable, pardon my saying...um, well I'll just finish sharing our proposal, Captain. We've planned for Oomb and Fafama - and Earth too, I might add; President Carey has already given the go-ahead to launch a protective laser mesh shield around Earth. He's got agreement from all other major world leaders, including sworn secrecy to avoid needless panic. So that brings us to the Smoke and Mirrors. Ideally, especially with what you folks learned on the maiden voyage, well I'm sure you'd like to redesign it in certain respects."

"There are certain respects, definitely," Helena nodded with authentic enthusiasm. Although she imagined what she had in mind varied dramatically from what Secretary Spinner was thinking.

"Regrettably, we might not have time for more than a few retrofits," Secretary Spinner said shaking his head.

"And maybe not even that long. You return to Oomb and Fafama next week, and you might find them already turned into vast meat-packing slaughterhouses. Or maybe we will even be attacked ourselves just a few days from now. Though in that scenario, I suppose we could send you back in time. You seem anxious to make that sort of cosmic end-run in any event.

"What it comes down to, I wish kids could wait longer before they hit adolescence. However, the Mrs. tells me no amount of genetic remodeling is enough, once those hormones start to rush, Ho! Ho! Ho!

"So this is what I suggest, Captain, priority three. Of course you've got those add-ons Officer Leung wants to make, to protect the Smoke and Mirrors from random space debris. We especially want to assure it never chokes, ever again, on some big asteroid caught in its throat. But in addition to those things I'd wager you agree with, I propose arming the spacecraft with retractable nuclear cannons, four in all, plus two laser knives. Those nifty toys could come in most handy, when and if you ever required surgical strike capability.

"Again, Captain, I'm sincerely in awe of what you and your skeletal crew accomplished on the first mission, and also with what you got away with, to be quite frank about it. But you can't count on bluffs working every time. Sooner or later someone out there will need to see a little more than just a firefly donut buzzing their pyramid, if you know what I mean. And you can't keep tucking your tail between your legs and fleeing, every time you detect a UFO within a light-year of you. That's all I'm saying, Captain."

His fingers laced together, President Carey turned from Spinner to Taylor and said, "Well, Captain?"

"Do I have a choice?"

"You have input."

"I am not comfortable giving our most advanced weapons technology to the Fafamans," Helena stated plainly, fighting down her strong desire to ask, instead, whether President Carey saw her heading up the second mission. "As I noted in my report, there is a resistance movement to the Fafaman central government. We don't know enough about them yet to say for certain whose values are closer to ours: the Fafamafalafama's or theirs."

"Oh, from your report, Captain, I know plenty. I know all I need to know," growled Secretary Spinner. "That giant spider attack you documented, that's the work of terrorists."

"Terrorists, agreed, but they don't necessarily speak for the bulk of the resistance. Yes, of course what they did was absolutely horrific. But I would be concerned the Fafaman government might turn our weapons against the general populace, to consolidate their power. I would be especially concerned about that, should the extraterrestrial invasion not actually materialize.

"As for your other priorities, Mr. Secretary, I fear for their possible consequences. What you're advocating for is the militarization of outer space across two other solar systems in addition to our own, against a threat that still appears more hypothetical than real. I'm haunted by the words of our best sociologists. Chaudry Malek said civilizations that do not set aside warfare as a solution to political problems inevitably self-destruct before they can spread their failing program elsewhere."

"Well talk about hypothetical! Hmph!" Spinner snorted. "These 'ologists, these 'experts' come up with this garbage in their luxurious seaside hurricane-proofed floatable mansions while gazing out their wall-sized windows. Meanwhile, why do we make historic first contact with an extraterrestrial civilization? They cried out for help regarding the menace posed by another extraterrestrial civilization! That's why!"

"Yes. And a spacecraft presumably engineered by that other civilization couldn't avoid fatally crashing into Fafama."

"Well, Captain Taylor, you certainly didn't crash the Smoke and Mirrors into Fafama *or* Oomb. And yet we still aren't rid of war on our planet. In fact here we are, on the verge of projecting military might across our neck of the galaxy. What's stopping US, hmm?"

On concluding his question, Spinner's Cheshire cat grin gave Captain Taylor an awful chill similar to when she realized the baby ahtpah eggs were hatching.

"Captain Taylor, if I might add something," said Louisa Entroper, looking to the president for a nod to proceed. "About arming the Smoke and Mirrors: Remember, it's like your hands."

"My hands?"

"That's right. You could put them round a neck to strangle someone, your husband for instance."

"Don't tempt me."

"That's the whole point!" said Entroper, leaning forward over the oval table.

"That sometimes I want to strangle my husband?"

"No," spoke Entroper in a don't-you-get-it tone, shaking her head reprovingly. "The point is you can strangle someone, but no one is saying you have to or even ought to! It's the same with these weapons retrofits. Nobody will force you to use them. But they're a nice thing to have along, just in case."

So I AM going to be heading up the second mission? Helena wanted to ask while settling with, "I understand what you're saying."

"Captain," said President Carey, "about Secretary Spinner's proposals, uh, maybe I'm completely misreading you. But I do sense some discomfort…"

"I'm *not* comfortable with the proposals, believe have already indicated that," Helena nodded.

"Then let's look at one of *your* proposals, think you know which. Captain Taylor, if it wasn't for Officer Leung insisting he will not continue aboard the Smoke and Mirrors with anyone other than yourself at the helm… Well I was ready to yank you off the mission, regardless, once I read *this*," said Carey gesturing contemptuously towards Taylor's report.

Here we go. Just how much more pissed would they be if they knew the idea came from a voice in my head?

"Captain Taylor, I want to hear what you have in mind in your own words."

"Those are my own words, Dr. Entroper."

"Yes, I know that. But I still want to hear you say them aloud, make sure we fully understand."

Captain Helena Taylor gripped the conference table edge, might as well have been hanging on at the edge of a cliff. This was it. "On our mission," she began, "Officer Leung discovered how to safely send objects back and forth through time. He used rifts produced in the four-dimensional shapes of living objects. With our perception limited to three dimensions, we experience those rifts as untimely deaths. For rifts large enough to traverse, the four-dimensional shapes of multiple creatures have to have been affected. You need something big, such as the Mars disaster.

"This discovery got us thinking, um, what if we could go back just before the Martian hurricane? What if we could warn everyone out of there in time? Of course if we succeeded, the rift would seal up, possibly before we could return to the present. Not the worst thing in the world, though a little strange for us were we to interact with our past selves until, um…

"Well, had we averted the Mars disaster, would have been interesting to see how the conundrum resolved itself. In that scenario, a time-travel rescue mission wouldn't have been needed in the first place. Hope you followed that. Of course Officer Leung tells me we are always surrounded by a plethora of smaller rifts, tiny nicks and cuts in the space-time continuum…"

"I didn't follow any of that, Captain, but go on," groaned Louisa Entroper with forehead leaned into her stretched-apart thumb and forefinger for support.

Helena Taylor wondered whether Louisa might be suffering a migraine as she nevertheless continued, "Officer Leung has figured out how to leave an anchor that brings time-traveling matter back to when and where it left. But the problem is a three-year margin of time error and hundred-thousand-cubic-mile margin of space error. We could get ourselves caught in the disaster, according to our present understanding.

"So I asked Buddy, um, Officer Leung, what if we went much further back? Say, half a century? What if we homed in on the ancestors of impoverished families who agreed to become Martian colonists? Back before the quarantine zones were erected? Could we, um, ask them to join us? Could we take them to Oomb for a new life?

"Officer Leung thought that might work, and be far less, um, noticeable than if, in the more recent past, a group of Martian colonists suddenly vanished. Also could provide the creatures of Oomb a measure of our good intentions, make them more favorably disposed towards us. That is, if the Tictoctic menace turned out real, and we needed to rally their support against it.

"And something else occurred to us, concerning my husband's great uncle on his mother's side, Pedro Perez. Pedro and his grandson perished in the Mars disaster. You may remember he made the news for being the oldest colonist, how he'd always been fascinated by astronomy and wanted to go into space. He must have been in his eighties when that dream finally came true. We thought we could round up him and his entire immediate family, back when he was a lot younger, um..."

Drs. Aquinas and Spritzer hunched their shoulders and winced. Where Helena was concerned, they might as well have been watching the entire Mars disaster unfold again right before their eyes, powerless to stop it.

The others exchanged looks accompanied by pronounced exhalations.

"In other words, this would be your own little do-it-yourself rapture, like some evangelicals have spoken of?"

"You could put it that way, Secretary Spinner."

"But you realize, of course, the lives you saved doing that would consign other poor families from the quarantine zones to a nightmarish fate on Mars. You would send others to hell as you bring one group to heaven, net decrease in suffering exactly zero."

"Not exactly, Mr. Secretary. There would be the relatives and neighbors who accompany them, who were never a part of the colonization project. In Mr. Perez's family alone, we counted at least ten other people who would be receiving a fresh start in the new world. And we learned from archives that some of them met violent fates not too far along in this world. Our actions, yes, would result in six new people going to their deaths in the Mars disaster. They would take the place of Mr. Perez and five others whose grandparents we remove from north Philadelphia. But we would also lift one-hundred-seventy other people out of there. Again, we learned some of them met horrible fates in their own neighborhood. Um, you might call their being brought along collateral benefit instead of collateral damage. And, and hopefully, as we better understand time travel, the day does come when we can avert the Mars disaster altogether, um…we have to start somewhere…"

"So you're talking about close to two hundred people."

"As you know, Mr. Secretary, the Smoke and Mirrors can comfortably sustain five hundred people; plenty of space left over for a full crew contingent as well as the personnel we'd need to help our settlers adapt to Oomb."

President Carey shook his head multiple times. "I can't believe what you're suggesting. I did read it, but listening to you actually saying it out loud, I can't believe it."

"That's what I was telling myself, Mr. President, when knocking that asteroid loose from the photon exhaust shaft came down to preparing a batch of chocolate chip cookies."

"Ah, yes," Spinner nodded. "The ephemeral dragon, that's supposedly still loose aboard the Smoke and Mirrors."

"My husband is preparing plenty more cookies to confirm Effy- uh, to confirm it is staying put. We actually have hit upon a lighting condition that allows you to catch fleeting glimpses of the creature. Officer Leung says it's almost like seeing a constellation come to life with what it's supposed to represent. For example, there's Scorpio, uh, the scorpion."

"Captain," said Sandy Warlor making a stop-already gesture, "what bothers me about all of this, and I hate to say it as I'm a big fan of yours, believe me. But your attitude; whatever you're telling yourself, whatever your husband and other loyal crewmates are telling you, you are essentially holding the entire second mission hostage to totally off-the-chart demands. Far as I'm concerned, we cannot train your replacements fast enough, replacements for you and Officer Leung both, to preside over mission three."

In other words, Helena wanted to paraphrase, *you've overruled your conscience so often, you've gone along so much, you're ticked off at me for not validating your choices by selling my soul too. So even though you and I are on the same wavelength, you want to be rid of my presence fast as possible.*

"General Warlor, if I may…"

"Of course, Mr. President."

"Whatever we might think of Captain Taylor's plan, clearly she is convinced it's in everyone's best interest. She's even willing to put her career and prestige on the line for it. Am I correct, Captain?"

"Mr. President, at this point I wouldn't mind being relieved of duty immediately. And I can speak with Officer Leung, try convincing him to stay on. However, if I am still viewed as indispensable for mission two, if I do indeed hold veto power, here's my final offer: Despite my huge misgivings about any further militarization of space, I am willing to preside over the deployment of the laser meshes around Oomb and Fafama, as well as the weapons retrofit of the Smoke and Mirrors. That is, if we can conduct our 'own little do-it-yourself rapture' as Secretary Spinner put it. The only deal-breaker in Mr. Secretary's wish list is offering missile launch systems to the Fafamans. There." Helena spread out her hands on the oval conference table, palms up.

"Well Mr. President, on the plus side I hear some movement closer together," said Secretary Spinner, stealing a wink at Helena to her disbelief.

Does he seriously believe he can con me into even toying with the idea we enjoy any camaraderie? Captain Helena Taylor wondered incredulously. But she resisted a strong temptation to observe that practically all the "movement closer together" had come from her. Far as she could tell, Spinner's wink and a few complimentary opening remarks were all the concession she'd been offered.

"You know, Captain Taylor, crew members have initiated a formal complaint against you," said President Carey, pointing his thumb over his shoulder like those members might have been standing right behind him. "Is that news to you?"

"No it's not, Mr. President." The only news to Helena was how long it took for her to receive word of Deborah Davis-Murphy's effort. "In fact, I probably know who they are and specifically what they complained about. Please understand, though, they performed outstandingly, in my estimation. I wouldn't want to embark on another mission without them. As much as dissent sometimes makes me squirm, don't like surrounding myself with yes people. That's why I'm so happy to be here among all you today."

Tension-breaking laughter erupted, but before it could erupt very long, President Carey quickly grouched, "With all due respect, Captain, I'm not sure what difference those dissenting voices make. Your very closest counsel seems exclusively 'yes people,' as you put it. Um," Carey shook his head like he was clearing it, finally emerging from a fog, "General Warlor, based on your talks with SHQ, could a whole new crew be rush-readied for when we finish retrofitting the Smoke and Mirrors?"

"A full contingent of special support staff is in training for mission two either way, Mr. President. As for rushing replacement officers at the top, ideally they should mentor first with people who have already experienced travel through deep space to other inhabited planets. But we don't think the simulators are worthless, so yes, if push came to shove, we could go with a whole new crew."

As General Sandy Warlor spoke, Helena pointedly stared her down, to confirm she was avoiding eye contact.

"Captain Taylor," said Louisa Entroper, flashing a let-me-handle-this look President Carey's direction. "You're making this a very difficult situation."

"Excuse me Dr. Entroper," reacted Taylor, "I would say the situation is very difficult without assigning blame. My convictions are very strong, your convictions are very strong, and those convictions clash. That's the reality we face."

"But Captain, we all want the same things, am I right?" asked Louisa, nodding around to everyone. "I mean, who doesn't want to travel back in time and fix all the crap that happened there? I know I'd like to. But what I'm not getting is the urgency you place on doing that now, while it's still a very risky proposition. Why not later, after more time for careful, research-based planning? Captain, the past isn't going anywhere. It will still be there two, three years from now. Hopefully by then, we'll all be done with this scary Tictoctic business.

"Mr. President," Louisa went on, turning President Carey's way, "in exchange for Captain Taylor's full cooperation now, can't we assure her sufficient resources for this past-modification experiment down the line? Or am I being too presumptuous?"

"Not too presumptuous in the least, Louisa. I think the needed players would come to a quick consensus on that."

"You see, Captain?"

"Two points," said Helena Taylor no sooner than Louisa tossed her hands in the air and gave everyone else an I-give-up glance. "One," she went on nevertheless, "Officer Leung has already laid the research-based groundwork for safe time travel, assuming certain easily manageable precautions. Second, with that time travel we can not only start to rewrite the Martian tragedy. We can also give people an alternative on Oomb to their lives being beaten down and wrecked, as we know from their archived histories. I see this as an enormous opportunity to spread something elsewhere in the galaxy that's not just a projection of our military might. Even further, this is a chance to stop repeating past injustices. Our settlers on Oomb will be grateful emigrants respecting the natives, rather than colonists scheming to dominate them."

"In other words," said Secretary Spinner, "they'll be space pilgrims set up for slaughter by the Tictoctic deerskins. I don't see how that's any bit better than what some of our more naive ancestors did, when you get right down to it."

Arguing any further feeling futile, Helena held her tongue despite having a lot to respond.

"Dr. Spritzer, Dr. Aquinas, you've both kept notably quiet. What are your thoughts?"

"Well, Mr. President- Oh, were you-"

"After you, Dr. Spritzer," Dr. Aquinas gestured.

Helena mused to herself that Spritzer and Aquinas might as well have been navigating who would walk through a narrow doorway first.

"Dr. Aquinas, I must insist," said Spritzer in no uncertain terms that made clear there was to be no turndown of his own most elegantly gracious gesture.

"If you insist," Aquinas grumbled, irritated over his politeness not ultimately triumphing. "Mr. President, I see a quantum element in the dilemma set before you. The various choices you could make, for now they all exist as real possibilities. They constitute a virtual electron shell enveloping in a sphere the nucleus of the problem. But once measured, the electron must take leave from its shell of possibilities to exist at only one discreet location. And likewise, your decision must reduce the possible outcomes to one. This is how I see it."

"Uh-huh. That's fascinating," President Carey nodded.

Helena could tell Carey was nonplussed to the point of dazed.

"Dr. Spritzer, would you like to add anything?"

"Oh Mr. President, I couldn't have put it any better than my most esteemed colleague. I say, 'Bravo,'" said Dr. Spritzer, applauding Aquinas. He clapped his hands with his elbows tucked close together.

Spritzer reminded Helena of a performing seal slapping its flippers together as it barked.

"Uh-huh."

Chapter 25 - The 5ᵗʰ Session

"Aydiomio, no!" whined Placido. "Por favor, is a big game tonight, Phillies against the New York Mets! I have been waiting for this all week!"

"Is always a big game you have been waiting for all week, mi bruto!" Rotonda shouted from the kitchen while stirring tomato sauce into a pot of kidney beans. "When you are NOT waiting for a big game, THAT you can tell me like it is news!"

Corona Lite beer in hand, Pedro unbuttoned his jeans and unzipped them halfway. He'd already unbuckled his belt. "Look, Papi," he said, "I tell you, those Mets need to start swinging their bats now. Santiago pitches so fast, they have no prayer of even a foul tip if they wait until the ball actually leaves his hands! I would love to savor every minute of his shutout. Believe me, that is the truth. But we have not seen Doña Galleta in many months; I am curious why she told Mami is so urgent to visit us now. You heard Mami on the phone, yes? She asked why not tomorrow afternoon, but Doña Galleta said no. She has to come here today. Maybe she finally discovered the strange pendant's origin."

"But why can't she wait until tomorrow? Dios mio, hijo, will we have to sit through more of her crazy tales in English about flying to another planet sixty years from now?"

"Listen, Papi!" Rotonda called from the kitchen. "At least that is something different from you belching at the TV screen while I rush around cooking and cleaning!"

"You forget I work road crew construction all day!"

"So cooking and cleaning are NOT work?!"

"

"I never belch," Don Típico waved his hand as in not-for-me, seated on the sofa beside Doña Norma.

Ah, yes, Pedro thought to himself, yet another of your proud accomplishments.

"You should not belch, especially in public," counseled Norma, giving Típico a gently reproving pat on back of his hand.

"Ay, caramba!"

"Think about this, Papi," said Pedro, wanting to defuse the growing tension. "Maybe Doña Galleta is bringing us the number of cookies required to compensate for all those months she has brought us nothing!"

"Yes, that is what you need! More cookies! Come here, Alexita! Let Mami give you a diaper change!" Ludi opened her arms.

"No!" Alexita squealed as she staggered down the hall into the living room. She circumnavigated Placido and Pedro, and reached the small dining area en route to the kitchen. Her diaper sagged to her knees, saturated with pee and poop.

Just then the doorbell rang, and Ludi let in Pedro's sisters, forestalling pursuit of her daughter.

"Is that Gloria and Jerri?!?" Rotonda called from the kitchen. "Careful, Alexita! The stove is hot!"

"Bela!" Alexita squealed excitedly in her truncated version of the Spanish word for grandma, *abuela.*

"Wait for Mami to make you more comfortable with a fresh diaper!"

"No!"

"Your two sumo wrestlers are here!" Jerri announced.

Jerri and Gloria toasted one another with their sixty-four-ounce soft-drink cups, and playfully bumped together their pregnant bellies.

"Ay," moaned Jerri, the belly bump not gentle enough. "My barón is kicking too much!"

"Ay, mine too. Listen, Mami," said Gloria referring to her own mom Rotonda, not Alexita's mom Ludi. "We saw Doña Galleta coming this way with a big tray of cookies!"

"Sí, hija, and she said you should stay here for her visit! Jerri also!"

"Okay," Gloria shrugged her shoulders. "At least there will be cookies," she then said for the benefit of Jerri still favoring her ballooned-out belly.

"Hola, tía!" Alex giggled as she slapped Gloria's tummy.

"Ay, no, Alexita, you have to be careful because a new friend for you is in there!"

"Ah-ha! Now we change that dirty diaper!" said Ludi triumphantly, having snuck up behind Alexita and grabbed her.

"NO!!" the year-old daughter shrieked to ear-piercing extent, thereby overwhelming her mother enough to wriggle free and run off again.

"You could help instead of just sitting there," Ludi complained as she lurched past Pedro's armchair.

"Excuse me if my back still feels like hell, especially after standing behind a cash register all day!"

"My day was no picnic either! I had to deliver groceries in this heat for three dollars an hour!"

"You need the exercise!"

"Sí, and how many months pregnant are you? Looks like you're carrying twins!"

"Stop! Both of you!" cried Rotonda storming out of the kitchen with a sauce-dripping spoon.

Thunk!

"Maaaa-miiii!!" cried Alex, having tripped and fallen flat on the floor.

Knock! Knock! Knock!

"I'll get it," said Pedro, wincing with pain as a mix of anger, frustration, and guilt propelled him too quickly out of his armchair. He hobbled bent over to answer the door. "Doña Galleta!"

"I can carry the cookies over to the kitchen," Galleta shook her head "no" to Pedro's outstretched arms. "You worry about carrying yourself. Mm," she added after lifting her nose for a sniff. "The beans smell delicious!"

Gray hair in a bun, the diminutive Galleta seemed once again to cut a mouse-y presence, in Pedro's estimation.

"Ay, Doña Galleta! Welcome back finally!" said Rotonda, finished wiping her hands on her stain-speckled apron as she moved to meet Galleta halfway, take the cookies off her hands. "You want to have dinner with us first before that thing with the pendant? Maybe you stay for a while?"

"We will see who stays."

As if on cue, Pedro thought, a distinct rumble of thunder punctuated Galleta's mystifying remark.

Given the sweat-drenching humidity made hardly more bearable by window fans, Pedro could easily believe an electrical storm threatened.

"There is not much time left."

"She is correct about that," Placido nodded his unshaven triple chin into his chest. "They are about to sing the national anthem."

"Should we move aside the coffee table to make room for you on the floor?" asked Rotonda, swiping the remote from her husband's hands and clicking off the TV.

"Aydiomio!"

"I have already finished preparations," Galleta shook her head no, "including mixing myself in as an ingredient." Then she shuffled her slight frame over to the sofa and sat beside Norma. And after giving everyone a gently cherishing regard, she stared off into space, announcing, "They will arrive here soon."

"Who will arrive here soon, Doña Galleta?" asked Pedro, equal parts thrilled and haunted.

"The crew of the Smoke and Mirrors is coming to take you away on their spaceship."

"To discover the significance of the mysterious pendant?"

"The voyage will bring you closer to that, yes."

"And they are coming now? We need to pack for travel?" Pedro couldn't contain his desperate excitement.

"Pedro," said Ludi, wanting to admonish her husband for not reigning in his gullibility. For instead, encouraging what were clearly the mad ravings of someone who lost her mind.

"You might want to gather up photos of family and friends. Other than those, you will be provided with all you need, and more. "

"Pedro," groaned Ludi holding hand to forehead as she gestured for her husband to remain seated, not gather up photos presumably. Thinking she better humor the crazy lady, though, she smiled faintly and said, "There will be time for us to prepare after they arrive, sí?"

"I believe so," replied Galleta plainly, staring off into space.

Her diaper finally changed, Alexita kept busy gnawing on one of Galleta's cookies. But no one else knew quite what to do or say, save Pedro. He strained his ears to listen past abrupt wind gusts and rumbles of thunder loud enough for hearing above the window fans.

What will a spaceship from the future sound like? Pedro wondered. *Will its crew quietly materialize in our living room like people materialize on Star Trek?*

For all Pedro's intense effort, his reward was the noise made by Jerri's straw scraping the bottom of her Super Large Requenchinator from a local convenience store.

"We could start eating while we wait, okay?"

"Ay, sí, Doña Rotonda! Am feeling the jitters again," complained Ludi, untypical for her.

"Bendito, chica, I will serve you first," said Rotonda. "Have one of Galleta's cookies with lots of chocolate chips in it. But very soon, we have to check with a doctor about your trembles."

Bang! Bang!

Where she sat on the floor with her cookie, Alexita broke into a totally unbridled wail, mouth wide open.

Screeching tires prefaced the roaring zoom of a car driven away at breakneck speed.

"Alexita?! Are you okay?!" asked Rotonda, hurriedly scooping up her grand-daughter.

"Here's where the bullets entered the wall," Gloria pointed. "Ay, no one was hit, yes? Please God, no one was hit?"

BOOM! went thunder from the closest lightning yet, as though in response.

With one flicker all the lights went out, and the fans decelerated to a stop.

Pedro had had enough. In meager twilight leaking through drawn curtains and between window fan slats, he confronted Galleta still seated beside Norma. "There's no spaceship coming for us, sí? SÍ?!?!"

That last exclamation jolted Galleta into a look up at Pedro towering over her.

"Pedro, please. You're terrifying Alexita."

Heedless of his daughter's cries and Ludi's imploring, Pedro Perez went on, "What somebody said about the pendant was right! It was just some piece of junk jewelry from a gumball machine, dropped on the roof by teenagers! But you made up this absurd story about it! To take our minds off our shithole life! About your spirit listening in on events sixty years from now! You think you make us a favor by promising some kingdom beyond the skies that is not there! But you are like those whore evangelists! They promise pie in the sky for believers while taking their money to build million-dollar churches! The only thing difficult to understand is what you get out of this; you give everyone your cookies, and are not asking anything in return! Maybe you sincerely believe this fantasy bullshit is good for us!

"However, all you are accomplishing is more suffering, more disappointment! After your cheap magic trick with that little flash of blue smoke over your navel, and after all your other science fiction bullshit, we are still stuck in our asshole existence where everything, EVERYTHING continually gets worse!! Here..." Pedro hobbled over to Galleta's tray and grabbed handfuls of cookies, crumbling and patting them together like a snowball. Then he made for the front door, greeted by howling wind when he opened it. "Take your puta madre cookies, AND LEAVE US ALONE!! LEAVE US ALONE!!" he cried tearfully, hurling away his cookie asteroid with all his might.

Pedro remained standing at the open door sobbing, everyone else shocked frozen where they variously stood, crouched, or sat. That is, save for Alexita still wailing, and Galleta quietly, slowly rising from the sofa for the exit, her head bowed humbly forward.

Only when Galleta finished shuffling past Pedro, back outside exposed to the gathering thunderstorm, did she pause to turn around, look up, and search Pedro's bleary eyes to say, "This is not how it happens."

*

"Not too creepy, is it, Captain?" Officer Kevin Smith-Park asked regarding how the Smoke and Mirrors' progress back to Earth rippled space ahead of them.

On the navigation bridge panoramic view-screen, a familiar blue sphere grew steadily larger in the foreground, blocking out more and more of its star field backdrop. But Earth and backdrop both were strangely distorted. They might as well have been seen through a layer of perfectly clear water while plopped-in tiny pebbles agitated that water's surface.

In the wink of an eye, the Smoke and Mirrors had successfully traversed the huge space-time rift close to Mars for returning to the past.

"It's going to get a lot creepier on Earth," cautioned Buddy Leung. "Of course what's happening is this: We are intruding on the geometric moment of space-time to where we've gone back. So we're displacing even the emptiness here, similar to how a sailboat displaces the water where it's sitting.

"When we left 2062, our sudden absence did the opposite, leaving an absolute vacuum. Had that happened in the presence of atmosphere, a deafening bang would have resulted from the vacuum instantaneously filling back in. Not unlike the thunder produced by rapidly expanding air when lightning raises its temperature thousands of degrees Fahrenheit."

"I'm not sure I understand, Officer Leung," barked Dr. Louisa Entroper seated beside the captain in her official capacity as mission observer. "And goodness gracious, my my my, I hope you've got this all straight. Seeing the Earth and stars rippled like that is making me dizzy. Are you certain we're not going to get ourselves stuck in- What is this? Already completed space-time? You're certain we're not going to be entombed like some ships had happen ages ago? When they tried plowing through the North Sea in wintertime, then were trapped and crushed by the seasonal ice shield?"

"That's why we are relying on our aft lasers to supply all the light for our mirror array propulsion presently," explained Buddy. "Those lasers are our ice breakers, essentially. And I did anticipate the visual effects being a challenge for some of us, Dr. Entroper. You might want to limit how long you attend the view-screen. But again regarding that 'already completed space-time,' please rest assured we will not experience the scenario you've described. I say that with especially high confidence, based on my guinea-pig time-travel experiment in a modified shuttle."

"You see, Officer, a lot of what you're telling us now would have been helpful, at least for me… Maybe I'm the only one," conceded Louisa, patting herself on the chest. "If this had been an agenda item at the last crew leaders meeting, Captain, maybe more of us would have had a better idea what to expect. Looking outside could have been less disturbing. Of course an agenda, period, would have been appreciated."

"I had an agenda," snapped Captain Taylor, hoping she sounded more assertive than defensive.

"A written agenda?"

"I asked each crew leader to report on his or her team's work. That's the same for most meetings. Don't need a written agenda for that."

"So you have minutes?"

Helena tried to shrug as nonchalantly as possible, responding, "I took notes on whatever concerned me enough to require follow-up. Other officers did the same.

"Um, Buddy, how are we looking with the timeline?"

Dr. Entroper crooked a forefinger under her nose and shook her head. She was trying her best to display, for anyone who might glance her way, her profound concern over Captain Taylor's management style.

All the same, Buddy replied, "We're back a few years earlier than planned, Captain. But 2002 is good enough."

"Expected disembarkation time, Officer Park?"

"We should reach our target orbit in forty minutes, Captain. We've already shut down the on-board lasers for momentum to carry us the remaining distance. You're good to go after that."

"Dr. Entroper, care to join me with the away team?"

"I have too much to learn yet about what's going on aboard this spaceship, Captain, since you don't believe in agendas and minutes. I'm sorry, FORMAL, WRITTEN agendas and minutes."

Helena bit her lower lip to keep from asking, *Could you tell me just exactly what you were so in awe of?*

"Captain, you don't think we could leave her behind as part of our space-time ballast?" asked Kevin while pulling his envirosuit up over his legs inside the shuttle pod airlock chamber.

"Now, now, the woman's motives are noble. She's just trying to help," responded Helena despite appreciating Kevin's sentiment.

"Actually, I thought she made a good point," pushed back Chief Medical Officer Deborah Davis-Murphy. "Had that been on an agenda, what to expect once we crossed over to the past, crew leaders could have made certain everyone else was braced."

Captain Taylor knew Deborah would sing Louisa's praises, first chance she got. Taylor put her on the away team nevertheless, as her expertise might prove invaluable for transporting so many people in the unique state they were expected to be found.

"Dr. Davis-Murphy," Buddy Leung laughed nervously, "I honestly didn't realize during my guinea-pig flight, um…maybe I was too focused on basic safety. But the space-time displacement effects didn't seem so pronounced despite calculations indicating they would be. I concluded we best go with a generic heads-up that everyone should brace for possible sensory input distortions."

"I concurred with Officer Leung. And I personally assured his cautionary note went out to every crew leader with explicit dissemination instructions. Am trusting that personnel under your supervision were alerted down to the last person, Dr. Davis-Murphy," Captain Taylor concluded, unable to help an edge in her voice. She was beyond irritated with Deborah's pointedly wistful talk of "an" agenda, as though "the" agenda had never existed.

Anyhow, as Helena finished suiting up, she thought to herself it was just as well that Dr. Louisa Entroper declined to join the away team. She probably would have asked: Why an envirosuit on Earth? Especially after the Oombian atmosphere was deemed safe enough for Chris to directly inhale so his golf swing wouldn't be constricted?

Buddy would have explained his calculations strongly hinted at life-threatening danger from trying to inhale past-time air. With the quantum wave having long since passed, that could have been like trying to breathe taffy. Then Dr. Entroper probably would have blown another fuse about how something like that also ought to have gone in the agenda.

To be sure, Buddy's warning that things would get a lot creepier on Earth proved too circumspect, if anything. During shuttle descent, Helena and company spotted cloud-to-cloud forked lightning frozen still between the cirrus and cumulus cloud decks. Helena imagined wiring for an elaborate mobile display, aglow as though constructed of neon light tubing.

A Boeing 737 passenger jet sat amidst the lightning, like it could have been one of the mobiles hung there.

"Holy Crappazoly, I'm getting dizzy just looking at that thing," Kevin complained, though he couldn't take his eyes off the jet. "Hey, Bud, are ripples from our displacement of the space-time continuum rocking that 737 back and forth? Like the wake from a bigger boat upsetting a smaller boat? Is that why it's looking all blurry?"

"What you said might be contributing," Officer Leung responded noncommittally. "But I suspect a majorly part of that blurriness is akin to what you see when waving your hand fast before your eyes. We've returned to one infinitesimally small geometric point in the past. However, our three-dimensional vision is going through the evolutionary growing pangs, baby steps if you will, of fourth-dimensional acuity. We perceive objects across a split-second-tiny period of the past, present, and future. When we're riding the quantum wave in present time, you don't particularly notice. Stuck in the past at one particular moment, though, is another thing altogether. Because then those past and future instants kind-of stick out."

"So freakin' crappin' hell, I'm getting a little glimpse of the aircraft's flight as a four-dimensional object!"

"Well put, Officer Park-Smith! And all of you should be aware that's how some things might look when we're on the ground."

Starlings frozen in mid-flight had to be dodged on the shuttle pod's touchdown course to the middle of North Hancock Street.

On exiting the shuttle, Captain Helena Taylor felt strangely drawn towards a frozen blur of a woman bearing a tray full of cookies. That woman appeared en route to where Don Placido and Doña Rotonda lived. But Helena resisted giving her any closer inspection, in favor of climbing the Perez residence's front stoop instead.

On entering Placido and Rotonda's home, Helena and company found more blurred figures. Alexita was the blurriest, one leg suspended in midair on her run through the living room away from her mother. Placido cut the least-blurred figure, sunk motionless into his Easy Boy chair.

"Captain, should I start with that baby girl on the loose? Make sure we can even budge these things out of their already-set fourth-dimension shapes?"

"Think so, Kevin, but I defer to Buddy and Deborah."

"This is all new to me," demurred the chief medical officer. "Far as I'm concerned, Officer Leung needs to lead the way."

So much for her invaluable assistance, Helena couldn't help thinking.

"Was hoping we could start with a dog or cat," said Buddy. "But without one of them, a child probably is the best place to start. I suspect that at first, it's going to feel like you're trying to latch onto a cloud, Kevin. Just keep moving your hands through the blur..."

"Okay." Kevin had already gone for it. "There's something solid, but weird. None of the muscle is tensing up like you usually feel from grabbing someone. Yet it's not like lifting a sack of potatoes either."

Buddy wanted to ask how many opportunities Kevin had had to lift a sack of potatoes in his envirosuit. And what a sack of potatoes had ever been doing in his envirosuit to begin with. But he knew they couldn't spare time for such foolishness. That is, if they were to complete their so-called rapture before their firefly donut anchor back in 2062 gave out and left them stranded. So he simply said, "Okay, now slowly dislodge her from completed space-time. If I calculated correctly, shouldn't take much more effort than flicking a switch. Then her blur should come into sharp focus, and she should feel as light as though she were a cardboard likeness."

Picking up Alexita went exactly as Buddy predicted. Cradling her in one arm like a watermelon, Kevin said, "This is too bizarre, Buddy. I prefer how time travel worked in those old movies like *Back to the Future*."

"If only it were that simple, but we can go nostalgic later; we've got to hurry."

"Aye, Captain," Kevin saluted with his free hand.

Of all the strange things I've been through on the Smoke and Mirrors, this has got to be the very strangest, Deborah thought to herself while carrying three people to the shuttle. They were so light-weight, she could have carried four or five. Only she wouldn't have been able to see where she was going. *The way we're piling them in back of the shuttle pod, they might as well be department store manikins.*

With the last bunch taken aboard on the third shuttle trip, Kevin ran over to Doña Galleta and said, "Hey, Captain! These cookies she's bringing look pretty good! Why don't we bring her, and them, with us as well?"

Helena slapped Kevin's envirosuited hand reaching for one especially big chocolate chip cookie. "According to Buddy," she warned, "eating one of these would likely kill you. And as for the woman,-"

"Not to worry, Captain; wasn't going to take a bite out of her!"

"Ho ho ho! Anyway Kevin, I'm not sure why, but we just have to leave her there."

"Okay, Captain," Kevin nodded agreeably, refraining from any second guess. But he wouldn't be able to help wondering what that was about.

Before re-boarding the shuttle with a final pile of raptured individuals, Helena took one last look at Galleta...and would have sworn she winked. As if she required that final confirmation this was the woman whose voice in her head directed her there in the first place.

*

Captain's Log, Smoke and Mirrors Second Mission, September 1, 2062:

Not going well with the hundred-ninety-one people we "raptured" out of their north Philadelphia tenement block from 2002. None of them have shown any signs of life yet. I still decided to take them back to the present with us before our space-time "anchor" could fail.

But at least another one of Officer Leung's predictions bore out. The "ballast" from the present we left dumped in the past measured close to the collective volume of who we "raptured." And so the "raptured" bodies are not "crowding" our universe and causing ripples. Of course their clothes are ethereally flimsy, shaved immeasurably thin off their four-dimension space-time reality. In case they don't "flesh out" once the quantum wave catches up to the life forms they enrobe, we've added hospital gowns.

About that quantum wave, Officer Leung has been poring over his calculations repeatedly. He's worried, we're all worried. Maybe he's missed something, made some major error. And this led to the incorrect conclusion that our intervention would force the quantum wave to backtrack, reanimating the "raptured" bodies.

The comparison Buddy invoked was to a spider squatting in one part of its web. When it feels an insect caught in another part, it rushes over to investigate. Buddy compared that spider to the quantum wave. He said our disruption of the past, spiriting off those bodies, should send the quantum wave back to investigate. Then just like the spider spins new webbing to further entrap the caught insect, the quantum wave spins new space-time webs. The original space-time webs shrivel away, like a tributary dries up when the stream feeding into it is diverted. Lives take a new course while the previous course, their original history, rapidly fades from memory. The only glimmers left from the previous course are déjà vu experiences, and occasional haunting dreams forgotten soon after waking up.

What Buddy fears may be the actual result involves the quantum wave not returning to the past, either partially or wholly. That is, not until and unless it reaches the end of time, or the end of someone's life. Then like a whittler's knife reaching the end of a strip of wood, it returns to the other end to carve off additional slivers.

I return to Chris's side in the room of Ludi and Pedro Perez, plus daughter, to wait. But am not sure how much longer our new mission can be postponed.

And the longer we wait, the more opportunity for Dr. Entroper to convince the president, the head of the Joint Chiefs, and the defense secretary to relieve me of my command.

*

"Great Grandpa, I'm scared!"

"Bueno, why are you still standing over there? You are looking at me, not a monster in his lair. Come closer."

Daniel Perez obliged Pedro Perez's request, albeit stepping tentatively to enter his grandpa's bedroom. But a sudden crack of thunder seemed to the elder Perez to practically kick Daniel into a running hop onto his bed, into his welcoming arms.

This cannot be good, Pedro thought to himself as the power went dead. *Especially when the dome is sealed, the thunder always sounds much more muted than that. And we never lose electricity. The trick here is going to be keeping Danny calm, when I am feeling so jittery about this myself.*

Pedro was jolted out of his late afternoon lounge-around, while Danny was napping, by his TV suddenly winking out with a distinct boink! At first he thought the set malfunctioned, blown a circuit or something. But when he left his room to check his transponder left in the kitchen, he found it disabled, and the lights out. Through the living room bay window he saw darkness gather beyond the enormous dome, blacker than any previous dust storm or thunder bumper he'd ever seen on Mars. Coming from the east, it made nightfall appear already upon them.

The dome was customarily sealed up each afternoon. Thereby the colony vegetation replenished oxygen levels inside the dome following a daily contribution to the more general atmosphere. Plants outside the dome also fed Martian air, mostly ferns and other primitive forms bred to survive on far lower carbon dioxide levels than on Earth.

A new crack of thunder, even louder than the first, prompted Danny to cling ever more tightly to his great grandpa.

"Hey, what's this?" asked Pedro with a forced chuckle. "What kind of He-Man Master of the Universe are you being?" he added, referring to Danny's favorite cartoon action figure. "You're acting more like He-Chicken, master of the buk-buk-buk!"

Danny giggled.

"How about you go back to being He-Man? Let go of me so we can check out this storm from the bay window! Bet we will see some of the most spectacular lightning displays ever!"

Two generations of unwed parents started with Alexandra Perez, mother to Olivia Perez, who in turn gave birth to Danny. Raising Alex had given Pedro reason to live after a diabetic coma took Ludi from him while Alex was still a teenager. Pedro had hoped to launch his daughter on a good enough path for a Perez to finally escape tenement life for the suburbs, permanently. Practically overnight, though, it seemed Alex went from responsible and hardworking to promiscuous and drugged out. She was telling Pedro he knew nothing. That he and she were two very different people, so he needed to stop trying to live through her what he couldn't obtain for himself. Pedro heard of other kids able to handle losing a parent, but she was not to be one of them. Her mother's untimely death clearly devastated her as much as his back-breaking car accident devastated him.

For a while, there, Pedro wished death would take him, maybe to reunite with Ludi and his mom. His mom, Doña Rotonda, didn't last much longer after Placido beat her up in a drunken rage, and then fled to Puerto Rico where he disappeared. So Alexita's father started gorging himself like there was no tomorrow, like he hoped there would be no tomorrow. But even the three-hundred-pound mark didn't budge Pedro's low blood pressure. He mused bitterly that were he a chain smoker, he would have been one of those rare nicotine addicts who outlived a century. Nevertheless, he kept trying to eat himself into an early grave, at least until Alexita brought over his grand-daughter, Olivia. Olivia's big eyes sparkled with all the hope and promise of future happiness. Her father who split before she was born, Pedro couldn't help thinking of him as the thief in a poem he'd read. The thief missed the real treasure: the moon in the window.

Over ensuing years, Alex's visits for Pedro to see his grand-daughter evolved into Alex dumping Olivia on him so she could do some death-wish fattening-up of her own. She would sink into a stupor of soap opera novelas and Krispy Kreme donut binges.

Pedro wondered at how this self-destruction thing seemed to have passed on from possessing him to possessing his daughter, like some migratory evil spirit. Helping raise a girl who so reminded him of Ludi, and suggested what Ludi would have been in her youth, had renewed his sense of purpose. And that in turn had helped him finally fend off his own suicidal urge.

Unfortunately, Alexandra's constitution proved not nearly as resistant to the ravages of a bad diet as her father's. She was found curled up in a fetal position on her couch, gone from a massive coronary before she even reached forty.

The same as for parents everywhere, Pedro outliving his daughter felt like hell. But the responsibility for Olivia's care was left squarely on his shoulders, no room for grief and self-pity to incapacitate him. A renewed death wish was definitely out. And Olivia made such determinations especially easy because, unlike her mother, she faced the loss of her mother with amazing resilience.

There was still an accidental pregnancy by Olivia's second year in community college, but Ricardo was a good boy. They loved each other, and wanted to have the baby. In fact Olivia and Ricardo planned to marry once they could move out of Pedro's two-bedroom tenement, and afford their own home.

However, returning from a church dance while Pedro was babysitting their three-month-old son Danny, both got gunned down. And they weren't even the drive-by shooter's intended targets. Rather, just another tragic mistake on the cusp of waves of gang violence in several major cities...waves of violence which finally gave mainstream political traction to a fringe movement intent on big walls and fences around poor urban areas. Only lacking was the final impetus of a disease pandemic.

Anyhow, his grand-daughter's horrific death finally brought Pedro Perez to a sort of peace. The bitter part regarded the huge hopes with which new life seemed always invested. Pedro was finally, absolutely if reluctantly persuaded that each birth constituted a dream-missile launch doomed to malfunction. Or it was doomed to be shot down before malfunction, in which case people could always delude themselves with thoughts of what might have been. How would Olivia and Ricardo's marriage have turned out, for example, had they lived long enough?

The sort of peace that went along with the bitter part, though, was a defiant conviction, really. Okay, existence might ultimately prove a total farce. But so long as Pedro's continued, he would smite the senselessness with love and compassion for whoever fell his way, that person presently being his great grandson Danny.

Not long after Pedro adopted Danny, a Sunday newspaper magazine article featured this eighty-plus-year-old man raising his three-year-old great grandson. Far from flattered, though, Pedro saw such attention as part of a guilt-salving bid by people on the quarantine walls' lucky side.

And there was plenty of guilt to be salved, Pedro believed, over trying to shut out the wretched of the Earth on such a grand scale. Where he was concerned, half the planet had been turned into a gargantuan-sized version of those gated communities he detested so much on his last trip down to Puerto Rico back in 2006.

The bigger part of that guilt-salving bid revolved around terraforming Mars. After humanity's first landing there in 2024, the red planet's transformation into a habitable world went faster than anyone predicted. So the question became: Why not train trustworthy persons from a quarantined area to join Martian colonization? Why not this as a dramatic first effort to break the poverty cycle? And why not select Pedro and his great grandson as that mission's mascot family? Especially considering Mr. Perez's long-abiding interest in astronomy and space flight?

So there they were after astronaut training, a months-long flight, and settling in on the slowly but steadily greening red planet. If only Pedro's excitement over this dream of a lifetime were not tempered practically to indifference by not being able to share it with Ludi. He still couldn't stop missing her.

"Why is it super dark over there, great grandpa?"

"Bendito, Danny, is sunset on the way! When you combine that with a strong thunderstorm, super dark is the result!" But in reality, too much time remained before nightfall for the approaching storm to have turned the eastern sky pitch black.

"What is that noise, great grandpa? Sounds more like a train coming than a thunderstorm!" shouted Danny standing on the sofa. He leaned forward with enthusiastic curiosity, nose smudging the window, because he so trustingly bought into Pedro's assurances.

Señor Perez resisted an impulse to become He-Chicken, protectively gathering his great grandchild back into his arms. Better that Danny not panic, not become terrified for as long as possible. Whatever would happen was going to happen anyway; they both might as well have been napping. So rather than do anything physical, Pedro Perez merely answered, "That must be a super strong wind coming. Thank goodness the dome will keep stuff from flying around and making a big mess."

No sooner did Pedro finish speaking, though, than two boulder-sized rocks and a truck-sized Mars all-terrain rover were hurled against the east-facing side of the dome. Big booms from their impact echoed across the land one right after the other. Then a flash of lightning was succeeded a split-second later by rolling thunder that shook the Perez cottage earthquake style.

Pedro braced for the worst because the lightning highlighted cracks in the dome where the big objects hit. He imagined those cracks being jagged, black lightning bolts.

"Danny, I think we need to go down to the basement, purely as a precaution."

"Why, great grandpa?!" Danny cried with sudden fear, from at last sensing the dread his grandpa tried so hard to conceal. "The dome isn't going to break, is it?"

"It should not break." Pedro was already picking up Danny in his arms. "But if it does, the basement has been built to protect us."

"But if the dome breaks, we won't be able to breathe!!"

"Aye, there goes He-Chicken, master of the buk-buk-buk, again! You know how they open the dome every day to spread the air? They couldn't do that if we would not be able to breathe! Besides, there are oxygen containers in the basement, in case we need them."

Pedro left out what could happen if a large-enough chunk of dome fell on their cottage. He did still hope the geodesic girder framework would prevent such an event. But if the chunk fell regardless, most likely it would crush the underground shelter and everything, everyone in there as well.

Once Pedro turned on the underground lights, run on a separate storage generator, he pulled shut the trap door. He hoped acoustic-dampening insulation would mute the storm's fury enough to ease his great grandson's fear.

But would Pedro and Danny survive the most extreme Martian weather phenomenon seen since they arrived?

For three minutes, shelter insulation did dull harsh noises from the storm's fury. However, Pedro ended up cursing to himself over the cruel false hope those three minutes provided. Better not to have enjoyed even one of them, he believed, since they suddenly gave way to the most awful cracking, splitting sound he'd ever heard.

Next thing Pedro knew, the storm went from something heard over a poor phone connection to something deafening loud, despite his location inside a sealed-off basement shelter. However, there was too much metallic quality to the cracking and splitting for thunder.

At least there were no thumps, what Pedro would have expected from steel girders falling on vegetation-covered Martian soil. He wanted to believe the wrenched-apart geodesic trestle work and transparent aluminum alloy got twisted together...too twisted together for anything to make deadly descent. He well knew, though, the far greater likelihood was that the winds blew so ferociously strong, they'd made that stuff airborne.

As Danny wrapped his arms around Pedro's neck and buried his sobbing head in his chest, the storm intensified, seeming closer and closer until a concussive noise like dynamite exploding.

Pedro could hear the cottage tearing apart, as well as human cries and shrieks. He wanted desperately to believe it was all just howling winds.

The metal alloy basement walls started buckling. "Ay, Dios!" cried Pedro as he realized the storm must have eroded dangerously much of the red Martian soil in which the shelter was embedded. Then there was the awful feeling of being lifted skyward.

Next thing Pedro knew, the floor was gone, and over Danny's shoulder he was looking down at rapidly receding ground. After he fell through the flying basement's empty bottom, persistent hurricane-force winds lifted him up past it into the general maelstrom. A piece of trestle smashing his skull caused him to at last let go of Danny. Before that he realized *God of love, this storm must be sucking the atmosphere off Mars!!*

*

Helena Taylor turned away, fighting an urge to double over from a stress-induced stomach cramp. What were they going to do with all those feather-weight - They weren't even bodies. They were more like rumors of bodies, making not the least impression on the mattresses where they lay. What if-

"Captain," said Deborah as sudden monitor beeps sent her into a swirl of motion. "His weight has abruptly gone from half an ounce to twenty-seven pounds!"

"Helena!" Chris couldn't help exclaiming. "His eyes are opening!" Chris was also struck by how Pedro Perez sank into the mattress, albeit not to the extent he would have were they at full rather than one-quarter gravity.

"Captain, I'm receiving word of comparable activity from several other cabins," Buddy weighed in with hand cupped over his earpiece, just in case Chris let loose with another exclamation. "Well, we won't have to wait for the re-creation of the universe for the quantum wave to pass through again, after all! It DID backtrack!" Officer Leung laughed like he'd told the funniest joke, from relief instead of nerves.

Helena laughed along as she rushed over beside Chris.

Pedro Perez slapped his arms around himself, trying to grab hold of, not let go of- Who? He couldn't remember. That was when he realized a man and a woman in sky-blue uniforms were smiling down on him with cherishing regard.

"You are," Pedro pointed up at Chris, thinking he recognized him. But he stalled out, losing his thread of memory again.

"I am Christopher Olsen-Taylor. My mother, Samantha, is your uncle's daughter, and one of your cousins. Mr. Perez, maybe you thought you recognized me because my grandpapa was that uncle. He used to drive us up from Maryland to visit you in Philly."

"Oh, I understand," Pedro nodded.

Chris knew as an intellectual abstraction that Pedro must have recognized him from their meeting on Mars with…Who? He couldn't remember. What had been the reality was already fading fast from memory, shriveling away now that Pedro's life had been rerouted.

Pedro impulsively sat up, looked around. His head started to swim, though. And the room seemed to spin, so he flopped back down.

"You're okay," Helena assured him, holding out a cautioning hand. "But adjusting to lower gravity will take you a little while."

"Lower gravity? Who are you? Where am I?"

"I am Captain Helena Taylor, and you are on board our light-propelled spaceship, Smoke and Mirrors. We propose delivering you, your family, and many of your neighbors to a planet in another solar system with ideal conditions for starting over. That will be with our assistance, and your permission, of course."

"My family?!?!"

"Pedro, cariño!"

"Ludi?!?!" exclaimed Pedro, nearly pulling a neck muscle as he turned and saw Ludi's long, beautiful, golden-streaked hair matted out wet against her pillow, like he remembered seeing it on the delivery table when she gave birth…

"Mami? Papi?"

Deborah gently unbuckled and cradled year-old Alexita out of her crib, and brought her over to Ludi's greedily welcoming arms. By then, Pedro was already clenching strands of his wife's hair, holding on for dear life.

"When you say my family, you are including Ludi's grandparents and my parents?"

Helena gestured for patience as she spoke loudly enough to assure she was heard where she needed to be heard over the intercom system, "Can I have an update from the other Perez family cabins?"

"This is Cabin Three C, Captain. There's some argumentative commotion in Spanish between spouses. But the women are assuring us they are fine with the settlement mission, and that their husbands will cooperate."

"Aydiomio!"

"Ay caramba!"

While Ludi laughed, Pedro gasped, "How can this be?" His voice echoed total perplexity, mystified bafflement as he turned to his loved ones and went on, "How can our Alexita be so young? And you so beautiful?"

"What?" Ludi laughed. "You're in a hurry to grow us old? But this is very strange, Captain Taylor, because one moment I am chasing my daughter through the house, and the next moment..."

Pedro shook his head. "I must have been having a nightmare daydream, maybe provoked by whatever you did to bring us here. But whatever it was is gone now." He left out the hauntingly inexplicable part, a comforting feeling that came over him concerning his great grandson. How he was going to be safe after all, somewhere, even though he wasn't born yet.

Helena nodded knowingly. "We have a lot of explaining to do, that's for sure."

"Pedro and Ludi Perez, I'm Dr. Deborah Davis-Murphy, chief medical officer," said Deborah, shaking hands with both. "Mr. Perez, it seems you have some back trouble. We should be able to take care of that in a few weeks."

"Only a few weeks?!"

Deborah winked. "We may have learned a thing or two in medicine since 2002."

"Since 2002?! What year is this?!?"

"Ah, yes, that. Mr. Perez, it is September of 2062."

"So Captain, you have taken us sixty years into the future?"

"That's with your permission. We can always take you back, maybe. Things might be a little tricky."

"And you are bringing us to a new planet?"

"Oomb is an island-strewn water planet. And its constantly shifting axis provides a temperate climate everywhere."

"Cariño," said Ludi, grabbing Pedro's hand and squeezing, "it's your kingdom beyond the stars."

"YOU are my kingdom beyond the stars," Pedro squeezed back.

*

Knock! Knock!

The two Jehovah's witnesses looked like they'd seen a ghost when Doña Galleta opened the door for them at the Perez residence.

"Where are they? Where is the family?" the shorter one asked as he stepped past the slight woman to peek inside. "What did you do to them?"

"I did not do anything to them. They were taken up in the rapture."

"The rapture?!?!"

"Apparently your fate lies elsewhere. Should I bake you some chocolate chip cookies?"

*

"How are we looking, Yoon-hee?"

"Advance guard fireflies have been accelerated factor nineteen to all four quadrants, Captain, and mirror arrays are full bloom fore and aft. Say the word, and I'll boost the EM field to full capacity."

"Then let's boogie," said Helena, though not feeling nearly as joyfully flippant as she made sound. *Forgive us the weapons we are carrying,* she prayed. *And bless our precious cargo from Alexita to Effy our ephemeral mascot.*

Have I answered to a higher calling? Or surrendered to a profound madness no one around me could garner enough resistance to successfully push back against? Who knows?

But my responsibility for the care and safety of these people from north Philadelphia seems certain. When I deliver them to Oomb, I am potentially placing them in the path of a civilization that might be bent on turning us into cattle...and possess the means to do so.

Just have to hope that Oomb will prove a far, far better place for these families from 2002 than they were otherwise to ever know, where they can live far, far richer lives than they were otherwise to ever live. May the planet of golfing trees be their pot of gold at the end of a light-years-long rainbow!

*

Samantha Santiago couldn't sleep. Lying facing one direction, she bothered over the light under her bedroom door from out in the hallway. Long as it stayed on, her mom or dad could yet be giving her one last peek before they turned in for the night. Lying facing the other direction, she confronted what kept her worried about that final parental eavesdrop. It was the golden cylindrical pendant attached to a bracelet chain. Handed to her by a mysterious old lady earlier that day,

Samantha was instructed to keep it secure for sixty years, about.

A secure enough place for the evening, at least, had seemed as a necklace around Samantha's beloved Bebop Bear seated atop her bookcase. Bebop already sported a miniature Orioles' baseball cap, so why not?

However, soon as Samantha flipped off the switch to her various lamps, she realized the pendant glowed pale green in the dark. And that glow proved all the spookier for setting off in such sharp relief, however teensy, the etched-in hieroglyphic-type figures.

One moment, Samantha was inclined to believe her parents wouldn't notice. And that if they did notice, they would just assume one of her friends at school gave her some goofball trinket.

Heaven knew there were enough goofball trinkets out there, such as carbonated candy that gave your mouth a bad case of the fizzles. And not to mention the keychain character showed her by pal María. When squeezed, a big purple booger oozed from its nose until you let go.

Were this as far as Samantha's thinking went, she could have drifted off to sleep in no time. But there was that pesky other moment when something else seemed probable.

Her parents had suffered lots of upset, her dad especially, from part of his family seemingly having vanished off the face of the Earth. Wouldn't this oddly glowing object with the cryptic engraving really set them off?

Maybe she shouldn't wait for her parents to start asking uncomfortable questions. Maybe she should tell them what the old lady said, about her dad's relatives being caught up in an adventure where they were celebrating- Wasn't that the word the woman used? If they were celebrating, they must be okay, yes? Wouldn't that make her dad feel better?

Or maybe it would just upset him more. He'd fear his relatives were murdered and then buried somewhere. So he would call the police, who would confiscate the pendant and arrest the frail-looking little old lady. Subjecting her to endless rounds of merciless interrogation, law enforcement officers would never accept her responses, would they? Wouldn't they find her responses too incredibly ridiculous, and go digging up her backyard for bodies?

Back and forth, back and forth, Samantha tossed and turned, debating herself sleepless over what to do. And pondering the mystery of the pendant only prolonged her insomnia.

The sliver of light under her door hinted at a big wide world beyond, including... Wow, wouldn't her science-fiction-obsessed brother go nuts over the pendant? What sort of world beyond was hinted at by its soft green glow?

One concern temporarily held back Samantha from relieving Bebop Bear of the pendant bracelet, and tucking it beside her under blanket. Namely, what if radioactivity produced its odd glow? Finally, though, she realized that little old lady, however mysterious, certainly would have apprised her of such danger. After all, said lady didn't even want an ant to come in harm's way.

On this comforting realization, Samantha slid from her bed quietly as possible. She removed the pendant from her favorite stuffed animal with the care of a thief trying not to make noise while stealing valuable jewelry. Then she slipped back under the covers, tucking the mysterious object into her pajama top pocket.

Samantha finally lulled herself off to sleep on two comforting thoughts. One, she could more clearly figure out what to do about her situation in the morning, after much rest. Second was a growing conviction she had been honored with a sacred trust she must do everything in her power to fulfill.

By next morning, a marvelous strange dream was already fading from memory. But exhilarating elation persisted undiminished.

In Samantha's dream, four trails of sparkling fairy dust heralded the arrival of an amazing interstellar spacecraft trailing the largest, thickest stream of sparkling fairy dust, its design inspired by a blooming rose, its destination a distant solar system…